THE CONTAGIUM SERIES BOOKS I AND II

CONTAGIOUS
AND DEATHLY CONTAGIOUS

EMILY GOODWIN

A PERMUTED PRESS BOOK
ISBN: 978-1-61868-517-9
ISBN (eBook): 978-1-61868-535-3

THE CONTAGIUM SERIES BOOKS I and II
Contagious and Deathly Contagious
All Rights Reserved

Cover art by:
Dean Samed, Conzpiracy Digital Arts

Permuted Press
109 International Drive, Suite 300
Franklin, TN 37067
http://permutedpress.com

THE CONTAGIUM SERIES: BOOK ONE

CONTAGIOUS

a novel by
EMILY GOODWIN

Acknowledgments

I would like to thank the many people who made this book possible by answering my many questions about 'medically realistic' zombies, survival skills, hunting, explosives, self-defense skills, weapons, and the workings of the military. Dad, thank you for helping me with 'zombie target practice' every weekend so I could learn how to shoot like Orissa. Thank you to everyone who supported and encouraged me to never stop writing and who read and reviewed this book. And finally, I'd like to thank my husband for always having faith in me.

To my husband,
Thank you for being my best friend and
believing in everything I do...as well as putting up with my weirdness.
I love you

"I shall set my face toward the infernal regions,
I shall raise up the dead, and they will eat the living,
I will make the dead outnumber the living!"
-The Epic of Gilgamesh

PART I

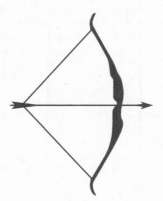

CHAPTER 1

I stumbled my way up the worn, carpeted stairs of Aunt Jenny's small apartment building. It was one-thirty in the morning and I was drunk. My hand slipped off the doorknob more than once and, realizing it was locked, I dropped my purse so I could dig through the jumbled mess for my keys. I finally fished them out from the bottom. I wobbled when I stood, teetering on tall, black heels. The door swung open just as I reached for the lock.

"Orissa!" Aunt Jenny cried, her hand flying to her chest.

"Sorry," I mumbled.

"It's ok," she breathed, looking relieved. "I just wasn't expecting you so early. Well, early for you." Echoes of muffled, angry voices floated down the hall.

"They've been at it all night," Aunt Jenny sighed and ushered me in.

"Did you wait up for me?" I asked, as I shakily removed my shoes.

"Yes, well, no. I told you I wasn't going to keep tabs. But I worry."

"I can take care of myself."

"Oh, yeah. And you can bail yourself out of jail."

I glared at Aunt Jenny. "That was over a month ago. Can't we please drop it?"

"Yes, sorry." She shook her head. "You should have called me though. I would have picked you up."

I shrugged. "Thanks, but I don't want you to go out of your way. Maybe next time." I tripped over the ottoman as I crossed the small living room.

"Had enough?" she asked, with just a hint of laughter in her voice.

"I," I began, standing up straight, "was doing my part to stimulate the economy." Well, I was doing my part to make sure others stimulated the economy. My money hadn't paid for any of the liquor I'd consumed.

"I should have opened a bar," Aunt Jenny joked. She gathered up her dishes from the coffee table. "Did you have fun at least?"

"Yes. I rocked karaoke. And I got two numbers."

"Two?"

I smiled and nodded.

Aunt Jenny just laughed and shook her head. "So how come you came home early?"

"There was a fight," I blurted, my filter turned off due to overindulgence in alcohol. There were always fights in bars. But this fight was…different. I had just talked to him, the tall guy in the blue shirt, before he snapped. We were having a good conversation—and he had bought me my third drink for the night—when he doubled over, holding his stomach, and complaining about being in pain. Not wanting to get puked on, I wandered to the other side of the bar where I could watch him from a distance. Then his pain had given over to rage, the kind of rage that brings to mind frothing dogs. No one knew what had caused it, but suddenly his hands wrapped around the bouncer's throat. It took three guys to pull him off. Blue Shirt was sputtering, screaming, clawing; he even tried to bite the guy. I skipped out right as the police showed up. From the parking lot I watched them tase Blue Shirt to subdue him. "And my abs hurt," I covered up, not wanting to discuss the fight.

"Your abs hurt?" Aunt Jenny raised an eyebrow incredulously.

"Yeah, I must have worked out too hard." I put my hand over my right side; briefly I recalled Blue Shirt. His madness had started with pain, too. "I'm feeling kinda nauseous, so I'm gonna go to bed."

"Ok, night. Remember I work in the morning, so I'll see you after, alright?"

"Ok. Night." I weaved my way to my tiny room, stripped out of my clothes, and collapsed onto the bed. Too tired to shower, I fell asleep, not waking until after ten the next morning—sick from more than a mere hangover.

The ER was so busy that I had to wait over an hour just to freaking get my blood drawn. Pissed, nauseous, and tired, I refused to put on the stupid paper robe. My nurse was old and it didn't take ESP to sense that she wanted to retire. I wanted to tell her to get over herself and be thankful she at least had a job. Since the Depression had hit, many were in need of gainful employment. Seeing the needle in her hand made me change my mind.

I'm angry, I thought, but not like Blue Shirt. Who wouldn't be angry? The ER wasn't exactly a fun place to be.

"There's no yes or no test," the nurse explained, when she came back with the results another hour later. "Your white blood cell count is high, so you may need to have your appendix removed."

The nurse then put in an order for a CT scan to confirm her suspicions. When she came back, after what felt like hours, she informed me that it was indeed appendicitis.

"Lovely." I didn't have health insurance and I sure as hell didn't want to pay for surgery, but what choice did I have?

"Put this on," she said gruffly, tossing the ugly robe on my bed. I rolled my eyes but obliged, wanting to get this whole thing over with. I was in a lot of pain by now, but I was also relieved to discover that it was only my appendix. I changed just in time for my crabby-ass nurse to retrieve me for surgery. I curiously looked around the hospital as she wheeled me down the hall. I made eye contact with a tall, dark haired man as he exited a room. I was instantly drawn to his big, blue eyes. He smiled politely at me, revealing perfect white teeth. I was so mesmerized by his beauty I barely noticed the green scrubs and lab coat he was wearing. If he was my doctor, surgery might not be so bad after all.

My mouth was dry. My head was fuzzy. I didn't know why I was in so much pain, and I was beginning to forget where I was. My eyes just wouldn't open so I listened and heard nothing. Every breath took effort and I tried to call out for help. But no one came. It felt like hours passed before I drifted back to sleep. When I woke up the second time, a young, dark skinned nurse was adjusting my IV.

"Good morning, Orissa!" she said brightly. "Surgery went well."

"Did I really need it out?" Damn it, even though I had just woken up from surgery, money was still my main concern.

"Yes. It was close to bursting," she informed me.

"Oh. Good, I guess."

"Your mom is waiting outside. Do you want me to get her now?"

"My *mom*?"

"Petite, short brown hair…that's not her?"

"No. She's my aunt. Yes, she can come in."

Aunt Jenny came in with a vase full of flowers. I wanted to glare at her and tell her it was a waste of money, but I only smiled, too weak to argue. She gushed over me for a bit, making sure everything was ok. She promised she'd be back after work even though I told her I'd be fine on my own. The hospital had cable, after all.

With the pain medication, my time spent in the hospital went by quickly. I caught a glimpse of the hot doctor again as I was leaving, making me wish I had come in my bar clothes rather than purple pajama pants.

For the next five days, I did nothing but park my ass on the couch or in bed. Since no new shows were being aired, I amused myself by watching reruns of *Family Guy*, flipping to the news stations during commercials.

I had nightmares about the broadcasts I had seen, many reporting a huge increase in unexplained deaths and small, and seemingly random, outbursts of violence across the country. Friends turned on friends, and one witness described her attacker's behaviors as being like those of Blue Shirt. It freaked me out and made me very glad I had insisted on taking martial arts lessons instead of ballet like my mother had wished.

In the small hours, it occurred to me that I might be like Blue Shirt, like the people on the news. Maybe it was just moving through me slower. *It*. Whatever it was…

Did I feel my temper rising?

Only all the time…

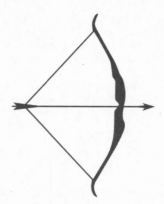

CHAPTER 2

A little over two weeks after my surgery I forced myself out of bed. I was no longer worried that I was like the people on the news since so much time had passed. I slowly cleaned the apartment and even made banana bread out of the browning bananas that had been forgotten on top of the refrigerator.

I had a follow up appointment at the hospital at two-thirty that afternoon. I hadn't dressed in anything but pajamas, done my hair, or worn makeup in the last two weeks. Deciding that putting effort into my appearance today would help cheer me up, I slipped into my favorite jeans and black t-shirt with a brown leather jacket over top. I traded the heels I initially put on for a pair of leather boots, tall and flat. Since it wasn't that far, I decided I'd walk; halfway there I felt so drained I wasted my extra cash on a cab.

Feeling pissy from pain, I hastily got directions to where I needed to go. I hated elevators. I was always afraid of getting stuck. And the hospital was more crowded than usual. All I needed was to get trapped inside an overly stuffed box full of strangers. Despite my pain, I took the stairs. Going slow, I was concentrating so hard on not acknowledging that I hurt that I didn't notice *him* until I was very near. Blood ran down a gash on his cheek. Hands bound behind him in handcuffs, he head butted his police escort and madly dove down the stairs.

We collided. I desperately reached out for the railing—without success. He brought me down with him and, when we stopped tumbling, he crouched over me, drooling and growling. There were collective shouts of panic as people watched, gaping open-mouthed at the lunatic above me. The only items in my possession were my purse and a notebook. My purse was somewhere underneath me, but the notebook was still clutched in my death grip. Not knowing what else to do, I slapped him across the face with the notebook, grimacing at the blood and drool that splattered.

While it wasn't my first weapon of choice, it worked. The guy was stunned, giving me enough time to knee him in the balls and roll away. I sprung up and kicked him hard in the side, immobilizing him long enough for the cop to recover his assailant. I backed away, my vision fading. A strong hand caught me just as I passed out. I remember seeing his big blue eyes and his mouth moving, but I couldn't hear what he said.

I came to in an exam room. My purse and notebook were on a chair next to the hard, foam bed. Stiffly, I got up, gathered my things and opened the door.

"Whoa, where do you think you're going?" a deep male voice asked in an alluring Irish accent.

I spun around; not a smart move at the moment. Blood rushed to my head and I felt dizzy again.

The doctor with the pretty blue eyes put his arm out, thinking I'd faint again, but I held my ground. He led me back into the room. After I was lying on the uncomfortable bed, he said, "You were just in here a few weeks ago for surgery, right?"

"Yeah."

"Appendectomy?"

"Yep."

He carefully touched my side. "Does this hurt?"

"I had my stomach sliced open and part of my guts ripped out. Of course it hurts."

He laughed. "Does it hurt anymore than it did before you fell?"

"No." I sat up. "It hurt before then too. But my back didn't."

"You seem to be healing fast," he said, as he inspected the incision site. "But I'd still like to run some more tests and do a CT scan to make sure the fall didn't damage you. You could be bleeding internally." He looked into my eyes. "Did you hit your head?"

"Uh, yeah, I think." It happened so fast. The guy diving down a flight of stairs. The blood. The primal growls rumbling in his throat. There was something else, too. It was in his eyes, well, kind of. It was more like there *wasn't* anything in his eyes. It was as if all the humanity was gone and all that was left was raw, animal instinct. I forced a half smile. That was a stupid thing to think. There is no way I could tell all that from the two seconds I'd had to look at the maniac.

"What was with that guy?"

"I'm not really sure," Dr. Blue Eyes said, looking at the floor. He was lying. "Why don't you change into a gown and I'll get you set up for a scan right away. Do you want anything for pain?"

"Yeah, I'd like that."

"Have any allergies?"

I shook my head. "Nope."

He reached into his pocket and pulled out a pill bottle. He filled a Dixie cup with water from a bottle and handed me the pills. He closed the door and left. Assuming the pills were strong painkillers, I popped them into my mouth, willing them to take effect right away. I carefully folded my clothes on the chair and put on the stupid gown. At least this gown was more substantial than the last one.

To keep from feeling freaked out, I rummaged through the drawers to find paper towels. Using hand sanitizer, I cleaned the bodily fluids from the notebook. When I was satisfied it was clean enough, I sat back down and opened it, flipping nostalgically through the pages.

Someone screamed.

It startled me, and I jumped. The quick movements hurt my recovering abdomen. Another scream was followed by a loud bang. Half tempted to get up and see what was going on, I reminded myself that this was a hospital and screaming probably wasn't uncommon.

I turned to the page in my notebook, smiling at what I was reading. I was starting to feel kind of sleepy from the pills; my mind felt at ease and my muscles were relaxed. Then, all of a sudden, something clattered to the floor outside the door. Someone screamed again: a long, harrowing, horror movie scream. Then a gun fired.

My blood ran cold. What the hell? I gripped the notebook tight and swallowed. The screaming started again, this time coming from multiple people. Three consecutive gunshots put an end to their shouts. I heard more panicked yelps as people ran up and down the hall. What sounded like heavy objects clattered to the floor. I tossed the notebook to the side and carefully put my legs over the edge of the bed. Slowly, I inched toward the door.

Something thrust against it and I jumped. Pain radiated through my side and I feared I had ripped my stitches out. I smelled it before the high-pitched beeping confirmed it: smoke. I needed to get out, even if it meant facing what was out there. I grabbed the cold round knob and twisted. The door didn't open; something had fallen in front of it, blocking its path. I was locked in. Smoke billowed in from the vents. Panic rose in my chest. Desperately, I slammed my body against the door. Every move hurt. Again and again, I tried forcing the door open. My vision blurred. My legs buckled. "Fuck," I swore, wishing I hadn't taken the pain pills. Then I lost consciousness.

———————▶

It was the emergency sirens that woke me. I sat up, a migraine threatening to form, and realized

I wasn't in the exam room anymore. I was in what looked like a basement, lying on a cot on the floor. Two backup floodlights were the only sources of illumination. I was surrounded by many other people, patients by the looks of it. Children cried right along with the howling of the sirens. I ran my hands through my hair trying to make sense of what was happening.

It was bad, that much I could tell. That was as far as I got, however, since the medicine still poisoned my veins. Then I saw him, looking all calm and professional in his scrubs and lab coat. A fire burned inside me, fueling my ability to get up. I attempted to angrily march over to Dr. Blue Eyes but staggered along the way.

"You!" I shouted. "You drugged me! What the hell is going on? What are you doing to us?"

Alarmed, he rose up and moved away from the crying girl he was soothing. "Calm down. It'll be ok." He put his hand on my arm. I jerked it away and shoved him.

"Be ok? What, after you surgically attach us to each other? Yeah, I've seen the *Human Centipede,* you creep!"

He took hold of my arms. I tried to fight him off, but I was too weak. My head pounded and any twisting hurt my side.

"Calm down and I'll explain," he whispered. "You're scaring everyone more than they already are."

"They should be scared. He's trying to kill us!" I shouted, able to break free from his hold. "He's going to kill us!"

"Quiet! They'll hear you!"

"Good! Hey! Hey!" I screamed, hoping someone would hear me. The exit sign loomed ahead like a mirage. If only I could get out, maybe I could get help. Come back and save everyone. Dr. Blue Eyes grabbed me again, this time with more force. He held me back, telling me to calm down over and over. Still, I fought. I might have been weak and drugged to all hell, but I wasn't going down without a fight.

"I'm sorry," he said, not meeting my eyes. Then I felt the needle pierce my skin.

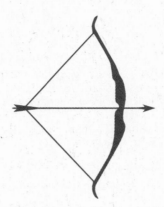

CHAPTER 3

Once again, I woke up from a drug-induced sleep—this time in restraints. It wasn't the first time it had happened, but this was very different than my wild night with Danny Merdock—a story for another time. A young nurse sat on the floor several feet in front of me. She hugged her knees, slowly rocking back and forth.

"Hello," I croaked.

She turned, tears streaming down her face.

"What...what is happening?" I managed to ask.

She shook her head. "'And there shall be signs in the sun, and in the moon, and in the stars; and upon the earth distress of nations, with perplexity; the sea and the waves roaring; men's hearts failing them for fear, and for looking after those things which are coming on the earth: for the powers of heaven shall be shaken.'" She turned away and went back to rocking.

Ok, not much help there. I pulled against the restraints, noticing for the first time that I was hooked up to an IV. How long was I out? Something moved next to me. I turned to see a small set of green eyes staring at me.

"Can I help you?" I asked the girl. She had to be no older than ten.

"I've been waiting for you to wake up," she told me. She clutched a stuffed animal close to her chest. Her ears were pierced; pink sapphires barely glinted in the dull light. Her hair and eyebrows were gone and she was very frail.

"Why?"

"You seem strong. I think you can save us."

"Maybe. You need to undo these buckles for me, though. Then I'll get us out of here," I lied.

"I don't want to leave here."

"Why?" I asked again.

"We're safe here!" she whispered.

"Safe? Safe from what?"

"The monsters." She looked around nervously. Heavy footfalls made her squeal and dart away.

A shadow fell over my bed. "You're not going to attack me again, are you?" There was no mistaking that Irish accent.

"Obviously not," I retorted.

"Promise and I'll let you go."

"Why, so you can drug me again?" I asked.

"I don't want to hurt you," he said and almost sounded honest.

"Please. Then why else am I trapped in a basement tied to a bed?"

"Let me explain," he said gently.

"Explain away."

I wasn't like Blue Shirt, I told myself. These people weren't like him either!

He sat at the foot of my small bed. "I'm sure you've noticed the violence." He didn't wait for a response before continuing. "There are...were things about it that we doctors were aware of that you—the public—weren't. The Center for Disease Control asked us to keep it quiet. They didn't want anyone to panic. They said they'd get it under control."

"Will you get to the point?"

"The point is that the violence is caused by a virus."

I wished I could sit up and dubiously stare down Dr. Blue Eyes. I wasn't buying his bullshit. "A virus?"

"Yes." He twisted so he could look me in the eye. "Have you ever heard of Phineas Gage?"

"Yeah," I said, getting a flashback to Psych 101. "The guy that got the railroad spike blown through his head."

"Good. And do you remember what was so significant about him?"

"Uh, he lived?"

"True, but the damage to his brain caused his personality to change."

"Ok, I remember that part. What does this have to do with anything?"

"The virus. It causes damage to the frontal lobes—"

"And then people go crazy."

"Right."

"Holy shit." Blue Shirt...the guy on the stairs! "Ok, but why am I down here?" I still hadn't fully decided to believe this crazy story yet.

"This is the part I'm sorry about." He cast his eyes down. "We're safe down here. Everyone else left."

"Why would they leave?" As the words slipped from my lips, I realized the answer. If there really was some crazy-making virus, everyone would leave. It would be mass panic, just like in the movies. "Never mind."

"I'm Padraic Sheehan," he said, getting up and unbuckling the restraints. In a swift fluid movement, the IV was pulled from my vein.

"Orissa." I sat up and rubbed my wrists, examining the room. We were definitely in a basement. There were several beds, a few cots, and mostly blankets scattered around the room. Old medical supplies, broken wheel chairs, and dusty boxes cluttered the already crowded room. The people occupying the makeshift beds were ragged, to say the least. A handful were hooked up to machines, many were bandaged, and others looked too old to move. Over in the corner, a couple sat huddled together, holding their new baby. I got why we were here. "Why didn't you leave?"

Padraic smiled softly. "I couldn't leave my patients," he said. An old man a few beds down from me started wheezing. Padraic got up and hurried over, doing his best to soothe the man's pain.

Trying to fathom what little information I had been given, I ran my eyes over every single person in the room. There seemed to be one other doctor: an old, gray haired woman who fell into the 'too old to run' category and three nurses. I counted forty-seven patients, including myself and excluding the baby.

The little girl was back. She set her stuffed cat on my bed and stared at me again.

"I'm Zoe," she told me.

"Hi, Zoe. I'm Orissa."

"That's a pretty name," she said, climbing up on my bed.

I shrugged. "It's a city in India."

"Where you born there?"

"Nope. Conceived there."

"What does that mean?"

"It means my parents were in India when...you know what, never mind. You'll figure it out when you're older."

"You don't look sick."

"I'm not, not really, I guess. I had my appendix taken out."

"That sounds like it hurt."

"Nah, it wasn't so bad," I promised.

"Did your mommy and daddy leave you too?" she asked. She walked her cat up and down the bed.

"They left a long time ago." Well, that was partially true. It was really my decision to stay behind. "Zoe, have you seen the monsters?"

She nodded and hugged her cat.

"Can you tell me what they look like?" I asked gently.

"They look like people, 'cuz that's what they are. But they want to eat your brains."

"Oh, thanks." This kid had obviously seen too many horror movies. I needed to talk to an adult, preferably one who'd seen the 'monsters.' I also needed my clothes.

A middle-aged woman walked over to us. She was dressed in pink scrub pants and a butterfly patterned shirt.

"Hey, Zoe Boey. Whatcha doing?"

"Hi, Hilary! I'm talking to Orissa. She hasn't seen the monsters yet."

"Ah. Hopefully she never will. Have you eaten yet?"

When Zoe shook her head, Hilary instructed her to find Jason and eat dinner. Without giving me a chance to ask any questions, Hilary led me to a small, dirty bathroom. It worked, she assured me, though the water in the shower never got hot. It certainly felt good to be clean. I begrudgingly put the hospital gown back on, happy Hilary had given me a pair of bleach stained scrub bottoms to go under it, and padded my way back into our little group.

A teenage boy handed me a sandwich and it was only when I looked at the plain, white bread that I realized how hungry I was. I scarfed it down, draining the bottle of apple juice that came along with it. Surprisingly I was tired, but sleep could wait; I needed answers first. I sought out Padraic, who was changing a bloody bandage on a sandy haired man. He saw me waiting and nodded in acknowledgment. I retreated back to my bed, which was really a gurney, and sat. A few minutes later, Padraic joined me.

"You need to tell me more," I pleaded.

"I don't know much more."

"Then tell me what you do know."

"Ok." He nodded. "A few weeks ago we started seeing odd, isolated cases of what seemed to be psychotic behavior. At the same time, an alarming number of people came in complaining of headaches and dying within twenty-four hours of admittance. We didn't see the connection then. We know now it's the same virus. It seems to do three things: make you insane, kill you, or do nothing."

"How is it spread?"

"We don't know for sure yet. I'm guessing through the water. It started on the west coast and now it's here."

My heart fell into a bottomless pit. "It's nationwide?"

"Yes."

"H-how long was I out for?"

"Almost three days," he admitted, sounding ashamed.

"What the hell, Padraic?" I jumped off the gurney, wincing in pain. "Why?"

He waved his hand at me. "That's why. I thought it would give you time to heal. You seem to be quite the fighter. I didn't think you'd rest."

"You're right I'm not going to rest! I want out of here!" I stared at him, for once in my life, unable to come up with anything to argue with. Sighing, I sat back down. "Tell me about these 'monsters'."

"It comes on suddenly, with very few symptoms. The victim might seem agitated or angry, but then they…they just snap," he snapped his fingers, "like that. And aren't human anymore. Like a rabid dog."

"Is there a cure?"

His blue eyes met mine. "No, we've only been able to autopsy a few of the bodies before the CDC took them away, but the virus completely kills parts of the brain."

"Then how are they alive?"

"It seems the virus doesn't affect the parts of the brain, right away, that control basic life skills, like breathing and eating. All aspects of humanity: drive, memory, and emotion are gone. The victims are never the same and never will be. See, the virus turns them into angry, raging monsters."

"And then what?"

"The central nervous system starts to shut down. I haven't seen anyone who has had the virus for that long, though."

"Lovely."

"Are you alright, Orissa? This is a lot of information to take in at once."

"Yeah," I said quickly. "I'm no stranger to horrible things."

"If you say so."

"How many?" I asked suddenly.

"How many what?"

"How many people got infected?"

"I'm not sure. After the outbreak, everyone panicked. We were told to stay in our houses and that the local authorities would send out buses to take us to quarantines."

"But you knew they wouldn't take us sick, injured people," I said bitterly.

"Right."

"So you stayed?"

"Yes."

"With the lot that's gonna die?"

He narrowed his eyes a bit. "You don't know that. Not everyone here is at death's door."

I looked around the room once more. True, there were several people who, like me, were on the mend. A few more didn't look sick or injured at all. Maybe they were here with someone, a family member perhaps, and couldn't stand the thought of leaving them behind.

"Could any of us be infected?" I asked, apprehensive to hear the response.

"No. It's been long enough; we would have known by now. My guess is that most of us are resistant to the virus."

"Good." I nervously twisted a section of my dark hair around my fingers. "So what's our plan?"

"Survive."

"I know that. We can't stay in this basement forever though."

"We have food that will last us…awhile. As long as the generators stay on, what is in the freezers will tide us over. The storage for the cafeteria is down here."

"And when the food runs out?"

"I'm hoping someone will come rescue us by then."

"Hopefully," I agreed ruefully.

The room we slept in was pretty secure. It was dark and cavernous, but it only had one exit and a heavy metal door guarded it. To get to the food storage, we had to walk down a dark hallway past the boiler room. To conserve what little power we had left, all unnecessary lights had been shut off. No one ever went to get food alone. Jason, a seventeen-year-old boy, had taken over the role of patrol guard. Armed with a twisted piece of metal, he made sure the coast was clear. As far as anyone knew, our little party had made it into the basement without being followed, shutting the main doors before anyone had a chance to come in.

Sonja, Jason's younger sister, had taken upon herself the position of keeping up morale. She organized activities for the kids and tried her best to entertain us. For the next week, I allowed myself to fade into the background. I was still weak, my body still in pain. I didn't want to think about anything or anyone. I didn't want to wonder what had happened to Aunt Jenny. I lied to Padraic about being in pain so he would give me more morphine. If I wasn't sleeping, I was talking to Zoe. She devised a storytelling game where we alternated adding words to some sort of epic tale. Maybe I was in shock. Maybe the truth of the matter hadn't hit me since I hadn't seen any of it. While others cried and prayed, I sat calmly by myself, sticking to my routine of eating breakfast, doing what little yoga my body could handle, and getting my morphine shot.

One night, Megan and Heath's newborn son wouldn't stop crying. No one could fault her or the baby, but she apologized again and again. I was trying to force myself to pass out when I heard it. The thick, metal door blocked out most of the sound. I sat up, closing my eyes. Yes, I knew I heard it.

"There's someone out there!" I whispered. "Shhh!" I added, when anxious murmurs broke out.

Some thought it was a rescue mission and we were saved. Others, myself included, didn't trust what was on the other side of the door.

Then a knock.

"Hello?" a female voice called. "Is anyone in there?"

Jason and Padraic slowly cracked the door. They looked at each other and nodded, stepping aside to let two ragged girls limp inside. One was dirty and worn, but otherwise unharmed. She helped her bloody friend walk. Hilary rushed over, taking the injured girl into the bathroom to wash out her wounds.

I seemed to be the only one who didn't trust them. Outsiders, I thought, we didn't know anything about them, but everyone else saw them as heroes, survivors. Rebecca and her injured friend Karli brought news of the outside world. It wasn't what any of us wanted to hear.

They guessed about half the population of the town had evacuated. The other people hadn't been so lucky. They thought that more than half of the remaining had either died or contracted the virus, leaving less than a fourth of the entire population alive. They spoke so mathematically that it was hard to envision the dead bodies that littered the streets. They had survived by hiding in Karli's little sister's tree house. Hunger forced them out of the trees. On their search for food, Karli was attacked by one of the 'monsters.' By a stroke of luck, they'd found the hospital. Exhausted, both girls slipped into a deep sleep.

No one bothered to keep track of time. There were no windows in the basement, so it was impossible to tell what time of day it was. I assumed my body kept with a fairly consistent cycle and I felt tired at night, around ten or eleven. The girls had shown up several hours past that. I had one quick nightmare about death and turning evil when I heard the slurping. I sat up, pissed that someone had gotten into our carefully rationed food, when I saw her silhouette.

She was standing over Mr. McKanthor, an eighty-something year old man who was dying of cancer. Padraic told me that Mr. McKanthor wouldn't make it much longer, even with the medications he had been taking. Something splattered on the floor. Thinking it was his IV bag and that Karli was fixing it, I turned over to go back to sleep. But there was something not right. The liquid was dark and thick. I sat up, eyes widening in terror.

Blood. It was blood that covered the floor.

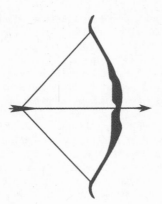

CHAPTER 4

Mr. McKanthor was dead. His head flopped back, lifeless eyes staring at the ceiling. Karli's hands were shining with blood. She reached down, rummaged through his intestines, and grabbed onto something that stretched and snapped. She shoved it into her mouth. Frozen in horror, I watched her do it again and again. She was infected. She had gone mad. Zoe calling them monsters wasn't an exaggeration. My mind raced. I needed to stop her, but with what?

As I mulled it over, Sonja sat up. "Hey, what are you doing to—" she began, her voice dying with a sharp intake of breath. Then she screamed. Karli growled at the noise and lunged for her. Without thinking, I leapt off my bed. Jason, who was next to his sister, startled awake. He used his body as a shield, blocking Karli from killing Sonja. I was by his side in two seconds, picking up his metal weapon and hitting Karli as hard as possible over the head.

She didn't react to the pain. She clawed and bit at Jason, who struggled to keep her at arm's length. I hit her two more times; nothing. It was as if I were hitting her with a pool noodle. Knowing Jason couldn't fight her off forever, I grabbed her hair and yanked her back. She snarled at me, thrashing blood covered hands into the air.

She crouched, reminding me of an animal stalking prey. Also adapting a predatory mindset, I was ready when she jumped at me again. My foot hit her square in the chest. She gasped for air and stumbled back, tripping over a cot. Her head hit the hard concrete with a thud. My fingers gripped the metal pipe so hard my knuckles turned white. She unnaturally pulled herself up, a rumbling growl coming from deep inside her throat. Her lips snarled and she flung herself forward. I dodged out of the way, grabbed her arm, and spun her face first into the wall.

"Nooo!" Rebecca screamed from behind me. Ignoring her desperate calls to spare her friend, I advanced on Karli. I didn't want to kill the girl. I grabbed a fistful of her hair and smacked her head into the brick wall again. She wobbled, attempted to wrap her hands around my throat, but finally sank to the ground.

I heard Rebecca's sneakers scuffing on the gritty floor. But I didn't see her launch herself in the air. She landed on my back, knocking the wind out of me. Paralyzed, I lay there in terror. Someone must have pulled her off of me. Padraic's hand grabbed mine and he yanked me out of the way. I scrambled to my feet, clutching onto Padraic for support. I gasped for breath and turned to see Jason struggling with Rebecca.

Like Karli, she was snarling and growling. Recovered, I sprang forward, pipe still in hand, and drove the pointy end into her stomach. Jason let her go and she collapsed, her body twitching as her blood poured out.

The metal pipe clamored to the ground. I slowly became aware that I wasn't alone. The children cried and the rest gaped at me in horror. My eyes refused to move off of Rebecca's dying body. Someone took my hand and gave it a gentle tug. Shaken from my reverie, I faced Padraic.

"I...I" My voice died as I spoke. Shaking my head, I robotically walked back to my bed.

Little Zoe tiptoed over. "You killed the monsters!" she practically cheered. "You are a hero!"

"No," I breathed. I hadn't killed two monsters. I had killed two humans, taking their lives and their souls. It had to be done, right?

Jason, Padraic, and two men I hadn't bothered to learn the names of moved the bodies out of our safe room. Though I was far from tired I laid back down, pulling the thin sheet over me. Clutching her toy cat, Zoe climbed in next to me.

"I feel safe with you," she whispered. I put my arms around her, suddenly feeling very protective of this sick little girl. We didn't move while the others went about cleaning the blood. They all left me alone and finally, after what felt like an eternity, I fell back asleep.

I didn't ask for my morphine shot the next morning. I went on with my usual yoga routine, showing Zoe the basics of the Sun Salutation. She stayed close to me while we ate breakfast, which consisted of a small bowl of cereal, powdered milk, and canned fruit. I could feel their eyes on me as I stuck the plastic spoon in my mouth. I couldn't say I blamed them; for many days I had been portraying a pathetic, weak girl, eating only enough to stay alive, getting my drugs and hiding under the covers. Jason looked at me with a doe-eyed expression I knew all too well. I smiled a tight smile and looked back at my meager meal.

Jason was a good kid. He tried to do everything he could to, not only protect his sister, but the others in the ragged group. I didn't want him getting mixed up with me *or* the monsters, as Zoe called them. He was too young, too innocent, to take on that much responsibility.

"Is no one gonna talk about this?" a strangled voice choked out. It was the young nurse, the one who spouted out biblical end of days shit. She stood, extending her hand and pointing at me. "She *killed* two people and no one seems to care."

"She saved us," Jason defended. "You saw it. Those girls we let in..." he shook his head. "They weren't human anymore. If Orissa hadn't killed them then they would have killed us."

"You can't refute that," Padraic agreed. "Nor forget that they killed first. And we...we can't let anyone else in. It's too dangerous."

"She's dangerous," the nurse said. The group had gathered in a circle, sitting on the cement floor near the heavy steel doors. An older man who was across from me rolled his eyes at her. He caught my gaze and winked. Jason and his sister Sonja were to my right, looking back and forth from the nurse to Padraic, waiting for his response.

"I'm more dangerous than what's out there?" I asked, looking up from my bowl.

"We don't know what's out there," she snapped.

Padraic held up his hands. "Exactly. Which is why we cannot let anyone else in, even if they knock like those girls did. It's not worth the risk."

That caused a hush of murmurs amongst everyone. Half seemed to agree, some objected, others doubted there was anyone left to let in.

"It shouldn't be too much longer until the rescue groups come and save us." Though he spoke confidently and smiled like he meant it, I knew Padraic was lying. No one was coming. Hell, maybe all of FEMA had died too.

I cleared my throat. "You all can thank me anytime." I stood, wishing I could make a dramatic exit as I marched away from the group to the corner of the room that housed old wheelchairs. I flopped down in one, bored, annoyed, scared, and on edge. I picked at the crackling foam armrest.

"You didn't ask for painkillers today," Padraic said, coming up to me.

"Nope."

"I'm gonna guess you never needed them."

"Nope," I repeated.

"Then why?"

I sighed and shrugged. "Why not? What else am I going to do?" I dug my nails into the foam. I didn't want to tell him that I hadn't taken the virus outbreak seriously until I saw it firsthand and until now my plan had been to get out of this Godforsaken basement. "I knew I needed that time to heal, so what better way than to do it in an almost happy, drug-induced coma?"

"You could be more social?" he suggested.

"What's the point?"

"It's good for you, for everyone, and I see Zoe's taken a shine to you."

When I didn't answer, he walked away. I stayed in that corner for the rest of the morning, busy being pissed off at everything.

<hr>

I accompanied Jason to the storage closet. At first glance, the large pantry seemed to house a lot of food. But when I mentally divided it up among fifty-two—well, now fifty-one—people eating three times a day, it wouldn't last us more than a week.

Since Padraic seemed to have taken on the leadership role, I pulled him aside after we ate our yummy lunch of microwaved, frozen pizza.

"You told me there was enough food to last 'awhile'," I said.

He only frowned.

"Why did you lie? We're lucky if we make it another week."

His shoulders sagged. "I know."

"Then why didn't you say something?"

"What was I supposed to do?" he begged.

"I don't know. Go find more?"

"I can't leave—"

"—my patients, I know," I finished for him, rolling my eyes. "Great plan. Stay here and medicate the shit out of them while they starve to death."

"Shh! Orissa, I don't want the kids to know." He put his hand on my shoulder. "If we just wait a few more days, maybe someone will come for us like they promised."

"No one is coming! Don't you get that?" I waved my hands around. "Don't you all get that? No one is coming for us, and we can't stay here forever." Megan's baby cried, as if he knew the truth my words held.

Jason nodded. "What should we do?" he asked.

"Get out of here, leave. This basement will be our tomb. The food will run out…and what about when winter comes?"

Padraic took my hand in his. "Orissa," he said, his accent heavy when he spoke my name. "Come talk to me out here." He took me out of the safe room and closed the door. "I know we will run out of food. I know it will be cold in the winter."

"Then why aren't you doing anything about it?"

"There's not much I can do; these people are sick, Orissa. They physically cannot survive without their medications."

"So you're just going to stay here and die with them?"

"Yes, I will take care of them for as long as I can."

Stupid, noble Irish man. "Let me bring food," I offered.

"From where?"

"Anywhere, I think a grocery store would be a good start."

"We don't know what it's like out there."

"Exactly. It might not be so bad," I tried.

"Don't be a fool, Orissa."

"We have to at least try," I pleaded, hoping to appeal to his empathetic side. "And I'm not your prisoner. You can't keep me here against my will."

"We're going to set it up so it's safe here…and safe for us out there, as safe as it can be. Then I'm going with you."

I rolled my eyes at his chivalry. Objecting might have been the decent thing to do, insisting that he was more valuable here than dead. But I really didn't want to go out there alone.

Padraic instructed a nurse, more than once, about which patients should receive which medications. He hesitated and stammered; always sure that he had overlooked something. In the end, I think he decided that getting his charges food was just as important as keeping them medicated.

"Let's go," I finally said, after Padraic had gone over his lists with the nurse for the hundredth time. She had been taking care of the patients for days. She knew what she was doing.

"Now?"

"No, we'll wait until the crazies go to sleep. Of course now. When else?"

He nodded. "Right. I'll go tell the others."

So far only the nurse knew. She didn't look happy about the plan, only resigned.

"Hurry up, ok?" I wanted to leave before fear stopped me.

"Alright." He scuttled back into the room. I leaned against the wall, wishing I was familiar with this town. Several minutes later, Padraic returned. He wasn't alone. Jason, Sonja, and the two guys who'd helped move the bodies accompanied him.

"They're coming too," he informed me.

"No," I replied shortly. Padraic seemed to be in good shape. I was banking on him keeping up with me. I was quick, a natural athlete, as my grandmother liked to say. I could take care of myself, but five others?

"Safety in numbers," one of the men said with a wry smile. The moment he spoke, I did a double take. It was as if my grandpa, the man who'd taught me so much, was right there with me in the hallway. Everything from his salt and pepper hair, strong jaw line covered in gray stubble, and green and black plaid shirt was familiar. His eyes were brown, reminding me he was just a stranger. I'd gotten my blue-green eyes from Grandpa.

Couldn't think about my grandpa now…

"Weapons," I sighed, "You need weapons." Annoyed no one had thought that far ahead, I went back into the safe room, pulling apart machinery to make spears and shanks. They weren't my first choice, but better than nothing. "Alright," I said, examining the two feet of metal I had in my hands. I fashioned a point at the end of the rod I had taken out of the IV stand. "Where is the closest grocery store?"

Jason and Sonja weren't from this town either. Padraic lived on the opposite side, away from the slums, but the two men were familiar.

"There's one block away," the older of the two men, the one who reminded me of my grandfather, told me. He had a firm grasp on his makeshift weapon, holding it as if he knew what he was doing. "On foot, it's just a few minutes' walk."

"Great, let's go." I wanted to know his name, but didn't ask. What was the point of getting chummy with people who might die? Though he seemed the most capable of the group and constantly looked around us for danger. I led the way up the dark stairs, unlocking the main basement doors slowly. Suddenly dreading leaving the safety of this dungeon, my hand shook as I pushed the door open.

Since I was in front, I peered around the door. This hall was dark as well; dull emergency lights cast shadows on the ransacked hospital. Tentatively, I moved out of the stairwell. I had no idea where we were. Knowing we had to be somewhere in the middle of the hospital, I went to the right. Muscles stiff with anticipation, my eyes darted madly around for any signs of life. Padraic nodded for me to continue. I rounded a corner and froze.

"What is it?" Sonja whimpered.

"Nothing bad just…" I motioned to the glass shattered all over the tile. I was barefoot.

"I'll carry you over it," Padraic offered. Knowing how this situation fared for Bruce Willis in *Die Hard*, I didn't balk at his proposal. We were a good ten feet past the glass when he finally set me down.

"Thanks. My clothes," I started, "where are they?"

Padraic didn't know what I meant.

"The exam room I was in. Where is it?"

"Orissa, I don't think it's a good idea," he advised.

"You can't carry me over every sharp thing," I added pointedly.

Jason butted in saying, "She's right."

"Thank you," I noted, pressing a smile.

With a sigh, Padraic directed us to the exam room. Bodies littered the hall. The smell was nauseating. Sonja clutched her brother's arm, not wanting to look at the decaying humans. I slipped into the room. My clothes were still there and I hurriedly got dressed. I dumped the contents of my purse onto the floor, only putting back what I really needed: the notebook, keys, a bottle of hand sanitizer, lip balm, a hair tie and my taser. I debated if I needed my wallet. Not wanting to just leave it here, I pulled out my ID and the little cash I still had, stuffing it into my leather bag. My cell phone had died days ago. Seeing it as useless, I left it on the floor. I slung the strap over my head, pulled on my boots, and dashed out of the room.

Padraic pointed to the right. Silently, we walked through the hospital, passing more bodies. Sunlight filtered through the dirt- and blood-splattered windows in the lobby.

Something scuttled behind the front desk. I whirled around, raising the piece of metal. Sonja let out a muffled scream. She was our weak link, I knew in that moment. And Jason would die trying to protect his sister. He stood in front of her, ready to defend.

"Shh!" I whispered harshly, shaking my head. Sonja pressed her hand over her mouth, tears welling in her eyes. Carefully, I advanced. Whatever was lurking behind the desk grumbled, moved quickly, and rumpled papers. Picking up what was supposed to be a decorative vase from the desk, I threw it as far as I could to the side. It clattered loudly on the ground.

The thing lurched out, seeking the source of the noise. Half of its face was burned and bloody, inhibiting me from guessing its sex or race. One leg was twisted, obviously broken. Still, it moved with impressive speed. At first it was too distracted by the noise. It abruptly skidded to a stop and sniffed the air. Slowly, it turned to look at us, salivating. It snarled and roared before coming after us.

Sonja screamed again, grabbing onto Jason for dear life. I circled around, raising my metal rod to crash it down in its head. The thing turned so fast it startled me. I recoiled, tripping over a fallen stack of medical files, my weapon bouncing out of my hand and rolling away from me. I pulled my knees to my chest and kicked, hitting the disgusting person in the chest. It staggered back. The older man in the plaid shirt that I didn't know hit it over the head with his weapon: a broken two by four. I was so thankful he came with us.

The thing dropped to its knees. I sprang up, grabbed the rod and drove it through its chest; blood weakly splattered out. I yanked my weapon back, panting. My eyes met the older man's. "I don't know your name," I spat out.

"Logan," he said. "I'm Logan."

"Orissa."

He winked. "I know. I think we all know."

"Ok." I nodded. My heart was still racing. "We need to go on."

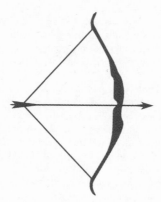

CHAPTER 5

The glass front of the grocery store had been broken, causing a small flicker of fear to rise up in me. So far, every place we passed had been quiet. The world seemed truly dead. But this was different.

From what I had been told, the virus outbreak came on so suddenly no one had time to prepare. I was banking on the notion that the stores hadn't been emptied, that people had left in a chaotic panic, leaving canned food and water behind.

The air was cold, characteristic of Indiana October. The sun beat down warmly upon us. If it wasn't for the surrounding decay, I could have said today was a picturesque fall day. I swallowed, nodded at Padraic and stepped inside the store.

The thick cobwebs confused me for all of two seconds. Halloween decorations colorfully decorated the registers. Stepping over a broken jack-o-lantern, I eased further into the store. A rusty squeak and a metallic clang sent my nerves on end. I spun around, almost slipping on pumpkin parts, only to see Sonja guiltily shrug as she pushed a cart.

"How else are we going to carry everything?" she asked apologetically.

"You're right," Padraic said, and got a cart himself. "There's no way we can carry everything back." He pushed his cart forward, realized the wheel stuck and rattled loudly, and traded it in for another.

"Sonja, Jason, Padraic," I said in a low voice. "Get water. That should be your first priority. If there's still room left in your cart, get juice, preferably the 100% kind, not the sugary crap." The other man Padraic had chosen to come with us had introduced himself during our walk to the store as Deron. He was young, in his mid twenties at best, and had black tattoos covering every inch of his exposed skin. He stood behind Logan now, so I decided that the three of us would group together. "Deron, Logan, and I will find food. Be quiet. Two of you load up supplies while the other watches. Scream only if necessary."

Without giving anyone a chance to dispute my plan, I strode forward, bypassing the deli section of the store, which I could smell. Sunlight illuminated the front of the store; its rays not reaching the back. In the dark, we fumbled with dumping boxes of beef jerky, dried fruit, and nuts into our cart.

"Maybe there's more in the back," I said, as I took the last box of beef jerky off the shelf.

"Maybe," Deron agreed.

"We need to find a flashlight first," I instructed, squinting to read the hanging signs. We detoured down the snack food isle; Deron suggested we get chips and cookies for the kids. Chips and cookies weren't healthy when you weren't trying to survive.

"If there's still room," I told him. "We need to save room for the important stuff." When we walked down the personal hygiene section, I pulled toothbrushes off the rack. My teeth felt absolutely disgusting. "Jack pot!" I excitedly exclaimed after seeing a display of batteries. I emptied it into the cart, telling Deron to open a pack to put in the flashlight he had picked up. Deron flicked on the light. Logan pushed the cart and I led, staying alert for infected people. We successfully raided the storage room. Our cart was now over flowing with jerky, nuts, yogurt covered raisins, crackers, and cans of fruits and vegetables.

We made it out of the parking lot before we noticed him, casually walking down the street. His arms swung at his sides and he appeared relaxed, head tipped slightly to enjoy the warm sun. Nevertheless, we halted, jolting our carts to a standstill so abruptly that a few cans of peas flew out and rolled away. The noise caught his attention. He dropped down to his hands and knees and screamed.

"I got it!" I shouted, brandishing my metal rod like a sword. I rushed ahead, waiting for the maniac to cross the street. He jumped up and down, looking like a crazed baboon, screaming. My heart thumped, my breathing quickened. What was he waiting for? *Just run across the street like a good insane person and get this over with.* His eyes darted all around. Maybe he couldn't see me? Apart from being a crazed, homicidal lunatic, something looked…off. His skin was pale and had a blue tint. I edged forward another foot. His eyes were void of color.

He leapt up, arms out, coming toward me. I swung the metal, hitting him in the teeth.

"Keep moving!" I yelled behind me. I hit the crazy over the head one more time before plunging the pointy end into his chest. Using my foot to pry him off my weapon, I turned and nearly screamed myself. Thick, brown blood oozed out of his wound. The crazy sat up, unfazed and still alive. What the hell? I had stabbed him right in the heart. He couldn't be alive.

Slowly, he rose and reached out at me. For good measure, I stabbed him in the heart again without success. He didn't so much as look down at the gaping holes. Hands shaking, I rammed the rod into his forehead. That did the trick. Instantly, he died, or re-died.

Heart thumping in fear, I stared at the body. What the hell was going on? I had just stabbed him— twice—in the freaking heart and he didn't die. That wasn't possible.

Distracted, I didn't hear the footsteps behind me until hands grabbed my shoulders. I twisted and came face to face with a giant crazy. He stood well over six feet and was solid. He wouldn't have been someone you wanted to mess with *before* he became infected.

He shoved me and I stumbled, tripping over the body. The piece of metal pipe fell from my hand. The crazy leaned over me, growling and showing his teeth. Shit. I was on the ground, legs tangled over the dead body, and this guy was freaking huge. I couldn't push him away.

Then Logan was there, right behind the crazy. I hadn't even seen him coming. With practiced grace, he closed in on the crazy, put his hands out, and grabbed his head. I turned away but not before I saw Logan snap the crazy's neck.

"Thanks," I said. Logan extended a hand and pulled me to my feet.

I looked across the street and, if possible, my panic increased. There were more crazies!

"Go!" I shouted.

Padraic whipped around and shouted. Sonja screamed. Jason pushed his cart forward, breaking into a sprint. "Go!" I shouted again. Deron slowly started forward with our heavy cart. Rooted in fear, I watched the maniacs lumber from the parking lot. Moving slowly and groaning, I doubted they could easily catch us.

There was no mistake: Zoe's monsters had become full-fledged zombies.

I hurried after the group. The loaded carts slowed them down. I needed to do something. Skidding to a stop, I desperately looked around for something, anything to use against the pursuing horde. Three cans of peas rolled to a stop in the middle of the road. I dove to get them, chucking the first can as hard as I could into the herd of seven zombies that stalked us. It missed and exploded in a waste of food on the ground. Actually aiming this time, I threw the second can into the face of a female zombie. It broke her jaw, her bones hanging on limp fragments of skin. She kept moving.

"Shit," I swore and blindly threw the last can, knowing it wouldn't make a difference. The zombies were gaining speed, catching the scent of their prey. We couldn't outrun them, not with the carts. Sonja's shouts yanked my attention away from the zombies. Another one limped forward, dragging a broken ankle. My mind raced. I wasn't about to die at the hands of these creatures. No, not today;

not ever.

"This way!" I shouted. "Leave the carts!" I darted around an abandoned car, weaving my way over debris to the back of the store. Without checking to see if any of my living companions had followed, I jumped and yanked down the roof's access ladder and frantically climbed up.

I startled when Sonja joined me, doubting her ability to move quickly. I pulled her away from the edge just in time for Jason to scramble out of the way. Deron came next, followed by Logan. Padraic was last, tumultuously pulling the ladder up and away from the grubby hands of the zombies.

"What the fuck?" Jason panted.

"Zombies," I breathed.

"No," Padraic said, catching his breath. "That's not possible."

Jason motioned to the edge of the building. "You wanna tell me *that's* not possible. What the hell else are they?"

Below us, the zombies gathered—almost two dozen by now—smacking the sides of the shopping center and moaning. The stench of death was heavy in the crisp, fall air.

"Can they get up?" Sonja asked, her voice quivering.

"No," Logan answered, precariously leaning over the edge. "The ladder is too high. They'd have to jump."

"But Orissa was able to get it down."

"She jumped," Logan went on. "I don't think they're smart enough anymore. And if they do come up, we can use it to our advantage." He held up his weapon, slicing it through the air. "Only one will come at a time. I think we can handle it."

I nodded, agreeing with him. He was determined to keep us safe, and I was so thankful for that.

Deron looked down. "I hope you're right."

I followed his lead and glanced down, too. I shook my head. "They came out of nowhere. Sons of bitches are faster than they look."

"Yeah," Sonja agreed. "Aren't zombies supposed to be slow?"

"Zombie's aren't supposed to be," Padraic remarked. His blue eyes met mine; he was scared.

"No," I agreed. "But they are now."

"Orissa," Jason asked. "What do we do now?"

I shook my head, running my hand through my hair. "I—I don't know." I was too fazed by the zombies to think it was weird he was asking me for advice. "Wait. I don't think they'll stay down there forever. Then we get back to the hospital." As much as I hated being trapped, it was safe.

"But they *can* wait forever," Sonja argued. "They're dead. We're the ones who can't wait."

"I know," I said, pacing around. "Ok." I sat back down. "We wait for now, hope they disperse. That's all I have for now."

"It's as good a plan as any," Logan said. "We have a vantage point up here. It would be suicide to try and escape now."

My plan seemed to go over, since everyone agreed, but it wasn't like we had a genius back up plan. Before we knew it, the sun was setting and the zombies still milled below us. Without the sun it was cold, really freaking cold. We huddled together, deciding to sleep in shifts. There was no way I would be able to fall asleep, no matter how tired I was. Turns out, neither could Jason or Logan. We took the first watch, each taking a direction to gaze blindly at.

"You two should try and get some rest," Logan said, his gruff voice cutting through the grumbling hum of the zombies' constant moaning.

"It's ok," I whispered. "I can't sleep knowing they're down there. I'll wake up in just minutes."

"Hyper sleep," he said quietly. "I got familiar with that when I was in Vietnam."

My heart skipped a beat. "My grandpa fought in that war too," I said so quietly I wasn't sure if Logan even heard me. I turned my head down, inspecting the blood crusted end of my metal pipe so he wouldn't see the emotion that was sure to be apparent on my face.

Somewhere in the hazy dawn of morning, I leaned against an air vent and drifted into a light sleep.

Not even twenty minutes later, I woke up, my heart pounding. Tiredness clung to me, urging me to close my eyes. Padraic spoke softly to Sonja. Deron walked around the perimeter. Ok, we were safe for now. I let myself get pulled back under. I woke up again not long after. My brain just wouldn't let my body relax. For the next two hours I repeated the irritating pattern of barely falling asleep and then startling awake.

This time, I got up. As I stood to stretch, Logan waved me down. Instantly, I dropped. Army-crawling over to him, I shrugged as if to ask: "what's going on?"

"The zombies are leaving," he mouthed.

I peered over the edge, my heart swelling with joy. They were yards away, moving on to find another source of food. No one dared move a muscle until they were long out of sight.

"What do we do now?" Sonja asked me.

I turned to Padraic. I hated the idea of using a car; cars were noisy, but I didn't see another option.

"Do you have a car? I mean at the hospital?" I asked him.

"Yeah I—"

"Good. Our new plan is to get back. We are not equipped to fight them. I'll go first, and when I say run, run. Got it? Logan, stay in the back. Make sure everyone is moving."

After being satisfied everyone listened, I climbed down the ladder. Not wanting to make any noise, I jumped the last six feet to the ground, the shock stinging my ankles. After checking to see if the coast was clear, I rounded the corner. "Run!" I loudly whispered. I sprinted forward, leaving everyone else in the dust, and passing the carts of food. I leapt over random crap that made the streets a freaking obstacle course.

A lone zombie meandered about with one of his arms missing. I pulled the metal rod from my boot and rammed it through his eye. Instantly he went limp. In the few seconds it took me to kill—or re—kill him—the others caught up. Nodding in approval, Padraic encouraged me to go on.

My lungs burned by the time my feet graced the hospital entrance. I put my hands on my knees, gasping for air. I was nearly recovered by the time the others made it in. Once everyone else was able to breathe normally again, we picked our way into the hospital. Adrenaline running, I jumped at every sound, expecting to see a zombie, or worse, a fast-moving crazy person.

But what we found was much worse...

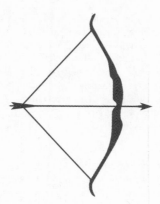

CHAPTER 6

The heavy metal door had been pried open. A horde of zombies stomped around the safe room and everyone inside lay dead on the floor.

"No!" Sonja started forward, tears streaming down her face. I shoved her aside, into Jason's arms, and slammed the door shut. "What are you doing?" she demanded.

"There has to be more than a hundred zombies in there and who knows what else," I told her.

"They could still be alive!" She reached for the door. Jason grabbed her around the waist, pulling her off her feet.

"Shut up!" I whispered. "They respond to sound."

"What do we do?" Padraic asked, his eyes filled with fear.

I felt a small twist of pity for him at seeing everyone he'd tried to save reduced to zombie food.

"Your car. Where is it?"

"The garage."

"Keys?" Sometimes I didn't need keys, but I imagined that Padraic owned a newer model car. If there was a way to hotwire a late model, I wasn't familiar with it.

His face went blank for a moment. "Third floor. In my locker."

"Ok, then, take me there," I said.

He nodded. My hands shook. I forced a stoic expression and eased away from the door. I had just put one foot on the basement stairs when I heard her call my name.

"Zoe!" I clamped my hand over my mouth.

"Orissa!" her weak voice carried through the dark hall. "Help me, Orissa!"

"Zoe, you need to be quiet!" I called as loudly as I dared. Padraic rushed forward, following her voice. I reached out to grab him, my hand missing the back of his lab coat by only an inch. The crazy person, however, was close enough to grab him around the throat. Having left my only weapon in the broken skull of a zombie, I dropped and spun, kicking the crazy's legs out from under him. He fell, taking Padraic with him. I hadn't counted on that.

Padraic scrambled to get away. The crazy snarled and hissed, trying with enraged might to bite into the doctor's flesh. His cacophonous screams were sure to get the other zombies' attention. Careful not to miss and nail Padraic in the face, I kicked the back of the crazy's skull, forgetting that they didn't react to pain. I needed to kill him before he killed Padraic.

I tangled my fingers in the crazy's hair and yanked. He growled, released Padraic, and turned on me.

"Get me something!" I yelled, annoyed no one was helping us. The crazy slunk on all fours, hissing. Misjudging his strength, I tried to counter his jump with my own weight. He slammed into me, whacking me against the wall. My head hit hard, sending black, sharp pain throughout my body. My legs threatened to buckle. The crazy opened his mouth, set on ripping his teeth into my flesh. Letting my knees give out was actually a good idea. I slid down the wall, darted in between his legs, got back on my feet, and kicked him into the wall in seconds. Padraic outstretched his hand, holding a broken brick. I took it, and, closing my eyes, brought it down on the crazy's head.

The brick fell out of my grip. It sickened me; the crack of his head, the way he still growled as his blood gushed out. Padraic took my hand and pulled me to him.

"Are you alright?" he asked, breathing heavily.

"Yes," I answered, too worked up to tell him, 'no, I wasn't alright, you freaking idiot, I just killed someone.'

"Thank God."

I heard Logan shout. He and Deron were fighting off zombies. At least their attackers were slow moving. I picked up the brick and ran over, smashing in the skull of one of the zombies. Its blood splattered and I slammed my eyes shut just in time to block out the infectious ooze.

"There're too many!" Deron panted.

"We have to get out of here!" I agreed.

Padraic objected. "Where are Sonja and Jason?"

"Zoe," I said under my breath. Sonja would have wanted to find her and Jason wouldn't have let her go alone. "Five minutes," I told him, though I had no way of tracking the time. "If we don't see them then we leave. Or get killed."

His blue eyes met mine. Begrudgingly, he nodded.

"I'm not dying in a basement," I said with finality. I wanted so badly to race up the basement stairs. But I knew I could never live with myself if I did nothing. I had to try to save them.

Logan took out another zombie. Three more took its place. Like an angry hive, zombies filtered out of the safe room. We couldn't fight them all. Even if we had proper weapons, there were just too freaking many.

"This way!" Padraic suggested, jogging ahead. Still holding the brain covered brick, I followed. We blindly crashed down the hall, hearts racing. Padraic stopped suddenly and I bumped into him. "Shh!" he said, instantly irritating me. I wasn't making a sound. His shushing was highly unnecessary. I pushed past him as if that would help me see into the darkness. Something sizzled behind me. With a pop, a match blazed alive. Logan held it up, casting the flickering light around us. The match stayed lit only long enough to illuminate the face of a mad woman. She babbled incoherently, repeatedly walking into the wall. She hid from the light, retreating away.

No one moved. I held my breath, hating how loudly it escaped from my lungs. Terror pulsed through my body. I couldn't help the tremors that took over. With hands just as shaky, Logan lit another match. The woman was gone.

"Maybe she's gone for good," I suggested quietly, knowing it wasn't true. "Let's keep going."

"Where are we going?" Padraic asked, his hand finding its way into mine. I gripped his fingers tightly, trying to will the shakiness from my muscles.

"We need out," I said. Then the match burned out. When Logan struck another, the woman was behind Deron. "Look out!" I cried, pulling my hand from Padraic's. I was fast; she was faster. She wrapped her arms around Deron's neck and sank her teeth into his tattooed skin. He yelled and staggered back. She released and clamped down again, blood spurting out of the first wound. Padraic grabbed my hand again.

"She severed an artery; there's no way..." he cut off. There's no way Deron can live was what he meant.

And just like that Deron was motionless...silent. His attacker hovered over him, and he was lost to us.

"Come on!" I shouted, racing forward in the darkness. I tripped over God knows what, falling hard on my knees. "Mother fucker!" I swore.

"Orissa?" a frail voice called.

"Zoe!" I shouted back.

"I got her!" someone, presumably Jason, yelled back.

"Where are you?" I asked, cursing myself for not grabbing a flashlight. "Don't move, just keep talking and I'll follow your voice."

Padraic—or at least I thought it was Padraic—helped me up. I took hold of his wrist.

"Hold onto each other," I instructed, not wanting to get separated. "Jason," I called. "Talk to me."

"Ok."

"I mean keep talking. Talk until I find you." Or until a zombie eats your brains.

"We are in the basement. It's dark. Uh, and cold." His voice grew louder.

"Keep talking," I instructed.

"Sonja and I came here with our mom. She had a headache and she—"

"Never mind, what's your favorite sport?"

"Football. I like the Colts."

Finally, I felt body heat. My fingers touched warm flesh. I was almost afraid to ask.

"Orissa?" Sonja whimpered.

"Yeah. Grab onto me."

"Orissa!" Zoe cried.

Thank God, I let out a breath. "Ok, everyone needs to be really, really quiet," I directed. "Logan, got any more matches?"

"Just three," he told me.

"Turn everyone. Then light one."

The match fizzed. For now, we were alone in the hall. Along with Zoe, Hilary and another young girl not any older than Zoe who had made it out of the safe room. I took the lead, finding my brick and holding it up, ready for a fight. I could hear the shuffling and moaning of the zombies as we darted around a corner. The new girl coughed loudly and wheezed. Great, we had a sick asthmatic with a cough loud enough to wake the dead. Literally.

The zombies' pace quickened. The girl doubled over, unable to catch her breath. The second to last match faded to its end just in time for me to see Padraic pick her up and toss her over his shoulder. Logan struck the last match; if we didn't find the hall with the stairs soon we were screwed. The fire came and went with no luck.

Running my hand along the wall in front of me, I led the group down another hall. Every few seconds I stopped, listening for the dragging of feet. I was about to give up when a very dull glow came into view. Dim illumination from the security lights shone above the stairwell. Once everyone was out, I slammed the heavy door shut, a moot attempt considering how many zombies were afoot.

After leaving the others in the safety of a reinforced closet with Logan promising to keep them safe, Padraic and I headed through the hallways toward his locker and the parking garage.

"What kind of car do you have?" I asked suddenly.

Padraic gave me a 'what the hell does it matter' look. "A Range Rover."

Figures. I rolled my eyes. "How many people fit in it?"

"Oh," he said, cluing into what I was getting at. "Five."

"I suppose we all will fit. It's not like we have a choice."

From inside a room, a crazy jumped out, knocking me to the ground.

"Get the keys!" I demanded. "I can hold him off. Go!"

The crazy hissed and snapped. Oddly, my martial arts instructor's voice rang in my head. *Remember that you are worth defending, Orissa.* We'd spent several months ignoring the traditional methods and had focused on self defense. I was confident I could get away with minimal harm from a human attacker. I knew the weak points, and I knew going for the eyes, nose, and throat were good ways to stop an attack. But that relied on inflicting pain, and the crazies didn't react to pain. The crazy's hands wrapped around my throat.

In a minute I would pass out.

With my free hand, I struck the crazy's face, shoving my palm into his nose, driving the bone up. Unable to breathe, he let me go. I scrambled out from under him. I had nothing to kill him with. A med cart sat a foot behind me. I grabbed it and shoved it at him. He fell back, tumbling over an overturned wheelchair. I had been trained how to fight, not how to kill.

You are worth defending. And so was everyone else. The madman crouched, saliva dripping from his mouth as he growled. My body hummed with adrenaline. A biohazard trash can had fallen off the med cart and cracked, spilling dirty, used needles all over the floor.

"Here goes nothing," I said, as I dove down to get one. I pulled the needle back and lunged, driving it into the man's chest. I pushed it in; the needle bent on his sternum, not killing him with a bubble of air as I'd hoped. Defeated, I backed into a room, gagging instantly at the smell of the rotting corpse that had been left behind. Expeditiously, I scanned the room. There was a small bathroom in the room across from where I was standing. I circled around the bed, knocking over the IV stand. The tubes pulled the corpse's arm, and I grimaced, not wanting to look.

My heart was racing so fast I thought I was going to have a heart attack. With my back to the bathroom, I stood completely still, hoping that the crazy would act as predictably as I assumed. I was relieved when he jumped. I dropped out of the way, spun and slammed the door on his hand. I wheeled the bed in front of the door and booked out of the room. Padraic was racing down the hall toward me, keys in hand, thank God. Thank God, because I knew the door wouldn't hold the crazy.

"Run!" I shouted and took off, not bothering to wait for him. I tore down the stairs. My thighs burned from the exertion. Forcing myself to use some grace, I slowed and tried not to stomp down the last few steps.

"We have to go this way," Padraic breathlessly told me, pointing away from the closet. "To the parking garage."

"Ok." For a minute, we caught our breath. Then I darted out of the stairwell to the closet. Silently, I waved everyone to follow Padraic. No zombies got in our way as we hurriedly jogged to the parking lot. They must all be in the basement, a fact for which I was both thankful and wary; why would the zombies stick together?

We piled into the Range Rover, sitting on top of each other. Padraic gunned it out of the parking garage, smashing through the motion-censored gate.

I knew exactly where we were going.

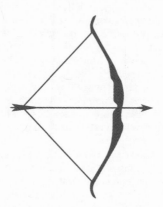

CHAPTER 7

When no overwhelming stench of death hit me, after unlocking Aunt Jenny's apartment door, I walked inside. Everything was where it should be. The banana bread I had made the day of the outbreak sat on the stove moldy, but untouched. Maybe Aunt Jenny had gotten out in time. A hard ball of guilt wound its way around my stomach, telling me that she would have tried, at the very least, to find me. I was her favorite (if only) niece, as she liked to remind me. There was nothing I could do about it now.

Along with locking the door, Jason shoved a chair under the handle. It was a good idea, but executed prematurely. We didn't know if we were alone. I crossed the living room into the kitchen, rustling around in the knife drawer for the biggest knife I could find. Something rattled the bathroom door. Sonja screamed and I wished it was humane to gag her. No one liked a screamer.

Logan looked at me. I nodded. I raised the knife, moving my feet as quietly as I could. He put his hand on the doorknob, mouthing 'on three.' I counted along with him. *One, two, three!* The door opened. A cat ran out.

"Damn it, Finickus," I swore, letting my hand fall to my side. What was he doing trapped in the bathroom? A big bag of cat food had been dumped on the floor and the sink and tub were filled with water. "Oh," I said out loud, feeling a bit of hope. Aunt Jenny had left him with plenty of food and water. That meant she had left with her mind intact and had also provided us with something to wash up with.

I peered into the living room. Hilary, Jason and Sonja sat on the couch. Zoe traded her pink stuffed cat for Finickus. Logan looked out the window and Padraic tried to help the asthmatic girl breathe normally.

"Take slow breaths, Lisa," he said, his voice calming. The girl gasped for air, tears rolling down her face. I felt bad for her because I had no faith in her survival. I walked into the room; a fuzzy feeling surrounded me when I saw Aunt Jenny's unfinished tea on the coffee table. Then I felt their eyes. Every one of my seven companions looked at me.

"What do we do now?" Jason asked.

"I don't know," I quickly answered. I didn't like the hope in his voice.

"I'm tired," Zoe whimpered. "And hungry."

"We should rest," Padraic suggested.

I couldn't disagree. My body ached and I was exhausted.

"Not all at once," I told him, leaving the living room to search for food. There was nothing readily available that offered much, if any, nourishment. I extracted a bag of pretzels and a box of Oreos from the cupboard. Aunt Jenny was a fan of canned soup, but without a microwave or range top to heat it on, it wouldn't be easy to choke down. Remembering that Finickus preferred tuna over canned cat food, I opened the cupboard under the sink and found ten cans. Perfect, one for each. I opened the cans, plopped one upside down on the floor for Finickus and delivered our less than tasty breakfast.

Zoe, Lisa, and Sonja curled up together in Aunt Jenny's bed after they ate and fell quickly asleep. I went into the bathroom and gave myself the coldest sponge bath ever, using water from the tub. I even managed to wash my hair. I stood in front of the mirror, staring into my green eyes as I brushed it out. We couldn't stay here. There was nothing left and too many zombies and crazies. I wanted to go north, to see if one of the only people I truly loved in this world was still alive. I put my bathrobe on and darted across the hall into my bedroom. I hadn't bothered to unpack anything except my clothes since I'd moved in with my aunt.

I'll be the first to admit my wardrobe was more than a little bipolar. The right side of my closet was full of 'going out' clothes: tight jeans, short skirts and dresses, low cut tops that showed off my boobs and the like. The left side housed practical clothing from summers spent at my grandparents' Kentucky farm: comfortable pants, thermal shirts good for layering, old tank tops that were meant for getting dirty. I changed into a clean pair of underwear before pulling on a pair of stretchy skinny jeans that would be good for running, but still offered more protection than thin athletic pants. I yanked a long sleeved shirt on before stuffing my arms into a fleece hoodie of brown. I pulled mismatching socks from my drawer.

I guessed Sonja to be about my size, though not quite as tall. I yanked a pair of loose fitting jeans so hard the hanger broke. Oh well. It's not like I'd be needing it. I picked out a thick hooded sweatshirt and another pair of socks. I could provide Lisa and Zoe with sweaters and hoodies too, but nothing I or Aunt Jenny owned would fit Hilary. And then there were the guys to think about. Padraic definitely couldn't gallivant around in thin scrubs.

I dragged a suitcase out from under the bed, throwing a few more long-sleeve shirts, another pair of pants, several more pairs of underwear, and socks into it. Without explaining what I was doing, I rummaged through the small apartment looking for anything that could be useful. I took minimal personal hygiene supplies from the bathroom, vitamins, a can opener, and the rest of the knives from the kitchen along with matches, candles, bleach, and duct tape. Logan was rooting around in the kitchen drawers, removing anything he thought could be helpful.

"Feel free to help," I snapped at the remaining three who sat dumbly in the living room.

"What are you doing?" Padraic asked, his voice level.

"Getting supplies," I replied, though I assumed it was obvious.

"How can I help?"

"Get supplies," I huffed, covering my nose as I opened the fridge. I poured the spoiled milk down the sink and rinsed the container with water from the bathtub.

"What are you doing?" Jason asked innocently, thinking I was cleaning. "I mean, does it matter anymore?"

"It's for gas," I explained. "We need to get as much as we can."

"How? I don't think the gas pumps work."

I chuckled. "Do you know how a siphon works?"

"I don't know what that is."

"You will," I promised. Together, we gathered up everything useful. I raked my long hair to the side, pulling it over my left shoulder, and braiding it. "You need clothes," I told Padraic.

I was about to suggest we go to his or Logan's house. Then it dawned on me that tons of other people lived in this apartment complex. Leaving Logan and Hilary to guard the sleeping girls, I led the others into the hall and to the neighbor's door. I knocked and pressed my ear to the wood. Nothing stirred. Stepping back, I kicked the center.

It didn't break. I kicked it again, right next to the dead bolt. The frame buckled. Two more kicks and I was in. When I caught Jason looking at me like I was Wonder Woman, I said,

"These are really cheap doors. They break easily."

The smell of decay hit us. I almost puked when I saw the dead bodies lying on the floor. Both had gunshot wounds to the head. I pried the gun from a wilted, dead hand, clicked on the safety, and stuck it in the back of my pants. "There has to be ammo in here somewhere," I said. "Look for a box of bullets. And take anything that could be useful."

Padraic and I left Jason and went back into the hall. Padraic kicked the next door in on his second try, revealing to me that he was strong. Another body lay on the floor, though this one must have died from the virus. We loaded up a bag with canned beans, tuna, and crackers. A set of keys hung on the wall. I grabbed them and went on to ransack the medicine cabinet.

"Padraic!" I called when my hands gripped something. "Will this help?" I tossed him the inhaler.

He read the label. "Yeah, I think so." He gawked admirably at me.

I told him to hurry and check the closet for clothes.

Eventually, we split up. I felt like I was burglarizing when I nosed through cabinets and drawers and lifted whole sets of keys. I kept looking behind me, both for crazies and for homeowners, as if they would show up any second. Even if they did, what would they do? I wondered if there were any police left. It certainly felt like we were the last ones in the city, which couldn't be true. If we had made it, surely others had.

"Preparation is the key to survival," I mumbled.

"What did you say?" Padraic asked, startling me. I hadn't heard him sneak up behind me.

"Nothing. It's just something my grandpa used to tell me." I looked at the unopened bottles of cranberry juice in his hands. "Awesome, that's my favorite," I said honestly.

"Mine too."

"Now if only I had a little Vodka…" I said with a hint of laughter, meeting Padraic's eyes. He had changed into jeans and a light blue T-shirt. Since his body wasn't covered up in baggy scrubs, I noticed for the first time that, though he was slender, he was firm and well built. A gray jacket was folded over his arm.

"We should get back and rest," he said.

"Sure."

We found Jason at the end of the hall, proudly carrying a box full of supplies. I noticed several video games stashed inside the heavy box. I opened my mouth to tell him it was pointless to bring games since we didn't even have electricity or the luxury of time to sit around playing them. I stopped myself, remembering that he was just a teenager and probably hadn't put a lot of thought into it. I gave him an approving smile and walked with him back to the apartment, making sure we didn't meet any unwelcome guests along the way. We dumped everything out in the middle of Aunt Jenny's living room, sorting the stuff into piles.

"So," Hilary asked, as she pulled a sweater over her scrubs. "What is our plan?"

I didn't like that she said 'our' plan. I had no intention of dragging them along, since my own plan was a shot in the dark and I knew it. "*My* plan, is to head a few hours north and see what it's like up there," I said, my face serious and neutral.

"Why north?" Hilary asked.

"There might be a quarantine at the college I went to," I calmly blurted and instantly regretted my sorry excuse for a lie. "It's a big school so something might have been set up."

"There were a lot of people here," Padraic interjected. "And nothing was set up."

"It's worth a shot," I said, my heart beating faster. He was right, which made me second guess my original plan. "And it's not that far. Since I have no traffic laws to abide by, it won't take long at all." He still didn't look convinced. "And if there's nothing I will try something else."

"You make it sound so easy," Padriac said. "I don't think it's a good idea."

I pressed my cold hands on my cheeks, red and warm from the rush of looting others' homes. "That's where I'm going. You guys are free to go wherever, you know."

Padraic actually leaned away with surprise. "Split up?"

I shrugged. "Why not? I don't want to drag you somewhere you don't want to go."

Padraic's pretty blue eyes widened. "I'd have no idea what to do without you," he admitted. Embarrassed, he smiled. "I'd figure it out eventually, but I'm quite out of my element."

"I think we all are," I said gently and returned his smile.

"You're right. Still, I'm hesitant to try anywhere that housed a lot of people."

"Then don't go," I told him. "You can stay here. If things don't work out for me, I'll come back and find you," I offered.

"Do you really think there's a quarantine there?" Hilary asked.

"Maybe," I lied since I had no idea. I was a decent liar. I could almost always look someone in the eyes while I did it and my stories always stayed consistent. Over the years I had discovered the best lies were the simplest. The less you had to remember, the less of a chance you had of messing up. "If we leave now we can make it there before nightfall."

"Leave tonight?" Jason asked, displeased at my haste.

"Why not? It's not like we have anything holding us back. The sooner the better anyway. It's only a matter of time before those, those *things* realize we're up here." I wrapped my arms around my body. "I feel trapped in here."

Padraic shook his head. "We're not rested. The five of us didn't get much sleep on that rooftop," he reminded me. Even though only a few hours had passed since this morning, the whole hiding on the roof from zombies seemed like it had happened days ago. I hated that he was right.

"You're right. We'll rest. It will give me more time to get supplies and find a good car. But as soon as the sun comes up tomorrow morning, I'm leaving and I'm not forcing anyone to come with me," I reminded him gently.

"We can't stay here," Jason voiced my earlier reasoning. "We will die."

"We will," Logan said softly, meeting my eyes. "Tomorrow morning it is, then. We will go north and see what it's like."

➤➤➤————————➤

I slept for a whole forty-five minutes, but I stayed in bed for another hour, trying not to think about zombies. Unsuccessfully, of course. Something didn't seem right. And it wasn't the obvious there-is-a-zombie-apocalypse thing happening. I threw back the covers, got out of bed, and prepared to interrogate Padraic.

Logan, Jason, and Hilary sat at the kitchen table, playing cards. Padraic slept on the couch. Damn it. I wasn't about to wake him up. I sat at the table next to Jason. My stomach growled. Jason nodded, silently telling me he was hungry too. Soup seemed appetizing, if only I could heat it up.

"I can," I said aloud. I got up, my chair scooting on the tile. I padded into the living room and took several candles from my 'candle and lighter' pile. I arranged them on the counter in between four glass cups. I set a pot on the cups, dumped several cans of soup into it, and waited.

"You're brilliant," Jason told me when I dished the warm soup into bowls.

"So I've been told," I said with a smile and devoured my soup. The girls woke up, the smell of food driving them out of their slumber. After they ate, I played several painstakingly boring games of Go Fish. Time passed slowly. But when the sun began to sink, I felt a hand of dread grip my heart. It would make sense that the crazies couldn't see in the dark. They were still human, after all. Like me, darkness left them vulnerable. I had a nagging feeling that it left me more vulnerable, too. The crazies had nothing to lose. I wished I had found a pair of night vision goggles.

I tossed my cards in the middle of the table, strode to the door, and removed the chair that had been propped under the handle.

"What are you doing?" Logan asked.

"I'm going to see what's up there," I said, pointing above me, meaning the third floor, "before it gets dark."

"I'll come with you." Logan stood from the table.

"Ok," I agreed. I wasn't too keen on going up there alone anyway.

Logan picked up a knife and joined me by the door.

➤➤➤————————➤

There was a zombie in the first apartment we forcefully opened. I think he had been old when the virus took him. It was hard to tell due to the decomposing state of his skin. My heart raced in fear and I struggled to hold the gun steady. Instead of rushing at us, opened mouthed and hungry, the zombie dragged his feet slowly in our direction, tripping over a rumpled rug. I looked at Logan, who stared back at me just as confused. I lowered the gun, not wanting to waste any ammo. Logan crossed the room and sunk the knife into the zombie's back, piercing the heart. But it didn't die.

"Haven't you seen any zombie movies?" I said, exasperated. "You have to get the brain." I held back a giggle, turning around just as the knife sliced through the air, piercing the bottom of the zombie's skull. I did a quick sweep of the apartment, finding nothing of significance. Wiping the bloody knife on a towel, Logan followed me down the hall.

"Wait," I told him, holding up a hand. "Do you hear that?"

"No," he said after a second.

"Well it stopped now." I shook my head. I knew I had heard something. "It was like a high pitched whine," I explained, moving forward. With the gun ready in my right hand, I pressed my ear against another door, three down from where we had been. I heard it again. "There!" I whispered. It sounded familiar and very non-zombie.

"Skip this one?" Logan suggested.

"Don't you want to know what's in there?" I asked.

"No. Let's go back and eat."

"We just ate. I know it's not much, but we have to get used to it." I shook my head and knocked on the door. A dog barked. "It's alive!" I exclaimed, realizing as soon as the words escaped my mouth that what I said was dumb and obvious. "Maybe others are," I added, knocking again. "Hello?!"

No one answered. I frowned and Logan shrugged. I stepped aside and let him kick the door.

Terror flashed through my veins as the Doberman jumped, putting his paws on me. Instead of biting me, he licked my face. The stub of his cropped tail waggled feverishly and he whined.

"Hi, buddy," I said, pushing the dog down. The place reeked of dog feces and urine. "Are your owners' home?"

Logan was looking around, seemingly unbothered by the smell.

"No one's here," I summed up and went back into the hall, gagging. Assuming the dog's owners had done what Aunt Jenny had done for Finickus, they were long gone. Before I could read the dog's ID tag, he took off. "You're welcome," I muttered.

"He was eager to leave," Logan chuckled. "Though I can't say I blame him."

"I know, right?" I turned to him. "Being locked in the basement, even though it was for our protection, was suffocating." I bit my lip and looked down the hall. "Though now we don't have a thick door to separate us from them. I don't know how I'm going to keep them safe." I closed my eyes, trying to hide my emotions.

"Orissa," Logan said softly.

Crap. He had seen the fear in my eyes. "I want you to know that I'm with you, that you don't have to do this alone. I might be an old man," he said with a half smile, "but I'm here. If you need a break, need to step away and take a minute to yourself, I'm here."

I felt as if my grandpa was standing before me, telling me that he was here for me, that we could get through anything together, just like we had during my parent's divorce. I looked up at Logan then quickly cast my eyes down. Stupid tears.

"Between the two of us, we might even teach them a thing or two along the way, right?" he said.

I turned my head back up and gave him a small smile and suddenly a weight was lifted. A pair of festering zombie hands, pulling me downward into hopeless despair let go. I didn't have to do this alone.

Logan put his hand on my shoulder. His touch was warm and reassuring. "You've got fire in you, kid. We'll make it. Together."

I put my hand over his and nodded. He was right. He had to be right. We would make it someway or the other.

I told Logan to check the end of the hall while I searched the rest of the apartments on this end. The next apartment I broke into was interesting.

He had to be the biggest movie nerd in history; posters of recognizable wizards and dragons covered the walls in the living room. The display case next to the couch housed several comic book figurines, a very fake looking machine gun, and a set of knives. Several swords hung on the wall and a bow rested on the coffee table. I wondered if it was even worth checking out the weapon replicas.

The first sword I removed from the wall was heavy, sharp, and impractical. The next one was shorter, just as sharp and maybe doable. I tossed it on the couch and contemplated whether or not I should take it. Running with a sword probably wasn't as easy to do as it looked in the movies. The knives were nicely made but dull, the leather carrying case they were in, however, could come in handy.

I picked up a bow, examining the gold swirls etched and painted into the wood. It was pretty, even I had to admit. I'd shot a bow many times; I preferred them when hunting since they were silent. But I'd never used a long bow like the one I was holding. I pulled back on the string with ease. Not even a twenty-pound pull, I thought and set it down. I picked up a metal knight's helmet, tapping my fingers to test its strength out of curiosity. I sighed, dropped it, and moved to the bookshelf behind me.

Along with books, DVDs, and figurines, the shelf held more replicas. I found two daggers that could be useful and one very sharp Samurai sword. These weapons could easily stab through anyone, but they still weren't ideal. You had to be close to something to stab it.

"Why couldn't you be some weird gun fanatic?" I spoke to no one. I rolled the weapons up in a sheet, found a case of bottled water and a jar of peanuts, shoved those in a bag and took the lot into the hall. I kicked open the next door to reveal an empty apartment. I was starting to feel the weight of not sleeping. I was relieved though. For the first time since this whole thing had started, I had someone to help us through, someone skilled. I had Logan...*We* had Logan.

Whoever lived here had taken everything useful, and the glass door to the balcony had been left open. Wind blew the pictures that had been scattered along the floor. I stepped on them as I went toward the balcony for some fresh air. The sunlight was fading fast.

It was unnerving how quiet the city was. No rush of traffic, no cars honking, no sirens, no people talking or laughing, no children playing. Wishing for binoculars, I looked out. I held out the gun, wishing I could fire and test for accuracy without wasting a bullet or drawing attention.

I grabbed the cheap plastic handle to the door and slid it halfway before coming to the conclusion that closing it was pointless. It was only a matter of time before the whole building became overrun by zombies or crazies.

A very pretty face beamed up at me from a photograph. I crouched down, putting the gun on the floor, and picked up the picture. The girl looked familiar. She was beautiful, with golden brown skin and perfect dark hair. I inspected another photo, trying to place the face that I knew I'd seen before.

"Collette Gravois," I recalled. She used to be a famous model. She'd had her own TV show and lingerie line a few years back. I'd wasted much of my hard-earned money on her sexy Brazilin lace designs. Then the Depression hit and frivolous spending came to an end. No one cared what your clothes, let alone bra, looked like when they couldn't afford food.

I wondered how she ended up in Indy and especially here. Or maybe she hadn't. Maybe these photos belonged to a friend. I thumbed through the remnants of an album of Collette at a theme park, wearing normal clothes and looking happy. She was probably dead.

Something flashed. I snapped my attention to the balcony door. It had come from outside. I waited for it to happen again. And then I saw his reflection, fading sunlight glinting off the knife in his hand.

"Jesus, Logan. You scared me." I held up a picture of Collette in a bikini. "Know who this is?" I turned, expecting Logan's eyes to bulge at the scantily clad model. He tipped his head down and stared, drool dripping from his mouth. Something wasn't right. My brain didn't have time to form a logical thought. Everything happened so fast. With a yell, Logan flew at me, knife raised. I tried to move out of the way. My feet slipped on the photographs, and I fell, sprawled on the floor. He was on me, pinning me down. I watched as he raised his arm. With horror, I saw the reflection of the knife cut through the air, and I felt it rip into my back.

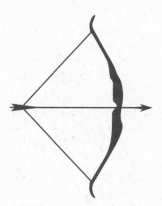

CHAPTER 8

I screamed and thrashed around, desperate to get out from under him. The wound hurt; pain rippled through my body, running up and down my spine. I didn't have time to focus on that if I wanted to live. Logan was bigger and stronger than me. Since I was face down, I was defenseless. I snapped my legs up, driving the heel of my boot into his back. It didn't work. Inflicting pain did nothing to the crazies.

I want you to know that I'm with you, that you don't have to do this alone.

The dog raced into the room. His body flew in a graceful leap and collided with Logan, knocking him off me. Growling, the Doberman circled him. Logan crouched down, knife raised. Running on adrenaline, I staggered up. I took hold of a lamp, yanking its cord from the wall. I hesitated. This was my friend...my...I couldn't do it. Not to him, not to the only person who promised our survival.

I had to. He was crazy, infected. I closed my eyes. Then with all the force I could muster, I slammed the lamp over Logan's head.

It didn't hurt him, I suppose, but it disoriented him long enough for the dog to jump. His jaws closed around Logan's arm, tearing his flesh instantly. I didn't want to kill Logan. Not Logan! Just a few minutes ago we were talking. He'd been fine. We'd come together in some way. We'd made a pact.

"Logan!" I yelled, hoping to spark some sort of remembrance. "Please don't make me do this! Logan! We are going to get through this together, remember?" He only growled at me, fighting against the dog. Afraid he might stab the Doberman, I kicked him in the chest. As soon as my foot made contact I fell, the stab wound throbbing. The knife slipped from his fingers, and my blood splattered the floor as his weapon clattered to the ground. Logan fell back, hitting his head on the balcony door.

The balcony.

I forced myself up. The dog stood by me, growling and showing his fangs. I closed my eyes and kicked Logan again, bracing for the pain that would surely follow. It hurt like hell, but my plan worked. He back stepped, taking himself out onto the balcony.

"Get him," I said to the dog, not knowing if it was a command he knew. The Doberman lunged again, sinking his teeth into Logan's arm. I pushed on the weak metal railing. Like Aunt Jenny's, it was loose.

"Good dog," I said and put my hand on the animal's back, hoping he wouldn't turn around and bite me. Thankfully he let go. I shoved Logan. He tipped backward and crashed into the rusting metal. It creaked and groaned and finally gave way. I grabbed the dog's collar, jumped back inside, and closed the glass door as Logan toppled down.

I sank to my knees, felt like I was going to throw up, and couldn't catch my breath or slow my pounding heart. The dog nosed me as if he wanted praise.

"Thanks," I said, unhappy with how high pitched and shaky my voice sounded. My hands trembled. My fingers didn't want to cooperate in grasping the chipped metal ID tag that hung from the dog's neck. "Argos," I said, finally reading his name. His whole butt shook with excitement at the sound of his name. He licked sweat off my face and trotted off.

I pressed my hand over my quivering lips and turned to the balcony. Tears blurred my vision and my heart thumped in my ears. "I'm so sorry," I whispered. "I'm so fucking sorry." A sob escaped from deep within me and I fell forward, the tears I had been holding back spilled down my cheeks and splashed onto the floor. I sucked in a breath and wiped my eyes, pulling myself up. Then I trudged back to Aunt Jenny's apartment.

"Orissa!" Zoe cried, practically falling out of her chair. She was the first to notice the blood. In the explosion of chaos, Padraic had woken. He was concerned over the amount of blood I had lost. Before anyone could drill me with questions, he took me into the bathroom and closed the door. He had to help me remove my shirt. As the shock wore off, the pain settled in. He pressed a clean towel to the wound, told me to hold it, and scuttled out to get medical supplies.

"Do you think you could stand to let me stitch it closed?" he asked.

The blood drained from my face at the thought of a sewing needle repeatedly piercing my skin. "Does it need it?"

"I'd say so."

"Ok then. Do it fast."

Padraic's hands were soft and gentle. He didn't have gloves but didn't balk at my blood.

"Were you strangled?" he asked, apparently seeing the red marks on my neck.

"Yeah, earlier back at the hospital."

"Why didn't you say anything?"

"I've been strangled before. It's no big deal."

"Oh, I beg to differ. Want to tell me what happened up there now?"

I didn't want to talk about it ever. The needle poked into my flesh. "Logan."

"He got attacked?"

"Not quite."

"He did this?" Padraic's hands stopped moving.

"He was infected. I...I had no idea. He was fine and then ten minutes later..." I felt tears form, whether it was from the pain or the horrible loss, I didn't know. I blinked them back. "I don't even know how he got infected. I thought you said we were all immune."

"Resistant," he corrected, pulling the thread up. It yanked my skin in a sickening manner. "Viruses evolve and change. One strand could do nothing while a slightly different strand could be fatal."

Padraic clipped the thread, rubbed some sort of salve on the wound and bandaged it up. He sat on the counter, wiping his bloody hands on a wet rag.

"You said you didn't think he was bitten, insinuating you think the virus is transmitted through saliva. Maybe that's not the only way," Padraic said.

"What do you mean?"

"Take AIDS, for example. If someone with AIDS bled on that fresh cut..."

"I'd get it."

"Exactly."

My eyes locked with Padraic's. He looked almost excited about his discovery, but terrified at the same time. This upped the 'we all get the zombie virus, go crazy, or die' factor. "How do we tell the others about Logan?" he asked.

"I'm sure they already suspect it." I unfolded my shirt, which I had wadded up and squeezed while I was being sewn shut. I stuck my fingers through the knife hole in my hoodie.

"Is he still out there?"

"Nope."

"Did you?"

"Yep."

"After he stabbed you?"

"No, I killed him and then he stabbed me," I jeered derisively. I shook my head. "I don't want to talk about it, ok? I took care of it, ok? I can't—" I cut off when my voice broke. Thinking about Logan was painful. Talking about him was even worse.

"I got that," he said quickly. "I meant that I'm a little impressed and a lot surprised you were able to put up a fight after going through that."

"Well," I said, standing and not mentioning the dog; I didn't know if my canine savior would ever come back. "It's not the first time I've been stabbed."

"You are an interesting girl, Orissa."

I'd been called a lot of things in my life, though interesting wasn't one of them. "I guess." I dropped my torn and bloody clothes on the ground. "Am I good to go, doctor?"

His blue eyes only looked at my chest for a second. "It's as good as I can get it with what I have. I'd like you to take antibiotics to prevent an infection."

"Well we don't have any," I spat, inhaling deeply. I hoped he understood that my anger was directed at our lack of supplies and not at him. He didn't look away from my eyes. Granted, I was wearing a plain, pink bra, not sexy in the least with no frills or lace. Did he not find me attractive? *I shouldn't care*, I mentally scolded myself. I turned in the mirror and discovered the back of the bra was covered in blood. My skin had been perfectly cleaned though. "Thanks," I added. "I guess having a doctor around during a zombie apocalypse is a good thing."

"As is having a girl who can kick some ass," he added.

------------------------>

Later, in the privacy of my room, I let myself wince at the pain. I held up a hand mirror to inspect the reflection in my big mirror. The knife had cut me to the left of my spine, but not too deep. Instead it dragged a three inch, nasty line across my shoulder blade. My skin prickled and tugged with every movement. Carefully, I stuck the bandage back to my skin and went to the closet.

It was agonizing to unhook my bra. It hurt so bad to reach behind that I considered not putting another one on in its place. The only front clasping bra I owned was my 'going out' bra. It was deep purple, lacey, and a ridiculous push up. Might as well look good if I die, right? It hurt like hell to pull the cream-colored camisole over my head and even worse to reach my left arm back to put it in the sleeve of a red, plaid shirt. I buttoned it halfway.

My jewelry box contained mostly cheap, costume jewelry, good for the bar scene but nowhere classier. I owned one real silver pendant. When the price of silver skyrocketed two years ago, I sold every piece of it I had to pay for school, except this. I draped the thin chain around my neck, biting my lip at the pain it caused my injured back, and closed the clasp. I turned it around so the little silver leaf rested under my collarbone. Once belonging to my grandmother, this necklace brought back memories. Memories were nice and all, but did nothing for survival. I dropped the lid on my jewelry box and went to join the others.

"Here," Padraic said, extending his hand. "This will help."

"Why are you always so eager to drug me?" I asked, taking the pills anyway.

"You said that before. But I didn't drug you."

"Yes, you did. Before everything happened. You gave me pills and everything went fuzzy."

"No. You passed out from the gas."

"Gas?" I sat cross-legged on the floor, once again sorting through our meager stash of supplies.

"They came through, the police or soldiers maybe. They were in all black." He shook his head. "Crowd control," he suggested with a frown.

"Oh." I thought back. Screams followed by gunshots. And then the smoke alarms going off. Obviously, the hospital hadn't burned down. "Why would they gas the place?"

"I don't know," he said absently.

Jason and Sonja sat next to me. "What's the plan?" Jason asked.

"We leave," I said shortly. "As soon as the sun is up."

"And then what?" Sonja inquired.

"We hope to find others and a place to stay and wait this out." Even if that were possible, I mused, what would it be like? Would we have anything to live for? Half the world was probably dead.

------------------------>

I sat at the table next to Padraic while the others slept. A circle of candles offered the only light, reminding me of a cheesy séance scene in a low budget horror film. I watched the flames bob up and down, hypnotized.

"So," Padraic's voice broke the laconism. "What's your story?"

"My story?"

"Yes. You've been strangled and stabbed before. Why?"

My story was colorful and not something I eagerly divulged. "I've made some bad choices."

"I think we all can say that," he chuckled.

"What about you? What's your story?"

I watched him lean back in the uncomfortable chair. "I was born and raised in Dublin, came here for med school, liked it, and decided to stay." He laughed. "There's not much to my story. I had a normal childhood, studied more than partied in college, and became a social recluse during my residency. I don't have much free time but when I do I like to read. The most exciting thing I've ever done in my life is go scuba diving."

"Oh," I said, imagining some grand, stone house in the Irish countryside. "I've been to the Hill of Tara, well, what's left of it."

"Really?"

"When I was sixteen. It was very…green." And enchanting and enthralling and magical. Padraic didn't need to know that. "I liked it."

"I've only been there once, and I was young. I was convinced I'd find a leprechaun," he admitted. "Why did you go there?"

"My stepdad, Ted, likes to travel."

"Where else have you been?" Padraic asked.

"All over, but mostly third world countries."

"Why is that?"

"Ted, my stepfather, runs mission groups," I said.

"Wow, that's a very compassionate thing to do."

"I guess, if you can say leaving your own country that's full of poor, starving children to go help people thousands of miles away is compassionate."

Padraic must have seen the resentment in my eyes because he promptly changed the subject. "So you're not going to tell me why you got stabbed before?"

I pulled on my braid, hesitant to tell Padraic about my shady past when his own teen years were probably spent eating perfect potatoes with his perfect family in his perfect house. "I got mixed up with some bad people who did bad things. I was majorly in the wrong place at the wrong time." Truth was, I didn't just get 'mixed up' with a drug runner. I purposely sought him out, hoping to piss Ted off. He and my mother had planned a mission to China that year and would be gone not only for my birthday but Christmas as well. I had hoped they'd be so upset they'd stay home and try to discipline me. I got to spend Christmas with my mom alright; she sat next to my hospital bed while I suffered a knife wound to the gut. It knocked me out of my 'befriend the druggies' scene at least.

I stood, needing to stretch my muscles, and paced around the living room.

"You should rest your shoulder and back," he told me, getting up as well. "To give it time to heal."

"I don't think I have the time," I sighed but sat on the couch. Padraic sunk down next to me. The candles on the table didn't offer much light.

"Why are you a doctor?"

"I wanted to help people. I grew up seeing my dad heal and cure. I thought he was performing miracles. One day he brought me to a lab and showed me cells and bacteria and viruses under a microscope. He said it wasn't miracles that saved lives, it was science. I was hooked."

I wanted to say something about science and the current virus but kept my mouth shut. "I wanted to be an actress or a Broadway singer," I informed him.

"You're pretty enough."

"Thanks. But Hollywood has no money anymore."

"Or audience, now." He laughed, and eventually, I did too. "So did you just come here from California then?"

"No." I came here from jail, another thing Padraic didn't need to know. "I dropped out of school last year and got a job waiting tables. That didn't work out so I moved in with my aunt."

"What were you going to school for?"

"Business, then theatre, then communications, then psychology. I couldn't make up my mind." I yawned.

He got up and rooted around in our medical bag. "Take two of these. It will help you relax. I'll keep watch."

I took the pills from Padraic's hand, about to pop them into my mouth when something scratched at the door. I jumped, the pills bouncing away on the cold tile.

Padraic didn't move. I sprung up, snatched my gun, and looked out the peep hole, though I knew perfectly well I couldn't see in the dark. Then I heard him whine.

"Argos," I whispered and moved the chair out of the way. The Doberman bolted inside as soon as the door opened. In his excitement, he jumped on me, pushing me into the door. The pressure on my cut radiated throughout my body.

"You know this dog?" Padraic asked, kneeling down.

Argos ran over to greet him.

"Kinda. He was upstairs. I let him out and he ran away."

"He seems friendly."

"He isn't friendly to the infected," I said in a way that conveyed what I had seen.

"What should we do with him?"

"I don't know." I put the chair back and took a bowl from the cabinet. Filling it with water from the bathtub, I set it on the floor for Argos to eagerly lap up. I gave him some of Finickus' food. I didn't want to leave the dog just as much as I didn't want to take care of an animal while running for our lives. "I think he can fend for himself."

"I'm sure he can," Padraic agreed.

I sat on the couch, pulling a crocheted blanket over me. With his mouth still dripping water, Argos leapt up next to me, curled into a ball, and rested his head on my lap. "He can see in the dark," I quietly added. "We can't."

"He'd be a good watch dog," Padraic suggested.

I thought about it, weighing the options. Padraic again urged me to sleep. With Argo's hearing and sight better than any humans', I felt as safe as I could and eventually drifted off.

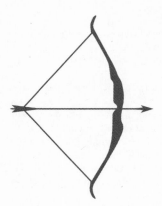

CHAPTER 9

The sun had fully risen. I was annoyed for sleeping so late, though even I had to admit it felt good. I woke everyone up, made them eat a lousy breakfast and dress in warm clothes. Nerves tingled throughout me at the thought of leaving. The apartment was warm and welcoming just as much as it was run down and crappy. I looked reassuringly at the three large duffle bags full of food, clothes, medical stuff, and miscellaneous things I thought we could use. In my purse were the 'emergency get away' supplies. Logan helped sort through some of this stuff. His face flashed through my mind. I hated that we were leaving him, even though he was infected. But we needed to get to safety. That's what Logan would have wanted.

I stiffly slipped my arms into a brown, leather bomber jacket. I had two sets of keys and needed to figure out which cars they belonged to. Of course, the easiest thing to do would be to hit the panic button. It would lead me, and the zombies, right to the appropriate cars.

Zoe ungracefully walked from the bedroom wearing a pair of my pajama pants. The hems caught under her slippers and she tripped, dropping Finickus, her stuffed cat, and a plastic bag of cat food. Argos took off, chasing the fat cat around the apartment.

"Argos, no!" I yelled, wondering if the dog would even bother listening to me. Somewhat surprisingly, he did. Since this complex didn't allow big dogs (and especially wouldn't allow 'aggressive' breeds) I figured his owners had made sure he was well trained. Lisa helped Zoe up, scooping up the spilled cat food, while Zoe picked Finickus back up, soothing him like a baby. I hadn't planned on taking Finickus. He had no value to us, wouldn't help us survive. How could I tell that to Zoe?

I rooted through one of the bags until I retrieved a pair of scissors. Careful not to clip her skin, I cut several inches off the hem of Zoe's pants. She needed to be able to run if she had to. I wanted to wrap Zoe in a blanket and tuck her in the backseat of the SUV. I was banking on Jason or Padraic carrying her, which wouldn't work with that stupid cat in her arms. As if he could read my mind, Finickus looked at me and meowed.

Padraic gripped a movie dagger that made him look out of place. He followed Argos and I through the hallways while the others waited inside the apartment. Our plan was to test the car keys I'd taken from the apartments on the cars parked in the lot. There was always the chance that I'd find a car or truck that I knew how to hotwire, but these were few and far between.

Down the hall and around a corner, Argos pawed at a door. I pressed my ear against it. Suddenly, something bumped on the other side. I jumped back. The thing clawed, making horrible gurgling growls.

"Zombie," I mouthed. I didn't know what to do. Should we bust down the door and kill it? It had probably been in there for weeks; I didn't see it getting out now. I took hold of Padraic's wrist and pulled him along.

"You're gonna leave it?" he asked, his mouth open in alarm.

"I don't think it will get out. Come on, we're wasting time."

The rest of the complex was zombie free. I stood guard while Padraic went back to get the others. I had wanted them to stay safely on the second floor in case something happened, but Padraic insisted we all be ready.

Too bad I was right.

A horde of zombies shuffled around the parking lot. I stood, transfixed on their jerky movements, rotten skin, and unified moan. A blur of black whizzed past me. I didn't have time to scream his name. Argos leapt onto a zombie, knocking him to the ground. The movement gained the attention of the others; soon six more dragged their feet in Argos' direction.

My heart ached for the dog. I pulled the gun, aimed, and shot. The scope was off. The bullet hit the zombie in the neck instead of the head. Its neck flopped back, arms flailing to the sides. Then it collapsed.

"What the…?" I muttered. I shot one more, this time in the ear, before telling myself not to waste any more bullets on a dog. My heart hammering, I pulled the keys from my pocket. Seeing no use in being surreptitious anymore, I hit the lock button. A small SUV beeped in response.

"Thank God," I whispered. This was exactly what we needed. I flew to the door, my hands shaking as I unlocked it. I jumped in, jammed the keys in the ignition, and started the engine. "Son of a bitch!" I hit the steering wheel. The 'check engine' light came on. Taking a car with engine problems isn't a good idea even if you're not running for your life. We couldn't rely on this.

The second set of keys didn't have a remote. The Chevy symbol was etched into the black top of the key, which helped narrow it down. The parking lot was nearly empty; only three Chevys were in sight. The truck would be too convenient. The Camaro, however, was the least practical. And it was a match.

I didn't know how to drive a stick. I had always planned on learning but the opportunity came and went. The engine roared to life. I forced the stick in any direction it would move. In reverse, the car jolted back, slamming into another car. Fumbling, I moved the stick one over. The engine squealed, but the car was moving.

Leaving the engine running, I jumped out and ran inside. "Go!" I yelled, waving them out. "Hurry! There are zombies out there!" I caught Padraic's arm. "Keys," I instructed.

He reached into his pocket.

"The Camaro's a stick," I explained shortly. "I can't drive a stick."

"I can," Hilary said. She hoisted her bag up on her shoulder and darted out.

My fingers closed around the Range Rover's keys and I was off again. I didn't want to look for Argos. I couldn't stomach the sight of zombies ripping flesh off his body, shoving it into their decomposing mouths. The Range Rover was close to the main doors; we snuck out through the back. I ran around the building, my thighs burning from moving so fast. I could barely breathe as I started the SUV.

I slammed on the break and swerved, threatening to tip the vehicle. There Argos stood, practically untouched, wagging his stump of a tail. I opened my door and called him. With ease, Argos jumped inside, stepping over me and into the passenger seat. I jumped out, almost forgetting to put the SUV in park, to help load the remaining bags and Zoe. By some miracle, Finickus remained wrapped tightly in her arms.

The zombies that had chased Argos were making their way back with disturbing speed. I scrambled to throw the heavy bag of food and water into the back of the SUV. Argos sniffed the air, showing his teeth and turning in the direction of the zombies. He tried to jump out the back of the open SUV. I reached out for him on impulse, my fingers wrapping around his collar. He jerked me forward, pulling my left arm which sent ripples of pain across my torn flesh.

I involuntarily cried out. Padraic appeared, getting Argos back in the Range Rover. He shut the door, put his fingers through mine and moved forward, only to get stopped by a zombie. Letting go of my hand, Padraic swung the dagger at the zombie, slicing its chest. Pale yellow pus and blood oozed out.

Argos barked and Zoe screamed. More zombies were coming. We were about to be surrounded. The zombie in front of us staggered, waving its hands blindly in our direction. The eyes were clouded over. I didn't think it could see very well.

"Drop!" I whispered to Padraic. His eyes questioned me, but he followed suit. I crawled under the running SUV, desperately moving away from the zombie. My hands burned from pulling myself along the pavement as I scrambled up. The zombie had just figured out where we had disappeared to. Padraic kicked it in the face and dragged himself into the clear.

I shot another zombie in the shoulder as I frantically got into the car. With no real destination in mind, Padraic gunned it. We tore out of the parking lot, past a herd of zombies, and onto the main road.

"The highway," I panted.

Padraic made a U turn (an illegal U turn, but who was gonna stop us?).

It was a little sickening to remember the full carts of food, water and supplies left to fester in the street. I told myself there'd be other stores to rob.

More zombies than I could count meandered around the chaotic streets, with absolutely no signs of human life. It was horrifying. And it confirmed my worst fear: we were the only survivors in the city.

Cars were pulled over on the side of the road with their doors left hanging open. Suitcases, bags, and other personal belongings lay scattered and forgotten amidst the occasional dead body. Where had everyone gone? Following the body trail seemed like a literal dead end. I kept my mouth shut. I needed to go north. I had to see if she was alive.

The number of zombies dwindled the farther we got from the heart of the city. I waited until we made it ten minutes without seeing the dead milling about to say that we needed to stop for gas.

"Where?" Padraic asked. "I don't think the gas stations will accept my credit card anymore. That and I don't have it."

I rolled my eyes. "We need to stop at a house, preferably one with a nice garden. Then, you'll see."

"A garden?"

"Yes."

"Can I ask why?"

"You'll see," I repeated. "Get off on the next exit," I told him. "And we'll try to find a neighborhood."

Every minute that passed without finding what I was looking for felt like a waste. I nervously wound my braid around my fingers, thinking about her, hoping she was somehow still alive. I had zoned out when Padraic said, "Is this ok?"

"It's perfect." I straightened, almost smiling at the sight of the large houses. We passed three massive brick homes and pulled into the driveway of an impressive colonial that was elaborately decorated for Halloween. "Stay here," I told Padraic. Looking back at Zoe, I added, "If anything happens, drive. I'll meet you at the front of the neighborhood."

"Orissa..." he shook his head.

"Keep her safe," I persisted. "Come on, Argos, let's go."

The decent thing to do was to knock, which was what I did. No one answered the door, as I suspected. I peered in through the big, living room window, kicking a fake gravestone out of the way. I knocked on the glass too, just in case. I looked, I watched, and I waited.

Nothing.

I picked up a decorative brick, red-hot pain searing through my stitched flesh as I did so, and threw it against the glass. It shattered, but not as neatly as in movies. Using a stupid plastic skeleton arm, I broke away the rest, allowing Argos and myself to get through without slicing ourselves open.

"Hello," I called out quietly. "If anyone is hiding in here, sorry I broke your window. And I'm not a zombie, so don't shoot."

Still nothing.

The house was incredible. The décor looked like something out of a magazine. Everything was grand and must have cost a fortune, but it wasn't overdone. Whoever lived here had good taste. And apparently a dog; Argos happily picked up a rawhide bone.

"Maybe I'll find you some food," I told him. My first priority was the kitchen and the garage.

Every nonperishable item had been taken, including all beverages. There was a small bag of dog food in the walk-in pantry. It wouldn't last Argos long, though it was better than nothing. With the food in one hand and gun in the other, I carefully picked my way into the garage. Argos followed.

"Yes," I whispered when my eyes feasted on the shiny, pearl white Cadillac parked in front of me. It was roomy, way better for a long road trip than the sports car Hilary drove. I went back into the house and began somewhat frantically looking for the keys. An odd feeling of dread and anxiety began to form in my stomach. I wanted out of the house. I was wasting time. That's all it was. I knew I needed to hurry.

Giving up and leaving the Escalade behind, I grabbed a pair of garden shears and exited through the back to find a hose. I pulled a few feet out and cut it. I bent down again. It could be helpful to have two siphons.

A gun fired behind me. I jumped, dropping the shears. I snatched up my own gun, expecting to turn and see a dead zombie and the person who'd saved me from it. My heart raced when I turned. There was no zombie, only a man.

And his gun was pointed at me.

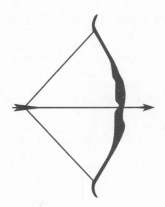

CHAPTER 10

"Don't shoot!" I cried, holding up my arms. "I'm not crazy or a zombie!"

"Like hell you aren't!" the man shouted, aim unwavering.

"I'm not. I promise! I haven't been bitten!"

"It's not the virus that's making you crazy," he said angrily, moving forward, rifle in hand. "Damn looters started already!"

"I'm not looting," I said back, though in all fairness, I had broken into someone's house. Where had this guy come from? And where was Argos? "No...no one lives here," I tried. I debated if I should raise my gun. I could drop to the ground, shoot him in the leg, take his gun and make a run for it. No, that was a crappy thing to do. The man came closer. I could see his hands shake ever so slightly. My heart pounded and my palms sweated. I swallowed hard and stepped in his direction. "What's it to you, anyway?"

"People lived in that house."

"Lived, see? No one does anymore."

He raised the gun so that the barrel was parallel to my forehead. Argos trotted around the house. He stopped and looked at me, assessing the situation. From what I knew about him, he didn't view humans as threats. If he could just stay quiet...

"No!" the man continued. "You shouldn't break into other people's houses, even though times are bad."

I nearly rolled my eyes. Was he going to lecture me or shoot me? I fixed my gaze on his, unblinking. I've always been good at reading people. It's partially why I'm good at getting away with crap. This guy was as easy to read as a highway billboard, and right now he was scared shitless.

"Zombie!" I yelled, diverting my eyes to the left. The man jumped, thankfully not pulling the trigger on impulse, and turned. I ducked out of the way, grabbed my gun and shoved it in his face. He staggered, crying out in pain, losing his grip on his own gun. I kicked it toward me and out of his reach.

And now it was in my possession.

"Listen here, you little prick," I said venomously. "Times are worse than bad. For all we know, we could be the only ones left. Don't waste a human life trying to be all 'above the law.' There is no law anymore."

He reeled back, terrified. Someone ran through the decorative planters along the house, feet crunching the lava rocks. I whipped around, my pistol aimed.

"Orissa!" Padraic called. "I heard the shot. I wanted to make sure you were alri—" he cut off, skidding to a stop. His eyes flashed from me to the man several times. Once he decided the guy wasn't crazy, he asked. "What is going on?"

"He," I jeered, "tried to kill me."

"Why?" Padraic blurted, having to be logical.

"Cause he's an idiot," I replied. "It doesn't matter. I got what we need so let's go."

"Wait," Padraic said. "Are there more? More people alive?"

"Maybe," the man said bitterly.

"That's great! You should get them and come with us. We're going to find the quarantine."

I clicked the safety on my pistol and stuck it in my waistband, refusing to wince at the pain in my shoulder. Switching the rifle to my right hand, I checked the remaining ammo; there were six bullets left.

"No," the man said firmly. "We decided to stay. We have supplies."

"It won't last forever," Padraic said gravely.

"I have enough," he said, putting his hand on his chin. I gathered up the hoses and the dog food, plopping them down in front of Padraic. That was when I noticed the sweat running down the guy's face. Sure, nerves could make you sweaty, but not on this chilly fall day.

"What kind of food do you have?" I asked.

"Uh, lots of dried stuff. It will last." His eyes moved to the left as he spoke.

"You're lying," I called him out.

Padraic shook his head. "Why would he lie?"

"I don't know. But he is." I aimed the gun at him. "Why are you lying?"

The guy shook his head. Blood dripped from his nose.

Padraic inhaled sharply. "You're infected," he alleged. "When?"

The guy twitched. "Yesterday."

"It's starting to set in, isn't it? You're having violent urges."

"Yes. I mean, no! I know it's wrong. I know she's wrong," he yelled, pointing at me. "She broke into that house. I had to shoot her. She broke the law."

Oh, was Padraic right. The craziness was setting in. Argos growled. We needed to leave, like yesterday.

After manipulating the near-crazy back into the house, Padraic carried the supplies and spare gun back to the car, getting in without saying a word. Later, on the highway, Padraic and the others watched as I used our new hoses to siphon gas from the many abandoned cars. We stored this in the jugs I had taken from Aunt Jenny's house.

➤

"Turn here," I instructed Padraic forty minutes later. I angled the map away from him, though I knew he could see the signs.

"Where are we going?" he asked, glancing at me.

"I went to school here," I explained. "There was a disaster plan. I had forgotten about it until now. It's worth a try checking out, right?"

"If you say so."

I hated that I felt guilty. I didn't want to feel anything towards Padraic. I wanted to find her—if she was alive—and go to my grandparents' farm. Padraic wasn't in that equation.

The campus was full of zombies.

"Damn it all to hell," I swore under my breath. Padraic drove slowly, hoping to sneak by unnoticed. I kept my eyes focused on the glove box in front of me. I didn't want to look at the faces, afraid of seeing someone I might know.

We reached the dorm, passing a dozen zombies. Hilary pulled up next to us.

"What's the plan?" Jason asked, too loud for my liking.

I didn't meet his eyes when I spoke. "Disaster relief planning. Might be inside. I went to school here." Damn it, I was giving myself away. "I'll go check it out."

"Not alone," Jason shouted.

"He's right, Orissa," Padraic had to agree of course.

"Anyone know how to handle a gun?" I asked.

"I've gone to the shooting range before, but that's about the extent of my experience," Jason admitted.

"I can shoot," Lisa's hoarse voice came from the back.

"No," Padraic and I said in unison, finally agreeing on something. The poor girl could barely speak let alone defend herself from crazies.

"I'm going alone," I said to appease my guilty conscious. That, and I really didn't want to see any of my companions get hurt. "If I'm not back in ten minutes, go on without me."

"Orissa, no!" Padraic hit the steering wheel. "You can't do this."

"Someone has to. And I know the layout of the building."

"Let me come with you," he insisted.

I raised an eyebrow. "Have you ever shot a gun in your life?"

"Once. A very long time ago."

"Exactly."

"Then let Jason go," he insisted.

"Fine." I unbuckled my seat belt. "Can everyone else fit in here? You know, just in case?" I turned to face Zoe, who had fallen asleep. "Argos will come with me, so there's more room. And seriously, Padraic," I said, putting my hand on his, "do not wait for us."

"Ok," he said. And then he hugged me. It was an odd sensation; his stiff, warm embrace and the pain it caused since his hand settled on top of the stab wound. "Don't make me leave without you," he begged.

"I'll try my hardest," I promised and got out of the SUV, calling for Argos to follow. I gave Jason the rifle, warned him there were only six rounds left and stood guard while the others piled into the Range Rover. It was weird, marching into the large, brick dorm, striding past a zombie that writhed on the ground, its legs apparently eaten off. It was such an epic moment, so dangerous and stupid yet here I was, going in without hesitation. I didn't have time to give an 'all or nothing' speech, didn't have time to prep myself for what I might find.

Argos had raced ahead again, wanting to be the first to check everything out. Luck must be on our side, I thought, since all was silent.

I fucking jinxed us.

The hall was full of zombies. I grabbed Jason, pulling him down on the stairs. Fear choked me, not of the zombies but of the realization that there was no way she had made it out alive. Not with this many. Oh God, what if she was one of them? What if her pretty face was rotting and deteriorating and her only drive in life was to shove human flesh into her festering, noxious mouth?

No. She was alive. She had to be. I had told her what to do. Ok, I hadn't told her what to do if the world is overcome with a virus that turns you into a homicidal maniac before you zombify, but she's smart.

Jason slid his hand up the barrel of the rifle. I flicked my eyes to him, watching him inspect the trigger.

"It will kick back," I whispered, "into your shoulder." He nodded, looking apprehensive. "Here," I said and took the rifle from him. I looked up; we were safely stashed out of view from the zombies, hidden in the stairwell. "Hold it like this." I put the rifle up, showing Jason where to put his hands. I handed it back. "Line up the front and rear sights. It will help you aim."

He held up the rifle, closing one eye to focus on the sights. He nodded and lowered the gun. "Thanks."

I counted thirteen zombies, groaning as they roamed the halls. And there had to be more that we couldn't see. It was dark, the only light coming from the windows at the end of the hall and the weak sunlight that filtered through open dorm room doors. Argos' short fur stood on end as he growled. I tried to shush him unsuccessfully. In theory, Jason and I could shoot every zombie in sight. And we'd be screwed and out of bullets. I needed to come up with a plan.

I bit down hard on my bottom lip and made myself bleed. Cursing, I swallowed the metallic substance.

"Blood," I whispered, wiping the inside of my mouth with my finger.

"What are you talking about?" Jason asked.

"We can distract them with blood, I think."

"So you want to bleed all over the floor and run away?"

"That's exactly what I want to do."

"That's a horrible idea," he told me.

"You got a better one?"

"Well, no. Do you really want to risk an open wound around them, though?"

"Who...who told you?"

Jason's dark eyes pierced mine. "I'm not stupid, Orissa. If this really is a virus, it will spread like one."

"Oh, right," I said, feeling bad for not giving him more credit. The fact that the zombie virus was contagious through blood wasn't my secret to keep. I had hoped that by not sharing, it would keep what was left of the calm.

"We need to do something. We're wasting time," I whispered.

"Ok." He crouched down, peering down the hall. "There's not really an emergency relief group in here."

"No."

"Who are we looking for? Your boyfriend?"

"Nope."

"Sister?"

"Nope."

"Brother?"

"Wrong again. I'll tell you later. Now shush before they hear us!" I hissed. My mind turned. I needed to come up with something, anything to get in the hall. Her room was in the middle on the left, right behind a fat zombie, munching on a crazy's' arm.

Sick.

"Upstairs," I whispered, holding onto Argos as we tiptoed up. A girl quickly walked out of a room, blood dripping down her face, growling. "Shit!" I cursed. "A crazy."

"Did she see us?"

"I don't think so. We have to take her out. We...we just have to."

We sank down on the stairs. The girl looked like a freshman, young and at one point, innocent. And now she was insane, covered with blood. I wondered if she knew it happened, like the guy back at the colonial house. What would it feel like? I'd want to die. If no one would kill me, I'd do it myself. But could I? Maybe my sense of right and wrong would get skewed too.

The girl muttered incoherent grumbles and crossed the hall. I struggled to take hold of Argos, who desperately wanted to bolt forward. In the two seconds it took the crazy to go from one room to another, I saw the bite marks on her arms.

Zombies went after crazies.

It made sense, why they would. Crazies still had beating hearts and fresh blood. They were in the process of dying, or un-dying, but they were one hundred percent alive.

"I have a plan," I said excitedly and whispered it to Jason. He took Argos, leaving me alone on the stairwell. This stairwell was dark and dreary without the threat of getting eaten alive. It was downright terrifying today.

I smelled him. That's how I knew a zombie had crawled up the stairs. I put my hand over my mouth to keep from screaming in frustration. Dammit Jason, I specifically told you to *close the door!* One of the zombie's eyes was hanging out of his head, flopping around with each jerky movement. His hands slapped the cold tile stairs. I couldn't shoot him. It wasn't time yet. Jason couldn't have made it to the other side; he needed more time.

Frantically, I pressed myself against the wall, praying he wouldn't see me. My body prickled with fear, every nerve on end. I wasn't sure I could move my feet even if I tried. This zombie was slow and I did, after all, have the gun, but he wasn't going to ruin my plan.

He kept moving, probably following the scent of fresh blood. I should have kicked it down the stairs when I had a chance. Idiotically, I didn't. And now it was above me, two stairs away from the top. The zombie turned; its only good eye bloodshot and dull. The pupil twitched. I didn't move. I didn't breathe.

It felt like a year passed. The zombie didn't continue on. He just stood there. I was afraid to blink; afraid the minute movement would set him off. The knock echoed through the stairs. I jumped. I needed to act, now.

And this son of a bitch was in my way.

"Fuck it," I said, and shot him in the head. I leapt past his finally dead body and burst through the doors. "HEY! Come and get me, you meat-eating freak!" I shouted. With a harrowing scream, the crazy took off after me. I sprinted down the stairs, my body jittering with adrenaline. I slammed into the doors on the second floor, drawing my gun. The crazy had tripped over the zombie body, acting as a perfect booby trap and allowing me to gain a few seconds head start. I shot her, the bullet hitting her arm like I planned.

Blood—fresh, juicy, and red—stained her already filthy Purdue University hoodie.

"Smell that, you stupid zombies? Come and get it while it's fresh!"

Zombies marched in our direction in a putrefying parade. The crazy ignored me, going for the bigger crowd. She was no match for them. Without further ado, I madly dashed down the stairs, across the lobby, the commons, and into another stairwell where Jason waited.

"It worked!" he said in disbelief.

I nodded, too winded to speak. I grabbed his arm and dragged him up to the second floor. Distracted with the yummy crazy girl, all the zombies surrounded her body, fighting to get a piece.

We reached her room; the door was still closed but not locked. If possible, I felt even more nervous as I opened it.

The room was empty. I didn't let myself think about it being good or bad. I couldn't just leave. Not after all we'd went through. There had to be something, some clue, like a note saying where she had gone.

And there was: the calendar on the wall. A big X was drawn through every completed day. The last X was on Friday, October 21st. She had at least made it until them. I didn't know what day it was. How much time had passed? A week? Two weeks? My appointment for a checkup had been a few days after the 21st. That's when the virus hit Indy. Had it hit the campus sooner?

'Seth's Party' was written in black and orange marker in the Saturday, October 22nd square. Yes! Seth, she'd be with Seth! And Seth lived…shit. He lived in a frat house. But which one?

"Betas," I said out loud.

"What?" Jason asked.

"Seth is a beta something. Or a something beta. Shit! I can't remember!"

"The Beta Theta Pi's?" he asked, picking up a flyer for the Beta's annual Halloween party.

"Yes! Oh thank God, thank you! She could be there. Let's go!"

———————▶———————

I caught a glimpse of Padraic's broad smile as we bolted from the dormitory. We dove into the Camaro, with me yelling at Jason to drive even before he got the keys back into the ignition. No sooner had the engine roared to life, than a dozen zombies ran outside.

Literally ran.

Full bellies must have given them an energy boost. Argos snapped and snarled at the window. Jason slammed the pedal down. The engine revved but we didn't move.

"Put it in first gear!" I shouted, pulse pounding. The zombies were close. "No, that's third, or second! Shit, I don't know!"

He moved the clutch, punched the gas and the car stalled. A fat zombie pounded on my window.

"Ok, ok," I ranted. I had a boyfriend once who drove a stick. I'd watched him shift gears before and vaguely remembered him explaining how to do it. I had driven his truck once; he had his hand over mine, shifting the gears for me. "Put it in neutral and turn the car off," I instructed. Two more zombies clawed at the car, their nails scraping against the metal. We were being surrounded. My hands shook. A newly turned zombie clambered onto the hood, roaring and desperately trying to claw through the glass to get us.

Argos jumped at her, saliva spraying as he barked. I struggled to push him back and out of the way. I closed my eyes, trying to remember what we had to do. The car shook when another zombie climbed on the hood. The young, female zombie climbed on top of the car, nails raking against the T-Tops. They wouldn't hold much longer.

The fat zombie made it around the car and was banging on the driver's side window, blocking out the sun. Jason turned the key; nothing happened. More zombies circled the car. We were going to die. There was just no way out of this. Trapped like sardines in a can, the zombies would peel back the lid that was the top of the car and tear us to pieces.

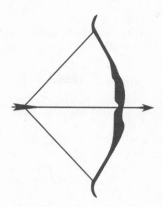

CHAPTER 11

The Camaro lurched, after being struck on the side. It threw me into Jason. Oh God, they were trying to roll the car! Horrified, I turned. Three zombies on my side withered down, thick blood streaking the window.

"Padraic," I said and watched the black Range Rover back up and jolt forward, pinning the zombies between his grill and the Camaro. They popped like zits, guts and pus oozing from every orifice. "Again," I told Jason, remembering that I needed to do something with the clutch. It was hard to shout out instructions over Argos barking. Jason heard me and the most beautiful sound of the engine rang out. "Please work," I prayed and shifted into what I hoped was first gear. The car lurched forward, running over several zombies. Jason jerked the wheel, hoping to knock off the bitch on the top of the car. He hit a stop sign, bashing out the passenger sidelights. The zombie girl flew off, rolling on the pavement, her rotten skin peeling off with ease on the rough street.

I forgot about going to the Beta Theta Pi house. My brain's only thought was getting the hell away and surviving. It took a minute of video game style driving through the abandoned streets of Purdue for me to break out of my timorous haze. I looked around, not able to fathom where we were logically. I had spent four and half years on this campus; I should know it well. Passing the Beering Hall of Liberal Arts and Education building jarred my memory.

"We need to get on State Street," I told Jason, knowing fully that he had no idea where that was. I gave directions. Some of the buildings had been burned down. My stomach twisted at the sight of them, at the sight of what our world had been reduced to. I debated if we should try the highway and sneak in the back. Afraid it would be another frozen traffic jam, I decided against it.

We drove through the perfectly manicured lawn, smashing over Halloween decorations and trampling the bushes.

"Maybe you should stay here and keep the car running," I said as my trembling hands gripped the door. My wide eyes scanned the yard. When I saw nothing, I got out of the car, Argos right behind me.

"No," he countered. "Hilary needs to drive. It's no secret I don't know how to drive a stick."

"Right." The Range Rover stopped next to us. Zombie parts stuck to the front. Without thinking, Padraic got out and rushed over. He put his hands on my shoulders, his blue eyes drilling into mine.

"Are you hurt?" he asked.

"Not really."

"Good." Still holding onto me, he looked up at the huge brick fraternity house. "What are we doing here?"

"Um, looking for supplies."

"You're not going in there," Padraic stated.

I turned to the house. The front door was open and most of the windows had been shattered. There was no hope, really, and I knew it. I had made it this far and I wasn't leaving. Not without exhausting every possibility. I had to find her.

$$\longrightarrow$$

Before I could come up with more stupid excuses, a crazy burst through the open door. Argos got to it first, taking it down and clamping his sharp teeth into its face. Four more took its place. Jason shot at one, hitting him in the shoulder.

The gunfire echoed across the lawn like a dinner bell, drawing more crazies and a few zombies from neighboring houses. I shot one crazy and two zombies in the head. Padraic had the dagger from earlier, and managed to decapitate one. Before I could acknowledge whether or not it was a bad idea, I shoved a new magazine into the .22 and traded him weapons. I didn't trust him in hand-to-hand combat and I didn't want to see him get hurt. His success with the zombie had likely been beginner's luck.

"Aim for the heart," I told him, hoping that if he missed the bullet would still have a chance of lodging in a stomach or face. I yanked the sheath off the dagger and rushed forward. "I've come here to pledge," I leered at the crazies. They whipped around at the sound of my voice, drawing some of the danger away from the rest of my party.

I crouched, waiting. It would have worked out better if one was a bit faster than the other but, no, they got to me simultaneously. Taking a stance, I leaned back and kicked the bigger of the two crazies in the stomach, planting my foot back on the ground and whirling in one swift movement, the blade slicing through the air.

It caught the other crazy across the chest. Any normal person would have fallen, shouting in pain, clutching their bleeding front in fear and agony. I leaned back, avoiding his blood crusted hands, swooping the dagger up and into his neck. Blood splattered and I closed my eyes, not wanting to get infected.

In that second, the big crazy jumped at me, his fat arms wrapping around my waist. We fell to the ground with him on top of me. Jostled out of my hand on impact, the dagger lay only inches from my fingers. Fatty licked the crazy's blood from my face, swallowed gratifyingly, opened his mouth and dove down. I caught his head with my hands. Meanwhile, the others were fighting their own battles nearby. Drool fell on my neck as I desperately tried to push his face away. On instinct, I kneed him in the balls. Crazy didn't even react. I tangled my fingers in his blonde curls and twisted.

It was revolting, the sound and feeling of a spine snapping. Revolting, but efficient. His body went limp. I rolled him off just in time to get attacked again. A slender, dark haired crazy boy growled at me, showing off his fangs.

What the fuck, fangs!? My fingers closed around the welcome metal of the dagger and I flipped myself onto my feet, ducking out of the way of his body as he dove through the air at me. He rolled to his feet and dove again, a predictable move I easily avoided. The first crazy I sliced crawled after me. He was running out of blood and wouldn't make it much farther.

I was ready when Fangy jumped. He stabbed himself, impaling his heart on the dagger, body twitching and then going limp. I crawled out from under him, eager to roll him over and look at his teeth. I pried his mouth open and laughed. The fangs were plastic, held onto his teeth by putty. Oh, right. Halloween. He was dressed up as a vampire.

I whirled around. Two zombies lay dead on the ground. I didn't recall hearing the guns fire. Obviously, they had. Jason stared at me with his mouth agape. I wiped my hands, which were covered in blood, on the grass and jogged over.

"I'm going in," I said. "I think they all came out already and are hopefully dead. Or deader, in the case of the zombies."

Padraic's eyes were filled with wonder. He slowly nodded, though I doubted he knew what he was doing. Leave it to him to go into shock.

"Guard the girls," I instructed. "There's a zombie across the street."

Jason immediately raised the rifle.

"No," I said, putting my hand on the long barrel. "It doesn't have legs." I watched it drag its pathetic body through the grass. "If I'm not out in ten minutes, go."

I didn't stick and around and wait for the others to protest.

<hr>

Something moved behind me. I spun, dagger raised.

"Argos, don't do that!" I whispered. He was absolutely disgusting, covered with blood and zombie skin. He whizzed past me. I heard his paws bounding up the stairs. The Beta house was big, really big, and elaborately decorated for a Halloween party. I pretended the dead humans in the hallway were merely props.

If she was here, she would be upstairs. Like Argos, I quickly ascended the stairs. The smell of death was so strong I gagged, retching up what little I'd had to eat that morning. My bloody hands did little to help when I covered my nose. "Hello!" I called, hoping to draw someone out—friend or foe. I couldn't be in this hall anymore. Not with the decaying bodies and the smell.

Argos had disappeared again. He was a bad ass when it came to taking down enemies; he was lacking on the loyal guard dog side. Forcing myself to not give up, I went to the end of the hall. Something moved behind a closed door. Its footsteps weren't clear. When I thought I heard dragging feet, I hightailed it out of there. It seemed closed doors were a challenge to zombies, and this one could stay in there.

Argos barked. My nerves jolted with electricity. He barked again. I took off, running past dead students, Halloween decorations, and disheveled furniture. Damn this house for being so big. I was panting by the time I got to Argos. He was looking at the ceiling. My eyes flew to it and I gasped.

"Hello?" I tried again. "Is anyone alive up there?"

"Orissa?" a muffled voice replied. The attic stairs creaked as she pushed them down. "Oh my God, Orissa!"

Tears pricked the corners of my eyes. "Raeya. You're alive." I couldn't help the gooney smile that broke out across my face. I couldn't believe it. Half of me didn't. Maybe I had died, and this was heaven. An arm was strewn a few feet from me. No, this was no heaven.

This would be hell.

I stumbled up the stairs, throwing my arms around my best friend. "I knew you were alive," I exclaimed.

"I've been waiting for you," she cried. "See," she said to someone behind her, "I told you she would save us."

We broke apart, Raeya still holding onto my hands. Two people huddled behind her; there was a boy I didn't recognize and a blond girl who looked vaguely familiar. Still smiling, I looked Raeya up and down, realizing that she was in costume.

"A sexy nurse?" I teased. "How original, though I have to say the 1980's yellow blazer puts a brand new spin on it."

"I was cold and it was the only jacket up here," she retorted. "And, please, do I have to remind you of some of the cliché costumes you've worn?"

"They fit my personality," I countered. "But this, this is so not you. I bet Seth picked it out in hopes of a little role playing later on." Then it hit me. Seth wasn't in the attic. "Oh God, Seth?" Raeya shook her head, tears rolling down her face. I hugged her again. "I'm so sorry, Raeya."

She sniffled and nodded. I looked around the attic; the junk had been pushed aside and blankets had been spread out, some covering the windows as makeshift curtains in an attempt to make the drafty room seem homey. That would have been Raeya's doing. The blonde girl was dressed up as Little Red Riding Hood, her red cloak wrapped tightly around her body. The boy had on dirty overalls and a stained white shirt covered with something that was supposed to be blood, except it was too bright red to be real. His pale makeup had been streaked across his face, making his costume indiscernible.

"What are you supposed to be?" I asked, though it was not important.

"A zombie," he replied gravely.

I burst into laughter. "Sorry," I muttered, trying to compose myself. "We need to go. Do you have any weapons?"

Raeya grabbed a tennis racket and a can opener, holding them up proudly.

"That's it? You have nothing sharp or pointy?"

"No," Raeya said quietly, her shoulders sagging.

"It's better than nothing. It's good, really good," I told her reassuringly. "Let's go."

The four of us had just made it to the exit foyer when one of the car horns honked. "Dumbass," I hissed, imagining Padraic honking impatiently. "Why doesn't he just tell all the zombies we're here?"

Turns out, he didn't have to. They already knew.

Jason stood on top of the Range Rover, rifle pointed. He shot, hitting someone somewhere. Blood splattered in the air. Still, they marched. There had to be dozens of them.

"Get in the car!" I yelled to Jason. I gripped the dagger, preparing myself. "Go to the cars," I shouted to Raeya and the others.

Our sprint was interrupted by a crazy and four zombies. The new guy yelled, throwing his hands in the air. He ran forward, desperately wanting to find refuge in the safety of a car and leaving the three of us girls to defend ourselves.

I heard the gun fire a few more times and I knew before I saw Jason swinging the gun like a baseball bat that he was out of bullets. I went for the closest zombie, eviscerating him in one quick swipe of the blade. His intestines fell out, darkened, rotting and foul smelling. The zombie kept walking, unaware that his organs were spilling with each jarring step.

His large intestine flopped out, hanging and swinging as he moved. It tangled around his feet. With horrified curiosity, I watched the zombie fall, tripping over his insides. Someone screamed. A slow moving zombie advanced on Raeya. Its skin was flaking off in chunks and most of its hair was missing. It came at her open mouthed; most of its teeth were gone. The few that remained hung limply on dangling roots.

"This is for Seth!" she shouted and swung her tennis racket. Like a rotten tomato, the zombie's skull popped. "Eww!" Raeya squealed, shaking her tennis racket. Bits of gooey zombie stuck to the nylon strings. "He's all gummy!"

Gummy, but easy to kill. I looked up just in time to see Jason slip and fall.

"Jason!" I screamed. Another gun fired. Padraic. I couldn't see what was going on. We needed to get to the car. The slow marching horde of zombies was getting closer every second. The crazy hissed, eyes on Raeya. Another zombie limped forward. It too was flaking apart. "Get that one!" I yelled to Raeya. She held her tennis racket out, at the ready.

"Which one?"

"That one!" I said, as I took on the crazy. "The gummy one!" This crazy must have been close to dying, or undying. Her skin was gray and she twitched uncontrollably. She grabbed my arm, nails digging into my wrist. Underestimating her strength, I yanked my arm back expecting to easily free myself. She countered, whipping me forward. My head cracked against hers. Little spots clouded my vision. I caught one foot on the other and fell.

With her death grip around my wrist, she fell too. She growled, opened her mouth and bit me.

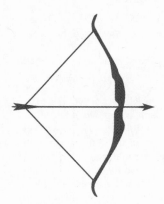

CHAPTER 12

It hurt like hell. I somersaulted back, breaking the connection. For my own pleasure, I kicked her hard in the ribs before sending the dagger into the nape of her neck. Raeya was beating a deteriorating zombie over the head. Chunks of its skull came up each time she raised the racket, splattering her costume with blood.

The Range Rover zoomed over, hitting a zombie on its way. Padraic was driving and Jason was in the passenger seat. He had made it.

"Raeya, let's go!" I shouted and looked around for Argos. "Argos!" I yelled. We didn't have time to wait. Sonja threw open the back door, beckoning us in. "Argos!" I shouted again. Raeya leapt in, cramming into the back next to Sonja and Zoe. As soon as I was in, Padraic pressed the pedal down, speeding away from the zombies.

I madly looked for the dog, heart sinking when he was nowhere in sight. The street was full of zombies. We couldn't hit them all without getting stuck. Padraic swerved onto the sidewalk, bumping over planters as we detoured around the zombies. We had driven almost a mile when Zoe yelled 'stop!'

There he was, running like wild, chasing after us. Padraic slammed on the brakes so suddenly that Hilary almost rear ended us in the Camaro. Jason opened his door and Argos jumped in, his stumpy tail wagging. Careful not to elbow Zoe in the face, I climbed into the very back, cargo hold. Raeya leaned out of the way to allow Argos to join me. He licked my face excitedly.

"Good boy," I breathed.

As the adrenaline wore off, the pain hit me. My stab wound was agonizing and I had a serious stitch in my side. Not to mention the bumps and bruises I'd received in the fights. Trembling with fear, I looked at my right arm. Little half moons imprinted the leather, but it had stopped her teeth from sinking into my skin. This was my new favorite jacket.

→

We drove north, speeding down the roads until there was nothing except barren cornfields. No one had spoken in the time it took us to get to this desolate place, and Jason had fallen asleep in the front. Padraic stepped off the gas and let the SUV coast to a stop. He turned it off and said, "Care to tell me what that was all about?"

I didn't need to lie anymore. I rescued Raeya. I didn't care if he hated me for the rest of my life (and the end of my life might be today). "I-I brought you an assistant," I said innocently. I watched Padraic's confused face.

"I was at a costume party," Raeya muttered through clenched teeth, pulling the ugly yellow blazer around herself. She narrowed her eyes at me before laughing.

"Orissa," Padraic began. "There never was a quarantine, was there?"

"Not that I knew of," I confessed.

Padraic shook his head and sighed, as if resigned to what had happened. Then he smiled. "You saved three people."

"Yeah. I did, I guess. And I'm sorry, alright? Really, I am. I have no idea if any quarantines or disaster shelters exist, though they usually are set up in school gymnasiums." I crossed my arms and snuggled into the seat, putting pressure on my wound.

Jason woke and cleared his throat. I looked out the window, not realizing that the others had left their vehicle to stretch their legs. Out of the dimness of the attic, I recognized the blonde as Lauren Hill. By some evil twist of fate we'd had at least one class together every year. I couldn't stand her. She came from an upper-middle class family that hadn't been touched by the depression, always had perfect hair, and acted like she was better than everyone else.

There was a minute of awkward introductions. Zombie boy introduced himself as Spencer and sounded like he might burst into tears at any second. He shook hands with me through the open window.

After introductions were made, we agreed to keep traveling, wanting to make good time before nightfall.

Things were easier during the next part of our journey. Padraic confronting me and me apologizing had eased the tension.

"How did you survive?" Padraic asked Raeya, glancing over his shoulder briefly to look at her as he drove.

"I had a list," Raeya replied, as if that was a normal thing to say.

"You had a list?" Padraic repeated.

"Well, not physically. Orissa helped me make it a while ago...it was a disaster plan for regular disasters. But I remembered what I wrote. And I did what I thought Orissa would do. If anyone could survive something like this, it's her."

"And Orissa," he continued, "how do you know how to...to *survive*?"

I looked at Raeya and smirked, remembering the years spent with my grandpa. "Trust me; I was put to the test."

Is that why you are so insistent that no one is coming?"

"No," I said, almost laughing.

"Give me something," he pleaded with a charming smile. "The way you fought back there... it was amazing."

"I've been taking martial art lessons since I was twelve," I supplied.

"That's the key to survival?" he asked, not convinced.

"Every battle is won before it is ever fought," I quoted the old Chinese proverb.

After a long silence, Zoe spoke up from her place beside me.

"Did you kill a zombie back there, Orissa?" her big green eyes alive with excitement.

"Yes," I said. "Two of them, actually."

"Don't lie," Padraic said, reminding me of the disagreement we'd had earlier. My heart actually skipped a beat. "She killed one and Argos got the other."

"Oh," Zoe said and hugged Argos. "Good dog."

Zoe had taken the ties out of her hood and fashioned a leash for Finickus. She tied one end around his neck and the other around her wrist. Amazingly, she held both the dog and the cat—neither animal showing aggression toward the other.

"W-what do we do now?" Jason asked.

"Well," I started, my brain turning on its survival mode. "There are ten of us plus Argos and only two cars. We need to find another vehicle, preferably one with four-wheel drive. And a hybrid would be nice, but beggars can't be choosers, right? We'll take what we can get."

Raeya grabbed my purse and extracted the notebook. She pulled the pen from the metal spiral and began to write.

"Ok," she said. "We need to first find shelter. Then another car and food." She quickly scribbled it down. "Then what, after that?"

"Head south," I answered, so used to Raeya's incessant list making it didn't strike me as odd. "We don't want to be here for the winter."

"Where in the south," Jason asked.

"My grandparents' farm," I said.

➤

Padraic and Spencer sat up front in the Range Rover, Raeya, Jason and Sonja sat in the backseats and I nestled down next to Argos in the cargo area. Using the sun as our guide, we headed south.

An hour later, we found a house—a white Cape Cod complete with picket fence and weed-filled flowerbeds. In its glory, the place could have been featured on the cover of one of those country life magazines. The windows on the first floor had been carefully boarded up and the shutters were closed upstairs; the owners intended on coming back. We quietly got out of the cars. We were probably in what had once been the heart of the town. Empty houses lined the streets, some preserved just like the Cape Cod in front of us. Argos sniffed the air.

Holding my breath, I waited. His head jerked to the right and he darted across the street. A raccoon shot out of an overturned trash can. My breath came out in a whoosh; at least it wasn't a zombie. Leaves covered the cobblestone path, filling the air with a sweet aroma. I signaled to the left, instructing Padraic and Jason to go around that side of the house while I took the other.

Everything was sealed tight. It seemed a shame to bash in the boards when they offered such good protection. With a shovel we found in the tool shed behind the house, Padraic and Jason carefully pried off three boards from the kitchen window. Padraic broke the glass and hoisted me up, his hands lingering on my waist. I shimmied through, trying my hardest to avoid the shards in the sink. I jumped off the counter, nervous that someone had been sealed inside the house, making it a zombie time capsule. I reached into my bag, pulling out and turning on a flashlight. With cautious steps, I weaved my way to the front door. I quickly unlocked it and threw it open, blinking at the bright sunlight.

Argos, giving up on chasing the raccoon, rejoined us. We let him explore the house, waiting in the safety of the foyer to see if the coast was clear. Like I suspected, it was. I waved everyone in. We had three flashlights and a decent amount of candles. The boarded up windows blocked out all natural light, kept intruders out, but also didn't allow us to see anything around us.

There were two small bedrooms upstairs facing the street with the master bedroom across the hall. The rooms were clean and the beds were made. A knot formed in my chest when I thought about the people who had lived here. Things only seemed bad then, when losing your job was your worst fear. And now, *now* there was a virus, a horrible, incurable virus. I sat on the bed in the master bedroom, pleased to find the mattress to be expensive memory foam, and buried my head in my hands. *We made it out of the city, Logan. Wish you were here to see it.*

I was determined to stay alive just as much as I was determined to keep Raeya and the others alive. And I thought I could. Now there were eight others to think about. I hated that they looked to me as their leader. I hated that the responsibility of their survival fell on my shoulders. Most of all, I hated that I didn't think I could do it.

"Rissy?" Raeya called. I jumped up, hardening my expression.

"Yeah?"

She came into the room. "I was just wondering where you were." She looked around, shining the flashlight on the walls. "This place was nice, once upon a time."

"Yeah, once upon a time."

She pointed the flashlight at me. I closed my eyes and turned away.

"Raeya, you're blinding me."

"Oh, sorry." She turned the light away.

I took my jacket off and threw it on the bed, marking it as ours for the night. Raeya sunk down next to me. "It's hard to believe this is happening, isn't it?"

"Sometimes," I agreed.

"I keep hoping I'll wake up from a horrible nightmare and realize everything is ok."

"Everything will be ok, someday." I felt like I was lying. How the hell could anything be ok after this?

"I thought it was a joke, at first," she said so quietly; it was almost a whisper. "I was at the Halloween party. Seth said his head hurt and went up to his room to lie down. I-I thought he had too much to drink. I was having fun. When the first guy wigged out, I thought it was a Halloween prank." She closed her eyes, remembering. "Then he punched someone. I don't even know who because the person had a mask on. My mind stopped thinking it was a prank; it had gone too far. I was sure he was on something, like bath salts or something that make people crazy. Then another one crashed through the window. Glass stuck into his skin, b-but I don't think he felt any pain. That's when I knew. I knew something absolutely horrible had happened."

My mind flashed to last year's Halloween. Dressed up as a sexy police officer, I dragged Raeya out to party. We got there early, wanting to snag good seats close to the bar. Raeya looked too elegant for the bar scene, wearing a short, black dress, her shoulder length, dark hair perfectly curled. She wore a beautifully hand crafted mask of black, done in a Venetian style. She looked like she belonged on the stage of some fancy ballet show, not sitting next to her slutty, drunk friend. I bought us our first drinks that night and downed my Vodka and Redbull in less than five minutes. Raeya sipped at hers, afraid of getting drunk too fast and feeling sick.

I was already buzzed when the bar began to get busy. I made eye contact with a guy with dark hair and dark eyes. He smiled coyly and eventually made his way over to us. He asked if I would dance with him, shouting over the music. I put my hand on his chest and told him I would if he bought me and my friend a drink. He obliged, ordered us something fruity and then proceeded to lead me to the dance floor. I put up with him for two songs before weaving my way through the crowd to find Raeya. I dragged her from her seat and made her dance with me. By the time she finished her second drink, she was shaking it on the floor.

We closed down the bar that night, getting a ride back to Raeya's in a Mustang full of frat boys. I dropped out of school the year prior, seeing it as pointless to waste money on a degree when no one could get a job. Raeya had just started working on her master's degree. I tried to talk her out of it only once; she insisted having two degrees would make her invaluable after the Depression was over. And, she reminded me, since she was a Residence Assistant, she had free housing.

"I went upstairs to find Seth." Raeya's voice pulled me out of my reverie. "I thought he was sleeping, but…" She couldn't finish her sentence. Big tears rolled down her cheeks. My heart broke as each one splattered on her lap, her head held down in pain. I hugged her again, trying not to think about Seth. She broke down in sobs. I kept my arms around her while she cried, wishing there was some way I could take away her pain.

She put her head on mine and, for just a second, I thought we'd be alright as long as we stuck together. "I made a list of places I always wanted to go or live someday," Raeya said after awhile. "I need a number five for my list."

"Go to Disney World and live in the castle?"

Raeya's body twinged with excitement. "Can we?"

"No. Well, maybe. I don't know what it's like there. A zombie Mickey Mouse would scar me for life. Let's avoid the theme parks."

"What's the point, Orissa? What's the point of going on living in a world like this?"

"We just have to, don't we?"

"I guess." She pressed her lips together and lightly knocked her head against mine. "There has to be more, right? More people like us?"

"I'm sure there are. And I'm sure there are real quarantines," I said, wanting to believe it.

"If anyone will get us there, it's you."

"I'm not going to let anything happen to you."

"I know," She whispered.

———————————▶

Lisa's coughing echoed up the hall. There was a scurry of movement followed by someone loudly stomping up the stairs. It was Sonja, asking me what bag the inhaler was in. I accompanied her back to the cars and dug through the medical bag until I found the little red thing. She sprinted back into the house, calling for Padraic. I rolled my eyes and shook my head. Sure, we *thought* this place was zombie free, but that didn't mean we should run around shouting. I opened up my suitcase, pulling out a pair of black athletic pants, socks, underwear, a black, long sleeved thermal shirt, and a hooded sweatshirt.

I folded the clothes over my arm and grabbed the strap of the food bag. The weight was too much for my injured back. Not wanting to appear weak, I grabbed another hoodie and socks from the suitcase for Lauren. With my hands full of clothes, I asked Jason to bring in the food.

Raeya was stripping the bed when I went back upstairs.

"I found clean sheets in the closet," she explained. "I already shook the dust out."

I held the clothes up.

"Thank God," she exclaimed, kicking off her heels. "I wish I could shower before changing."

"Me too, but I don't think we're gonna find a working shower anytime soon."

"I know." She pulled her blood stained nurse costume over her head and looked around for a hamper.

"I don't think it matters," I said, trying not to laugh. She nodded and quickly changed. Since it was dark, she didn't notice the details of the sweatshirt until we got into the fairly well lit living room.

"Hey! This is mine!" She looked down at the screen print of an elephant. "From the sanctuary. I'm surprised you still have it!"

"You must have left it. I knew I'd get it back to you eventually."

Jason spread the food out on the table, sorting it into categories. We had soup, bread, peanut butter, a variety of fruit, and a medley of junk food. As far as beverages, we had about two cases of water, several bottles of juice, two gallons of Gatorade and a few cans of pop.

It wouldn't last long.

Reminding everyone that we'd had a small lunch not that long ago, I refilled the pistol's cartridges and laid out the few weapons I had. Two guns—one with no bullets—two daggers and a sword. It was pathetic.

"Should we look in the other houses tomorrow?" a male voice came from behind me. There was no mistaking that accent.

"Maybe," I told Padraic. "I don't think we'll find much though. The people here had time to gather what they needed and wanted."

"Would it be a waste of time?"

"Maybe. We won't know until we try." I unloaded the gun, deciding I should try my best to clean it.

"How do you know how to do that?" Padraic asked, watching me take apart the pistol.

"My grandpa taught me how to care for guns," I replied flatly, focused on what was in my hands.

"I've not fired a gun often," he told me.

I nodded, not knowing what to say. I put the pistol back together; it was new and didn't need cleaning. Plus, I had nothing to clean it with.

"How many bullets do you have left?" Padraic sat next to me, his leg brushing against mine.

"Not many." I shook the box of bullets.

"Where'd you learn to shoot?"

"My grandpa."

"Sounds like an interesting guy."

"He is." I stuck the loaded cartridge back in the gun and clicked the safety on.

"So, you guys just shot for fun?"

"Sometimes."

"Were you close to him?"

"Yeah. I spent every summer at his farm since I was old enough to walk."

"Sounds nice."

"It was." I stood, shoving the gun in the back of my pants. "I'm gonna patrol around, see what's out there before the sun fully sets." I didn't even make it out of the kitchen before Padraic objected.

"Orissa, really?"

"Really, what?"

"You shouldn't go out alone."

"I'll take Argos."

"I'm coming," he told me.

"Stay here," I suggested. "Do doctor things."

"Doctor things? I think you're grasping at straws now." He stood. "You're not in charge of me, Orissa."

"Fine, come with. But if you get hurt or killed, don't complain to me."

Raeya wasn't happy about me going out looking for trouble either, but she knew better than to object. I advised her to lock the door and only answer when I knocked a rehearsed, repetitive knock.

The fire red trees were alive with birds, loudly chirping and chattering. Seeing the Range Rover parked on the curb brought a question to mind.

"The GPS in your car, it doesn't work, right?"

"Right," Padraic said. "It says the satellite signal was lost."

"That doesn't make sense." I pulled the band from my braid, combing out my hair with my fingers. "Are there zombies in space? There's no reason satellite signals would be lost."

"I don't really know how that stuff works," Padraic said, his blue eyes fixing on mine.

"Me neither," I admitted. "It just doesn't seem right."

"Does any of this?"

"Hell no." I sighed, scuffing my feet along the pavement, kicking leaves as I did so. Argos trotted ahead, following a scent trail into someone's yard. We walked in silence until we reached a fork in the road. I stopped in the middle, looking to my left and right. More houses lined the street to my left. Turning right, a park came into view. Swings blew slightly in the breeze, displaying rusty chains and peeling rubber seats. We passed through the overgrown baseball field, emerging onto what used to be the main street.

"When did you move to the city?" Padraic asked, unable to keep quiet.

"Uh, about a month or so ago."

"Looking for a job after college?"

"Not exactly." I walked faster, less than eager to talk about my reasons for moving in with Aunt Jenny. The windows of the post office were shattered, though it didn't look like virus infected people had done it. Stones had been thrown through, and cigarettes and beer bottles littered the dusty, tile floor. We hiked up and down the street, finding everything to be empty. The stitch in my side came back and I clutched it, trying to push the pain away.

"You doing alright?" Padraic sounded concerned.

"I'll be fine," I said through gritted teeth. I took a deep breath and dropped my hand, marching forward with as much dignity as I could muster.

"Why do you do that?"

"Do what?"

"Act like nothing can touch you."

"I'm not acting," I retorted.

"Orissa," he exhaled, reaching out, his fingers wrapping around my wrist "Stop. You're in pain. Just stop for a minute."

"Fine." With his hand still on mine, Padraic led me to a bench. Sitting felt good. I let out a deep breath, wishing I could relax.

"This must have been a nice town at one time," Padraic noted.

"Yeah, seems like it."

"Maybe we could stay here awhile."

"We don't have enough food to stay. And remember what happens in the winter?"

"Yes, I know it gets cold," he said, smiling. "It's a nice day today, as far as fall days go, wouldn't you say?"

"I guess."

"Look," Padraic pointed to the sunset. "My gran used to tell me that red sunsets are a sign of good things to come."

"It reminds me of blood. Like not even the sun can shine through all the blood and death anymore." I spoke hoarsely, vaguely aware of the concerned look Padraic was giving me. "The sun shines on us and the sun shines on them. Human, zombie, or crazy, we are all under the same sky."

"Hmm." He ran a hand through his hair. "I can't figure you out, Orissa."

"There's not much to figure," I assured him.

"I disagree. You put up this 'I'm too tough to give a shit' front, but underneath it, I can tell that's not who you really are."

"You're wrong."

"Am I?"

"I said so," I urged, trying to sound sure.

"I disagree." A faint smile pulled his full lips up. "I bet I can crack you."

"Take your best shot." I leaned back, painfully stretching my abdomen.

"Just tell me true or false, alright?"

"Sure."

"You had your heart broken."

I snorted back a laugh. "Who hasn't?"

"Ah," he nudged my leg with his, "the truth comes out."

"Next question."

"You were really close to the person who broke your heart."

"True."

"And you didn't see it coming."

"True."

"Your world shattered after they broke your heart," he said softly.

"True."

"And you had to start all over because everything you thought you knew was gone."

"True."

"You thought you'd never love anyone again."

"False."

His winning streak broken, Padraic frowned. "They hurt you so much, you closed off your heart to anyone else."

"False," I said after a moment's consideration.

"It's hard for you to trust new people."

"Very true."

"And that's because of what happened."

"True."

"You gave everything to this person."

"True."

"You thought you'd be together forever."

"False. And come on, what am I sixteen? I know better than to expect forever."

"Hah! Expect. Expectations. You don't get close to people because you're afraid of them not living up to your expectations."

"Saying true will make me sound like a horrible bitch. I might be a bitch at times, but not a horrible one...I like to think at least."

Padraic softly laughed.

"What about you?" I asked. "You seemed to be drawing from personal experiences there."

His smile disappeared. "It seems we both have our secrets." His blue eyes misted and he looked above me, pretending to examine the courthouse across the street. I wondered how someone could break his heart. He was a hot, Irish doctor. Isn't that what girls want? But I knew his type: a do-gooder. When you wear your heart on your sleeve, it's easy to break.

"Why aren't you mad?" I blurted.

"Mad?"

How could he be so clueless? "I lied to you."

"Orissa, I thought we resolved that."

"Still, don't you hold some sort of resentment toward me?"

"No."

"I would be mad at you," I assumed.

Padraic crossed his arms. "It was wrong of you to lie, there's no way around that. But you did it to save someone you care about. And you did."

I couldn't pinpoint why his understanding bothered me. Maybe, deep down, I was mad at myself for being so selfish. I supposed, really, it didn't matter. I needed to get through this alive before I started worrying about my inner self.

Padraic didn't speak on the walk back. Argos met us halfway to the house, proudly carrying a dead rabbit. I pushed the gate open and walked up the cobblestone. Padraic stopped short. I spun around, fear grasping my heart. Instinctively, I drew the gun, moving into a defensive stance.

"What is it?" Padraic asked.

"Did you see something?"

"No," he answered.

"Why did you stop so fast then?"

"Oh." He looked down, blood tinting his cheeks. "I-I just wanted to tell you something."

"Couldn't it have waited until we were inside?" I asked.

He laughed. "Yeah, I'm sorry. Anyway, I wanted to let you know that I'd follow you anywhere."

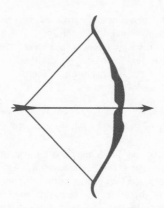

CHAPTER 13

The following morning, we loaded up the cars. Padraic and Spencer would be in the front seat of the SUV, with Padraic driving. Raeya, Lauren, and Lisa called dibs on the back. The others headed to the other car.

Padraic's eyes were full of worry when he looked at Zoe, who had caught Lisa's cough, making a lump form in my throat. He wrapped her in a blanket, placed her beside Raeya in the back, and put Finickus on her lap. She tied the leash to her wrist again. I got in the very back of the Range Rover, cargo hold, next to Argos. This SUV was packed this time, but most of our things had been put into the car to allow everyone to sit where they pleased.

"Do you have any music?" I asked Padraic as he steered down the country road.

"I listened to satellite radio mostly. But I have a few CDs under the passenger seat."

Raeya dug them out and handed one to Spencer, who popped it in. Padraic liked coffeehouse music, totally not my style but it was better than nothing.

Three hours later we pulled over next to a vast field of nothingness, still nowhere near the highway. Everyone got out, using the break to stretch and pee. I inspected the flat land on either side of us. It was quiet and still, with no signs of zombies or humans. I took Zoe from the SUV and took her to the Camaro where she would be more comfortable. Hot from being wrapped up in blankets with the heater on, she removed her extra layer of pants and sweatshirt. Her arms were covered with bruises. When she caught me staring she said, "I bruise easily." She put her hand over her arm. "Look! It's a hand print!"

I smiled along with her but it really made me scared. Padraic gave Zoe and Lisa a bottle of water, telling them he wanted the water gone by the time we got to Kentucky. I admired the way he was with them: patient, caring, and so calm. He made them peanut butter sandwiches with the last few pieces of bread. The rest of us snacked on junk food.

"After eating nothing but Twinkies and beer for two weeks, I would have loved a sandwich," Lauren scoffed under her breath. I met Raeya's eyes, telling myself it wasn't worth it to get into it with Lauren.

"Twinkies and beer?" Padraic inquired.

"It was a frat house," Raeya explained. "But we did have more than that."

"Oh yeah," Lauren said with a wave of her hand. "I forgot about the thawed frozen pizzas."

"Maybe we'll find food in Kentucky," Sonja said hopefully.

"Yeah. Kentucky," Lauren spat and turned away.

Shaking his head, Padraic shot me a glance and smiled. I returned the smile. We piled into the cars again—some people switching up for a change of environment. We wasted another hour looking for the highway. Once we found it, we drove steadily, making good time. Of course, we had to run into a pileup. I stopped counting the cars involved after thirteen.

"Hang on," I said as Padraic put the Range Rover in reverse. "I don't see any zombies, do you?"

"No," Raeya answered automatically. "No!" she said louder. "Orissa, please don't get out."

"This is the perfect place to find a car. There's a ton of them!"

"They probably don't have gas. Or keys."

"We won't know—"

"Until we look," she finished. "Fine."

"Um," Padraic started. "No. We can't see through the cars. Anything could be out there."

"Just let me check," I offered.

"Here," he said, motioning to the sunroof. There was a moment of jumbled movement as Raeya and I traded places. I shimmied my way through the sunroof, climbing onto the sun-warmed roof of the car. I stood, carefully placing my feet on either side of the opening. Shielding the sun from my eyes, I scanned the crash. Many of the doors had been left open in peoples' mad rushes to escape. Those weren't worth trying; the batteries had long been drained. The gas tanks, however, might have something to give. Maybe there was something that I could hotwire.

I knelt down, sticking my head over the window. "I don't see anything moving. We need gas at the very least. Keep the car running if it makes you feel better. I need one person to siphon gas with me to speed up the process."

"Is it safe?" Raeya asked.

"As far as I can tell."

"I'll help," she said. "We should look inside the cars too. I'd love a pair of shoes."

I grinned, reaching inside for my bag. As soon as I jumped off the SUV, Padraic turned it around and cut the engine. Hilary pulled up next to him and rolled down the window. I quickly explained my plan. She nodded and got out to help. Sonja took my place on top of the Range Rover, acting as our lookout. Lauren sat, stretching out her legs, on the Camaro's hood. It was too low to offer a good vantage point, though I didn't say anything. I didn't trust Lauren enough to rely on her to keep a watchful eye for the rest of us.

Cautiously, we combed through the cars. Spencer and Jason, after a brief lesson or refresher on how to siphon, were in charge of getting gas, filling up both cars and hopefully gathering enough to fill a third. Feeling anxious pressure to get on our way, I rummaged through cars that looked the most promising. Several were locked and the ones that weren't were missing keys or had built in protection against hotwiring. Purses, food, books, phones, and wallets were left behind. Where had the people gone? I imagined a camouflage bus rolling up, whisking everyone away to some heavenly quarantine. Or, more realistically, everyone became infected and took off in search of fresh blood.

A dead, rotting corpse leaned against the window of a rusty, old pickup. I could smell him through the closed windows and doors. I went around an upside down minivan, trying to avoid seeing the passengers who'd died in the crash. At least it was over for them. A red sedan sat with the door ajar on the shoulder. The body of what I guessed to be a woman—based on the long hair, blood-crusted and stiff—flopped out, her face chewed off.

Shuddering, I hurried past. After many more failed attempts, I found a decent car with the keys on the driver's seat. I put them in the ignition and fired up the car without a problem. I looked behind me: there was my problem. I was boxed in.

"Son of a bitch!" I hit the steering wheel. I shut the car off, mad I hadn't considered maneuvering the car before. Feeling like I was dragging my feet, I trudged back to the Range Rover. "See anything?" I asked Sonja, pulling the strap of my bag over my head.

"Nothing," she answered, sweeping her eyes over the highway. "Argos ran away."

"He'll be back," I assured her, only feeling mild panic. I sat on the bumper, wishing for a glass of water. My mouth was so dry.

"Can we go now?" Lauren asked loudly.

"Soon enough," I said shortly. I stayed in my spot, taking over Lauren's job as watchman. Spencer and Jason found three gallons of water with the safety seals still around the caps. Ecstatically, I ripped one off and put the jug to my lips. Water ran down my face as I drank. I passed the jug to Jason, who drank and passed it to Sonja. After Spencer took a long drink, he offered it to Lauren.

"Ew, I'm not drinking that after you four just did," she scoffed.

Sharing drinks never bothered me. I knew it grossed some people out—Raeya included—and I respected that. Given our current situation, fear of cooties needed to be overcome.

"Sorry we didn't pack cups," I spat.

"Can't I have a bottle of water?"

"Can't you just drink from the jug like the rest of us?"

"Zoe and Lisa got their own water bottles."

"Zoe and Lisa are very sick children who can't risk getting sicker from other people's germs," I reminded her.

"So you admit to having germs then."

I threw my hands up. "We all have germs."

Padraic and Raeya joined us.

"Who has germs?" Raeya asked.

"Everyone, apparently," Lauren pouted.

"We do," Padraic told her. "Why is that a problem?"

Lauren pointed to the plastic gallon of water. "They want to share from that. I think it's gross."

"I think we should only open one at a time," I interjected. "The others have seals. We should keep them that way until we need them."

Padraic shrugged. "I suppose it's a good idea. As a doctor, I normally advise against sharing food and drinks, but I think we have to bypass what we normally do." He picked up the water and took a drink. "And you can pour it into your mouth, if that makes it less gross."

"I want my own bottle," Lauren insisted.

"Oh my God," I vented. "Just take a damn bottle and shut up." I grabbed a small bottle from inside the Range Rover and chucked it at her. She barely caught it, shrieking that she'd broken a nail.

Raeya called me over to show me that she'd found a pair of purple Pumas that were her size, as well as more snack food. Hilary was the last to return, setting her armload of sustenance on the hood of the Camaro. Argos trotted to us in time to jump into the back of the Range Rover. We stuffed the extra water and food in the back.

Zoe woke up when Hilary started the engine. She said she had to pee and couldn't hold it. I told her I'd come and keep watch for zombies. She was shy and didn't want anyone to see her so we ventured farther from the cars than I would have liked. I took her behind a semi, promising her the boys couldn't see.

She had just pulled up her pants when I heard the gargling snarl.

➤━━━━━━━━━━━━━►

I took Zoe's hand, whispering for her to be quiet. We weaved our way around the semi. My heart was racing. The crazy banged on a car window nearby, scaring Zoe. She jumped and whimpered, clutching onto me. I put my finger up to my lips and shook my head.

Zoe nodded.

Her slippers skidded with each step, sounding incredibly loud. I picked her up and instantly wished I hadn't. Though she didn't weigh much, my battered body couldn't handle much at the moment. Keeping my eyes on the crazy, I didn't pay attention to what was in front of me. My foot caught on something metal. It scraped the street, echoing like a beacon.

Shit.

I froze. We were several yards from our cars. Our companions could no doubt see us. I set Zoe down, holding onto her hand so tight I had to be hurting her. My bag was in the car. I had nothing. I looked at what I had kicked. It was a bent tire rim, which had probably been popped off in the accident. I picked it up thinking I could use it as a shield.

Poor Zoe covered her mouth. Her eyes bulged and her body convulsed. She was trying not to cough. Tears filled her big, green eyes. The crazy spotted us, lips curling to reveal her teeth. Like an animal, she growled and lunged forward.

"Get to the car," I instructed. "Now! Go!" She took off, tripping and falling. Hands bloody from the asphalt, she scrambled up. Raeya, who was in the driver's seat of the SUV, opened her door. I glimpsed Zoe climbing in right as I swung the rim.

It hit the crazy in the jaw. It seemed to only anger her and she came at me with even more fury. I was sore, so sore. Every muscle was stiff. It felt like the stitches ripped out of my shoulder as I leaned back and kicked her in the chest.

She caught my foot.

I had only a moment to see Padraic, Raeya, and Argos running in my direction. Jason was out of the car fending off a crazy of his own.

I wasn't counting on any logic coming from my crazy. She yanked and I fell, the wind getting knocked out of me on impact. She was over me, sniffing as if sizing me up. The horn honked. The crazy's attention snapped to it, long enough for me to grab her hair and twist her head.

Her neck didn't snap. She flopped to the side, off of me. I crawled away, reaching for the tire rim. Her grubby hands closed around my ankle. I thrashed wildly, breaking her hold. I forced myself up, grasping the rim. The rusty metal sliced open the palm of my hand as I whipped it around. It broke her nose. Blood dripped down her face but did nothing to slow her.

Argos flew over me in a flash of fur and fangs. His teeth sunk into the crazy's jugular. He shook his head, tearing open her flesh. She clawed at him, not reacting to the pain. When her body finally went limp, I weakly slipped my unbloodied hand under his collar and limped back to the SUV with the support of Padraic and Raeya. Raeya jumped into the car and stomped on the gas as soon as Argos, Padraic and I were in. I pressed my thumb on the cut on my left hand, trying to stop the bleeding. We raced down the highway, getting off at the first exit. Not bothering with the map, Raeya turned to the right.

"Pull over," Padraic told her.

"No way. We're too close." Raeya's eyes were wide and her knuckles were white from gripping the steering wheel.

"Orissa's bleeding," he reminded her.

"It's just a flesh wound," I said with a horrible British accent.

Raeya laughed, turning to me. Her humor disappeared as soon as she saw the blood.

"Really, it's ok. It's just my hand." At least the pain of this wound made me forget about the agonizing gash on my back and my recently cut open abs.

"You're already injured, Orissa," Padraic told me as if I'd forgotten. "And even though it's just your hand you can still lose a decent amount of blood."

"I know," I agreed. "When we find a clearing we can pull over."

The next few minutes passed painfully slow. Raeya pulled into an empty church parking lot. We let Argos out first; he was proving to be more and more badass as the days went on. Padraic grabbed the first aid supplies and met me around the side of the car. He unfolded my hand, pouring water over it to wash away the still oozing blood. I watched as he scrubbed out the dirt and carefully extracted little shards of metal.

"Have you had a tetanus shot recently?" he asked.

"Yeah, I have actually. A few months ago."

"Good," he said, exhaling. Tiredness hit me and I leaned on the car. "Orissa?" he asked.

"Yeah?"

"You doing alright?"

"I'm tired," I confessed. "That's all."

"Do you want to try to find a place for the night?"

"No. I want to go home," I said without thinking. "I mean, Kentucky," I added quickly. Padraic didn't mention my slip up as he bandaged my hand.

"I know you'll hate this, but I think it would be best if we found some sort of rubber gloves to put over your hand to keep zombie blood out."

Yes, I hated that idea. Nevertheless, it was smart. "Sure."

Zoe was next, crying as Padraic cleaned her cuts. She hugged me once she was patched up.

"Thank you for saving me, Orissa."

"You don't have to thank me, Zoe. I'd save you anytime."

"You got hurt because of me."

"No, I got hurt because of the monsters. That's not your fault."

"I'm not worth saving," she cried.

"Don't ever say that!"

"But I'm not. My mommy didn't come back for me."

I kissed the top of her head. I wanted to tell her that her mother was a douche-bag asshole who didn't deserve to have children. "I'm sure she tried," I lied.

"No," Zoe objected. "They were with me. In my room at the hospital. They left when the monsters showed up. They went to get my brothers but didn't take me."

I held her tightly. I wished I could punch her mother in the throat. How can you leave your own daughter, no matter how sick? "Are you hungry?"

"Yeah," she said. I took her hand and led her back to the car, leaning over the backseat to pick out something for her to snack on while we drove. This trip could not end soon enough.

<hr>

After deciding to not drive on the highways again, we detoured through town. I closed my eyes, enjoying the heat blowing on my feet. The Range Rover slowed, jerking me back to reality. I looked around, trying to discern the reason for stopping.

"What are you doing?" I asked.

"It's a stop sign, Rissy," Raeya said, looking at me like I was crazy.

"Ray, it's ok to blow through stop signs."

"Oh, right." She pressed the gas pedal. "If a zombie cop pulls me over, you are so paying the ticket." She grinned and we both laughed.

"You girls have an odd sense of humor," Padraic observed.

I shrugged, knowing it to be true. I closed my eyes and sighed.

"Go to sleep, Orissa," Raeya said quietly. "I know you're tired."

"I'm fine."

"You are such a liar."

I felt safe while we were moving, and it didn't take long before I drifted to sleep.

"Rissy!" Raeya hissed, shaking me. "Rissy!"

"Huh?"

"Look!"

In the distance, a set of headlights grew bigger and bigger.

"People!" Raeya said.

I jolted awake. "Oh my God, you're right!"

"People!" she repeated. "In a car!"

Sonja stirred. "What's going on?"

"There are people! Look!" Raeya said excitedly.

Sonja elbowed Jason. "Jason! There's a car up ahead!" Padraic and Spencer had come to consciousness now, and they were thrilled to see signs of life.

The car wasn't moving. The people driving were probably just as excited to come across us as we were to see them. Raeya turned the brights off when we were a few feet away. A shadowy figure got out of the pickup. I rolled down my window and leaned out.

The man held his hand up, blinded by the headlights. Argos growled. Padraic held him back, not wanting him to scare off the only human we'd seen in over a hundred miles. Leaving my bag in the car, I eagerly got out, temporarily forgetting my pain.

"Hi!" I gushed. Nothing logical flowed into my brain at the moment. "I-I'm so glad we're not the only ones alive!"

The man nodded, looking from me to the car. He looked shocked to see so many people alive.

I moved around, extending my hand in a businesslike fashion. "I'm Orissa. There are ten of us."

He held out his hand, a sharp machete limply held in his fingers. He cocked his head, examining me. My blood ran cold, tensing every muscle. A nasty, infected bite wound festered on his neck. I didn't even have time to scream. The machete sparkled in the headlights before it came slicing down.

I ducked, barely missing the blade. I dropped to my knees, reopening the gash on my hand, and crawled away. "Go!" I shouted to Raeya.

The crazy looked for me. I made it to his truck, slamming the door and hitting the lock button. He grabbed the handle, jerking on the door so hard the truck shook. I shifted the car into 'drive' and slammed on the gas. Speeding past the Range Rover and Camaro, I pulled a squealing U-turn. I plowed right into the crazy. He clanked against the hood before getting sucked under. Even though he was a day or two past human, it was revolting to feel the truck bump over his torso. I let off the gas, my body shaking from the close encounter.

"Can't I fucking catch a break?" I asked myself. Something moved in the back seat. I looked into the review mirror, complete terror paralyzing my body. The zombie stiffly sat up, dumbly reaching for me.

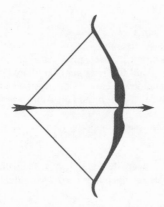

CHAPTER 14

I screamed and slammed on the breaks. The truck swerved, veering off the road and into a drainage ditch. Since I hadn't bothered to put a seat belt on, I flew forward, cracking my head on the windshield. I frantically pulled on the door handle. The zombie had been tossed forward too. He growled and groaned, his rotting face inches from my body. Finally, the door opened and I fell out of the truck, hitting my knees on something sharp. I grabbed handfuls of dried grass, trying to pull myself out of the way. The zombie toppled out of the truck.

Somehow I forced myself upright. Blood dripped into my eye. I fell again as I tried to make it up the ditch to the road. The zombie had my foot, pulling it toward his mouth. I kicked and screamed. I didn't see her coming. But she was there, standing over the zombie. Raeya hit him on the head once, twice, three times before he let me go.

"Why won't you die?!" She yelled, striking the zombie on the head with her tennis racket. Argos jumped on the zombie, fangs tearing into his leg, easily ripping off the rotting flesh. Hands slipped under my arms. I screamed and jerked away before realizing it was Padraic. He pulled me back. I kicked my feet, trying to get them to work. Once I was on the road, he released me, raising the gun.

"No," I tried to yell. My voice had no volume. "No," I repeated. He was likely a bad shot and Raeya was there. "Ray!" I attempted to shout. She heard, and after one more whack over the head, she ran up the embankment to us. Padraic put his arm around me, helping me to the car. He whistled, calling Argos. The dog didn't listen. I took the gun from Padraic, exhaled, aimed, and blew the zombie's brains out. When it stopped moving, the dog rejoined us.

As we tore down the country road—Raeya driving—I realized that my head was bleeding. I reached up, wincing as my fingers grazed the fresh cut above my left eye. The front seat was a jumble of chaos and body parts, but I made it to the back. Padraic turned the overhead light on and inspected the cut.

"You'll be ok," he told me and set to work cleaning my wounds. Sonja had taken my front seat, leaving a spot for Argos in between Jason and Spencer. The dog sat, stretching his blood and flesh covered paws across the boys. I started shivering, from fear, cold, or blood loss, I didn't know. Padraic unfolded the blanket he had been using as a cushion and draped it around my shoulders. I wrapped it tightly around myself, unable to stop shivering.

Raeya was forced to slow down as the road began to wind. We were only an hour away from the farm. The lights shining in on us from the Camaro were blinding. Looking out the back gave me an instant headache and I felt like I was going to puke. I closed my eyes, unaware that I was slowly falling to the side until I rested on Padraic's shoulder. I startled back to reality.

"Thanks for helping back there," I told him. "And Raeya, you totally had the game point. Thanks."

"I was so scared, Rissy," she said, looking back at me quickly. "So I did what I thought you would do."

"You thought I'd hit a zombie with a tennis racket?"

"Not exactly. But you would do something."

"Yeah," I agreed, nausea worsening. I closed my eyes again, leaning against the backseat. The SUV rounded a curvy hill. A curvy hill that was very familiar. This incline used to excite me as a child. It marked the start of my countdown. How much time had passed? Had I fallen asleep?

"Raeya," I spoke, my voice hoarse. "Sorry it took me so long to thank you for saving me. You too, Padraic."

"You already thanked me," Padraic said, sounding concerned.

"I did?"

"Yeah."

"Oh, I don't remember." My eyes were heavy, so heavy. They closed of their own accord.

"Orissa," Padraic said, loudly. He put his hands on my shoulders and gave me a gentle shake.

"Yeah?"

"You have a concussion."

"I do?"

I heard Raeya whimper something incoherent. "Do you remember what happened?" she asked, her voice full of worry.

My brain was black for a second—black and blank. Then I remembered the headlights, the hope in my heart when I thought we had stumbled upon another living soul. He'd been crazy and he'd had a pet zombie stashed in his car.

"I hit my head on the windshield."

Padraic said, "Yeah, definitely concussed."

"No, I remembered."

"It took you almost a minute to recall that."

"No it didn't," I insisted.

"Yeah, it did," Raeya hesitantly agreed. "Will she be ok?"

"Probably," Padraic answered, running a hand through his hair. "Orissa, other than your head hurting, how do you feel?"

"Tired. And sick. I feel like I'm gonna puke." The more I thought about it, the worse I felt. "Actually, I am gonna puke. Can you pull over?"

I barely made it out of the car before everything came up, burning my throat and nose. The rush of blood from leaning over made me dizzy, increasing my nausea three fold. This fucking sucked. Raeya held back my hair with one hand while the other gently rubbed my back. If I wasn't so disgusting, I would have hugged her and told her she was my best friend in the whole damn world. I slumped against the Range Rover, and was annoyed when Padraic carried me into the back. I rested my head against his chest. He gave me a little bit of water. It felt good to wash the taste of vomit away.

"You can close your eyes but I'm going to wake you up every few minutes, ok?" he said quietly.

I mumbled a response and was sucked into unconsciousness.

───────▶───────

The next time I woke up, the glorious site of my grandparents' farmhouse was in front of me. My head hurt like hell, not to mention the rest of my body, but I was able to wake up. The house was still standing, for one. Two, there were no zombies in sight. I groggily got out of the car, telling Argos to look for danger. I took a long drink of water and inhaled the cold night air, feeling more awake. The headlights from both the SUV and the sports car illuminated the white house. I slung my bag over my shoulder, taking the gun in my hand.

The big iron bars from the horse stalls had been removed and nailed over the downstairs windows, making the house appear like a jail. It was brilliant. My feet shuffled up the wooden porch stairs, which still creaked and groaned like before. I ran my hand over the bars. They had been expertly attached; no one could pull the bars off and get inside. My grandfather had taken extra measures to protect the house.

No lights were on inside, and I willed myself not to let that upset me. I hadn't *really* expected my grandpa to still be here. The front door had been reinforced. Leaving the car running, Raeya joined me. She put her hand in mine, knowing my worst fear. She had already retrieved the hide-a-key. I gripped her fingers tightly as she pushed open the door.

The smell of death didn't hit us.

"Grandpa?" I called. We waited, neither dared breathe. When nothing responded, we sent Argos through. He didn't bark or growl. "The coast is clear!" I called. "Bring the stuff in," I suggested to Raeya. "I'm gonna fire up the generator. Well, I'm going to try it. Who knows if it will work."

It was running low on fuel, but it started. The house came to life with lights. Though the brightness still hurt my concussed head, it was a beautiful sight. The soft yellow glow spilled out to the yard, casting funny shadows due to the bars on the windows.

I walked along the wraparound porch. Everything was quiet and still, like it used to be, like it should be. I paused before the front door, looking inside at the worn, wooden floors. With a deep breath, I crossed the threshold.

Suddenly, I was eleven-years-old again, walking through the front door of my grandparent's house. It was two summers after my parents' divorce. I remembered my grandmother crying when she found how I had to take care of my drunken mother. My grandpa was angry; angry at my mother and angry at himself. He shouldered some of the blame, saying if only he had been home more things might have turned out differently.

I missed my mother. I had been so excited to see her again, though I had nightmares about her stumbling around the house with a glass bottle in her hand, passing out on the floor. How many times had I sat by her, crying, not sure if she would ever wake up? I knew she missed me too. I was more than her drink mixer, really, I had to have been. I was her daughter. My grandparents said they wouldn't let me go back with her unless she cleaned up her act. And I had stayed with them a whole summer, thinking she would miss me, thinking she would change.

And she did. She turned completely around. Our house was clean, even redecorated in bright colors, and ridded of all liquor. I remembered that moment so well, a moment I thought I would cherish in my heart forever. I recalled the old pickup truck rolling to a stop. My mother flying down the driveway to hug me. Her hair had been curled and smelled like lavender. Her eyes—aquamarine like mine—had sparkled. She had changed.

Just not for me.

It was Ted who'd turned her life around, and Ted who'd pulled her out of the darkness. It had taken him only two months. I'd spent two years taking care of her, bringing her drinks, cleaning her vomit, cooking us dinner, attending to her every need, but *I* hadn't been enough. I couldn't make her happy, couldn't make her smile, couldn't make her see that I still loved her and desperately wanted her to love me back.

But Ted could make her see everything.

I couldn't find any real faults with him. He was kind, though stern at times, and accepted me like his own daughter. He'd had a good job, a nice house, and had bought me a puppy for Christmas. He was good to me, and even better to my mother. He was everything she wanted and needed and I hated him for it.

That summer was the last good summer I'd had with my grandpa. We went hunting and fishing, camping and hiking. He taught me how to survive if I got lost, which plants to eat, and which to avoid. I learned how to track, how to sit perfectly still in a deer stand for hours, how to make traps, and how to rely on only myself.

"Orissa?" Padraic's voice pulled me to the bloody present.

"Yeah?"

"I think you should sit. You look like you're gonna fall."

"Oh. I feel fine."

Sonja turned on the foyer lights. My stomach churned. I barely made it outside before I retched up nothing. I tripped going up the stairs. Padraic caught me, lifted me up, and carried me to the living room couch. He gently brushed my messy hair out of my face and looked into my eyes.

"Stay with me, Orissa," he said when my eyelids got heavy. "Orissa, try to stay awake."

"Ok," I mumbled. "The lights hurt."

"I know, but I'm afraid if you close your eyes you'll fall asleep."

"And why is that bad?"

"I think you hit your head harder than I initially thought."

"Ok." I closed my eyes.

"Orissa," he began.

"I'm not sleeping. See I'm talking."

"Ok, keeping talking then."

"Ok." I was aware of the shuffling going on around me. I heard Zoe's little voice asking what was wrong with me and Raeya gently telling her I'd hit my head, but not to worry as I'd be ok.

"You're not talking," Padraic said.

"Thank you, Captain Obvious." I opened one eye to glare at him.

He laughed softly.

"What is your name?"

"And I'm the one with the head injury? You know my name."

"Not your full name."

"Orissa Lynn Penwell."

"How old are you?"

"Twenty-four."

"What is your favorite color?"

"Black."

Argos' wet nose pressed against my face. I reached out to pet him. Someone closed the front door, the sound hammering my eardrums. I felt sick again. I didn't even bother to mention it; I had nothing left to come up.

"Black's not a color," Padraic noted.

"Yes it is."

"It's the absence of color."

"No," I argued. "White is. Black is all colors mixed together. And it's my favorite."

"How did you hurt your head?"

"I chased the gnomes through the magic mirror." I let Padraic suffer a few seconds before I opened my eyes. "I'm fine, ok? I know who I am, my age, where we are, and what happened. I just want to shower and sleep."

"Shower?" Lauren was eavesdropping. "We can shower?"

"Assuming the water pump still works, yes," I replied tartly.

"I call dibs on first shower," she said hurriedly.

Padraic interjected. "I think Orissa should be the first to shower. This is her house, and she needs to rest more than anyone right now."

I think Lauren actually stomped her foot. "I haven't showered in God knows how long. Do you know how oily your skin gets from eating junk food?"

I tugged on Padraic's sleeve. I opened my eyes just enough to look into his. "The water takes forever to warm up in this house," I whispered.

He smiled deviously.

"Fine," he said with authority. "But we have to agree to a two minute limit on the showers, since we all want to take one. Lauren, go ahead, be first. Remember you only have two minutes."

I asked Raeya to take Lauren into the master bedroom's bathroom and make sure there were towels. She led Sonja upstairs to the second bathroom with a shower. I hadn't been in this house in over a year. I wanted so badly to walk around and let the memories come back, see everything I had missed so much. At the moment, I wasn't sure I could move. Someone padded into the room. A cold hand gripped mine.

"Will she be ok?" Zoe asked.

"Yes, she will be just fine. She hit her head and is very tired," Padraic summed up. Zoe began asking something else and was overcome with coughing. There was a quick shuffling of feet; Hilary must have rushed over to help her. No sooner did they leave than someone else came into the room. A body sank down on the couch by my feet.

"How ya feeling?" Raeya asked.

"Peachy." I tried to sit up and look at her, but gave up when the movement brought another bout of nausea. "What's the house like?"

"In order. Well, as orderly as normal."

"We'll have to check the barn in the morning," I said.

"Of course."

My brain fuzzed out. Raeya and Padraic were having a conversation, the words sounding foreign. Raeya shook my foot.

"Rissy," she spoke. "Wake up."

"I'm awake," I told her, thinking I was speaking clearly. "I just closed my eyes for a minute."

"More like five."

"Nah-ah."

"Yeah," Padraic agreed. "You can sleep, but I have to wake you up every half hour, alright?"

"Ok," I agreed. I think I would have agreed with just about anything at that point.

Raeya moved off the couch, getting a blanket from the closet. She took my boots off before draping the blanket over me. "I want to sleep in my bed," I requested. I had been looking forward to it for a while.

"Where is it?" Padraic asked.

"I'll show you," Raeya told him. I didn't object as he carried me upstairs. But I did object to getting under the covers of my childhood bed covered in blood, dirt, sweat, and zombie parts. Padraic and Raeya insisted I rest right away. I forced myself to sit up, opening my eyes. When I saw the photos on the dresser, it was easier to pull myself out of the haze.

The room hadn't changed in the twenty-something years it had been mine. The blue floral wall paper was faded, pictures of Raeya and me as teenagers were still pinned to the bulletin board above my desk, which still housed notebooks, magazines, colored pencils, and markers that were sure to be dried out and worthless.

My grandma had picked out the bedspread. It was light purple with little blue and yellow flowers winding their way across the fabric on little vines. It was pretty, I supposed, but extremely girly. With the four-post bed, dresser, desk, bookshelf, nightstands, and armchair, the room was crowded. The floor creaked just as I remembered when I wobbled my way to the closet. The only clothes in there were too small for me. Thinking they might fit Zoe or Lisa, I reached for the hangers. I faltered, leaning against the doorframe for support.

I wanted to shower.

Raeya helped me into the bathroom. She was afraid I was going to slip in the shower and hit my head again. She stayed, sitting on the counter, and talking to me periodically to make sure I was ok. I hated that she was worried. I felt, somehow, that I'd let her down. I wanted her to take care of herself, to worry about her own survival—not mine.

When my time was up, I gingerly wrapped the towel around my battered torso and went back into my room, where I was surprised to see Padraic.

He was surprised too. After letting his eyes linger over my barely covered body for a whole second, he turned away.

"Sorry! I-I wanted to rebandage the cut on your back a-and make sure your stitches didn't come out."

"Ok," I simply said and sat on the bed. At this point, I didn't care if he saw me naked. I just wanted to sleep. I reached behind me to pull the soaking bandage off my back.

After Padraic tended my wounds and found me a pair of pajamas that still fit, I fell into a deep sleep and the night passed in a blurry haze. I remember Padraic waking me, asking me questions, and letting me slip back into sleep. At one point Raeya crawled under the covers next to me.

The next thing I remember is Raeya gently shaking me awake. Through the closed, ivory curtains weak sunlight filtered into the room. Good. I was up before the sun rose.

"What time is it?" I asked her, slowly sitting up.

"Probably after five."

"I haven't been up this early in a long time. We should get an early start today though."

"Oh, Rissy, it's five in the evening." She bit her lip, looking guilty.

"I slept all day?"

"Yeah. You needed it." She sat next to me. "I made dinner. It's not a good dinner, but it's warm and filling."

The talk of food reminded me how hungry I was. I stood too fast and my vision blacked out. Raeya grabbed my arm, steadying me. "I'm ok," I assured her. "This has happened before, you know. It's not from the concussion."

"Ok," she said with a pressed smile, not looking convinced. "I can bring dinner up to you, if you'd like."

The offer was tempting, mostly because it meant I could stay up here and not have to deal with anyone. Knowing I would have to face them eventually, I followed Raeya down the stairs which emptied into the family room. I began to feel a little dizzy as I walked through the room, past the bathroom, and into the foyer which then led to the dining room where everyone had gathered. The breakfast table had been set in there too, so that all ten of us had a place at a table. The aroma of dinner was strong, making my stomach growl.

I sat at the head of the table; the spot had been reserved for me, and dug into the bowl of rice and beans in front of me. Raeya had done well, making the best of what we had. We ate in awkward silence. Conversation seemed so trivial now. I noticed that Lisa's cough had lessened while Zoe's had worsened. Hilary asked Lauren to help her clean the kitchen after dinner. Lauren objected, wrinkling her nose at the piles of dirty dishes in the sink.

Deciding to leave the room before I smacked Lauren, I opened the basement door and headed down. My bare feet had just graced the cold cement when Padraic plodded after me.

"Anything good down here?" he asked.

I pulled the string to turn on the single light bulb at the base of the stairs. "See for yourself." To our right, shelves were lined with cans of beans, home-canned veggies, and bags of rice. "We'll have to check the dates. I'm sure more than half expired years ago. My grandpa liked to be prepared, but the last few years weren't good to him."

I crossed the basement, my heart speeding up in excitement. I ran my hand along the wall, feeling for the switch. Bright, fluorescent lights hummed to life. To the untrained eye, only my grandfather's model train collection sat before me, displayed on pine shelves. I picked up a red boxcar, unlatching a secret lock. It strained my weak body to pull the hidden door back.

"Holy shit," Padraic swore.

I couldn't help but smile at the awed shock on his face. When I turned back to what was in front of me, I felt like I was looking at an old friend. I reached out, running my hands over the cool metal.

"You really aren't a government agent?" he asked, unable to take his eyes off the weapons.

"You've seen too many cheesy American action movies," I said as I ran my eyes over my grandpa's impressive collection. "The M240 is missing," I muttered to myself.

"Is that bad?"

"It was one of my grandpa's favorites. If he took it, then he must have killed a lot of zombies before he got out of here."

"Got out of here?" Padraic asked.

"To a quarantine—a real one."

"You think he's there?"

"He better be. He's a veteran. They at least owe him a safe place to live out his last years after all he did." I eyed several other empty spots. Along with the machine gun, an assault rifle, two handguns, a machete, and several knives were missing. At least my grandpa was well armed. I picked up a Berretta M9, the lights gleaming off the shiny black metal.

"Is it legal to have some of these?" Padraic asked, eyes fixed on a machine gun.

"Hell no. It doesn't matter anymore though, does it?" I loaded the handgun, clicking on the safety. It was a habit to stick it in the back of my pants. Forgetting that I had on ridiculous pajamas, I reached behind me. With a sigh, I set the gun down and scanned over the selection of handguns, looking for one for Padraic. "I'll start you with a .22, ok?" I grabbed a box of bullets and extended them both.

"Ok...uh...what is this?"

"Aren't doctors supposed to be smart? It's a gun."

"I know that, Orissa. Why are you giving it to me?"

"Shit, I must be concussed," I said laughing. "I'm going to teach you how to shoot. Target practice."

"In the dark?"

"There are flood lights out there. And zombies attack at night."

"You want to teach me?"

"Yes." It would be so much easier on me if I wasn't the only one who could shoot a zombie in the head from farther than a foot away. "I think it's a skill we all need to learn now."

→

We didn't make it to target shooting. Just simply getting up, eating, and walking around had been too much for me. I became disoriented, and Padraic insisted that shooting practice could wait. We agreed that we wouldn't tell the others about the weapon cache just yet. I didn't want any gun happy novices shooting their feet off. Raeya already knew about the guns, of course, but she'd never tell. Finally, I allowed Padraic to help me up to my room where I spent the next three days on bed rest. No one dared to venture outside without me, and Padraic only let Argos out a few times a day, always keeping him on a make shift leash to ensure the dog wouldn't run off. With help from a concoction of painkillers he gave me, I was able to sleep almost twenty-four hours a day for the first two days. I was convinced that he overdosed me on purpose to keep me calm and in bed. By day three, I couldn't reason taking any more medication and was bored out of my mind.

Raeya spent the morning with me. We talked and caught up on everything we'd missed since the last time we'd seen each other.

Zoe kept me company in the afternoon. She seemed nervous, her eyes constantly shifting to the doorway like she was afraid someone was going to pop in and yell 'boo.' Wanting to save gas, we had the heat set low. It was uncomfortably cold in the house. Zoe got under the covers, sticking her cold feet under Argos' warm body. She had unearthed my grandma's scrapbooks. There was a scrapbook for each year of my life until I turned eighteen.

Starting from my baby book, we flipped through them. I hadn't looked at the books in years. They brought on a happy pain, reminding me of how simple things used to be.

"You look sad this year," Zoe told me.

"Yeah, I guess I kinda do." I closed the book, noticing for the first time that my 'sad photos' coincided with my parent's divorce. "It was a rough year for me."

"What happened?"

"My dad left us."

"Oh. That would make me sad too."

"It hurt my mom more. But, hey, it was a long time ago. And look," I opened the next scrapbook. "I'm smiling here."

"And on a horse! Can you still ride?"

"Yeah. It's been a while but it's something you don't easily forget."

Zoe turned the page.

There I was again, sitting on the back of a scrawny, buckskin horse, beaming up at the camera with an oversized cowboy hat sliding over my eyes. I put my finger on the picture. "That's Sundance. He was my first horse. I went with my grandpa to the auction that spring. He let me pick out a horse and I picked the skinniest, ugliest, most pathetic looking horse there."

"Why would you do that?"

"I wanted to show everyone that you can turn something hopeless into something beautiful."

"Did you?"

"Turn the page." I waited while Zoe skimmed the pictures.

"He is beautiful!" she gasped.

"He really was. He was a huge brat though. I got thrown off of him more than any other horse." I laughed at the memory. "But my grandpa always told me it made me stronger, getting up after each fall. He never let me give up and just put Sundance away. I was sore and scared and I thought he was being mean at the time."

"But he was, wasn't he? If you fell from your horse, you were hurt."

"Yes, but never that badly. You see, Sundance was lazy. He didn't like being worked. Every time he bucked me off, it was in hopes of getting to go back to the barn. If I put him away after I fell, he'd learn that bucking equals not being ridden."

"Oh." Zoe turned to the next page. "Is that your mom?"

"No, that's my aunt."

"She looks like you."

"Yeah, I look more like my Aunt Jenny than I do my mom. She's my mom's younger sister." I felt a knot form in my chest when I thought about Aunt Jenny. I closed my eyes for just a second and prayed she was alright.

"She's pretty, like you."

"She is. And thanks." We continued looking through the books. Zoe loved the pictures of Raeya and me as awkward teenagers; she couldn't stop laughing. Then her laughs turned into coughs and soon she was tired. She objected when I suggested she take a nap. She got out of bed and told me she had something important to do and that I needed my rest. She shut the door when she left the room.

"Strange," I said to Argos.

Not able to sit still any longer, I showered, put the stupid pajamas back on, and set out to find real clothes. Along with my room, there were two other rooms upstairs. At one point, my mom and Aunt Jenny had lived in those rooms. They had long since been turned into guest rooms with empty closets. Well, mostly empty. I went across the hall and into the nearest spare room. Stashed behind closed doors was a box of odds and ends that my grandma didn't want to part with and old toys that were too good for attic or basement storage. There was an ironing board, a sewing machine, old purses, backpacks, books, and lots of scrap material. I went through the purses and backpacks, thinking it would be useful for everyone to have their own bag to fill with survival supplies.

The next closet housed my grandpa's hunting clothes. The camo jacket I had worn years ago still fit, though the sleeves were a little short. Nevertheless, I pulled everything from the hangers and carried clothes back to my room. I was sure the boys would be able to fit into this stuff. I imagined Padraic as being preppy in style. I don't know why, since I'd only seen him in scrubs and clothes he'd found in the apartment complex. I didn't think he would so much as roll his eyes at the camouflage and boots; no, he was too agreeable for that. Still, I didn't think he'd like wearing something like this.

"These clothes are more substantial," I said aloud to Argos as I shook the dust out. My stomach growled. I tossed the heap of clothes onto the hope chest and called Argos to follow me downstairs. My muscles were stiff from doing nothing for the last three days. It was hard to keep up with my yoga with so many rips and tears in my skin.

My foot didn't even hit the first stair when Zoe dashed up. Panting, she held out her hand.

"Is everything ok?" I asked, feeling minor panic.

"Yes," she said as she gasped for air.

"Come sit and catch your breath," I suggested and led her into my room. I picked up the towel—which I had lazily dropped on the floor—and rubbed it over my wet hair. My pajama shirt was now damp and making me colder.

"You have pretty hair," Zoe told me.

"Thanks."

"Can I brush it?"

"Of course." I wrapped a blanket around my shoulders after I gave Zoe the brush. I sat on the hope chest so she could kneel on the bed. She carefully brushed out the knots.

"My hair used to be blonde," she said, running the bristles through my long, dark hair. It made me sad to think about the implications. "Can I braid it?"

For the next twenty minutes, Zoe brushed, braided, unbraided, brushed and rebraided my hair. Finally she was satisfied with two French braids that were tight and neat. I stood and admired them in the mirror.

"You did a good job, Zoe." I ran my hand over my hair. "They are really smooth."

She beamed. "Thanks. My mom taught me how to braid."

Lisa came into the room, smiling but not meeting my eyes. She whispered something to Zoe, who giggled and told me to stay put. I heard them loudly run downstairs and then up again, both coughing and out of breath. Zoe took my hand and, without explaining, pulled me after her.

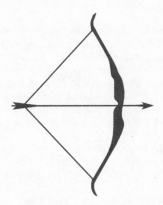

CHAPTER 15

"Surprise!" everyone shouted.

Lauren crossed her arms with a sour smile.

"What is this?" I muttered, the smell of fresh baked brownies distracting me.

Raeya laughed. "Orissa, don't you know what day it is?"

"No." Thinking Padraic would accuse me of still being concussed, I quickly added, "I haven't kept track of what day it is since we were holed up in the hospital basement."

"It's your birthday."

Oh. She was right. "You made me brownies?" I asked, feeling so appreciative of her gesture.

She blushed and nodded her head. "I couldn't make a cake. And we don't have eggs so I don't know how good they are."

I bit my lip to keep the smile from my face. I wanted to hug Raeya and thank her for being the most thoughtful person on the planet. "They smell wonderful. Let's eat!"

Despite the missing eggs, they were the best damn brownies I'd ever had. The ten of us quickly polished off the entire pan.

"I bet I can get you some eggs," I told Raeya as I helped her clean up the kitchen.

She turned to me, hands plunged in soapy water. "Do you think the chickens are still alive?"

"I'm sure some of them are. Only if they got out, though. Knowing my grandpa, I'm betting he let all the animals go."

"I've been too scared to look at the barn. I don't want to see any poor, helpless animal starved to death."

"I don't want to see it either," I admitted. "I found some hunting clothes upstairs. It's mostly outerwear, but it's at least warm. I'm gonna take a look in the barn and bring in firewood. It'll be nice to have a fire going."

"We're almost out of food," she whispered, eyes darting around. "I don't know if anyone else but Padraic is aware."

"Don't worry. I'll get more," I promised.

She nodded and faked a smile. "I know you will. I...I just...I'm worried and scared. Really scared."

"We'll make it somehow," I promised, feeling it was best not to tell her how scared I was too.

After clean up, Raeya, Padraic, Jason, and I changed into clean clothes. Raeya had done laundry and I was so grateful that she'd been able to wipe most of the blood off my favorite jacket. We decided to investigate the barn. Jason, I thought, mostly wanted to go with us because he had a crush on Raeya. He was always looking at her in that way and constantly trying to take the lead as we walked across the backfield.

Everything was how I remembered it: over grown gardens, junk cast behind the shed, the roof caved in on the old barn, the rusted out tractor stuck in the mud as it had been for the last decade. The barn we referred to as the 'new barn' had been built almost fifteen years ago now. The large doors had been left open and none of the stalls were closed. No animals, alive or dead, were inside. The knot loosened in my heart. Of course I didn't want to see anything—human or animal—in distress or dead. But more so, it was a sign my grandpa had time to get things in order.

We walked behind the barn and a familiar sound filled the air. Chickens clucked as they milled about the half plowed cornfield, pecking at bugs and pieces of spilled corn. Raeya grabbed my hand and smiled.

"At least we will have eggs!" she exclaimed.

"And a nice, plump chicken for dinner," I added, already dreading plucking the feathers off.

"That all sounds delicious," Padraic agreed. "But do any of you know how to, uh, butcher a chicken?"

"I do," I said flatly, turning to explore the far pastures. Ducks swam in the shallow, wide part of the creek, which I had called the 'pond river' for as long as I could remember. The creek cut through the property, almost exactly down the middle. It flowed into the woods; it was the perfect spot to hide in the trees and wait for deer. I was seven the first time my grandpa took me hunting. I can still hear my mother's angry voice when she found out I'd shot and killed a rabbit. A small yelling match had taken place between her and my grandfather. She insisted it was wrong for a young girl to take a life.

"You are full of surprises, Orissa." Padraic looked at me with a slight smile.

"I guess." It wasn't that surprising if you knew my grandpa. It was more surprising I turned out as normal as I did. I walked to the edge of the creek, the small pebbles crunching under my feet. The soft, rippling of water was peaceful. The forest was alive with birds, their chirping almost deafeningly loud. Geese honked, flying in the tale-tell V, signaling the end of fall and the beginning of winter. "Hey," I said suddenly, whirling around.

"What?" Raeya asked, gripping her tennis racket.

"Nothing bad, sorry. I just had an idea." I strode through the pasture, Ray and Padraic following without question, and Jason lingering behind to inspect the stalls. I went into the new barn. It was weird seeing the stalls taken apart. It looked wrong, so different than how I remembered it. "Dammit, there are no lights in the tack room," I mumbled to myself.

"What's that?" Padraic asked. Ok, maybe he hadn't grown up in a charming country cottage with a quaint, stone barn in the backyard.

"Tack is the stuff you put on a horse, you know, like saddles. The tack room is where you keep the stuff."

"Oh, ok. What could be in there?"

"A lead rope to use as a leash for Argos," I explained.

"Good thinking."

I ran my hand along the wall, my fingers getting covered in dust and cobwebs. I knew there used to be a flashlight on the top shelf to the right of the door inside the tack room. I knocked several things off the shelf before I found it. The light flickered and turned on. I slowly circled the room.

"Ah-ha," I said when the yellow light illuminated a shot gun. I picked it up, blowing the dust off.

"Jesus, how many guns does your grandpa have?" Padraic asked.

"You don't want her to answer that question," Raeya told him. "Look boots!" She picked up a pair of my old riding boots. "Maybe they'll fit," she said hopefully and tried them on after shaking out the dust. They were a little tight, she told me, but better than the Pumas. I grabbed a lead rope for Argos, we exited the tack room, and made our way to another pole barn; this one deemed 'the workshop.' I pushed the heavy door open and light spilled in, highlighting the little specks of dust that floated in the air.

There were several trackers, my grandpa's old truck—his new Ford was gone—and three ATVs crowding the cement floor along with other odds and ends. The most important thing in here was the thing I almost ran to.

"It's full," I breathed, and the knot in my stomach loosened even more. I wanted to hug the gas tank. It was huge. At one point I knew how many gallons it held. I couldn't recall the exact number anymore, but recalled being shocked by the storage capacity. "There's another one outside." We went out through the back of the barn. This gas tank had about a fourth of a tank left, which, considering its size, was plenty.

Firewood, enough to last us the whole winter, was stacked along the outside of the workshop. We had fuel and firewood, but no food. My grandparents didn't have a ton of livestock. When I'd stopped by for a too short visit last summer there had been a small herd of seven cows, four goats, the chickens, and three horses. The knot tightened when I thought of the horses. They weren't pedigree horses by any means; they had all come from the auction. But they were well trained and taken care of. And most of all...they had meant a lot to my grandpa.

"Have you ever ridden a four-wheeler?" I asked Padraic, rubbing my hands over my thighs. The stupid, striped pajama pants were no match for the cold November wind.

"Never."

"You're about to." *If they start,* I added in my head.

Only two started and Raeya automatically took the blue ATV, motioning for Jason to join her on the back. It was the one she had ridden when we were kids. I got on a larger red one, waving for Padraic to sit behind me.

We crossed the creek at the pond river, crossed through a thin tree line and emerged into the pasture. The rusty, metal gate had been left open. Argos ran alongside us happily. He barked, darting forward with more speed.

"Ohmygod," I whispered. "They're still alive." One by one, cows came into view. If the cows were still here, then the horses had to be. My heart sped up as I scanned the pasture. I learned to ride the same time I learned to hunt. I enjoyed it, and I loved Sundance, but I never became one of those horse obsessed girls. My grandma was the horse person in the family. Aunt Jenny had shown Quarter Horses as a girl, competing in barrel racing. My own mother must have been the odd one out in this farming family as she never took to the animals or the lifestyle. I hadn't either, thinking I would be much happier in the city where there was this indescribable energy flowing. I liked the city, loved it even at times.

But you never realize how much you miss a place until you come back. This farm was home. In the back of my mind I think I knew I'd end up here. I slowed the ATV, not wanting to spook or upset the cows. They seemed in good shape; not skinny or beat up. I hadn't bothered to check the hay barn. If there was any hay left, we should bring a few round bales out here before all the plants died in the winter.

This pasture was about fifty acres. I accelerated quickly and Padraic grabbed onto my waist to keep his balance. We didn't find the goats or the horses, which could be good, I reminded myself. With limited daylight left, we drove home. The keys to the old pickup were hanging where they should be. I fired it up and drove around to throw firewood in the back. Reminding me again that I hadn't healed, Raeya, Padraic, and Jason did all the heavy lifting while I kept the truck running.

This was the happiest I'd been since the world had died.

→

Everyone crowded around the fire place that night. Finickus purred loudly on Zoe's lap, enjoying the warmth as much as she did. Raeya and I kept first watch and she laid out several pieces of paper on the coffee table. I picked up the closest one.

"You made a pie chart about zombies?"

"We need to know what we are dealing with. See," she said and grabbed a paper. She explained the 'phases' of the infected—crazy, zombie, gummy.

"They get all gooey and gummy, remember? I think it's safe to say they are the least threatening. And, given what we've seen, crazies don't live that long, if you can call that living. The longest phase is the zombie one. And I don't know how long the gummies last. I'm assuming they will fall apart."

"You are very thorough," I complimented.

"Thanks," she beamed. "I figured it doesn't hurt to know the facts."

After awhile we went upstairs to wake Lauren. It was almost one in the morning and her turn to keep watch.

Lauren dragged her butt out of bed and grumbled something about how she wasn't good at keeping watch and someone else should do it. After reminding her that all she had to do was wake us up if she heard anything, a job that a monkey could do, I sighed and went into my own room.

⟶

The next morning, after breakfast, Raeya and I planned to take smaller gas cans into town and siphon enough fuel for the larger tanks outback. We were also running low on food. Padraic protested of course. I was getting tired of the whole 'a man should go with you' argument. Even Jason took the news that we wanted to go alone as the most deplorable thing he'd ever heard. Spencer only looked relieved that nothing was expected of him. He was a big guy, standing over six feet—muscular but overweight. Sometimes I wondered if he was still in shock. He never said much and kept mostly to himself. At least he didn't complain all the time like Lauren.

In the end, Raeya and I got our way.

⟶

'Town' consisted of two bars, a funeral home, a gas station, a general store, a post office, a barber shop, an antique store full of junk, a feed-slash-hunting supplies shop, and Bob and Barb's diner. Leaving the truck running, we parked in front of Lee's General Store. The front door was ajar. I clicked the safety off the gun, my finger poised over the trigger.

Shelves were knocked over, food strewn about, carts on their sides. The place had been madly picked over. Raeya held the flashlight as we walked deeper into the store. It wasn't that big and normally enough sunlight would shine through the glass front. The clouds made that impossible today. Raeya suggested we hit the hygiene aisle and try another store. She took off her backpack and stuffed it full of anything useful.

The feed store was in a similar state, though it was obvious human survival was the top priority. We piled several bags of chicken feed, three bags of dog food, dog treats, and a big bag of cat food into the truck. There was absolutely nothing left on the side of the store that housed the hunting supplies.

Feeling disgruntled, we went back to the house. We weren't even able to find any fuel.

It was disheartening to share the food and gas situation with everyone. Raeya spread a map of Kentucky on the breakfast table and pointed to the closet grocery store: it was an hour away.

"How do you people function out here?" Lauren scoffed.

"You people?" Raeya and I said in unison.

Not seeing the ignominy of her question, she continued. "Yeah, so far away from everything. I mean, where do you buy clothes?"

There was no way in hell I would admit that the same thing used to bother me.

"We got along just fine, thank you very much," Raeya said through clenched teeth. Though she wasn't born and raised here like most of the townspeople, Raeya didn't take kindly to harsh words about our little town. "Anyway," she pointed to a spot on the map, "this is our best bet."

"Great," Jason said, his eyes scanning over Raeya. "When do we leave?"

Raeya looked at me for an answer.

"Right away," I said. "Though I think it's best if it's just the two of us again." I waited for the chaos to begin. Why anyone would want to willingly leave the protection of the house was beyond me.

"Maybe," Padraic said over the censure, "you should think about it more. Orissa, what if you got hurt? Raeya would be left on her own. And you're going much farther away this time."

Dammit, now Padraic was figuring me out. "Right. Three of us then."

"I'll go," Jason offered. "I'll keep Raeya safe. And you too," he added quickly, his cheeks turning red. Sonja grabbed his arm.

"I don't want you to go," she whimpered. "What if you don't come back?"

Jason's face softened. "I will come back."

"You don't know that for sure," I stated. "We don't know what's out there. This town is near where that crazy almost got me. Where there's one, I'm guessing there are two. Or hundreds." I eyed the nine others, splitting them up into groups in my head. Lauren, Lisa, and Zoe were definite no's.

Spencer, Sonja, and Hilary...I wasn't sure. I remembered that Sonja was fast. Hilary had enough sense to get Lisa and Zoe out of the basement alive and unscathed. Spencer was big and presumably strong. That had to be useful one way or another.

In the end, I decided Raeya, capable with my crossbow, should stay behind. I chose Padraic and Jason to come with me, despite Sonja's persistent protesting. Her tears did no good, my decision had been made.

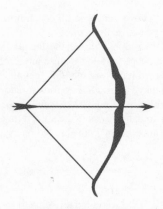

CHAPTER 16

"Am I ever going to know why your grandfather has so many weapons?" Padraic asked only ten minutes into our journey. Along with the M9, I brought two rifles, a shot gun, a .22 pistol for him and Jason, and a bow and arrows for myself. I sat beside Padraic as he drove. Jason, as usual, remained quiet in the backseat.

"Hunting," I said stiffly.

"You hunt with a hand gun?" Padraic raised an eyebrow.

"You can."

"Sure." He sighed, drumming his fingers on the steering wheel. "I didn't know bows looked like that. I imagined them a lot simpler."

"You're thinking of a long bow then," I assumed.

"What is that called?" Padraic asked, eyeing my black bow.

"A compound bow."

"Is it better?"

"In some ways. This can shoot farther. You can draw and hold back the arrow while you wait for prey. It's just more modern, in my opinion. A long bow is lighter."

"Hmm. So you've shot both?" Padraic glanced away from the road to look at me.

"Yup. We used bows a lot when hunting. It's quiet, and you can get your ammo back."

"You know," Padraic said and stole another glance at me. "I thought you were going to turn out to be prissy and girly. Sorry."

I shrugged. Why did he feel the need to voice that out loud and apologize? "It's ok. You're not the first person to think that."

"You're kind of bossy," Jason piped up from the backseat.

"You say bossy, I say great leadership skills," I said with a smile, since I couldn't refute that either.

A peaceful half hour passed before Padraic started the question game again. This time it wasn't true or false.

"Did you hate living in the city?"

"Nope," I answered honestly.

"Even though you grew up in the country?"

"It was a fun change." And I didn't always live with my grandparents.

"You're grandpa was in the Army?"

"Nope."

"You said he was a veteran."

"He is. Air Force."

"I wanted to join the Air Force," Jason said wistfully. "I'll turn eighteen this summer, not that it matters anymore. Do you think any laws really matter?"

"Not right now," I speculated. "I suppose inside the quarantines the government will want to maintain order. And I would hope people wouldn't cause any problems. Maybe they're threatened into good behavior, like act up and we'll put you out with the infected, starving rest of the world."

"They don't know about us, do they?" Jason leaned forward, not wearing his seatbelt.

"No, I'm sure they don't," Padraic answered. "They would have sent someone by now."

"Oh yeah," I interjected. "Sent someone to save the sick, dying people they left at the hospital." The ramifications of my sentence hung heavy in the air. No one spoke again until we rolled into the town.

"Holy shit," I swore.

Zombies milled about the streets. There weren't a ton of them—at least not that we could see—but enough to give me goosebumps. A few could be classified as being in Raeya's 'gummy' phase. They perked up when they saw the movement of the truck.

Seven. I counted seven. I could easily take them out, especially the slow moving ones. I wasn't sure if the echoing gunfire would draw more in, if there were more of course. I could attempt to shoot them with the bow.

We bypassed them all together, wanting to get to the store. The truck slowly rolled down the street. The closer we got to the grocery store, the fewer zombies we saw. When we pulled into the parking lot, there were none. Something wasn't right—other than the fact that zombies existed—about that. I had a bad feeling. We needed to use the lull to our advantage.

The parking lot wasn't empty, nor was it full. It held enough cars to leave me with the impression that the outbreak had happened during normal business hours, much like it had in Indy. Padraic pulled up to the motion activated doors. They didn't open, but it's not like I expected them to. I got out and tried to push them but to no avail.

"Locked," I told the guys when I got back into the pickup. My eyes scanned the lot. I found what I was looking for right away. "Go over there. I have a plan."

Padraic backed the truck up and away from the door. "Keep the safeties on your guns, too."

"What are you doing, Orissa?" Padraic asked, his blue eyes clouded with worry. Jason leaned over the seat and squinted through the windshield.

"Getting us into the store. Be ready." I opened the door and sprinted out to a brand new truck. I hopped in the back and used the butt of my rifle to knock the lock off the toolbox. I grabbed what I needed and ran to an old crappy car. As I hoped, the door wasn't locked; no one locked their doors in small towns like these. I crouched down in the front and got to work. It had been awhile since I'd done this. Though like riding a bike, hotwiring a car was not something you easily forgot to do.

I backed the car out and lined it up with the front doors of the store. Gripping the steering wheel, I pushed the gas pedal all the way down. The engine roared and the tires squealed. I closed my eyes as I crashed through the front of the store. Glass and metal rained down. I slammed on the breaks before I hit the registers. With a lot of crunching under the tires, I backed up and out of the store. I waved Padraic in, circling my fingers to signal for him to back into the store so we could load food easier.

I killed three zombies on our hunt for food. I put my foot on their decaying bodies and yanked the arrows out, wiping them clean on whatever the zombies was wearing. We each took a cart and hit an aisle. In no time, the bed of the truck was full, an extremely satisfying sight.

Thinking luck was—for once—on our side, we got back into the truck. There was a clothing store the next street over. We all needed winter jackets and if I could, I wanted to grab a pair of better fitting boots for Raeya. We heard the screaming before we saw the horde of zombies.

"Janey Mac," Padraic swore, his accent heavy.

I put my hand over my mouth. Whoever was screaming was alive, very alive. So this was why there were no zombies or crazies at the grocery store! They had followed someone else.

The screaming stopped.

Without thinking about what I was doing, I rolled down my window and opened the front door. Using the open window to steady the gun, and support my leaning body, I found the huddled zombies, aimed, and fired, sending three bullets into three heads. Too busy with the fresh meat, the gunfire was ignored by the remaining monsters.

But not by the three living people who were hiding under a car. One of them shouted. My mind raced and my heart pounded. I struggled to keep my hands from shaking so I could keep dropping the zombies.

"What do we do?" Padraic frantically asked me, raising his gun. He forgot to flick the safety off.

"I-I don't know," I stammered. The people were yards away. A shit ton of zombies and a drainage ditch separated us, making driving to their side impossible unless we went down the street to cross a bridge. I emptied my cartridge. "Drive to them."

Padraic put the truck in reverse and spun us around. In the mirror, I caught a glimpse of someone running and waving.

"No!" I shouted. She must have thought we didn't see her. She must have thought we were leaving. She was young; her blonde curls blew slightly in the cold air. She shouted something incoherent, which quickly turned into a strangled cry.

A crazy was on her, doing its best to sink its teeth into her skin and rip open her stomach. Padraic slammed on the brakes. I jumped out of the car, raising the M9. I pulled the trigger, forgetting it was empty. Jason handed me a rifle.

I held it up, aimed, and didn't fire. The crazy's head was now close to the girl's. She was putting up a good fight, using something she had found on the ground to keep the crazy's face away from her skin. I exhaled, telling myself it's now or never. The crazy's head bobbed in and out of view. If it would just hold still!

I fired.

I missed.

I aimed again.

This time I shot at its side, which was a wider target than the head. I hit it, though it had no instant effect. Before it had the chance to bleed to death, three zombies did their death march to the site. I shot again, hitting one right between the eyes. Padraic and Jason were shooting at the infected now too. I didn't bother to tell them that their .22s didn't pack any punch at this distance.

Where one zombie went down, two took its place. We were horribly outnumbered. The only hope the girl had at this point was getting away. She was still fighting the crazy. If she had any sense, she would reach down, stick her fingers in the bullet hole and rip open his flesh even more. The fucker was taking an awfully long time to bleed to death.

Another scream pierced the air. The zombies had found the others' hiding place. A fat zombie in overalls dragged a little boy out by the ankle. I fired my last round into his face. I had to stop and reload. "Dammit!" I yelled, terrified and frustrated. Jason and Padraic didn't know how to load the cartridges. I fumbled with the bullets, my fingers going numb in my anxious haste.

I was too late. Another zombie was on the little boy in seconds. It bit a chunk of his skin off, using its rotting hands to shove the gore into its mouth. There was one more person under the car. I dropped the cartridge. I wanted to scream. I wanted to personally kill every single zombie in this parking lot. When the M9 was finally loaded, I emptied it in seconds, killing seven zombies.

The little boy was still screaming. The zombies circled around him. Padraic must have watched me load the cartridge a few seconds ago because he was busily working on filling another. I stuck it into the gun with a click and looked for the girl.

A gruesome circle of death and filth surrounded her. I felt sick. I froze, unable to look away.

"Orissa!" Jason shouted, jolting me back to the here and now. "Look!"

The zombies that had feasted on the first victim were dispersing, coming toward us. Running toward us. Running?

"Get in!" Padraic said. We dove back into the truck. Padraic sped off. We flew down the road and over the bridge. The third person had made it out from under the car. He was running toward us. He wasn't fast enough. There were so many of them, coming from all directions. I shot at anything that moved.

But they got to him first. I watched in horror as the zombies tore into his body, eating his organs, and drinking his blood. When it sunk in that there was nothing left, Padraic turned the truck around. No one uttered a word the entire way home.

We parked near the front door, backing up to the porch so we could easily get the food out. Padraic cut the engine and looked at me and then at Jason.

"This didn't happen." I knew my lips were moving and sound was coming out, but I wasn't fully aware of what I was saying. "No one needs to know about this," I spoke slowly. "There's no need for them to know that the only living people we've encountered just got eaten alive."

"Yeah," Padraic agreed. "We got the food and came right back. There were zombies but not that many."

"Yes," I affirmed.

The three of us were quiet and distant the rest of the evening. We blamed it on the trip and no one questioned us. Hilary and Raeya organized the food while Sonja and Lisa made dinner. Spencer kept watch and Lauren was upstairs doing God knows what. Zoe wanted to help us carry stuff in.

She was so weak. Her cough had worsened and she was running a fever. Padraic told her she should stay out of the cold and rest until someone could bring her dinner. She asked me to lay down with her because she was scared to be upstairs alone. She carried Finickus up with her, tucking him under the covers. The cat stayed for a few seconds as if to humor her before leaping away.

Padraic had made a clean sweep of the pharmacy inside the grocery store. He brought up a handful of pills and a glass of water. He told Zoe to drink the whole thing. She nodded and took the pills one by one.

"I'm tired, Orissa," she told me, cuddling with her pink stuffed cat.

"Close your eyes. I'll be right here," I promised.

She tried to say something but was overcome with a coughing fit. "And my lungs hurt."

"Padraic will take care of you." I forced a smile. "Want me to read you a story?"

She nodded.

I went to the bookshelf and picked out a book about a rich girl falling in love with a poor stable boy. Zoe was almost asleep when I finished the first chapter. I set the book down and turned off the bedside lamp.

"Orissa?" she asked sleepily.

"Yeah, Zoe?"

"Are you scared to die?"

Maybe it was odd, after all I had seen today. But I answered without hesitation. "No."

"Really?"

"Really," I promised. I wasn't afraid of death. If I died, it would be over. My worst fear wasn't of dying, it was of living. Living, while everyone around me had their flesh savagely torn from their bodies to be shoved into the festering and ever-hungry mouths of zombies. It terrified me, right down to my very core, to be alive while the rest of the world was dead.

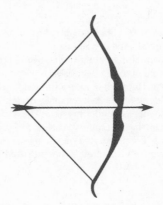

CHAPTER 17

We spent the next few weeks acting like a dysfunctional family. Raeya had drawn up chore charts. I felt like I was seven-years-old again, but the charts kept us organized and on task. I was scheduled to hunt every other day, alternating with teaching the others how to shoot. We drove ten miles away so the echoing gunshots wouldn't draw the infected our way.

Today was a hunting day. A fresh layer of thin snow covered the earth. It was one of those mornings that could take your breath away. Everything was frozen and still, cast in beautiful and soft morning light.

I hunkered in my tree stand, bow and arrow at the ready. I knew I was safe in the tree. And I knew I would most likely have the upper hand, literally, in killing anything beneath me. If there was a place to relax, this was it. My own safety wasn't my main concern anymore. I was constantly worried about the others. Zoe's health was rapidly declining. Realistically, it was a miracle she'd made it this long. Padraic and Hilary were with her around the clock, doing anything and everything they could to prolong her life.

Snow crunched underfoot. Slowly, I sat up, pulling the arrow back. I silently exhaled, eyes locking on my target. The arrow flew into the head of a buck. He collapsed, red blood staining and melting the glittering snow. I couldn't look at the deer. I grabbed it by its feet and hauled it through the trees. I was exhausted, sweaty, and panting by the time I got to the ATV. With much difficulty, I hefted the heavy carcass onto the back, strapped it down, and drove to the workshop.

As requested, I went inside to tell everyone I was okay. Jason stayed with me while the others dispersed. I wanted to teach him how to gut and clean the deer. I was fast. It was something my grandpa was proud of me for. Once he killed three does just so he could show me off to his friends. I could do it in less than ten minutes as long as I had a sharp knife and saw.

I hated doing it. I hated hearing the skin rip. I hated seeing the dead, black eyes. I hated the frozen innocence on their faces. I hated the way the blood splattered and the way their organs spilled out. I wanted to get it over with as soon as possible.

This time around, I went slowly for Jason's sake. It was different, I had to admit, when we were relying on the meat for survival. We each carried a large chunk of meat into the house to be made into jerky. I set it on the counter and began cutting the fat off.

"That is disgusting," Lauren said, wrinkling her nose.

I didn't respond.

"Don't you feel bad, killing an innocent animal for no reason?"

"For no reason?" I stuttered. "There *is* a reason. We're going to eat it. We would starve to death if

I didn't hunt for us, and you know that."

"Ugh. Whatever. Look, there are little hairs all over it."

"Yeah, it happens when you skin it." And it was Jason's first time. It was a little sloppy, but better than my first attempt at skinning something, though I had bawled my eyes out then.

"I'm a vegetarian," Lauren reminded me.

I had nothing against vegetarians. But with our very limited food supply, refusing to eat meat was just stupid. She had been picking at me for the last ten days, saying little things about me hunting and killing. As much as I tried to not let her get under my skin, I was close to snapping.

"Good. More for me," I said, referring to Lauren's earlier comment.

Lauren huffed and stormed away. I concentrated on slicing off the fat so I wouldn't get angry.

"Jason said we shouldn't piss you off," Padraic's voice drifted behind me. "He told me you are scary good at cutting things open."

"Yeah, I guess," I said quickly.

"I didn't mean to offend you, Orissa."

"You didn't," I assured him. "I'm just annoyed at Lauren." I let out a breath and shook my head.

"What are you making?"

"Jerky. It will keep for a long time."

"Want to teach me?"

"Sure. It's not hard."

Padraic was good with a knife. He had impressive accuracy and control. There was just something about the way he moved his hands, the care and grace in which he held the knife. "Were you a surgeon?" I asked, feeling slightly ashamed that I'd never bothered to ask what kind of doctor he was.

"Yeah, how can you tell?" he asked, his blue eyes flicking up to mine.

"The way you cut that."

"You can tell just by the way I'm cutting a slab of meat?"

"I guess." I turned back to my strips of deer. "You should gut the next kill then."

"I can. I won't enjoy it, but I can. If you want me to," he offered. We put the slices of deer into bowls of marinade to soak overnight. I washed my hands, sat at the table, and unbraided my hair. Zoe had done it again into tight French braids. My dark hair fell in even, smooth waves around my face, cascading over my shoulders and down my back.

"You look pretty with your hair down," Padraic said shyly, joining me at the table.

"Thanks." I put my hands on the table. "I used to never wear it up."

"Funny how things have changed, isn't it?"

"Yeah. A year ago I was living it up, partying without a care in the world. It was all about me then."

"You're doing a good job."

"Thanks. Wait, with what?"

"Orissa, you…you are fantastic. Ok, you're a little bitchy and blunt, but you've kept us alive."

I yawned and deflected the compliment.

"Tired?"

"Couldn't sleep last night. I had that dream about killing Logan again."

He reached out and put his hands over mine. His skin wasn't as smooth as before. I looked into his blue eyes. Lauren came back into the room. She opened the fridge and rummaged through our little bit of cold food.

"It's not lunch yet," I reminded her.

"I know," she sighed. "But I'm hungry."

"Breakfast was only a few hours ago."

"I'm so sick of eggs. I can't eat them anymore."

"I'm sick of eggs too. We are all sick of eggs, trust me," I said evenly.

"Then you understand."

I pulled my hands back from Padraic's. "No. We have a limited amount of food. We eat three times a day and that's it."

She slammed the fridge closed. "Fine."

"Oh my God. I'm going to kill her," I vented to Padraic once she'd stomped out of the room.

"One less mouth to feed?" he joked with a wink.

I laughed. "I can use her for zombie bait."

"Everyone handles stress differently," he logically defended. "She's focusing on other things to keep her mind off what is really going on."

"No she's not. She's always been that way. But at least she 'out bitches' me."

Padraic laughed. "That's quite an accomplishment."

———————————→

Zoe, suited up in my old winter clothes, sat on the couch next to me. "Can I ride the four wheeler?"

"No, Zoe. It's cold out there."

"But I've never ridden one."

"In the spring. When it's warm."

"But I want to ride it now."

"It's too cold. Stay in here where it's warm," I insisted.

"Please, Orissa?"

"Zoe, no. I'll read you another chapter."

"No. Reading is boring. Everyone else gets to go outside except me. It's not fair!"

I was not in the mood to hear another hissy fit. And I was not going to let Zoe go outside in the cold when she was fighting a very bad upper respiratory infection. She shouldn't even be out of bed. "I said no." My voice came out too stern for my liking. Zoe's green eyes filled with tears and she ran away.

Later, I relented when Padraic bluntly told me just how sick Zoe was.

"Orissa," he said, "would you rather spend three days actually living or three weeks locked in a room?"

When I didn't answer he went on.

"Life's about quality, not quantity. We could all die tomorrow. Does that mean we should give up on happiness?"

He was right, and Zoe deserved to be happy. I found her, wrapped a scarf around her frail body, and zipped up her coat. Padraic, Raeya, and Argos came with us, taking turns keeping watch and racing against us. I let Zoe drive and she had a blast. We rode through the creek, over the hill that leads into the large pasture, and through the trees. Zoe stopped and pointed out everything beautiful, from the frost covered branches to the tiny bird footprints in the thin snow. Instead of seeing the world as the horrible place it was, she saw nothing but wonder and beauty.

The happiness of being outside made her forget about her attenuating health.

Later, she was still in high spirits. She danced around the house and helped Raeya make dinner.

"That smells wonderful," Hilary praised when Zoe took the chicken from the oven. "Oh, be careful not to burn yourself, Zoe."

Zoe pressed her lips together and glared at Hilary. "I know what I'm doing," she said with so much sass it made both Hilary and me laugh. Along with the chicken, we were having another treat tonight. Zoe excitedly set a basket of sweet rolls on the table and covered it with a cloth napkin.

And we had cake for dessert.

It seemed trivial to be celebrating Thanksgiving while zombies roamed the earth. It was Raeya's idea. I disagreed at first, arguing it was pointless to carry on with cultural traditions.

"The group doesn't have very much to look forward to," she reminded me. "All of our families and friends are dead or worse at this point. When we make it through a twenty-four hour period without being attacked by flesh eating freaks, we call it a good day. People can only take so much; the little things matter now more than ever, Orissa. Celebrating something, even a meaningless holiday like turkey day, could really brighten everyone's spirits. We need this."

We crowded around the dining room table. The spread was nothing like I was used to on Thanksgiving, but, for us, it was a feast.

"I think," Raeya said as she passed the basket of rolls around the table, "we should all think of one thing we are thankful for. I know times are worse than hard, but if we could all find one small thing, it will be good for us."

"That's a wonderful idea," Padraic agreed.

"Yeah," Jason said quickly. "It is."

"Thanks!" Raeya beamed. "I'll go first. I'm thankful for everything we have: food, shelter, friends. It might not be ideal, but we're alive and pretty comfortable." She turned to her right, looking at me.

I hated the 'giving thanks' part of Thanksgiving even before the zombies attacked. I always felt awkward sharing how I felt. "I'm thankful for my best friend, Raeya, and all she's done for us," I said shyly and smiled at her.

Padraic was next. "I'm thankful Orissa's appendix needed out when it did," he said, winking at me. "Without her, none of us would be here."

"Yeah," Spencer agreed when our eyes fell on him. "I'm thankful she saved us from that attic. I know she only came for Raeya."

The thanks continued with a similar theme until only Lauren was left. "I'm thankful for this innocent animal Orissa slaughtered."

I gripped my fork. Silence fell over the table. Raeya cleared her throat.

"It's really good," Raeya said. "Thank you, Rissy."

"Yeah," Lisa agreed, angrily eyeing Lauren. "Thank you for putting food on the table."

"You're welcome," I said.

<hr>

After dinner, I attempted to read. I hadn't read for fun in God knows how long. I had only made it through two pages when Lauren sat on the couch next to me. She began chattering to Padraic, who was in the recliner across from me, about her life at school. Along with annoying the piss out of me for the last several days, she made it a point to openly flirt with him. He was only half listening, too polite to tell her to shut the fuck up.

When she told her story—one Raeya and I had heard many times—about how a modeling agency 'practically begged her to sign' I couldn't take it anymore.

"Oh my God, Lauren," I spat, slamming my book shut. "If you don't shut up, I'm going to find a spray bottle, fill it with zombie blood, and spray you in the face!"

"Geeze, psycho much?" Lauren snorted.

"Yeah. I'm crazy. *Real* crazy. And you're the first person I'm going to fucking bite!"

"Rissy?" Raeya asked softly, peeking around the corner. "Are you alright?"

"Fine. I'm fine. I'm just an animal killing, crazy dunce."

"Ok." Raeya nodded. "As long as you're ok with that."

I dropped the book and stormed out of the room and onto the porch. The cold night air hit me, making me shiver. Raeya stepped out after me.

"Rissy? What's going on?"

"Nothing. I'm fine."

"Don't lie to me."

"Sorry. I can't stand Lauren."

"Me neither. Try being stuck in an attic with her for days. Several times I contemplated pushing her out."

I smiled. "I probably would have."

Raeya shivered.

"I'm fine now. That freak out was good for me. Let's go back in."

Padraic and I were on first watch that night. It was windy and the old house creaked and groaned with each gust. We sat together on the sofa.

"Where did you learn how to hotwire cars?" he asked.

"Juvie."

"They teach you that in juvenile detention?"

"Of course not," I laughed.

"Then how…?"

"I met someone in juvie. We exchanged lots of fun information."

"Why were you in juvie?"

"I, uh, beat someone up," I admitted shamefully.

"Why?"

I shrugged. "They insulted Raeya."

Ted had given me a speech about how I should demonstrate nonviolence even when tempted. I didn't anticipate getting arrested. And I really didn't *beat up* the guy. I punched him in the face, breaking his nose, after he had called Raeya fat. After that, I lived with my grandparents.

"I really don't get you." He ran his hands through his hair, tousling it. "Every time I think I can see through the cracks in your tough-girl exterior, you fill them back up. I think I know who you are and then you slip through my fingers."

"I don't even know who I am." The words slipped from my mouth of their own accord. Suddenly, I felt naked. I got up and made a deal of looking through every window for zombies. I avoided talking to anyone but Ray for the rest of the night.

→

The horses—all three of them—came racing across the pasture the next morning. Nostrils flaring, they stopped, huffing for air. I couldn't help the fondness they stirred in my heart. Too excited to ponder what had spooked them, I raced into the house to get Raeya. Lisa, Sonja, and Zoe were giddy with excitement. Like most girls, they loved horses. They rushed to get their coats on.

Zoe was saying that she was going to find treats for them when she slipped. I thought maybe she'd stepped on her scarf. She tumbled down the stairs, landed at the bottom and didn't move. Terror coursed my veins as I rushed over.

"Padraic!" I screamed, my voice threatening to crack. "No, no, no! Zoe!" I shook her then felt for a pulse. "Padraic! Hilary! Help!" Tears filled my eyes. "Zoe, Zoe!"

Padraic and Raeya arrived first. I moved out of the way to let Padraic work a miracle. Raeya grabbed my hands. I choked back a sob. She hugged me. Everyone else had rushed over now. Sonja held on to Lisa, both staring with fear in their eyes.

"She's alive," Padraic said, gently scooping Zoe's body up. He looked at Hilary, their eyes passing a message. Hilary nodded and turned away, tears streaming down her face. Padraic carried Zoe up the stairs and laid her down in my bed. We tucked her under the covers. "Let her rest," Padraic told us, his face grim.

Zoe's eyes fluttered open.

"Zoe," I whispered, moving to her side.

"I saw the horses." Her voice was a faint echo. "They are beautiful."

"Yes, yes they are."

"The white one is my favorite."

I looked at Raeya. How did Zoe know...she hadn't seen them? Raeya's mouth opened in awe and she shook her head.

Padraic knelt next to the bed. "Do you want anything, Zoe?"

"I'm kinda thirsty," she answered.

"I'll get you a drink," Raeya said and rushed out of the room, pushing past everyone. She brought the water to Zoe, who barely had the strength to hold the glass. We all took a turn sitting and talking to her.

"Orissa?" she feebly called.

"Yeah?"

"Will you sit with me?"

"Of course, Zoe." I carefully sat next to her. She lifted the covers for me to stick my feet under. Painstakingly, she sat up and rested her head on my shoulder. I wrapped my arms around her and fought off tears.

"I'm tired," she whispered.

"Go to sleep. I'll stay right here."

"Ok."

As if he knew what was going on, Finickus gracefully leapt onto the bed. He rubbed against Zoe, purring loudly. Padraic told everyone that Zoe really did need to rest. I don't know where they went or what they did, but the room emptied.

"Orissa?" she said.

"Yeah?" I answered.

"I can't sleep."

"Want me to read to you?"

"No. Will you sing me a song?"

"Of course." I nodded, closing my eyes. "What song?"

"Something pretty."

"Ok." My brain raced. The music I listened to would never be classified as 'pretty.' I sang the first song that came to mind, a song my grandmother used to sing.

Tears spilled from my eyes, running down my cheeks. Struggling to keep my voice level, I had to pause and take a breath. I wasn't able to finish the song, though it didn't matter. Zoe's eyes were closed. Her breathing was shallow and weak. I kissed the top of her head, crying even harder. It wasn't fair. She had escaped certain death and had defied the odds. She was so young, so innocent. I closed my eyes and prayed to trade places with her.

"Take me," I whispered. I'd had my chance. I'd pissed away my life, making bad decisions, and doing things to purposely hurt and anger people. I wasn't a good person. I lived for myself and had never given a damn about anyone.

I moved Zoe off of me and got up to get another blanket to keep her warm.

"You have a beautiful voice."

I didn't see Padraic sitting in the dark hall. His voice startled me.

"Thanks," I responded and wiped my eyes, not wanting him to see my tears. In the dim light, I could see that he had been crying as well.

"Is there anything we can do?" I asked.

"Stay with her," he whispered.

I nodded, my heart breaking. I pulled a quilt off the bed in one of the guest rooms. I laid down next to Zoe, pulling the quilt over both of us. I held onto her little hand all night, waiting for a miracle.

Sunlight sparkled through the frosted window.

And Zoe never woke up.

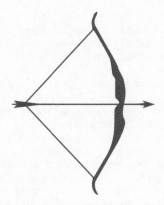

CHAPTER 18

I don't remember calling Padraic's name. His arms wrapped around me and I buried my face in his chest, crying.

"I don't want to do this anymore," I admitted.

"Do what, Orissa?" he asked, smoothing my hair.

"Live in this world." I sniffled. "You think I'm tough but I'm not. I'm not at all."

"Yes you are, Orissa."

I wiped tears away, showing him the proof. "Obviously not."

"You're human." He pulled me in and rested his head on mine. "*Dá fhaid é an lá tiocfaidh an tráthnóna.*"

I had no idea what he said. I let him hold me for a minute longer, willing the pain away. He ran his hand over my cheek, turning my face up to his. When his lips pressed against mine, I broke away.

"We need to bury Zoe," I said, still crying. My vision blurred. I numbly walked out of the room and found Raeya.

Spencer and Jason dug the grave. Raeya and I gently wrapped a soft white sheet around Zoe. The funeral party marched through the cold November wind to the top of the small hill. Raeya held my hand, and Lisa found a bundle of dead, dry flowers. She dropped them into the hole one by one.

We piled rocks on top of her grave as a marker and to keep zombies from digging up her frail body. I knelt next to the grave, taking slow, controlled breaths to keep from crying. Wind rattled the dead branches. I bent my head, letting the tears fall.

Sonja screamed. I looked up to see a dozen or more zombies crashing through the forest. I swallowed my pain, twisting it into rage. I grabbed the shovel, my body flying over to the nearest zombie. Using the shovel like a spear, I shoved it into the zombie's face. I held the handle and kicked the rotting body, decapitating the monster. I spun around, taking the side of another's face off and destroying his rotted brain.

I was vaguely aware of someone calling my name. All I wanted to do was kill the sons of bitches. They were everywhere. Surrounding us. Closing in. A few had fresh blood on their faces. They moved fast.

Argos yelped. I wasn't losing him today. I grabbed the back of a zombie's shirt, yanking it off my dog. It fell to the ground and I used the heel of my boot to break its skull. Since it was in the gummy phase, my foot sank into putrid mush.

"Rissy!" Raeya screamed. I whirled around, ready to defend her. She was standing a good twenty yards away, madly waving for me to follow her. I swung the shovel one last time. It hit a zombie in the head, its ear smashing and sticking to the metal. I dropped the shovel, grabbed Argos by the collar, and sprinted toward Ray.

When we got back into the house, I realized Hilary and Spencer hadn't made it. We had no time to grieve. Knowing we had mere minutes until the zombies pounded down the front door, we scrambled to pack up what we could. If there weren't so freaking many we might have tried to fight them, but there were hundreds.

I raced up the stairs to grab the Berretta and my bag. Zoe's pink stuffed cat was tangled in the blankets. I shoved it into my bag.

Padraic took Lauren and Jason downstairs to load up the weapons. Raeya, Lisa, and Sonja frantically threw food into bags. We didn't have time to get blankets or fuel. With Finickus tucked under my arm, I bound out the front door. Zombies groaned, only feet away. I fired, taking one out and scaring the cat. He jumped out of my arms, scratched my stomach, and bolted.

I couldn't think about it. We were lucky the cars were close to the front door. Our meager supplies were thrown into the back of the truck. Padraic, Jason, Sonja, and Lauren got into the Range Rover and Raeya, Lisa, Argos, and I piled into the truck. I was in the driver's seat.

As if someone had shaken the hive, zombies swarmed, moaning and searching for food.

We drove south.

After several miles, Padraic pulled up next to me. His blue eyes were bloodshot and he was shaking. "What do we do?" he asked, his voice on the verge of breaking.

"We keep going. Find open land, um, a safe place so to speak. Hole up, then...then keep going."

"Can't we go back?" Lisa asked, her voice hoarse from crying. I turned around to look at her. Her eyes were red and puffy and her cheeks were still wet from tears. My chest tightened and emotion made tears sting in my own eyes. Argos, as if he could sense Lisa's pain and read my mind, let out a whine and nosed Lisa's face. She put her arms around the Doberman.

I shook my head. "No. Maybe later, like days later. You saw how many there were."

"Where did they come from?" Raeya asked distantly. She sat unmoving beside me, her brown eyes fixed on nothing.

"I don't know. They must move around, looking for food."

"There were so many," Raeya whispered, her lip trembling.

I raked my hair to the side and started braiding, needing to do something with my hands. "Maybe they...they join up or something." I pulled the hairband from my wrist and wrapped it around the braid. "Drive. We keep driving."

And we did.

After several miles, the low fuel alarm ominously dinged. I knew Raeya heard it and could feel her eyes on me. I bit my lip but kept driving. We were on a stretch of country road, with nothing but fields on either side. I prayed, we'd come to a small town or a gas station or a truck stop. The siphons were still in the Range Rover. We'd be able to get gas and be on our way.

We found a small town alright—a ghost town with no cars and no gas. Deciding it was as good a place as any, we stopped. Not bothering to unload any of our stuff, the seven of us got out. The houses were run down even before being abandoned; there were open doors and broken windows.

I went into the first house on the street, gun raised. The place smelled old and forgotten but not disgusting. It would work. We had no candles and no matches. I had kept the one, small flashlight in my bag. Before sunset, I went back to the truck to sort through our meager supplies.

Padraic had done a good job rounding up the weapons. It was a good thing I decided against keeping them loaded; they had been haphazardly thrown into canvas bags. A box of bullets spilled, rolling everywhere. As I picked them up, I swore each one would end up in the head of a zombie.

Raeya had kept two 'emergency bags' ready under the counter in the kitchen. Each bag contained enough food and water to sustain us for two days, and that was when there were ten of us. If we rationed it carefully, we'd have five or six days before we started to starve. More than anything, we needed to find a source of clean water. I wasn't going to risk letting anyone drink out of a lake or pond.

We ate, we slept, and we left. I was forced to take gas from the Range Rover, which made me sick. If we ran out of fuel out in the middle of nowhere...there'd be no hope.

After a few hours of mindlessly outrunning the setting sun, we came to a zombie infested parking lot. Both vehicles were running on less than a quarter tank, but the cars in the lot were the first automobiles we'd seen in hours. It was now or never. Sonja was fast. I entrusted her to get the gas while I distracted the zombies.

I probably looked like a terrorist, with a rifle slung over each arm and a pistol in each hand. My pockets were weighed down with bullets. It was a horrible plan.

But it worked.

I was able to get the zombies' attention and opened fire with deadly accuracy. Atop a school bus, I was out of their reach. It brought me sick satisfaction to see their brains splatter as the bullets pierced through their rotting skin.

Raeya ran two over with the truck. I jumped into the bed, rolling my ankle and twisting my wrist in my hurried attempt. We sped away, stopping when we couldn't see, hear, or smell them anymore. I clambered into the truck, Argos excitedly greeting me.

The days blended together. Even Raeya stopped keeping track after a week. We were tired, ragged, hungry, cold, dirty, and losing hope. By constantly moving we were able to avoid zombies and crazies. We slept in the cars, feeling safest with two pairs of wheels underneath us.

Down to our last bit of jerky, I made a desperate stop in a small Kansas town. Like my hometown grocery, this one had been looted. There was nothing left. We explored a tiny pizza parlor, coming out with nothing but cans of olives and tomato sauce.

That's what we had for dinner that night.

I hadn't slept in days. I would doze off for a few minutes and then startle awake. I promised myself that I would do whatever it took to keep the others alive. I lied to Raeya, telling her I'd already eaten and passed my 'leftover' raisins to her that morning.

It was a dreary and cold morning. Wind blew through the weak slats in the barn where we were hiding. Half the roof had blown off in a storm. It was shitty protection from the elements, but it allowed us to see our surroundings. It was temporary, I reminded everyone. We were all sick of being in the car. Our muscles were stiff from sitting, our spirits low—if we even had spirits by this point—and our tempers were high.

We were in the hayloft. Even Argos. It was a pain in the ass hauling his eighty-something pounds up there. Everyone had grown fond of him as a pet and no one could argue his practicality. He was resting with his head in my lap, dozing off as I scratched behind his ears. Raeya shivered. Trying not to disturb Argos, I took my jacket off and tossed it to her.

"Ris, it's too cold for you to not wear a coat." She frowned and held it out to me.

"I'll be fine for a little bit. Argos is keeping me warm."

"I'll warm up my hands. Then you're putting it back on," she said and stuck her hands inside the sleeves.

"Deal."

Suddenly, Argos growled. Frantically, I grabbed his leash. His fur stood up and he showed his fangs.

"Holy shit," I whispered when I saw what he was looking at. I peered through the high window frame...

Zombies. More zombies than I'd ever seen in one place. The ground trembled under their undead feet. We were fucked.

We couldn't stay here. If the next gust of wind didn't blow the dilapidated barn over, the herd of marching dead certainly would.

"Get against the wall and don't move, speak, or breathe," I instructed. I gave Argos' leash to Padraic, who could handle the dog's strength the best. Padraic pulled the dog close to him and clamped a hand around his muzzle to keep him from barking.

I grabbed a rifle, sticking my head through the strap. I slung the quiver of arrows and the bow over my shoulder, stuffed an extra magazine in my pocket, and stood.

"What the hell are you doing?" Padraic asked, over Argos' muffled growls.

"I'm going to bring the truck around."

"No!" Raeya objected. "Rissy, you'll die! You...you can't go down there with them!"

"They're still far enough away I can get to the car."

I didn't stick around to argue. There wasn't time.

My feet hit the cold cement, shock stinging my ankles, and I exited the barn. I pulled an arrow, ready to shoot. My breath clouded around me as adrenaline coursed through my veins. The zombies were closer than I'd anticipated. They surrounded the cars, passing them without a second look. Hungry, they followed our human scent. I released the arrow. It zipped through the air, passed through a mushy zombie skull, and continued its lethal voyage into another's eye.

I couldn't do that again if I tried. I ran around the barn, clambering onto the roof of an out building. I fired the rest of my arrows. Two fast zombies raced in front of the others, stretching their arms out when they caught sight of me. I dropped the bow, jumped down and held the rifle like a baseball bat. I whacked one in the head and kicked the other in the chest.

Its skin slimed off, making the bottom of my boot slippery. My foot skidded out from underneath me. The zombie I kicked grabbed my foot, bringing it to his mouth. He couldn't bite through my boot. The M9 was wedged in my waistband, hurting me like hell when I landed on my back. I madly thrashed around, retrieving it. I held it to the zombie's head and pulled the trigger.

Spoiled bits of brain and thick blood splashed across my face. Thank God I remembered to close my eyes. Wiping zombie blood from my lips, I rolled over, shooting the other in the cheek. *Dammit*, I thought, *a wasted bullet.* I fired again, this time hitting between the eyes. Yellow brain matter oozed from the hole. I scrambled back onto the roof of what had to be a chicken coup, based on the feathers. I emptied my magazine, burying each round deep into the skull of a zombie.

Though they dropped like flies, my kills couldn't dent the horrifying number that lumbered toward the barn. I switched to the rifle, shooting anything that moved. I needed to get off the roof before I was completely surrounded. I dropped the rifle, shoved another magazine into the M9 and jumped. I sprinted to a silo, climbed six feet up the ladder, twisted and began shooting.

One particular zombie moved through the crowd with sickening speed and grace. I had one bullet left. I aimed carefully, lining the scope up with his eye. I paused, thinking he was the best looking zombie I'd ever seen. His eyes met mine. There was something human about him. I aimed my gun away from him and shot a different zombie.

The zombie whose eyes were alive put his finger to his lips and walked through the flesh eating monsters, leaving them behind. He looked up at me from the bottom of the silo's ladder. He wasn't a zombie...he couldn't be.

I swallowed, not knowing why in the world I would trust this person or how the hell he was walking amongst the zombies. I shoved the empty M9 in my waistband and climbed down the silo's ladder, hands trembling uncontrollably.

As soon as my feet hit the ground, he pressed himself against me, pinning me between his body and the silo. Over a black, long sleeved shirt, he was wearing a moldy vest made of leather. It was wrinkled and rotten in parts. I wanted to shove him off me when I realized it was made out of zombie skin. Fingers, tied to strings like freaking decorations, hung from his neck. A hand was tied to his belt. I didn't know what part of the zombie was stitched onto the baseball cap he was wearing.

It was disgusting, having zombie parts rubbing against me. It smelled revolting. Regardless, I closed my eyes and buried my face against his chest.

As if we didn't exist, the zombies milled by. I was grateful for this stranger but I wanted to help my friends. A gun fired. My body tensed. I worried that one of my friends had gotten a hold of a weapon and was shooting at the guy who was trying to save me...shooting and thinking he was really a zombie.

He put an arm around me, obviously thinking the echoing shot scared me. My fingers closed around the material of his shirt and I peeked from beneath my savior's arm. A zombie stopped and eyed us hungrily. I pulled the guy closer to me, holding my breath. The zombie moved on.

The rapid fire of machine guns was the most beautiful sound in the world. I wanted to watch the zombies fall, but all I could see was my stranger's chest. I read the dog tag he wore: UNDERWOOD HAYDEN J stamped into the metal. Under his name, blood type, and social security number were the letters 'USMC.'

Voices echoed, male voices, deliberately shouting over the zombies' death moans. Hayden leaned back so his eyes could meet mine. He looked to the right and then at me. Ever so slightly, I nodded. Clinging onto each other, we took the smallest step to the right. We froze, waited, and took another step. Painfully slow, we continued our game of stop and go until we were on the opposite side of the silo.

With an imperceptible movement, Hayden reached behind me and pulled the M9 from my jeans. Not taking his eyes off mine, he unloaded it, dropping the empty magazine. Just as surreptitiously, he extracted something from his pocket. It clicked into place. He put the loaded gun into my hand and drew his own. He nodded again, a devious smile flashing across his face. He cocked his weapon and stepped away. There was a rusty piece of metal lying by our feet. I grabbed it. Hayden covered me while I shoved it in the open mouth of an approaching zombie.

Hayden quickly emptied his magazine, hitting a zombie in the head with every shot. *Finally, someone who knows how to handle a gun*, I thought to myself. He kicked a zombie in the chest then crushed in its skull with his combat boots. He reached behind him, grabbing my hand. We ran toward the barn, bypassing the zombies. An engine revved and a black truck sped into view, running over three zombies. Hayden jumped in the back, extending his hand to help but I was already in.

"Turn around! My friends are in there," I panted as the truck sped off.

"Not anymore," Hayden informed me. He pointed to another truck, yards ahead of us. "We got them out."

PART II

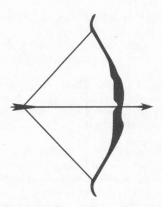

CHAPTER 19

By the time the truck slowed, we had put several miles between ourselves and the zombies. In that time, I joked with Hayden, almost convincing him that I knew he was a Marine because of psychic abilities. I also took a moment to study the mounted machine gun at the center of the truck bed. Hayden complimented my shooting skills and I reiterated.

We turned off the country road and onto a broken paved drive. Rusty, metal gates limply hung on hinges. A large stone building of gray loomed ahead of us. Our driver parked the truck near the front.

Jason, Sonja, and Argos were inside the black truck I rode in. I hadn't seen them because of the darkened windows. Lauren, Lisa, Padraic, and Raeya got out of the bed of the other. Raeya rushed over and hugged me. Four soldiers or Marines dressed in camo, boots, and vests got out, surveying our surroundings. Hayden jumped out of the truck and took the skin vest off. He handled it like it was just any other piece of clothing. He tossed it and the rest of his zombie wardrobe into the bed of the truck and pulled the black shirt off. He had a full sleeve of black Polynesian tribal tattoos on his right arm, running up to his shoulder, and down on his chest. I ran my eyes over a line of spearheads that were woven into the design of waves, shark teeth, and other Polynesian symbols that I didn't recognize. The dark markings on his skin moved, reflecting what little sunlight shone down on us, each time he flexed his muscles.

I watched him, wondering if it was wrong to be admiring his six pack and muscular arms when zombies, not all that far away, limped across the field in hopes of ripping our organs from our bodies and feasting on our flesh.

He ducked behind a truck and changed into combat ready attire, matching his comrades. Argos jumped up at me, trying to lick my face. I knelt down to pet him. I had to count my friends twice just to make sure everyone was really with me.

One of the Marines clapped Hayden on the back. "Nice job fitting in with the zombies. See, I told you, all we had to do was pick someone whose intelligence equaled their own and they'd never know."

"It's a good thing we didn't pick you then. They'd instantly kill someone dumber than they are," Hayden countered.

The Marine—Brewster was his last name, as it was stitched into his jacket—laughed, showing off perfectly straight, white teeth. He was tall and muscular, with beautiful dark skin and buzzed hair. His dark eyes sparkled when he laughed. "Oh, I got thirteen."

"You did not," another Marine named Callias argued. "Machine gun takedowns don't count."

I looked at the guys curiously. Were they counting how many zombies they'd killed?

"Hi," Callias said to me. "I'm Brock. You were incredible out there."

"Forgive him," Brewster said. "But it's not that often we find anyone who can take down zombies like that."

"I know the feeling," I said with a slight smile. "Uh, thanks, guys, for helping out back there."

"Helping out?" Lauren snorted. "They *saved* us. And you'd be dead if it wasn't for them."

"I had a plan," I spat.

"Oh, sure. She always has a plan," Lauren said to Hayden, smiling coyly. I wanted to tell her that her attempts at flirting sucked ass even when she hadn't gone days without showering. Her hair was a greasy mess, but so was mine. I kept my mouth shut.

Padraic stepped close to me, taking my hand in his. "Are you alright, Orissa? You didn't get hurt did you?"

"I'm fine. Really. Hayden…Hayden saved me." I didn't want to be a damsel in distress. I didn't want to admit that I needed saving, though in all honesty I knew we'd been in a situation beyond my control. Now, if I had weapons like the Marines had, it would have been a different story.

Padraic squeezed my hand, his blue eyes drilling into mine. I was reminded of his kiss. I pulled my hand back, set on not giving him any mixed signals, not that I thought I had before.

"Thank you," he said, looking at Hayden. "For saving Orissa. And us," he added.

"It's what we do," Hayden said. "Come in. We have a camp set up in there."

Brock Callias went in first, rifle ready just in case. I knew where we were as soon as I entered the lobby. Of course we would come to a place like this—an old sanitarium.

We walked down a hall, up a flight of stairs, down another hall and into a large room, it made sense why the guys had picked this place. There were bars on the windows, the walls were cinderblock or cement, and the doors were steel with multiple locks. Even though it was as creepy as all get out, it was designed for keeping violent, crazy people in. And, in our case, it would work to keep them out.

"Let's see that cut," Brewster said to another Marine. A young looking redhead yanked his pant leg up. He had a four inch gash on the back of his calf. It was dirty and jagged and looked infected. "I told you to watch that farm equipment," Brewster sighed and inspected the cut. "I think you need stitches. We can go back to the compound—"

"No," the young Marine argued. "We have orders—"

"Orders to come back when wounded," Brewster reminded him.

"It's not that bad," he countered.

Padraic stepped up. "Maybe I can help."

The incredulous look 'Ginger' gave Padraic sparked something inside me.

"He's a doctor," I bragged for Padraic.

"Really?" Hayden asked, his eyes lighting up. "You're a doctor? A *real* doctor?"

Padraic nodded.

Hayden's excitement grew. "Thank God. Our medical staff consists of two veterinarians, a few nurses and 'an almost' neurologist who never finished med school. And she's crazy, not zombie virus crazy, but locks herself in her room writing scientific formulas on her wall crazy."

"Medical staff?" Padraic asked, bending down to tend to Ginger's cut.

"At the compound," Hayden explained. "It's where we, uh, live, so to speak. There are about three hundred people there. It's safe from the hostiles—"

"You mean zombies?" I inquired.

"Yeah," he agreed, giving me a look that let me know 'hostile' was the politically correct term to use. "Anyway, you can come back with us. We're trying to find survivors. We haven't come across a group this big since it first happened." He looked out the window that faced the front. "You said you had cars?"

"Yes," I responded.

"Are they in good condition?"

"The Range Rover is. The truck is old," I confessed. "And full of ammo," I said bitterly to myself.

"Really?" Hayden was suddenly interested. He turned to Brewster. "We should go back for them. We're in need of good vehicles."

Brewster initially nodded, stopping short and looking at the seven of us. "We can't leave the civilians."

"It will only take two of us," Hayden pointed out. "That leaves three to guard these guys."

Brewster considered, then looked at Ginger. "Rider's in no condition. He probably should keep weight off that leg, right, Doctor?"

Padraic looked up, blood on his hands. "Yes. He does need stitches; you were right. So until then, he needs to take it easy."

"I can go," I said bluntly.

"No," Raeya, Padraic, and the Marines said in unison.

"Why not? Obviously, I'm capable of taking care of myself. And it's my choice. It doesn't seem like we are being held hostage here, so I think I can leave if I want."

I looked at Hayden.

He nodded.

I rode shotgun in the black truck. Country music quietly drifted from the speakers.

"You're not scared to go back there?" Hayden asked, turning away from the passing field to look at me.

"No," I answered automatically.

"Not at all?"

"Are you?" I countered.

"No," Hayden said.

"See. That makes two of us."

"Yes but you're—"

"A girl? Ohmygod, don't even go there."

"You're not trained for stuff like this," he finished.

"Oh. Right. Not formally. But who really was formally trained for a zombie outbreak. Were you? Did the government know about this?"

"No, we had no idea," he promised me. "What kind of training did you have?"

"My grandpa used to take me shooting."

"That's it?"

"More or less."

"Hmm." He turned on the heater. "Is that Irish guy your boyfriend?"

I laughed. "No."

"He seems protective of you."

"He tries to be. We're all pretty protective of each other," I told him, thinking I'd do anything for any one of my friends back there...except for Lauren. "But he doesn't need to protect me."

"You don't like someone looking out for you?"

"No, well, yeah, it's nice. But I don't need it."

"Obviously," Hayden said with a grin. I didn't know if he was joking or being serious. Neither of us spoke until we were back by the barn.

A zombie lay dead—or deader—a few feet from me. An arrow stuck out of his face. I put my foot on his chest and yanked it out, wiping the goo on the zombie's shirt. I looked around in the fading light and located another arrow.

"I never got into archery," Hayden said as he handed me two arrows. "Always wanted to, though."

"I like it," I told him and easily pulled an arrow from a gummy's head. "My grandpa preferred it when hunting because it's silent." I looked around. "Where is my bow?" I didn't remember dropping it. Hayden walked with me back to the barn, retracing my steps. "Where did they all go?" I asked, looking around for the zombies.

"I have no idea. I've wondered about it too. Sometimes I think it would be interesting to follow them, you know, like those people that observe animals. And then I remember what they really are and I want to blow their fucking brains out."

"My friend, Raeya, made this list of all—" My words died in my chest as the wind got knocked out of me. Something lunged, landing on my back and pushing me to the ground.

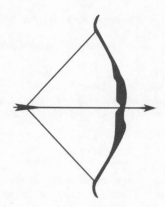

CHAPTER 20

Hayden pulled her off before I knew what was happening.

Another crazy screamed and limped at me, her ankle obviously broken. I picked up an arrow and went after her. A shot rang out and the first crazy collapsed. Hayden fired at the second before I was even close.

"You alright?" he asked.

"Fine," I answered automatically. I saw them just as Hayden heard them. Responding to the gunfire and screaming, and now the scent of human blood, the herd of zombies shambled out of the trees and weeds.

The barn was close. We scrambled up the loft ladder, laying flat on the rotten, hay covered boards. If we died, it would be my fault. My fault that I wanted to get my stupid arrows. Hayden had said it would be an 'in and out' mission and it would have been.

Dammit.

The zombies passed us, busily eating the two fresh bodies at their disposal like hand delivered Happy Meals. I scrunched my eyes as if that would help me see better through the settling darkness.

We decided to stay in the loft and wait for sunup. Then we might be able to find my bow.

Hayden turned the volume down on the walkie-talkie and explained our situation. He had to insist more than once that we didn't need backup. The zombies didn't know we were up here. Since they were still distracted by fighting over the bodies, Hayden used the time to shine his flashlight around our little loft. He moved a few of the rain dampened hay bales to the side, creating a barrier to stop the cold wind. He unzipped his backpack and pulled something out.

"I only have enough food for one person," he said, opening a small bag. I took it as his polite way of saying he wasn't sharing, which was fair enough. It took me by surprise when he pushed it in front of me. "I'm going to go off on a limb and say you haven't eaten in awhile."

"No," I admitted, my mouth already salivating at the thought of the unseen food. He handed me the bag. Inside was a sandwich, a banana, sweet potato chips, beef jerky, and chocolate chip cookies. "We can share. This is plenty." Though the soft bread on the sandwich was tempting, I hadn't had fresh fruit in so long. I pealed the banana open and took a bite. It was so good. I must have looked like a pig but I didn't care.

While we ate, Hayden told me all about the compound. It had been built nearly fifty years ago as an underground bomb shelter, disguised as an estate with rolling farmlands. The only way inside was through the main house.

"The first thing I'm gonna do," he said as he tore the sandwich in two and passed me a half, "when this is over is park my ass in the sand in Mexico with a bottle of tequila."

"Ugh, that sounds so good. If you go, I'm coming with you. I'd kill for a beach and a margarita."

"Me too. Literally. But no matter how many I kill, I'm no closer to that beach." He sighed and ate his half sandwich. I finished mine and leaned against the thin boards.

"Imagine my surprise," Hayden said. "I came home after two tours in Afghanistan to this."

"Oh God. I'm so sorry."

"I should have figured something was wrong." He stretched out his legs and leaned back. "I still had a little over a month left when they pulled us out. All I could think about was going home. I didn't want to question something good."

"So they brought you guys back to fight here?"

"I guess. I never found out. I expected my family to be there waiting when I got off the plane. When they weren't there…that's when I knew something happened." His voice grew quieter as he spoke. "When I got back to my hometown, I saw them for the first time. Just walking around looking normal."

He didn't tell me the fate of his family, and I didn't want to ask.

"Then a fight broke out. It was Mr. Harris from the bank attacking little, old Gina Phelps. When I pulled him off, Gina bit me."

"You've been bitten!?"

"Yeah," he said, proudly holding up his arm, revealing a shiny, crescent moon scar. I ran my finger over the smooth tissue. "I'm immune."

"Resistant," I said, echoing Padraic's words. "Go on."

"I didn't know what was going on. I thought they were drunk or something. But there were others. Most were in the S1 stage, attacking each other. I saw some horrible things overseas. *Really* horrible things. But seeing people you know ripping into the stomachs of others isn't something you can easily forget." He shook his head. "I never found my mom and sisters. I don't know if they got out or…I-I don't know. My dad skipped out on us when I was a kid. I took care of them. I wanted to make something of myself so they could be proud. So I joined the Marines. I moved up fast. I was good. And I wasn't there when they needed me most."

"You can't blame yourself," I told him, though I felt just as guilty. "I was staying with my aunt. She's the most passive person ever. And I don't know what happened to her either. By the time I got back to her apartment, she was gone. It sucks, not knowing."

"I wish I knew. Every town we go into, I hope I find them. It's stupid, I know."

"No. You wanna know stupid? I'm totally hoping my grandpa is at your compound." It surprised me how relieved I felt after saying that out loud. "I don't know what happened to him either. I couldn't get to his farm until, God, weeks after the outbreak."

"You're from around here?"

"No. I don't even know where we are, honestly. We—" I closed my eyes. "—we had been staying at his house in Kentucky. But we had to leave. The last place I remember was this small town in Kansas."

"You're in Oklahoma. Or what used to be Oklahoma."

"Oh. I had a feeling we weren't in Kansas anymore." I pulled my knees to my chest. Eventually, I slept.

I woke up with my head on Hayden's shoulder and his jacket draped around me.

The zombies had moved on by morning light. Hayden and I gathered up the arrows, I found my bow covered in zombie brain bits and transferred the weapons and ammo from the truck into the Range Rover. As we collected these things, Hayden told me about the S1, S2, and S3 classifications. A crazy was an S1, a zombie was an S2, and a gummy was considered an S3. Likewise, I told him about Raeya's more humorous classifications of the three. His jacket, still draped over me, kept me warm.

We sped back through the field, and I never thought an old insane asylum would look so welcoming.

Forgetting I was still wearing Hayden's jacket, I didn't understand the look Padraic gave me. Was that jealousy in his pretty, blue eyes? Raeya looked more like her normal self. She told me that the

Marines had debated about going back to the compound this morning since they had seven people to look after. They had orders to go farther and Brewster thought they should continue on. She said they were looking for something, but they talked in hushed voices and didn't seem to want her to know what they needed.

I told her I'd talk to Hayden about it. For some reason, I trusted him. Everyone else had already eaten breakfast by the time Hayden and I got back. They saved us some bland oatmeal and apple juice. Hayden said he was going to sleep for a few hours before we left for the compound since he had stayed up all night. He advised me to try to get some shut eye too.

I kicked off my boots and crawled into a sleeping bag that was beside Hayden's.

I slept for three hours. I woke, warm for the first time in days. Hayden was still asleep. He was facing me. He looked oddly innocent when he was sleeping.

The guys packed up their stuff with impressive speed. We loaded the gear into the back of the trucks. The Marines wore their uniforms and I couldn't help but notice how good Hayden looked all suited up, weapons strapped to his fit body, and a gun slung around his shoulder.

Raeya, Argos, and I rode with Hayden. We were headed back to the compound. In mere hours, I would be able to shower. Hayden said there was even warm water. Raeya was ecstatic. We put several hours behind us before we stopped to stretch our legs. Hayden, Brock, and Wade got out first, guns ready, and gave us clearance. My M9 was loaded and an extra clip nestled safely in my pocket.

I went with the girls to a ditch on the side of the road to pee. Raeya grumbled how unfair it was for the guys when it came to stuff like this. Lisa had a coughing fit again; I guess there was mold in the hayloft that had triggered her asthma. Even Argos was fed. Hayden told me they had several German Shepherds back at the compound that had been military dogs at one point. A few were trained to find cadavers. They were also being retrained to find living people. He promised me Argos would be well taken care of.

I didn't want to say anything. I wanted to pretend I didn't see it. We were only three hours (give or take) from the compound. Raeya, Hayden, and I were reminiscing about our favorite childhood toys, laughing for the first time in weeks. If I ignored it, I would feel guilty. And I was trying to change. *Sonofabitch.*

"Is that smoke?" I asked, thinking maybe I was seeing things.

Hayden braked. Yep, it was. Speaking through the walkie-talkies, he told the others what was going on. The Marines told us to stay in the cars. Ginger, I mean Rider, was forced to stay behind as his injury slowed him down. Hayden gave me two more clips and whispered that there was more ammo in the silver box in the bed of his truck.

The smoke was coming from an official looking brick building. A chain link fence surrounded it, bent and pushed down in parts, telling me it was not zombie proof. For our safety, the trucks were parked a good fifty yards away. I nervously watched the four Marines disappear inside the fencing. The minutes ticked by.

Argos growled. Thinking he'd caught a glimpse of Hayden or Brock exiting, I shushed him. Then I realized he wasn't looking at the building.

"Crazy," I whispered, grabbing Raeya's arm. "Don't move. Maybe she'll pass us."

And she did.

She went through a break in the fence. I wasn't even worried; one crazy wouldn't be a threat for the four, well armed Marines.

But the herd of zombies that followed her would.

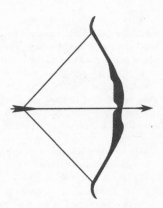

CHAPTER 21

I had to do something.

"Come on, Hayden," I whispered, nervously pulling on my braid. "Come *on*." I stared at the door, trying to will the guys to emerge before the zombie herd entered the building. My mind raced trying to figure out what to do. The Marines needed to know. Rider had a walkie-talkie. Surely he had warned his comrades. I looked through the Range Rover, past Padraic's worried blue eyes, and into the other truck. Yes, Rider held the device to his mouth and his lips were moving.

Brock exited first, opening fire on the herd. He could have made it back to the truck. He could have guaranteed his life. We could have sped away to safety leaving Hayden, Brewster, and Wade inside. But he was a Marine and he would never do that.

And neither would I.

Brock shot the crazy between the eyes and gunned down a few zombies. The herd moved in. Brock closed the gate, reeling away from the zombies' reach. Their skin peeled off as they stuck their arms through the chain link fence. I caught a glimpse of Hayden before a wall of zombies blocked him from view. He was carrying a child.

The fence wouldn't hold much longer. Rider had started shooting the trailing zombies; it was too risky to shoot at the ones that posed the biggest threat without being able to see the guys behind them. The infected didn't even turn and look at Rider, more concerned with the perspective group meal trying to get away.

It was now or never. I looked around, my eyes settling on the building next door. It was close by and under construction. Before Raeya could object, I got out of the truck and ran to it. I climbed up the scaffolding, just out of the zombies' reach. I turned and shouted, "Hey! Stupid zombies! Come and get me!" My voice was drowned by their moans. "Hey! Zombies!" I screamed. Again, my voice just blended in. I needed to catch their attention somehow. Screaming wouldn't work but maybe… it was worth a try. I took a deep breath, closed my eyes and sang the same lullaby that I had sung to Zoe before she died.

My voice floated out over the groaning and creaking of the rusty fence. A few zombies turned. Oh my God, it was working. But not well enough. A very dirty box cutter lay forgotten a few feet away. I didn't want to think about the risks. I picked it up, resumed singing and held out my arm.

I pulled up my sleeve and sliced my skin. The scent of blood on the wind did the trick. One by one, the zombies turned. The blood slowly trickled from the cut. I squeezed my fist, twisting my arm to let the blood drip ten feet down. Then it really started bleeding.

Shots echoed and zombies dropped. Hayden and the three others made it to the cars with two children and an adult. The realization that I was stuck set in at the same time I realized I'd sliced open a major vein.

The scaffolding shook under the zombies' desperate attempt to get me. Like the fence, it wouldn't hold. I scrambled up and into an open window, blood trailing. The faster I ran the more I bled. I was feeling woozy when I made it to where the stairs should have been. A crash came from outside.

The scaffolding had come down. I clasped my hand over my gushing wound. I went to the window on the other side. It was zombie free, and a three story drop. Dammit. Why had I gone up another story? I looked around, trying to find something to ease my jump. An orange extension cord was covered in dust. A saw was still attached. My bloody hands couldn't get a good grip on anything. It took longer than it should have to tie the extension cord to a wall frame. It wasn't long enough to shimmy down to the group.

I wiped my hands on my pants and held onto the cord, hoping to ease my way down the hole that should have been the stairwell. I lost my hold halfway down and landed hard. My hip took the brunt of the fall. I think my blood splattered. I wasn't sure of anything at that point. I crawled toward light and grabbed a plastic dust curtain to hoist myself up. It tore out of the wall, showering me with sawdust and bits of drywall. On my knees, I dragged myself over and left bloody handprints on the wall. I attempted to stand.

I had lost too much blood. I was already weak from lack of food, water, and sleep. My vision blacked. My legs buckled.

"Orissa!"

Had someone really shouted my name? I struggled to remain conscious. I slapped at the ground since I had no strength left to scream.

"Orissa? Where are you?"

Yes. That voice was real. I didn't recognize it at first. It was strong and deep and full of concern. The ground vibrated.

"Oh God, Orissa." Hayden scooped me up, closing his hand over my still bleeding cut. I went in and out of awareness as Hayden carried me down a ladder and out to the truck. He jumped in the bed, still carrying me, and the tires squealed. I remember him taking off his jacket and wrapping it around me just like he'd done at the barn. He held me close to him, trying to keep me warm, again, just like last time. Then everything blacked out.

→

Searing pain brought me back. I opened my eyes, vision fuzzy. Padraic was leaning over me, pressing on my arm. He poured something on it that I swear fizzled and smoked like holy water on a vampire. I yelled.

"Try to hold still," he said gently.

"Easy for you to say," I mumbled.

Hayden laughed, making me aware that my head rested in his lap. "Did we win?"

"Win?" Padraic asked, setting the bottle of pain down. He rolled gauze around my arm.

"The zombies. Back there?"

"Yeah," Hayden said. "I guess you could say that. We got away, thanks to you."

"It was a piece of cake," I said sarcastically. "All I had to do was almost bleed to death."

"You were brilliant," Hayden said admirably.

"You were stupid," Padraic spat. "You could have died."

"Well I didn't." I turned to look at him, only able to move my head.

"What were you thinking, taking on all those zombies?" Padraic said and wrapped tape around my arm.

I shrugged, then realized it made me move suggestively on Hayden's lap. "I told you, if I go down, it's gonna be fighting."

"You are one of a kind, Orissa," Hayden said. "We got three people back there, thanks to you."

"Yes, that is true," Padraic argued. "But she shouldn't risk her life like that. It's not her job."

"Oh, it's mine?" Hayden interjected.

"No, well, yes," Padraic stated.

I sat up. "It doesn't matter, ok? I'm alive I'm—" I cut off, searing pain in my arm. "What the hell did you do to me?"

"I didn't have anything to stitch it with," Padraic said apologetically. "So I used safety pins."

"What?" I felt a little sick. "That-that's…inventive. Thanks."

"You're welcome. Try not to move your arm, alright? I don't want you to rip your skin. You cut yourself deeply and lost a lot of blood. You'll need proper medical care once we get to this compound."

"I'll see to it," Hayden promised. He wrapped me tight in his arms and stood. As ashamed as I was to admit it, I was too tired and weak to fight him, too tired to insist I was capable of moving on my own. I wasn't sure if I actually would be. He put me in the backseat of the truck where it was warm and comfortable. I closed my eyes and rested my head on the cool window. Raeya rode up front. Hayden drove while Padraic and Argos joined me in the back. I wanted to stay awake but failed.

"Home sweet home," Hayden spoke in the darkness. The headlights illuminated a narrow gravel driveway cut into thick woods. We drove maybe a hundred feet before stopping. He got out and opened a heavy iron gate. Another hundred feet after that was another metal gate. On either side were two masonry towers that reminded me of the watch towers of a castle.

"Back already?" one of the guards shouted to Hayden.

"Got ten civilians," Hayden answered. The guard nodded, pressed some buttons and the gates swung open. We drove through a winding tree lined path and emerged into a large field. The brick estate wasn't just big. It was fricken huge.

Hayden was right. It looked like a rich family lived here, raising expensive race horses or something of the like. There were armed soldiers and Marines at every entrance.

Hayden jumped back in and we drove to a large, white barn. He parked the truck, told us to stay put, and got out. The other Marines followed suit. After what felt like an eternity, Hayden came back.

"You guys have to be quarantined for twenty-four hours." He held up his hand before we could object. "We do too. If anyone leaves the compound, they have to go through it. It's not that bad, I promise. I'll take Argos inside and give him to the dog handlers. Orissa, someone will come and take care of you. See you in twenty-four."

I wanted to be mad at him for not telling me earlier, though I agreed it was a smart idea. More soldiers or Marines ushered us into the barn. It had been transformed from horse barn to holding barn. Each stall was set up with a cot, sleeping bag, and bucket. I didn't understand the bucket at first. Then it dawned on me that we would be stuck in here for twenty-four hours and needed something to go to the bathroom in.

My stall smelled strongly of bleach; I guessed its last occupant hadn't made it out alive. Sheets had been nailed to the sides, offering little privacy. Something buzzed and clicked. A hot wire had been weaved around the metal bars on the stall's sides, electrifying the entire thing.

I stepped willingly into the stall. I sat on the cot—as instructed—and waited for a medic to come stitch up my arm. She was dressed in a homemade hazmat suit. Her face was pretty behind the protective plastic mask. She smiled at me and opened a first-aid kit. I wish I could have taken a picture of her face when she undid the bandage and saw my Frankenstein arm. It hurt like hell when she opened the safety pins. As iron stomached as I am, I had to look away.

When my medic left and the stall door clicked shut, I felt panic creep into my heart. I wanted to talk to Hayden to find out more about this place. Would I be trapped like this forever? Not in the stall, I knew that wouldn't be true, but would this place be run like a jail? Maybe it was a mistake letting him take us here. Maybe we could have gone back to Kentucky and made things work.

I paced back and forth, wearing myself out. When I couldn't take it anymore, I sat on the cot, shivering. For the time being, there was nothing I could do.

Sometime in the night a lunch bag of food was delivered. I devoured the sandwich and apple and downed the water in minutes. Without taking off my boots, I eased my aching body into the sleeping bag and tried to sleep.

I was beyond bored when the sun came up. Raeya was next to me and we talked back and forth for awhile until she fell asleep again. I watched the soldiers guarding us. They walked past each stall, inspecting us and assessing for zombie symptoms. Based on the position of the sun in the sky, I judged the time. We got one more meal before we were released.

Everyone passed, even the three others we'd saved. A female soldier with US ARMY stitched onto her jacket told us we could shower before going inside to 'learn the ropes.' We would even get clean clothing. We followed her into a room inside the barn. It had once been a washing area for fancy horses. The smell of soap and shampoo was wonderful. I had just unzipped my boots when another soldier opened the door.

"Orissa?" he called.

"Yeah?"

"Come with me, please."

I looked at Raeya. She reached out for my hand.

"It's nothing bad," he promised. "You can meet up with your friends later."

I nodded and left the shower room feeling grosser than ever. The soldier was dressed in greens and had an official looking ID tag hanging from his neck. I only caught a glimpse and learned his last name was Jones. We went up a well lit path and into the house. The first floor was set up just like a normal living space. Hayden *did* say that the house was a great cover. I would have no idea we were over a top secret bomb shelter. We went to the middle of the largest room. Two soldiers stood next to a door that led into the basement. My guide used an old fashioned skeleton key to open it.

We went down normal looking stairs into a hallway with three doors; there was one on each side and one in front of us. Jones unlocked the center door, held it open for me and relocked it once we stepped in. Inside was another set of doors. These were thick, shiny steel that required a pass code to get through. The doors closed with a whoosh. Another set of steel doors was ahead of us; these required a pass code and a hand scan to open. One more door had to be unlocked with a regular key before we could go down another set of stairs.

The shelter wasn't cave-like at all. The halls were tiled, the walls painted white, and the lights were ultra bright. Not cave-like, but maze-like. I would get lost in here for sure. We weaved through a hall. Some of the doors were open. They reminded me of dorm rooms when I looked inside.

My head hurt from the fluorescent lights. My guide knocked on a closed, unmarked door. An older man in formal military garb answered instantly.

"Orissa," he said with a nod.

"Uh, yeah?"

"Please, come in." He waved his hand.

His office was painted in earthy tones, a nice break for my eyes from the sterile white of the halls. I sat on a leather armchair. Everything in here was clean and tidy, making my dirty state very salient. I felt like I was in trouble. I knew, this time at least, I hadn't done anything wrong.

"I'm Colonel Fuller. I'm more or less in charge of things around here." He closed the door and sat behind his desk. He smiled warmly at me. "Hayden vouched for you. I have to say, I'm quite impressed. And I heard you've had no formal training."

"Uh, no. What do you mean, vouched?"

"I've never done this before. Hayden insisted it would be a waste for you to be anything but A1."

"A1?" Was that like S1? No...it didn't make sense.

He chuckled. "No one's explained the rankings to you?"

"No. I don't know much of anything about this place."

"My apologies. I'll let you rest and clean up, then see to it Hayden fills you in on everything. You should know that being an A1 is something to be proud of. I hold all my A1s in high regard. You have expectations to live up to, Orissa."

"Uh, ok."

He uncapped a pen. "What is your last name? Mind you, it can be anything now. But choose wisely, for it will be yours from now on."

"Penwell," I said honestly. As soon as I was old enough, I had my last name changed from my douche-canoe of a father's to my mother's maiden name.

"And your age?"

"Twenty-five."

"Birthday?"

"November 10th."

"Thank you," he said as he jotted down something else before getting up.

Jones was waiting for me outside the door. It was just as much of an ordeal to get out of the basement as it was to get in. We went upstairs to the second story. Jones told me that due to overcrowding, the A1s got moved upstairs. He sounded a bit jealous as he spoke.

The house reminded me of Seth's frat house in its size and design, though it was much, much cleaner. Each heavy, oak door had two name plates nailed onto it. We went to the very last room in the hall. UNDERWOOD was etched onto the top plate. The plate under it had been removed. I could only guess what had happened to Hayden's roommate. Jones knocked on the door. It took Hayden a minute to answer.

Dressed in gray athletic pants and a black hoodie, Hayden looked completely normal. Normal, and attractive. He pulled out his earbuds, turned off his iPod, and smiled.

"Orissa...come in," he said.

I mumbled a thank you to Jones and went into Hayden's room. It was tidy and orderly and almost pre-zombie looking. Two beds were pushed up against opposite walls. Hayden's was to the left of the door. A large dresser was across from them with a nice sized plasma TV resting in the middle. The closet was open, revealing more clothing than I expected and an impressive display of weapons. A fairly full bookcase was next to the dresser.

"You're supposed to explain things to me," I said simply.

"Oh, yeah. Do you want to shower first?"

"Am I that disgusting?"

"Well, I wasn't gonna say it," he laughed.

"You have no idea how much I want out of these clothes."

"There's stuff for you on your bed," he said, pointing.

"My bed?"

"You don't know? We're, uh, roommates."

"We are?"

"If you have a problem with it, I'm sure we can get it changed. Maybe they can put you in with the other women or—"

"It's fine. I can handle it if you can." I went over to the bed. A towel, a little bag of toiletries, a brush, and a bottle of lotion had been set on it. "I need clothes."

"Oh, I guess Ender assumed you picked out your own. I can grab you something if you want."

"That would be wonderful."

"What size?" he asked quietly, as if he knew that was a rude thing to ask a woman.

"I'm not sure anymore." I had lost a lot of weight since my surgery. "I used to be medium." Giving him actual numbers might be pushing it. I knew guys weren't good with stuff like that.

"I'm sure I can find something," he said. "I'll show you where the bathroom is."

I couldn't describe how good it felt to shower even though there was only 10 minutes worth of hot water. I scrubbed my body with soap, shampooed my hair twice, and slathered on conditioner, letting it soak in while I shaved my legs for the first time in weeks.

It took forever to brush out the tangles in my hair. I towel dried it the best I could before I pulled it to the side and braided it. I wrapped the towel around myself, brushed my teeth for probably ten minutes, and gathered up my filthy clothes, thinking burning them was a grand idea. I cracked the door and looked down the hall for Hayden. I waited a few more minutes. The bathroom was getting cold fast. Giving up, I dashed down the hall in just my towel.

Hayden wasn't in our room and neither were the clothes he'd promised. Maybe it was because I was nearly naked with wet hair, or maybe it was just cold in the room. I shivered, causing goosebumps to break out across my skin. I investigated Hayden's stuff while I waited for clothes. He had an interesting collection of books, most of them in the sci-fi genre, along with a variety of movies. The closer I got to the window, the colder I felt.

The window, which was by the foot of my bed, had bars across it. It brought up a mixed feeling of safety and being trapped. I couldn't see much of what was outside. The exterior of the house was well lit and, in the pool of light, it looked like a normal yard.

The door opened and I whirled around. Hayden's eyes slid over me before he quickly cast them down. He held out a pile of clothes.

"Finally," I said trying to suppress my smile. It had been a long time since anyone had looked at me that way. I took the clothes and held them up. He had brought me a pair of jeans, socks and a blue, plaid shirt. "And I'm supposed to go bra-less and commando?" I raised an eyebrow and half smiled. Hayden looked embarrassed.

"I-I didn't...even t-think about that," he stammered, still staring at the ground. "I, uh, can go back."

"It's ok." I put my arms through the shirt, wincing as the fabric caught my bandaged left wrist. When I pulled my legs through the jeans, I was reminded of how sore my body was. It took effort to put on the socks.

"Do the clothes fit?" Hayden asked, pretending to read while I got dressed.

"Yeah. The pants are a little big, but that's ok because I want to gain back the weight I lost."

"Wouldn't most women be happy about losing weight?"

"Most women haven't spent the last few weeks starving and running from flesh eating crazy people."

"Very true. Hungry?"

"That is an understatement," I told him.

"Good, me too. I can explain everything while we eat."

After painfully putting my boots on, I followed Hayden down the hall, paying extra attention to where we were going. We went into the basement, through the security doors, and down the stairs. We turned left and walked along a quiet hall that seemed to stretch forever. The kitchen and cafeteria reminded me of something seen in a school. Like the rest of the shelter, it was a blinding white and smelled like cleaning products. Hand drawn pictures, obviously done by children, were taped up along the wall giving the place a more personal feel.

Hayden opened an industrial sized fridge. "What do you want?"

It was strange, how exciting it was to pick something to eat. "I don't care. As long as it's not tuna or some plants I found in the woods, I'm fine."

"There's left over lasagna," he suggested.

"That sounds incredibly satisfying right now." My stomach grumbled.

Hayden plopped a large piece on a plate and stuck it in the microwave.

"You really survived on plants?"

"Not entirely. We had venison jerky and so much canned tuna. I don't think I can ever eat it again."

"How do you know what plants are edible?"

"My grandpa taught me," I explained.

"He seems to have taught you a lot."

"Yeah, he did." I sat at a table.

Hayden poured two glasses of milk, set them down, and brought over the lasagna. He turned away to heat up another piece for himself.

"Where did you get the venison jerky? It's not something you come across in stores very often."

"I shot the deer and made the jerky myself before we had to leave."

"You're like one of those wilderness guys from TV," he joked.

The microwave beeped. I had devoured most of my food by the time Hayden sat across from me. It was the blandest lasagna I'd ever had. But it was warm and filling and didn't come from a can. I could feel Hayden's curious gaze while I finished my meal. I pushed the plate aside and drained my milk. "So, what do I need to know?"

"There's a lot," he said with his mouth full.

"I got that, genius. What's an A1?"

"It's a ranking. Everyone is sorted into either A, B, or C, categories. A is for soldiers or Marines, B is medical, and C is domestic, which entails things like cooking, keeping the place clean, inventorying supplies, and taking care of the farm elements. A and B categories have numbers one through three. An A1 is what you and I are. We go on missions. A2s patrol the fields and farms where the animals are since they aren't inside the shelter's fencing. A3s are guards, like the ones by the gates and doors."

"So an A1 is kinda like the highest ranking?"

"I guess you can say that," he said, trying not to sound like it was a big deal. "And the Bs have three ranks: doctors, nurses, and medics. 'Medics' is used broadly for anyone with a medical background, like the veterinarians or anyone who's worked in healthcare. We didn't have any B1's until now."

"And the C group? They don't have numbers?"

"No, work within that group is divided up as seen fit. Children, old people, or anyone with any sort of condition don't leave the shelter's protection. The fields are pretty safe and are always patrolled, but we don't want to risk it."

"Does everyone have to do something?"

"Yes and no. It's not fair to make others do all the work so yes. But if someone can't, we won't make them."

"Who is 'we'?"

"Us. I can't say this without sounding like a tool, but without us soldiers and Marines, this place wouldn't exist. We make the so called laws. But nothing is horrible, I promise. You need laws and structure to keep a place like this going and under control."

"So is there like a real leader?"

"You met Fuller, right? He gets the final say, I guess. He's not interested in ruling or having power or anything of the like. He wants us to survive."

I nodded. "So, how do you decide who goes into what category?"

"Everyone is given time to rest after coming in, usually about a week depending on what condition they come in. Then they are tested."

"Tested?"

"To find strengths and weaknesses. Really, Orissa, I know how this sounds. We want to put the most capable people in the right spots. Everything is done for the good of the community."

"What if someone has no skills?"

"Everyone can clean."

"Ok. And once tested and sorted, who organizes, who does what?" I asked.

He laughed. "They've been nicknamed 'overseers.' We have nine right now but need more. It's a tough job," he admitted and crossed his arms. "They have to make sure everything gets done on time and that there is someone there to do it."

"Why didn't I have to test?"

"I talked to Fuller."

"He told me, but...why?"

"I saw you out there. You fought valiantly. You risked yourself for us and...and succeeded. You're smart, cunning, quick, a real fighter. I know a warrior when I see one."

"Thanks," I said, unable to look at Hayden. Those weren't the compliments I was used to. "So everyone with me will be tested in a few days?"

"Everyone except Patrick."

"Pad-rick," I corrected. Hayden nodded in acknowledgement. "Tired?"

"Among other things."

He washed the dishes, grumbling that the 'kitchen ladies' get pissed when dirty dishes are left in the sink.

We mazed our way back through the quiet halls. It freaked me out at how silent everything was. I felt dumb once I realized it was the middle of the night and everyone was sleeping.

"Where are my friends?" I asked.

"They have rooms," Hayden responded. We went through a door into a dark room. Hayden slid his hand up and down the wall, feeling for the light. It flickered on. "You'll need more clothes," he said and waved his hand at the shelves in front of us.

A lot of the clothes were new and still had price tags. I speculated the guys raided a clothing store. I was too tired and sore to give a damn about clothes at the moment. I got only what I would need for that night.

He took the clothes from me as if they were too heavy for me to carry. We went back into our room, and I took the pajamas to the bathroom to change.

"It gets cold in here at night," Hayden said when I came back into the room. "There's something wrong with the heating system for the house. We had hoped to find an HVAC guy."

"Instead you got me." I crawled under the covers.

"I think it's a fair trade." He smiled and turned out the light. For the first time in months, I felt safe. I slept soundly. That is, until a loud alarm sounded.

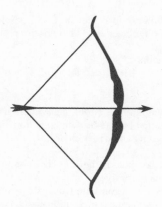

CHAPTER 22

I sat up. The beeping echoed throughout our room. Something was wrong. Had zombies gotten in? Were we under attack?

"It's ok," Hayden said sleepily, seeing my fear. "It's my alarm."

My heart was still racing. He picked up the little clock from his nightstand, turned it off, threw the covers back, and begrudgingly got out of bed.

"Do I need to get up too?" I asked.

"No. Not yet at least."

"Thank God." I flopped back down and pulled the blankets closer around myself. "What do you have to do?"

"Workout," he mumbled. "You can go down for breakfast whenever. Soldiers and Marines don't have a scheduled time like the others."

"I think I'll stay in bed," I informed him. It felt good to get several straight hours of sleep, and I could tell my body would hurt if I moved.

"Ok. I'll be back in awhile. You can, uh, do whatever I guess."

When Hayden came back into the room around noon, I couldn't believe how long I had slept. I washed my face, brushed and rebraided my hair, and got dressed. Brewster was in our room, talking and laughing with Hayden.

"Welcome to the A club," Brewster said when I entered.

"Thanks, I think." I flashed him a smile.

"Ivan Brewster, at your service," he joked and shook my hand. Ivan was a few inches taller than Hayden, will full lips and defined cheekbones.

"Am I supposed to call you by your last names or address you as Private or Sergeant or whatever?" I asked and sat on my unmade bed.

Hayden shook his head. "We don't keep up with the formalities anymore."

"Makes it easier for me."

"Orissa Penwell," Ivan said slowly. "I want to know everything about you."

"Uh, everything?"

"Why not? Coming across someone like you doesn't happen every day. You've sparked my interest." His voice was smooth.

"I can handle a gun and I don't want to die. That's really it," I simplified.

"I don't buy that for a second."

"My parents are ninjas," I supplemented wryly.

Ivan smiled and turned to Hayden. "I like her."

Hayden smiled and nodded, appearing oddly shy.

Later we headed to the Cafeteria. Ivan and Hayden were dressed in combat boots and camo pants with black shirts tucked in. They looked like Marines: put together in an effortless way, confident, and muscular. Ivan was making a joke about someone he referred to as 'Crazy Cara' when we walked into the cafeteria. It was packed, with a line of people waiting to get their trays. A little boy saw us enter. He tugged on his father's shirt and pointed. The dad looked up and elbowed his wife. They put their hands to their hearts and nodded with respect in our direction.

Others noticed us, and had a similar reaction. A hush fell over the room, and an old man saluted. Then, as if on cue, everyone burst into applause. I didn't know what to do. Looking at Ivan and Hayden for direction, I, too, smiled. We walked to a table in the back, getting stopped and thanked along the way.

"Does that happen all the time?" I asked once we were seated.

"Yeah," Ivan told me. "I always said people would clap for me someday. I thought it would be for my mad guitar skills and not my hostile takedowns, though."

After the awe wore off, I spotted Raeya running in our direction. I jumped up and wrapped my arms around her.

"Raeya! H-how are you?"

"Peachy," she said with a laugh. "I was so scared they took you away for some reason." She brought her tray over, Lisa trailing behind, and joined us. She had been told the same things about being sorted and the ways of the compound as I had. She and Lisa were sharing a room with a middle-aged woman who'd lost everyone. She said those in the C category thought of the A1s as the new celebrities.

"I'm gonna hang out with Raeya," I told Hayden when we finished eating.

"Ok, see you tonight," he said with a slight smile.

"What are you guys doing tonight?" Raeya asked as we walked into her room. "Top secret soldier stuff?"

"No," I said, crushing her excitement. "We, uh, are roommates."

Her eyebrows went up. "You are?"

"Yeah." I waited for her reaction.

She pressed her lips together and let it go. Her room was small, set up like a dorm room in some ways. It had a bunk bed and a single bed, two large dressers, a desk, and an uncomfortable looking chair, ugly and pale pink. We sat on Raeya's bed—the bottom bunk—and talked about the compound. The C's had a strict schedule. Raeya supported it and thought it was needed to keep a place like this in order. She was nervous about her sorting test, afraid she'd end up a dishwasher.

Scarlett Procter was the self-appointed Welcome Committee. She was one of the first occupants in the shelter, along with her husband, two children, mother, sister, family dog, best friend and best friend's family. She even had time to pack up her valuables. The high heels, skirt, and silk blouse she wore would look good on a news reporter. On someone hiding underground from crazy, carnivorous humans, the outfit looked stupid. Her ID badge hung from a beaded necklace. She was chipper and thankful and had no idea what it was really like out there or what it felt like to lose the ones you love.

She took us on a tour, showing us the large 'game room,' which was painted—wait for it—white. There were tables and chairs and bookshelves filled with books and games. She showed us the 'theater room' that was very much like the game room but with a large TV and couches. She showed us the supply rooms and then took us down another level.

The second basement, as she called it (though technically it was the third) housed the hospital ward, offices, weapon supply, and more living quarters for the A2s, 3s and Bs as well as some spill over C's. She only had access to the living quarters.

She led us back into the theater room, where kids were watching a cartoon. I was happy to see Lisa sitting next to several girls her own age. Scarlett told us the shelter was full of gossip since there wasn't much to do other than talk.

"I heard about the new A1," Scarlet gushed, leaning in and lowering her voice. "Apparently, he really made an impression on Hayden Underwood and Ivan Brewster."

"Why are those two so important?" I questioned, avoiding Raeya's eyes. The girl couldn't keep a poker face to save her life.

Scarlett smiled, pleased to know something I didn't. "They are the best. And cute too, don't you think?"

"How did this noob impress those two?" I asked.

Scarlet leaned forward. "You didn't hear it from me, but my girlfriend Minnie's son is an A3 and he overheard the A1s talking about the new A1 and how he just pulverized the hostiles. And get this: he almost killed himself saving ten civilians and some of our guys."

"Wow. Do you know how this brave, and awesome, and probably good looking A1 did it?"

Confusion muddled Scarlett's face for a brief second. "I guess he drew the hostiles away so everyone could escape."

"Wow," I repeated. "Simply amazing!"

Raeya elbowed me. Scarlett went on to tell us about the plans for the shelter that couldn't be executed until the spring, such as planting crops.

I surveyed everyone in the room as Scarlett spoke, pointing this way and that. Those who weren't watching the movie chatted quietly, read, or drew. An old lady sat near the children working on a cross-stitching that might have been needlepoint.

It's a funny thing about the human race, how we crave normalcy so much we're able to adapt to almost anything.

"…and then he burst through the door," Scarlett said breathlessly, putting her hand on Raeya's arm. "Oh, my! Speak of the devil!"

"Orissa," Hayden called. I stood to face him. He tossed something to me that I instinctively reached out to catch. I yanked my left arm to my side, wincing in pain. "Oh, sorry, I forgot." He picked up the ID badge. The A1 status looked so good next to my name. I pulled it over my head, patting it against my chest.

Scarlett's eyes bulged. "*You're* the new A1?" she asked incredulously.

"Yep," I replied.

The look on her face was priceless.

"Hi, Hayden," Raeya said politely. Hayden said hello back but I could tell he had forgotten her name, just like he'd forgotten Padraic's in the cafeteria.

"Orissa," he said, "Fuller wants to get you programmed in and give you the pass codes."

I said bye to Raeya and followed Hayden down to the next level. We went through one of the doors Scarlett wasn't authorized to go through and into a high-tech room. My hand got scanned into the computer and I was given a list of codes to remember. I was warned not to lose the list, since reprogramming the codes was a pain in the ass.

When we were done I wandered around until I found Raeya's room. I found her refolding her clothes and sorting them into color groups.

"Want to find Padraic?" she asked. "I haven't seen him since the quarantine."

"I'll pass."

"Why?"

I sighed. I had hoped to avoid him until things wouldn't be awkward. "He kissed me."

"What?" She smiled. "When?"

"Before we had to leave. It was…weird." I wrinkled my nose.

"Weird? Are we thinking about the same hot doctor here?"

"I'll admit he's hot—"

"—and kind and caring and smart."

"No." I shook my head. "It's still weird."

"Why?"

"I don't know," I lied. "Ok, I do. He reminds me of Ted."

Raeya put a sweater down and sat next to me on the bed. "Your stepdad?"

"Yeah."

"The last time I checked, your stepdad was overweight and balding. How in the world can you even compare those two?"

I folded my arms. I hated deep conversations like this when I was forced to admit something that made me feel like scum. "You know I'm not Ted's biggest fan. And you know as well as anyone that I had no reason for giving him hell. He'd done nothing but make my mom happy. And I say I hate him, but really I can't think of any good reasons why I do. He's a good person, I have to admit. He does the right thing; he puts faith in people who don't deserve it. People like me." I looked up at Raeya and shook my head. That crap about getting a weight off your chest was true after all.

"So since Padraic's a good person you don't like him?"

"It sounds bad when you say it like that."

"No, this is good. I think we're coming to a breakthrough."

"We are?" I asked, playing with a button on my shirt.

"Yes. Why do you hate Ted?" she asked.

"He took my mom away from me."

"He did something for her that you couldn't do and you never let that go," Raeya analyzed. "And you've overcompensated by excelling physically."

"I'm good at killing. Hunting. Being a glorified hillbilly raised by my paranoid, Post Traumatic Stress Disorder grandfather." I'm twenty-five years old and have nothing to show for it."

"A lot of things that used to be important seem really dumb now," Raeya said, likely thinking about her degrees.

I nodded.

"Yeah, things like Black Friday," she said.

"Black Friday?"

"The after Thanksgiving sales? I used to love getting up at three a.m. to hit the stores. Now, I can see how much of a waste of time and money that was."

I laughed and shook my head. "Yeah. That one is pretty stupid. People getting hurt or killed over material items. It puts things in perspective, doesn't it?"

"So what are you going to do about Padraic?"

"You know I'm not one to put up with any sort of thing like that. I like him as a friend, really, I do. There's just nothing more. And I don't want to hurt his feelings, so I plan to avoid him until he forgets about it and moves on."

Easier said than done.

I was sent to the hospital ward to have my cut checked. At least we weren't alone. There were several injured people lying in beds. Padraic told me he'd had to fix two botched surgeries already. Apparently he didn't get a week off to rest. He was also trying to put together a training class for the B3's and a simpler one for anyone interested. He smiled when he told me he'd always wanted to teach.

I could read him easily. It was a lie. He was tired and stressed and busy and the only one with the know-how to heal these people. He assured me that one of the nurses used to work in the ER and was wonderful and she gladly spilt the main responsibilities. They all looked up to him, as they should, and trusted his professional opinion.

He told me my arm looked good and that I was every doctor's ideal patient because I healed so fast. Before I could hop off the exam table, he put his hands on my shoulders.

"How are you really, Orissa?"

"Grand."

He removed his hands from my shoulders, ran one though his dark hair, rumpling it. Then he sat next to me. "I need to thank you for everything you did. I know you're aware that none of us would be here if it wasn't for you."

"You're welcome," I said.

"You...you are an amazing young woman," he began.

Here we go, I thought.

"You are so...so full of fire. I always thought I was alive before," he trailed off.

I concentrated on the floor.

He shook his head and started over. "I used to be only concerned with other people. I took my duty as a doctor seriously. As long as I could help other people, I'd be fine. But I was wrong. I forgot about myself, I forgot that I, too, wanted and deserved to be happy."

"You do, Padraic. You are a good person, a really good person."

After escaping the awkward moment, I hurried up to my room. Hayden was lying in bed watching a movie. He wore sweatpants and a T-shirt with a blanket draped over his knees. I sat on my bed, eyes glued to the TV. I had seen the movie *Ted* many times and found it to be unintelligibly funny every time I saw it. Since I hadn't watched TV in months, it was the best movie ever for the time being.

"Donating blood?" I asked Hayden, seeing the little ball of cotton bandaged on the inside of his elbow. He didn't look away from the movie.

"Yeah."

"Why?"

"The doctors like to make sure we're healthy."

"Do they take everyone's blood?"

"If they want to," he said quickly.

"Uh-huh."

I knew he was lying…

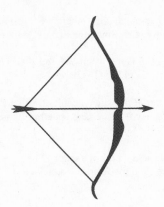

CHAPTER 23

I spent my days healing, getting to know the A1s, walking around being bored out of my mind with Raeya, exploring the fenced in parts of the shelter, which weren't much, and playing with Argos. I ate breakfast and lunch with Hayden and the other Marines and dinner with my old group. Some days Hayden had a new puncture in his arm, cotton, and a bandage. I was curious but didn't ask about it again.

Not all of the A1s were welcoming. The five guys who saw me in action were thankful to have another on their team. Others didn't find it fair since I hadn't gone through boot camp like they had. Brock said they weren't convinced I was good enough but they'd get over it once they saw me in training.

When my first day of training arrived, Hayden assured me that it was nothing more than working out, mock zombie situations, and learning new fighting techniques. And, since I was the only A1 who knew how to use a bow and arrow, Fuller wanted me to teach the others. I used to work out regularly. Then I couldn't afford my gym membership so I cut my routine down to running, yoga, and exercising in my room. I was looking forward to getting back on a treadmill as I followed Hayden down the basement stairs.

We entered a rather extensive workout room. I was to do a cardio routine and then go through a list of strength training exercises. I would be assessed by Hayden on where I needed improvement. After a short break, we moved outside for target practice. Though the shelter had plenty of ammo, we didn't want to be wasteful.

There were a handful of new, modern weapons that I hadn't used before. It didn't take long before I was hitting the bull's-eye. When we finished, Hayden took me around the quarantine barn to his truck. He retrieved the bow and arrows.

"Can you show me how to use it? I want to know what I'm doing before you play teacher," he said with a cheeky grin.

"Yeah," I told him, knowing I would want the same. He looked around, set the arrows back down and pulled his keys from his pocket.

"Want to go for a drive?" he asked.

"We can just leave?"

"Orissa, this isn't prison."

"I know; it's just…" I thought about the bandages, about them taking his blood—his and no one else's. Was he sick? "If we leave, do we have to be quarantined again?"

"No. Not if we go to the fields. You haven't been there yet, have you?" When I shook my head he smiled. "Perfect. It's patrolled so it's relatively safe." Because I'd been so hurt and groggy last time

I'd been in his truck, I hadn't noticed the details—there were roll bars on the back, USMC emblems on the dash, and a leather steering wheel. Someone had put a lot of money into this truck. Hayden pressed play on his iPod.

"Spice Girls?" I asked, trying not to laugh when *Say You'll be There* rang from the speakers.

"Oh, I'm a *huge* fan," he said with a flick of his hand.

I laughed.

"Not really. I, uh, started collecting iPods since I can't download new music anymore. I got sick of what was on mine." He went to change it to the next song but I stopped him.

"I like this song."

"You do?" he asked with a smile.

"Yes. Don't tell me you don't at least think it's catchy?" I turned the volume up so I could sing along. "I went through a short dress and platform sneakers phase," I told him.

"You did?"

"My stepdad hated it."

"Which made you want to do it more," he guessed.

"Of course, now shut up and let me sing," I said with a smile. When *Wannabe* came on next, Hayden sang the refrain along with me. We were both laughing when the song finished. "It's been a long time since I've done that," I admitted.

"Done what?"

"Sang. For fun, not to distract zombies."

"That was a genius idea, by the way." He glanced at me with a wry smile.

I sang a few more songs before we parked near a large barn. Hayden waved to the patrolling A2s and got out of the truck. I carried the bow and he carried the arrows. I walked ahead of him, curiously surveying my surroundings. I could see the herds of cows and could smell the chickens. At one time this must have been a real working farm. About two feet away from the wooden fence that corralled the cows was a single wire, electric fence.

"This is supposed to keep the zombies out?" I asked, reaching for it. Hayden dropped the arrows and pulled me back. My foot caught on the uneven ground, causing me to stumble. He caught me with ease.

Still holding onto me he said, "Not the zombies. But the S1s. It has enough juice to stop a human heart."

"Oh," I said, straightening. "Thanks for, uh, saving me then."

"No problem." He looked behind him. "Let's go over here. I don't want to accidentally kill something."

We rigged up targets using hay bales and empty feed bags that I turned inside out and drew circles on.

"It'd be nice to have an arm guard," I mumbled.

"Why is that?"

"It's helpful. Sometimes the string hits your arm when you release it. And it keeps loose clothes out of the way."

"Oh," he said and held up the bow.

I laughed. "Sorry." I covered my mouth.

"What?"

"You're doing it all wrong. Watch. Pay attention to how my body moves."

"I think I can do that," Hayden joked.

I rolled my eyes, pulled an arrow, aimed, and released.

"You're good," he told me. "And you make it look easy."

"I've been doing this for a while," I said honestly. "I sucked at first."

We spent the next hour going over parts of the bow, what they did and finally how to shoot. Hayden paid attention and caught on quickly.

The next day we had one-on-one combat training. Ivan was my partner. I hadn't mentioned my years of martial arts lessons.

I kicked his ass.

Hayden didn't go to training the following day. He seemed to have disappeared. We woke up at the same time, ate breakfast with the other Marines, and walked down the hall together. But when I got into the workout room, he simply wasn't there. I gave my compound bow shooting demonstration that day; I didn't think Hayden would want to miss it.

That night, I sat on my bed brushing my wet hair, having just showered. Finally, Hayden came in and looked alarmed to see me. I knew something was up by the way he pressed his left arm to his side and tried to weasel in unnoticed.

"Are you sneaking off to see a vampire?" I asked.

"Huh?"

"You've been donating a lot of blood," I said seriously. This was the fourth time I'd noticed the cotton ball and Band-Aid on his arm.

"Oh, uh, no."

I got up and closed the door. "Hayden, I know you're lying."

He sighed, ran his hand over his head and sat on his bed. "I am."

"Why?"

"I'm not supposed to tell anyone."

"Tell anyone what? And where were you today?" I knelt on the bed next to him. I grabbed his left hand and extended his arm. "And what is this all about? Are you sick?" Suddenly, I was scared. I didn't want anything to be wrong with Hayden.

"No, I'm not sick."

I raised my eyebrows, wanting an explanation.

He twisted his arm so his hand was resting in mine. "You can't tell anyone, ok?"

"Promise."

"Remember how I told you that I got bitten?"

"Yeah?"

"That crazy doctor I also told you about is trying to make a vaccine."

"A vaccine?" I echoed incredulously.

"Yeah."

"Can she do it?"

"I don't know." Hayden took his hand away. "We don't know anyone else who has been bitten and not infected so it's not easy. She told me she needs to test it on people but there's no way we can do that."

"But why does she keep taking your blood?"

"She—and your *friend* Patrick now—are trying to figure out what's different about my blood."

"Have they found anything?" I asked. Hayden was still referring to Padraic as Patrick, but this wasn't the time to correct him. Again.

"Nothing substantial. I guess I have more white blood cells. But not too many, like in cancer patients. I've always had a good immune system. Patrick thinks we need more than blood samples."

"What do you mean?"

"I don't speak doctor, but he said something about needing to do neurological testing. Obviously, we can't do that here."

"Or ever," I spat, surprised at the emotion it sparked in me. "What if they fuck up your brain?"

"It's already pretty fucked up," he said dryly. "You can't tell anyone though, alright? Only Cara, your *friend* Patrick, and Fuller know about this."

"I won't tell," I promised. "And his name is Padraic!"

Hayden shrugged. "We don't want anyone knowing because it will be disappointing if it doesn't work," he explained.

"I understand."

He leaned in close. Gently, he touched a scar on my forehead. "How did you get this?" he asked quietly, his face only inches from mine.

"Car accident. Well, kind of. I stole a truck from a crazy and there was a zombie in the backseat."

"Now that's an interesting story."

"Sadly, it's true."

He smiled and pushed a loose strand of hair out of my eyes. A knock at our door made him jerk away. It was Fuller. With a grave look on his face, he pulled Hayden out of the room. I did my best to eavesdrop. From the bits and pieces I was able to gather, the group of A1s that were on the mission hadn't come back that morning as scheduled.

One more day and they'd be here, Hayden was sure. But I could tell by the worry in his voice that Hayden didn't believe a word of what he was saying.

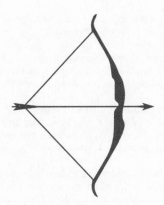

CHAPTER 24

The missing A1s did come back that evening, as Hayden predicted. They were quarantined and given one day to rest. Then another group would be sent out. And that group consisted of Hayden, Ivan, Brock…and me.

I was excited for my first mission. It was a supplies run, as Ivan called it. We had a list of needed items. If a town was overrun with infected, we were to leave. If we spotted signs of human life, we were ordered to assault and rescue. This was true on any mission.

We headed to Louisiana. Ivan and Brock led the way and I rode with Hayden in his truck. We didn't stop until we crossed the border. The first big town we drove through was overrun. And so was the next, and the one after that. Daylight was running out.

"We're not going to find one that's clean," Hayden spoke over the walkie. Ivan agreed. We sped along a country road, bumping our way into a smaller town with considerably less zombies. We circled around, getting to know the area. Following the movement, the zombies chased after us.

"Teams or singles?" Hayden asked over the walkie.

"Teams," Ivan's voice said after a moment's consideration. His truck lurched forward and hit a zombie. "And I believe we are in a two point lead."

"It's not dead. And, if it was, that was an S3. One point," Hayden argued.

"You keep score?" I asked.

"Yeah. S1s, the most dangerous, get three points. Two points for an S2 and one for an S3."

"Gotcha. We will win." I smiled. I was a competitive person and this was the perfect contest for me.

Ivan swerved and hit another zombie.

"Kicking your ass is easy!" he teased over the walkie. "I haven't even broken a sweat!"

"There's one," I pointed out, thinking Hayden would run it over. He gripped the steering wheel and didn't say anything. "What?"

"The truck. I-I don't want to hit anything."

"You are such a typical man." I rolled my eyes. We drove a few miles away from the town in search of a place to set up camp for the night. A hayloft had proved a good hideout before. A new barn with a sturdy loft would be even better. We hauled our heavy gear up the ladder. This loft was three times the size of the last one. We pulled apart several fresh bales of hay, making an almost comfortable bed. We ate, checked over our weapons, and settled down for the night.

Hayden and I slept first. Though we had gone south, it was still freaking cold. I moved closer to Hayden in my sleeping bag solely for warmth. I felt vulnerable away from the protection of the shelter. Though this time, I was with three people who could take care of themselves and actually cover me. I wasn't tired but I closed my eyes and forced myself to sleep.

"Mmhh," I mumbled when Hayden gripped my side. "You're hurting me."

His fingers dug into me. "What are you doing?" I cried.

He didn't answer. My eyes flew open in fear. Before I could turn, the crazy grabbed me.

Stupid, fucking sleeping bag. I flailed around trying to get out of the way. I screamed for Hayden. He sprung up and saw what was happening. Brock and Ivan raced over just as Hayden kicked the crazy off me. I scrambled up, snatching a knife, and sank it into the crazy's eye, blood pooled down its face and away from my hand.

"What the hell?" Hayden said, clenching his fists in anger. "Who was keeping watch?"

"We were," Ivan said flatly, not able to take his eye off the crazy. "We were just over here." He looked at Brock. "Two minutes ago. We've been going back and forth from that side to the windows."

"It either had impeccable timing or it waited," Brock said. "S1s can't think. They're not supposed to be able to think."

"They can, and they can talk," I said, remembering the guy in the fancy neighborhood back in Indy.

"No they can't." Brock's voice faltered, turning his argument into a cry of hope.

"We came across one. He had been bitten and knew it. He was confused but still able to carry on a conversation."

"And by confused you mean?"

I told them about the crazy who tried to shoot me for looting his neighbor's house and about the S1 who had been able to drive.

"Crazy Cara will want to talk to you," Ivan told me.

"She's not that crazy," Hayden defended.

"How cute. Hayden's got a crush on the socially inept med student," Ivan jeered.

"Shut up," Hayden began.

"Uh, guys," I interrupted. "Who's gonna help me chuck the body out the window?" Hayden picked it up easily. The crazy was female and young. I didn't want to look at her face. I hated that they were alive.

Though no one was tired after that rush of adrenaline, Hayden and I took over watch and let Ivan and Brock sleep. Eliminating the chance of another crazy coming up, Hayden and I hoisted the heavy ladder into the loft. We stood guard looking out the small window. It was nearly worthless in the dark.

We heard the groans in the purple haze of twilight. Hastily, we gathered up our stuff, woke the others, and raced out of the barn. I shot the first of maybe a dozen, nailing it in the head. The four of us hammered the zombies, the boys calling out scores for each kill. If it didn't sound so twisted, I would have said I had fun.

"So," I said over Ivan and Hayden's bickering about points. "I think that a 'rekill' by arrow should be worth more points than by bullet."

"Fair enough," Ivan said. "But you're the only one with a bow."

"Lucky me," I said with a wink.

We drove back into town. The zombies that lurked yesterday must have been the ones we'd taken care of at the barn because there were only a few wandering between abandoned cars and ditches. The first items on our mission list were tools. Ivan and Brock went to a drugstore while Hayden and I hit the hardware store. Three zombies milled about. Not wanting to waste any bullets, I shot two with the bow. A gummy, or S3, limped toward us. I passed the bow to Hayden.

"Take your best shot," I said.

He missed a few times. When he finally hit it, the gummy was only ten feet away.

"It takes getting used to," I assured him.

We cleaned the shelves of anything useful and took only the heavy items that were on our list. We loaded bags and deposited them in the back of the truck. We went back in to finish.

Empowered. That's how I felt. Cocky was probably the better word. Hayden was fast, strong, and could hit a zombie from yards away. I was his equal with my bow. And I didn't have to worry about him lagging behind, not being able to load the gun, or make a stupid mistake that landed a bullet in his foot. We milled through that small crowd of zombies like we were in a video game, as if it was nothing at all.

We had let our guard down.

When enough zombies pressed against the windows and doors to block out the sunlight, I thought we could handle it. The sound of the glass shattering sent shivers up my spine.

We *couldn't* handle it.

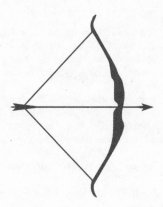

CHAPTER 25

I couldn't count the number of zombies that filtered into the store. True, between the both of us, we had enough ammo to take them all out. But we didn't have enough time. Hayden grabbed my hand and ran, pulling me into the stockroom.

"There has to be a back door," he said in the darkness. Dressed in a military issued vest, I patted my many pockets until I found the flashlight. I locked the door knowing it wouldn't hold. I moved the light around the room. There was no back door. We were stuck in this room.

"Fuck," Hayden swore. "I'm sorry, Orissa. I thought we could get out."

"We will," I breathed. My heart raced. Nothing about this was fun anymore. We were in a world filled with monsters. It didn't matter how well armed we were, they outnumbered us.

A zombie slapped at the door causing me to jump.

Calling Brock and Ivan wasn't an option. They'd be zombie bait, not back up. My eyes scanned the dark room. There had to be something we could use. We were in a large supply closet, not the stockroom like Hayden had hoped. Mops, rags, and cleaning products cluttered the shelves.

My heart raced, my palms sweated, and my cheeks burned.

"Burn. That's it!" My eyes focused on the cleaning products, chemicals that were sure to be flammable.

"What's it?" Hayden asked.

I snatched a bottle of bug spray from above me and cleaning rags from another shelf. "Do you have a lighter?"

"Yeah. Why?"

"We're going to burn them."

"That's great and all, Orissa, but won't we burn too?"

"We shouldn't."

"That's reassuring. We'll come up with something else."

"No, there is nothing else." I forced myself to take a deep breath. Using my knife, I ripped the rags into strips. I tied the strips, mop style, around the tip of an arrow. "Hold this," I told Hayden.

He held it at arm's length while I saturated it in bug spray. "Shoot a hole in the wall," I said.

Hayden handed me the arrow.

"Where?" he asked.

"Uh, high enough to keep them out. For a while at least. But low enough for me to shoot through."

The door frame threatened to give in from the pounding of zombies. Hayden opened fire on the wall, speckling holes in the drywall. He dragged a table over to stand on. Using the butt of his rifle, he punched the remaining particles of the wall away. I wrapped another piece of the rag around a second arrow and jumped up next to him.

"There," he said, pointing to a clearance display of barbecue accessories. "Can you hit it?"

"I think so." Zombies shoved each other, blocking my target.

"I have an idea," he said and looked at the bug spray can. "Get it."

I jumped off the table, shocking my ankles, and grabbed the can.

"Throw and I'll shoot," he told me.

I tossed it in the air above the hungry, manic crowd. Hayden hit it. The can exploded. Several zombies turned at the noise. Hayden lit the first arrow. I carefully drew it back, the heat of the flame hot on my face. I could still see the brightness etched into my vision after I let the arrow go. It sunk into the chest of the zombie that had been doused with the most bug spray. She was too soggy and rotten to burst into flames.

Her clothes caught fire, burning just enough to create a diversion. The zombies moved toward her, attracted to the heat and light.

Hayden lit the second arrow. I aimed. I didn't have time to see it nail the target. Hayden used his body to shield me from the explosion.

The blast knocked us off the table. He had to be in as much pain as I was, but he cradled my head, protecting me. Flames shot through the hole in the wall. I felt the hot fire above us. In a flash, it was gone. We got up to inspect the damage.

"Holy shit," Hayden swore. Charred zombies blundered about. Some writhed on the ground unable to move since their skin and muscles had been burned off. Smoke hung in the air and the entire place reeked of barbecued road kill.

It was now or never.

While the zombies still tripped over each other, Hayden and I made a break for it. Moving so gracefully he could almost be dancing, Hayden sliced his knife through the air, cutting through a gummy's skull. He spun and sunk the knife into the eye socket of an S2. He looked behind him and kicked a zombie in the stomach, knocking him over. Before the creature hit the ground, a bullet made a home in its rotten skull.

We jumped over bodies, dodged burning merchandise, and sprinted to the truck. As soon as our asses hit the seats I locked the doors. Panting, I turned to Hayden.

"That was fucking brilliant," he told me, grinning as he took in air. Suddenly he leaned in close, his eyes fixed on mine. His hand had just landed on my cheek when Ivan's voice came over the walkie. He had heard the explosion.

A flaming zombie raced at us in a blur of smoke and fire. I watched it, hypnotized by the crepitating flames.

A gunshot echoed and he went down, collapsing into a pile of burning flesh. Hayden started the truck. I tossed my bow in the back and didn't bother with my seatbelt.

Ivan and Brock had cleared out the drugstore and were halfway done emptying a small electronics store, since we desperately needed space heaters for our rooms, when a small group of S3s moved in.

No big deal, right? It wasn't, until Ivan slipped in gooey brain matter and twisted his ankle. He was pissed more than anything. He could still walk, though the pain he was trying to cover up was obvious through his limp.

We were all assembled in front of Hayden's truck, the S3s no longer a threat after Brock and Ivan had taken them out.

"Let's call it," Brock said, almost sounding relieved to have an excuse to go back to the shelter.

"No way," Ivan argued. "We only got half of our supplies."

"Clothes are on the list," Brock interjected. "I think they can survive awhile longer with what they have."

"We were given orders. I plan on following through with those orders," Ivan said sternly.

"Ivan," Hayden suggested, coming out of his lean against the truck. "Your ankle is sprained at least. You're in no condition to carry out a mission."

"I'm fine! I've been worse. Hell, you've been worse!"

When Hayden brought up a bad situation that had happened to the guys overseas, I stepped away respectfully. I hadn't known Hayden and Ivan had served together. I rested against the side of the truck, scanning the horizon. Smoke billowed from the hardware store. There must have been a tank or two of propane along with the dozen or so bottles of lighter fluid. I was a little pissed that I'd lost two arrows.

"Orissa," Hayden called, motioning me to come around. "How do you feel about finishing the mission with just me?"

"Fine," I said casually, approaching the group.

"See," Hayden assured Ivan. "We will be fine. I'll be smart. I won't take on what we can't handle."

"They just blew up a building," Brock said with a smile. "Don't worry about it, Ivan."

It took more convincing, but finally Ivan agreed to go back to the shelter with Brock to get his ankle checked out. We put everything we had gathered, so far, into their truck, and Hayden and I spent the rest of our daylight hours driving around looking for a place to spend the night.

I had never been this far south. Moss hung off trees, making the landscape seem foreign and mysterious. We passed numerous swamps. Great. Now along with zombies, I had to watch out for alligators.

We drove down a lonely road for a mile or two before something caught my attention: a historic plantation house that had been converted into a bed and breakfast. Raeya would love a beautiful place like this.

It was free of infected, and we chose a room that had a balcony—just in case we needed to make a quick escape. I spotted a trashcan that was filled with empty pop cans just outside the back door. Hayden looked curiously at it. He had a plan. We strung the cans on electrical cords, hanging them across the stairs. If anything tried to get up, we'd hear them before they made it to the door. Hayden walked around the house while I put together a crappy dinner.

Something buzzed and roared to life. It scared the shit out of me before I realized it was a generator. Hayden came back inside, looking victorious. Not wanting to draw attention to our hideout, we turned every light off except for two: one above the stairs and one in the room we were bunkering in.

"Oh my God, it feels so good," I said when I stuck my hand under the running hot water. "Keep watch while I shower?"

"I can do that," Hayden said. He watched me take my outer layers off, his eyes hungrily wanting more. He blinked and shook his head. He showered after me, both of us dressing in our spare clothing. I grabbed blankets off the bed across the hall and haphazardly threw them on the bed, nervously eyeing a porcelain doll. Her eyes were as blue as the dress she wore and perfect blonde curls surrounded her painted face. I suppressed a shiver.

"How do you want to do this?" I asked Hayden when he opened the bathroom door. He looked at me, lying in the bed, wide-eyed.

"Do what?"

"Sleep. Are we gonna go one at a time, keeping watch?"

"Uh, sure."

That wasn't the answer I was hoping for. "Do you think we need to? I mean, this house has been ignored for awhile and we would hear if anyone tried to get in."

"True," Hayden said and sat on the bed. "I guess we could both get some sleep."

"Yeah," I agreed. "Are you tired?"

"Not really."

"Me neither. It's like my body is but my mind isn't. I have a hard time sleeping in this dead world."

"Me too," he agreed.

"We can be insomniacs together then," I offered.

"Deal."

We had everything ready in case of an attack. Hayden turned off the light and got under the covers, his body heat instantly reaching me. I wanted so badly to be close to him, but we turned our backs on each other.

I lay in bed shivering, trying to sleep and not notice the cold. The generator was running, but it wasn't powerful. At about one in the morning, jerking movement woke me. It was Hayden. His breathing was heavy.

"Hayden," I whispered. "Wake up."

He didn't respond.

"Hayden! You're having a nightmare. Wake up."

Still he thrashed.

"Hayden!" I said again, sitting up and gently shaking him.

He woke with a start, grabbing my arms forcefully.

"Hayden!"

He stiffened, still breathing heavy. "Orissa?"

"Yeah."

"Oh. Sorry." He let his hands run down my arms. "Your arms are like ice!"

"Yeah, it's cold in here."

He didn't let me go.

"You ok?" I whispered.

"I-I, uh. Yeah." I could barely see the silhouette of his head shake. "I have this dream sometimes. About Ben."

"Ben?"

"My best friend. He joined the Marines with me. He died when an IED went off."

I didn't know what that was but my heart ached for him. I couldn't imagine losing Raeya.

"It's so real. Everything just replays. I saw it happen…" he trailed off.

"Hayden, I'm so sorry." I twisted and put my hand on his shoulder.

"Then, Ben came back as a zombie. Not really. Just in the dream." He put his hand over mine. "You're still cold."

"I am."

He took my hands in his to warm them. "And I have to kill him, again and again, 'cuz he won't die. It feels like I'm really doing it." Still holding my hand, he laid back down. "It's just a stupid dream, I know that."

I lay next to him, pulling the blankets up to my chin. "My mom used to be an alcoholic. I don't know how many times I found her passed out in her own vomit. I still have nightmares about going to wake her up and she's stiff and cold and dead."

Hayden took his hand off mine and shyly put it on my waist. His body was so warm. I snuggled close to him, almost spooning, not wanting to acknowledge that his presence brought me more than physical comfort.

"What did you do? When you had the dreams, I mean?" he asked.

"If I was home, I'd go check on her. If I wasn't, I'd get up. I'd tell myself it was just a dream and do something else. Or sing. I sang myself to sleep many times."

"You have a beautiful voice," he complimented.

"Thanks."

He held onto me a little tighter so that his lips brushed against the back of my neck, giving me butterflies, something I hadn't felt since the seventh grade when Bobby Warner had taken me on my first real date.

When I woke the next morning, Hayden's arms were still around me.

I moved in closer, turned and rested my head against his firm chest.

I closed my eyes, feeling safe, warm, and something else. Something that filled me in a way I hadn't been filled in a long time.

"Hayden?" I whispered.

"Yeah?"

"That doll is creeping me out."

"What doll?"

"You seriously didn't notice it? Look at the dresser."

"Ah, you're right." He let go of me, sat up, and cocked his gun. The shot echoed in my ears. "Better?" he asked with a smile. Bits of the doll's face fell to the floor.

"Yeah, but now the evil spirit that lives inside the doll will kill us."

He laughed. "Ok, sure it will. Wait, do you really believe that?"

"Of course not. I made that up years ago to scare Raeya. Her dad wasn't very involved so he never knew that she hated dolls like that. She, of course, didn't have the heart to tell him. So, year after year guess what she got for Christmas? One year, she got a clown porcelain doll. I mean seriously, a clown? Whoever made that should be shot. Anyway, she purposely dropped it so it broke and had to be thrown out. That's when I made up the evil spirit story. She didn't sleep in her room for a week after that."

"She believed you?"

I laughed. "Yup."

"So you've known her for a long time then."

"Yeah, but I told her that when she was fifteen."

"You're joking."

"I wish I was."

Hayden pulled me close and for a moment I forgot that most of the world had died.

We ate not so tasty protein bars as we threw everything into the truck, Hayden cracking jokes and making me laugh the entire time. I went over the remaining items on the list as we drove.

"Do you think Brock was right? I mean, do people really *need* more clothes?" I asked him.

"No. Not for survival. But to feel normal, yes."

"What is normal anymore?" I folded the list back up. "I mean, even after all this—when the zombies are all gone—nothing will be normal."

"No," Hayden agreed. "It won't be."

"We'll have to reset normal."

"Yeah," he said as if the idea had never occurred to him.

"And when we do, people will be fined for being rude or stupid."

"Fined for being rude? Isn't that a little extreme?"

"Obviously you've never worked retail," I told him.

"No, I haven't. Is that what you did before?"

"In high school."

He took his eyes off the empty road. "Tell me more about the pre-apocalypse Orissa."

"She's not that interesting."

"Really? 'Cuz I think a hot girl who can shoot almost as well as me is pretty interesting."

"*Almost* as well as you? Need I remind you of the arrow that blew up a building?" I teased.

He laughed. "Give me time and I'll be better."

"Oh sure." I rolled my eyes, laughing as well.

"How did you learn how to shoot like that?"

"I told you, my grandpa."

"When are you going to stop lying to me?"

"I'm not lying," I insisted.

"Ok, not lying, but not telling the whole truth?"

I bit my lip. Talking about my grandpa was painful. I felt guilty that I hadn't seen him in so long, and it was sickening to think of what might have happened to him. I was reluctant to talk about him for other reasons too. What he put me through was less than orthodox, but everything he'd done to me had been done with the best intentions, wanting me to be strong and capable. I wasn't mad at him for it.

"My grandpa came back from Vietnam with more than just a Purple Heart," I began, choosing my words carefully. "He had severe PTSD. With medication and therapy, he got it under control by the time I was born, so I didn't know about it right away. He was always into the whole outdoors thing. We went hunting and fishing and camping all the time, just like normal.

"And it was normal, for me. I didn't see the slips. I didn't think it was odd he insisted I know how to handle a rifle by the age of ten. When my grandma got sick, the stress pulled it out even more. When I was thirteen, he dropped me off in the back woods of God-knows-where Kentucky with a water bottle, matches, and a bow and arrows. It took me three days to get home." I looked at Hayden, gauging his reaction.

The truck slowed, and he looked at me.

I folded my hands in my lap, remembering those three days. I was terrified. I cried for the first six hours, wasting all my daylight. I was convinced it was a joke and that he'd come back for me. I didn't move an inch, wanting him to be able to find me. Then night fell and I knew he was serious. I curled up under a tree, waking with spiders in my hair and enough mosquito bites on my arms and legs to play connect the dots. I was so hungry and thirsty. Not thinking, I drank all the water.

Kentucky summers are hot. In a matter of hours I had sweated all the water out in an attempt to run to the road. I didn't know I was running deeper into the woods. I was exhausted and nearly dehydrated when I found a creek. Again not thinking, I drank from it. It would take until the day after I returned home for the E. coli to make me sick.

I wasn't numb to hunting yet. I cried when I shot a squirrel and almost vomited when I skinned and gutted it. Luckily, I had mastered making fires so I was able to cook the meat. I savored it, eating bits at a time. I was unsure of which plants were edible and which were poisonous, so I ate only dandelion greens.

Assuming the creek was the same one that ran through our pasture, I followed it. It forked some miles later and I chose the wrong branch to follow. It took the rest of the day to double back. I was dirty, tired, scared, and utterly pissed when I made it home.

But my grandpa was so proud of me. He went on and on about it. He took me out for ice cream. We went shopping—I got my very own compound bow—and then saw a movie. I sighed at the memory.

"Why did he do that?" Hayden asked in a level voice.

"He thought we might have to hide in the woods from…I don't even know…the government I suppose. The next time we went even farther. It took me six and a half days to get home."

"And your grandma never noticed you were gone for a week?"

"She was in the hospital during that week. She had lung cancer and was in the hospital a lot."

"Oh, sorry."

"It's ok. The sicker she got, the more unhinged my grandpa got. He started buying guns that weren't traditionally used for hunting. And well…you can figure out the rest."

Hayden didn't say anything for a minute. And those sixty seconds were excruciating. I wondered what kind of thoughts were going through his head. He probably pitied me, feeling bad that I had been raised by such a backwoods, crazy, and hillbilly grandpa.

"Did you always live with your grandparents?" he finally asked.

"No. I lived in Ohio with my mom and dad. I always spent the summers with my grandparents. My mom didn't handle the divorce well—or at all—and that's when she started drinking. My grandparents wouldn't let me live with an alcoholic so I kind of unofficially moved in then. But she met my stepdad and sobered up. My stepdad, Ted, was into going on missions and helping other countries end hunger. Apparently he forgot about the homeless here. I refused to go with them most of the time. So I lived with my grandparents while they were away."

"You are interesting," he said with a smile.

"What about you? When did your dad leave you?"

"When I was thirteen," he said without hesitation. "It was my birthday. He woke me up extra early and said he had a present for me. I was really excited because I knew we didn't have much money. I had wanted a dirt bike for years. I couldn't believe he really got me one. I rode it for hours…when I finally stopped, he was gone. Just like that. When I realized he was never coming back, I sold the bike and got a job. It was my responsibility to take care of the family then."

"That really sucks. I'm sorry."

"We both had fucked up childhoods."

"That's for sure."

"So," he said, changing the subject. "That beach can't get here fast enough."

"Tell me about it." I took a deep breath, thinking of the warm sun and sand between my toes. "I want to spread a towel in the sand and relax, listening to the ocean so bad."

He turned to me, raising an eyebrow and smirking. "You better find a bikini unless you plan to lay out in the sun naked."

I bit my lip, tipping my head to him. "You'd like that, wouldn't you?" I teased.

He wrinkled his nose. "Nah. Not one bit. Nope. Not at all." He laughed and I noticed the smallest amount of red blushing his cheeks. He drummed his fingers on the steering wheel and flipped through songs on the iPod.

We took the back roads into Shreveport. Almost everything had been burned down. It was gut-wrenching to see the occasional charred body. "Who set the fires?" I asked, knowing it was a rhetorical question. "The people who lived here? Why?"

"Maybe it was so overrun they had no choice," Hayden said.

"I suppose we could check the intact cars for gas."

"Fine with me." We stopped in the parking lot of a windowless, gothic themed bar and emptied the tank of a red corvette. The windshield had been crushed and cracked. Hayden was muttering something about it being a shame since it was such a nice car. After our gas cans were filled, we went into the bar, stepping through the broken door. Stupidly, I let out a slight gasp. Hayden whirled around, gun at the ready.

"Where?" he asked.

"No zombie," I said quickly. "Come on, do I make noises of surprise at zombies? You should know me better than that," I said, pretending to be offended. "I just had a realization. The first crazy, or S1, that I ever saw was in a bar. I had no idea at the time."

"Oh, ok."

"And hah. I said I'd get you back."

"Jerk," Hayden said, unable to keep from smiling. Bodies were piled up in the middle of the dance floor. It was odd and wrong, well no more wrong than a pile of bodies can be. Someone had messed with them. The body of a waitress festered on the top of the pile. Crumbled dollar bills spilled from her apron. It was weird how money had no value anymore.

I hopped over the bar, looking for anything useful. "Yes," I said when I saw the bottle. "This shit is top shelf!" I cradled the unopened bottle of tequila. Hayden joined me, picking up a cardboard box. He shook out whatever crap was inside it and placed a bottle of Captain in it, smiling up at me.

"No one ever said we can't take things for ourselves," he told me.

A bottle of Jack clanked in next. We carefully selected the most expensive bottles. It was tempting to sit in the truck, blast the radio, and take shots, but neither of us was stupid enough to follow through.

I impressed Hayden with my hotwiring skill, repeating my drive-a-piece-of-shit-car-through-the-store-doors act. I was also forced to tell him how I learned that, which in turn, forced me to explain about getting arrested for the first time. We drove into the department store. Hayden stood in the truck bed, keeping watch and shooting the occasional zombie employee in the head while I got clothing. I shoved things into plastic bags, not caring about color or style.

I drove so Hayden could move displays out of the way. I rolled my eyes, annoyed at how presumptuous it was to be worried about scratching your truck when the world had gone to shit.

"There are no shops to take it to anymore. And I don't have anything to fix it with," he argued.

I suggested he get a crappy truck to drive around for missions. Of course, that wouldn't work since he had gone through 'a lot of work' mounting the gun in the back.

I hit the woman's section while Hayden went to get stuff for the guys. I had always been a fan of lace myself. I filled a bag with sexy undergarments just for me. I justified that I wasn't being selfish because I was risking my life. Like Hayden said, no one said we couldn't take things for ourselves.

And having a few things for myself was a little like being with Hayden. As I filled my bag, I wasn't thinking about the end of the world.

We had just crossed the Texas border when we noticed the smoke. We got out of the truck, examining the small bonfire.

"Unless S1s retained the ability to logically build a campfire, there were people here," Hayden said, kicking a smoldering log. "And not that long ago."

"Should we look for them?"

"Yeah," he said enthusiastically.

"Ok. How?" I could track something through the woods. I looked around at the vast nothingness that threatened to swallow us whole. "They could be anywhere."

"And they probably are. Anywhere that's not here." He stepped back. "We can canvass the area in a…a ten mile radius. If we don't see any signs we can call it."

We didn't find anything. It was frustrating, knowing that somewhere out there were people. I told Hayden about our days of being gypsies, always on the run. If these people were like us, they were long gone.

And, I reminded him, a campfire can burn for hours. We hadn't bothered to put out our fires; there was no point. It might do the world a favor if a huge fire broke out and burned some infected bastards.

"Let's go. It's almost dark and we need a place to stay for the night," I suggested.

Hayden agreed.

We didn't find a safe shelter before the moon took place of the sun. So we drove toward the compound. Hayden called it 'home' but I just couldn't bring myself to call it that. Around two in the morning, Hayden could barely keep his eyes open. I offered to drive since I had fallen asleep earlier.

Hayden stopped the truck, put it in park, and hesitated with his hand on the door handle.

"Maybe you shouldn't get out," I suggested. It was dark and we didn't know what was around us. "I can just climb over and you can go under."

"Sounds kinky," he sleepily joked.

"You wish."

"Maybe I do," he chuckled. I felt that weird, warm feeling in my heart again. I shook my head and forced it away. Without much grace, we switched places. Following the map, I drove us back to the compound.

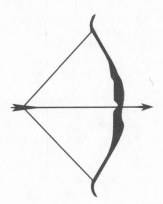

CHAPTER 26

"This is the soldier and Marine quarantine?" I asked, looking around the room.

"Yeah," Hayden said, unlacing his combat boots.

"It's freaking nice!"

"It is. Don't, uh, tell anyone, ok?"

"Why? 'Cuz you know it's majorly unfair?"

"After going out there and risking our lives, I'd say it's plenty fair," he chuckled.

"Can't argue with that." I took my shoes off as well. "It's so warm in here." We were in the basement of the estate, in the room across from the weight room. It was large, well lit, and homey. A huge TV was centered against a wall, surrounded by comfy couches and armchairs. There was a pool table behind all that, next to the kitchenette. Two beds were pushed against the opposite wall, and there was a full bathroom.

"Do you want to change? I can go get clothes," Hayden offered.

"That would be wonderful. You can leave?"

"I can run upstairs and come back."

"Then, yes. I want my pajamas," I informed him.

"Me too. I'll be right back. You can take the first shower then."

And I did. The water stayed warm longer than ten minutes. The Bs and Cs might be stuck in dungeon-like rooms but at least they got warm water. And a heater. I stretched out on the couch, enjoying the warmth. I was so freaking sick of being cold.

Hayden joined me, his skin red from taking a hot shower. He put a pillow against me and rested his head on it, closing his eyes and sighing.

"What's wrong?" I asked.

"Nothing," he lied.

"It's those people, isn't it?"

"What people?"

"The ones who built the fire in Texas. You're thinking about them."

"Yeah," he admitted and opened his eyes. "I feel guilty for not finding them."

"Why? It's not your fault they wandered away."

"We should have looked longer."

"We needed to get back," I reminded him.

"One more day wouldn't have hurt anything."

"Hayden, you can't feel bad about not rescuing everyone in the world. There are how many people here because of you?"

"You're right," he said, not sounding convinced. We watched a movie, ate a bland meal of rice and beans, and retired to the couch. Hayden pointed to a blinking light on the ceiling and told me it was a camera. Someone would occasionally glance at it and make sure we weren't going crazy.

We played cards, watched another movie, talked about our messed up childhoods some more, and eventually fell asleep. When Fuller came in to talk to us the next day, I was surprised at how fast the twenty-four hours had gone.

⟶

While Hayden filled Fuller in on the details of our mission, I went to find Raeya. She was in her room, refolding the new clothes I'd brought her. Upon seeing my face, she dropped a sweater and ran over, her arms flying around me.

"Ohmigod, Rissy!" She squeezed me tight. "I was so worried! When I saw those other two soldiers you left with come back without you I thought something terrible happened."

I hugged her back. "You should know it takes more than zombies to stop me."

"How was it? The mission I mean." We sat on her bed while I recanted the story, leaving out the part about finding traces of human existence in the Lone Star State.

"Oh!" she exclaimed as soon as I shut up. "I got my ranking!"

"Ranking?"

She shook her head. "From the tests."

"Oh, oh yeah. What did you get?"

"I," she said proudly, "am an overseer!"

"Really? That's great! Congrats, Ray!"

"Thanks. I suggested they redo the test. It just plain sucks."

"You would suggest that," I said with a slight giggle.

"Anyway, I'm helping reorganize a lot of stuff. I'm making lists. Oh, and Jason is an A3."

"Really?"

"Yeah. Sonja's not happy about it. Though, I don't think she has to worry. A3s don't go anywhere, do they?"

"I don't think so. From what I got in training, they have the chance to move up to an A2 and eventually an A1."

Someone knocked on the door. Raeya got up to open it. A familiar pair of blue eyes widened in delight.

"You're back," Padraic said with a smile. He strode in and hugged me. "How was your first mission?"

"Not too bad. We got everything we needed." I hugged him back, happy to see him again.

"What's it like out there?"

"It hasn't changed in the few weeks we've been here," I said with an equivocal half smile. "I blew up a building."

"Seriously?"

"Yeah. It was awesome."

"Nice, I guess. Are you going out on any other missions?" he asked apprehensively.

"I'm sure I will. That's the point of being an A1, remember? I'd like to go to Florida. I'm sick of the cold."

"Oh, if you go I'm coming," Raeya told me. "Can we go to Mexico?"

"That's where Hayden's going as soon as this is over," I said with a laugh. "We have this plan to find a yacht and live safe and sound in the ocean. Zombies can't swim, ya know."

"Ohmygod," Raeya exclaimed. "What the hell is wrong with us? Why haven't we all packed up and gone to Hawaii? Why are we *here* when we could be there?"

"It's not that easy, Ray," Padraic said, not understanding Raeya's sense of sarcasm. And since when did she let him call her by her nickname? He sat next to me, wanting to be all chatty and social.

"How's Ivan?" I asked suddenly.

"His ankle is sprained. He'll be fine in a week or two. It's not a bad sprain at all," Padraic responded.

"Oh, good." I stood up. "I'm gonna find Argos. I miss that dog."

"I'll come with ya," Padraic offered. I had gotten used to his company and didn't mind him tagging along—as long as he didn't try to kiss me or hold my hand or any of that stupid middle school romance crap.

There was about an acre fenced in outside for the dogs to roam in. The bigger dogs seemed to like the space and weren't bothered by the cold, so they stayed out as long as they liked. The dogs all belonged to people at the compound and lived with them just as they did before zombies roamed the earth.

"Why do you think people brought their dogs?" I wondered out loud, looking at a small toy poodle.

"You know people love their pets," Padraic supplied. "And, I was told, dogs are able to sense the infected people. Even that little thing over there," he said, pointing to a Chihuahua. "Its owners told me that he basically saved their lives."

"That thing? He's a sad excuse for a dog. He's wearing a sweater."

"Maybe, but he alerted them to the zombies lurking about their house at night. Gave them enough time to get away."

"I guess." I picked up a tennis ball and threw it.

"Argos missed you."

"He did?" I asked, my heart almost hurting for the poor dog.

"Yeah. He looked around whining, thinking you'd be coming to see him."

"You come out here and play with him?"

"Every day. Well, not out here, but when they're inside."

"Oh." I had no idea. "Uh, thanks."

"You don't have to thank me. I like that dog. He's saved us many times."

"He has."

We played with the Doberman for awhile longer before going back inside. I spent the rest of the day with my old gang. Sonja was happy she was assigned to caring for young children because that meant she was with Lisa. Raeya and I snickered behind Lauren's back at her job as dishwasher.

Lauren had found herself a new group to be with, which was more than fine with us. Sonja, Jason, Raeya, Padraic, Lisa, and I sat together at dinner. When I saw Hayden come in, my face lit up and I waved him over. He said something to the Marines he was with, grabbed a tray, and joined us. Sonja blushed when she caught his eye.

Jason drilled us about our mission. He was convinced he'd go up in the ranks from A3 to A1 quickly. Hayden bragged about how many zombies we killed, joked about being a better marksman than me, and told everyone how awesome blowing up the building was—and that we narrowly avoided getting blown up as well. I wasn't in the social mood anymore so after dinner I went up to bed.

⟶

The next morning, Hayden brought up the personal things we'd looted. He also managed to unearth the purse I'd arrived at the compound with.

"You can shove my purse in the closet too." I yawned and stretched. "Or toss it. There's nothing useful in it."

"You sure?"

"Yeah."

"Ok." Hayden opened the flap and looked inside. Grinning, he held up a stuffed animal. "Care to explain this?" he asked. "Please tell me you didn't sleep with this thing."

"Oh, God." The blood drained from my head fast. I sunk onto my bed. The vision of the pink cat was like a sucker punch to the face. Zoe. I hadn't thought about her since that day. I buried my memory of her when I buried her body. It was too painful, too sad. It wasn't fair. The image of her frail body lying at the bottom of the stairs flashed through my brain, the memory searing a gaping hole in my heart. An odd sound escaped my mouth as I tried not to cry. Tears blurred my eyes. I didn't remember seeing Hayden rush over, but suddenly he was there, right in front of me.

"I'm so sorry, Orissa. I didn't mean…it's ok." He put his hand on my shoulder. My head shook as I tried to force back the tears.

"It's not mine," I tried to explain. A tear snuck out, rolling down my cheek. Hayden hugged me. His muscular embrace was warm and comforting. One sob escaped; I inhaled quickly to cut it off.

"It's ok," he whispered, stoking my hair.

"Zoe," I told him. "It's Zoe's. S-she's dead." And then I cried. I forcefully wiped the tears away. "I'm sorry for crying," I told him.

He wrapped one arm around my body and used the other to pick up my legs, putting me on his lap. "I'm sorry about your friend," he whispered, hugging me. Being enveloped in Hayden's arms wasn't anything new. We had cuddled before under the cover of darkness. I felt so vulnerable and exposed right now, with my heart on the table.

I thought of Zoe's last few days: her smile, her eagerness to find joy in this horrible world, her love for that stupid cat. And then I felt a wave of guilt for letting Finickus run away. I should have held onto him tighter, made sure he was taken care of. I remembered the zombies crashing her funeral. It sickened me to think that they might have used their fingernails to dig up the freshly disturbed earth to eat away at her lifeless body. I held onto Hayden, pressing my face against his chest.

"It's okay," he soothed. When I looked up, his face was only an inch from mine. Our eyes locked and that feeling came back.

"Zombies didn't kill her," I said, casting my eyes down. "She was sick long before the virus." I took several deep breaths to get my emotions under control. "Sorry I cried," I repeated, feeling ashamed of myself.

"Orissa, stop."

"Stop?"

"Yes, stop." His tone was stern and his face was set. "Stop acting like you're doing something bad by showing that you have feelings. The world has gone to hell. It's more than a little upsetting."

"Crying doesn't solve anything," I told him.

"No, but holding it in isn't going to help either."

"Okay, thank you, Dr. Phil."

"Seriously, Orissa. It took me a long time to come to this conclusion. After all I'd been through in Afghanistan, after Ben died…"

"Crying doesn't solve anything," I repeated, my voice a distant echo of my past. My mother spent two years after the divorce crying and drinking. I swore I'd never be like her. I'd never be weak. I'd never let anyone damage me.

"Get it out and get over it," he said a little gruffly. "Especially now."

I'd rather feel nothing than feel pain; I could go through the motions. I closed my eyes, gripping Hayden tighter. "She was innocent. And young. Before she died, I prayed that we could somehow switch places. It would have been better that way."

Hayden didn't say anything. He ran his fingers through my hair. I saw her face, her big green eyes, and her pink earrings. And then Logan. I trusted him, liked him even, thought of him as our best asset for survival. And I killed him. Seth. It wasn't fair that he had to die. It wasn't fair Raeya had to lose someone she loved. Aunt Jenny. My grandpa. My parents. Like vomit, the tears came involuntarily. I wiped my eyes.

"I do feel better," I confessed.

"Good." He brushed a loose strand of hair from my face, tucking it behind my ear. His hazel eyes met mine and I was suddenly aware of everything about him: the warmth of his skin, his heart beating, his chest rising and falling as he breathed, his muscles underneath me. Part of me wanted to jump up and run down the hall. And part of me never wanted to get up.

The A1s had a meeting after lunch. Another group was going out tomorrow to search for more survivors. When they came back, a second group (that included Hayden and me) would go out on what Fuller called a 'destroy mission.' He told us that the zombies weren't deteriorating into the third stage as quickly as at the beginning of the outbreak. His eyes met Hayden's several times in an unspoken conversation.

After the meeting I decided to go upstairs. Only As went upstairs. I had never been told that I wasn't allowed to bring anyone up with me. It seemed, from listening to the soldiers' and Marines' conversations, that some of them had brought girls up on a few occasions. Still, Raeya and I whispered as we trotted down the hall that night.

"I am so jealous of how normal your room is!" she exclaimed as she looked around. "You have windows and drywall. We have cement walls."

I laughed. "There are bars on the windows, if it makes you feel any better."

"And you have a closet!" She opened the door and looked inside. "This isn't fair! You have hangers!"

"I'd gladly give you my hangers. You know I hate hanging shit up. I'd rather throw it in a drawer."

"You do have drawers. You have a closet and a dresser."

"Oh, I have to show you something!"

Hayden kept a box of junk food and booze in the closet that I snuck into freely. I dragged it out now. "You can't tell Hayden I showed you though."

"Ohmygod! Now this…this is *so* not right!" She bent down, sifting through the candy. "And you're just now cluing me in? Some friend you are!"

I laughed. "It's Hayden's secret stash. He only told me about it…uh…like over a week ago." I grabbed a box of Oreos. "Take what you want and I'll put it back before he comes up."

"Speaking of Hayden," she said, opening a bag of cheese flavored chips. "You guys have been spending a lot of time together."

"Yeah, we're partners."

"You know what I mean," she raised her eyebrows.

"No I don't."

"Come on, Orissa, you so do."

"No."

"Well, I've seen the way he looks at you. I think he likes you."

"Nah. He's just…he…I'm the only attractive female he spends time with. Hence the looks."

"There are plenty of other good looking women here," Raeya pointed out. "Why do you act like it would be a bad thing?"

"What would be the point, Ray?"

"Don't you want to be happy?"

"Oh yeah, be happy in a world filled with the living dead."

"What about the living dead?" a male voice spoke from behind us. Shit. It was Hayden. Had he overheard us?

"Nothing," I said quickly, feeling unnerved.

"You," Raeya said, standing. She picked up my pillow and threw it at him. "How dare you hide candy from me!"

"You told her?" Hayden asked, trying to look pissed.

I shrugged. "She forced it out of me."

"I'm sure she did," Hayden said, crossing the room to sit next to me. He took the Oreos from my hands, opened them and ate one. I had a disturbing urge to lean against him. I jumped up, striding to the closet.

"Shots, anyone?" I said, holding up the tequila.

"Oh my God, yes!" Raeya squealed. "This is so overdue."

"You're telling me," I agreed.

"Do you have shot glasses?" she asked seriously.

"Yes, Ray, 'cuz I always carry them with me." I said sarcastically.

She wrinkled her nose. "Shut up."

"I'm sure we can find something," Hayden said. "Go look in the kitchen."

"Can't you go?" I asked him, smiling innocently.

"I don't feel like it."

"Fine. Lazy-ass," I teased.

"I am. Now get in the kitchen, woman!" he joked.

I grabbed the Oreos from him, snatched the pillow, and threw it at him again. Laughing, Raeya and I took off down the hall. We ran into Padraic on the way to the kitchen.

"Orissa!" he said happily. "I'm glad I ran into you. I'm blood typing all of the As. Do you know your blood type?"

"A positive. Or negative. Or maybe O. Shit. I don't remember. Wasn't it on my chart at the hospital?"

"Yes, but I didn't look over your chart. Can you come to the hospital ward in an hour or so? I can take a sample and find out."

"Yeah. I'll see you in awhile then."

"Alright." He smiled warmly and said goodbye. We went into the dark kitchen, flicking on the lights. While Raeya looked for three small cups, I opened the freezer and dug out frozen limes. I put them in a bowl, filled it with water and stuck the thing in the microwave while I looked around for a salt shaker.

After we collected everything, we ran back to my room. Hayden had changed out of his military issued clothing and into athletic pants and a T-shirt. Country music quietly filled the air.

"You weren't kidding when you said it was cold in here," Raeya commented as the three of us settled on the floor.

"I can solve that," I told her, opening the bottle. I poured more than a shot's worth into each of the three glasses. We held them up. "To us," I said. We clinked the glasses and took the shots. The tequila burned on the way down and I coughed.

Soon we were playing the drinking game Never Have I Ever.

We sat in a circle on the floor with the bottle, limes, and salt shaker in the middle.

"Never have I ever had a one night stand," Raeya said.

Hayden and I drank. He poured more into our cups. "Never have I ever kissed someone of the same sex," he said.

I took a drink.

"Shit," I said, shaking my head as the tequila went down. "Crap. What haven't I done?" I smiled deviously at Raeya. "Never have I ever color coded my closet."

"You're a bitch," Raeya said and took a drink, recoiling at the taste.

I laughed. "Here," I said, grabbing the limes and salt. I used a pocket knife to cut the still frozen limes up. "Your turn again, Ray."

"Good. Never have I never been in jail."

I drank.

"Never have I ever," Hayden began, "had a fake ID." I drank again.

He laughed. "Maybe you should sit this one out. You're gonna be sick soon."

"I'm fine. I'm only sipping it." I could already feel the buzz set in. "I don't like this game anymore. All it does is make me sound like a slutty bad person."

"You are a slutty bad person," Raeya giggled.

"Never have I ever," I said loudly, "made notes about zombies."

Raeya scowled and took a drink.

"Never have I ever lied about my birthday to get free desserts at a restaurant," she said.

Hayden and I drank.

"Never have I ever had a fear of porcelain dolls," Hayden said almost shyly.

"Orissa!" Raeya snapped and took a drink.

Hayden and I laughed.

"Never have I ever enjoyed listening to country music," I directed to Hayden.

"This is getting personal," he said and took a drink.

I laughed like that was the funniest thing in the world, evidence I was getting drunk.

"It is," Raeya agreed. She leaned toward me. "Never have I ever had bruises I couldn't explain."

Hayden and I drank.

"Where's that lime?" he asked.

"Right here." I tossed it to him. "Ok," I started, filling up the glasses again. I stood and made my way to the iPod. I flipped through the songs until I found one I liked enough to dance to. I tried to pull Raeya up to dance with me. She laughed but refused. Hayden tossed his drink back and stood. I grabbed his hands and made him dance with me.

"You're a horrible dancer!" I told him, laughing. He put his arms around my waist and pulled me to him. I hooked mine around his neck.

"Sorry I'm not a pro like you," he laughed back, leaning in, his hazel eyes sparkling.

"Watch and learn," I said. I finished off what was left in my cup and went to the middle of our small room, showing off what I thought were my impressive dance moves. After a song passed, Hayden picked me up, spun me around, and fell back on the bed.

"Ok," he said, still holding onto me. "What do you miss most?"

"Miss most?"

"From before the zombies?"

"Hmm…everything?" I said loudly.

"I miss privacy," Raeya pointed out. "We have next to none here."

"Yeah, I miss that too," Hayden agreed. "And football and chocolate milk."

"Chocolate milk. What are you, five?" I teased. "I miss cookies, going to bars, having fun, and sex."

"Sex," Hayden repeated. "You're telling me."

"Oh yeah!" I unscrewed the bottle and took a swig. "You came straight here from overseas. You haven't gotten any in a *long* time, right?"

He took the bottle from me. "Maybe."

After Hayden returned from walking a stumbling Raeya to her room, we collapsed on the bed, then decided to watch a movie.

I had to pry his arms from me to get out of bed. Dancing along with the still playing music, I picked out a horror movie. We didn't finish before we were drinking again, on the bed and almost falling off.

"Salt, drink, lime!" I shouted. I licked my hand, ran it over my chest, and sprinkled salt on my cleavage.

"You want me to lick the salt off of you?" Hayden said, his words slurring.

"Yeah."

"Ok." Hayden more than licked me. I shrieked and laughed as he bit at me, dropping the lime as I pushed him off.

"Your turn." He salted his abs.

"And yours again!" I said as I sprinkled salt on my boobs. Right as Hayden licked me, the door opened. "Padraic!" I shouted, attempting—for some drunken reason—to say his name with an accent.

Padraic's blue eyes were wide with shock. "O-Orissa?"

"Come have a drink with us!" I offered.

Hayden's hands were still planted on my waist. His tongue wasn't on my skin but his head was still nestled in my breasts. "Hello Doctor," he said, also speaking with an accent.

"What are you doing?" Padraic asked Hayden.

Hayden blinked, sitting up. In a moment of general confusion, he looked at me. "Shots."

"Take one!" I held up the bottle and then put it to my lips. As soon as the alcohol touched my mouth, Padraic took the bottle.

"I think you've had enough," he said softly.

"No!" I stood to take it back. My foot caught on Hayden's. He attempted to catch me but ended up falling on the floor too. We, of course, laughed.

"You both are drunk," Padraic stated.

"Your face is drunk," I retorted, laughing even harder.

"This is pathetic," Padraic scoffed, watching Hayden and I try to get up.

"Then why did you come?" I questioned. I rolled onto my back and stared up at Padraic.

"You were supposed to get your blood typed. When you didn't show up I thought something bad happened. Obviously, I was right."

"Nothing bad…wait, I love this song!" I started singing along with Journey while Hayden got to his feet.

"Nothing bad happened. I won't let anything bad happen to Orissa," he slurred.

"Yeah, you can really take care of her," Padraic jeered. "You're doing a bang up job."

"I can take care of myself," I reminded both of them, taking a break from *Don't Stop Believing*.

"No you can't," Padraic said, waving a hand at me. "Obviously!"

"Oh come on, Paddy. I'm an adult. I can do what I want."

"You're not acting like an adult. Not at all. Look at you, drunk and writhing on the floor. You're an A1 for Christ's sake. Have some self respect!"

"I am an adult!" I nearly shouted. I realized my argument would be more credible if I wasn't lying on the floor. At that moment I doubted my ability to stand. "And just because I'm an adult doesn't mean I can't have fun!"

"Orissa, you have drill tomorrow morning. And, Hayden, you're seen as a leader. Maybe expectations for Orissa are a shot in the dark, but you should know better."

My world might have been spinning, but I could still be insulted. Hayden defended me, reminding Padraic we'd been through a lot and that we all deserved a break. Maybe Hayden wasn't as drunk as I thought he was. I faltered in my attempt to get up. Padraic offered a hand to help me.

"No thanks. I don't want to not live up to your expectations," I snapped, knowing that didn't make sense. Just to piss him off, I took another shot.

"I'm sorry," Padraic said. "I didn't mean it like that."

"How did you mean it?" I stumbled back to Hayden's side, sinking down on the bed next to him.

"I-I didn't mean it as anything. I was mad, ok. And I'm sorry."

"Prove it by taking a shot," I suggested.

Hayden took the bottle, poured a small amount into a glass and offered it to Padraic. "Loosen up," he said, shaking the glass.

"Fine," Padraic said and tossed it back.

His face made me laugh.

"How can you stand that?" He asked.

"Drink more. It'll taste better," Hayden suggested, taking another drink.

Hayden climbed into his bed.

"Bed time," Padraic suggested. My stomach flip flopped and I knew sleep was a good idea.

"Ok. Night," I told him, kneeling on Hayden's bed, trying to push him over so I could join him under the covers.

"Whoa, missy. Your own bed," Padraic said, taking my hand.

"I want to snuggle."

"Well, you, uh, can't." Padraic gently pulled me.

"But it's cold!" I argued. "And I like to cuddle."

"I always cuddle with Orissa," Hayden drunkenly confessed.

"Sure you do," Padraic said. "Come on, Orissa; get into your own bed."

"Do you want my blood?" I asked him suddenly.

"Not right now, alright?"

"Ok." The last thing I remember was Padraic tucking me in.

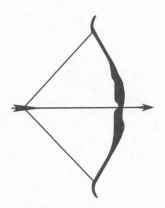

CHAPTER 27

The following evening, I watched *Toy Story* with Lisa and Argos. Then I walked Lisa to her room and hugged her good night. I was slowly making my way upstairs when someone crept up behind me.

"Can I have your blood?" she asked.

I whirled around and was face to face with a thirty-something year old woman. Her brown hair stuck out in a frizzed mess around her face, and her gray eyes were half hidden behind wire rimmed glasses. She wore an oversized sweatshirt with silk screen butterflies printed across the chest and a long yellow skirt. She held up a syringe.

My first thought was that a crazy had gotten in. Or that someone was infected and we didn't know it. My heart raced as adrenaline pumped through my body. I took on a defensive stance, wide-eyed and ready. Then I remembered the descriptions of Dr. Cara.

"Uh, why do you need my blood?"

"Blood typing," she said as if it was obvious. "I'm Dr. Cara and I'm blood typing."

"Right. Um, yeah. Sure." I followed her through the hall into the hospital ward. "Where's Padraic?" I asked.

"Not here," she told me. "Sit. I only need a little bit. More if it's good like Underwood's."

I rolled up my sleeve and extended my arm so Dr. Cara could tie the rubber band around me.

"You have nice veins," she commented as she slid the needle into my skin.

"Thanks, I think," I replied.

She pressed gauze over the pinprick sized hole and walked over to a counter. The exam room was dark and sterile. It reeked of bleach and cleaning products. I watched as Cara divvied my blood into different wells on a plastic dish. She then added some sort of chemicals, gently shook the dish and waited.

"AB positive," she told me. "Lucky you."

"Lucky?"

"You can get blood from anyone," she explained. She took her gloves off, snapping the rubber. "Dr. Sheehan said you heal fast."

"Yeah."

"I'll keep the rest of this blood," she said, looking at the vial on the counter. "I might need more."

"All right." I stood, unrolled my sleeve and exited the room.

"She's not that weird," I told Hayden when we I met him in the hall. "I'm disappointed, really. I was hoping for a full on mad scientist."

He laughed. "No, she's more socially awkward I guess."

"And doesn't know what a hairbrush is," I said, again making Hayden laugh. "Has she found anything else in your good blood?"

"Not that I know of."

"What blood type are you?"

"B negative. I don't think it really matters though, in terms of being immune," he said.

"Right." I again remembered Padraic telling me that he thought no one was fully immune since the virus could mutate. It made me worry that Hayden would do something careless, thinking he was immune and end up infected. The following day, the five of us loaded into our cars, Hayden and me in his truck and Rider, Wade and Brock in a silver SUV. We were on a seek mission—the destroy mission had been postponed—looking for survivors. Our orders were to go east, but no farther than Pennsylvania. I thought it was odd but Hayden told me that going farther was just too far. I also tried to convince him to ask Fuller to change our mission to exploring the Florida coast. Obviously, that didn't happen.

We were given ten days. None of us were too crazy about being away from the compound for that long, since it meant ten days of no showers, cold food, cold weather, and constant stress.

Orders were orders. None of the boys questioned it. Our plan was to drive eight hundred miles or so and end up somewhere in South Carolina. Depending on what we found, we'd use the rest of the time to canvass the state. It would be a twelve-hour drive and we planned to drive straight through. Since we didn't want to reach our destination in the dark, we left at nine that night.

Hayden drove first. Every now and then we'd see the glowing of eyes in the headlights. As if it was a sick game, I'd lean out the window and bury a bullet in the skull of a crazy. Zombies milled about as well, but their eyes had died so long ago that there was nothing left to catch a reflection. We sped along in the dark, passing bodies, ruined towns, and remnants of human life.

"Maybe it was better," I said quietly.

"What was better?"

"Maybe it was better Zoe went the way she did." I opened the window, catching glimpses of body parts scattered along the road, a bloody trail leading to an ever-hungry monster, munching on human flesh. "This world isn't...won't...ever be the same."

"Someday. It will end someday."

"So will we," I said hoarsely.

"They will go first."

"Are you sure?"

"No. But I want to believe it," he said.

We passed what was left of a church. The sign out front spoke of God's mercy on the holy. There was no mercy left. Everything felt weird. I closed my eyes, letting the cold air smack me in the face. Hayden pressed the button to close the window.

"Are you alright, Riss?"

"Yeah. It's just pointless. I mean there are how many of us left? We will never repopulate the country. We will never be able to get things back to normal. There's just not enough left. And it's weird to think about, but what if there really isn't anyone left. Would the zombies be around forever? No one would be here to kill them. They'd have free run.

"And if there is a God, why isn't he doing anything? How can he sit up there and watch us starve and be scared and have dead fingers rip open our bodies and eat our insides? And, even if we kill every single zombie, we will still lose people. We will dwindle down to nothing. People get sick; we don't have good medical care. And getting old? Yeah, can't stop that. Sure, we can all pop out a few, but that takes time. It takes time to get pregnant, it takes time to grow a baby, and even longer for that baby to have a baby. I just don't see it working. And why? Why live? What do we have to live for?"

Hayden opened his mouth to say something but stopped. His face was set on the road ahead. "I don't think anything I say will change your mind. We have to keep going. We have to believe things can get better because we are left. We can't lay down our weapons, spread our arms and welcome death. We found you, we've found others, and we will keep finding others. I won't go back until we do. I promise you, Orissa, there are more people out there. And I will find them for you. I want to make you happy, Orissa Penwell. And I will do whatever it takes to do so."

I curled my fingers around his free hand. "I almost believe you."

We reached what was left of Greenville, South Carolina, around ten the next morning. By this time, I was driving. There were zombies—lots of them.

"Hopefully that means there are no crazies," I mumbled. "Some silver lining, I know."

"Time to start the count," Hayden told me with a mischievous smile. I put the truck in park, retrieved a high powered rifle from the back, opened my window, and took down three S2s. Rider came over the walkie-talkie saying those didn't count. Hayden laughed, told him to stop being a baby and that the two of us would still beat the three of them.

We drove up and down the streets, picking them off one by one. Hayden said it would take forever to make this part of Greenville safe enough to explore, and that he had an idea. He radioed Rider and told him to follow us. We drove into the middle of downtown, stopped, and opened the windows. Hayden turned on his iPod and cranked up the volume.

The zombies snarled and groaned, limping and dragging themselves in the direction of the music. I fired rounds into four zombies, emptying the magazine.

"Hang on," I said, getting out of the truck, my arms full of guns and ammo. I jumped in the back, loaded the machine gun and fired. It was a rush, using a gun with that much power. Brock and Wade crouched in the back of their SUV, shooting zombies through the back window. When they drew too close for comfort, Hayden drove forward, gunning the gas too hard and making me misfire. I waved at Rider to get him to drive in front of us; I didn't want to accidentally shoot them.

Bullets showered the crowd, zombies dropping, others tripping over their secondly dead bodies. A tiny piece of dread disappeared from my heart every time blood and brains splattered from a zombie's rotten skull. I could hear Hayden cheering from inside the truck as he watched the blood bath.

"Hold on!" he yelled and made a sharp U-turn, stomped on the gas, and sped right past the zombies. He held his left hand out of the window, pulling the trigger on his pistol, hitting a fast moving S2. We rocketed down an alley, the obnoxiously loud country music drawing out zombies like fan girls to a boy band concert.

A gaggle of zombies pushed against a chain link fence, one that had been put up in hopes of keeping the infected out. The wire acted as a cheese grater, slicing the flesh from their soggy, festering arms as they reached through. Hayden kept driving and I kept shooting. If anyone was alive and bunkering in this desolate town, they'd know we were here. Once the numbers dwindled, Hayden followed Rider to a mall parking lot.

The mall seemed nice; when I saw a sign for Pottery Barn, I was tempted to go in and grab some décor for Raeya. I didn't think the guys would go for it.

"Hey," I said, jumping out of the truck. An idea hit me that I couldn't ignore. "Have you ever seen that movie where people hide in the mall from zombies? Maybe we should look inside."

"Why not?" Brock agreed. He slugged a backpack on, loaded his rifle, and nodded.

"While we're in there," Wade began, as he adjusted the scope on his gun, "we need more movies. I'm getting sick of what we have."

"Yeah," I said with enthusiasm. Looking at Hayden I said, "We watched the same comedy three times last week. And I'm getting insoles because these shoes are really uncomfortable."

"Why don't you get new shoes?" Hayden asked, raising an eyebrow.

"I suppose. I like the boots though; they're more or less bite-proof." I looked down at my poor leather boots. I had spent a whole month working extra shifts (back when I had a job) to earn the money to buy them. They were scuffed to hell and stained with God knows what.

The five of us walked into the mall without trepidation. Again, I was feeling cocky. Last time I felt cocky, Hayden and I came close to being blown up. The glass doors weren't locked, nor were they broken or streaked with bloody hand prints.

That had to be a good sign, right?

We walked through Macy's. It was startling to see that the emergency lights were still on. A lot of bigger companies and stores switched over to solar power during the Depression as a way to save money, so it probably wasn't that uncommon. As tempting as it was to check out the shoes, the store was too big and too full of displays to feel safe. Rifles raised and ammo at the ready, we silently slipped out of Macy's and closer to center court. We stood at the mouth of the store, looking down the long mall halls. To my right was a Coach store.

"Oh!" I exclaimed and strode over. Raeya's birthday was a few months away. It would be silly not to get her something. Rider's eyes had fixed on an Apple store.

"One hour of looting," Hayden said. "You three—stay together. Walkies on, one always as the look out. Get out if it's too much."

"Sweet," Wade said and sped off with Rider and Brock.

Hayden jogged to catch up with me. I took purses off the shelves, inspecting them like I was a regular customer.

"Really?" he asked, skeptically watching me.

"It's not for me. It's for Raeya. She loves shit like this." I ran my hands over a smooth, leather bag. "Ok, and I do too." I picked up a pair of shoes and went behind the counter. Emerging with two large bags I asked Hayden, "Is it wrong I'm having fun?"

"Hell no. I say we do whatever the fuck we want." The devilish glint in his eyes made me feel warm. I smiled wildly and turned back to the beckoning designer leather.

We went down the hall and into an Abercrombie and Fitch where a zombie employee slithered along the floor.

Yes, slithered. His legs had been gnawed off. Hayden took his knife from his belt, stabbed the pathetic thing in the head and wiped it clean on a hanging polo shirt. I yanked things I liked off the hangers while Hayden kept watch. After a bag was full of things for me, I started one for Hayden, avoiding anything overly preppy.

Preppy reminded me of Padraic, but I did grab polo shirts and sweaters for Padraic.

Leaving my multiple bags in the empty hall, Hayden and I went into a diamond store.

"I've always wanted to do this," I said. Using the butt of my rifle, I smashed the display case of diamond bracelets.

"Someone didn't hug you enough as a child," Hayden teased and picked up an expensive watch.

I took a display of diamond tennis bracelets from inside the case. Shaking off the broken glass, I dumped them into a bag. I hit the case of necklaces, grabbing jewels and precious stones.

"Hey Bonnie," Hayden called. I looked up and he tossed me something. "Marry me."

"Holy shit that's huge!" I exclaimed when I looked at the engagement ring. "Sorry, Clyde, I'm gonna pass on the proposal but I'm keeping the ring."

We laughed and shoved more jewelry into our pockets. I promised Hayden I'd be fast in Pottery Barn. Like a normal guy annoyed with a female shopping, he sighed and complained he was bored. He shut up once he saw a display of down blankets.

A gunshot echoed. I froze, the eco-friendly rug, rustic and striped, almost slipping from my fingers. Rider quickly came over the walkie, telling us that a lone S3 was in the dressing room of the store they were in. Arms loaded, we hauled our stuff to the hall with the rest.

Rider told us they already hit up GameStop, gathering up everything they possibly could. That was the only store Hayden was interested in so he followed me into Victoria's Secret, making faces and jokes about seeing me in black lace as I rifled through the merchandise.

"Anywhere else?" Hayden asked.

"I think we have enough. And I don't want our luck to run out."

"Good thinking." He relayed the message to Rider. I made a detour on our way through Macy's to get a new and more comfortable pair of boots. We loaded up the stuff, feeling like kids on Christmas morning.

We drove around the town once more and found nothing. Disheartened, we left Greenville, driving east. We spent the rest of the day slowly rolling up and down the roads, looking for signs of life. When there were no zombies, it was almost boring. Hayden was good company, and by the time we decided to find shelter for the night, I had learned a lot more about him.

We bunkered in a newly abandoned house. The neighborhood we were in showed signs of panic yet no signs of life. Staying in our teams, Hayden and I took the first shift. It was warmer here than back in Arkansas, but still cold. I huddled close to Hayden on the roof, my breath clouding the air as we talked. We were both frozen to the bone when our duty as watchmen ended. Worried about getting caught, we closed the bedroom door and snuck into bed together. Though, if anyone were to see us we could easily convince them we were just snuggling for the warmth.

→

Cold rain pelted the truck, its sound soothing. Not having seen any zombies, Hayden and I were playing an abridged game of Never Have I Ever, which was really nothing more than asking each other questions without the liquor. After an hour we ran out of questions. We were close to the Catawba River when I noticed the footprints.

Hayden radioed the guys as the truck bumped off the main road, following the muddy tracks. We wound our way through trees. A run down, crappy RV was parked in the middle of a small clearing. It had two flat tires and was sunken deep into the earth, making me think it had been there before the outbreak.

But the campfire dwindling under the awning was new.

A young, dirty boy flew through the RV door, brandishing a shotgun. His hold on it was shaky and he lowered it once he saw our faces. He called over his shoulder and a middle-aged man emerged from the woods. Hayden got out of the truck, holding his hands up in a 'we come in peace' sort of way. I stayed back, letting the boy and man introduce themselves and giving Hayden a chance to explain to them the plan of rescue.

But I didn't trust them one bit. The boy, Parker, was only twelve years old. Evan, his father, had been on the run from the infected since the outbreak. They were with four other people but became separated two days ago while attempting to hunt.

"The January trees did little to stop the cold rain from falling down on us. We huddled inside the RV," the man said.

"There was a house we were supposed to meet up at," Evan explained. "I was being so careful, marking the trees as we went. But somehow we got turned around and ended up here."

By this time the SUV had pulled up and Wade was standing with Hayden.

"Have you come across any zombies?" Wade asked.

"No, that's why we decided to try our hand at hunting. We thought it'd be easy along the river."

I stifled a laugh. When everyone looked quizzically at me, I diverted my eyes. Surreptitiously, I ran my eyes over Parker and his dad, looking for bite marks or fresh wounds. Maybe it was unorthodox, but I thought it would be a good idea to make them strip and prove to us that they had no open cuts or scrapes. After Karli and Rebecca back at the hospital, who could blame me?

"How did you find us?" Parker asked. He had a look of awe in his eyes as they swept over the faces of the Marines. Dressed in their military garb, they did look straight out of an action movie. I had on stretchy jeans over Underamour leggings, a sheer, black turtleneck under a navy cable sweater, and a jacket. I looked normal, to say the least.

"Orissa saw your footprints," Hayden told him.

Parker smiled. "I'm glad you found us."

"Me too," Hayden responded. "Now, this house. Do you have any idea how far you are from it?"

Evan folded his hands and sighed. "No. I didn't think we were that far, but—"

"Obviously you are," I retorted. "Was the house along the river?"

"Not right along. It's close by, though. It's a big house, with a lake in the backyard."

Thinking it would be shitty to tell him the lake was mostly likely a big pond, I disregarded his wrong word choice. "How close? Like less than a mile?"

"Oh, a lot less than a mile."

"North or south of here?"

"Uhh…"

"With or against the river's flow?"

He looked at his son. "We walked with."

"Ok, I should be able to find it," I said, getting out of the truck.

Hayden pulled me aside. "Do you really think you can find it?"

"Maybe," I said honestly.

"How?"

"I was planning on walking along the river, following their tracks. If they left from the house, there should be a trail."

"Can't we just drive up and down the roads?"

"I do my best work in unfamiliar woods. And I was just going to go on my own," I admitted.

"As your superior, no."

"My superior?" I raised an eyebrow.

"Yes."

I shook my head and rolled my eyes, all the while trying to keep the smile from my face.

———————▶

It was late afternoon by the time we finally found the house.

It was big and nice. It must have been someone's vacation home—clean and stocked with comfy furniture, cozy beds, and plenty of books. The house offered a homey feel that we all had missed. The four missing friends were nowhere to be found. We ate dinner, heating up Spaghetti-O's in the fireplace. Meant to offer breathtaking views of the forest surrounding us, the large windows leered instead, with their ability to easily be broken.

Parker and Evan gobbled down the food, not having anything to eat in the last twenty-four hours. They asked endless questions about the shelter, told us what we already knew about zombies and the world being a hopeless, shit-filled place. We lit a few candles and drew the blinds, not wanting the flickering light to summon any zombies.

Hayden and I took first watch again that night, circling the house, waiting and listening. Upon hearing nothing, we went in, moving from the front to the back, both uneasy about being surrounded by trees.

When it was our turn to rest, we settled on the couch near the fire. It warmed up the room considerably. Evan and Parker were asleep in front of the fireplace. Wade, Rider, and Brock were patrolling outside. Hayden and I were alone, for now.

I rested my head on his shoulder and he put his arm around me. He ran his fingers through my hair and I relaxed, stretching my legs out on the couch. I was nearly asleep when I heard Parker's voice.

"Can she really track things?"

"Yes, she can," Hayden whispered, thinking I was sleeping. "She's good at it too."

"Do you think she can find my friends?"

"If anyone can, it's Orissa."

"Good." With a shuffling of the blankets, Parker sat up. "Is she your girlfriend?"

Hayden hesitated. "Well, she's a girl and she's my friend."

"Oh, I get it. Do you want her to be?"

It felt like forever passed before Hayden answered. "Yeah."

Zombies breaking through a window would have been a welcome distraction. How awkward. It took effort to keep my body from tensing up.

"Does she know?" Parker pressed.

"I don't think so. I hope not."

"That seems silly. Why wouldn't you want her to know?"

"I...I don't think she likes me the same way. Look, aren't you a little young to be so interested in this stuff?"

"Young? Have you met today's generation?" he asked, making Hayden softly chuckle. "I think you should tell her."

"Maybe later."

"What if there isn't a later?" the boy inquired.

"Well, then that would really suck."

"There's this girl with us—Joni. She's fourteen but she's just...wow."

I could feel Hayden trying not to laugh at Parker. "Is she now?"

"Yeah. She has blonde curls and beautiful blue eyes. She's fourteen, but I think I have a chance."

"Probably. There's not too much competition anymore, is there?" Hayden asked.

I wanted to pinch him.

"Anyway, I'm going to tell her that I love her. Life's too short to hold back. You should consider it."

"You're a smart kid, Parker. Go back to sleep, now. You need your strength to, uh, impress Joni."

"Right. Night, Hayden."

———————————→

In the early light of dawn, the four lost people returned. Like Evan and Parker, they were dirty, tired, hungry, and defeated. Along with Joni, the group consisted of Jane, Joni's twenty-something sister, an older man named Austin, and Lydia, a middle-aged woman. We went through introductions, information about the compound, and then ate breakfast.

The six had traveled together in a van. They had minimal supplies and no food left. The four who had just joined us were anxious about leaving right away. Brock suggested they rest while we were in a safe place. No one disagreed.

While the others were sleeping, Hayden and I walked around the house. The sun was shining and the temperature had to be around fifty degrees. Birds chirped loudly, making this place seem almost beautiful. I expected to feel awkward around Hayden, knowing what he'd confessed to little Parker.

But I didn't. We talked and laughed like normal. I traded my rifle for my bow and arrows, thinking I'd shoot a squirrel or rabbit if I got the chance. A large quiver had been rigged up for me out of a backpack that was able to hold three times as many arrows as normal.

I passed the bow to Hayden. "Want to practice?"

"Sure." His fingers brushed mine as he took the bow.

I refused to let myself feel anything.

"What should I hit?"

"Hmm," I said, turning around. "How about there," I pointed, "at that big, whitish tree."

"Alright." Hayden pulled back the arrow, released, and missed. I was busy watching his stance and posture.

"You need to drop your shoulder. It should help with your accuracy." I took my jacket off, dropping it to the ground. "Watch," I said, taking the bow from him. "See how my shoulders are?" I hit the tree dead on.

"Show off," Hayden said.

I slung the bow over my shoulder and walked forward to retrieve the arrow. Hayden had to yank it out of the tree for me. "Orissa," he began, putting the arrow in the quiver.

Something washed over me. But it wasn't dread. It was anxiety.

"Hayden," I said with a slight smile.

"There's something I want to tell you."

I stepped closer to him, the smile growing.

"There's a zombie behind you!" He grabbed me, pulling me out of the way. A zombie with an arrow sticking out of its chest rushed at me. Hayden drew his gun and shot it in the head.

"That's what you wanted to tell me?" I asked, almost furious.

"No, but you should know there are more." He took a step back.

That's when I heard the horrible moans…shuffling feet cutting into the first beautiful morning we'd had in weeks…

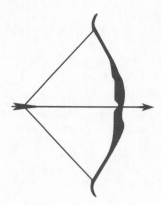

CHAPTER 28

In horror, Hayden and I watched a herd come into view from inside the forest. Hayden emptied his magazine. Rider raced across the backyard, having heard the shots.

"Holy shit!" he swore. "We have to get the civilians out of here."

"Yes, go!" Hayden yelled.

Rider went.

The zombies swarmed us. Hayden grabbed my hand and sprinted to the house. I scrambled to gather up our things. Hayden ordered me to leave it so we could book it to the cars before the zombies closed in.

We *were* too late. A crowd of zombies blocked the cars.

Everyone stood frozen on the covered porch. We could make a run for it into the woods but no one knew their way around. I wasn't going to die by their hands. And I wasn't going to let Hayden die either.

"Cover me," I told Hayden.

"What? No!"

"See that tree? I'm gonna climb it."

"Climb it, no!"

"You have a better idea?" I desperately pleaded.

"Yes! Gun them down!"

"There are too many."

I started for the tree. I had no time to argue.

Because he couldn't stop me, Hayden shouted for the other Marines to cover me.

A well fed zombie ran at me, arms stretched and mouth open.

I pulled the knife from my belt, throwing it into its skull. A second later I whirled around, my foot landing in the center of the chest of an S3. It crumpled backward, tipping and falling. Ooze and puss splattered out. Hayden and Rider fought back the zombies who tried to gain the porch and the civilians, while Wade and Brock covered me. I got to the tree, madly pulling myself up. It had been years since I'd climbed a tree and was reminded of how hard it was on the hands. I was four feet up, not nearly high enough to be safe from the zombies. I kicked one in the head; the effect was similar to kicking a rotten pumpkin.

I scrambled up another branch, finally daring to look at the porch. Everyone was still there; the boys were hitting zombies, decreasing the numbers slightly.

"Hey, you pieces of shit!" I screamed at the top of my lungs, praying that would be enough. I didn't feel like singing and almost bleeding to death again. I hooked my leg around a fat branch and leaned on the trunk, pulling my bow off my shoulder. I fired an arrow into the skull of a child zombie. "Up here!" I screamed. "Free food, come and get it!"

I gained a few more zombies' attention. Damn it, it wasn't working. I smacked the tree, watching the zombies close in on the porch. Hayden held his arm out defensively, in front of everyone, ready to go down fighting.

I wasn't going to let him. With more care this time, I used the point of an arrow to slice open my index finger. I milked the blood out, shouting. The first drops hit the ground. A female S2 dove at it, licking it off the ground. I smeared the blood all over an arrow and shot it below me. That got everyone's attention.

"Go!" I shouted to Hayden. "Get them out of here!" I used the rest of my arrows, pissed I wouldn't get them back. Engines roared to life. The van and the SUV peeled out of the gravel drive. Hayden's truck made a sharp turn. He revved the engine once and floored it, running into the pile of zombies that desperately reached for me. He reversed and ran over them again. Blood crusted zombie hands slapped the truck's tires.

My plan was to jump into the tree next to me. On the ground, it had seemed like a fool-proof idea. Up here, the ground seemed a long way down. I put the bow over my shoulder and across my chest, slowly moving away from the trunk. *Here goes nothing,* I thought and jumped. The branch snapped, and the flesh on my hands tore as I slid down. My face caught the fat, gnarly branch. Blood instantly gushed from my nose but I wasn't falling anymore.

Any hope of Hayden distracting the zombies died. The steady dripping of blood from my face brought them back to me. I was still twelve feet or so in the air. With one hand over my nose, I scrambled down another set of branches. The truck came to a stop under me. Then it rolled back, running over a zombie. And then forward, stopping.

I knew what Hayden was hoping for. I swung my legs over a branch and jumped. I landed hard on the roof of the truck. I pushed myself into the bed and hit the back window. Hayden floored it again and took off, leaving the zombies in a trail of dust. I removed the bow from around me and collapsed against the cold liner.

Hayden stopped before we were far enough away. Leaving the truck running and his door open, he flew out and jumped in the bed. One arm went around me, pulling me to his chest. The other gently tipped my head up.

"I'm ok," I assured him, spitting out blood.

"Yeah, you look ok," he joked. His smile was genuine and his voice was calm but his hands shook. "I'll get a towel or something."

I leaned against my shopping bags, not caring if I got blood on the new clothes. My heart was hammering and my nerves were alive with electricity. Hayden gave me a clean rag to hold to my face. I didn't know the proper procedure for taking care of a nose bleed. I'd only had two in my life—one from a dodge ball incident in middle school and the other when Mindy Croswell punched me in the tenth grade.

Hayden sat behind me, stationing me between his legs. I let my body fall back against his and I could feel how fast his heart was beating.

"Lean forward," he said. "You won't get blood in your mouth then."

"Ok," I said, my voice sounding funny. Grimacing, I pinched my nose to try to stop the bleeding.

"Is it broken?" he asked.

"I don't know. I don't think so."

"Good." His arms tightened around me and his lips brushed my neck.

I made a strangled noise of surprise and pointed.

The herd of zombies had caught up. Hayden extended his hand for me and helped me over the side. The walkie-talkie got caught and flew off my belt. I dove for it.

"Forget about it!" Hayden yelled.

My fingers closed around it just as he landed on me, the force separating me from Hayden. I didn't see him coming. I didn't even know where he came from. If I was a screamer, now would have been a good time to scream.

Half the zombie's face had been burned. Blackened bones were exposed, teeth, not hidden behind lips, bit at the air. The wind had been knocked out of me and my nose still bled. Covered in my own blood, my hands slipped off his rotten face as I tried to push him off.

This is it, I thought. The zombies were surrounding us. If Hayden had any sense, he'd leave.

The shot rang out and brains splattered my face. Hayden's hand reached for mine. My fingers laced with his just as a festering row of teeth clamped down on Hayden's skin. I punched the zombie in the side of the head, sprang up, and kicked it off Hayden before falling into his arms. Hayden managed to shoot another and we scrambled into the truck, both entering through the driver's side door.

Hayden floored it.

I felt nauseous from swallowing my own blood. Knowing there were bloody teeth marks on Hayden's arm was too much. He was immune before, but what if the virus had mutated or grown stronger?

"Stop," I said.

Without questioning me, Hayden slammed on the breaks.

"Let me see it." My voice came out hoarse and weak.

"It's ok," he reminded me. "I'm immune, remember?"

"Then why do you look so freaked out?" With shaky hands, I took his left arm, pushing his sleeve up. "Where's the first aid kit? Even if you don't get the virus, this can still get infected."

"It can wait. You're still bleeding."

"My nose is fine. You can't do anything for nosebleeds but wait till they stop anyway." I got the first aid kit from the back, cleaned and bandaged his wound.

"If you suspect *anything*, you have to shoot me."

"I will," I promised.

His arms went around me and mine went around him.

The distant roar of a car drove us apart. Rider stopped next to us, horror and worry taking over his face as he took in the sight of me. Catching a glimpse of my reflection in the side mirror, I could see why.

Blood had dripped down my face, all over the front of my shirt, mixing with zombie splatter. Hayden picked a chunk of something from my arm. The skin on my palms had suffered horrible tree-burn; I flinched when I wiped the blood on my jeans.

"Jesus Christ," Rider whispered and got out of the truck. "I want to ask if you guys are alright but I think I know the answer to that."

"It's worse than it looks," Hayden assured him.

Rider looked me up and down. "You're kinda amazing, you know."

"Thanks," I said. My stomach flip flopped from the taste of blood. Afraid I was going to puke, I walked to the other side of the truck. I listened to Hayden and Rider's plan of going straight back to the shelter since we had six people and I was injured.

Cold, I got back in and turned the heat on, my hands hurting when I moved them.

"We're gonna find a clearing," Hayden informed me when he took his seat. "Then I will take care of you."

"Thanks," I said.

"Really?"

"Uh, yeah. Why?"

He smiled. "I expected you to protest."

I shrugged. "Meh. I've done my share." And I was tired and sore and scared. And it would be nice to have someone take care of me.

Hayden put his hand on my leg. "Rider was right; you are amazing."

By the time we reached a clearing, my fresh cuts were nearly scabbed over. I closed my eyes and gritted my teeth, holding out my hands for Hayden to clean. He had to break open the dried blood to disinfect my cuts and scrapes.

"Did you touch that S2 with your hands?" he asked as he picked out pieces of bark.

"No, I fought him solely with my feet."

"Orissa, this is serious. Did you touch him?"

"Yes. I kept my hands closed though."

"Are you sure?"

"Yes. But I mean, I suppose it's possible…" I trailed off.

"Great. Now we will both be infected. Ten dollars says I kick your crazy ass first."

"Psh! No way. I'd out crazy you any day! And neither of us are infected. I most likely didn't get any zombie parts on my cuts and you—"

"Had teeth sink into my arm," he reminded me.

"You're fine." I did my best to wash the crusted blood off my face. Not caring who saw me, I took off my sweater and then the turtleneck, throwing them on the ground.

The bandages on my hands made it hard to ruffle through my bag. I should have gotten the new shirt out first. I yanked a brown sweatshirt over my head and plopped back in the truck. Wade suggested we find a place to hide for the night before we ran out of sunlight. Hayden instantly disagreed. He wanted to get back to the compound right away.

I knew why: he wanted to get himself in the quarantine.

He drove the first half and the conversation was sparse. Having pulled a muscle or two in my back while climbing (and falling from) the tree, I was sore and very uncomfortable in the seat of the truck. Hayden was tense, gripping the steering wheel tightly, sitting straight up.

Unlike last time, Hayden didn't waste time getting into the quarantine room. Fuller wasn't there to greet us, which was a relief to me since Hayden wanted to tell him that he had been bitten—again. I wanted to keep the information just between us. I didn't want Hayden taken away from me. I went up into our room to get clothes. Ivan hobbled into the hall at the sound of my footsteps.

"How did it go?" he asked before taking a good look at me. "Whoa, what happened to you?"

"Half jumped, half fell out of a tree," I said with a shrug. I was eager to get back to Hayden. Someone needed to make sure he didn't go crazy. "We brought back six people," I told him quickly.

"You'll have to explain the tree thing to me tomorrow," Ivan said with a smile.

"Sure will." I hightailed it into my room, grabbed comfortable clothes for myself and Hayden and jogged down to the quarantine room. I took the first shower. I toweled my wet hair and pulled it to the left and into a braid.

"Do I look crazy?" Hayden asked me after I entered our quarantined room.

"Kinda," I replied. And he did. His brown hair, which was in need of cutting, was messy. His eyes were wide with fear and lines of stress wrinkled his forehead. "You are fine," I repeated firmly.

"Ok, I'm fine."

"Hayden," I whispered, putting my hand on his shoulder. "Stop it. You're freaking yourself out and you're starting to freak me out!"

"Right, sorry. You said the virus can change and I-I'm—"

"It's ok."

"Yeah. It will be." He sprang up. "Hungry?"

"Sure."

After Hayden showered, we went into the kitchen area and warmed up the dinners that had been prepared for us. Brock joined us at the little table, making small talk about random, non-zombie related things. After everyone had showered, changed and ate, we decided to gather around the TV and watch a movie. Hayden and I sat next to each other on the couch. I pulled a blanket over the both of us, whether or not it looked suspicious to Wade, Rider, or Brock, I didn't know or care.

Halfway through *The Dark Knight* Hayden fell asleep, his body limply leaning in my direction. Not wanting to wake him, I carefully got up after the movie ended and resituated the blanket to keep him warm. The boys, trying to be chivalrous, said I could have one of the twin beds while they bickered over the other. It felt good to lie down and stretch out. My eyes had just closed when someone sat at the foot.

"Orissa?" Hayden whispered. "Are you asleep?"

"Not yet." I sat up. "You ok?"

"Yeah. I'm cold."

"Come here," I said lifting the blankets for him to crawl under. He did, and his skin was anything but cold. I pressed the back of my hand to his forehead. "I think you have a fever," I told him. I could feel his body tense up.

"I need to get out of here before I snap," he pleaded.

"No, Hayden, you're fine."

"Not if I have a fever!"

"That's not a symptom. You're sick. Just regular sick."

"How can you be sure?"

"I-I don't really know. But it's what I want."

"You want me to be sick?" he teased.

I could imagine his cheeky smile through the dark. He let out a deep breath and settled down, pulling the blankets closely around him.

"Of course not. But I'd rather you be regular sick than zombie sick. And," I said, remembering the times when my grandma would take care of me while I was sick, "you shouldn't bundle up if you have a fever."

"But I'm cold," he protested, sounding like a stubborn child. "And maybe your hands are just cold so that's why you think I'm hot."

"No," I said, checking his skin again. "You're feverish."

"I do kinda feel sick."

Once Hayden was back asleep, I moved to the couch. I didn't want to explain to the others why we were snuggled in bed together and I didn't want to draw attention to Hayden being sick.

People got sick all the time, I reminded myself. Just because we were on a mission didn't mean anything. Did it?

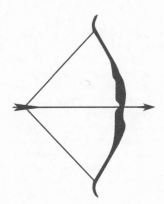

CHAPTER 29

When the digital clock finally showed it was eight in the morning, I woke Hayden to tell him he hadn't turned into a raging lunatic. He smiled weakly, told me his throat hurt, and went back to sleep. I played a game of cards with Brock, watched another movie, and paced around the room.

"You look like shit," Wade told Hayden when he finally got out of bed.

"I feel like it," Hayden agreed, plopping down in a kitchen chair. He put his head in his hands.

"You know," Rider chimed in, "I'm surprised we don't get sick more often. With all the stress and dirty shit we deal with. I guess it was only a matter of time before one of us came down with something."

I sighed. No one was going to accuse Hayden of being infected. Feeling rather domestic, I made Hayden breakfast. Ok, I didn't make him breakfast. I put cereal and milk in a bowl.

When we were finally released, Hayden was obviously sick. I accompanied him to the hospital ward. A young B3 was on duty; she smiled and blushed when she saw Hayden.

"Is Padraic around?" I asked.

"No, he's off tonight."

"Shit," I swore, looking sideways at Hayden.

"Do you think you can get him?" I asked the B3. "It's official A1 medical stuff. He wanted to document any injuries we had personally and," I held up my bandaged hands, "I have a lot of injuries. They're pretty deep too, won't stop bleeding."

"Oh, my, yes! I'll go get him." She scuttled away. Something told me she wasn't too keen about blood.

Hayden rested his head on mine. "My head really hurts. I can say that now," he admitted.

"How long has it been hurting for?"

"Since we got here. I didn't want to worry you."

We made our way to an exam room. I sat on the foam bed next to Hayden. He leaned against me with his eyes closed, resting his hand on my thigh. A few minutes later, Padraic came through the door. He was dressed in navy blue pajama pants and a black T-shirt.

"Orissa, are you alr—" he stopped mid-sentence, looking at Hayden with a bit of surprise.

"I'm fine," I said quickly. "Close the door."

Padraic obliged, though his confusion was apparent. I rolled up Hayden's sleeve.

"I got bitten," Hayden said weakly.

Padraic recoiled. "When?"

"We went through the twenty-four hours, Padraic," I snapped. "Don't be dramatic. He's just regular sick."

"Can you move aside, Orissa? I need to examine him."

I jumped off the table. "I tried to disinfect the bite, but I didn't get to it right away."

Padraic unwound the gauze. The bite marks were red, puffy, and definitely looked infected. "I can't imagine the mouth of a zombie is very clean," Padraic said seriously.

The sentence was so odd that it made me laugh. Padraic raised an eyebrow, shutting me up. He left the room and returned with a little case of medical stuff. He injected something into Hayden's arm, had him lie down, and set to cleaning his wound. Then he did a full exam and concluded that Hayden had some sort of flu-like virus, but was worried about how rapidly his fever had gone up.

Padraic thought it would be best to keep Hayden in the hospital ward until he was better. He would receive more care and wouldn't expose the rest of us. Hayden seemed too tired and too weak to care. I offered to stay with him and keep him company, but Padraic objected, saying I needed to let Hayden rest and I should rest myself, especially after a mission. I hadn't spent a single night at the compound without Hayden. Leaving him behind was harder than I ever would have suspected.

I was lonely by myself that night, which reminded me of what Raeya had said about privacy, which reminded me, of course, about my best friend. Though it was late, I slipped down the stairs and quietly knocked on her door. She was over the moon excited that I was back. We tiptoed to the cafeteria so we could talk.

She was ecstatic that we had found people. It gave her hope that more were out there, just waiting to be rescued.

I told her minimal details about the narrow zombie escape and nothing about the mall looting. I wanted to surprise her in the morning with a Coach purse. I walked her to her room, hugged her goodnight and went farther down the hall to find Argos. Happy to be with me again, he didn't leave my side all night.

I slept through breakfast the next morning. Hungry, I stuffed myself with junk food. Raeya was doing some sort of overseer project so I hung out with Sonja for awhile before visiting Hayden. Really, I was stalling, afraid that Hayden was sicker than Padraic had first thought. But I found him hooked up to an IV, which looked scarier than it was. He was feeling better already, he promised, though he still seemed weak and tired. Word had leaked that he was sick, and his hospital room was filled with homemade get well cards.

Training picked up right where it had left off. I was put in the group that trained the A3s, and not all the A3s took me seriously, since I had no military or law enforcement background. Little did they know I had been shooting since early childhood…a lot longer than most of them.

We ventured out into a large field for target practice. I had to work to keep my patience and remember that not even I started out perfect.

"But I was never this bad," I muttered under my breath, having to walk away from a teen boy named Jay. He was cocky, thinking that his glory days playing Call of Duty had taught him how guns work. He was horrible and unwilling to take any advice from me.

Jason wasn't bad. He really tried and took everything I said to heart. He kept calling me over, asking me to show him how to hold each gun to make sure he did it right.

"I keep missing," he sighed, lowering the gun to reload.

"It's ok," I assured him. "I still miss…just not very often."

Jason turned around, scowling at my smile. "You make it look so easy."

"I've got *years* on you, Jason. Really, don't worry." I shook my head. "Ok, worry a bit since we're pressed for time."

"Thanks, Riss. Way to make me feel better."

I laughed. "You'll catch on. You're a hell of a lot better than him," I added under my breath, flicking my eyes to Jay. Jason laughed and turned back to the target in front of him. "Take a breath and relax."

"I won't have time to do that when zombies are chasing us," he argued.

"Hey," I said, reminding myself to be patient with him. "That's true but you'll never learn if you don't take the time now."

He grumbled and fired again. I looked up and down the line of trainees. They were wasting an awful amount of bullets. I moved among them, giving tips along the way. By the time I went back to Jason, he had hit the inside circle around the bull's eye.

"I'll be as good as you in no time!" he exclaimed. I bit my tongue, not telling him that a moving target made things ten times worse. "Maybe I can go on missions!"

My stomach dropped. I blinked, forcing a smile to my face. "Maybe." I didn't want Jason to go on missions. I wanted him to stay here, guarding the perimeter where he could run to safety if need be. He had grown on me and the thought of anything bad happening to Jason was more upsetting than I expected.

Later, Raeya practically bounced with excitement during lunch. All the noobs had made it through the quarantine. After their allotted time to rest, they would be tested for jobs. She had come up with a new (and better, as she reminded me twenty times) test.

"You need to bring more people," she said, shoveling a forkful of canned beans into her mouth.

"Yeah, I will, just so you can put them through your tests."

She laughed. "You know what I mean. But yes, I'm very happy with this test. It really will showcase everyone's strengths."

After lunch, I pretended to take Argos out, wanting to run to the truck and bring in our stuff. Padraic caught me on the way out. He motioned for me to follow him. We went down to the B level, through a hall and into his room. Like the Cs', his room had colorless walls and harsh tile floors, but was twice as big. And—this would really make Raeya mad—he had the room to himself.

"Who else knows that Hayden is resistant to the virus?" he asked.

"I'm not sure. I assumed some of the A1s and you guys."

"He wasn't supposed to tell you."

"I kinda saw him get bitten," I reminded Padraic.

"I know that. We talked. He told me that he told you he was immune."

"Yeah, he did. And I know about the vaccine. And," I said quickly so he wouldn't interrupt me, "I know not to say anything."

"Good." Padraic nodded. He sighed, dropped his professional air, and sat on a loveseat. "It's not looking too promising," he confessed.

I joined him on the loveseat. "Why not?"

"Well for starters, we only have one person who we know for sure is resistant. I'm assuming most of us here are, but I'm not willing to test that."

"Remind me again why you think we're resistant."

"Everyone was exposed to the virus at around the same time. It was a pandemic, sweeping across the country in days. I find it hard to believe that we, meaning everyone here, didn't come into contact with it."

"It makes sense," I told him. "Though I wish we knew how the virus got out in the first place."

"Me too. And if it's worldwide," he added quietly.

"Oh," I whispered. I felt like an ass. I was so concerned with myself and saving the people I wanted to save that I never even thought about the rest of the world. Padraic's family still lived in Ireland. He had no idea if they were alive, dead...or undead.

"I think it is," he speculated. "If it wasn't, I believe some other country would come in on a rescue mission."

"My mom and my stepdad are in Papua, New Guinea," I said, my voice coming out in a harsh whisper.

"What are they doing there?"

"Forcing their religion down the throats of people who clearly don't want it. And feeding hungry children or something like that."

"Oh," he said shortly, not knowing what to say to my mini rant. "Well, that's a pretty secluded area; maybe they're still alive."

I leaned back. "If...no when this ends, what is the first thing you are going to do?"

"Probably still be a doctor," he said logically.

"You are *so* lame!" I joked.

"What about you?"

"I am going to a beach—any beach—with a drink in my hand, and I'm gonna soak up the sun. I'm not gonna move either, except to roll over to tan my ass."

"That does seem nice."

"Ugh! Better than nice! Imagine the warm ocean air, the smell of salt and sand and coconut, the sun shining down on you, the crashing of the waves." I closed my eyes.

"Birds chirping, tropical birds of course," Padraic added.

"The feel of sand between your toes, the way the refreshing breeze blows your hair."

"Sunburn."

I opened my eyes. "You suck at this game."

"Well, you didn't mention sunscreen."

"Fine. I'm slathering it on myself now, ok?"

"Ok. I am a doctor, I'm just watching out for your health," he teased. "I better check on my patients. It was nice talking to you, Orissa. I've missed you."

I shrugged. "Yeah, sorry, busy doing A1 stuff."

He stood. "Don't be a stranger."

"I won't," I promised.

<hr>

I visited Hayden who was sitting up reading. He explained to me that Cara had taken a lot of blood, enough to classify him an anemic.

Immediately I was upset. "No! She shouldn't do that! That's not—"

"Orissa, it's fine. If I wasn't ok with it, she wouldn't take any. I'm not being forced, remember?"

I sat on the edge of his bed and he closed his book.

"I-I just don't like seeing you not like yourself."

His hand settled on top of mine. "I don't like not being myself." He blinked several times, making me think he was tired.

"I had a dream about you last night," Hayden told me.

"Really? What kind of dream?"

"Oh, you know," he trailed off, raising his eyebrows. "Not really. Well, not last night at least," he joked. "We were just killing zombies."

"That's a nightmare," I corrected.

"I guess so. We were awesome in the dream."

"We are awesome in real life."

"Hell yeah," he said and we both laughed.

Then two teenage girls came in; one was carrying a plate of cookies and the other had a large glass of milk.

Milk Girl scowled at me for a millisecond before turning her pouty lips into a broad smile. "Hi, Hayden," she spoke with practiced charm. "We brought you cookies."

Cookie Girl held up the plate and smiled, her cheeks turning beet red. "They're still warm," she said quietly.

"Awesome, thanks. They smell wonderful," Hayden praised. Milk walked around the bed, her blue eyes flicking to me, and set the glass down. Cookie held out the plate. Unable to reach out since his arm was tethered to an IV, Hayden couldn't take it from her. I extended my hand and she jerked back, not wanting me to take the cookies. Once she realized what I was doing, she blushed and gave me the plate. I picked up a cookie, which was still warm, and held it up for Hayden to bite into.

"Mmh," he said with his mouth full. "They are good. Thanks, ladies."

The girls practically squealed with delight.

"I'm so glad you like them," Milk cooed. "Did you get my card?"

"Oh, uh, yeah. Thanks for that too."

I could tell Hayden didn't know who these girls were. His eyes scanned the cards, looking for clues.

"I'm Orissa," I said to get them to introduce themselves.

"We know who you are," Cookie giggled. "Everyone knows who you are."

"Is that good?" I asked.

"I guess," Milk said with a nonchalant shrug.

"Joni told us you saved everyone," Cookie added.

"Yeah," I admitted. Looking at Hayden, I said, "I couldn't have done it alone though."

Hayden finished the cookie and put his hand on mine. "She's amazing. You should have seen her."

"Ok, now I know you're hopped up on drugs."

"No, I'm not. What I am is honest." He grinned at me.

"Is it true you climbed fifty feet up the tree?" Cookie asked.

It was more like twenty at the highest. "Pretty close to it," I lied.

"I'm glad there are more female As," she said, earning an elbowing from her friend.

The girls introduced themselves as Megan and Felicity.

"Is there anything I can get you?" Felicity asked, batting her eyelashes at Hayden.

"No. I'm good. Thanks though," Hayden yawned and leaned his head against the pillows.

"Well, thanks for bringing Hayden cookies," I started. "He needs to rest though."

Felicity shot me a look as if to question why I wasn't leaving but kept her mouth shut and retreated with her friend.

"I can go too, if you want to sleep," I reminded him.

"You can stay."

"You won't hurt my feelings. Tell me to leave if you want me to."

"I will. When I want you to. I kinda miss you. You know, since I'm used to being with you all the time." He ran his fingers over my left hand. "Are the cuts healed?"

I opened my palm to show him the scabs. "Almost."

"You do heal fast."

"I suppose. It seems normal to me."

"I guess it would." His eyes closed.

I stretched my legs out on the bed. Hayden's fingers closed around mine. The words he spoke to Parker about wanting me to be his girlfriend echoed in my head.

I woke the next morning with a sore throat. Austin turned out to be a great person to rescue: he had the know how to fix our heater. Warm and comfortable, I begged off training and fell back asleep.

Sometime later, the mattress sunk down. I knew someone was sitting on the bed but didn't care. When his voice spoke my name, I opened my eyes.

"What are you doing?" I asked Hayden, looking into his hazel eyes.

"Sitting."

"No shit, Sherlock. That's not what I meant."

"They let me out early on good behavior. I'm still on bed rest, but at least now I can watch TV."

"Hmm," I mumbled and pulled the blankets over my head.

"What's wrong with you?"

"I think I caught what you have," I grumbled.

"Shit, I feel bad. Sorry, Orissa."

"It's not your fault. Ok, it is. You should feel horrible and do everything it takes to make it up to me."

"And how can I do that?" he asked, trying to sound coy, which utterly failed considering he had a sore throat and scratchy voice.

"Let me sleep."

He laughed. "Sounds good."

Maybe it was the warmth of the room or merely Hayden's presence that made me sleep like a baby. I took it easy the rest of the day, staying in bed, occasionally talking with Hayden and napping. Padraic checked on me once, took my temperature—which was slightly elevated—and then he left.

The next day, I felt slightly better. We had thousands of dollars worth of diamonds—or what used to be thousands of dollars worth. I put a necklace, a tennis bracelet, and two pairs of earrings into a wallet, wrapped it up in a shirt, and stuck it in a Coach purse. Raeya would get a nice surprise later.

Though the heater was back on, the room didn't warm above sixty-five, which, by my standards, was still cold. I shook out one of the down blankets and spread it over Hayden, who was asleep. I put the other on my bed.

I sorted through the mass of clothing next, putting stuff in our closet. We had built-in shelves, which worked out nicely since I didn't think to get hangers for all the new items. Along with clothes, shoes and the box of junk food, candy and booze, the closet held various weapons and ammo, just in case we needed it.

Everything for Raeya went into bags next to the door. I'd take them to her in the morning, I told myself. The shirts and sweaters I had picked out for Padraic were folded as neatly as I could get them and had been placed in a bag as well. After letting Argos out one last time before bed, I got back under my covers and slept until Hayden woke me up for breakfast, which had been brought up.

I showered, got dressed, and braided my hair. I wasn't fully recovered, but wanted to give Raeya her presents. Hayden offered to help me carry the gifts.

We found Raeya in the game room, talking to a very tired looking Padraic. Not wanting everyone else to see what they wouldn't be getting, I waved Raeya and Padraic out into the hall. "I have presents for you!" I gushed.

"You two shouldn't be out of bed," Padraic said flatly.

"We got bored," Hayden explained.

"Yeah, and shut up," I said, holding up a bag. "I brought you things!"

Padraic took his bag, smiling when he saw inside.

"Raeya, try not to scream," I warned.

She had to clamp her hand over her mouth as she sorted through the clothes and décor. "Oh my God! I-I can't believe you—ohmygod!—a rug! The tile floor in my room is so ugly!" She hugged me. "Thank you, Riss!"

"You're welcome. I would have gotten more if we were able."

"This is wonderful! Ah! I'm so happy to be able to dress nicely again!"

"Yeah, 'cuz it matters so much here," Hayden teased.

"It does to me," Raeya rationalized with a laugh.

"You have expensive taste," he continued to heckle her.

"I guess I do," she said, holding up a pair of drop earrings that sparkled with diamonds.

"You always have," I reminded her. "You were the only one at our high school with designer shoes."

"And one of the few who even knew who those designers were!" she reminisced.

I laughed. "Not all of us had a rich research scientist for a father!"

"I hate to break up the fun," Hayden said. "But we should probably get this stuff out of eyesight."

"You're right," Padraic agreed. "Thanks, guys. Really. It was very nice of you to think of me." His blue eyes lit up when he smiled.

"Why wouldn't I think of you? You're a good friend," I admitted. And he was.

"Well, thanks." He picked up the bag. "And, Hayden, since you're down here, wanna come into the lab for a, a, uh, check up?"

"Sure," Hayden said, knowing the checkup was really to see how much zombie virus he still had in his system.

"Thanks again, Orissa. I'll see you later, Ray," Padraic called over his shoulder as he strode off.

"Ray? You let him call you Ray?" I asked, helping Raeya gather up her stuff.

"Yeah, so?"

"That's your nickname. I thought you didn't like being called it."

"It doesn't bother me," she said with a shrug.

"It does, unless that person is a close friend," I continued.

"Well," she began, hauling the bag down the hall. "He is. You said so yourself. He is a good friend."

"Have you been hanging out with him a lot?" I asked, trying to keep judgment out of my voice.

"Not really."

"What does that mean?"

"He's the only B1 we have; he barely has time to sleep. We just talk occasionally when we're lonely. Padraic and I don't really have anyone else when you're out on missions. We're friends that's all. Why do you ask, Rissy?"

"I was just wondering."

Raeya stopped short, turning to me with an eyebrow raised. "Orissa, that's crap. You know you have feelings for him. Why else would you care if you didn't feel something for our favorite Irish doctor?"

"I don't have feelings for him. I just don't want you to have a new best friend," I confessed.

"Oh, Riss! I could never replace you! Don't worry!"

"Good, because I'd probably have to kill you if you did."

"See, that's exactly why I'd never replace you! Who else would pose such idle threats? I'd miss it dearly. I promise."

We entered her room and she put down the bags. I closed the door after us and leaned against it.

"There's something I want to tell," I whispered, "but you have to promise you won't tell anyone."

"Promise," she said.

"It's about Hayden."

"Oh, I know about him being resistant, if that's what you were going to say."

"How did you know?"

"Padraic told me," she said with a nod.

"What? He just made a big stinking deal about me not saying anything to anyone and he told you!"

Raeya shrugged shyly. "I told you, we talk. He feels a lot of responsibility for making a vaccine."

"Oh! And you know about the vaccine too! What else has he told you?"

"Nothing. Why? Is there more?"

"No. Well, not that I know about." I shuddered, and thought about Hayden being bitten.

"Wait, you *saw* it happen, didn't you?"

"Yeah, he was right in front of me. I was fighting off a gummy. I had cuts on my hand so I couldn't do much without getting infected. He reached down to pull me up. And it bit him."

"He's so brave," she said with a bit of a swoon in her voice, reminding me of a teenage girl. "And reckless." Good, my Ray was back. "Though I'm glad. He saved you."

"He did. It wasn't a good situation at all. There were so many. I don't get why they have to travel in herds like that."

"You guys should get tanks."

"Hah, yeah. Oh, how I'd love to blow up zombies. Do you think bookstores sell books about bombs?"

"No, I think they stopped selling those a few years ago," she mused.

"Damn."

"Do any of the A1s know how to? I mean, I think they would since they've been in the military."

"I bet they do."

"You should ask Hayden," she suggested.

"He's not too eager to talk about his time overseas." I looked down. "He lost his best friend. I can't imagine what he went through."

"Do you know what he did?"

"Infantry. In the Marines. He's told me that much. And I know he was, or is, a sergeant," I informed Ray.

Ray shrugged, I said my goodbyes, and went off to my room.

➤——————————➤

The guys were crowded in Ivan and Brock's room down the hall playing video games when an A3 knocked on my door. It was pretty late at night, so his appearance made my heart speed up.

"Orissa?" he asked sheepishly.

"Yeah?" I called, looking up from the book I was reading.

"Dr. Sheehan requests you and Underwood's presence."

"Dr. Sheehan? Oh, Padraic? Right. I'll find Hayden." I sprang off the bed. "Did he say why?"

"No, he just wanted me to tell you to come to the lab as soon as you could."

"Alright, thanks, Brian," I said, reading his name off of his ID tag. I rarely wore mine; everyone knew who I was so what was the point? When I entered Ivan and Brock's room, the guys tried to get me to join in on their game. I declined and snaked my way through the crowd to Hayden, who was sitting on one of the beds near the TV.

Not wanting to announce what was up to everyone, I put one hand on Hayden's shoulder and leaned close so I could whisper the message in his ear. His hand gently rested on the small of my back. The gesture was small but it made me feel something. I refused to think about it, too worried about what Padraic could want.

The Marines cat-called when I told them I needed to borrow Hayden for a few minutes. A slew of inappropriate jokes filled the room as the two of us exited together. I brushed them off, laughing, but couldn't meet Hayden's eyes, afraid they would be full of hope. When we reached the lower level of the old estate house, I confessed my fears to Hayden.

"Maybe it's good news," he suggested. "About the vaccine."

"I hope."

We walked into the hospital section, hoping for the best. But nothing could have prepared us for what we saw...

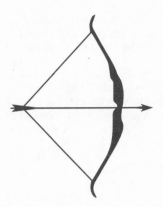

CHAPTER 30

Sitting on the hard, foam bed, was little Parker. His shirt was off, revealing a nasty looking scab on his side. When I got closer, I could see the half moon teeth indents.

"Hi, Hayden!" Parker said enthusiastically.

His father stood behind him, looking grim. "I've been bitten too," Parker explained.

Evan closed his eyes, as if the information was too much.

"I see that," Hayden said. He pushed up his sleeve and showed Parker both of the bites. "When did you get bitten?"

"About two weeks ago," Evan spoke, his voice heavy with worry. His eyes scanned Hayden dubiously. "You've really been bitten twice?"

"Yeah. By an S1 and an S2," Hayden explained, forgetting no one else knew the proper terms for crazy, zombie, or gummy.

"What's an S1?" Parker asked.

Hayden expatiated about the stages of the virus. Parker had been bitten by an S1. He hadn't known the girl was infected when he found her wandering around the streets of an abandoned city. She seemed almost normal, he told us. Then she bit him.

Padraic and Cara came into the room and told Parker and Evan about trying to create a vaccine. They explained that they wanted to take a few samples of Parker's blood to study. Padraic assured Evan more than once that they wouldn't force him or Parker to do anything they didn't want to do.

"Could this work?" Parker asked.

"We're hoping it will," Padraic said, barely able to keep the equivocal tone from his voice.

"Then I want to help. If there is a chance, then I'll do it."

"Parker," Evan blurted. "Think about this!"

"It's nothing bad," Hayden chimed in. "It doesn't hurt or bother me. I give blood every now and then. That's all."

"I want to be like Hayden," Parker begged to his father. "If I can help, then I want to."

Evan looked at Hayden with contempt, as if he wished Hayden would have spoken about how awful donating blood was and made Parker not want to do it.

"Who else knows?" I asked, not fully understanding why I was needed.

"No one," Evan noted. "I didn't tell a soul. And neither did Parker, right?"

"Right," the kid agreed. "I didn't tell anyone."

"Well then," Padraic said, clasping his hands together. "Parker, I will have Dr. Cara get a quick blood sample from you, and then you can be on your way."

Dr. Cara's hair was frizzier than the last time I'd seen her. She wore a purple sweater and red leggings. The potato soup we'd had for dinner was splashed down the front of her, and her socks didn't match. She snapped on rubber gloves and told Parker to hold his father's hand.

Padraic motioned for us to follow him into the hall. He closed the door and looked both ways to make sure no one was in ear shot.

"I know this is asking a lot," he started. "But now that we have two samples to draw from, it looks more promising. If we can find anything similar, then we may be on to something."

"What are you asking?" Hayden said with impatience.

"We need blood samples. From zombies. All three stages if possible."

"Ok," I said with indifference. "That shouldn't be a problem. I can shoot them first, right?"

"Yes," Padraic told me. "As long as you get the blood right away from the crazy stage. I don't think it will make a difference for the other two. Also," he said, looking at Hayden. "A sample of your lymphatic fluid *could* provide useful information."

"Sure," Hayden agreed.

"Wait." I put my hand up. "How do you get the lymphatic fluid?"

"A simple procedure," Padraic explained. "One I've done before. It's called a lymph node biopsy. I'll start with a needle biopsy; all I'll do is take out fluid with a needle. Hopefully that will be enough, though it's only a small sample of cells."

"And if it's not enough?" Hayden reluctantly asked.

"An open biopsy would be next, but again, only if you want to do it."

"Yeah," Hayden agreed again.

"Doesn't he need his lymph nodes?" I questioned.

"Yes, he needs them," Padraic said. "But biopsying one will not cause harm."

"Sure. I'll do it," Hayden stated. "Uh, how do you do it?"

"The needle biopsy takes less than ten minutes," Padraic began. "A needle will be inserted into the lymph node and the fluid is pulled out. Kind of like getting your blood drawn. And an open biopsy is the actual removal of the node. Normally I'd numb my patients, but I don't have any anesthesia."

"Oh, yay," Hayden said with less enthusiasm.

"I can give you morphine. It will at least help."

"It's better than nothing."

"And," Padraic said, "I'd like to do yours first, since I can't guarantee favorable results."

"Fine with me," Hayden said. "I don't want to put the kid through it if we don't have to."

"Great. And again, don't mention this to anyone. I will talk to Fuller tomorrow." Padraic forced a smile and went back into the lab.

"Are you not ok with this?" Hayden asked as we walked up the stairs.

"I am," I told him.

"Then why are you so quiet? You're never quiet."

"I'm thinking," I admitted. "About what it would mean if we really did have a vaccine?"

"It would be awesome, for one thing. And I think it would offer a lot of hope."

"Yeah, it would." I smiled at him. I didn't like the fact that creating a vaccine might cause Hayden pain. It was horribly selfish, that much I knew. I should be thinking about the greater good here.

Hayden went back to the video game party, leaving me to go to sleep by myself.

I didn't see much of Hayden over the next few days. He was busy talking with Fuller and the other 'officials' about expanding the shelter. I ran another session on yoga with the A1s and then again with the A3s. Jason had come up with some stupid story about me being in the CIA. He told me he hated seeing me disrespected.

It was odd, having someone stick up for me like that. I wasn't sure I liked it. They just needed to see me in action, he went on, and then they'd know. I thanked him nonetheless, wishing he wouldn't have gone with such an overused agency. Homeland Security was more modern.

Hayden, Ivan, Brock, and I were going on the next mission, leaving in two days. It was a unique mission, Fuller explained. The first thing we needed was feed for our livestock. One of the veterinarians made a list of vaccines that were needed for both the livestock and the cats and dogs we had at the shelter. Our next task was to find a farm with healthy looking animals. Finally, we had to find a trailer. A commercial semi truck and trailer would be ideal, though none of us knew how to drive a semi.

Come spring, the plans for expansion would be put into action. The addition would rely a lot on farming and wouldn't have electricity. The plan was to start bringing in livestock slowly and have enough to sustain us by spring. The cows and chickens we had were used solely for milk and eggs; it would be nice, Fuller told me, to have a burger for dinner.

That night, we met with Sam, a middle-aged man who drove trucks for a living. He painstakingly went over everything we'd need to know about driving the rig. Personally, I thought it would make more sense to find the animals and truck, come back and get Sam, and have him drive the truck while we made sure nothing happened. And semis were big; he'd be able to crush any zombies that tried to get him.

I didn't pay much attention, figuring that even if I did have to drive, Hayden would show me. Sam left and the guys hung around the table in Fuller's office, talking about their time in the war. Brock joked that he missed the desert heat, and Ivan said he was glad the zombies couldn't work guns or detonate bombs.

Though I couldn't contribute, I stayed, finding their tales both horrifying and interesting. At half past eleven, we said goodnight and headed to bed. I fell asleep quickly that night, dreaming about having my own little cabin on the compound ground.

Hayden's thrashing and groaning woke me. He was having another nightmare. I swiftly got out of bed and rushed over to him.

"Hayden," I said quietly. "Hayden, wake up." I put my hands on his shoulders and gently shook. "Hayden!"

He jerked away, his hands harshly grabbing onto me. His eyes darted all over the room, not able to focus. His body trembled and he let out ragged breaths.

"Hayden," I repeated, my voice soothing. "It's ok, I'm right here."

He nodded, pulling himself out of the hell his mind was stuck in. "It feels so real," he said breathlessly.

"It's not real," I told him. "I'm real. And I'm right here, listen to my voice. This is real."

He pulled me to him. I cradled his head against me, running my fingers through his hair. "Breathe. It's ok."

"Orissa," he whispered. "It felt so real. One minute Ben was there, the next he wasn't. The IED went off and he...he exploded with it." His body began to shake again. "Just bits of teeth and hair. Not even half a helmet left. Nothing to bring home. I feel like I'm there. I can hear the bombs. I can feel their heat."

I held him tighter. "You're not there. You're right here, in your bed at the compound, with me."

"Right." He took several deep breaths. "You are here. I'm not there right now."

I continued running my fingers through his hair. Then I let them drop, tracing the contours of his neck and shoulder, down his arm and through his fingers.

"You're cold," he said.

"I'm ok."

"You feel cold." He nestled his head against me. "And real. You feel real."

"That's 'cuz *they* are real," I joked.

Hayden became aware that his head rested against my breasts. His body stiffened as if he wasn't sure what to do. Then he relaxed.

Light from the full moon spilled into our room. "Stay with me?" he whispered.

"Of course," I said softly. We resituated and Hayden pulled me onto his chest, wrapping his arms around me.

"I don't want to go back to sleep," he confessed. "I don't want to go back there."

"I'll wake you up if you do. I promise. I won't leave, ok?"

"I don't know what I'd do without you."

"Hopefully you'll never be without me," I told him with a half smile. It had been awhile since I'd fallen asleep in Hayden's arms. Even though I was supposed to be the one comforting him, it felt good to be protected.

The next morning, Hayden hit the snooze button twice. We were still tangled together. When it went off for the third time, he turned off the alarm altogether.

"Orissa," he softly called my name. "Can we talk?"

"We are talking," I informed him with a smile.

"I know," he chuckled. "There's something I want to tell you."

My heart sped up, and before Hayden could get one word in, the door flew open. I flattened myself, squirming into the crack between the wall and the bed. Hayden threw the covers over me and sat up.

"Rise and shine, Underwood," Ivan said merrily. "I know you're just as eager as I am to sweat your ass off in training."

"Uh, yeah," Hayden agreed, trying to inconspicuously put the pillow over my head. "Where's Penwell?"

"Don't know. Breakfast probably. She likes to eat with her friend, Raeya."

"Mmh, Raeya. She's hot. So is Orissa but I know that you—"

"—let's go to breakfast," Hayden interjected, springing off the bed. "I'm starving."

"You gonna get dressed first?"

"Uh, oh yeah. See you down there, then."

I imagined Ivan's quizzical stare. A few horribly slow seconds passed before the door clicked shut. I didn't move until Hayden told me the coast was clear. He quickly got dressed and said he'd get Ivan to go down to breakfast with him. I waited a few minutes before getting up and doing the same. If Ivan questioned me, I'd say I was in the bathroom.

There wasn't a seat open next to Hayden. I felt more disappointed about that than I was willing to admit. I sat next to Ivan.

"Hello, Special Agent Penwell," he leered.

"You heard about that?" I stabbed my spoon into the oatmeal.

He laughed. "Yeah. That little A3 has a crush on you."

"No, I'm too much of a bitch for him. He has it for Ray."

"That makes two of us," Ivan told me, raising his eyebrows.

"Oh, you should bring her a porcelain doll. She *loves* them."

"She does?"

"Yep. Can't get enough. She used to have a huge collection. She's really heartbroken they got destroyed," I said seriously.

"Then I'll have to get her one," Ivan said. "Where do you, uh, find dolls like that?"

"I have no idea."

"Damn. I'm gonna find one."

Hayden, having overheard our conversation laughed. His hazel eyes met mine and that stupid feeling came back, making my stomach flip-flop and making me not want to eat. I pushed it aside and forced myself to finish breakfast. Training went by fast that day. I had gotten back into shape quickly and was pleased to be able to push myself. And seeing the male A1s shirtless and sweaty wasn't so bad either.

Later, Padraic gave me a little bag with empty vials. They were already marked in his messy, doctor handwriting.

"Don't risk your life over this," he pressed. "We can get samples anytime. I don't want to lose you, ok?"

I promised to be careful, put the bag of vials in Hayden's truck, and dashed in from the cold. Hayden was in bed already. I padded down the hall to shower and when I returned Hayden had sprawled out, looking peaceful and comfortable. I got under the cold sheets of my own bed.

In the middle of the night he had another nightmare. I woke him up again, though this time he didn't seem so confused.

He smiled right away. "Orissa," he whispered my name, and it almost sounded alluring. "Stay with me?"

"Of course," I promised and got under the covers.

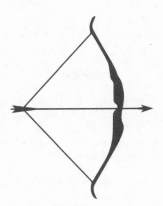

CHAPTER 31

We set out first thing in the morning. Since we had hopes of bringing a semi full of animals back, Ivan and Brock rode in Hayden's truck along with us. The vials were stashed in the glove box. Ivan rode shotgun, annoying Hayden by putting his feet on the dashboard. He was recanting a funny story about strippers in Mexico when we saw them.

A herd of twenty or so zombies blocked the road. With the frozen ground, we easily could have avoided them. Hayden turned, a wicked smiled on his face. We were all thinking the same thing. The zombies, most in the S3 stage, didn't notice us until we got out of the truck. Ivan yelled 'go' and we started firing, shouting out our points as the zombies hit the ground.

Trying to get a higher score, I picked out the S2s. We easily mowed through the herd. No one could agree on fair scores. S3s became S2s, and Ivan swore there was an S1 in there that he shot and killed. Brock was ready to drop it and move on, but Hayden and Ivan kept bickering about who had the higher score.

"Give it up, guys," I said and got back into the truck. "You both know I kicked your ass and will continue to kick your ass. You're lucky I don't have a bow and arrow, since that's worth double points."

"Teams," Hayden said. "There has to be a hunting store along the way to get another bow and some arrows. She's on my team."

"That's not fair," Brock complained. "Neither of us knows how to use a bow."

"Your loss," Hayden teased. "Find another weapon to use for double points."

I rubbed my hands together. "Can you turn on the heat? I'm freezing."

"Thanks," I said after Hayden turned it on. "Why are we going north in February?"

"That's where we were told to go," Ivan said casually.

"We should go south," I said.

"We were told to go north," Ivan reiterated.

"We should go south. No one would know. And besides, cows in Florida aren't any different than the cows in Ohio. In fact, they'd probably be healthier since they've had more nutrition. See, that settles it. Let's go south."

Ivan skeptically looked at Hayden, his eyes saying something I couldn't interpret. Brock stared straight ahead.

"Orissa," Hayden said in a level voice. "We don't disobey orders."

"Technically we won't be. We were told to bring home animals. No one will even question us on where we got them. It's not like you can bite into a steak and go 'mmhh, this tastes like an Indiana raised cow. So much better than those damn Georgia cows'."

"That's true and all, but we were told to go north. So that is where we will go." Through the rearview mirror, his eyes met mine, silently pleading for me to shut the hell up.

"Right. North it is then."

We drove nonstop for four hours. Sitting in the back of the truck wasn't as bad as I thought it would be. The extended cab offered more legroom than a normal truck would have. After eating, peeing, and a walk to stretch our muscles, we got back inside, arguing over what kind of music to listen to.

Brock didn't care as long as it wasn't jazz or classical. Hayden liked his awful country music and Ivan and I wanted hip hop. We tried to use the two-against-one angle, but since this was Hayden's truck, he reminded us, he got to choose. I also learned that this really was Hayden's truck—his before the world became overrun with infected cannibals. He had invested a lot of time and money into it, hence the not wanting to mess it up at all. And, though he didn't admit it, I was sure it reminded him of home and of a time where things weren't so fucked up.

It was snowing when we stopped somewhere in Missouri late that night. It would have been wiser to stop in the daylight, but we were all eager to make good time and get back to the safety and warmth of the compound. Doubting we'd get lucky and randomly find a house with a generator, our next best hope was finding a place like a school or hospital that would for sure have one.

We avoided the big cities and drove through the unplowed streets of small towns; the truck slipping on ice every now and then. No one said anything, but we all had to be thinking it: driving a semi full of animals back to the compound seemed like a horrible idea in this weather.

Soon the roads were covered in black ice. The four wheel drive did nothing to help with that. When a small, brick elementary school loomed in the glow of the headlights, Hayden slammed on the breaks, purposely making the truck spin in a circle. Though doing donuts in the empty parking lot was fun, it made me realize that a jump-in-the-car-and-drive-like-the-wind getaway wasn't possible.

"We should stay here tonight," Hayden said, putting the truck in park.

"We have no idea what's inside," Brock rationalized.

"I'll go check," Hayden said.

"No, you won't," Ivan interjected. "It's too big."

"That's what she said," Hayden said.

Ivan playfully punched Hayden's arm. "You wish, Underwood. And no. It's too big of a place to investigate at night when we have no reason to."

"I can wear the vest. If any zombies are in there, I can pretend I'm one of them."

Ivan shook his head. "Underwood, that's the dumbest thing you could do."

Hayden grinned. "Obviously you never met my high school girlfriend."

"There are no tracks," I interrupted. "At least none I can see from here. And apart from the snow that's currently falling, I'd say it hasn't snowed in awhile. See the top layer? You can tell it melted and froze again. It's been that way for at least a day, probably two."

The guys' eyes settled on me, as if I'd stated something profound. Then Ivan nodded.

"Right," Ivan stated. "No tracks. So nothing's gone in or out."

"There's only one way to be sure," Hayden pointed out. He shut off the truck. We zipped up our coats, cocked our weapons, and left the warm cab, stepping into several inches of snow.

"I've never seen this much snow," Brock told us, awe in his voice. "I'm from southern Texas," he explained, easing the incredulous looks he was getting.

"You'd love North Dakota then," Hayden said under his breath. "We get lots of snow up there."

"You know," Brock said, turning around with his rifle raised. "I always wondered why anyone would live up north. It's so cold."

"I thought the same thing," Hayden admitted. "I always wanted to move where it was warm. Now, I'd give anything to go back."

"I'm from New Jersey," Ivan said. "We had the best of both worlds: hot summers and cold winters."

"Arkansas isn't so bad," Brock mused. "It's still colder than what I'm used to, though."

"I can't wait to go to Mexico when this is over," I said with a sigh.

"Me neither," Hayden agreed. He advanced a few steps, looking through the scope of his high tech gun. Once we made sure the coast was as clear as it could be, we ran to the front doors. Because the doors were chained and locked, the boys had to get tools from the truck to cut through the metal. "That's a good sign," Hayden suggested. "At least nothing new got in."

CONTAGIOUS

"Not through the front at least," Ivan corrected.

Staying together, we quietly slipped inside. A cutout skeleton hung on the door to the principal's office. "I thought schools weren't allowed to decorate for Halloween anymore," Ivan questioned.

"If this place is as rural and backwoods as my hometown, then they still would," Hayden said quietly as to not draw too much attention from an unknown lurker. "Especially after President Samael cut funding by more than half and most of the teachers lost their jobs."

"My aunt was a teacher," I whispered, feeling a wave of nausea when I thought about Aunt Jenny. "She lost her job two years ago and was reduced to waiting tables with high school kids at a low class dinner."

"The world was bad before the zombies," Brock affirmed. "I couldn't find a job. Even with the military experience. There was nothing."

"I know the feeling," I told him. "That's why I dropped out of college. It didn't matter anymore. The economy was too crappy." It still pissed me off when I thought about it. President Samael promised a lot of things: a revamped healthcare system, money for public schools, an economic stimulus. He was compared to JFK, young, good looking, and offering hope for our country. But all that changed the moment he got into office.

Our troops had officially been out of the Afghan war for less than two years when Samael sent them back in. That was the turning point of our tanking economy. The housing market, which was already in a slump, plummeted. Things went from bad to worse at a scary speed. The stock market was a joke, foreign countries were skeptical to trade with the US, and banks ran out of money. What started as peaceful protests turned into full-on riots and uprisings. People were gassed, tazed, and eventually shot.

I still remember walking to class when the first shooting happened. Students at a digital arts school in Florida held a protest against the government's shut down of funding for all public school art programs. Supposedly, the protest grew violent and the students refused to listen to police orders. The televised interview with a female student was abruptly cut off the air.

Raeya speculated it was because the freshman was making too much sense. She raised some really good points and found flaws in the government's tactics, she told me. President Samael put our country deeper in debt by 'fixing up' America's hotspots. California and New York were the most well known states. If anyplace in the United States could bring in tourist dollars, it was those two, he promised.

I stopped following the train wreck our country was on. It was too depressing and there was nothing I could do to change it. Raeya was optimistic and thought things would get better. We survived the Depression from the 1930s, she often reminded me.

The school was empty and all the doors had been chained. It was safe but had no generator. Funding must have *really* been cut in this small Missouri town. We set up camp in a room that looked like it had been a music room at one time. It held old desks and office supplies now. Located at the center of the school, it was the only room besides the library that was windowless.

Brock messed with the smoke alarms—Hayden quickly explained that Brock used to be an engineer of some sort—so that they wouldn't go off when we built a fire. We carefully built one under an air vent, not wanting to choke on the fumes. The four of us huddled close together, giving Hayden and me a reason to be near.

Hayden and I took the first watch, patrolling the halls for awhile and going back to warm ourselves by the fire. I went into a kindergarten room and examined the artwork on the walls. I shined my flashlight all around. A name list hung by the door with each kid's name spelled out in sparkly stickers. Their pictures were next to their names.

"Sasha," I said aloud to no one, running my fingers over the pink letters. A little girl with blonde curls framing her face smiled up at me with a missing tooth. I wondered if she was dead, alive, or undead. "And what about you, Mrs. Hefty?" I asked when the light hit the teacher's name plate on the desk. "Did you make it out alive?"

Four hours later, Hayden and I switched with Ivan and Brock. Though I hated it, I slept with my boots on, ready to jump up and defend myself and the guys if need be. We lay down close to the fire. I wrapped my sleeping bag tightly around me, not bothering to take off my gloves since I was so cold. I would have really appreciated Hayden's warm body pressed up next to mine.

As if he could read my mind, he reached out and held my hand. That was as close as we could get with the two others around. Still, somehow, it was enough to comfort me. I didn't wake up until morning.

→

Hayden let Ivan drive, which surprised us all. He claimed he hadn't slept well last night and didn't feel like concentrating. Brock called shotgun, forcing Hayden to sit in the back with me. We hit a ghost town, making us all feel like we were wasting precious daylight hours. By lunch, we found another small town. Zombies struggled through the deep snow drifts.

Careful not to get stuck ourselves, Ivan stopped the truck. Not wanting to trudge through over half a foot of snow, Hayden and I didn't care that Ivan and Brock would rack up a ton of points when they leaned out the windows to shoot.

The farther north we went, the deeper the snow got. At one point we weren't sure we were even on a road anymore. It was the most anxiety I'd felt on this mission. All I could think about was crashing through a lake and freezing to death.

Resisting the urge to yell 'I told you so,' we turned around and headed south. It was after noon by the time we made it through the town with the school. The snow fell harder, slowing our already slow-going trip. Hayden unbuckled, rolled up his jacket and used it as a makeshift pillow, leaning on me.

"Wake me up if anything exciting happens," he said with a slight smile before closing his eyes.

Two hours would pass before it did.

→

"Stop!" I yelled.

Ivan slammed on the brakes; the truck fishtailed.

"Go back and down that driveway," I said.

"Why?" he questioned.

"There was a fancy looking sign for a Clydesdale farm."

"A what?" Brock asked.

"A draft horse. You know, like the Budweiser horses."

"Ok, and you want to stop and pet the pretty ponies?" Ivan asked, looking at me through the rearview mirror.

"No, smartass. Big breeder barns like that usually have their own truck and trailer. And since these are big horses-"

"There's likely a big truck and trailer," he finished.

"Exactly."

And I was right. The truck started without a hitch, the diesel engine loudly coming to life. Ivan and Brock would take turns driving it; Brock seemed almost excited to test his skills at driving a big rig. I didn't see any of the horses and I didn't want to look for them, afraid of what I might find. Several miles later, the snow thinned.

A large barn looked promising ahead. Brown cows dotted a distant pasture. Stupidly, none of us thought about what rounding up the animals would entail.

"I doubt they've had grain in awhile," I said, an idea forming. "If there is some in the barn we might be able to lure them into the trailer."

"It's worth a try," Hayden agreed, his breath clouding around him as he spoke. I stuck my hands in my pockets, wanting my fingers warm so they would be able to pull the trigger. The barn was boarded up. It didn't strike us as odd until something crashed into the door.

All four of us whipped out our weapons. We waited and the things bumped into the door again. The unmistakable sound of fingernails scraping on metal echoed across the snowy farm.

"Zombie," Hayden announced. He pressed his ear up to the door. "Sounds like there's more than one."

"Are there any windows?" Ivan asked, moving back to examine the barn.

"Skylights," I said, pointing. "Help me up and I'll tell you how many are in there."

"How?"

I looked around. The barn was nice, but nothing spectacular. It was large but not tall. "Actually, if you pull the truck around, I can climb onto the trailer and then onto the roof easily."

Ivan agreed and jogged off. The snow that was stuck to my boots made the roof of the trailer slippery. I almost lost my balance. Clicking the safety on my machine gun, I handed it down to Hayden. I wouldn't need it to look through a window.

Rather unsteadily, I climbed up the snow-covered roof. Using my arm so my gloves wouldn't get wet, I brushed off the snow and peered inside. It was too dark to discern much of anything. Carefully, I moved to the next glass window and brushed off the snow, allowing more light to pour into the barn.

"I can see three," I called down, moving to the third skylight. This one was frosty and required some scraping. "There's something…weird."

"What's weird?" Hayden yelled up to me.

"I can't tell; hang on." I cupped my hands around my eyes and peered in. Something big lumbered about. It was too big to be a zombie, I thought. I tapped on the glass, trying to get its attention. "I might be able to shoot them from up here," I told the guys, not looking away from the large creature.

"What?" Hayden asked. "I can't hear you, Riss."

"I said," I shouted, sitting up so my voice would travel down to the guys, "I might be—" I didn't get to finish telling Hayden what I might be able to do. The glass cracked and I fell through, landing on the cold barn ground.

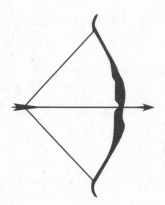

CHAPTER 32

The wind had been knocked out of me. I reeled, trying to breathe. I had landed in a stall. A stall full of dirty bedding and uneaten hay. I never thought I'd welcome a stall full of frozen horse poop and urine soaked wood shavings. The debris had prevented me from breaking something.

The guys yelled, frantically, outside the barn. Someone banged on the door. It caught the attention of a few of the zombies. The smell wasn't as bad as it should be. They could barely move since their limbs were frozen.

"I'm ok," I tried to shout. My voice was only a weak wheeze. I pulled myself up, grasping onto the metal bars of the stall. There were five zombies, all in the gummy stage or worse. Brushing the glass from myself, I slowly moved to the front of the stall. I drew my gun and fired four times.

The big thing I saw was nowhere in sight. The barn was still fairly dark. I wished the guys would stop yelling and trying to break through the boards; it would make it a hell of a lot easier to hear where the bastard was hiding.

The stall was locked and there was no way to reach through to let myself out. Sticking my M9 back in the holster, I climbed over the stall, my cold feet stinging when I jumped down. My hands trembled with adrenaline as I rushed over to flip the metal latches on the sliding door. It flew open. Ivan and Brock rushed inside, rifles at the ready. Hayden's arms wrapped around me.

"Are you alright?" he asked, letting me go.

"Yeah. Well, I'm sore. But nothing is broken."

"That scared the shit out of me. Don't do it again."

"Trust me, I don't plan on it." I looked up. "I don't know why it broke."

"The glass is cold. It weakens it. I-I should have thought of that before." Hayden shook his head, looking guilty.

"Me too. And I should have been smart enough to not sit on it, but we live and learn, right?"

His hazel eyes were still filled with worry, making his attractive face appear older.

I put my hand on his chest. "I'm ok, Hayden. Really."

"Orissa, I—" Three shots rang out. We rushed inside. The big thing and one more gummy lay dead on the ground.

"Look at that big mother fucker!" Ivan exclaimed. The big thing had been a huge person at one point, standing well over six feet tall. Broad shouldered and built like a bull, he would have looked intimidating as a human. As a zombie, he was downright terrifying.

"I don't think they do well in the cold," I said. "Which would explain why we haven't seen very many."

"It makes sense," Brock said, nudging Fatty's leg with his boot. "He's frozen in some parts."

"You ok, Penwell?" Ivan asked.

"Yeah. Frozen horse shit broke my fall."

"You're cold. You might not feel it right away but you could be hurt internally."

"I don't think so," I stated, though, come to think of it, I didn't feel anything.

The zombies didn't start off as zombies trapped in a barn. By the looks of it, six guys bunkered up in here, thinking it was safe. One of them must have been infected. A tent lay in ruin, covered with blood stains, and moldy food was frozen to the cement floor. When we went into a room full of feed, I felt the pain shoot through my hip.

"You're limping," Hayden observed.

"No I'm not," I brushed him off. The adrenaline gone, my hip hurt so much it nearly brought tears to my eyes when I moved.

"Yes, you are. I can see it," he insisted.

"That's just my pimp walk."

"Very funny, Orissa," he said, unable to keep from laughing. "You're really something, ya know."

"Thanks." I wasn't sure what he meant. Instead of thinking about it, I went to the feed room. I shined my flashlight around, trying to look busy so I wouldn't have to lift any heavy bags.

"Hey," I said, when the light hit a stack of papers. "Look at this vet bill."

"What about it?" Ivan asked.

"The address. It's on Mill Road. We passed a Mill Road only five miles back."

"Sweet. Let's get the cows, get the medical shit, and go home."

"Sounds like a plan," Brock gladly agreed.

The guys loaded up all the feed. We got into our vehicles and drove to the pasture. Not bothering to close the gate, we drove in. The cows looked up hopefully at the sight of the trucks.

Going with the pretense of being a lookout, I stayed in the truck while the guys opened a bag of feed. It was slow going. The cows didn't recognize us, though they were familiar with trucks that came through with food.

Finally, we had the trailer loaded with cows. I felt a little bad for the long, cramped ride they would endure. I made myself feel no guilt when I remembered that they would be going to a new, better home.

I stayed outside, guarding our trailer full of livestock while the guys went into the vet's office. I thought it was strange how Fuller told us to go north in February. He was a smart man; he would know that this was one of the coldest months for many states and that we would most definitely run into snow. And it didn't take a genius to figure out that no humans meant no one to plow the roads. Yeah, Hayden's truck was big and had four-wheel drive. But that did no good on ice and didn't make us invincible to big drifts or sliding off the road.

We drove straight back to the compound, taking turns driving. We stopped once to refuel; finding diesel was a pain in the ass. Hayden lied about not being tired, thinking it wasn't right to make me drive since I was hurt. I gave him crap for going easy on me just because I was a female and he let me take the wheel for awhile.

The A2s and a few Cs in charge of the animals greeted us around midnight when we entered the compound. They would handle getting the cattle settled into their new home. Ivan and Brock piled into the back of the truck and Hayden sped to the shelter.

I turned the water on in the quarantine bathroom. It was painful to strip out of my layered pants. A huge bruise had formed on my right hip. Stupidly, I pressed it, wanting to measure the pain.

It was a lot.

I pulled my three layers of shirts off to reveal a bruise on my shoulder as well. My neck was stiff and it hurt to walk. This was just effing great. I stepped into the steamy shower, feeling my muscles relax almost instantly. We hadn't collected Padraic's blood samples this trip, but we'd be heading out again soon. There was still plenty of time since Dr. Cara was still setting up for the tests.

The next morning, Hayden and Ivan were eating oatmeal while watching a movie. They informed me we had run out of milk, butter, and brown sugar. They added syrup to their breakfast to help with the taste.

I took a bowl, heated it up in the microwave and sat between the boys. Their eyes latched onto me.

"What?" I asked Ivan.

"Sorry," he said, suddenly flustered. "I'm not used to seeing that much feminine skin."

"And I'm not used to seeing it all bruised up," Hayden added.

"Oh." I looked at my shoulder. "My side is even worse. Even the pressure from my waistband hurts."

"Want me to inspect it?" Ivan joked.

"It's fine. It's just a bruise. Ugly, but nothing threatening."

"Maybe you should have it looked at," Hayden commented, concern in his eyes once again. "You know, to make sure you didn't crack your bones."

"It'd hurt more if I did," I assumed.

"Suit yourself. You could at least get something for the pain."

"Actually," I said. "That isn't a bad idea. I bet Padraic would give me something that would knock me out for the rest of the time in here too."

"You think he'd do that?" Ivan asked.

"Sure. He has before. Well, not in the same situation, but close enough."

"How did you two meet up? Was he your friend from before like Raeya?" Ivan questioned.

I found myself telling Ivan the whole story, everything from my appendix to being gassed to the horror that had befallen the hospital's basement.

"Gassed?" Hayden asked, raising an eyebrow.

"Yeah. Padraic told me that some sort of law enforcement agents—he couldn't tell what kind— came through to save the healthy people. They had knock out gas. He thought it was for crowd control, but that doesn't seem right to me."

Hayden and Ivan exchanged glances.

"I suppose," Ivan said, though he didn't sound convinced.

"You're kind of crazy; you know that, right?" Hayden asked me, smiling.

"Yeah. Always have been." I smiled back and our eyes met. I felt that thing again, this time I didn't want it to go away. Ivan loudly cleared his throat, and Hayden dropped his gaze.

"Do you still want some pain meds?" Hayden asked.

"Sure."

He got up and stood under the camera, waving. After a minute, he was still waving. "I thought someone was watching us at all times," he huffed, annoyed. It took five more minutes before a voice came over the intercom. Hayden explained the situation, and assured the voice that none of us were feeling infected.

Padraic came in mere minutes later. He had bags under his eyes and looked pale.

"You need a vacation," I told him with a wry smile.

"So do you," he said when he saw the bruises. "What happened?"

"I fell. Slipped on ice. Nothing too bad. I'm just sore and wanted something to help me sleep, if you could do that for me." I smiled an innocent smile.

"Of course. It's, uh, the morning though. Do you want it now?"

"Yeah. What else am I going to do?"

"We need to talk about your drug addiction," he joked. "I'll get you something."

"Ok, thanks. Oh, and Padraic," I said before he could turn to leave. "Thanks for saving me at the hospital."

His eyebrows pushed together as if he couldn't quite figure out why I had brought that up. "You're welcome. If I didn't, I wouldn't be alive." He smiled, his blue eyes as bright as a clear sky. "I'll be right back."

Whatever Padraic gave me was disgusting. I think it was some sort of cough medicine that failed at trying to taste like grapes. Half an hour later, I was feeling sleepy. The guys were watching *The Simpsons* on DVD. I took a blanket from the bed and curled up next to Hayden, careful not to put any pressure on my bruises. Ivan and Brock were in armchairs set at an angle in front of the couch. If they turned around, they would see us. Since we were out of their line of sight as they stared at the TV, Hayden put his arm around me.

I stayed drugged up on the horrible cough medicine the next day. I really didn't hurt that bad. I was impatient and hated being held back by a stupid injury. Hayden told me Raeya threatened to drag me to dinner if I didn't get my lazy ass out of bed. I got dressed, braided my messy hair, and followed him down.

"I've been waiting!" Raeya said impatiently. "I have something for you. It's not as good as designer purses or diamonds, but it's something."

"What is it?"

"It's at your spot on the table. There's one for you too, Hayden."

A little, white laminated card was upside-down in my spot. I picked it up and read aloud, smiling. " 'Zombie Kill Squad: killing the undead.' I like it Ray!" My name, class, and division were under the title.

"I thought you'd like it better. Maybe you'll actually wear it like you're supposed to," she said brightly.

"I will," I promised. "But I don't have one of those string things."

"A lanyard," she informed me. "I'm working on making some."

"Then I'll always wear it."

The next day Fuller pulled Hayden and me into his office after training. Two detailed lists were on the table. One was alphabetized and the other ranked items in order of importance. That would be Raeya's doing, for sure. He told us that the compound was running very low on vitamins. Since we had a craptastic diet that consisted of mostly canned food, it was important to take vitamins every day. Other things were needed, mostly hygiene items, that we could get at the same place we found the vitamins.

"Now," he said, folding his hands. "I'm going to leave this up to you two. I know you just got back and I would never send you out again. However, those samples are important. It will not be held against you if you decline this mission."

I looked at Hayden. He shrugged, telling me he didn't care. Great, now the decision was up to me.

"It's fine. But I have one condition," I stated.

"Name it," Fuller said and crossed his arms.

"We get to go somewhere warm, like out west."

Something flickered across Fuller's face. Was it fear? "How about Texas? That's not so far and it's a hell of a lot warmer than it is here."

"Good enough," I agreed.

"Is leaving tomorrow too soon?"

"No, sir," Hayden said automatically. "Oh, Riss—"

"I'm fine," I replied quickly.

"Fine?" Fuller questioned.

"I fell on ice," I smoothly lied, though I had no reason to keep the truth from Fuller. I had already lied about it once, might as well stay consistent. "It's nothing major."

"Rest tomorrow," Fuller ordered. "No training. Then leave the following day."

"Sounds good," I said over Hayden's formal 'yes, sir.'

Raeya met with the other overseers. She told me that the supplies needed to be better inventoried so we wouldn't run out of things again.

I didn't tell her that eventually we *would* run out of things. The world would run out of things. There was no one left to work in factories. We would have to go back to an old-fashioned lifestyle, harvesting our own food and hunting. The compound had solar and wind powered generators, but we still relied on gas for transportation.

Jason stopped me on my way back to our rooms.

"Hey, Orissa," he said shyly. "Tomorrow is my first day on duty."

"Yeah, I'm excited." I smiled, proud of him for making it into the A group. "I'm sure you'll do great."

"I hope so," he said, returning the smile. "Can you teach me how to use the bow and arrows?"

"I would but I don't have any arrows," I said bitterly, still upset over losing my arrows.

"Oh, never mind then," he said, dejected.

"We'll get more," I assured him. "And then I'll give you lessons. Just the two of us."

"Awesome!" Jason exclaimed. "Thanks!"

"No problem."

Later, Hayden and I visited with some of our friends. Parker drew pictures for us, and the kid was a pretty good artist for his age. He gave me a picture of a girl in a tree, shooting arrows down at a pile of bloody zombies. Hayden's picture was of everyone on the porch with Hayden in front, blocking everyone from harm.

Hayden and I stayed together for the rest of the day. We played with Argos. We drove to the fields to see how the new cows were settling in, and Hayden attempted to teach me how to play poker. After dinner, we went up to our room to watch a movie.

Hayden munched on potato chips while I chose the movie. I was really getting tired of watching movies. I was looking forward to our mission, though. It was simple, just the two of us, and we would go somewhere warm.

"Since we don't have to get up early tomorrow," I said and shook the bottle of tequila in the air. My stomach churned at the thought of taking a shot of it. I traded it for a bottle of Captain Morgan and sat at the foot of Hayden's bed. Unscrewing the lid, I pressed the bottle to my lips and took a swig. Hayden took a drink and passed the bottle back to me. I took another drink, accidentally swallowing too much. I coughed and reached out for my apple juice.

I didn't realize I was drunk until I got up to pee. The room spun and I almost fell.

"You alright there?" Hayden asked, not affected by the alcohol.

"Yeah. I'm, uh, fine." I staggered down the hall, running my hand over the wallpapered drywall for support. I decided to wash my face and ended up splashing water down my front. I didn't think to dry it.

"Fall in?" Hayden asked when I crawled over him. I must have looked confused because he added, "You're shirt is wet."

"Oh, yeah. It's just water."

He laughed. "I figured so."

I had a tank top on under the brown, long-sleeved hooded sweatshirt. I pulled it off, the hood getting caught around my head. Hayden laughed again and helped me take it off. I felt incredibly tired and really wanted to snuggle up next to him. My drunken mind was thinking very inappropriate things about the muscular Marine.

To distract myself, I unbraided my hair. I shot the elastic hair band across the room and smiled when it landed on my bed. I tipped my head over, shaking out my hair. I pitched forward, losing my balance. Hayden grabbed my arm, catching me. I sat up and fell against him, my head on his chest. He brushed the hair out of my eyes. I stared up at him, feeling something warm travel through my body. He moved his head toward mine. Without thinking, I parted my lips, wanting to pull him to me.

Somebody slammed the dryer closed, the noise echoing throughout the hall and making me jump. I moved away from Hayden, laughing. I blinked several times, pushing all romantic thoughts out of my head…for now.

"You kinda look like Elle Wilson," he said. His eyes went to my breasts. "Well, with better, uh assets then her."

I sat up, pushing my hair back. "Who?"

"Elle Wilson."

I shook my head. "No clue who that is."

"Oh. She was on The Voice a few years ago. Didn't win, but was in the finals."

I burst out laughing. "You watch that show?"

Hayden smiled, reaching for my hand. "What if I did?"

"I wanted to be on it, you know. Well, thought about it, really."

He pulled me to him. "You do have a beautiful voice." I nestled up against him, finding comfort in the beating of his heart. I think he said something else. I didn't catch it before I fell asleep.

The next day, I spent time with Raeya, who wasn't happy about us leaving again. I assured her it would be an easy trip. Hayden and I would avoid places that were too crowded with the undead and we wouldn't risk anything for the samples.

Hayden and I left right after breakfast. The other A1s hadn't known about our second mission. I wondered how Fuller would explain that one.

"Have you ever taken blood before?" Hayden asked once we started the drive.

"Nope. You?"

"No. How are we gonna know how to do it?"

"It can't be hard. Especially if they're dead. Oh, maybe we can cut them open and suck up the blood that pours out."

"Do you think that would work?"

"Maybe. I can find a vein on a crazy, but I'm not sure about the zombies. Do their hearts even beat anymore?"

"Yes."

"What?!" I don't know what surprised me more: the answer or the fact Hayden knew it.

"Very, very slowly. Medically, they are dead. A human couldn't survive with a heartbeat that slow. Their blood is thick, as you know, but it still goes through their system."

"How the hell do you know this?"

"Dr. Cara told me."

"So are they technically alive?" I asked.

"No. It has something to do with the central nervous system and random firings of neurotransmitters or something that makes muscles spasm. I didn't follow everything she said. It sort of makes sense."

"In what way does that make sense?"

"If you had no blood flow, your tissues would die. And they wouldn't be able to move. They'd crack apart," he said.

"Too bad they don't."

"Yeah, that'd be too easy."

Parts of the highway were deserted. If we came to a blockage of stalled cars, we'd exit, turn around, or go off-roading. I was loading magazines when Hayden suddenly jerked the wheel. We were about five hours into our journey, and it was time we saw some action...

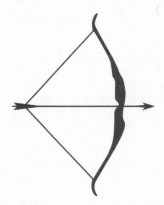

CHAPTER 33

"What is it?" I asked, when I saw nothing but emptiness.

"You'll see," he told me with a grin.

"I'll see what?"

"A surprise."

"Really, you have a surprise for me?" I asked dubiously.

"Yes. I can't say I planned it, though."

"Ok." I loaded another magazine before it came into view. I felt like a kid going to a candy store. I stashed the bullets away and unbuckled, eager to get out and explore the huge outdoor sporting goods store.

"This is genius!" I exclaimed, rolling down the window. We were in a fairly populated part of Texas. The lake behind the store eliminated some of the threat at least; we didn't have to worry about zombies rising from the water.

The parking lot was as full as it would have been during normal business hours. That was good and bad news. The good news was that no one had time to loot and leave. The bad news was that people, or what used to be people, were inside.

We parked close to the doors, which weren't locked. Guns at the ready, we got out of the truck. Nothing jumped out or staggered over to eat us. I looked at Hayden. He nodded ever so slightly and approached the door. He waved his hand and I followed.

The doors opened easily, allowing the horrible smell to escape. We both balked at it, covering our noses in disgust. Along with festering zombies, rotting corpse parts, and decaying food, the huge fish tanks were full of dead fish and skuzzy water.

Zombiefied customers meandered around. Some were so far into the S3 stage that it would be a waste of ammo to shoot them. The bag of vials was around my neck. This might be a good time to get some good S3 samples.

When a rather deteriorated S3 caught scent of us, she limped forward and tumbled down the stairs. With a snort of laugher, I shot her in the head. The shot echoed throughout the building.

"It's go time," Hayden said with a wicked smile. A dozen zombies stumbled my way. Bullets rained down, finding new homes in the squishy skulls of what used to be people. Hayden went up the stairs and took out everyone up there. "It's clear!" he shouted.

"Same here," I called back. The zombies had done most of the work already. In the crazy stage, they must have killed most of the patrons. I pulled my shirt over my nose, gagging at the smell of death. It was so strong it burned my eyes. Hayden and I met in the hunting section.

"We should have come here a long time ago," he said, his eyes feasting on the glorious display of guns and ammo.

"You're telling me," I said, kneeling down and removing the bag.

I couldn't be sure if the zombies were in the S2 stage. By the way they smelled, all were rotting from the inside out. I jammed the needle into the arm of what used to be a gray-haired, old woman. I pulled back on the syringe without success.

"Here," Hayden suggested. In one swift swipe, he slit open her wrist. Brown, chunky blood oozed out. He nearly gagged and looked away. "That is so freaking nasty!"

I'd never smelled anything worse. Holding my breath, I tried to suck up the goo.

"It's too thick," I said, retching.

"There has to be a bottle we can put it in somewhere. But we don't have to do it now." He looked around. "I don't know what to take first."

"I know, me neither," I exclaimed, standing up and away from the nasty S3. "Weapons. I really want to get my hands on a Benelli 12 gauge."

"I love it when you talk like that," Hayden joked. "This is better than Christmas," he said, carrying an armload of shotguns. "I wish we had more room."

"We can come back, can't we? I mean, it's not that far. We can make a twenty-four hour mission out of it."

"Yeah. We can. We will," he said. He looked me up and down when I emerged from behind the counter with three pistols and a .45. Blushing ever so slightly, he looked away. "I'll get ammo. Why don't you get arrows and any other archery thing you want? Keep an eye out."

"Will do." I hauled as many arrows as I could carry to the front door, putting them in the pile with our guns. Hayden, having already filled bags with bullets, was in the camping section. After bringing down several compound bows, three crossbows, and more arrows, I met up with him.

I had to run down to the registers and get more bags. We loaded them with camping gear. Leaving Hayden to get food, I went over to look at footwear. As stylish as my tall, leather boots were, they were not comfortable at all and had minimal traction.

I put on a pair of combat style hunting boots. They were comfortable and fit well over my jeans. Having left my good jacket on the forest floor in South Carolina, I was currently wearing one that came from the compound's supply. I stripped it off, decided I hated the ugly sweater I had on and went shopping for something new.

The red plaid shirt was soft. I put it on, liking how similar it was to my old shirt. It reminded me of the farm in Kentucky. I buttoned it halfway, slung the crossbow over my back, and picked up the M9.

"You look hot," Hayden said, appearing behind me.

I looked down at my redneck fashion. "Oh yeah, so hot." I smiled, thinking he was joking. I checked the sizes of jackets, hoping to find my size in the black Columbia coats I was looking at. "We should put this stuff in the truck and see how much room we have left."

"Good idea." He turned and strode off. We were able to go back for a few more weapons. I got more arrows and a few accessories, like arm guards and arrow rests. Hayden picked up a set of carbon arrows.

"Now I see why you like to get your arrows back. These are expensive," he told me.

We packed as much as we could into the truck, leaving room to work the machine gun if need be. Sitting on the tailgate, Hayden opened a bag of freeze dried cheesecake. He mixed it with water and waited.

"It has to sit for awhile. Want to go get our S3 blood while we wait?" he asked.

"Yeah, 'cuz that'll make me hungry."

We laughed, but went back inside to the camping section. Hayden handed me a rubber container with a tight fitting lid. He returned to my old woman.

I set the bowl down, pulled my knife and stopped. If I touched her, I would get covered in zombie ooze. *Really, Hayden should do this since I know he's immune*, I thought. After finding a pair of thick, leather gloves, I cut open the other wrist, holding it up by her fingers. I slid the bowl under and waited for the revolting blood to slime out of her dead veins.

I snapped the lid on the container and wiped the drips with the gloves. I put both containers inside a plastic shopping bag, tied it, and put it in another. We took our cheesecake to the dock behind the store. It was almost peaceful, sitting by the water next to Hayden, eating in silence.

"This isn't bad," he told me. "Maybe we should go back for more."

"Fine by me." I said, finishing my share. "And you're right. It's not as bad as I thought it would be."

Hayden took my hand when we stood. I felt something that was close to nerves when he looked into my eyes. Slowly, we walked down the dock. It was warmer here than at the compound, but still cold. Wishing I had put the jacket on instead of leaving it in the truck, I shivered. Quick to notice and respond, Hayden wrapped his arm around me.

"Orissa," he began.

"Hayden," I said in a similar tone, looking up at him with a smile.

"Orissa I want to te—"

I pushed out of his embrace, yanking the crossbow from around my neck. A crazy jumped out of a docked boat and ran full speed at us. Hayden drew his gun and fired before I had the chance. The crazy took one more step before splashing into the water.

"Dammit," I swore. "Couldn't he have died *on* the dock? I could have at least gotten a sample."

"Yeah," Hayden said, clicking the safety on his gun and putting it away. He ran his hand through his hair. "Too bad."

"What were you saying?"

"Uh, nothing. I don't, uh, even remember," he said distantly.

"Ok. Let's go."

"Yeah, we should find a pharmacy."

"Good plan. I want to get back to the compound and play with our new toys."

"Want to find a place to stay tonight?" he asked.

"Ideally."

"Something tells me this isn't a good place. It's too…too populated."

I nodded.

<hr>

We drove a few miles west trying to find a small and unpopulated town. When we didn't find one, Hayden said the truck would have to do for the night. We drove two hours south before pulling into an empty parking lot.

It was late and we were both tired. We kept the keys in the ignition so we could make a fast getaway. We couldn't rationalize why one of us would need to stay awake. It wasn't like we could easily see outside in the darkness anyway.

Bright sunlight woke me up. Hayden was still sleeping so I moved quietly. I scanned our surroundings for zombies. Not finding any, I opened the door and snuck out. I wandered a ways down, not wanting Hayden to wake up and see me squatting to pee.

We were in the parking lot of some sort of industrial building. It looked pretty new and high tech. Curious about what it was, I walked around to the front to read the sign.

"Charisma Industries," I read the sign out loud. "Don't be too descriptive, Charisma."

The sun was bright and warm. I rolled up my sleeves and walked through overgrown weeds around the rest of the building. I felt something that could only be described as warm and fuzzy when the black truck came into view.

Then the warm and fuzzy feeling turned into terror when I saw the truck ajar…without Hayden inside.

"Hayden!" I yelled, not even thinking of the repercussions of screaming.

"Orissa!" he shouted back and came running from around the building. "What the hell were you doing? I woke up and you were gone!" he spat, angrily.

"Sorry, I didn't want to wake you up."

"Oh, yeah, that's nice. Just sneak out in the middle of nowhere with God knows how many zombies milling about."

"I'm fine, ok? Chill."

"Don't tell me to chill. That was stupid!" he yelled.

"Well I guess I'm stupid then." Like a child, I got in the truck, slammed the door, and pouted. After a few seconds passed, Hayden opened the door.

"I shouldn't have yelled at you. I-I was scared. Scared something happened to you." He put his hands on my thighs.

"It's ok. I guess getting out like that was kinda dumb."

"Kinda?" he said with a half smile. "You're good, Riss, but you're not invincible."

"I beg to differ," I teased. "Want breakfast? I can make us some delicious freeze dried pancakes!" He nodded.

We ate, enjoying the sun, and quickly hit the road again. We both agreed to find a pharmacy sans zombies since neither of us felt like having to deal with a herd.

$$\longrightarrow$$

We were further south than we planned and came into a town that looked promising. The local drug store was family owned, and had big, glass front windows that weren't broken. A few zombies roamed the streets. Reminding me we hadn't gotten any S2 blood, Hayden shot them and extracted the syringes. The blood was thick, but not as bad as the S3. We were able to fill up two vials.

"I'm actually wishing for an S1," he said with a smirk.

"And now we won't find any."

"That's the trick then, we just have to want them to come."

"That's how life goes," I agreed. Hayden emptied the shelves of vitamins while I got the hygiene items. We loaded up the truck, relieved we had all the items on our list. We traveled around again, this time looking for S1s to kill.

The nice sized town we went into was full of zombies. Zombies ate S1s, so with this many, we figured it wouldn't be worth it to get out and look. We were thinking about stopping for lunch when I saw the weird symbol spray-painted on a door.

"What is that?" I asked Hayden, pointing to the black design.

"It looks like a house. Like something a child would draw."

He was right. The 'house' consisted of a square with a triangle roof. It was odd, but not worth investigating. Not until there was another symbol two houses down. It was the same black house. Hayden shrugged, not thinking it was important. Further down the street was a house with more markings on the door: two blue, squiggly lines. Two houses across the street and the one next to it had the same markings.

"Ok, now this is weird," Hayden admitted. He put the truck in park and looked at me. "Want to check it out?"

"Of course," I said, already unbuckling. "Keep driving. I see a red mark on that door," I told him, pointing to a house a few yards down the street. This one had a red X on the door. "They have to mean something," I speculated.

We went into the first house with the black marking. There was nothing out of the ordinary. It had been abandoned during the outbreak, stuff had been left behind and the doors unlocked.

"Hello?" I called out apprehensively. "Nothing, I hear nothing," I told Hayden, in case it wasn't obvious.

"Let's try the next house."

We walked down the street to the house with the blue squiggly lines. It was the same deal; nothing stood out. We went across the street. An empty bag of pretzels and several Coke cans littered the table. I went into the kitchen to have a closer look while Hayden stood guard out front.

I picked up the can and shook it. Little remnants of pop hit the side of the can. Someone had been here recently. I thought I heard something move above me. I waited, listening, annoyed with the dripping sink.

Wait! The sink dripped?

"Hayden!" I called and he came running. "Look!" I went over to the kitchen sink and turned on the faucet. Clean water poured out. As if it was something spectacular, we were unable to take our eyes from it. "It doesn't smell."

"Water isn't supposed to smell," Hayden stated.

"No, I mean the pipes. When you don't use water for awhile it smells."

Our eyes met. "Someone has been here." Hayden flicked on a light switch. The fan slowly started to turn. "There's power."

"Solar power?" I suggested.

"I didn't see any panels."

Again mesmerized, we watched the fan blades spin faster and faster. "Do you think they're still here?"

"Maybe."

We raced through the house to the streets. Hayden fired one shot in the air. If anyone was around, they'd hear it. We got in the truck and waited, drove a few miles down, fired, and waited again. Disappointed, Hayden let the truck coast to a stop.

"Hang on, go back," I said.

"Why?"

"I have a theory."

"A theory?"

"About the symbols."

We left the tuck; I took Hayden's hand, and excitedly pulled him into another house with blue lines. We went into the kitchen and turned on the sink. Fresh water came from the tap. "Blue lines mean water."

"You're right."

"What about the other markings?" I asked.

"I have no clue," he said as he ran his hand through his hair.

"There has to be people around, organized people, right?"

"I'd think so," he said. "People organized, armed, and smart enough to avoid getting eaten."

"Unless they died recently."

We walked around the house. Hayden stopped and looked around. "Something about this doesn't settle right. Let's get the S1 blood and go home."

"Ok," I agreed.

We had exhausted as much effort as we could looking for the makers of the marks. Back in the truck, we had to go over the map before we took off toward Arkansas. As good as I was in the woods, I failed at driving directions. Once we ran out of daylight, Hayden asked if I wanted to keep driving or stop for the night.

"I don't care," I told him. "We can stop if you'd like."

"Yeah," he said, smiling. "I'd like to."

Dinner was eaten on the tailgate under a clear Texas sky. It was so peaceful, if you didn't think about the virus plagued population. The night air was chilly, so we retreated back inside the cab and cranked the heat.

"Beer or wine," Hayden asked suddenly.

"Huh?"

"Which do you prefer?"

"Oh, beer."

"Showers or baths?" he asked next.

"Showers." I sighed. "What I wouldn't give to be naked and wet in a long, hot, steamy shower right now. Especially one that lasts longer than a few minutes." With a wistful smile, I turned to Hayden. He had an odd expression on his face. "What, no more questions?"

He cleared his throat. "No. I, uh, can't think of any."

"Ok," I laughed. "Maybe I can think of a few," I added, thinking he was playing this game to distract himself from thoughts of that campfire we'd seen in Texas not long ago. I knew it bothered him to think that there were people out there, wandering around in hell on earth when we could have brought them to safety. That didn't bother me as much as the weird symbols on the door. I thought of questions for a moment before asking, "Did you play sports in high school?"

"Football and wrestling."

"Were you any good?"

"Yes, but it was a small school. It was easy to be good. Did you do anything besides cheerleading and martial arts?"

"Not in school. I showed horses a few times. I never had much time, between going back and forth from my mom to my grandparents and being dropped off in the middle of nowhere."

Hayden chuckled. "I guess you have a point." Suddenly, he shot up.

"What is it?"

"I thought I saw something. Behind us, in the moonlight." He paused Tim McGraw on the iPod.

"How close behind us?" I asked, watching him study the review mirror.

"Close. Within reach of the tailgate close."

"Zombie?"

"It was fast."

"Oh! Maybe it's a crazy! We can get our blood samples."

"Maybe," he agreed.

"I'll check. I have to pee anyway."

"Riss, not yet. Hang on a second. There could be more than one."

"There's only one way to find out." I opened the door against Hayden's protests. "Hello?" I called to the darkness. I heard nothing but the sounds of the night. Hayden stepped out of the truck, his gun cocked.

"Do you see anything?" he asked.

"No. Nor do I hear anything."

"Get back in the truck. We can turn around and shine the brights."

"Let me pee first!"

"Fine. Don't go far. Stay on your side and keep the door open."

"Don't watch," I added.

"Wasn't planning on it," he said. Hayden relaxed considerably once I was in the truck and the doors were locked. We turned around, the headlights shining cones of white across the land. "Nothing," he mumbled. "I know I saw something."

"I believe you," I promised. "Anything infected would be coming at us right now. Maybe it was an animal."

"Maybe. It was tall and thin, though, like a person."

"Are there bears in Texas?" I suggested.

"I have no idea. And I'd know a bear when I saw one, Riss."

"Then maybe it was a ghost."

"That is the most logical explanation," he teased. "I bet it was from those dolls. It's followed us all this way. Now that we are alone, it's going to kill us."

"Damn it, I left my ghost killing kit at home."

"What's in a 'ghost killing kit,' dare I ask?"

"Uh, stuff you kill ghosts with, duh."

We laughed again.

"Want to go a few miles and stop again? I don't like not knowing what that was."

"Totally fine by me," I agreed.

We drove another few miles northeast. Since there was something questionable roaming about, we slept in shifts. Hayden took first watch, staying in the driver's seat in case we needed to make a fast getaway. Not wanting to squander fuel, we cuddled in our sleeping bags and cut the engine. We had about seven and half hours until the sun came up and agreed on four hours of sleep apiece. Six hours later, Hayden woke me up. I gave him crap for letting me sleep an extra two hours. He said he lost track of time and then changed his story to not being tired.

He climbed to the back before I moved into the front. I tossed my sleeping bag into the front and stood, ready to crawl over the center console. Something moved behind the truck, reflecting in the rearview mirror. I spun around so fast I lost my balance, hands flying out to catch myself. One hand landed on Hayden's shoulder.

"I thought I saw something," I whispered, looking out the rear window. Hayden's hand shyly landed on my back.

"I don't see anything now. Do you?"

I looked out front. "No." I turned back to Hayden, looking into his eyes. Suddenly, I didn't want to go into the front.

"Riss," he said and gently pushed me back. I could feel his heart speed up beneath my fingers. "Yeah?"

He moved his face up, as if he was going to kiss me. "There!" he said and quickly pulled away, hand flying to his gun. "There's definitely something there." I moved into the front seat and peered out the window.

"It's a zombie," I told him. "Just one...I think." I leaned forward and touched the keys, making sure they were dangling in the ignition before I cracked the door. The zombie looked up, attracted to the light. Hayden got out and knifed it in the head. We waited, making sure the zombie had really been alone.

About twenty minutes later, we settled back into the truck. Because Hayden quickly drifted to sleep, I knew his excuse of not being tired was a lie. Once he was sound asleep, I felt a little lonely. I pulled on my braid as I scanned the darkness, not liking that I couldn't see very far. I mentally kicked myself for not getting a pair of night vision goggles from the hunting section of the sporting goods store.

In the early light of morning, we took off, driving around until we found a promising looking town. It had been awhile since we'd crossed the Arkansas border. The parking lot of the movie theater wasn't overly crowded. The big, glass doors were broken; dry, brown blood streaked the insides.

"When this is over, no place of business is allowed to have glass doors," I told Hayden. "You know, since we will be in charge and all."

"Of course. Anything else you want to add to Orissa's Rules? What was the first one? Rude people will be fined?"

"Yup. Ooh! This is a good one. If you abuse an animal, the same exact abuse will be inflicted on you. Same goes for neglect. Leave your dog chained up outside with no water or shelter on a hot day? Well, now you can see how it feels."

"Eye for an eye, eh? You scare me," he joked.

"What would you change?" I asked as we carefully stepped over broken glass.

"Driving tests every ten years. Yeah, it's a pain in the ass but people seriously forget how to drive. Everything about healthcare and insurance. Ban all smoking. Zero tolerance for drinking and driving. No nuclear weapons. Oh, and make prostitution legal." He grinned. "I'm joking about the last one."

"You've thought about this."

"I haven't been happy with this country since Samael came into office." He stopped moving and put his finger to his lips. "Hear that?"

"Yeah. Behind the counter," I whispered. Weapons raised, we crossed the lobby and found rats in the popcorn. "Sick," I said. "I was hoping we could make some but not after this. Don't people get really sick from rat poop in food?"

"I would think any poop in food would make you sick," Hayden said so seriously it made me laugh.

My eyes fixated on the nest of rats. I didn't see the spilled stack of plastic lids until I slipped on them. Hayden caught me with breakneck speed. I wrapped my arms around his neck and let him pull me close. "Orissa," he began. "I might as well just spit it out now."

"Spit what out?" I asked.

I never heard the answer.

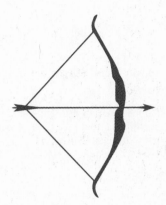

CHAPTER 34

A crazy came running at us, diving ungracefully over the counter. With one hand, Hayden cradled my head to his chest. With the other, he drew his gun, shot, and killed the bastard.

"Thanks," I said, almost breathless. It wasn't a close encounter by any means, but I wasn't ready to let Hayden go. After a few seconds, I forced myself away. "We should get the sample while it's fresh."

"Right. We should." He let me go and removed a vial from his pocket. "I'll do it," he offered. "Since it doesn't matter if I get blood on my hands."

"I have gloves," I reminded him.

He waved his hand, brushing me off and strode over to the body. He tipped his head, curiously examining the S1.

"You know, she looks *healthy*," he said.

"She's dead. How the hell is that healthy?"

"Look," he instructed.

I walked over. The crazy was a young adult female with blonde and pink hair, gauged ears, and a choker necklace. She was filthy and her clothes were worn and torn, but Hayden was right; her body was in good condition, well, aside from the hole in her head.

"How long do you think she's been infected?" I asked, nudging her leg with the crossbow.

"Going by her clothing, awhile. Going by her firm skin and rosy cheeks, not long."

"Maybe she was on the run and recently got bitten," I suggested.

"She's not wearing a coat," Hayden observed.

True, the girl had on a short, pleated skirt of black and red, ripped leggings, and a black, graphic T-shirt.

"I lost my coat in South Carolina," I reminded him.

"Right. I suppose it doesn't matter since she's dead."

"Yeah. Let's get the blood." I couldn't stop thinking about it. How had she remained in the S1 stage for such a long period of time? Based on Raeya's notes—and our general observation—crazies had a short shelf life. Hayden gripped her arm and shoved the needle in.

"You're not in a vein," I told him.

"Can't I pull the blood out from anywhere?"

"Maybe. Stick it in that blue line in her elbow," I suggested. During my drug-runner days, I saw my 'boyfriend' shoot up more than once. It was disgusting and terrifying and I still couldn't wrap my head around the idea of anyone doing something so stupid.

"Success," I said when Hayden capped the vial.

"Is this enough?" he asked.

"I'd say so. There will be more missions if it's not."

"Good, let's go."

"Do you want to see what's in there?" I motioned to the theater rooms.

"Not really." He put the vial in his vest pocket. "Come on; let's go."

"You're eager to leave," I commented.

"Aren't you?"

"Yeah, I guess." And I was. I liked the safety of the compound. I liked having a bed to sleep in, a shower to use, and my friends surrounding me. But I liked being alone with Hayden just as much. He winked at me and shot the glass front of the candy display.

"Going around was too much effort," he explained, reaching through the broken glass. "What's your favorite?"

"Sour Patch Kids."

He tossed me three boxes. With our arms full of candy, we walked back to the truck. "Do you smell that?" Hayden asked, looking alarmed.

I sniffed the air. "Yeah. It smells like cigarettes."

He dumped the candy in the bed of the truck and drew his gun. "Someone's here."

I followed suit, spinning in a slow circle. "I don't see anyone."

He got into the bed and scanned the horizon. "Neither do I. Hello!" he yelled. His voice echoed across the abandoned plaza.

"We come in peace!" I added. I held my breath as I waited, positive someone would come running, white flag waving.

But no one did. No humans at least. A massive herd of zombies staggered out of the shadows.

Hayden sprang to position. He fired up the machine gun and rained a storm of metal death on the zombies. I fired every magazine I had. There had to be fifty or more. They just kept coming. When they were less than twenty yards away, we got in the truck. Hayden reached for the ignition.

The keys weren't there.

"If you lost the keys, I'll kill you," I threatened, watching with wide eyes as the herd was just feet away. Frantically, he felt his pockets. I let out a breath of relief when he fished them out. The horses revved to life. He stomped on the gas and we took off.

"I can breathe now," he only half joked when we were a safe distance away. "Actually, I'm getting used to these close calls."

"Me too, sadly."

"We should leave sooner next time," he told me.

"Yeah," I agreed. "Though it's hard to stop killing them."

"Eliminating the virus, one zombie at a time," he said in a funny, deep voice. Only a few miles away from the compound, we decided to stop and have one last meal together in the openness. We stopped in the middle of a forgotten field, overgrown with weedy, dry grass. Hayden pulled the tailgate down. We hopped up, sitting on opposite sides of the mounted machine gun. The field reminded me of Kentucky. It wasn't huge—only ten acres at the most and was surrounded by trees. The sun warmed the cold air and birds noisily chattered in the neighboring trees.

We polished off another freeze-dried cheesecake and sat in silence, enjoying each other's company and the freedom the farmland offered. Hayden gathered up our dishes, debated on whether or not to toss them on the ground, and ended up shoving them to the side of the truck bed. Littering seemed so minor compared to everything that was happening, but it was something neither of us wanted to do. Someday, this would be someone's field again, we hoped.

"Orissa," Hayden said, his hazel eyes locking with mine as he stood. That familiar feeling sent a chill down my spine. This time, I wasn't anxious. I knew what he was going to say and I wanted to hear it. I smiled when I realized what that feeling entailed.

Being with Hayden gave me hope and made me see that the world wasn't a worthless piece of shit after all. With him, I had a reason to keep living. If anyone could make me feel that, it was him.

And only him.

He moved closer and my heart sped up. "Orissa, I shouldn't have waited…" his voice trailed off and a look of horror spread across his face.

A red dot hovered over my chest. I froze, abhorrence radiating through my body, heart pounding. My eyes flitted to Hayden. For a split second, he held my gaze, unmoving.

And then he jumped.

If anyone was going to die, it should have been me. I was no hero, no warrior. I had no true importance to the compound, could never make a big difference. I would not let him take a bullet for me.

But I was too late. The shot rang out, echoing through the barren field, splattering Hayden's blood across my face.

TO BE CONTINUED…

THE CONTAGIUM SERIES: BOOK TWO

DEATHLY CONTAGIOUS

a novel by
EMILY GOODWIN

To Megan:

You are a wonderful friend. The world needs to know how amazing you are.

"The belief in a supernatural source of evil is not necessary.
Men alone are quite capable of every wickedness."
-Joseph Conrad

Zombie Notes
by Raeya Kingsley

Stages:
Crazy (S1) – Still alive but possess little human emotion. Fast, strong, and sneaky; pose the biggest threat.
Zombie (S2) – Slower than crazies but can still run after prey. Rot and decay has set in; you can smell them before you see them.
Gummy (S3) – very deteriorated zombies, are usually so slow and rotten they are easy to kill

Helpful notes:
Crazies can be used to distract zombies, it seems that zombies are unable to tell if an individual is infected or not. Crazies (luckily) are loaners where zombies and gummies travel in herds. A crazy can be killed in any way a non-infected human can but zombies and gummies can only be killed with brain damage. Tennis rackets are effective in taking out a gummy.

PART I

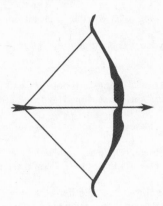

CHAPTER 1

A red dot hovered over my chest. I froze, abhorrence radiating through my body, heart pounding. My eyes flitted to Hayden. For a split second, he held my gaze, unmoving.

And then he jumped.

If anyone was to die, it should be me. I was no hero, no warrior. I had no true importance to the compound, could never make a big difference. I would not let him take a bullet for me.

But I was too late. The shot rang out, echoing throughout the barren field, splattering Hayden's blood across my face.

"Hayden!" I screamed, my body frozen in absolute terror. "Hayden!" I pulled my gun and blindly fired in the direction the shot came from as I clutched his body. "Hayden!" I cried. Unable to hold him up, I sunk to the ground. His warm blood gushed and stained my skin. The bullet had hit him between his shoulder and his neck. "No, Hayden…Hayden!" My body shook. I emptied my magazine, dropped the gun, and wrapped my arms around my Marine's body, crying.

I repeated his name between sobs as if that would make things better. I nuzzled my head against him, barely able to breathe. I didn't want to go on without him. I didn't think I could. All I wanted was to feel my fist crush every bone in the face of the person who shot Hayden. Then I wanted to die too.

I had no idea Hayden was alive until his fingers tightened around my wrist. In a true panic, I flipped him over. His eyes were open and locked with mine.

"Ohmygod, ohmygod," I stammered. "Hayden." There was so much blood. The entire front of his jacket was red. With shaking hands, I unzipped it to find the bullet hole. I screamed when another shot was fired. It ricocheted off the tailgate.

"I have to get you in the truck," I told him, tears still falling down my face. "You're gonna be ok, you're gonna be ok," I incoherently repeated over and over.

"Orissa," Hayden mumbled as he reached for me. His fingers brushed my cheek. He tried to sit up but winced. I was completely hysterical. Feebly, he put his right arm around me and tried to help me hoist him up. Finally, I got him to his feet. I wrapped both arms around Hayden and dragged him to the passenger side. I opened the door and he fell into the truck. I slammed the door shut and dove around into the driver's seat.

The keys were in the ignition. I slammed my foot on the gas as soon as the engine revved. We needed to get away. I needed to stop the bleeding. I looked at Hayden, forgetting that I was driving.

"Riss, drive," he muttered. "Don't let them follow you!" And then he was silent.

I drove with one hand and kept the other pressed to the bullet wound. He had been shot between his neck and his shoulder on the left side. A sob escaped my lips.

"You're gonna be ok. I'm not going to let you die," I promised, my voice coming out uneven as I tried to breathe.

Breathe? It didn't look like Hayden was breathing...

We were almost there. Hayden was going to be ok. He had to be. The gate came into view. Stopping to open it would waste precious time—time Hayden didn't have. I slammed the pedal down and drove right through it.

The A3s at the second gate didn't know what to do. I laid on the horn, yelling at them to open the gate. I rolled down the window.

"What the fuck is the matter with you? Open the goddamn gate!" I clamored. Jason's familiar face flashed in the tower. The gate opened and I sped past. I could see them running after me but didn't care. I needed to save Hayden.

Cars weren't supposed to drive close to the old house. Maybe it was because of the compound underground. I didn't know; I didn't care. I stopped just feet away from the front door. Leaving the truck running, I got out and raced to Hayden's side. I tore open the door and put my arms around him, trying to ease him to the ground.

His body was cold. I felt like I was going to puke. Why wasn't anyone helping me? I wanted to scream. I made it five feet before I collapsed under Hayden's weight. I struggled to my feet, cradling him against me.

"Orissa," a voice called from behind me. I turned to see an A3 running at us.

A3s were different than A1s. Everyone in the 'A' group was trained to defend the compound in some way or another. A3s did basic guard duty—not too dangerous but very necessary. They stood watch around the fences and the gate that led in and out of the shelter. A2s patrolled the farm and fields, a job with a bit more risk than the A3s. And A1s—which Hayden and I were—faced the most danger. We went on missions, leaving the safety of the compound, in search of food and supplies, taking in other survivors, and killing as many zombies as we could.

"Help me get him inside!" I demanded, on the verge of hyperventilating. Someone put their hands on my shoulders. Thinking the two guys might lift him, I backed off. The A3 rushed to Hayden, dropping to the ground and looking at his body. Jason pulled me a few feet back.

"Orissa, I...let's get you in...inside," he stammered.

"No, I have to save him!" I cried out, pulling away from him. Jason tightened his grip.

"Let them," he suggested quickly.

I sunk to the ground, crying. The whole thing played through my mind. If Hayden had time to jump in front of me, then I had time to move away. It was my fault. I was mad at him for being so stupid. I wasn't worth dying for.

"What a shame," the unknown A3 said to his buddy. "Underwood was the best."

"Yeah, should we tell Fuller now? He'll want to know before we burn the body."

My blood boiled. "What?" I screeched, madly rising to my feet. Jason tried to hold me back, but I easily elbowed him in the ribs. "He's not dead!" I stumbled over, protectively holding onto Hayden's body. "He wasn't bitten! He's not dead!"

"Orissa," the first A3 started. He looked like he might burst into tears at any second. "I'm so, so sorry."

"No!" I yelled. "Go get help! Go get Padraic. He can fix this. Hayden's not dead!" The two A3s didn't move. I pulled a small pistol from Hayden's ankle holster and pointed it at them. "Go!" I shouted. "He's not dead!"

Jason moved over, his hand extended. "Oris..."

"No!" I screamed, turning the gun on him. "Don't touch him! He's not dead!"

Jason put his hands up and froze. I turned back to Hayden, burying my head against him, unable to catch my breath. I had no sense of time. Seconds or minutes could have passed before they came running out. Ivan got there first, dropping to his knees next to Hayden.

"He's not dead!" I yelled at him, though he wasn't telling me otherwise. He pressed his fingers to Hayden's neck. I looked at him; his eyes were wide as he desperately attempted to find a pulse.

Without explanation, Ivan and Brock lifted Hayden up. Wade put his arm around me, having to help me walk since my legs suddenly turned to noodles and could hardly hold me up. Padraic ran down the hall, meeting us halfway. He ushered the guys into the exam room, closing the door in my face.

I pounded against it, demanding I be let in.

I heard Padraic bellow, "Start compressions."

"Why?" a frantic voice asked incredulously. "He's gone! Padraic, he's...he's gone!"

I banged on the door harder, drowning out their voices. I *needed* to go in. I *needed* to know what was going on with Hayden. He couldn't be gone. No...he wasn't. My fists dropped to my waist, and I suddenly felt weak.

How the fuck did this happen? How did we come to this?

I took a step back, blinking away the dots that speckled my vision. If my stupid appendix didn't need to be removed, I wouldn't have met Padraic, Jason, Sonja...or Zoe. Zoe! The little girl who had died of cancer right in the middle of the apocalypse. Unwelcome tears stung the corners of my eyes. All the people we had lost—including a man who reminded me of my grandfather—and now Hayden!

If I hadn't gotten sick I wouldn't have had to wait to go to Purdue University to rescue my best friend, Raeya. I wouldn't have to wonder what happened to my aunt Jenny or my grandpa. We could have gotten to the Kentucky farm in time and been safe from the zombies that roamed the earth. We would have never ended up with a band of survivors holed up in an underground base run by military personnel—Marines and army who had come together under a united entity along with a group of civilian survivors.

But if none of these things had happened, I never would have met Hayden...

I looked at the door. *Hayden*. He was bleeding to death—if not dead already—and it was my fault. I wrapped my bloodstained hands on the handle and turned it, trying to bust the lock. Wade tried to subdue me. I pushed and swatted him away. Ignoring my attempts to seriously hurt him, Wade patiently let me scream and hit the door for a few minutes before he put his arms around me and picked me up. He carried me into another exam room where Dr. Cara was waiting with a syringe. Before I knew what was happening, she plunged the needle into my shoulder. Something cold rushed into my vein, burning as it coursed through my body. I screamed and protested, hitting Wade in the face more than once. Then everything went black.

------------------------->

When I woke, I immediately knew what was going on. My brain was fuzzy and I had little control over my body. I swung my legs over the hard, foam bed and fell onto the floor. Ivan, who was sitting in a chair by the door, got up to help me.

"Freak out and you'll get another shot," he warned me. "Doctor Cara's orders, not mine," he added. His face was grim. I felt sick.

"Is he ok?" I asked, my voice barely above a whisper.

"He's still in surgery," he responded. "Another surgery now. He just keeps..."

"What does that mean?" I asked as Ivan helped me back on the bed. I hated being drugged.

"He lost a lot of blood."

"But...?"

"But he's not conscious yet. We don't know if that much blood loss...losing that much blood can mess up a lot of things."

"No shit, Ivan. What are you getting at?"

"They don't know."

"So he's ok?"

"I don't know, Orissa. I'm waiting, just like you." He sat next to me and sighed heavily. "What happened?"

"We were eating. Someone fired at us from the trees. I...I don't know where they came from."

"This wasn't an accident?" he asked, taken aback.

"You think I shot him?"

"Well...no, I didn't think...I'm sorry I even possessed that thought. What happened?"

"We thought we saw someone that night. I think we were followed."

"Followed?"

"Oh God," I breathed, suddenly realizing the importance of Hayden's last request: *don't let them follow you.* I closed my eyes in a long blink and the memory of sitting on the back of Hayden's truck flashed before me. We had just collected the samples for Dr. Cara and were headed back here. We should be in the quarantine room right now, not in the hospital ward. Maybe then I'd know what Hayden was trying to say. He'd been trying to tell me something, just before he was shot.

"The guys that shot him…they could have followed us," I said. Horrified, I looked at Ivan. He jumped up, told me he'd be right back, and raced out of the room.

The samples we'd been trying to collect for Dr. Cara were blood from the S1, S2 and S3. These were the names assigned to zombies based on certain criteria. A freshly infected S1—or crazy, as Raeya liked to call them—were the most dangerous. They were very much alive, and liked very much to rip into human flesh and eat fresh meat. The virus made them into homicidal cannibals. Pain and fear didn't register in their infected minds anymore. The only way to fight them off was by killing them.

The virus progressed into the zombie stage, more properly called S2s. Then, as they deteriorated, their skin slothed off and their movements slowed even more as their bodies rotted. Raeya liked to call the S3s 'gummies' since they were, in fact, usually sticky and gummy.

I wiggled my toes, trying to force feeling and control back into my legs. I got to the point of being able to extend my knees when Ivan came back in.

"Rider, Brock, and Wade are taking care of it," he told me. "If anyone followed you here, they'll be dead soon."

"Save them for me," I sneered, attempting to get up again. I wobbled, my legs unsteady as if they were asleep. What the hell did Doctor Cara give me?

"Sit back down," Ivan said shortly.

"I can't just sit here while he's in there."

"It's hard, I know."

"No, I don't think you do," I spat, suddenly annoyed at how calm he was. "You don't know what it's like to—"

"Orissa, he's my friend too," he stressed. "If we go in there, we'd be in the way. Padraic will get us when Hayden's stable."

"When," I repeated. Not *if.* Hayden was going to be ok. Padraic might be the only doctor I really knew, but I had no doubt in him. I nodded and leaned against the bed. Hayden was going to be ok, I told myself again. He was. He had to be.

I should have moved out of the way. Instead, I sat there like a dumbass deer in headlights. I felt like a failure. I let Hayden get hurt—possibly lethally. If he died, I'd never forgive myself. A hard ball of fear formed in my heart as well as my stomach. I realized that simply avoiding a lifetime of guilt was not the only reason I desperately wanted Hayden to live. The thought was almost equally as terrifying.

Ivan stood, distracting me from my complicated thoughts. He walked over to the counter, opened one of the cabinets, and tossed a thin, white sheet to me.

"You're shivering," he stated. "I think you're in shock."

"No, I'm just cold," I retorted but gladly took the sheet.

"It's ok, ya know, to admit you're scared."

"I'm not scared," I said, knowing that it was a horrible attempt at a lie. "Ok, I am."

"Me too," he said softly. He leaned against the bed and sighed. "The tunnel's open," he said rather suddenly.

I looked at him dubiously.

"Oh, you don't know," he went on. "There's a tunnel that goes from the weapon storage room out to the fields. It was blocked off. Now it's open."

"Don't try and change the subject. It won't work."

"Alright," he said softly.

Neither of us spoke while the minutes painfully ticked past. When I heard someone grasp the door knob, I jumped off the bed. Thankfully my legs were functioning again.

Fuller looked stricken when he walked in. He nodded at Ivan and frowned at me. I felt like someone dumped a bucket of ice water over my head. My heart plummeted to the ground. My ears rang and I felt weak.

"He's alive," Fuller informed us, taking in our horrified faces. "He's alive...for now."

I had to put a hand on the bed to keep from falling.

"Barely," he continued. I could tell Fuller was working hard to choke back his own emotions. He cleared his throat. "Orissa, come with me."

"No," I said simply.

Fuller's face twitched slightly. "That's an order."

"I'm not a soldier or a Marine," I countered. "I'm not leaving."

"I'm not taking you away," he affirmed. "I need to know what happened."

"I can tell you here," I pointed out. Without waiting for him to argue I said, "We were eating, sitting on the tailgate. Someone shot at us. Hayden got hit. I got Hayden into the truck and floored it all the way here. We didn't see anyone. They were hiding in the woods."

Fuller nodded and swallowed hard. "Do you have any idea why someone would shoot at you?"

"A necrophiliac wanted a fresh body? I have no clue. As I said, we didn't even see them."

Fuller nodded again, taken aback by my statement. He made a big deal over looking at his watch. "You need to go to the quarantine room."

"Fuck off. I'm not going."

"Excuse me?"

Ivan stood. "Sir, I think she's in shock. She's obviously not thinking clearly."

"I can see that," Fuller said. "Orissa," he said gently. "It is a rule. You of all people should understand."

"I'm not going," I repeated. "I'm staying here until Hayden's ok."

"That...that might be a while." Fuller's eyes became glossy.

"I can wait."

"You can wait in the quarantine."

"No. I wasn't bitten. Here," I said, unbuttoning my shirt. "Look me over. You'll see."

Afraid I was going to get myself into trouble, Ivan stepped in again. "Orissa, how about we wait and talk to Padraic, then go into the quarantine?"

"Maybe," I agreed just to get them off my case. "Yes. I can do that." I watched Fuller and Ivan exchange worried glances. Finally, Fuller agreed. He pulled Ivan aside, spoke quickly and quietly to him, and left the room.

"You sure you're alright, Penwell?" Ivan asked again.

"Are you really asking me that right now?" I said incredulously.

"Sorry, dumb question. It's just I've never seen you...freak out like this."

I was too worried to be embarrassed. "Well, what would you do?"

"I'd probably wig out just as much. But I'd never tell Fuller to fuck off," he said with a chuckle.

I shrugged and started picking at the dried blood I was covered in.

"You want to shower?" he asked.

"No," I said. "I'm not leaving. I want to be here when Hayden wakes up."

Ivan nodded, his eyes narrowing in question. "You really care about him, don't you?"

"Of course. He's my friend and partner."

"Just that?" he asked suggestively.

I shook my head and sunk down in the chair. I didn't look up or speak until the door opened again...

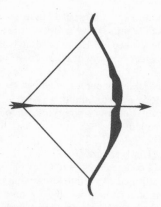

CHAPTER 2

Dressed in bloody scrubs, Padraic smiled weakly at me. "Riss," he breathed.

I rushed over to him. I wasn't expecting him to envelope me in his arms the way he did. The warmth from his body was comforting. I hugged him back, feeling emotional.

"Is he ok?" I asked with my head against Padraic's firm chest.

"He's not stable," he responded. "I can't keep him stable."

I let him go and blinked. "And that means?"

"He's not conscious. I can't do a full assessment yet. His vital signs aren't what they should be and...I...I did the best I could."

"The best you could?" My heart raced again.

Padraic stepped into the room and faltered. I reached out for him, catching him before he fell.

"Sorry," he mumbled. "I had to give blood."

I led him to the chair and knelt down next to him. Once he was sitting, I continued. "You gave your own blood?"

Padraic nodded. "So did Jason. We're the same blood type. I didn't trust anyone else's blood to be clean enough."

I put my hand on Padraic's knee and waited for him to continue.

"I got all the bullet fragments out. I did the best I could given what I have."

"What does that *mean*?" Ivan asked. I felt him pacing behind me, wanting to hear and not wanting to hear.

"This place isn't equipped for surgery. I can't tell if nerve damage was done just by looking. I'd normally order an MRI plus a slew of other tests and labs. There aren't even IV pumps here. I can't tell you the extent of the damage because I don't know."

"Can I see him?" I asked suddenly.

"He's not awake."

"That's ok."

Padraic's blue eyes met mine for a second. "No."

"Why not?"

"First off, he needn't be disturbed. And," he said before I could protest, "you're dirty. After a normal surgery in a sterile environment, we keep outside contact to a minimum. The conditions here are less than ideal."

I couldn't argue. "What if I shower?"

"Tomorrow, alright?" Padraic mumbled, looking too tired to fight with me.

"I want to be there when he wakes up," I admitted, feeling my cheeks redden. "To thank him for saving my life."

"*If* he wakes up…it won't be for a while. *If*!" Padraic told me. "These first few hours are the most crucial. Orissa, I want you to be prepared for…"

"He's strong," Ivan said. "He's strong and…" He didn't finish, but continued pacing.

I nodded, not knowing what else to say.

Ivan strode over to Padraic. He extended his hand. "Thank you," he said seriously and shook the Irish doctor's hand. "We are lucky to have you with us."

Taken off guard, Padraic dumbly nodded.

Ivan said he'd be right back and slipped out the door.

I extended my hand to Padraic, pulling him to his feet. We walked to the door.

"You look exhausted," I told him.

"I am," he sighed.

"You should go to bed."

"You should too."

"You know I can't sleep when I'm stressed," I said with a wry smile. I slowly walked down the hall with Padraic. "Are you gonna be ok?" I asked.

"Yes," he assured me. "I'll be better in the morning."

"Ok." We stopped in front of his room. "Padraic, thank you."

He smiled slightly. "It's what I do, Riss."

"I know, but…all I could think about was getting him back here to you. I knew you'd be the one to save him."

Padraic didn't look at me. "Thanks, I suppose." He cast his eyes to the ground. "He asked for you," Padraic said softly.

"What?"

"The first time he was stabilized before…before he crashed again. He asked if you were ok."

Something sparked inside me. The corners of my lips twitched as if they wanted to smile. I shook my head and scraped blood from under my fingernails.

Fuller gave me permission to take my best friend Raeya with me to the quarantine room that night, and he gave us a few minutes to gather our things. Raeya and I detoured to her room. We walked slowly, avoiding the curious stares from the compound residents.

"What happened, Riss?" she asked when we got to her room. I eyed the door. Taking my hint, she opened it. She flicked on the light and sat on her bed. Since I was covered in blood, I remained standing.

"It started in Texas," I confessed. "We found these houses with symbols on them. And they had electricity and running water." I closed my eyes, vividly remembering the fan blades moving. "We knew someone was around so we went looking but didn't find anyone. That night, Hayden said he thought he saw someone outside the truck."

"What do you mean?"

"A shadow or something. I didn't see it." I shook my head. "But then nothing happened, well, nothing with humans. We got the samples—which are still in the truck—and were on our way home. Wait," I paused, going over the memories.

"What is it?"

"Smoke. We smelled cigarette smoke." I closed my eyes again, mentally cursing myself for being so incredibly dumb. "They followed us and waited until we were vulnerable."

"How were you vulnerable?"

"We were eating and talking. That's when I saw the laser."

"Laser?"

"You know, like in movies when the gun has a laser pointer?"

"Oh, yeah."

"It settled right over my heart. I didn't know what to do. No matter which way I moved, I was dead,

I just knew it. And then Hayden jumped." Tears pricked my eyes. I felt so guilty.

"I'm glad you're ok," Raeya said. "He was very brave, saving your life."

"Yeah, and stupid," I added. I sighed. It was a relief to admit the whole truth to someone. I took in a ragged breath.

Raeya put her hand on mine. "He didn't take a bullet for you just to die," Ray tried to convince me. She smiled broadly. "I told you he liked you."

"Shut up, Ray," I said, struggling to stay serious. "Hayden is a Marine. He'd do that for anyone."

"Ohmygod, Riss, will you just adm—"

I closed my eyes and shook my head; I was losing it. "I should go shower," I said and made an exit, motioning Raeya to follow. She accompanied me to my room to get my pajamas.

She was impressed and slightly jealous of the quarantine room. She played around with everything in it while I showered.

It surprised me how tired I was when I sank down on the couch after showering. It wasn't long before I fell asleep.

$$\longrightarrow$$

I was bombarded with questions during my first meal with the rest of the compound. I was polite to the first three people who asked about it before I snapped and told everyone to fuck off and leave me alone. After I ate, I went up to my room, picked out clean clothes, and showered, scrubbing myself thoroughly with soap. Then I marched down to the hospital ward.

"Hello, Orissa," a nurse said. She was the same nurse who had taken care of me the first time I set foot in the compound. I glanced at her name badge.

"Hi, Karen. How's Hayden?" I asked nervously, pulling and snapping the band around my braid.

"No change," she told me.

"Can I go in there? I'm clean," I added.

"Actually, that would be nice."

I eagerly nodded and followed her into the sick ward. She stopped inside the room and motioned to the sink. "I know you said you're clean, so don't take offense. But can you please wash your hands?"

"Yeah," I easily agreed. "Where's Padraic?" I asked as I scrubbed my hands clean.

"Sleeping, hopefully. He was up all night."

"Oh. It's ok for Hayden…if he wakes up and Padraic isn't here?" I asked, not caring if I offended her.

"Yes," she said patiently. "I'll be there and, honestly, there isn't much else we can do other than wait and see."

Karen led me down the row of beds. Hayden was at the end, and the curtain was pulled around his area. When Karen pulled it back for me, I was shocked. Hayden just lay there, looking gray and lifeless. The head of the bed was slightly elevated, and Hayden's left arm was taped in place to his bare chest and resting on a pillow. Gauze covered the incision and an IV was hooked up to his right arm. His eyes were closed and his skin was pale; he looked nothing like the way I was used to seeing him. I made myself go forward.

"You're alright with blood, aren't you?" Karen asked me. I nodded. "Good. I'm going to clean the wound before he wakes up."

I simply nodded again and pulled up a chair. My fingers graced Hayden's hand, careful to avoid the IV line. His skin was cold. I watched as she took the gauze off the bullet wound. My stomach churned when I saw the damage done to Hayden.

I linked my fingers with his and closed my eyes. After she was done, Karen looked at her watch. She smiled, told me she'd be nearby, and left us.

Gently, I ran my fingers through Hayden's hair. There was so much I wanted to say to him when he woke up. I wanted to tell him that he was stupid for letting himself get shot because I would have been alright. I smiled to myself, thinking of the dubious stare he'd give me when he heard that.

"Hayden," I said softly. "Can you hear me?" I continued to run my fingers through his hair until Karen came back in to take his vital signs. She jotted them down on a clipboard and told me his blood pressure was too low again.

"You can talk to him," she suggested. "I've had a lot of patients tell me that they remember voices when they were in comas."

"Ok," I said, not really knowing what to say. "Hayden," I spoke quietly. "It's Orissa. Thanks for saving me, though it was really stupid. You shouldn't have gotten hurt just for me; I'm not worth it. And I would have been fine on my own, you know." I put my hand over his. "Everyone's really worried about you," I went on to say. "You better heal fast, cuz I don't want to get stuck with someone stupid. You and me, remember? We're the best zombie killers."

I smiled and blinked back tears. "You'll be okay," I told him. "You have to be." I ran my fingers through his hair again, unable to keep a tear from rolling down my cheek.

Wake up, Hayden. Please. Why won't you wake up?

→

Brock, Wade, Ivan, and Rider came back that evening. They had found the guys who were following us. Along with Ivan, the five of us crowded into Fuller's office. I sat across from Fuller with Wade at my back, Brock sat beside me and Rider leaned against the far wall with his head in his hand.

"There were four," Brock explained, raising his head, "in a black Mustang, '69 by the looks of it. Nicely restored but odd to be driving given the zombies. We found them ten miles from here." He paused, looking at Wade and Rider.

"They opened fire right away," he continued. "We had no choice but to take them down. One got away, but he got clipped in the leg first. He won't make it long; I bet he's dead already. Especially on his own, since he was used to running with others. When we examined the bodies, all three had the same tattoo of a skull wearing a crown. It was painted on the door of the Mustang as well."

"Gang members," I speculated.

"Yeah," Rider said. "One of them had 'Imperial Lords' tattooed on his back."

"Now what?" I asked, mad I didn't get to feel my fist crush the cheek bones of the bastards who shot Hayden.

"They're dead," Wade said, giving me a look like I just asked the world's dumbest question.

"We've come across gangs and small groups before," Brock explained. "They've never shot at us, and they've never wanted to come to the compound. Can you think of anything that would have made them want to shoot you guys?"

"The back of the truck is full of weapons," I stated. "We raided a hunting and camping store. Maybe they were...desperate for supplies or something. Plus Hayden's truck...you know, with the mounted machine gun? It does come in handy."

There was a murmur of agreement. Fuller sat up and looked at Ivan. "Bring in the weapons and have them inventoried. Have someone check the fuel supply and report back to me."

"So that's it? We just carry on as if nothing happened?" I interjected.

"Yes," Fuller ordered. "They *are* dead, Penwell. But we aren't. We have to carry on if we want to keep it that way."

I crossed my arms. I didn't know what I expected Fuller to do, but leaving the bodies of Hayden's shooters on the side of the road to get eaten by zombies was just so anticlimactic. I stared Fuller down and left the room.

Four members made a small gang. What if there are others?

→

Since I wasn't allowed to see Hayden again, per Padraic, I spent the rest of the evening with Raeya. I stayed with her until she was ready to go to sleep; I didn't want to be in my room alone. Seeing Hayden's empty bed—yes, as A1s the two of us had been assigned to share a room—was something I wasn't ready to do.

I didn't go to training the next day. I wandered the halls, stopping by the hospital ward enough to annoy Padraic. This stop, his brow was furrowed with worry as he rooted around through the dwindling medications.

"What's up doc?" I asked, leaning against the counter.

"Orissa, hi," he said in a monotone voice. It was the third time I had stopped by to check on

Hayden that morning. He still hadn't opened his eyes. According to Padraic, if Hayden hadn't woken by now, there was a good chance he wouldn't. But I didn't want to believe that. I *refused* to believe that.

"What are you looking for?" I had also become incredibly nosy; I wanted to know what was going on with Hayden at all times.

"Medication, a certain medication." He moved one box aside and tore through another. Then he went for the cabinets.

"Morphine?"

"No," he said shortly, taking a bottle down and reading the label. "Antibiotics."

"Hayden?"

"He...I don't..." Padraic stopped and sat down hard on one of the boxes. "Orissa, I'm sorry. Hayden is sick. I don't have what I need to take care of him. I...I think it's best if you stay close, just in case..."

No. No fucking way I believed that. There had to be another way.

"An infection is the last thing he needs," Padraic sighed and ran his hands over his face. Dark circles were prominent under his eyes.

"You need to sleep," I told him,

"I need to take care of my patient."

"Can I help?"

"Yeah, if you can get me some Cipro," he said with a slight laugh.

"I can," I said, straightening up. "I can get anything. Just tell me where I'd find it."

Padraic looked at me unblinking. "You shouldn't go out on another mission right now."

"Why not?"

"You went on two in a row."

"So?"

"So," he said exasperated, "maybe you should stay here a while. Luck hasn't been on your side."

"Yes it has. I wasn't the one who got shot. And I don't think luck has anything to do with anything anymore, Padraic." I stared him down. He shook his head and sighed again. I strode past him and uncapped a pen. "Tell me what you need. I'll give the list to Fuller. He's the one who has the say on if I'd go or not." I didn't care what Fuller said. I was going no matter what. I would be faster than everyone. I would make sure they hurried. I would do it for Hayden.

Padraic hesitated. "Fine. Cipro," he said. "And benzodiazepine." He had to spell that one out for me and went on to rattle off a few more medical items. "There's actually a lot we could use here," he started. "Equipment, like IV pumps and vital sign monitors."

"I'll write them down too," I told him and listened intently as Padraic described what we needed. I was unable to pronounce most of the items.

I folded the list and stuck it in my pocket. "Can I see him?"

Padraic shook his head before giving in. "Five minutes. He needs to rest." He stood and took my hands in his, "Orissa, listen...If you go on this mission, I can't promise that he'll still be here. I don't know that he'll still be alive when you get..."

"No!" I shook my head and pulled my hands away. "Just no!"

I went to the sink, rolled up my sleeves, and washed my hands before going into the sick wing. I walked around the curtain, still angry at Padraic. How could he say something like that? Hayden was going to make it. I was going to get him medicine, and he would get better.

"Hey," I said softly and sat on the chair by the bed. I put my hand on top of Hayden's. His skin wasn't as cold as before. But he still looked awful. I swallowed the lump that was rising in my throat.

"I'm going to get you medicine," I told Hayden. "It won't take long. Padraic told me what to get and it will clear the infection. You'll be able to wake up and start healing."

I ran my fingers up his arm, tracing the outline of his tattoo. I wiped away tears with the back of my hand, feeling guilty and heartbroken. I hated seeing Hayden like this.

"I miss you," I confessed when a wave of emotion crashed over me. "Please be awake by the time I get back."

I sat with Hayden for a few more minutes then got up to leave.

I ran into Dr. Cara on my way to the C level. The underground compound was broken up into floors. The 'C level' housed our living areas and most of the sleeping quarters. The next level down was called the 'B level' since anyone working in the hospital ward was assigned to the B category.

"Thanks for the samples," she said, her voice monotone.

"Oh, yeah," I told her. I had forgotten about them until now. "You got them already?"

"Yes. Blood doesn't stay fresh. I had to test them right away. I might need more."

I nodded curtly and took a step forward, but Cara grabbed my arm. She flipped it over and ran a finger over the vein in my wrist.

"Can I have some blood?"

"Uh, sure."

Her thin lips pressed into a smile and she motioned for me to follow her back into the hospital ward. My eyes scanned the door that separated me from Hayden.

"Hayden won't last too long with that infection setting in. The vaccine is in jeopardy."

I didn't try to hide my 'why the fuck would you say that?' expression. Hayden was right: Dr. Cara was so socially awkward. She snapped on rubber gloves, hastily rubbed a cotton ball of alcohol over my arm, and slid the needle into my vein. I watched the deep scarlet blood rush into the vial.

"Are you getting any closer to finding a vaccine?" I asked, knowing the answer would most likely be 'no.'

"Possibly. I've found some similarities between Hayden and Parker's blood, but they're not identical. I need both. I'm gonna need both for quite awhile. When I have the samples to compare it to I might know more, too. Of course, having someone to test the vaccine on would help." She scribbled my name on a sticker and wrapped it around the vial. "Can you bring me a monkey?"

"Huh?"

"A monkey. You know…" She imitated a monkey, complete with scratching her head and jumping up and down while making a horrible noise.

"Yeah, I know what a monkey is. Why do you want one?"

"Primates share most of our DNA. I might be able to infect one."

"Oh, yeah. If we don't have enough problems on our hands already, let's throw in a crazy, homicidal zombie-monkey."

"I'll let you shoot it in the head if it goes crazy."

"Gee, thanks." I raised my eyebrows. "If I find a monkey, I'll bring it back." I shook my head and left, pondering where the hell I'd even find a monkey. Chances are every animal in a zoo was dead; there was no one left to care for them.

It was easy to convince Fuller to let me go. The other group of A1s were leaving on a supplies run. I was going to tag along and get the medicine. Then I would turn around and leave on my own, getting back here as fast as possible. I didn't share the last part of my plan with anyone. If Fuller knew I wanted to venture out on my own, he wouldn't let me go. I didn't trust the other group to be fast enough. It had to be me.

But after getting his permission, I was no longer sure if I could leave Hayden. What if Padraic was right? What if I came back and Hayden…no. He would make it.

Fuller also thought it would 'do me some good' to get my mind off of everything that had happened. As if I would be thinking of anything out there other than Hayden, but I packed a bag and hugged Raeya goodbye. Like Padraic, she didn't want me to go.

I snuck into the hospital ward and explained everything to Hayden, who still hadn't opened his eyes. I doubted if he heard a word I said. He didn't so much as squeeze my finger or flutter an eyelash.

Karen didn't smile anymore. Her face looked grim, and in the corner near the medicine cabinets two young girls wept—I recognized them as the two volunteers who had brought him cookies a few weeks back when he had the flu.

Walking off the ward…leaving Hayden behind was the hardest thing I'd ever done.

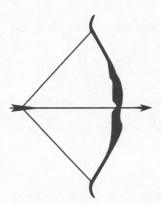

CHAPTER 3

I hadn't interacted much with the six other A1s: Gabby, Jessica, Alex, Mac, José, Noah. I wasn't sure who I'd get paired up with, and, frankly, I didn't care. Besides Hayden, I preferred to work alone.

Since this was supposed to be an easy supplies run, only Alex, Mac, Gabby and I were going. Like Hayden, Alex had served multiple tours overseas. He had intense gray eyes and dark hair. His strong jaw was set and he was the self-appointed leader. I instantly didn't like him.

I wanted to get to the nearest hospital, get the stuff Hayden needed and race back to the compound. We spread out a map and starred every hospital in a fifty mile radius. Hell, if we hit up a close one, we might even make it back tonight.

I had gone over the list several times with Padraic so I would get exactly what we needed. He had even told us what parts of the hospital to go to first. This really would be an easy mission, I reiterated to myself.

Against my suggestion, Alex drove north. I told him that we had *just* come from a mission where we went north and it was cold and snowing and miserable. He said that he'd rather deal with the snow than zombies, since zombies don't fare well in the cold.

I had to work hard to bite my tongue. I hated the way Alex tossed his rank around like it mattered. He was a specialist in the army; Hayden had been a Marine sergeant, which was a higher rank. But Hayden had never used his rank with us. We were past that. Not wanting to make this trip any worse, I kept my mouth shut. Plus, I was too preoccupied with the nagging feeling I was missing something crucial to care much.

What if there were other gang members? What if they followed us?

It didn't seem right that only four gang members would have an entire street marked off. Why would they need so many houses?

"Get off on this exit," I told Alex, following the route with my finger on the map. "The hospital is only a few miles after that."

The front doors of the hospital were open, spewing out unknown danger and darkness. Silently, we got out of the SUV and suited up. I had a holster on each side holding an M9, a machine gun strapped to my right thigh, and the compound bow and arrows hung from my shoulder. Extra clips weighed down my pockets.

We silently stepped into the lobby. Daylight filtered through the open doors and cracked windows. Gabby gagged at the smell of rotting humans.

Farther in, feet limply dangled out of a once grand fountain; the rest of the body was disintegrated under putrid liquid. Brown and tan foam floated on the water's surface. The stench only got worse the farther we went in. I traded my M9 for the machine gun, using the night vision scope to see through the dark halls.

Alex took the lead. I wasn't going to fight with him on that; if we got attacked, at least he'd be the first to go. Glass crunched under his boots. Someone had broken open the case that held the fire axe. I cringed as the rubber soles of my camo-colored combat boots crushed the glass, the breaking sound echoing down the dark, empty hall.

Well, the *used-to-be* empty hall.

Three zombies limped their way out of a waiting room. Alex motioned for me, but I was already a step ahead. An arrow whizzed through the air, sinking into the rotten eye of a female S2. Ignoring the sting of the string slapping my unguarded wrist, I shot two more, dropping the other zombies. I clicked on my flashlight and looked with disgust at the kill.

Careful not to press too hard, I put my foot on their festering chests to pull out the arrows. I shook off the lumpy parts and wiped them clean on the zombies' dirty clothes before sticking them back in the quiver.

"Nice work, Orissa," Gabby said, her smile barely visible in the dim light. I smiled and nodded. We stepped over the corpses and continued down the hall, pausing to look at the directory.

Alex had just opened his mouth to bark out an order when we heard the moans. My hand flew behind me, my fingers grabbing onto an arrow. My heart skipped a beat when the shuffling of feet drowned out the moans.

I went for the M16 instead and saw shadows along the far wall. The owners of these shadows turned the corner... and blocked our way

A hoard of zombies!

They snapped their dead faces in our directions, opening their decaying mouths hungrily at the sight and smell of us. We opened fire, dropping the first line. It offered little help; the zombies that tripped, those that hadn't been shot in the head, only crawled toward us. Death calls came from behind. Damn it, we were being surrounded.

"Fall back!" Alex yelled.

No. We were so close. I wasn't leaving empty handed.

"Cover me!" I yelled, eyeing a doorway.

"No, get out, Penwell!"

"Twenty minutes! If I'm not back in twenty, assume I'm dead and go on without me. Now cover me!" I strapped the gun back to my leg and sprinted through the open door, the rapid fire blinding me...deafening me. I tripped over a fallen IV stand, sending painful shocks into my wrists as the heels of my palms smacked the cold, tile floor. I kicked the door closed and madly looked around.

I was in a lab. I scrambled up, shoving a file cabinet in front of the door. There was another exit; I assumed it led to a waiting room or, if I was lucky, a hall behind the exam rooms. It did both, and I raced through the waiting room into the narrow pathway, running past the exam rooms. I slammed into the automatic doors that led to the ER.

Several gummies moaned and made feeble attempts to come at me. I buried an arrow in their mushy skulls.

Holding the flashlight in my mouth, I yanked back curtains. A nearly deteriorated gummy had oozed onto a hospital bed, permanent bed sores sticking him to the material. The smell choked me and I gagged.

He reached for me, biting at the air. He had no teeth left.

"You give 'gummy' a whole new meaning," I said as I fired an arrow into his head. It went all the way through and pinned him to the wall. I wrinkled my nose at the globs of brain matter that oozed down his forehead and decided to leave my arrow behind.

Padraic told me to look for a machine that dispensed meds. I frantically looked all over but came up empty handed. Refusing to leave with nothing, I filled a pillow case with IV bags and antiseptics. I shot a zombified EMT in the skull with the M9 as I made my way to the exit. I kicked open the doors, rushed past an ambulance, and jogged into the parking lot.

"Seventeen minutes," Alex said when I got into the SUV, hardly able to keep the smile from his face.

"Told you," I said, adding extra smugness to my voice on purpose.

"Three more and I would have left you. What did you get?"

"IV fluid and that chlorhexidine stuff Padraic wanted. I couldn't find the meds."

"The next hospital," Mac promised.

I nodded and tossed the bags into the back of the SUV. "Where did you go for that stuff?" he asked.

"The ER," I told him.

"Was it full of zombies?"

I shook my head. "Not yet."

Mac looked at Alex and Gabby. "We should go get the monitors and pumps."

Alex grumbled, not liking the idea simply because it wasn't his. After a moment's consideration, we pulled the car around and went back into the ER. Alex and Gabby took on half the list while Mac and I found the rest of the items. We filled up the back of the SUV in less than an hour. And we got everything on the list...except the most important medicine.

<hr>

We were running out of daylight and then the blizzard started. Alex wanted to keep going and so did I, but when thick snowflakes blasted down from the dark clouds, we turned off to the back roads in search of a town. Visibility was near zero and the SUV continually skidded toward the ditches and hopped curbs.

"We have no choice, Orissa," Gabby said. "If we spin out or crash, Hayden will never get his medicine."

I knew she was right, though I hated it. I wanted Hayden to have his medicine yesterday!

It was the tall gates that drew us in. They were unscathed and made of cast iron. The town seemed ghosted, though the litter that blew atop the powdery layer of pristine white snow led me to believe it had been abandoned only recently.

I was too busy scanning our surroundings for the undead to read the town's name on the sign as I passed it, though the paint was flaking off so badly it would have taken a second glance to discern what it said anyway.

I lowered my rifle and examined the house Alex had chosen. Painted a forest green with dark gray shutters, the Victorian must have been beautiful at one time. The wooden boards creaked as we walked up the porch, barely able to stand in the face of the swirling snow. I half expected a creepy girl dressed in a white lace dress to pull back the ivory curtains and stare at us before disappearing. I rolled my eyes at my own thought.

"No," I told Alex when he raised his foot to kick the door in. I set my rifle down. "I'll get it."

"You're good and all, Penwell, but I'm stronger than you," he stated. That was almost a compliment.

"Chill, Hercules. If you kick down the door, we can't close it tonight."

"Then how are we supposed to get in?" he demanded, waving his hand at the door.

I pulled a bobby pin from my hair. "Uh, pick the lock." I straightened the pin and yanked the rubber ends off. I did the same to another, causing my bangs to fall into my face, knelt down, and got to work. Only a minute later, I turned the knob.

"I've heard you are quite the criminal," Alex sneered.

"Lay off, Alex," Gabby snapped. "She got us in. Thanks, Orissa." She glared at Alex and stepped inside. I dropped the bobby pins and followed her.

The first thing I noticed was the stuffed dog. It wasn't a cute, fluffy, stuffed dog. It was a *real* dog—taxidermy at its finest—in a sitting position, set at the bottom of the stairs that spilled into the foyer. The light from Gabby's flashlight reflected off the glass eyes.

"That's disturbing," she said and cast her light elsewhere.

"Not as disturbing as that," Mac said, motioning to where his flashlight illuminated.

"What the hell?" I asked, tipping my head. I looked around and felt the slightest bit of fear. "We're in a fucking wax museum." I stepped forward to the life-size wax figure of Abraham Lincoln that Mac's light still shone on. I pulled my glove off and scrapped at his face with my fingernail.

"What a lovely place to stay," Gabby said sarcastically. She took her backpack off, letting it drop to the floor with a heavy thump. "Hey," she whispered, turning to me. "Do you think there's a psycho in the basement waiting to dip us into a big vat of wax and turn us into dolls?"

I looked at her quizzically. "Uh, no."

"Never mind, I guess you never saw that movie."

We explored the rest of the house. Each room was a different theme with coordinating wax characters. We shoved the dolls out of the living room and broke chairs apart to use as firewood for the fancy, cast-iron fireplace, which did little to warm the frozen room.

We slept in shifts. Like usual, I took the first watch. I was too cold to settle down so I walked around the building, jogging up and down the stairs to keep warm. There was an old newspaper in the recycle bin inside the closet of an office. It was dated four years ago. This place had gone out of business before the town even ghosted out.

At 2:00 AM, Gabby said she'd switch with me. I crawled inside my sleeping bag but was unable to warm up. But cold and tired, I drifted to sleep easily. I dreamed that we made it safely back to the compound, but as soon as I stepped inside the faux brick estate, I was taken back to my grandparents' Kentucky farm. Raeya was sitting in the living room crying. I walked past her and slowly ascended the stairs.

Hayden was lying in my bed, his eyes cold and lifeless.

I startled awake, my heart racing. "Stupid nightmare," I mumbled to myself, as I rolled over to try to get comfortable. Hayden wasn't dead. Well, he wasn't as far as I knew. Only one person had died in that house, and I refused to think about Zoe.

I got only a few hours of on-and-off sleep that night.

<hr/>

The next morning the blizzard was gone and there was little accumulation. I dozed off in the car while Alex drove. I had no idea where we were when Mac shook me awake. I instantly became alert when a large hospital loomed ahead. There was a fresh dusting of snow over the parking lot.

"There are no footprints," I stated.

"You don't know that," Alex spat.

"Yes, I do. There either are or there aren't. And I don't see any. The snow isn't that deep, but footprints are still obvious."

"That doesn't mean anything."

"I didn't say it meant anything. But I'm telling you, I do not see any footprints." I clenched my fists. If it came down to it, I'd so trip Alex if zombies were chasing us.

As far as we could tell, nothing new had left or entered the building since the snowfall. The hospital looked new. The lobby was big and thankfully bright and open. There was a large atrium off the lobby, with high glass windows and a glass ceiling, giving a full view of the thick forest that sat behind the hospital.

Weapons raised, we eased our way through the hallways, making our way to the oncology floor. Bodies littered the hall, but these people had not been killed by zombies. They were neatly laid out with sheets covering them, all with the same bloodstain on the forehead; they had been executed.

I stopped counting after fifty. The smell was horrendous; we covered our noses and did our best not to gag. We reached the end of the hall. Mac pushed on the doors revealing that they had been chained off from the other side.

"Son of a bitch!" Alex swore, glaring at me as if it was my fault. I opened my mouth to say something catty back when we heard the growl.

The smart thing to do would be to kill the sole S1 silently. Dressed in bloodstained scrubs and a dirty lab coat, the crazy doctor bared her teeth when she saw us. Her ankle was twisted and broken and two of her fingers had been chewed off. She wasn't even worth an arrow. I pulled the knife from its sheath on my belt and ran forward, prepared to send the blade deep into her damaged brain.

The bullet was faster.

Faster, and louder. Once the crazy dropped, I turned to stare down Alex, who had his pistol raised. He had a smirk on his face, satisfied he had gotten the kill before I did.

"What the hell?" I yelled, seeing no point of keeping my voice down now.

"Three points for me," he said smugly.

"Yeah, three point for being a dumbass!" I waved my arms at the end of the hall. "Why the hell would you do that? We are at the end of a *locked* hall!"

Alex's face twitched when he realized that. "You could thank me for saving you."

"You didn't save me. You just endangered us all, you moron!"

"Stop being so dramatic," he jeered. "Obviously we're fine."

Mac and Gabby exchanged nervous glances. They agreed with me. "Let's get the stuff," Gabby suggested. "It's cold and I want to go home."

"Good plan," Mac agreed. We doubled back, going down a different hall to get into the ER. Adrenaline coursed through my veins and my hands almost shook. I kept expecting something to jump out at us. We made it to the pharmacy without running into anything.

It wasn't right. It was *too* quiet.

But who was I to wish for zombies? We had to break open locks, rip cabinets apart, and pry open the drawers of the computerized medication dispenser. I hit the lock on a medical refrigerator several times with the butt of my rifle before it broke. The only good thing about it being so freaking cold was that the medications that needed to stay cool did. I dropped bottles of insulin as I madly rooted around.

"I found it!" I exclaimed, holding up a little glass vial of Fentanyl. I also found Cipro! We spent another few minutes gathering up more meds, including a tablet form of the Fentanyl. Since it worked the first time, I grabbed another pillowcase and held it open for Gabby to dump in medications. We grabbed more dispensers and even IV pumps. Once it was full, we high-tailed it out of the hospital. I stayed in the rear of our line, glad the others couldn't see my smile. I would be back soon, back to see Hayden. I got that annoying fluttery feeling in my stomach when I thought of him and shook it away.

Bright light from the atrium shone like a beacon. We marched for it, so close to going back to the compound. The smell hit us first. The four of us stopped, crouching into position. Then we heard the moaning and the shuffling of feet.

A pack of zombies blocked our exit. There were dozens of them, mouths gapping and arms reaching. No! We were so close. I had the medicine. I wasn't letting this stop us now. We spun around to flee in the opposite direction.

More zombies filtered into the hall on that end. Where the hell were they coming from? Gabby fired first, sending a bullet into the head of a child zombie. It dropped, tripping the S3 that was behind it. We all opened fire, raining down metal death on the herd that marched closer and closer. My magazine emptied from the M9 and it made no difference in the numbers.

We needed to get out if we wanted to live. We were being swarmed. I shoved the M9 back in the holster and yanked the M16 free. I jumped onto an overturned sofa in the lobby and sprayed the windows with bullets, causing the glass to shatter. I grabbed the vials and medicine from my pocket, pressed them into Gabby's hand, and yelled, "Twenty minutes! I'll lead them off. If I'm not back, go, get back to Hayden!"

She opened her mouth to object, but I took off, using the rifle as a baseball bat and hitting an S3 in the face. His teeth slimed out on impact and clanked onto the floor, splattering bits of blood and rotten gum particles over the tile.

Seeing I had little choice, I picked up a piece of the broken glass, rolled my sleeve up and dragged it across the top of my wrist. "Hey, you motherfuckers!" I screamed, whipping my hand back and forth to get the scent of blood in the air. "Dinner time!" I climbed on top of a table, kicking over a colorful display of pamphlets on how to deal with a loved one's illness.

Gabby, Mac, and Alex continued to fire at the zombies. A few caught the yummy scent of my blood and roared as they lumbered over. Damn it! It wasn't working well enough.

"Hey!" I screamed again. I really should invest in a fog horn. I threw a dead pot of marigolds across the atrium, hitting the glass, though not hard enough to break it. A few more zombies turned their attention to me.

Gabby screamed when a fast moving S2 jumped on her. Mac kicked it off, shooting it in the head and pulling Gabby to her feet. I screamed again, my voice getting lost in the zombies' moans. I shook with the fear of us dying and not getting back to Hayden.

Hayden and Raeya and Padraic.

I wanted to see them again. I wasn't going to die. Not by the hands and mouths of zombies. *It worked before*, I reminded myself, and took another deep breath.

I sang a few bars of the Styx song "Renegade" as loudly as I could. I grabbed an arrow, wincing in pain as I rolled the cold metal through my blood dripping cut. I sang louder. The arrow flew through the air, grazing the arm of an S2. The others around him pounced, following the smell of blood.

It worked. I smiled triumphantly, eyeing my fellow soldiers. Alex waved for Gabby and Mac to go while he covered them from behind. His eyes met mine and I nodded, letting him know it was ok. He took off. Right as I was about to jump down, sprint out the broken window, and race around to the SUV, a well fed S2 lunged at me.

We collided. I slid off the table, and the wind was knocked out of me. The M16 bounced out of my grip. He pinned me down, saliva dripping from his open mouth. Bits of flesh and hair stuck to his teeth. I struggled to get away, kneeing him in the balls instinctively. Of course it had no effect. I rolled back and sat up quickly, elbowing him in the nose.

His grimy hands thrashed the air, recoiling from my blow. I scrambled away, kicking him in the ribs before I stomped on his head. I dove for my rifle only to get attacked by another zombie.

"Son of a bitch!" I swore and flipped myself to my feet, pulling the knife out at the same time. I kicked the zombie in the chest and drove the blade into its head through a soggy eye socket. The eye came out with the blade. I didn't have time to wipe it off before another grabbed my hair.

Using form so perfect that my martial arts instructor would have been proud, I softened my knees and sprung up and around, my fist landing square in the middle of the zombie's face. It didn't hurt him of course, but the blow made him stagger back. I dropped down, kicked his feet out from under him, and jumped on his neck while at the same time slicing through the spinal cord of another, younger zombie.

I leapt through the broken window, taking off as soon as my feet hit the frozen ground. The sound of the glass breaking let me know without looking back that I was being followed. I slipped on a patch of ice and fell, only staying on the ground for a split second. I was up and running again, but this time slower. I had twisted my ankle and it hurt like hell. I doubted it was broken or even sprained. All I needed was to rest it for a minute to let the pain subside.

Desperately, my eyes scanned the trees in front of me. About twenty feet to go and I could climb to safety and wait until the herd dispersed. I couldn't resist shooting two more in the forehead before I climbed up and away. I stopped once. I was ten feet up, just out of the reach of the festering, grabbing hands.

"Come and get me," I jeered. "Oh wait, that's right. You can't." I emptied the rest of my magazine, pocketing the empty magazine while I traded it for another. I quickly fired every bullet into the heads of zombies before I tested the branch above me. Deciding it was strong enough, I climbed up and sat, leaning against the truck of the tree. I grabbed a handful of snow and pressed it to the cut on my arm, which was starting to sting.

I struggled to maintain balance as I extracted a bandage from my pocket to tie around my wrist. My ankle hurt too, so I forced myself to slowly extend and bend it, trying to get the blood flowing so it would feel better.

The sun reflecting off of the snow was blinding. I wished I had sunglasses. I closed my eyes, almost relaxing as I waited for the zombies beneath me to give up and move on.

More than twenty minutes passed before *she* came wandering out of the pine trees.

Ice hung in clumps from her hair and she was not dressed for the weather. Black patches of frostbite covered her exposed arms and face. She was carrying something, something warm that oozed and steamed in the cold, winter air.

With more curiosity than I should have had, I leaned over my branch and watched the crazy struggle through the shallow snow, slipping every now and then. When she saw the herd of zombies clawing at my tree, she clutched her object to her chest and hissed.

As if she was suddenly afraid that the zombies might get whatever the hell she was holding, she bit a chunk off and chewed. And then I realized she was holding a stomach.

I wouldn't have known it if I hadn't had years of experience cleaning and gutting deer. Except by the size of it, I didn't think Ms. Frostbite had killed a deer. She had ripped it out of something smaller than a deer, and I instantly wondered how she'd managed to hunt anything with her damaged skin cells and diseased brain. It was a stupid thing to think about. I shook my head and carefully stood, precariously placing my feet on the branch.

I ignored the pain that putting weight on my ankle caused. Slowly, I edged to the end of the branch, keeping hold of the one above me in case it snapped. I didn't feel like falling to my death just yet. A few zombies noticed the crazy, who stupidly stood there hissing and snarfing down her stomach.

It was now or never. The zombies milled away from my tree, going for the crazy. She let out a harrowing yell and took off, leading the zombies away from me. I didn't want to go through another failed Evel Knievel act of jumping from tree to tree. My face hurt just thinking about the last time I'd attempted that.

Seeing that I didn't have much of a choice, I snaked my body up another level of branches. I hated being so high up, but the branches were much closer up here. I resituated the bow over my shoulder, held my breath, and jumped.

My hands burned from grasping the branch so hard but I made it. I shimmied through that tree, paused as an S3 limped under me, and jumped to the next tree. The twigs snapped and I tumbled down, hitting every limb on my way.

I landed on my ass. It hurt like hell, but it was the best thing to land on. I pushed up, not allowing myself time to register the pain, and attempted to run before the zombies noticed me. It was a feeble attempt and I knew that if it wasn't for the impeccable timing of that crazy wandering amidst the forest, I wouldn't have made it.

I jogged around the hospital, slowing only when the street came into view. I expected Alex to give me crap for taking a long time. I was thinking of something extra bitchy to spit back at him when my feet hit the pavement. My eyes darted around the street, looking for the SUV.

I didn't expect this.

They were gone!

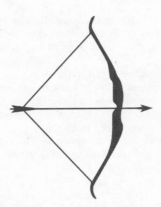

CHAPTER 4

No, I thought. They just drove off to distract the zombies. That was all. They wouldn't really leave me. I had told them to leave, but I didn't expect them to actually do it. Panic tried to bubble in my heart. *No*, I repeated in my head. They will be right back.

I stood, rooted in the spot for several minutes as I waited to hear the distant roar of the engine. But all I heard was the distant moaning of zombies. The distant moaning that was gradually getting louder and louder.

Damn it.

I couldn't stay here. I had to find somewhere safe to wait. Abhorrence made my heart race. What if they came back and I wasn't here?

"No," I said out loud. I had to move. My ankle was stiff from standing still for so long in the cold. It cracked painfully when I took a step. I let out a breath and limped down the street. It took effort to climb on top of the ambulance where I laid down out of sight from zombie eyes. If I just waited, if I just stayed right here, Alex and the others would come back.

The sun set and I was still alone. Alone, hungry, and cold. I had to face it; they had left me, truly left me. My twenty minutes was up, and they assumed I was dead. I slid down the front of the ambulance. This sucked, but it wasn't the end. I took comfort in knowing that they were on their way back to the compound and Hayden would get the medication he needed. And I knew that I would get back to him…to them eventually, and when I did, I would knee Alex in the balls and remind him about what happens when you assume. Using the sinking sun as my guide, I started walking south in the general direction of downtown. The forest gradually thinned, torn down to make room for the modern buildings. My plan was to find a safe place to stay tonight, get a car in the morning, figure out where the hell I was, and go to Arkansas.

Easier said than done.

The herd of zombies emerged from the woods. I ducked behind an overturned car, holding my breath. They marched back toward the hospital, thankfully, and I took off running, my boots hitting the pavement with too much noise for my liking. My ankle screamed, but I ran until I couldn't stand the pain anymore, passing neat little houses and cute store fronts, abandoned and trashed by the undead. Reluctantly, I stopped and unlaced my boot.

"Great," I muttered upon seeing my swollen ankle. There was nothing I could do for it so I laced up and limped off again. The scent of decay hit me and my blood instantly turned into ice. I looked around but didn't see any zombies. I held my breath; I didn't hear any either.

"What the hell?" I asked myself, taking another step, following the sickening smell of death. Maybe I shouldn't have cared. Maybe I should have let dead things lie.

But I knew it wasn't right. I knew passing the house that reeked like an unplugged fridge full of meat would mean a surprise later. I pulled the bow off my shoulder and pulled an arrow back. I kicked the door open, the hinges squeaking in protest. The smell was so bad I gagged. Holding my breath, I took a tentative step inside.

Light spilled in through the windows. Blood trailed in a very particular path on the hardwood floors. And it looked like more than one body had been dragged through this small house. I entered the living room, my eyes darting around like crazy, and my heart beating a million miles an hour. Every breath that escaped my lungs seemed too loud. Never in my life had I wanted to blend in or be so invisible. It would be so freaking practical to be that now.

The living room was set up like a living room should be. Thick dust covered the magazines on the coffee table. A cup of purple juice had been knocked over, staining the light blue rug. I had to pull the collar of my black turtleneck over my nose. The smell grew even more pungent as I neared the kitchen. And it was obvious why.

About half a dozen bodies were haphazardly discarded on the floor. Tangled up with one another, their lifeless faces displayed twisted horror. Terror and curiosity forced me to look at them longer than what was psychologically healthy. Images of festering, gapping mouths burned into my memory.

I snapped out of the nightmare reverie and told myself to think logically. Ok, there was nothing logical about a pile of dead bodies in the kitchen.

"Dead," I whispered. "All dead, but no bullet wounds." At least none to the head. I walked around the disgusting pile and noticed the torn open abdomens with missing guts. "Stomachs," I said to the bodies.

Something banged against a wall deep inside the house. I jumped and positioned the arrow in the bow and left the kitchen, following the source of the noise. I went down a hall, which, of course, didn't have any windows.

The scurrying came from behind a closed door. Not wanting to free my hands of my weapons, I kicked it. The door swung open, revealing a healthy looking S1. He was tall, fit, and at one point he had probably been kinda cute. He didn't even have time to get up before the arrow cracked open his skull and pierced his brain, sending little bits of skin and bone splattering on the wall behind him. I hung the bow over my shoulder and yanked the arrow free, having to pull extra hard to get it out of his head.

This room smelled putrid too. The guy I had just killed had been feasting on a stomach. I kicked it out of his hand, nearly retching at the scent.

Behind him was a pile of more stomachs.

"What the fuck?" I asked nobody. They were neatly laid out and...sorted? No, crazies weren't that smart. Along with human emotions, their intelligence was damaged by the virus. Covering my mouth and nose, I looked at what was in front of me. I thought the stomachs were divided by size or even species.

The one the crazy was eating leaked contents over the floor, smelling like a dead animal that had been shoved up someone's ass and then shit out. I took one last look; it appeared he had ripped it open and was eating whatever was inside. Ok, that was just gross, even for me.

I quickly left the house. A few stragglers meandered down the street. I pulled back an arrow and shot two S2s. I retrieved my arrows, wiped off the goo, and trudged forward. After another mile of walking, I knew I needed to stop for the night. The last rays of sunlight were almost gone and my ankle was killing me. I needed to rest it in case I needed to make a fast getaway, which was only inevitable.

I looked up and down the street. Most of the store fronts had been broken, giving the impression that this town had been looted. Hunger drove me to limp inside a mini mart. Everything edible was gone. Not giving up just yet, I took out my flashlight and made my way into the break room.

I held my breath when I opened the fridge. An unopened bottle of water sat on the bottom shelf. Someone's yogurt parfait had molded and dripped over it. Grimacing only slightly, I took it out and wrapped the bottle in a napkin. Then I found a can of chicken noodle soup along with a box of expired crackers in a cabinet covered with mouse droppings. Both the soup and the water were frozen.

Feeling the mini mart didn't offer enough protection, I crossed the parking lot and stopped in front of a pet store. The glass windows and doors where still intact. I put my hands on the cold glass and pushed, forcing the automatic doors open. Leaving them ajar, I stepped inside.

The place seemed orderly, although I didn't find it surprising that no one had looted the pet store. As much as Americans loved their pets, I bet many were left behind and forgotten when the virus struck. Without making a sound, I moved to the back of the store.

A big S3 in a blue jacket slithered around the floor. He was so far gone he wasn't worth an arrow. I picked up a can of dog food and chucked it at his head, which popped open like a rotten pumpkin. I stepped over the body, turned on my flashlight, and took a look in the storage room. Besides the norm, it was empty.

This was as good of place as any to bunker down in for the night. I went back to the front of the store to close the doors. There was an office behind the registers and it had a steel door that seemed sturdy enough. I didn't like the idea of locking myself in a room. As long as they quietly shuffled in, I could open the door to a zombie surprise party.

I grabbed a dog bed, a big metal bowl and a bag of small animal bedding. I heaved it all up onto a shelf then climbed up myself. I shoved bags of dog food onto the floor; they split open and kibble rolled out on impact. I sat on the bed and dumped the wooden shavings into the bowl. I pulled a box of matches from my pocket and struck one, dropping it into the bowl.

It took a few attempts to get the fire going. I took the can of soup and placed it in the middle. Careful not to melt the plastic, I held the water over the flames. My appetizing dinner had only halfway thawed when the fire went out. Not wanting to waste anymore matches, I decided it was good enough.

"Goddammit," I swore when I looked at the can of soup. I had no way of opening it. I was just about to throw it angrily on the ground when I had an idea. I wedged the can between two bags of food and pulled out my M9. Regretfully wasting a bullet, I pulled the trigger.

I shook the can before putting it to my lips. The warm broth spilled from the bullet hole and into my mouth. Careful not to swallow any metal fragments that might have fallen into the soup, I ate as much as I could, knowing that this could very well be all I'd get for a while. My ankle throbbed, but I didn't want to take my boot off in fear I wouldn't be able to get it back on. I loosened the laces and leaned against the wall.

I was tired, physically and mentally. And I was pissed, so pissed that I had been left behind like a piece of garbage. I ripped open a bag of dog food and spent the next several hours throwing it into the aisle. I couldn't stop shivering. I unbraided my hair, hoping I could gain a little bit of warmth from its length. I closed my eyes, wanting to fall asleep. My brain wouldn't allow it; every little noise made me jump to alertness, my heart instantly racing.

Sometime in the hazy purple dawn, I drifted into a restless sleep

---

I woke only an hour or so later. I eased off the shelf, stretched, and gathered up my things. My first order of business was finding a car. I only had two clips left for my Beretta plus the arrows. Finding more weapons was my second priority. Food and water was third, though, if I got a car and drove straight to the compound, going a day with no food or water wouldn't kill me.

My ankle didn't hurt as badly as before, but it still wasn't healed. Ignoring it, I set off into the parking lot. There were three cars still in it and they were all new. I couldn't hot wire anything hybrid. Moving on, I went back into the street. I kept my hand poised over the bow, ready to send a black arrow flying into the face of anything that got in my way.

And that's exactly what I did when a lone S2 came around a corner. He saw me, turned away and let out a high pitched yell before he dropped to the ground. I thought it was strange, the way he almost let out a call when he saw me. It didn't matter anymore. I stepped on his puffy chest—something snapped and popped under my weight. I grabbed my arrow, and pulled. It slid free from his rotten brain with ease. I was shaking it clean when five zombies ran around the same corner. Mouths gleaming with fresh blood, they had full bellies and were wicked fast.

Using the arrow as a spear, I drove it into the open mouth of the closest zombie. I kicked another in the chest; she staggered back, tripping over the curb. I knocked another to the ground before I could stomp the S2 that reached for my feet. I pulled the M9 and shot two more in the head.

More zombies staggered out into the street. The herd hadn't dispersed after all. They were all here, coming after me. There was no way I could take them all down. Not alone. I finished the magazine, shoved a new one in and took the M9 in my left hand. I pulled my knife out with the other and set off to freedom, killing as many undead bastards as I could.

Two zombies tag teamed me. I spun around, my foot landing in the face of the shorter one while the knife sliced the other's neck open. His head flopped back, sending him off balance. His arms were still held out in front of him and he blindly grabbed for me. I dropped and rolled out of the way just in time for him to fall, his skull bursting like a water balloon filled with rotten pea soup when it hit the pavement.

I fired a round into the nose of a young zombie, whose white dress was stained with pus and blood. They just kept coming, tripping over each other as they pushed their way to me. I jumped over a car, sliding over the hood and out of reach of a fat S3. I plunged the knife into his forehead.

I slipped on ice, as I sprinted down an alley behind a stretch of stores, and I ran across a field and entered the woods again. I kept running until I was out of breath. I had outrun the zombies—for now. I stopped, doubling over as I panted, and pulled the water bottle out of my pocket, thankful all the running increased my body heat and further melted the ice. I drank what I could, recapped the bottle and pushed forward, sure I would come to a road soon enough.

I was wrong. Hours later, I was still in the forest. Ice coated snowflakes burned my already frozen cheeks. I zipped my coat up as far as it would go. Shivering, I lifted my legs higher than necessary as I marched on, hoping to increase my blood flow and warm my limbs. I rubbed my arms, flinching in pain when I touched my wrist. I had forgotten about the slice I'd made there. I pushed my sleeve up; the skin around the cut was red and puffy, sure signs of an infection. I scooped up a handful of snow and pressed it against my aching wound. I wiggled my toes, desperately wanting to gain the feeling back in my feet. It didn't help so I forced myself into a jog.

I quickly ran out of breath and my heart hammered in my chest. I stopped, feeling suddenly weak and dizzy. I sank onto the cold ground, the hard snowflakes panging against my face.

Which felt hot.

Damn it.

This wasn't happening. I didn't have time for this. I pulled my sleeve back and looked at the cut again. Yes, it was definitely infected.

"No," I told myself. "You do not have blood poisoning." If I did, I'd be dead in a day. I forced myself to my feet and made it another half an hour before the nausea hit. Dragging my feet, I continued. There was no stopping now, not if I wanted to live.

My body broke into shivers, which only worsened the horrible feeling in my stomach. The snowfall increased, decreasing my visibility. A crazy could easily sneak up on me, even if I saw it a mile away, all I could do was shoot; I was in no condition to fight. "Hah," I said to myself. As if I could hold the pistol steady enough to get a good shot. I stopped to pee as the sun set, realizing that it was the first time I'd had to go to the bathroom all day. I knew that it was partially because I hadn't had much to drink, still, I couldn't help but worry that my organs were shutting down due to the poisonous bacteria that floated in my blood.

I trudged forward, slipping and falling. The jolt sent my queasy stomach over the edge and I threw up what little food I had eaten. Unable to get up, I crawled forward. I don't know how much time passed. My hands and knees had gone numb. I was so weak I could barely move.

When I saw the light ahead, I figured it was some sort of reverse mirage. Instead of seeking cool, refreshing relief from a hot desert, I wanted to be warm, warm and well. Somehow I managed to pull myself to my feet. In a state of delirium, I fell several times as I emerged from the forest and plodded up the gravel driveway.

I might have been talking to myself…muttering, maybe. There were a few moments when I didn't remember where I was. I couldn't figure out why I was heading up this driveway, going toward a house I'd never seen.

Hayden!

Where was he? Was he in that house?

He was supposed to be with me.

Always. With. Me.

I couldn't keep my eyes open. I stumbled along the uneven driveway, my boots catching on heaps of frozen gravel. I wanted to collapse on the ground. But I had to keep going.

For a moment I was a kid again, trudging through the woods in Kentucky after my grandpa dropped me off in the middle of nowhere. My alcoholic mother turned born again Christian was too busy with my stepdad, Ted, to notice that my grandpa's PTSD was slowly taking over. I was only twelve years old and he was training me on how to survive on my own in the wilderness.

I never thought I'd actually need to know those skills. I blinked my eyes open and pushed forward up the driveway.

The driveway...it had been plowed; I could tell because security lights blinded me.

Lights?

I felt wasted, fighting to stay conscious and alive with every breath. It was so hard to get my feet up the stairs and onto the porch.

I took a deep breath and pounded on the door.

My eyes widened when a young boy answered, holding a shotgun in his hands. And then the world went black.

When I woke up, I was on a sofa, but I didn't know where I was or remember, at first, how I'd gotten there. A boy stared down at me.

"Ma!" he hollered, without looking away. "Ma! Get over here fast! It's...she's awake."

I heard the shuffling of feet. My vision blurred.

"Oh my! You're awake!" a gruff female voice spoke. "Dear, have you been bit?"

"No, not bit," I mumbled.

"Beau, Casey, get in here!"

I held up my arm, mumbled the words, "blood poisoning" and passed out again.

This time, I was only out for a few minutes.

When I woke up, a pretty red head was scrubbing my wrist. Her green eyes displayed fear and were filled with tears. She looked at me with what I could only say was empathy.

"Hi," she said shyly, looking over her shoulder as if she was nervous or afraid of being overheard. "I'm Olivia. As soon as you're better, you need to leave," she whispered harshly.

"I'm planning on it," I promised.

"Good. Because you can't—" she cut off as soon as a guy came into the room. Her body tensed up and the tears that brimmed her eyes spilled over.

"You taking care of our guest now?" he asked.

Olivia nodded slightly.

"Good. We want her healthy." He knelt down next to the couch and examined me. "I'm Beau," he said. My vision was too fuzzy to fully take in his appearance. His hair was cut in a mullet style and he chewed on a toothpick. "We're gonna getcha all fixed up now."

I nodded and mumbled, "Thanks." Olivia poured something over my arm that burned like hell. "Sorry," she told me before gently wrapping my wrist in gauze.

"So," Beau said, rocking back on his heels. "How did you end up here?"

Something in Olivia's eyes begged me not to tell the truth.

"Got lost," I said, which was ambiguous enough to be safe.

"You got others looking for you?"

Olivia's skinny fingers dug into my arm.

"No," I said. It was probably true. Everyone assumed I was dead anyway. "They got eaten."

Beau smiled for a split second. "Well, now. I'll let Olivia patcha up." His eyes slid over her body, and he smacked her butt. "Come up to bed when you're done, darlin'," he told her.

Even with my nonfunctioning brain, I knew something was off. He didn't ask who I was or how I was feeling. Wait, it didn't matter. I was inside, I was slowly warming up, and I wasn't going to die of sepsis. It didn't matter if he asked for my name. I leaned back against the couch and slept.

"I don't think this one's gonna make it," a female voice said, her face so close to mine I could smell her stinky breath.

I opened my eyes to see a freckled woman staring down at me. She straightened up and pressed a smile. Her hands settled on her swollen belly. She was either pregnant or had one hell of a beer gut.

"I'm fine," I told her.

"You don't look fine."

"I'll be fine," I corrected. Olivia put my arm down and unzipped my coat. I sat up and helped her pull the sleeves off my arms. The older woman who greeted me at the door came into the room carrying a tray. She set it down on the coffee table, which was cluttered with empty pop cans, a golden statue of a six point buck, and random wrappers and crumbs.

"Here ya go, sweetie," she said and lifted a cup to my lips. I took it and eagerly drank the warm broth. It felt good to have something in my stomach, but I instantly felt nauseous again. My face must have shown it because Olivia took the cup from me and guided me through piles of clutter into a bathroom.

I remembered to pull my hair back as the broth came back up. Olivia whispered something to me, but I didn't hear it over the sound of my own retching. The older woman and Olivia helped me up the stairs, past more piles of clutter and into a bedroom. The room was oddly neat and clean compared to the rest of the house.

I took off my boots and fell into the bed.

"Your ankle is swollen," Olivia observed. "I'll take care of you so you can leave," she said harshly again. I wanted to tell her that I didn't plan on staying, but I was just too weak. As soon as my head hit the pillow, I was asleep.

I woke up sometime in the morning. My head pounded and my throat was on fire. A soft hissing sound scared me and then I realized that someone had plugged in a humidifier next to my bed. I had been stripped of my clothes as well, and I wasn't sure how to feel about that. Yes, they were dirty but that meant someone had removed them for me…and did God knows what else.

It was probably the strawberry blonde girl, Olivia. I sat up, feeling dizzy all over again. Feebly, I got out of bed and searched for water. There was a bathroom attached to the bedroom and I stumbled my way to it. I turned on the faucet, running it for a few seconds before cupping my hands and getting a drink. I got a good look at myself in the mirror: my hair had been brushed out and I was dressed in a pink cami with lace straps and silk pink pajama pants. My bra was missing but at I least still had my underwear on.

A wave of chills and nausea hit me and my knees buckled. I laid on the linoleum floor for several minutes until I had the strength to pull myself up. Every breath hurt my lungs. Everything inside me hurt as if it was being pinched. I felt like I was dying. I got to my feet, tripped over the bathroom rug, and fell again.

The older woman rushed in, having heard the commotion.

"Oh, deary, what are you doing out of bed?" She linked her arms through mine and helped me up and into bed. I got under the covers without hesitation.

"Thirsty," I croaked, surprised at how weak my voice was. She nodded, clucking to herself before she scurried out of the room to return with a glass of water. I sipped it and then collapsed back into a sickly state of dementia-like sleep.

Time had passed in an indescribable way. It seemed only yesterday I was alone in the woods, shivering and delirious from blood poisoning. And then it seemed I had been here forever—in reality it had only been five days. Grateful as I was for the strangers' hospitality and eagerness to nurse me back to health, I wanted to go back to the compound.

Someone knocked on the door, waited a second and opened it. The pregnant Freckle Face held a steaming bowl of buttered rice. She set it on the nightstand and touched my forehead.

"Your fever's gone down."

"Oh, good."

"I'm Jaylyn."

"Orissa."

"Nice to meet you." She rubbed her stomach. I doubted that she was caressing an accumulation of fat, and I knew she was pregnant.

"When are you due?" I asked.

"Probably the end of July," she said casually. "We don't know for sure since I can't get one of those inside picture thingies done."

I nodded, not knowing what to say.

"Eat," she instructed. "Sue Ellen gave you some antibiotic injections the last few days. You should probably put some food in your stomach."

Sue Ellen must be the older woman. "She's a doctor?" I asked, feeling hopeful.

"No."

"Oh."

"Don't worry though, I've taken them before. Cows aren't that diff'ernt than humans. You just gotta cut the dose in half."

I nodded again, this time feeling a little horrified. I imagined Padraic's reaction when I told him I had been given animal medicine.

"Eat and rest." She faked a smile and left.

I slowly ate the rice.

Olivia came in later that evening with more food and a cup of juice.

"Hi," she said weakly. Her eyes met mine for a millisecond. "You're Orissa?"

"Yeah."

"It's a pretty name. We both have 'O' names," she said, though I think it was mostly to herself.

"Yeah, I guess."

She put a bowl of soup on the nightstand. She had a bruise on her right forearm and a black eye. I didn't remember seeing these injuries before.

"Where did you come from?" she asked, dropping her voice and looking over her shoulder at the door.

"South. From the south."

"By yourself?"

"Not entirely."

"You have to get out, Orissa. Before it's too—"

"What are you telling the new girl?" the young boy asked loudly, appearing in the doorway.

"Nothing, I'm just asking her if she's alright." Olivia trembled. "Harley, this is Orissa. You need to let her rest."

"You can't tell me what to do," he sneered.

"Harley," Olivia pressed. "Beau told you to let her rest."

"No he didn't," Harley snapped. "I came here to supervise." He looked to be about ten.

"You don't need to," Olivia went on, straining to stay calm. Tears formed in her eyes again.

"Yes, I do. I'm one of the men in this house," he said, puffing out his chest. "I have to keep an eye on the women."

"The women?" I questioned. Olivia gave me a please-don't-say-anything look, and Harley crossed his arms.

"Yes. The women."

"Alright," a deep voice said from down the hall. "That's enough." The guy who introduced himself as Beau stood behind the boy. "Get on, go help Ma." He pushed past the boy and came into the room. "Don't mind my 'lil brother," he said with a chuckle. His clothes were dirty and he smelled like unwashed hair and body odor. I knew hygiene took the back burner when it came to surviving in this hell of a world, but the house had running water. It was gross.

"Yeah," I mumbled.

"Rest up," he told me. "We'd like you ta eat with us and meet the rest of the family." He leaned against the door frame, crossing his arms. "Olivia, why don't you'n get Rissa here something to wear tonight."

"Ok," she said weakly, jumping off the bed. "Take a shower, Orissa. I'll be right back with clothes," she told me before she scuttled out of the room.

"Need help?" Beau asked.

"No," I retorted.

He smirked and turned away. I shut the door and went into the bathroom and showered. The water felt wonderful and stayed warm the entire time. I towel dried my hair, brushed it and re-plaited it in a side braid going over my left shoulder. I wrapped the towel tightly around my body and opened the bathroom door.

A short blue and white polka dot dress was neatly laid out on the bed.

"You have got to be kidding me," I breathed, holding it up. The only other clothes that had been provided were a pair of thigh high, white socks and a thong. If I hadn't worn the pajamas for five days in a row, I would have put them back on. I gritted my teeth and pulled the ugly thing over my head. Just a few more days, I told myself, and I'd be good enough to trek out on my own.

Later, at the dinner table, I noticed that everyone, except Olivia, had muddy brown hair. She sat next to me, nervously tearing her napkin. On her other side sat Beau. Across from him was a man I hadn't met yet, though he looked like a younger version of Beau. Next to him was Jaylyn, and to her right was another young man. I remembered seeing him the first night I arrived here. By the way he put his hands all over Jaylyn's body, I assumed he was the father of the baby.

Sue Ellen sat at one end of the table, with Harley crowded in next to her. An older man, with greasy, graying hair pulled back into a pony tail, sat at the head of the table. He winked and smiled at me, showing off his tobacco stained, crooked teeth.

"I'm Bart," he said gruffly. "Glad you stumbled into our neck of the woods. Lucky you did."

"Yeah," I said back, not wanting to be ungrateful. "I'm feeling much better, thanks."

"Now you'n take your time and heal up properly," he told me with a nod. "You sure is pretty," he added quietly, causing Jaylyn to huff jealously.

"Oh, where are my manners?" Sue Ellen asked, her hand flying to her heart. "Deary, you've already met Beau, Olivia, Jaylyn and my baby, Harley." She seemed way too old to have a little kid. "This is Casey," she said, pointing to the thin guy groping Jaylyn.

Casey nodded and said 'hey' dumbly. "And this is Delmont," she introduced.

"Nice to meet you, Orissa," Delmont said almost shyly. Beau whispered something across the table to him that made both guys erupt in giggles. Sue Ellen glared at them and Bart cleared his throat. Dinner consisted of canned vegetables and venison that Bart and Delmont had killed yesterday.

My stomach still couldn't handle much; I could only eat half of what was put on my plate. I pushed the food around while watching everyone interact. Bart was older, probably nearing sixty and I think he was Sue Ellen's husband. Jaylyn and Harley called him 'dad' while Beau and his brother Delmont called him uncle, and Casey called Sue Ellen his aunt. I couldn't wrap my brain around their messed up family tree.

But what really confused me was how Olivia fit into this. She seemed on the verge of tears again. When she lifted her fork to her mouth, I could see a bruise that looked very much like a handprint on the inside of her arm. She also had a thin, short dress on. Like my polka dot nightmare, her hideous dress had seen its heyday ten years ago and was incredibly impractical—not only for the zombie apocalypse but also for the winter.

As soon as dinner was over Olivia sprung up and started cleaning. Delmont came around and placed his hands on my chair, scooted it out, and extended a hand. Not taking it, I pushed myself up. A twinge of rage showed on his face.

"Orissa," he said.

"What?"

"Come with me."

"Why?"

"Let's talk. We should get to know each other."

The red flag went up at the same time the nausea came back. I closed my eyes and ignored the spinning sensation. Delmont put his hand on my arm. If I wasn't so dizzy, I would have jerked away. He pulled me forward and I stumbled, my reactions paralyzed. He caught me and held me close to him, crushing my breasts against his body. Like Beau, he reeked.

"She's still sick," Olivia's quiet voice came from behind me.

"No she's not," Delmont argued.

How the hell would he know? This was the first time we'd met.

"Orissa," Olivia pressed. "You don't feel well, do you?" It was more of a statement than a question.

"I feel like shit," I said quickly, going with my gut and trusting her.

"Fine," Delmont spat. "Rest up."

"I'll take her to bed," Olivia offered.

"No!" Bart interjected. "Jaylyn will."

When I was alone in the room, after Jaylyn had left, I flicked on the bedside lamp and slowly opened the dresser drawers. There was nothing in them. I threw open the closet door: nothing. Ok, maybe that wasn't entirely odd. I looked under the bed and in the cabinets in the bathroom and didn't find anything there either. I sat on the bed, shivering.

Dammit, I was still sick. I stood, trying to shake the horrible feeling that stabbed me in the gut. Something wasn't right about this situation. Deciding I needed to get to the bottom of it, I put my hand on the door, set on finding Olivia. But I couldn't leave.

The door was locked.

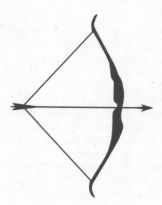

CHAPTER 5

What the fuck? Why did they lock me in? I strode to the window, my anxiety making the dizziness worsen. I pulled the ugly brown curtains back; it was a clear two story drop.

Son of a bitch.

I sat back on the bed, thinking. Whatever they were planning, they picked the wrong girl to mess with. I wanted out, and I had no doubt that I *would* get out.

I closed my eyes and forced myself to think. And that's when I heard it—the obvious sounds of someone having sex. Though only one person was enjoying it—a male moaning and groaning, but the female? She was crying, muffled whimpers. But I still heard her.

My blood ran cold.

For the first time since Hayden had been shot, I felt helpless. My heart pounded in my chest as I sat there in shock, too horrified to sleep.

My brain lost the not-sleeping battle as fatigue took over. I don't remember falling asleep. I only remembered waking up.

The next day repeated the same nightmare. Olivia woke me up—wearing another short dress, the bruise on her thigh was obvious.

She gave me a horrible yellow sundress, advised me to shave my legs, and trudged out of the room. I did twenty minutes of yoga and felt considerably better after that. I showered, braided my hair, and put on the ugly dress.

Delmont was sitting on the bed when I stepped into the room.

"Wow," he said, licking his lips. I wanted to punch him in the face. The hot shower made me feel a little lightheaded so I just glared.

"How do you keep the zombies away?" I blurted. I had been curious about that for quite some time.

He shrugged. "Seems they haven't crossed over this way much. Only seen a handful on the property."

I nodded. I knew it wouldn't last. Maybe I'd get lucky and zombies would attack. I could get away then.

"Want to see the shop?" he asked.

"No," I replied flatly, not caring what kind of 'shop' he was referring to.

His eyes narrowed. "Rest up," he said.

That phrase was really starting to annoy me.

"I'll have Ma bring you somethin' to eat."

He didn't lock the door. Using it to my advantage, I padded out and peered into the room next to the one I was in. It was a mess and smelled like a hillbilly frat house. I wrinkled my nose, moved on, and found Olivia on her hands and knees scrubbing the bathroom floor.

"Olivia," I said quietly, not wanting to startle her. She looked up at me, eyes widening in terror. She dropped the sponge and crawled over.

"You shouldn't be here! Quick, go back to your room!"

"What, why?"

"Please, Orissa! Just go before they see you. I-I'm not supposed to talk to you."

"I'm not leaving until you tell me what's going on."

"That's the thing, you c-can't leave now. You should have gone before...when I first told you."

"What are you talking about?" I asked, my voice was calm but my heart raced.

"They won't let you. They won't let me...not that I could survive out there." She cast her eyes down. "Maybe I *should* be grateful."

"Grateful? Olivia..." I didn't know what to say. I shook my head, causing the headache to worsen. "What happened to you last night?"

Tears filled her eyes and her body trembled. A creak came from the stairs. "Go!" she whispered. "Please!"

I nodded and quickly trotted down the hall. I sat on the bed feeling dizzy again. Who the hell were these people? What did they want with Olivia and me? A moment later, Sue Ellen came into the room carrying a tray.

"Hello, dear," she cooed. The steaming bowl of vegetable soup actually smelled good. She handed me the bowl and a spoon. "How are you feeling?"

"Not so good," I lied. "I feel like I'm getting sick again."

She pressed her hand against my head. "You don't feel hot."

"My stomach. It hurts."

"Oh, well, you'n lay down. We wantcha as healthy as possible."

I smiled, playing along. Really, I was wondering why, and I had all night to wonder...

------------------------→

The next day when Delmont brought me breakfast, I agreed to go with him to the junkyard. I had to know the lay of the land. I had to know what was out there so I could plan my escape.

It was really just a warehouse full of odds and ends with a workshop at one end. Behind that were acres filled with rusty cars and other discarded pieces of unwanted crap. It had snowed more since my arrival, and a path had been shoveled from the house to the shop. My combat boots had been 'misplaced' so I was forced to wear only a thin pair of slippers.

The shop was huge. There were rows upon rows filled with random junk. Dishes, old lamps, pieces of broken furniture, heaps of clothes, a black and white TV, and a rocking horse with a cracked head that threatened to tumble off the shelf and onto me at any second. I shivered and wrapped my arms around myself to try to keep warm and to cover up my breasts; I still hadn't been given a bra.

My eyes darted all around the shop. There were plenty of objects I could use as weapons. I just wasn't sure how to grab one unnoticed. It wasn't like I had a lot of clothing to hide anything in. Delmont was talking, or had been talking I supposed. I hadn't been paying attention to a word he had said.

"Orissa?" he asked, sounding ticked off.

"Huh?" I replied, furthering his annoyance.

He wheeled around, stepping close. "You listen when I'm talking to you!"

I raised an eyebrow.

Taken aback by me not cowering, he looked utterly perplexed. He sneered, grunted and turned away. What I wouldn't give to kick his legs out from under him, slam my heels down on his fingers, and stomp on his face.

Just a few more days. A few more days and I would have the strength to get out of here. Maybe I was already strong enough, but I didn't want to risk it. I knew I'd only get one shot. Possibly...there were four grown men to get past and I had no weapons. I could do it. I'd figure it out, one way or another. Until then...I put my hand on the shelf and pretended to faint.

Delmont caught me. It took everything not to grimace when his hands tightened around my waist.

"You alright?" he asked.

"Oh, I-I feel so weak," I stuttered. "I need to lay down."

"Right. Gotta get you ready."

"Ready for what?"

"Uh, I mean healthy. Gotta get you healthy."

"Yes, I want that," I agreed. He let me go and stepped in front of me. A baseball bat lay covered in dust on a bottom shelf. I made a mental note of that and went with Delmont back into the house.

I made my way upstairs, and heard voices coming from the bathroom as I walked down the hall.

"…it's your own fault, you stupid bitch," Jaylyn scolded. "We all know there's something wrong with ya." She stopped talking when she saw me. Olivia was standing by the sink, mopping up her bloody nose. My eyes widened and I stepped in her direction. Jaylyn slammed the door shut before I could enter the bathroom. I shook my head and ventured back into *my room*.

I felt a little better after I did another Sun Salutation. I dropped to the floor and did a set of crunches, then pushups, and squats. I ended with more yoga and laid down, wishing I could fall asleep and force my body to heal.

Delmont came in once the sun set. He brought me a plate of cooked venison. I ate it eagerly, purposely shoving it in my mouth in a way that mirrored a zombie. I smacked my lips and chewed with my mouth open, wanting to be as unattractive as possible.

When I was done eating, Delmont stretched out next to me.

"Rub my feet," he ordered.

"No," I said instantly.

"Do what I say, woman!"

I glared at him. God, how I wanted to hurt him. "No," I repeated.

He sat up. "Do it or I'll…"

"You'll what?" I inquired, angering him further. He raised his hand as if he was going to hit me but stopped, huffed, and stood.

"You'll learn your place around here. Just you wait." He stomped out of the room, slamming the door shut. I paced around the room. It didn't matter if I still had a headache and was weak. I had to get out of here.

I ate breakfast with the 'family' the next morning. Bart and Beau were going on a hunting trip tomorrow, they announced. That was perfect. Casey whined like a bratty child that he wanted to go too, but Jaylyn clung to his arm and begged him to stay. Annoyed, he pushed her away.

"Casey!" Bart scolded. "Is that any way to treat a lady who's carrying a child?"

"No sir," Casey mumbled, looking at the ground.

"That's right, my boy." Bart nodded and winked at me.

Having lost my appetite, I had to force myself to shovel a spoonful of stew into my mouth.

Olivia was sitting on the edge of her bed when Harley led me to my room. He waved me in, smiling like he knew something was up.

"Have fun tonight," he jeered. Laughing, he took off down the hall. As soon as he was out of earshot, I snuck into Olivia's room.

"Orissa!" she whispered. "Don't let them—"

"I know what you're going to say. And I'm not leaving until I hear the truth so you better tell me. What is going on here?"

"They won't let us leave!"

"Yeah, I kinda figured that out when they locked me in a room at night. Cut to the chase."

"We're all that's left. It's our duty. Really, I should be grateful for them."

She sounded brainwashed. The floor creaked downstairs. I cast a nervous glance over my shoulder. "What are they doing to you?"

"It's my fault," she said, sounding like a distant echo.

"What? Are you talking about your bloody nose?"

"Yes."

"Beau hit you," I speculated.

"Yes," she answered again, tears filling her green eyes.

"How is that your fault?"

"Because I'm not pregnant," she said shamefully.

"Wha—" I started. Then it hit me. "Beau's trying to knock you up?"

"Yes. It's my duty as a woman to repopulate the earth. We are all that's left."

"No," I promised. "We're not. There are more people."

"Where are they?"

"I can take you to them," I said quickly, fearing someone would come up the stairs. "I promise. I will get us out of here. Tomorrow. When they leave for the hunting trip. We will go."

"We'll die," she whispered, trembling.

"I can take care of us."

"How?" Tears rolled down her face. "How can you keep us safe from zombies? You fainted yesterday."

"I faked it. Just trust me; I can take care of us. I'm leaving tomorrow. Are you coming with me?"

"Yes," she said, not sounding too sure of herself.

"Ok. I'm gonna need your help. Do you know where they keep the keys?"

"Keys?"

"Yes, keys. To a car."

"Uh, yes."

"Get them."

"I-I don't know if I can."

"You have to."

Her hands shook as she pushed her strawberry blonde hair behind her ear. "Ok. Are you sure you're well enough?"

"Yes. I might not be one hundred percent, but trust me, I've been worse. We have to leave tomorrow, as soon as Bart goes hunting. It's now or never."

"They go hunting once a week. We can wait until next week when you're better."

"No," I said too loud. "Do you want to stay here another week?"

"No," she cried. "I don't."

"Ok, then, tomorrow...be ready. Signal me when you have the keys." I looked around the room as I thought up a signal. "Cough, really loud, three times in a row."

She nodded. The distinct sound of someone coming up the stairs made me jump. My eyes met Olivia's for a second before I ran back into my room. I pulled the covers over myself just in time for Delmont to walk in.

"Orissa," he cooed.

I pretended to be asleep.

The mattress sunk down from his weight. My heart began beating quickly. I was scared of what he was going to try to do to me. He lay down, sticking his feet under the covers. His hand settled on my waist. I wanted to throw up. When his lips planted a kiss on the back of my neck, I acted like it woke me up.

"Oh, Delmont, hi," I said groggily.

"Hey, baby," he whispered.

I had to hide my gag. *Stay calm,* I told myself. I couldn't blow my cover. "How are you feeling?" he asked.

"Still sick."

"Know what can cure that?" he jeered. I knew my heart was racing in anger and fear. I took deep breaths to try and slow it down.

"Letting me go back to sleep?"

"Wrong," he told me, running his hands down my leg. I couldn't blow it now, I knew that. But I wasn't going to let him fondle me. His fingers moved under the hem of the stupid dress I was wearing. I twitched and his grip on my waist tightened.

"I feel sick," I blurted, adding a moan for effect.

"You're fine." He put both hands on my waist and flipped me around. He pressed himself against me and I could feel his intentions through his jeans.

Gross.

"No, I don't think I am. I think I'm gonna barf."

"You're fine," he repeated, annoyance obvious. His hands trailed up my waist, over my stomach and onto my breasts. He rubbed against me, breathing heavily.

I didn't want to do it, but I didn't think I had a choice. I rolled over, pretending to be interested in Delmont. He was dumb enough to think I actually wanted him. I sat up and put my hands on his chest.

"Yeah, baby," he said.

I half smiled, narrowed my eyes and leaned forward, as if I was going to kiss him. Then I doubled over, moaning. My hands flew to my mouth as if I was covering it up but really I stuck my finger down my throat, forcing myself to throw up all over the floor.

"Ah! What the hell?" Delmont shouted and shoved me off of him. "Ma!" he shouted. "Ma! Get in here!" He backhanded me across the face. It took every single ounce of self control not to react. "Clean that up, bitch."

Beau came running in first. He looked at me and then the vomit. "What did you do to her?"

"Nothing," Delmont bellowed. "I didn't get to do *nothin'*,"

Sue Ellen hobbled in. "Oh!" she exclaimed.

Delmont stomped his foot and pointed at me. "I want a new one!"

"Calm down, boy," she instructed. "What happened?"

"She fucking threw up!"

"Well," Sue Ellen said with pressed lips. "She got blood poisoning. I thought it'd be outta her system by now, but I guess not."

"She's broken!" Delmont continued his temper tantrum.

"No," Beau butted in. "Mine's broken. I'll trade ya."

"No," Delmont said, shaking his head. "Mine at least has nice tits. Yours barely has any."

"Yeah," Beau agreed. "But yours is too muscular. Mine's softer."

They were talking about us like we were animals to be traded. I imagined the kinds of pain I wanted to inflict on them.

"Give her a few more days restin'," Sue Ellen assured Delmont. "Then, Del, she'll be ready."

"Fine," Delmont said pointedly. The three left the room, shut, and locked the door. I got a towel from the bathroom and threw it over my vomit. I wasn't allowed to eat much and I had barfed up what little food I had in my stomach. Now I was going to be hungry.

Shaking with anxiety, I got into bed and I laid there for hours, waiting for the sun to come up. My heart ached for Hayden.

➤

An hour or so after the sun rose, a Jeep roared to life, the loud engine echoing off the cold glass of my window. I jumped up and felt like luck was on my side. I saw Beau, Bart, Casey, and Harley get inside the vehicle and watched as it sped away.

I did yoga, sit ups, and drank a lot of water; I wanted my body ready. I was starving when Jaylyn unlocked my door. She had a dress folded over her arm and a smug look on her face.

"That's pretty," she said, looking at my chest. My hand flew up to the little silver leaf that hung from a chain. "Give it to me."

"No."

"Do what I tell ya."

"No. It's mine."

"I don't care. I want it."

"No," I repeated. *Would I be a horrible person if I hit a pregnant woman?*

She laughed, threw the dress at me, and went out of the room. The yellow dress I was wearing smelled like vomit, since some had splattered down the front. I took it off, carelessly throwing it on the floor, and put on the new one.

It was the worst dress by far. Light pink and very short, the thing had lacey cap sleeves and a bow on the back. It was belittling, the way they made us wear the dresses. It wasn't right, by any means, the way they thought they could do whatever the hell they wanted just because rules and laws couldn't be enforced. I closed my eyes and took a deep breath.

The door opened, startling me just a bit. Sue Ellen glared at me, dropping all pretenses of being nice and concerned with my welfare. I knew now that she saw me as a baby maker and nothing else.

"Come downstairs and eat," she said dryly.

I followed her down the hall. A door on the left was open; my eyes curiously looked inside. It had to be Jaylyn and Casey's room. An old wooden crib was pushed up against a wall. I slowed my pace and did a double take. I almost didn't see them since a dirty pair of pants covered one up, but my heart fluttered and my eyes widened at the site of the familiar camo pattern. My combat boots!

"Oh no," I groaned. "I'm gonna be sick." I turned around and scuttled into the bathroom. I made gagging sounds and flushed the toilet. When I got back into the hall, Sue Ellen was gone. I dashed into Jaylyn's room and grabbed my boots.

The stairs emptied into the very cluttered living room. An old, tattered chair housed various forms of crap that should have been thrown away years ago—crushed beer cans, torn magazines, used napkins, and dirty pillows. I tucked the boots safely underneath the chair, out of sight but easy to grab.

Olivia didn't meet my eyes when I went into the kitchen. She had a fresh bruise on her cheek, and she dished out a watery stew. When she took her place at the table, she coughed three times.

"Ah hell," Delmont cursed, pounding the table with his fist. Soup sloshed out of his bowl. "You better not be gettin' sick now too."

"No, just a tickle in my throat," she muttered.

After we ate, Sue Ellen demanded Olivia and I clean the kitchen to perfection while she went to her room to watch recorded episodes of Judge Judy.

"You got them?" I asked quietly, the sound of running water drowning my words from unwanted ears.

She nodded. "Yeah."

"Ok, do you know what they go to?"

She nodded again. "The old Ford truck outside."

"It works?"

Another nod. "It's Del's truck. I've seen him drive it before."

"Perfect. Where is it?"

"Probably in the driveway. The garage is full of junk so all the cars are outside."

"Even better. When I say run, we run."

"Ok."

I stepped away from the sink, looking through the kitchen doorway. In the living room, I could see Jaylyn and Del making out. What the fuck? I *knew* they were related. I wanted my boots, but I wasn't going to risk getting caught over them. I opened every drawer in the kitchen, looking for the sharpest cutlery. I decided upon two small yet effective vegetables knives. I gave one to Olivia.

I shouldn't have been surprised when I looked into the living room again. Jaylyn was on her knees, her mouth and hands busy with Delmont.

"Ew," I said under my breath. Wait...that was a perfect distraction. Del's eyes were closed and his head was back. I took a deep breath and carefully stepped into the living room. All Del had to do was open his eyes and he'd see me. I took another step. And then another, and another. I was almost to the chair. His breathing quickened. Shit, he was almost done. I snatched my boots and ran out of the room.

"I think the baby's his," Olivia stated once I skidded to a stop on the kitchen floor.

"Sick," I said and sank to my butt to lace up my boots. I stuck the knife inside my sock. "Do you have shoes?"

"No."

"I'll get you some." I stood. "Ready?"

"You have no idea how ready I am."

"Ok, then, run."

Leaving the water running in the sink, we raced out the back door, pausing in the snow-covered yard to find the truck. Olivia shivered. She had just raised her hand to point to a truck about fifty yards away when a shot rang out.

She screamed. I grabbed her hand and sprinted forward. The shop was closer than the truck. I flung the door open and jumped inside, pulling Olivia along with me. I don't know how he saw us, or how he pulled his pants up and grabbed the shotgun so quickly, but I caught a glimpse of Delmont chasing us.

We ran down an aisle of junk, bumping into overhanging shit that loudly toppled over. We ran through a break in the aisle before going down another one. This place was a fucking maze.

"You can't hide from me!" Delmont yelled. "I *will* find you!"

I slowed to a stop, pulling Olivia close to me. We huddled next to a shelf full of doll parts. Arms, legs, and broken heads stared up at us. I needed a weapon. I looked around; next to the dolls were their clothes, children's building blocks, and a bag of dingy stuffed animals that looked like they had spent too much time on a day care floor.

Olivia shook with fear. I took her hand and nodded reassuringly even though my own bravery had been replaced with trepidation. I heard Delmont's boots clicking the next aisle over. Olivia put her hand over her mouth. I held my breath, waiting.

"You're dumb, you know, trying to run away. You can never make it out there. You will get eaten in a matter of hours," he threatened.

I rolled my eyes. If only he knew…

My muscles tensed and I squeezed Olivia's hand. She shook her head, eyes darting in the direction Del's voice was coming. I nodded encouragingly and yanked her forward. We silently slipped through the aisle. There had to be a back door to this place.

I picked up a broken iron. I wrapped the cord around it to get it out of the way. I motioned to an empty spot on a shelf, trying to nonverbally tell Olivia I wanted her to hide there. It took her a few seconds to understand. With shaking hands she crawled in, hugging her knees. I ran to the break in the aisle, listening for Delmont, feeling as if the tables had turned.

His footsteps echoed loudly throughout the vast warehouse. I picked up a clock and threw it as hard as I could down an aisle. It clanked and skidded to a stop. Del fell for it and raced over, shotgun raised.

He dumbly looked at the clock, not able to put two and two together. I crept up behind him and struck him in the head with the iron. The gun flew out of his hands. I kicked him in the back and he fell to his knees, whacking his kneecaps on the hard cement floor. The gun was in my hands in seconds.

A smirk broke out on my face. Using the gun like a baseball bat, I hit him over the head. The scuffling of feet made me whirl around, pumping the shot gun. Olivia held her hands up. I flipped the shotgun around and extended it to her. She looked at it fearfully.

"Keep your finger off the trigger," I told her. "Only shoot if necessary. And trust me," I said, turning back to Delmont. "It won't be."

He staggered to his feet. I stood back and waited, allowing him time to regain what little composure he had. He took a swing at me. I easily ducked out of the way. When he swung again, I caught his fist, twisted his wrist, and in one swift movement, kicked him in the balls. When he doubled over in pain, I brought my knee up to his nose and shoved him back. I yanked a box of old books off a shelf, ripping the cardboard. They fell out, each one landing hard on Delmont's body. I pulled the knife from my boot.

"Don't kill me!" Delmont shouted, holding up his hands. Blood oozed from his nose. I laughed.

"Kill you? No, that would be doing you a favor. I'm not letting you off that easy." I held up the knife, the overhead florescent lights glinting off the metal. "Let's see…I could…cut off your balls, shove them in your mouth and sew your lips shut." The corners of my mouth pulled up in a sadistic smile. Delmont quivered. "Eventually you'll bleed to death. Or maybe choke. Either way, we will be long gone before anyone finds your cold, lifeless body, you disgusting, cousin-fucking prick."

I took the shotgun from Olivia and hit Del over the head, knocking him out. Then I yanked another box—this one filled with random junk—down on top of him, rammed the butt of the shotgun down on his balls, and grabbed Olivia's hand. She whimpered as I pulled her along. I pushed the back door. It only moved a few inches. Something was jammed against it from the outside. Dropping Olivia's hand, I used my body to force it open. I had to slam into it several times, no doubt creating nasty bruises on my shoulder, but it opened enough for us to squeeze through.

We weaved our way through the junkyard, all the while I was hoping Olivia wouldn't step on something sharp or rusty. The entire property was surrounded by a six-foot wooden fence.

"We're trapped!" Olivia cried.

"No, we're not," I promised. I walked along the fence, looking for a weak spot. I kicked it; the board cracked. I kicked it again and my foot went through. Feeling like a zombie, I painfully forced my body to fit beneath the small opening. Olivia clambered along behind me, her hair getting caught on a splinter. She yanked it free, leaving several strands blowing in the wind.

Sue Ellen was waiting for us on the other side, holding a buck knife. Olivia made a strangled noise of fear, but I eagerly marched forward. I pumped the shotgun once more and terror washed over Sue Ellen's face. I wickedly smiled and raised the gun.

I didn't want to waste bullets on her—she just wasn't worth it. But she didn't need to know that. She held her ground until I was six feet away. Then she dropped the knife and fled. As much as I wanted to punch her in the throat, taking the time to do so wasn't worth it either.

"Let's go," I told Olivia. I wanted out of there right away and, more importantly, I wanted out of there before a truck full of people with rifles and bows—and who knows what else—got home. We ran to the truck. I held out my hands for the keys. Olivia didn't move.

"Orissa, wait," she spat. "We-we're safe here, from the zombies. I don't want to die."

"I told you I'd take care of you," I reiterated.

"How do I know that's true?"

"Would you rather stay here?"

"No," she squeaked, her body trembled. "I don't want to get eaten."

"Neither do I. But I'd rather face zombies than get raped."

"They'll stop once I'm pregnant," she stated.

"That is so messed up and probably not true. Give me the keys before I force them from you!" I threatened, hoping it wouldn't come to that. This poor girl had been through enough.

She whimpered again but pulled the keys from inside her dress. I unlocked the truck, jumped in, and stuck the keys in the ignition. Olivia got in on the other side. It was cold and the truck hadn't been driven in a while. The engine sputtered.

"Come on," I encouraged it, turning the key again. Finally, it revved to life. "Thank God!" I sped down the driveway, fearing that we would run into the returning hunters. They had turned left onto the road; I turned right. I hated that there was several inches of snow. It made us so easy to track. The truck slid and fishtailed, but I didn't dare slow down. I was gripping the steering wheel tightly, so much adrenaline coursing through my veins that I didn't even realize it was cold until Olivia turned the heater on.

"What do we do now?" she timidly asked.

"Get out of these fucking lame-ass dresses," I bitterly spat. As if holding us hostage wasn't enough, they had to objectify us with frills and lace.

"You certainly have a way with words," she said, a faint smile evident on her pale face.

"Yep. I'm a fucking poet." We drove in silence for several minutes. The country road seemed endless. Snow drifted in front of us, challenging the old Ford truck. I didn't let up on the gas, and I kept throwing nervous glances at the review mirror. The tire tracks in the snow taunted me.

I almost missed the turn; I spun the wheel sharply and the truck slid around in a complete circle. We skidded to a stop on the side of the road. I pressed the pedal down and the engine groaned. We were stuck.

"Come on," I urged, putting the truck into reverse. I slowly rocked it back and forth, terrified of not getting away before Bart and his bastard, inbred children stumbled upon us.

"Should I get out and push?" Olivia asked, earning major points in my book.

"Possibly," I replied honestly, though I knew I was the better candidate for pushing. We rocked back and forth one more time before we were freed. Going slower this time, I started down the remnants of a snow covered, two lane highway.

"Do you think they'll come looking for us?" Olivia questioned, her voice full of fear.

"I'm sure."

"What do you think they'll do if they find us?"

"They won't find us. I promise."

"How can you be so sure?"

"I just am."

"That's not very convincing," she mumbled, picking at the hem of her dress.

"I'm not gonna let them find us. And if they do, I'll kill them. Each and every one of them. I want to see my friends again, and I'm not going to let some back-woods, *The Hills Have Eyes,* family stop me from going home."

Olivia said something, but I didn't pay attention. As soon as the word slipped from my mouth, I knew it was true.

I had never considered the compound home. I thought it was odd when Hayden called it his home. But, that was what it was. Everything...everyone I had left in the world was at the compound. Though it was far from ideal, the place housed a few people who just happened to mean the world to me. It *was* home, and that was where I wanted to go.

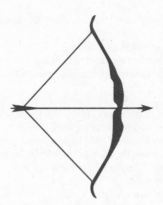

CHAPTER 6

We continued in silence for another twenty miles. Shops and restaurants dotted the highway. I eyed them, debating whether or not it was too soon to stop. We needed fuel. New, warm clothes and food would be nice, but we could survive without them for a while longer. And, most of all, I needed to know where the hell I was.

A motorcycle store loomed ahead. At the last minute I stopped, doing a donut in the parking lot. When the truck finally stopped sliding, I put it in park and opened my door.

"I'm gonna check it out, stay here and keep the engine running," I told Olivia. Her green eyes held back terror but she complied. I peered into the backseat, looking for anything useful. Along with a lot of crap was a large flashlight. It worked, though I wouldn't need the light just yet. It was metal and heavy and good for bashing in a brain.

The cold air stung my skin and was painful to inhale. I slowly approached the front door of the store. It wasn't broken, but it wasn't locked either. I pushed it open, making a stupid bell jingle. I reached up and yanked it down. Then I waited.

Nothing happened.

I waved for Olivia to open her window. Nervously, she leaned out of the truck.

"I'm gonna get us clothes and hopefully a map. Keep an eye out for zombies. Leave if it gets bad. I'll catch up, ok?"

She shyly nodded. I went back in the store. The first half was filled with motorcycles; some of them were really nice. I admirably ran my hands over chrome handlebars on a custom Chopper. I had an on-and-off boyfriend throughout most of high school who had a motorcycle. My mother hated it.

Past the motorcycles were accessories and parts that meant nothing to me. And past that were displays of clothing. There was only one small round rack of woman's clothes. I ruffled through the leather pants to find one my size. I took off my boots and yanked them on. They were surprisingly comfortable.

I threw the ugly dress to the ground and put on a black, long sleeve t-shirt. I zipped a tight fitting, black leather jacket up over that and picked up my boots, set on lacing them back up when I heard scuffling behind me. I spun around, ready to use the heel of my boot as a weapon.

"Sorry!" Olivia cried, holding her hands up protectively over her head.

"It's alright," I told her, trying not to sound pissed. The girl reminded me of an abused dog; as soon as someone raised their hands, she assumed she was going to get hit. "What are you doing?"

"I got scared out there. I left the truck running though, just in case."

"Oh, ok. While you're here, quickly get something to wear. I'm gonna look for a map or something."

I searched the whole store but didn't find a map. When I returned to Olivia, she had put on a pair of dark jeans, a Harley Davidson hooded sweatshirt, and biker boots. She wobbled when she walked in the low wedge heels.

"Not used to wearing heels?" I stated the obvious.

"No. I've never worn them before," she admitted. She tripped, nearly twisting her ankle.

"What shoe size are you?" I asked, thinking I couldn't have her slowing me down any more than she was bound to.

"Eight and a half."

"Try these," I said, sitting down to unlace my boots. "They're a nine, so they might be a little big, but it's better than the heels. I need you to be able to run if need be."

I exchanged my boots for another pair of motorcycle boots. They looked better with the leather pants anyway. I grabbed a pair of gloves for each of us before going back into the parking lot. A silver SUV caught my attention. I told Olivia to get in the truck and wait while I raced back inside the store. I emerged with tools and a devious smile.

"You're kinda scary," Olivia told me with just a hint of awe in her voice after I hotwired the SUV.

"Aren't you glad?" I asked, straightening up. "Let it run for a few minutes before we get in." I pulled down the visor and looked in the glove box. "Yes!" I said out loud when I pulled out a pack of cigarettes and a lighter.

"You smoke?"

"Ew, no way. But this," I held up the lighter, "can come in handy." We let the SUV run for over five minutes before turning on the heater. Another five passed and the car was filling with warm air. Declaring it good enough, I went back into the shop one last time.

I ripped the hem off of the horrible dress I was forced to wear and shoved it inside the gas tank of Del's truck. I drove the truck into the middle of the road, got out, lit the dress on fire and walked away. I didn't look back when it exploded. Olivia gaped at me for the next thirty miles, unable to believe everything I had done.

"I feel safe with you," she told me, her green eyes shining. Suddenly, an image of Zoe flashed through my brain. I pushed it away, but not before it could affect me.

No matter what, I was going to take care of Olivia.

I pulled into a parking lot of a grocery store. I assured Olivia that I had no intentions of going in. A few gummies milled about. I leapt from the SUV and struck one in the head with the flashlight and he dropped, his mushy brains leaking out onto the pavement. I smashed car windows, setting off an alarm on two, in search of an atlas. I found it in car number six.

We were in southern Iowa and I judged our time from the compound to be eight hours or less. My heart fluttered and my stomach did that stupid flip-flop when I thought of seeing Hayden.

After three hours of problem free driving, we ran into a pile up. Going on past experiences, I didn't want to chance it. But, we were hungry and running low on fuel. If I could find something to eat or a gas can, then it would be worth it.

"Stay here and keep your eyes peeled, ok?" I instructed.

"Ok."

"I mean it. If something comes, honk and I'll come running. As soon as I'm in, drive. Got it?"

"Yes, got it," she promised.

I slowly picked my way through the cars. Dead bodies scattered the road, most of them gnawed to the bone by zombies. I opened the door to a minivan and nearly retched when I saw the car seat in the back. Something really terrible must have happened to make the parents leave their baby.

Moving on, I thought luck struck when I climbed up the steps of a school bus. Coolers had been packed and stashed on the front seats. The cold kept the smell of rotten food to a minimum. I dug through it, looking for something edible and hopefully not full of E Coli. I pulled out a jar of peanuts. It wasn't much, but it was enough to get us through the next few hours. A case of water had busted and bottles rolled all over the bus. I grabbed four and jogged back to the car.

We devoured the nuts and drank our water within the hour. I should have known my luck would run out. The SUV suddenly started shaking and the engine overheated, I had no idea what to do.

"Piece of shit!" I cursed, hitting the steering wheel.

"What do we do?" Olivia whimpered.

I looked around; we were on another stretch of country road with nothing ahead or behind us. "Get out and walk until we find another car." I gathered up the map and the flashlight and got out. Olivia nervously gripped the shotgun.

"What's the compound like?" Olivia inquired as we walked.

"It's…it's nice. And safe. It used to be a bomb shelter so most of it is underground. There's food, water, medicine, and clothes. And even heaters and warm water for showers."

"Is it like a big room with cots set up?"

"Not at all. You'll have a roommate, or two or three maybe. The rooms look kinda like dorm rooms. And there's a cafeteria and a couple of game rooms."

"Is it run by the government?"

I almost laughed. "No. Well, maybe you'd call them that now. It's run by American soldiers and Marines."

"Oh, that does seem safe."

"It is. It's the safest place I know of, or can think of."

"So," she said quietly. "Why aren't you there?"

"We go on missions. To look for people or get supplies. I got separated from my…my friends," I explained, though I didn't consider Alex a friend at all. Along with reuniting with my real friends, I couldn't wait to punch Alex in the face.

A high pitched scream echoed behind us. Olivia froze in fear. I spun around, taking a defensive stance. The crazy had a piece of a metal pipe through his leg, but he raced toward us as if it was nothing. He wouldn't have been a problem. But there were a shit ton of S2s behind him…

"Motherfucker!" I yelled, really hating the way S1s were zombie magnets. My eyes darted back and forth from Olivia to the zombies. She was defenseless. Yeah she had the gun but I doubted she be able to hit the broad side of a barn. Besides it wouldn't be long before it was out of ammo. I took her hand. "Run!"

We raced down the road, across a field and into the woods. The zombies would eventually catch the S1 and hopefully he'd be enough of a distraction. All we had to do was get to another road with a pile up, a town with cars, or even a safe place to be bunkered in for a while.

Olivia couldn't keep up with me. She wheezed and gasped for air, putting her hands on her knees and bending over. I had to work to keep my patience with her, especially when I realized she had dropped the shotgun while we were running. I pushed her forward yet again, not feeling safe enough to slow down. Finally, when the trees became thinner, I slowed to a walk. She had just caught her breath when we emerged from the forest into an overgrown field. A large building that looked like an old hospital loomed ahead.

"Can we stop and rest?" she asked, pointing to it.

"Sure," I agreed. "But only for a little bit." Without speaking, we crossed the field. Soon, we came to a heavy metal door. I pulled it open, turned on the flashlight and stepped into a graveyard.

"What the fuck?" I said to the darkness. The door shut behind us with a rusty screech. I moved the flashlight around the room. Light reflected off tombstones and a coffin lay open in front of a crypt. Olivia tripped over a grave. It snapped under her weight.

"Oh," I said as I helped her up. "Right."

"What's r-right about this?" she stuttered.

"We're in a haunted house," I explained.

"And that's right?!"

"A *fake* haunted house," I continued. When she still didn't get it, I went on. "The virus struck in October. The country is frozen in a permanent Halloween Town."

"Oh, that makes sense. Can we get out of here? I hate haunted houses."

"Sure," I said. I wasn't scared of haunted houses, but I didn't feel like weaving my way through the maze of props. I shined the light on the door. "Uh oh," I said.

"What is it?"

"There's no handle on this side. I can't open the door," I told her as I pried at the edges.

"What are we going to do?"

"Go through the house."

She shook her head, making a whimpering noise.

"It'll be fine. We'll just go straight through."

She extended her hand. "Can I hold your hand?"

I took her hand, which was sweating already. I kicked a plastic skeleton out of the way, and slowly slid the light over the room; there were two doorways on each side of the indoor graveyard. We were closer to the one on the left. I guided Olivia through it.

We entered a hallway. Strips of rags, stained with fake blood, hung down, brushing against our faces as we walked. I put my hand out, feeling what was in front of me. The hallway gradually narrowed until Olivia couldn't walk next to me.

Then the ceiling dropped, and the feeling of being trapped made my heart race. Crouching down, I rushed through the shrinking hall, not being careful with the light. I smacked into a wall; Olivia smacked into me.

"What's wrong?" she whispered.

"Nothing, we just went too far." I scanned the area with the flashlight. "There!" I pointed to a hole in the wall. "We have to crawl through."

"No, I don't want to," she cried, clutching my arm.

"Olivia, we have to."

"I know, but I still don't want to."

"I'll go first." I slipped through the hole, turning to help Olivia. We were in another room; this one was supposed to look like an evil doctor's office. Fake brains and hearts in jars lined a shelf that also housed medieval-style surgical instruments. The blood-stained gurney had been knocked over.

We stepped over it, and I pushed aside the plastic curtain that hung in the doorway of yet another narrow hall. We had to go up a few stairs before we emerged into another room. This one was the biggest yet, and was filled with glass panels and mirrors.

"Seriously?" I said under my breath. We stepped into the maze. And something moved behind us.

The metal scraping on concrete instantly terrified me. I whipped around, right hand curling into a fist. The stethoscope still hung around his neck, but he was worse than an evil doctor; he was a zombie. I thrust the flashlight in Olivia's hands, not wanting to break it by using it as a weapon. Her shaking hands couldn't get a grip and she dropped it.

I jumped out of the maze, took my stance and kicked him in the face. His jaw broke and he staggered back from the impact. I had practiced the 360 style kicks relentlessly but was never allowed to kick someone in the face that way. With a smile on my face, I jumped up and around, my foot making contact with the zombie doctor's skull.

In the end of the S2 phase, his skull easily broke. When he hit the floor, I drove the heel of my boot down into his head. Brains spattered and a putrid smell filled the room, much like cracking open a rotten egg.

"Alright, carry on," I said with a wicked smile. Olivia's mouth was open and her eyes were wide. She didn't move when I walked past. I had to grab her hand and pull her out of whatever the hell kind of reverie she was stuck in.

Shining the light as we walked helped me know what was ahead of us; it reflected off the mirrors and the glass like I expected. But it didn't stop us from making a wrong turn and coming to a dead end. Twice we ended up in the same spot. Finally, we took the correct turn and moved forward.

And then we realized we weren't alone.

➤————————————————➤

I grabbed the flashlight and covered it with my hand, shushing Olivia. I smelled them but couldn't see them so I had no idea how many were in here with us. But the echoing death rattles and the shuffling and dragging of zombie feet let me know there were many—too many for me to single handedly take on.

If I released the light, they'd be more apt to get us. And we'd never get out of this fucking maze. They already knew we were here…I uncapped the light and raced forward. Olivia's breath came out in sharp, loud gasps. She was hyperventilating.

"Keep it together, I'm gonna get us out of this," I promised and gave her the flashlight so she'd feel like she had some control over the situation. We slammed into a glass wall. Olivia screamed.

"There's one on the other side! We're going to die!" she cried.

"Stop being so dramatic. We didn't get this far just to die. Come on!" I yanked her forward. My heart hammered and I couldn't get my breathing to slow. I too was scared, though I wasn't going to let Olivia know it.

We slowly made our way through another section of the maze. I squeezed Olivia's hand to keep from shaking. A zombie crashed into a glass panel. We both jumped. With trembling hands, Olivia shined the light on her.

Her lips hand been torn off and the tip of her nose was missing. One eye dangled out of the socket. She groaned, dragging her nails on the glass.

"Can she break through?" Olivia asked.

"No," I said, putting my hand on the panel to taunt the zombie. "This is Plexiglas, not real glass." Real glass would have been too easy. I could have easily broken it and walked in a straight line to the opposite end of the room. "But she—and the others—can catch up."

We staggered into a fork in the road of the maze. We circled around, unsure of which way to go. Behind us, the herd groaned. Well, that eliminated one direction. Suddenly remembering I had a lighter, I reached into the jacket to pull it out.

A fast S2 raced up behind us and grabbed me around the waist. His teeth tried to sink into my shoulder but the leather stopped him. I easily flipped him over my head and kicked him in the face. Before I could pull my leg back and end his after life, Olivia raised her foot and stomped on the zombie's head. She cracked the skull and then slipped and fell back on her butt. I extended a hand and pulled her to her feet.

"Good job," I complimented.

We sprinted forward, getting stuck at another dead end. It wouldn't be long before a zombie or two caught up to us. I could only hope they were having as much—if not more since they couldn't think logically—trouble with the maze as we were.

"This way!" I shouted, a few feet ahead of Olivia. We rounded a corner and slammed into a wall. I turned and was face to face with a mirror, which was situated at the center of the exit. We went around it and stumbled into another narrow hall. A door with a red X painted on it loomed ahead. *Please be the way out*, I thought. Without hesitation, I opened it.

We were in a large, open room. Maybe it was an empty, unused room. Olivia took my hand again, the flashlight shakily casting a cone of yellow light around the room.

"Don't move," I said. I took the light from her and illuminated my field of vision. Large, multi colored spots had been painted all over the floor and the walls. Oh, shit. I knew what room we were in; the one I despised the most in any haunted house. I heard him growl just as the rotting smell made me gag.

A zombie clown limped over, his spotted outfit camouflaging him with the spotted walls. His red nose was crusted with blood and drainage from the festering wounds had cracked and peeled the white makeup he was wearing. The rainbow wig was matted into a pus-covered sore on his forehead.

Olivia started shaking uncontrollably. I rushed forward and kicked the son of a bitch in the chest. He was big, and, having no sense of pain, didn't react optimally to my efforts. He clawed at the air, lips pulled back in a snarl.

Fucking clowns, I swore to myself. I dropped to the ground, extended my leg and knocked his feet out from under him. The heels on my boots came in useful yet again when I drove it into his eye socket. Something hung from the ceiling, wrapped in rainbow striped material. I pulled Olivia along and right as we walked past it, the thing wiggled to life, laughing an evil, harrowing laugh. She screamed and my heart skipped a beat.

It was a motion-activated, battery-powered, life-sized doll. Nevertheless, I punched it and ended the wiggling. I cast the light around the room until we found the door. With no time to second-guess it, we fled through it and into another room; this one was filled with giant spiders and rubber snakes.

Stepping on the props, we hurried through the room and crawled through another narrow hallway until we were thrust into a room that was set up like an old fashioned insane asylum. It oddly reminded me of Hayden, since the first safe house I stayed at with him was in an old mental hospital.

Something crashed into the fake jail bars, causing Olivia to scream again. She covered her mouth and whimpered. Still dressed in the strait jacket, the zombie looked fittingly insane. I didn't know if the bars would hold. We continued on, hearts racing and hands shaking. We went through one more room—this one set up like a demonic sacrifice—before we bolted into the fading daylight.

I kept running, wanting to put more distance between us and the literal hell house as possible. When Olivia couldn't go any farther, we stopped for air.

"I...used...to...like...Halloween," she panted.

"Me too." Though, I mostly liked the excuse to wear slutty costumes. I shook my hands and put them on my head, trying to open up my airway as much as possible. I walked in a slow circle, willing my body back to normal.

As soon as Olivia caught her breath, we walked down the road. After half an hour or so, a traffic jam came into view. There were no cars in the ditches, no bodies scattered along the ground, and no stench of death in the air. And, best of all, there wasn't snow anymore.

"Help me check the cars," I told Olivia.

"What am I looking for?"

"Keys. Or tools."

"Ok," she nodded and hesitantly strode off on her own. If people were fleeing for their lives, they might leave the keys, right? I hoped so. I pulled on the door of a BMW. Of course, it was locked. We wasted precious daylight checking the rest of the cars with no luck.

Sighing, I leaned against a new Chevy truck. I nervously scanned the stores that lined the road. When I read the sign, I excitedly gasped.

"Olivia! Come here!"

She raced over, looking scared shitless.

"Nothing bad, look," I said, pointing.

"Yeah?"

"It's a pawn shop, a pretty big one by the looks of it."

"Uh, I don't get it."

I shook my head. "Pawn shops usually have weapons." I smiled and took off in the direction of the store, Olivia trailing behind. I had to climb up on a dumpster and break in through a window to get inside.

Olivia scrambled in after me, falling as she jumped in from the windowsill. She got up right away and shook herself off, nodding to let me know she was ok. Behind the register was a display of guns. I picked up a twelve gauge.

"I don't know if there are bullets here," I mumbled. I strapped a nice, ivory handled Glock to my thigh.

"There are a lot of knives over here," Olivia called.

Setting down an antique revolver, I went over to the display and used the rifle to break the glass.

"Are you sure it's ok to just take things?" she innocently asked.

"Yeah. Who else is gonna use this? Everything belongs to everyone," I rationalized.

"Oh, if you say so." She looked around and excitement sparkled in her eyes.

"Hah," I said, picking up a device. "I always wanted one of these." I buckled it around my wrist, and, with a flick of my arm, a knife shot out of the little box.

"I changed my mind," Olivia stated, speaking more confidently than ever. "Instead of kinda scary you are *really* scary. And I'm glad."

I smiled and shrugged. "You have to be in order to make it in this world."

She nodded and pocketed a hunting knife. I was able to find ammo for the rifle and the Glock. But what Olivia found was even better. Hanging up on a labeled bulletin board in the office were four sets of keys. She selected the keys under the "Mustang" label, smiled, and tossed them to me.

We slipped back out the window. I looked around for zombies, almost disappointed when I didn't see any. I wanted to test out the new weapons. I unlocked the black Mustang and fired up the engine. We let it run for a good fifteen minutes this time before getting in. I cut apart a hose and filled up the tank with siphoned gas from parked cars. Olivia looked over the map as I drove.

Once we were on our way, Olivia messed with the MP3 player that was hooked up in the car. She flipped through songs, eventually deciding upon a Taylor Swift album. We were hungry and thirsty but didn't dare stop. In just hours, I'd be home.

I imagined Raeya's face when she saw see me walk through the doors. And then I thought of Hayden and wondered if he was okay…if he had made it. No, he had and he was okay. He had to be!

"What are you thinking about?" Olivia asked, turning down the radio.

"Nothing," I said automatically.

"You're smiling."

"No I wasn't."

"Yes, you were," she said, a hint of laughter in her voice. "Were you thinking about your friends?"

"Yeah. I'm excited to see them."

"I bet. I'm excited to meet everyone. You're one of the soldiers, right?"

"Sure."

"Sure?" she questioned.

"It's a long story," I said, although it really wasn't. I just didn't feel like explaining it. "You'll like it there, though, after what you've been through, anything would be nice. And I know someone who would be a good friend to you," I said, thinking of Sonja. "How old are you?"

"Sixteen."

My stomach churned. It was tempting to get my trusted A1 friends, load up a truck with weapons, and drive back to Iowa.

"Who are you excited to see?"

"My best friend, Raeya. And my friend Padraic. And…" I couldn't help the smile that formed when I said his name. "Hayden, my partner."

"Oh, so she's like your girlfriend?"

"What? Wait, no, no, not at all. Hayden has a penis. *He's* my partner, like we go out on missions and kill zombies together kind of partner."

"Oh, sorry. Is he the one you got separated from?"

"No. That's a long story too. You'll learn it all once you get there."

Thankfully, she took my hint and shut up. Time passed so slowly. When the landscape became familiar, my heart beat rapidly with excitement. I gripped the steering wheel, dumbly smiling. Observing my excitement, Olivia sat up straight and peered out her window.

I was home.

$$\longrightarrow$$

I turned onto the drive. The first gate came into view; it had been repaired since I ran Hayden's truck through it. I got out and hurriedly opened it, not bothering to shut it after the car passed through. The A3s scuttled around in a panic when they saw the Mustang roll to a stop. Jason's familiar face peered out of the watch tower.

I leaned out the open window and smiled. "Open the gate!" I yelled, only half joking. Jason stared at me for a few seconds, disbelief obvious on his face. Then the gates slowly opened. He flew to the car, opening the door.

I got out and let him hug me. I put my arms around him too, taken aback by the emotion I felt to be around my old friends again.

"Orissa! W-we all thought you were dead. I can't believe this! I-I think I'm dreaming."

"Nope. I'm here and it's real," I said with a gooney smile plastered on my face. "Where is Hayden? How is…"

"I-I just can't believe it!" he said breathlessly. The other A3s circled me, more than one shouting into their walkie-talkies.

"Hayden," I blurted. "Is he ok?"

"Yeah," Jason answered right away. "H-how did you…did you bring someone back with you?"

"Yeah, I did. I should get her inside."

"Right," he agreed, still dumbfounded. "You…you are…the best, Orissa."

"Thanks, Jason." I got back in the car and floored it to the estate. I shut the car off and got out, impatiently waiting for Olivia to follow. Brock and Padraic came running out of the house. My heart leaped in joy and I took off toward them. Padraic got to me first. He wrapped his arms around me, picking me up and spinning me. I hugged him back, feeling annoyingly emotional.

I felt his body shake. I pressed my head against his chest and let him hold me for a minute.

"I didn't believe it," he said.

I forgot how much I missed his accent.

"When they came over the radio….But you're here."

"Duh," I said.

He gently let go and held me at arm's length. "Are you alright?"

"I'm hungry, but I'm fine."

He pulled me to him once more and kissed my forehead. "We all thought…" he trailed off. "But I *knew*. I knew you were still alive. After all, you always told me you did your best work on your own."

"Ah, I did say that."

"Orissa?!" a female voice called.

I broke away from Padraic. "Ray!" Ivan and Raeya exited the house. She ran to me, her arms flying around my neck, and immediately broke down in sobs. I blinked back tears and squeezed my best friend.

"I'm so sorry, Ray. I didn't want you to worry."

"Orissa…I…I…you're…" she incoherently cried. I held her, stroking her hair.

"It's ok, Ray. I'm here now."

She sniffed. "I should b-be comforting you. I c-can't believe it! They said you died, that you got eaten."

"I told you it takes more than zombies to kill me. And apparently more than blood poisoning and inbred, psychotic, womanizing pigs."

"What?"

"I'll tell you later."

Ivan stepped up next to me and encased me in his muscular arms. "You are the most badass person I know," he told me as he squished me. "We all thought you were dead."

"Yeah, sorry about that," I joked.

"Seriously, Penwell. I never thought I'd see you again." He let me go and Brock stepped in, also hugging me. I looked around. Someone very important was missing. Had Jason lied to me?

"Where's Hayden?" I asked, fearing the answer I might get.

Brock looked at Ivan, his mouth open.

My heart stopped beating.

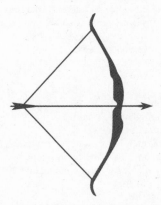

CHAPTER 7

For a moment, seconds that stretched on forever, it seemed no one wanted to answer me. They just looked at one another.

"Sleeping," Padraic finally answered, not easing my horror. He stepped closer. "I just gave him a dose of Fentanyl maybe an hour ago."

"He's ok? And the meds work?" I was almost stuttering. "Then he…he's been awake. He did wake up?"

"Yes and yes. The Fentanyl blocks out his pain," Padraic explained.

Tears pricked the corners of my eyes and relief washed over me. To mask the emotion, I turned to Olivia, who had gone unnoticed. "This is Olivia," I introduced.

"Ohmygod," Raeya exclaimed. "Sorry, where are my manners? Hi, I'm Raeya Kinsley."

"Hi," Olivia shyly stated, her cheeks turning bright red when Ivan walked over.

"You were left for dead, survived for almost two weeks on your own, *and* you bring back a civilian?" Ivan asked incredulously.

I shrugged like it was no big deal.

"Over achiever," he teased and we all laughed.

The door opened and Fuller stepped out, a smile on his usually stoic face. He strode over and shook my hand. "I didn't believe it. I had to see for myself."

"It was nothing," I said, brushing off the extent of my circumstance. As much as I liked being the center of attention, I wanted to go inside and see Hayden.

There were a few minutes of chaos as we walked into the compound. Everyone was asking questions at the same time. Olivia snaked her way through the small crowd and took my hand. I smiled at her and nodded, letting her know everything was going to be ok.

Ignoring the shocked stares from random residents, we went down to the C level and into Fuller's office. He looked at Ivan and Brock, nodded and turned to me. Raeya linked her arm though mine and said she was never going to let me go. Olivia still had a hold on my hand and Padraic stood behind me touching my shoulder.

The door clicked shut; Ivan and Brock left. Fuller circled around his desk, obsessively straightening a stack of papers.

"You're quite the soldier, Penwell," he complimented, looking at me proudly.

"Thanks," I said.

He looked at my friends and cleared his throat. Only Padraic got the hint. He dropped his hand off my shoulder and placed it on Raeya's back. When she turned to look at him, he motioned to the door. She shook her head in protest and held onto me tighter. I imagined the look he must have given her. She let me go, smiled sweetly at Olivia, and extended her hand. Reluctantly, Olivia let go of me and took Raeya's hand.

Then the door shut and I was alone with Fuller.

"What happened?" he inquired.

"They left me."

"I know that. Why?"

"Because they're impatient?" I tried.

Fuller frowned at me. "That's not what Alex said."

I crossed my arms. "Really? What *did* Alex say?"

He narrowed his eyes. "You took on the hostiles single handedly."

"Yep. I saved their asses. But go on, I'm dying to know the rest of Alex's story."

Fuller sighed and leaned against his desk. "You went against his orders."

"I don't take orders from anyone," I spat.

He took a deep breath. "Be respectful."

"How about you be respectful?" I countered, my temper rising. "I was *left*. I saved *their* asses. If not for me, we'd all be dead! And…and Hayden wouldn't have gotten the medication he needed!"

"Orissa!" he scolded, sounding very fatherly. His eyes darted from mine to a picture on his desk. I curiously followed his gaze and was startled to see a photo of Fuller and Hayden. I blinked. No, it wasn't Hayden; it just looked like him. The guy in the photo was younger and his hair was just a shade darker. His smile matched Fuller's. He had to be his son.

I snapped my attention back to the matter at hand. "What?"

"That's not how we function. You were part of a *team*. You shouldn't have gone off on your own."

"Oh, and they were such a great team to be on, leaving me to die!"

"You shouldn't have gone off on your own!" he reiterated.

"I had to."

"You shouldn't put yourself in danger like that."

I rolled my eyes. "Obviously, I can handle it."

He angrily shook his head. "You are a self-centered, reckless brat at times."

I shrugged. "I've been called worse."

He ran his hand over his head. "I didn't bring you here to reprimand you. Just go," he said with a wave. "Get something to change into and go to the quarantine room. You've earned your rest."

"Uh, hell yeah I have. But I'm not going to the quarantine room."

"We've been over this, Penwell. It's protocol."

"Fuck protocol. I'm. Not. Going." I almost stomped my foot. "You have no idea what I've been through. I want to be around my friends and sleep in my own bed. You damn well know that if I was bitten I'd tell you. I might be reckless, but I'm not dumb." I turned on my heel and marched out of the room. I slammed the door shut in his face. Pissed, I stomped down the hall, my boots echoing with each angry footfall. I went down to the B level and, luckily, Dr. Cara was leaving the hospital ward just as I got to the door.

"Welcome back, Orissa," she said with a warm smile.

"Thank you," I said sincerely, appreciating her politeness.

"You didn't get a monkey, by chance did you?"

And there went my appreciation. "No, I was too busy trying not to die."

"Oh, well. Another time then." She nodded and moved on. I slipped in through the door, stepping carefully so the clicking of heels wouldn't disturb Hayden.

The hospital ward was dim and empty—empty, except for Hayden. The curtain was pulled around the bed, the same one he was in before. A smile subconsciously settled on my face as I drew nearer.

He wasn't hooked up to IVs and he was wearing a pair of blue pajama pants and a white t- shirt, looking more like the Hayden I was used to seeing.

"Hayden," I whispered. He didn't move. I sat on the edge of his bed and put my hand on his cheek. His warm skin sent a chill through me. "Hayden," I repeated. "It's me, Orissa. I'm back and I'm sorry

I was gone for so long. I-I missed you."

His head moved in my direction. I ran my fingers through his hair hoping he'd wake up. When he didn't, I stayed there a while longer. I pulled the blanket up to his chest, wanting to make him as comfortable as possible, wanting to protect him, and willing him to heal.

Raeya and Ivan were walking down the hall when I left the hospital ward.

"Told you," Ivan said to Raeya. I didn't think I was supposed to have heard that.

"Rissy!" Raeya cried and hugged me again.

"Where's Olivia?" I asked.

"Quarantine," Ivan answered.

"No," I argued. "That girl's been beaten and raped repeatedly for the last three months. Get her out."

"What?" Raeya asked, horrified. "Riss, what—"

"—Penwell," Ivan interrupted. "You've caused enough trouble, don't you think that—"

"No! I don't care. Neither of us were bitten! I promised I'd take care of her."

Raeya put her hand on my arm. "Riss, you're scaring me. Were you—?"

"No." I closed my eyes and shook my head. "Almost but no. I got Olivia out just in time."

"Got out from where?" she hesitantly asked.

"I'll explain after she's out."

Ivan bit his lip. "I'll see what I can do." Since I didn't have my badge or keys, he let us upstairs. I opened the door to my room and looked around; everything was as it should be. Hayden's bed was neatly made; mine still had the covers lazily thrown about. I crossed the room and sank down on the mattress.

"What's with the leather?" Raeya asked, a cheeky grin on her face.

I extended my leg. "It suits me, dontcha think?"

"Yeah. I like those boots."

"Thanks," I said with a smile. "They're good for smashing zombie brains."

"Lovely." She sat down next to me and rested her head on my shoulder. "I'm glad you're back, Rissy."

"Me too. But stop thinking about what could have been. I'm here and I'm fine."

"Ok."

My stomach growled.

"Hungry?" Raeya asked.

"Starving."

"It's dinner time," she informed me. "I'm sure you'll get extra helpings today," she added with a wry smile. "Do you want me to bring you something?"

"Yeah. I don't feel like dealing with everyone."

"You sure you're alright?" she joked.

"Hah, yes. I want to shower first. I feel disgusting."

"Ok. I'll bring you a tray." We stood and she hugged me one more time before forcing herself to leave my side and get food.

I showered, brushed my teeth and braided my hair in a tight, French braid. Padraic joined Raeya and me for dinner; I was curious as to which A1 gave them access to come up here but didn't care enough to find out.

After we ate, we sat around talking for a long time. They both wanted to know what had happened. I gave them a cliff notes version of Delmont and his inbred family, knowing the fine details would upset them both.

I woke up sometime around two in the morning. Hayden was the first person I thought about. I swung my legs over the bed, grabbed my badge and keys and tip toed through the darkened compound and into the hospital ward.

I slowly pushed the hospital door open. Voices floated through the ward. I disregarded them at first, wanting to get to Hayden.

"...not as potent in his blood...after the transfusion," Dr. Cara spoke to someone. I froze, rooted to my spot in the walkway in front of Hayden's bed. Something else was said that I couldn't make out. I strained to hear.

"...test the vaccine. Then we wouldn't have to worry," Dr. Cara spoke again. I felt like I had been yanked down into a pool of ice water.

But it made sense. Hayden always had some form of the zombie virus in his system. His body was able to fight it off and not become infected. Then he got shot—because of me—and needed a blood transfusion. His body couldn't fight off the virus anymore.

Dr. Cara had the vaccine...possibly. She needed to test it. And I knew just the person she could test it on. I raced back to my room, changing into combat ready attire. I caught sight of Hayden's camo jacket. I pulled it off the hanger and put it on, my fingers running over his embroidered last name. I got as many weapons as I could carry and took off to B level again. I opened the weapon storage room door and flicked the light on.

The tunnel doorway easily opened. It was creepy in here, but the drive to keep Hayden uninfected and alive pushed me forward without hesitation. It had to be a mile long—or longer. The entire thing was cemented and smelled like a musty basement. Water dripped in from vents in the ceiling. Cobwebs hung from the halls. Bugs crunched under my boots. Every twenty feet a single light bulb gave off an eerie, yellow glow. I emerged out of what was designed to look like a root cellar of the barn. The doors locked from the inside; I couldn't sneak back in the way I came.

It didn't matter; I had a mission to carry out. I jogged to the road, planning on walking until I found a car. Rain misted down on me. I kept walking. Then, as if someone turned on a faucet, it started pouring. The loud rain masked the sound of the car until it was only a few yards away from me. I half turned and was blinded by the headlights.

Dammit. Ivan or Brock must have heard me leaving. I considered making a break for it and running into the trees near the road or pretending to be a zombie. Since either of my genius plans was sure to get me shot in the head, I kept my eyes on the ground and didn't stop walking, not even when the car rolled up next to me.

"I didn't take that bullet just so you could run away and get yourself killed," he said.

Gravel crunched under my feet as I abruptly skidded to a stop. "Hayden!"

PART II

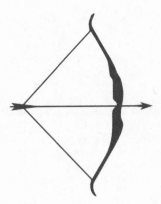

CHAPTER 8

He smiled at me. "Get in the truck, Riss."

"No. I-I have to do something." I didn't want to tell him what I overheard. What if he didn't know? He put the truck in park and got out. My heart sped up when he came close. "Hayden, you shouldn't be here. You could get hurt." The sound of the rain and wind nearly buried our conversation.

"Orissa," he said, his hazel eyes locking with mine, as he blinked back rain. "Losing you would hurt worse than getting shot a hundred times. "I lost everyone, Riss. Everyone I cared about. And then I met you. I'm not losing you."

"Duh," I blurted. "Then you'd be dead and wouldn't feel anything." I said. "Hayden, you shouldn't be out here."

"I won't let you go anywhere alone," he said. "I'm…" He smiled and stepped closer. "Orissa," he said again, though this time there was something alluring in his voice. "Every time I try to tell you, something horrible happens, so…" He put one hand on my waist. The other gingerly cupped my face. He tipped it up toward him then slid his hand back. His fingers tightened around my hair in desperation.

Then he kissed me.

And I kissed him back. My hands flew around him, pulling him closer. Suddenly, the pent emotion came flooding out. His tongue slipped into my mouth and his grip on me tightened. I yanked the M16 from my shoulder, let it clatter to the ground, and wrapped my arms around him, bringing him closer to me.

Hayden spun me around, pinning me in between himself and the truck. I wrapped a leg around him, desperately wanting him closer. We were drenched and the rain continued, relentless. He stopped kissing me only to put his lips on my neck. I shivered and let out a deep breath of pleasure. He moved his mouth down, unzipping the jacket as he did so. Then he kissed me again, pressing every inch of himself against me.

I put my foot back on the ground and grabbed him by the waist of his pants. My fingers quickly unbuttoned his jeans. He moved his mouth to my neck again, sucking and kissing my skin in a way that I couldn't resist. One hand went under my shirt, and the rough skin of his palm felt wonderful as he ran it over my stomach.

I put both hands around his face and kissed him hard, feeling such a strong pull of desire. A moan escaped my lips when his hands found their way under my bra. I stopped for air, moved to his jeans, and unzipped his pants. I stuck one inside, this time making Hayden let out a satisfied breath.

He melted against me as I worked my hands. He pulled one of his hands out from under my shirt and unzipped the jacket the rest of the way. Rain poured down, but neither of us cared. I continued stroking him until he stopped me, wrapping his hand around my wrist and pulling it out of his pants.

He picked me up and my legs automatically wrapped around his waist. He gave me a deep, passionate kiss. Desperate for more, I dug my nails into his back and pressed against him, feeling a tight coil of desire wind deep inside of me, desperate for a release. With me still in his arms, Hayden opened the truck door.

We ungracefully got in; I laid down on the back seat and Hayden was on me. He unbuttoned my pants and yanked them down; they got stuck on my boots and I sat up to hurriedly take them off. Having switched positions, I straddled him. Hayden ran his hands up and down my thighs. The desire wound tighter and tighter. My body wanted him, *needed* him. Not able to take it anymore, I unlaced his boots, tossed them to the front and removed his pants and boxers.

He grabbed a sleeve of my jacket and pulled it down. I shimmied out of it easily. He took my shirt and bra off next and cupped his hands around my breasts.

"You're beautiful," he whispered before he nestled his head in my breasts. I rubbed against his hardness, pressing it between my legs. The buildup was getting to be too much. I unbuttoned the flannel shirt he was wearing, carefully removing the sleeve from his left arm.

I gently touched the bullet wound. It had scabbed over, but still had to be painful. I lightly pressed my lips against it and let one hand fall from his shoulder, tracing down his abs and into his lap. He arched his back when I wrapped my fingers around his hardness. He enjoyed it for a few seconds before suddenly flipping me over.

On top of me, Hayden slipped his hand down the front of my panties, rubbing me with his fingers. He removed my underwear and laid over me, every inch of him pressing against my bare skin. I brought one leg up and curled the other around him, raising my hips to align with his. My desire for him was too much. I needed him. Now. My heart hammered and I ached for him.

We kissed again, and finally resituated with Hayden's hands on either side of me. I clung to him and he slid into me. Electricity rippled across my skin. Slowly, he thrusted back and forth. I loudly moaned, and he moved in deeper. My nails dug into his back. I sat up just enough to kiss him.

His breathing quickened, and he slowed his movements, biting at my neck. It sent me over the edge, and I grinded against him. I moved my hands to his muscular butt and pulled him to me, willing him in even more. He thrust faster and deeper. My back arched and my muscles contracted. Pure ecstasy took over. I opened my legs so Hayden could penetrate even deeper. I moaned loudly in pleasure as I came.

I ran my nails up and down Hayden's back then over his biceps. I opened my eyes to look at him and was hit with another wave of pleasure. Hayden was too, and he pulled me to him while he finished. He collapsed against me, breathing heavily. I combed my fingers through his hair.

He tightly wrapped his arms around me, holding me close as if I was the only thing that mattered. Hayden's weight on me was heavy, but I didn't care. I always enjoyed being wrapped in his embrace; being naked and wrapped in his embrace was so much better. It was safe, warm, comforting, and just so *right*.

When our hearts finally stopped racing, Hayden sat up, pulling me with him. I shivered. Though warm air was blowing from the heaters, the cold air that rushed in through the open door was stronger. He had to let me go to reach up and close it. Remembering that there was always a sleeping bag stashed in the back, I grabbed it and unrolled it. When Hayden moved back next to me, I draped it around our bodies.

"Orissa," he whispered.

"Yeah?"

He nestled his head against my neck. "I have been madly in love with you for quite some time now," he confessed.

I couldn't help the smile that broke out on my face.

"I wish I told you sooner."

"Why didn't you?" I asked softly.

"I was scared you wouldn't feel the same." His muscled tensed suddenly. "You do, don't you?"

"Of course."

He didn't look convinced.

I snuggled closer to him. "Hayden, when I thought you were dead, I wanted to die too."

He ran his fingers through my hair. "And when I saw the laser over your heart, all I could think about was how I didn't want to live without you."

I listened to his heart beat for a minute before I asked, "How did you find me out here?"

"I saw you come into the hospital ward. I heard what you heard and put two and two together. That and I followed you."

"So you know?" I sat up, fear radiating through my body once more.

"Yeah," he laughed. "And I'm not gonna get infected." He was able to discern the doubtful look on my face in the dark. "They were talking about the pain meds in my blood, not the virus."

"But I heard Dr. Cara say something about the vaccine," I countered.

"She did, but it had nothing to do with what she said. She does that—randomly switches the subject when she talks; it's irritating." He caressed my face. "Everything's gonna be ok. Somehow, it will, now that you're back."

His fingers traced my face, making me shiver, but not from cold. I put my leg over him and slid onto his lap until I was straddling him again. Hayden put his hands on my waist and smiled deviously.

"I don't like you going on missions without me," he said, his hands moving up my waist and onto my breasts. "Especially a long one like that."

My brow furrowed. "I wasn't on a mission," I said carefully. "Not the whole time at least."

"What are you talking about?" he asked and squeezed my breasts.

"You don't know?" I looked at him in disbelief.

"Know what?" He was more interested in what was in his hands. How could Hayden not know what had really happened? He put his mouth to me and when his tongue circled my nipple, I didn't care anymore. I held him tightly, crushing him against me. He flinched slightly and broke away.

"Are you ok?" I asked, worried I hurt him.

"Yeah. It just, uh, hurts sometimes," he said, shooting an annoyed glance at his shoulder. "What don't I know?" he asked again.

"I was left."

"Left?"

"Yeah. On that mission. They left me."

"What?" he demanded. He was mad, though not mad at me.

"The hospital we went to was overrun. I distracted the zombies and by the time I got away, Alex and everyone were gone. That's why it took me so long to get home." I figured I'd tell him the rest of my adventure later; this was upsetting him enough on its own. His face was set in such a way he looked scary.

"We should get back before anyone realizes we're missing," he said quietly, though I thought he wanted to get back and beat the shit out of Alex. I would love to watch.

I nodded. Silently, we got dressed in our rain soaked clothes and moved into our seats.

"You feel far away," Hayden said, the smile returning to his face. The center console separated us. I leaned over it and rested my hand on Hayden's thigh. He sped back to the compound, waving at the A3's who patrolled the watchtowers.

We were both cold from wearing wet clothes. By the time we got to our room, I was shivering. I kicked off my boots and yanked off my jeans. My underwear was still in the truck; I hadn't been able to find it in the dark. Hayden stripped out of his clothes too.

With the light on, I was able to finally openly admire just how good Hayden looked sans clothing. I removed my shirt, dropping it on the ground. Hayden put on a pair of blue boxers and a black t-shirt that said 'Semper Fi' on the chest in white letters. I put on the pajamas I'd been wearing earlier.

We got into my bed, snuggling close together. I stayed on his right side, careful not to put any pressure on his injured shoulder. I rested my head on his chest.

"Can you promise me something?" Hayden asked as he ran his fingers up and down my arm.

"Possibly."

"Don't try to go off on your own anymore."

"Ok," I said simply.

"Really, Riss. I mean it. I-I can't handle losing anyone else, especially you."

"I won't. Not anymore. I promise."

He sat up and kissed me. I pushed myself up and onto him, kissing him back. My hand slid over his chest and abs and under the waistband of his boxers. It didn't take long until he was hard again. The desperation wasn't as intense this time, but the desire was just as great.

Our clothing came off in a matter of seconds. Hayden tried to get on top of me again. I forced him away, pushing him down onto the mattress and climbed on, guiding him into me. I started out slow, wanting to draw it out for Hayden. His hands explored my body and I had to cover my mouth to keep from being heard. I rocked my hips, gradually moving faster. Then I stopped, and Hayden desperately wanted more.

I took his hands from my chest and moved them up, wanting to pin them above his head, but stopped, afraid it might hurt his injured shoulder. Instead, I pushed them down on the mattress so he was unable to move them. He breathed loudly and rapidly as I started moving again. The headboard hit the wall. I let go of Hayden's hands to shove a pillow behind it, which only muffled the sound a little bit.

Not caring, we didn't stop. Hayden bent his knees up, hitting me at a different angle, which felt incredibly good. I leaned forward, my breasts in his face, bit his neck and lost control. Once my muscles started working again, I straightened up and moved faster than before. In just a few seconds, Hayden came as well.

Hayden fell asleep soon after and didn't even put his clothes back on. I pulled his shirt on over my head and snuggled in. Later, he mumbled my name and put his arm around me. Feeling the happiest I had in a very long time, I drifted into a peaceful sleep.

Around ten AM, someone knocked on the door.

"Underwood, you alive in there?" Ivan's muffled voice called.

"Yeah," Hayden sleepily answered. Then we both realized how close we were to getting caught. Hayden jumped out of bed. "Pretend you're sleeping," he whispered and frantically looked for his boxers. He moved to the door, reaching for the knob.

"Your bed!" I whispered, pointing to his neatly made bed. He threw back the covers and opened the door.

"Why's the door locked?" Ivan asked, wiggling his eyebrows suggestively. "What—or who—are you doing?" he teased.

"Be quiet," Hayden said softly. "She's still sleeping."

Ivan must have looked at me. "You're right. She does sleep like a porn star."

I wanted to sit up and immediately question Hayden. Instead, I didn't move. I heard Hayden sink down onto his bed.

"Raeya was looking for Orissa, and your girlfriend wants you. She didn't like waking up with you not in bed next to her."

"Shut up," Hayden said, trying to sound serious, but I could tell he was holding back laughter.

"Dr. Cara really was looking for you."

"Is that all?" Hayden asked, obviously wanting Ivan to leave.

"Yeah," he replied. "Well, no. Raeya's bringing Orissa breakfast. I guess I'll tell her to bring up some for you. I'm glad you're ok, Underwood. And I know how this is gonna sound since you're half naked, but you look…good, like you've gotta clear head for once."

"Thanks," Hayden said awkwardly. When the door clicked shut, I opened my eyes.

"I sleep like a porn star?"

Hayden shrugged. "Yeah, the way you put your arms above your head reminds me of one."

"You watch me sleep. That is so creepy."

He nodded. "Yup. Every night. I steal your underwear too."

"I knew it." I laughed. Hayden crossed the room, and laid next to me. He turned on his left side and flinched.

"Hayden, you ok?"

"Yeah," he lied.

"The pain meds wore off," I stated.

"They tend to do that. It's fine. I don't like taking them; they make me tired and confused."

"How bad does it hurt? I don't want you to be in pain."

"It doesn't feel good, but it's not that bad," he tried to convince me. "You're a good distraction."

I sat up and gently touched the bullet wound. The horrific scene flashed through my mind. Where had those guys come from? Why did they want us dead? I rested my head on Hayden's chest. It didn't matter now. Hayden was alive and well and the guys that shot him were dead and gone.

But what if there are more? More gang members?

"I'm gonna take a shower," he said, getting up. "I wish you could join me."

"Me too," I agreed, already thinking of ways we could sneak it. Once Hayden left, I got up and put my pajama pants on. A minute later, Raeya appeared in the doorway, carrying a very full tray.

"I hope you're hungry!" she said.

"Starving!" I exclaimed. "Ohmygod, is that butter?"

"Yes! Jordan figured out how to make it from the cows' milk," she told me excitedly. I didn't know who Jordan was, but I wanted to give him or her a huge hug. I dug into the pancakes.

"Your room is a mess," Raeya observed. "Well, only your side is. How does Hayden put up with you?"

With my mouth full, I shrugged. I finished my plate and then Hayden came back into the room. I chatted with Ray while he ate and promised her I'd watch the Friday night movie with her. Hayden accompanied us downstairs, grumbling about going to see Dr. Cara.

Argos, the dog that had been with me almost since the beginning of the outbreak, was in the game room, chasing the ball Lisa was throwing for him. He snapped his head up at the sound of my voice and raced over. His butt wiggled with excitement as I cooed over him. When he calmed down, Lisa ran over and hugged me.

"Everyone said you were dead!" she cried. "I was so sad, Orissa. I told them that if anyone could make it, you could. I've seen you. You saved us, remember?"

I hugged her back. "Thanks for having faith in me, Lisa." Lisa had been around for a long time, too. She was one of the survivors from the hospital, a little girl who was adjusting well.

"You're welcome, Orissa!"

Ray and I sat at a table where half a puzzle had been put together. I picked up a piece and looked for its counterpart. I knew who came into the room by the clicking of heels on the tile floor. She dramatically gasped and the clicks got faster as she rushed over.

"Orissa! Bless your heart, you're alive! I just didn't believe it! And here you are and you look... well!" Scarlett, the self-appointed gossip queen, gushed. I half smiled. My hair was no doubt a mess and I was still wearing Hayden's t-shirt and my yellow and orange stripped pajama pants. "You *have* to tell me everything! How did you feel when you realized they had left? Do you really think they thought you were dead?" she asked seriously. Maybe she really had been a TV news anchor; she definitely dressed the part.

"It was a pretty rough situation," I vaguely summed up. "I'm sure the guys assumed the zombies were ripping me apart and feasting on my fresh, warm, internal organs."

"Oh," she grimaced. She pulled up a chair and sat next to me. "And then what? How did you feel when you realized you were all alone?"

"Pretty pissed," I went on. "And then all I wanted to do was get back here. And I did. It's not an interesting story," I lied.

"What about that girl you brought back with you? How did you find her?"

I abruptly stood. "Olivia," I said, feeling horrible I hadn't thought about her. "Uh, sorry. I'm going to go find her."

Raeya followed me down the hall.

"Who are you and what have you done to Orissa?" she teased.

"What are you talking about, Ray?"

"You were polite to Scarlett."

"I can be from time to time."

"I know that," she said, shaking her head. "The woman even annoys me. I'm just surprised, that's all."

I shrugged. I was in a *very* good mood, thanks to Hayden. I felt blood rush to my cheeks when I thought of him. We walked down the hall, through one of the heavy, security doors and into another hall. I punched in the pass code and opened the door to the soldier's quarantine. Olivia wasn't inside.

Rider came through the door, smiled, and gave me a friendly hug before I had a chance to get angry. "Glad you're back, Penwell. We were all devastated to lose such a good teammate."

"Aw, thanks," I said sincerely. "Hey, do you know where the civilian is that came in with me yesterday?"

"Yeah. She's in the hospital ward, but don't worry, she's ok, well mostly. I heard what happened to her. I would have beaten the shit out of the guy too. You're kinda my hero," he blurted then looked embarrassed.

"Yeah, sure," I said, feeling almost awkward myself.

Rider walked with us to the B level staircase. I was a little disappointed to see that Hayden wasn't in the hospital ward anymore.

Karen smiled warmly at me. "It's a miracle," she said softly. "I remember what it's like out there… and you found your way home."

I looked at Raeya. "I had good motivation. Is Olivia here?"

"Yes, she's asleep. Poor thing." She shook her head. "She thinks the world of you; you're all she talks about."

"Is she alright?"

"She's pretty torn up *down there* and just covered with bruises. Physically, she'll heal. Mentally…" she trailed off, becoming emotional. "She's on antibiotics to keep an infection from forming. And I put in a request for her to not be roomed with or near a male." She shook her head again. "I can't help but ask. Is everything she said true?"

Raeya, who had patiently been listening in the dark, stepped closer. We moved out of the sick ward, closing the door. Karen recapped what Olivia had told her about Beau. Raeya covered her face with her hands, horrified when I confirmed the truth.

"You really are that girl's hero," Raeya said, looking at me with admiration.

I shrugged it off. We slowly walked back to her room. Several people stopped me and expressed happiness that I was back. I smiled and thanked them, sharing only minor details about my time spent elsewhere.

———————————————————►

I turned on the little CD player that sat neatly centered on the dresser in Ray's room, tapping my foot to music.

"I like you being in a good mood," she commented. "I haven't been around the old, carefree Orissa in a long time. I miss her."

"I do too," I said with a sigh. "Hey, remember that time I tried my grandpa's moonshine?"

She laughed. "How could I forget? I spent the rest of the night holding your hair back as you barfed."

"I'm never doing that again," I laughed too. Raeya looked at the clock and frowned.

"I have to go over inventory. I haven't done it since you…you didn't come home."

"Want me to come with?"

Raeya raised an eyebrow incredulously. "I'd love that." We went into the supplies room. Raeya picked up a clipboard and sat on the edge of a table. "We're running low on sweets, which I guess isn't a top priority," she spoke out loud. She jotted down items that needed to be gathered on the next mission.

"You have a pretty serious job. Thanks for keeping this place in order, Ray," I told her.

"Thanks, Rissy," she said with a smile. I sat on the table next to her, swinging my feet. "What else do you need to do?"

"Luckily, Lupe already counted everything, all we have to do is decide what is the most important and write up a list of what we need and give it to Fuller."

"You should put oranges on the list."

"Oranges?"

"Yeah, so we can go to Florida to get them. I'd kill for a day on the beach," I joked.

"If you go to Florida, you're taking me!" Raeya laughed. "And Riss…are you really thinking about going on missions already?"

I shrugged. "Not anytime soon. Hayden's better, but not good enough to go out on one. He's a good partner; I don't want to go out without him. Especially since the last time I did, I got ditched. Hayden would never leave me. Ivan, Brock, Wade or Rider wouldn't either."

"No, those guys wouldn't either. I know for sure," she said seriously. "They were really upset when you didn't come back."

I sighed. "I feel bad; I didn't want anyone to worry."

"Trust me, plenty of people did."

"So," I started, trying to suppress a smile. "How many tears were shed over me? I'm assuming gallons, if not more."

Raeya laughed. "Oh, definitely buckets."

The door slowly creaked open, and we looked up to see Lauren, the most spoiled person I had ever rescued, poke her head in.

"Hi, Orissa," she said with the slightest smile.

"Hello, Lauren," I said with complete indifference.

"It's, uh, nice to see you again. I'm glad you're alive."

"Thanks," I told her.

"Yeah, everyone said you were dead. Maybe you'll stop trying to be such a dramatic hero now. You wouldn't want to actually die. And you're luck will run out someday" she said as if she was giving me legit advice and then looked at Raeya. "The bathroom in my hall is out of toilet paper."

"Oh," Raeya exclaimed and jumped up. She grabbed two rolls and handed them to Lauren. She took them, turned to leave, and stopped.

"Orissa?" she asked.

"Yeah?"

"When you, uh, go out on your next mission, do you think you could get hair dye? I hate my roots showing."

I shrugged. "Maybe, if I remember to."

Without thanking me, she nodded and left.

Raeya closed the door and hopped back up on the table next to me. She set the clipboard down and folded her arms. "What has gotten into you, Rissy? Lauren annoys the crap out of me, was rude to you, and you're being nice to her. You either got into Hayden's candy stash or his pants, cuz you are in a freakishly good mood."

I bit my lip and looked at the floor.

"What?" Raeya squealed.

I nodded.

"Finally!" she said with a huge grin.

"Finally?"

"Well, I'm assuming you also admitted that you have feelings for him."

"Yeah." I smiled at the memory. "Finally."

"So," she continued. "How was it?"

"Good. Really good."

"Even though he's injured?"

"The bullet hit his shoulder not his di—" I cut off when another overseer came into the storage room. I said hello and made my exit, promising Ray I'd find her later. On my way up the hall, I ran into Padraic.

"Hey, Orissa," he said brightly. "How are you doing?"

"I'm...I'm good," I said honestly. "Glad to be back and get back to normal."

"Me too." He beamed.

"I have a question for you," I said quietly, stepping to the side of the hall. "How come no one told Hayden I was missing?"

Padraic sighed. "It was Fuller's idea; Hayden was in critical condition...he didn't want to take any chances. I don't know if you're aware that Hayden suffers mildly from PTSD. The trauma of getting shot triggered his symptoms. No one, not even Fuller or Ivan, knew what he had been going through.

We were worried he'd become more upset if he found out you were dead. Physically, he was too weak to risk it. And he would have…I think he would have tried to go after you."

I nodded, feeling horrible that I wasn't there to help Hayden get through his nightmares. "You look tired, Padraic."

"I am," he sighed. "But that will change, I suppose. I haven't been able to sleep since that night the A1s came back without you. None of us could."

I felt awkward. "Well, I promise I'm one hundred percent ok. No worries about me anymore, promise?"

"I won't worry until you go back out again," Padraic added with a half smile. "Ray too. She was a wreck."

"I kept thinking about what you guys must have thought. I hated being sick and trapped."

"Sick?"

"Oh, right," I scuffed my shoe on the floor. "I guess I haven't told anyone yet. Walk with me?" We went down to the B level and into Padraic's room, which was one of the few places that provided privacy. "I got blood poisoning and found these crazy hillbillies who took really good care of me and I thought they were just nice, but it turned out they only wanted to use me as a baby maker for their inbred son," I said in one breath. "Once I was better, Olivia and I escaped, ran into a bit more trouble with a haunted house full of zombies, but now we're here."

Padraic opened his mouth but was at a loss for words. "Blood poisoning?"

"Yeah," I extended my left arm and showed him the scar. "They gave me medicine. It was medicine for cows but apparently it worked."

He ran his finger over the wound, looked at me in horror, and laughed. I looked at him like he had gone mad. Then a smile broke out on my face and I started laughing too. It felt good to laugh.

Someone knocked on the door, which had been left open. Still chuckling, I looked up to see Hayden. His lips moved into a smile. He looked from me to Padraic.

"Come in," Padraic called, taking a deep breath.

"Hi, Hayden," I said. Butterflies fluttered inside of me.

"Hi," he said almost shyly.

"Are you alright?" Padraic asked, going into doctor mode.

"Yeah, I feel great," he responded, still standing in the doorway. "I was leaving the hospital ward and heard your voice, Riss." He looked embarrassed. My eyes met his and I stood.

"Olivia was asking for you," Hayden said.

"She was?"

"Yeah, she's moving into her room."

"I'll go find her. I'll see you later, Padraic. Oh, and don't tell Ray what I told you. She doesn't need to worry about something that already happened."

He frowned. "I hate lying," he reminded me.

"Don't lie, just don't mention it. Please?"

"Fine," he agreed. "I'll see ya later."

Hayden walked with me back to the hospital ward. I stepped close to him, remembering what Raeya had said.

"What does he know that you don't want Raeya knowing," Hayden asked, his voice level.

I shook my head. "Nothing important."

"Really, Riss?" he said, stopping short.

"No, not really. You don't need to know either."

He opened the door for me. Once we were in the semi-privacy of the hospital ward, he put his hands on my waist. I instantly felt warm. "Don't lie to me."

"I don't want to lie. It's just…just I think it will upset you and I don't want you upset." I put my arms around his neck, careful to avoid putting pressure on his left shoulder.

"I'll be fine."

"Ok. The reason it took me so long to get back was because I got sick and stumbled my way to this house. I thought it was a miracle because they nursed me back to health, but they had an ulterior motive."

His hands gripped me tightly. "Go on."

"That's where I found Olivia. They treated her like a breeding cow, thinking it was their duty as men to repopulate the earth."

"And they wanted to do that to you?" he asked.

"Yes."

He squeezed me so hard it almost hurt. "Did they?"

"No, no. I promise. Trust me, I wouldn't let them. We got out of there in time."

He kissed me. I pulled myself closer and kissed him back. We quickly broke apart, went into the sick ward, and found a B3—B was the category given to anyone who worked in the medical areas of the compound—who directed us to Olivia.

Polly Ender was helping her pick out clothing. She was more or less in charge of keeping the little *compound store,* as she called it, in order.

"Oh, this would look lovely on you, dear," she said and held up a short, baby blue dress. I knew the feelings it evoked in Olivia right away.

"It's still pretty cold. How about some pants?" I quickly butted in.

Hayden leaned against the door frame, patiently waiting while Polly and I helped Olivia gather what she'd need. We went with her to her room, which was on the opposite side of the C level as Raeya's. I'd yet to see Sonja since my return, and when I finally hunted her down, she threw her arms around me.

I let her gush for a few minutes before telling her I had a favor to ask.

"Of course, whatever you need!" she replied.

"I don't know if you heard about the girl I brought back," I started.

"Yeah. I think everyone has. You know how word gets around here."

"I do. Anyway, she really could use a friend. And she's close to your age and I think she'd really look up to you." Though Sonja had annoyed me at times with her constant crying and screaming while we were on the run from zombies, she really was a sweet and caring person. I trusted her and hoped Olivia could too.

$$\longrightarrow$$

Hayden and I went back up to our room. He closed the door, sat on my bed, and I straddled him.

"Hayden," I began.

"Orissa," he replied, his voice alluring. He put his arms around me and leaned back until we were lying down.

"You know what you said yesterday?"

"Possibly. I remember saying a lot."

"About me? Well, I do too." I sucked at this. My cheeks flushed and I looked away.

"Could you be any more ambiguous?" he teased. "I have no idea what you're talking about."

"I'll tell you later," I said and pressed my lips to his.

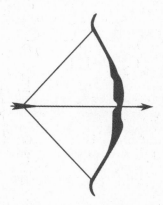

CHAPTER 9

Later in the cafeteria, Hayden and I got our trays and walked to the back to sit at our usual table. There weren't any assigned seats, but the back two tables had unofficially become reserved for the A1s.

Wade and Rider joined us, along with Raeya, Olivia, Sonja, and Jason. Raeya kept looking at Hayden and blushing; I rolled my eyes and kicked her under the table.

We were conversing like a normal group of friends when Hayden suddenly jumped up. Without explanation, he marched to the serving line. Alex had just gotten his tray. He was saying something to Noah, not paying attention to anything around him.

And then Hayden punched him.

The tray went flying from Alex's grip, food splattered the floor, and he crumpled to the ground. Noah jumped in to restrain Hayden. A hush fell over the cafeteria and all eyes were on my Marine. Wade was by his side in seconds, helping to pull him back.

Alex jumped up and took a defensive stance. Noah took his hands off Hayden and stood in between him and Alex, doing his best to stop a fight from breaking out. I watched, in stunned awe, still holding my fork with several green beans skewered on it. Was Hayden having another flashback?

And he was still hurt. He shouldn't be fighting anyone…yet.

"We *never* leave a comrade," Hayden spat, his face full of anger. Wade let him go, and Hayden walked calmly back to our table.

"What the hell?" I whispered when he sat next to me.

"He left you," Hayden said, not minding the volume of his voice. "We never leave a fallen comrade. He didn't even see you die…he didn't know. He assumed and left you."

I put my hand on his arm. "I know, but it's ok. I'm ok now. And thanks. I wanted to do that the second I realized the asshole drove off without me," I told him quietly, aware that everyone in the cafeteria was listening. He faced me, his hazel eyes drilling into mine. My heart hammered.

I let out a breath and went back to eating. Conversations slowly started back up amongst the residents. It was hard to stomach the rest of my flavorless lunch. I was eager to go up to our room and pig out on junk food. I devoured the rest of what was on my plate so we could get out there.

Fuller and Gabby's father, Hector, came into the cafeteria just as we were putting our trays back. Fuller's eyes met mine sternly for a brief moment. I wanted to give him a big 'I told you so' about not needing to be quarantined. I took a deep breath, not wanting to publically disrespect him.

A second hush fell over the cafeteria, though this time it wasn't as obvious, as eyes went from Alex to Hayden, everyone wondering if Alex was going to report the incident. But Alex kept his head down, concentrating on his food. Fuller came up to Hayden, a smile behind his stern eyes.

"It's good to see you up and around," he told him sincerely.

"It's good to be up and around," Hayden responded with a slight smile.

"How are you feeling?"

"Better. A lot better, sir."

Fuller failed at hiding his smile. He nodded curtly. "Good."

➤

Later, Hayden, Raeya, and I lounged around the game room. I felt caught up on the latest, finally, and Hayden asked Raeya what she'd been studying in college when the world went to hell.

"I was getting my master's in business. I wanted—or still want I guess, though it's pointless now—to be an event planner. Planning weddings would be so fun. I had this whole plan to open an all-inclusive event planning store." She sat on the floor in front of a coffee table. Hayden lay on the couch tossing back popcorn and catching it in midair with his mouth. I was in the recliner with my legs curled up.

"And what would that entail?" Hayden asked.

"I'd plan the events, make decorations, take pictures, make cakes. I even thought about designing and selling dresses." She laughed. "I really thought I'd do it someday. Even when the economy tanked. I thought somehow it would get better and I'd own my store."

"You would have," I told her. "You're good at everything you do." I looked at Hayden. "She would have been amazing. You should have seen all the sketches she did. She had both of our weddings planned since we were sixteen."

"That's...that's kinda scary," Hayden joked. "What did you want?"

"It was more what Raeya thought I'd want," I teased.

"That is so not true!" she butted in. "You helped! We spent hours going through bridal magazines." She turned to Hayden. "I planned a charming country wedding with an outside, daytime ceremony at the Lost River Cave Park," she gushed and continued to bore Hayden with every last detail she had carefully thought out.

"That's really detailed," Hayden observed.

"I'm not done," Raeya informed him. "We haven't even gotten to the reception yet."

"It is pretty awesome," I admitted, remembering the pictures.

"Do you know what Lost River Cave is?" Raeya asked Hayden. He shook his head. "Well, it's a cave, obviously. They have this amazing part set up for events. You are actually inside a cave overlooking water. It's perfect for Orissa, isn't it, Riss?"

"Yeah, I did like your idea."

"Anyway, it would just be so amazing."

"It sounds like it," Hayden said, his eyes locking with mine. "Maybe someday you'll get to live your dream."

Raeya made a squeaking sound of excitement. I nudged her foot under the table. "What about *you*, Ray? Remind me of all *your* wedding plans."

"Oh, yes!" she squealed, waving her hands like she does when she gets excited.

I smiled; that was one of the many things I loved about her.

"It is going to be so elegant."

"And expensive," I added.

"Shut up, Riss. But yes, it could possibly get a *little* pricey."

"You're very thorough," Hayden concluded after Raeya gave a detailed description of the wedding.

"What about you?" Raeya inquired. "Do guys ever think about weddings?"

"I never did," Hayden told her. "I was in and out of the Middle East for years. I never had the chance to think about it."

"So you never thought you'd get married?" Raeya pried a bit further.

"I wouldn't say that," he admitted.

"Why not?" I asked, trying to decide whether or not I was jealous.

"I was with this girl, Clara, for a while." He shook his head. "I didn't want to marry her, though. My mom loved her. She seemed like a nice, country girl. But the long distance didn't work out while I was in Afghanistan. That put an end to it. What about you?"

Raeya cast her eyes down. "No," she lied.

Hayden, able to sense it was a touchy subject, looked at me.

"I supposed I would get married, eventually. I never dated anyone I thought was good enough," I said with a smile.

"You just never found the right one," Raeya said, the smile returning to her face. She was so obvious. She waved to someone; I looked up to see Padraic come into the room. He strode over and pulled up a chair. Talk of weddings continued, and Padraic hinted that he had almost married.

"You've planned a wedding?" Raeya asked, looking up at him. Padraic's face grew grim. Suddenly, I was afraid of what he was going to say.

"My fiancé did most of it," he said with a distant smile.

"You were engaged?" Raeya and I asked at the same time.

"Yes," he said simply.

"Oh, man, I'm sorry," Hayden said, assuming his fiancé died at the hands of zombies. "Did she… was it…zombies?"

"No, no." Padraic shook his head.

"What happened?" I asked carefully.

"I knew her since we were kids but never thought of her as anything but that annoying girl my gran forced me to play with until I went home for Christmas during med school. She was at the family party and it was as if I saw her for the first time." A smile settled on his face.

Raeya leaned forward, her eyebrows pushing together in worry since she knew this story wouldn't have a happy ending.

"We started seeing each other," Padraic went on. "She flew here when she could; I'd fly back to Ireland when I could. Two years later, we were engaged." He smiled again. "I had three years left of my residency. We were going to get married that summer."

His sky blue eyes got misty and he let out a deep breath. "Three weeks before the wedding, she called and said she had cold feet. I thought it was normal and nothing to worry about. I flew home a few days later. And then…then she told me she didn't want to follow through with the wedding."

Raeya put her hand on his. "I'm sorry, Padraic."

"She's a dumb bitch," I blurted. "Any girl would be lucky to have you."

"Yeah," Raeya agreed. "You're a hot doctor," she added with a laugh and blushed.

"That was the problem," Padraic said bitterly. "I wasn't there for her; I was too busy with school."

"I thought Seth was going to propose," Raeya said so quietly I could barely hear her. I clasped my hands together. I knew something she didn't and it was eating me up.

Seth was a year younger than Ray; he would have graduated with a degree in engineering this spring. About a month before the virus killed him, he called me and told me that the next time I came to visit he wanted to take me ring shopping with him since I knew what Raeya liked. He made me swear I wouldn't tell Raeya. It was so hard not telling her, I just didn't talk to her much. It was hard, not being in contact with my best friend, but I was so excited that even I would have had a hard time keeping that from her. I hadn't thought about it until just now. I swallowed hard and decided never to bring it up.

"Well, this is fun," I said to break the tension.

"Have you had any nightmares?" Padraic asked Hayden in an attempt to change the subject. His question hung awkwardly in the air.

"Uh, not last night."

Raeya coughed. I glared at her.

"That's good," Padraic said. "Things are looking up."

I raised an eyebrow. "Yeah," I said sarcastically.

"Really," Padraic told me, the familiar gentle smile returning to his face. "You came back, against all odds, Hayden pulled through and we're here—together."

"Together," I repeated and looked into the eyes of each of my companions. I felt a tug of emotion again. I shook it away and stood. "Well, I'm gonna go shower, since I, uh, haven't yet today."

"And I'm gonna go lay down," Hayden said quickly. "I'm tired."

"Sure you are," Raeya suggested. I wanted to throw something at her.

I said a quick goodbye and Hayden and I went up to our room. As soon as our door closed, he and

I were kissing. We tumbled backward onto my bed, Hayden on top of me.

"I want my shirt back," he said deviously.

"You don't think it looks good on me?" I asked innocently.

"It does, but it looks even better off."

I laughed. "That is such a lame line."

He kissed my neck. "Did it work?"

"I suppose." I squirmed out from under him and pulled the shirt over my head. Hayden leaned back and looked at me. "What?"

"I...I just want to look at you. You are beautiful."

Desire coursed through my veins, and a warm tingle settled between my legs. I wrapped my arms around Hayden and pulled him to me. His hazel eyes locked with mine. I felt so vulnerable and exposed. I didn't hold back, I didn't hide anything, I wasn't on guard. I was just myself—flaws and all, and Hayden was alright with that.

I kissed him, drawing him in. He flinched ever so slightly when he enveloped me in his embrace. I pulled away and pushed him down on the bed, removing his pants. Carefully, I took off his shirt, not wanting to hurt his arm. I kissed his lips, his neck, then his collar bone, slowly making my way down.

A short time passed before Hayden stopped me, switched positions, and did the same to me. As much as we'd both love to keep the slow burn going, we knew we only had a short time before someone knocked on the door. Hayden laid back down and I got on top. He held onto my sides, quickening my movements. In only minutes, we were both finished.

He pulled me onto his chest. I stretched out my legs and snuggled close, pulling the comforter around our bodies. I traced the swirling lines of his tattoo with my finger.

"That was stupid, wasn't it?" he asked.

"What was stupid?"

"Having unprotected sex three times in twenty-four hours." He reached up and tucked a loose strand of hair behind my ear. "Not that I think you have anything," he added quickly. "Cuz I don't. I-I don't want to knock you up."

I laughed. "Thanks. I don't want that either." I rested my head on his muscular chest. "I thought you were gonna say you regretted sleeping with me or something," I admitted.

"No. The only thing I regret is not doing it sooner. Really, Orissa. I love you."

"Why?" I blurted, the word coming out of my mouth of its own accord.

"What's not to love?"

"Hah. A lot."

"Really?" he asked.

I shook my head. "Never mind."

"No, tell me."

"Where do I start?" I asked with a slight laugh.

"Orissa, you're beautiful. You're brave. You would do anything for the people you care about. You've risked your life—multiple times—for complete strangers. You are a fighter, a survivor."

"I love you too." I tightened my grip on him.

"I have a confession," Hayden told me. "That last time you woke me up from a nightmare, remember?"

"Yeah."

"I faked it. I just wanted you to get in bed with me."

"Well, now we're even."

"Huh?"

"You're not the only one who can fake things, Hayden."

He lifted his head off the pillow to stare at me. "You faked that? All three times?"

I laughed. "No, I'm messing with you."

"That's not funny, Riss."

"I think it is," I laughed.

"So you didn't fake it?" he asked again, needing reassurance.

"No. I promise. It's...different with you."

"That doesn't' make me feel any better."

I slowly let out my breath. "It feels good, *really* good, physically. But it feels good…inside too. I can't explain and please don't make me, but I've never felt that with anyone else." I closed my eyes. "And even this…this talking. It's like I can tell you anything."

"Do you think we would have met if there weren't any zombies?" he asked quietly.

"I…I don't know. Probably not. I don't think I'd ever end up in North Dakota. We should thank the zombies next time we go out."

"For sure," he said with a chuckle.

"Speaking of zombies, I saw something…interesting while I was out there."

"What was it?"

"A crazy, well two crazies really, eating stomachs. One was just wandering around munching on it and the other had this whole system set up: dead bodies in the kitchen, stomachs in the bedroom. And he was sorting them by size."

"That is interesting. Dr. Cara would like to know about it."

"Yeah, I forgot she likes to know info on zombies."

"She knows a lot. We got to talk a lot while I was stuck in the hospital, getting my daily sponge bath from Padraic," he joked, "which I thought was awesome."

"You would."

"He's very gentle."

I laughed.

Hayden kissed my forehead. "We better get dressed."

I sat up, pulling the Semper Fi shirt back on. "Now I really am going to take a shower."

"And change your sheets."

"Later," I said and wrinkled my nose. I yanked on my bottoms, picked out something to wear and scurried to the bathroom. I took my time shaving away all the unwanted hair from my body, brushing my teeth, and towel drying my hair. I even clipped my nails. Feeling almost like a normal girl, I got dressed in gray yoga pants and a blue long sleeve t-shirt. I gathered up my stuff and stepped into the hall.

"Orissa," someone called.

I spun around to see Alex, with a black eye. I stared at him, waiting.

"Look, I'm sorry, alright?"

"Gee, what a great apology."

"I-I am, ok? And, for what it's worth, I really thought you were dead. There was no way anyone could have taken on all those zombies and lived to tell about it. H-how did you do it?"

I wanted to make up some idiotic story to tell him about how I killed every son of a bitch. But I wanted to get back to Hayden more. "I climbed a tree and waited until they left."

"Oh, that's simple…and smart. If I thought you had a chance, I wouldn't have left. Sorry," he repeated and stuck out his hand to shake. "Truce?"

"Truce? Uh, no. A truce would mean I did something wrong and we agreed to stop fighting. I was the victim. I was the one that had to find my way home with no food, water, ammo, or car."

He dropped his hand. "Fine. Sorry." He brushed past me. I let out a breath, not wanting to get angry. It was so tempting to throw my bottle of shampoo at him. I hurried to our room and found Hayden sprawled out in his own bed. I dumped the armload of stuff on my bed and sat next to him.

"Are you sleeping?"

"Hmm," he responded.

"Hayden," I whispered. "Wake up."

He opened his eyes for a brief second and laced his fingers through mine. "I can't."

"You can't?" I laughed.

"I took the pills," he mumbled.

I realized he meant the pain medication and remembered him saying he didn't like taking it because it made him tired. "Oh, ok. Does your shoulder hurt?"

"Yeah…no, I mean no."

I brushed his hair back. "You don't have to pretend like it doesn't hurt. I already know you are manly and tough," I told him with a smile. "Go back to sleep."

After doing laundry and going out to play with Argos, I ran into Fuller in the hallway. He was just walking out of his office. I almost spun on my heel and walked away. He caught my eye, stopped walking, and waved me into his office. With a roll of my eyes, I followed him.

"Yes?" I asked, already impatient.

"Sit," he said, beckoning to the chair. He leaned on his desk. I sat, hating having to literally look up at him. "I think things got off on the wrong foot the other day. You had gone through a lot, and I failed to see that side. However, you have to understand the importance of protocol. I know the way things are run is less than normal, but it is incredibly important to keep order. You know how hard it is to keep the compound going."

I nodded but didn't say anything.

"Take some time off—until the bruises heal—and then you are to get back to your routine. I know you didn't ask to be a role model, but as an A1 you are. You are seen as the person who provides the food, brings back other living people—which gives hope—and eliminates the enemy. If the compound is attacked or surrounded, you are our first line of defense. If you don't follow the rules, then who will?" He crossed his arms. "Orissa, this has been hard on all of us. And I want you to know that I do give all twelve of you credit for going out there. You might not think I care, but I do. I don't want to lose any of you. I've lost enough—even before the infection." His eyes flew to the picture on his desk. "But, you must follow orders."

"Or what?" I asked slowly, knowing there was more to come.

"You won't be an A1 anymore. There are several A2s that would be great out there."

I felt my heart speed up. It wasn't like I enjoyed going out and risking my life. But being trapped inside...*that* was scarier than zombies. "Fine. I'll do my best."

"Thank you. Underwood is an excellent Marine; I suggest you follow his example."

"I think I can do that," I said with a half smile, thinking about how Hayden was excellent at so many other things. "Uh, bye...sir," I added the last word and it sounded forced. I quickly exited his office, wondering what kind of bruises he was talking about.

Raeya wasn't in her room. I wandered around until I found her in the theater room, sitting with Ivan, Brock, Sonja, and Olivia. I waved to her as soon as our eyes met.

"Hey Rissy!" she called.

I sat on the arm of the couch. "Hey guys."

"Where's Underwood?" Ivan asked.

"Upstairs. He sorta passed out."

"Wear him out, did ya?" he teased.

I laughed. "No, his pain meds make him tired."

"Sure they do," Ivan continued.

Raeya laughed which gained an odd look from Ivan.

I quickly changed the subject and suggested we go outside since it was finally sixty degrees.

Ivan cleared his throat and looked at Brock. "Penwell, you're not supposed to do that."

"Why not?" Sonja asked. "I thought we'd all be able to go outside when the weather got nice."

"You will, eventually," Brock continued. "Once it's safe. We don't have a secure area."

"The compound's not secure?" Olivia looked panic stricken.

"No, it is," Brock assured her. "You're safe down here; trust me, it would take a hell of a lot more than zombies to get through the concrete and metal. The premises are surrounded with fences, and we added a very high voltage wire around that. It will kill anything with a heartbeat."

"So how's that not safe?" Sonja asked.

"We are secluded out here. But that doesn't mean zombies will never wander. We've seen them and they have always passed. With everyone underground, there's nothing here for them."

"We can't say that anymore," Ivan mumbled. "Don't forget about the livestock now."

"Right," Brock said. "But the problem isn't so much just the zombies seeing us. What happens if everyone is outside and a herd comes by? It would be mass chaos getting back inside. Someone could get hurt."

"What if small groups went out one at a time?" Raeya suggested.

"That's a good idea," Ivan complimented. "Still, I'd feel better with a tall fence surrounding everyone."

"Will it look like a jail?" Olivia asked.

"Yes," I answered honestly. "But you're not trapped here," I explained, recognizing her fear. "You're not trapped in, they are trapped out."

"That makes sense," she told me with a small smile.

"Let me talk to Fuller," Ivan said to me. "Then we'll see about going outside."

"Alright," I agreed, sitting back on the arm of the couch.

Later, I went and woke up Hayden for lunch. Groggily, he followed me down the stairs. I was a little worried he might trip and fall in his dizziness. He sat heavily next to Ivan; I said I'd bring him a tray because Hayden was still pretty out of it, and he laid down as soon as we got back to our room. I changed into my pajamas, popped a movie in the DVD player, locked the door, and snuggled close to him.

He put his arm around me. "What if someone sees us?" he slurred. It wasn't the first time he had asked me that.

"I don't know. Tell them the truth?"

"No," he said, taking me by surprise. "I've been thinking about it. If Fuller knew, he might assign us to different partners. And probably different roommates."

"Oh. I don't want that."

"Me neither."

"Ray knows."

"I thought so. She was acting odd."

"Yeah, she can't keep a secret to save her life, but she'll be quiet if I ask her too. And I don't keep any from her. She's one of the only people I have a hard time lying to."

"Am I one of those people?"

"Yes," I said honestly. "You are."

"Good. Will I always be?"

"Of course, Hayden. Always."

——————————▶

A week after I came back, I went to training. Even though I hated getting up early with a passion, it felt good to be active again. Later that day, Brock, Ivan, Wade and Rider left on a supplies mission. I could tell it bothered Hayden to not be able to go out with them. He was healing well, but he wouldn't be ready to go on a mission anytime soon.

Lisa asked us to watch a movie with her that night. Hayden and I sat close together on the couch. There weren't too many people in the theater room; several had come down with the flu. We had all been reminded of the importance of hand hygiene, getting plenty of rest, drinking lots of fluids, and staying in our rooms if we felt ill.

I rested my hands on my lap. Hayden shyly took one, pulling it in between us. I glanced at him and he nodded, letting me know he didn't care if anyone saw. A week of being secret lovers wasn't fun or romantic; it fucking sucked. Being afraid of getting caught didn't make sex more exciting like it does in the movies; it was rushed and Hayden constantly had to remind me to be quiet so we wouldn't be heard.

Sonja, Olivia, and another girl—I think was named Felicity—walked past us to take seats on the couch behind ours. Felicity smiled coyly at Hayden and her eyes flicked to his hand in mine. Her eyes widened and she stared at me, not paying attention to where she was going and walked into Olivia.

"Hi, Hayden!" someone said excitedly. We turned to see Parker waving madly. Hayden took his hand from mine and waved back.

"Hey, Parker, how are you doing?"

"Better now. I was sick for a few days. Now my dad has it." Parker was a little boy Hayden and I had rescued awhile back. Like Hayden, he had been bitten and not infected. They both had a kind of immunity that I didn't understand.

"Oh, well glad you're doing better."

"And I got to help out more with…with…Operation Bulldog," he said with a wink.

"Awesome," Hayden told him with a smile.

"Are you better?" Parker asked. "You look better. I brought you a card in the hospital."

"Thanks, Parker. I remember your card. And yeah, I'm feeling better."

Parker beamed. He looked at me and then Hayden. "Did you tell her yet?" he asked quietly.

"I finally took your advice."

"And?"

Hayden linked his fingers through mine again. Parker's smile widened, and he gave Hayden a thumbs-up.

"Way to be inconspicuous," I whispered.

He tightened his grip on my hand.

"Hello, Orissa." There was no mistaking that accent. I yanked my fingers from Hayden and turned to see Padraic coming into the room. "And Hayden. Good evening."

The dejected look on Hayden's face stayed for a second before he said hello to Padraic. "Are you watching the movie with us?" I asked.

"Yeah, I promised this one I would," he said endearingly to Lisa. He sat next to her, leaving little room for Ray, who, surprisingly, was running late. She rushed into the room right as Sonja pressed play.

"Sorry," she breathed. "We were making blue prints for the cabins! Fuller wants to start building them soon!" she whispered excitedly. "Maybe we can get one together!"

The thought was exciting. We all squished together on the couch, which was fine with Hayden and me since it meant we were forced to be very close. Hayden put his hand on my thigh and I stiffened. He raised an eyebrow and removed it. He leaned away from me and crossed his arms.

Once the movie was over, we walked Lisa and Raeya back to their room. Their third roommate was lying in bed.

"Does she ever do anything?" I quietly asked Raeya.

She shook her head. "Every night when I come in, I'm scared I'm going to find her dead in her bed. She makes me so sad."

I nodded in agreement and hugged Ray goodnight. Hayden snatched up my hand on our way down the hall.

"Am I allowed to touch you now?" he only half teased.

I slowed my gait. "You can touch me anywhere, anyway you want, baby," I said with a coy smile.

"Well in that case…" he pulled me to him and kissed me. "What was that all about in there?"

I shook my head. "Nothing, I just, uh, don't want to risk being separated from you."

"Bullshit."

"Padraic kissed me," I blurted.

Hayden stopped walking and gaped at me.

"It was a long time ago, before I met you."

"Do you have feelings for him?" Hayden asked.

"No. Well, like friendship feelings. But nothing more. He's like family."

"But he still has feelings for you," Hayden speculated.

"I'm not sure. It's been a while. I tried to avoid him after it happened. I didn't want to hurt him. Padraic's a nice guy."

Hayden nodded.

"Are you upset?" I asked carefully.

"No. I just didn't think I'd have to fight for you. I thought you'd fall head over heels for my good looks and charm," he joked.

"You won't have to. Unless you're fighting zombies and crazies. I'm all yours."

"Good."

"What about you, am I gonna have to chase you down?" I asked.

"Nope. I'm not going anywhere."

"Promise?" I tested with a smile.

"Of course."

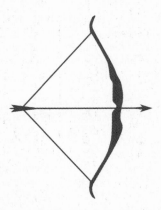

CHAPTER 10

Four days after they left, Brock, Wade, Rider, and Ivan came back with a truck full of everything on their list. Hayden had been eagerly awaiting their return; I knew he was worried about their well-being but I think he mainly was looking forward to hearing the details of their mission. He spoke quickly with Ivan before he trudged into the quarantine room.

"What did he say?" I asked Hayden when he came upstairs.

"The mission went smoothly. They ran into one herd but were able to avoid it. And Ivan swore he killed over a dozen S2s with a bow."

"I'll believe it when I see it," I said with a laugh. "How's your shoulder?"

"Sore," he admitted. Padraic had given Hayden medical clearance to start lightly working out again, though the first day Hayden didn't take it too light. "I just want to be back to normal."

"You will be, just give it time. You're healing pretty fast," I reminded him.

"Not as fast as you would," he said with a grin.

"That might be true. Hopefully we never find out."

"Hopefully," he echoed. "Want to go downstairs with me?"

"Sure."

We ran into Steven, the A2 that Fuller thought was ready to advance to A1. I hadn't spoken to him much, but I knew he used to be a firefighter, took his A2 duties very seriously, and was polite every time we spoke. I didn't want him to advance, and my reasoning was more than not wanting to change what was currently—more or less—working for us.

Steven had a wife and kids. His oldest daughter, Maryanne, was Lisa's age. His identical twin boys had their fourth birthday at the compound. It was too great of a risk; he had a family that emotionally depended on him being there.

But Fuller didn't care.

I exchanged a few words and went on to the game room to find Raeya while Hayden and Steven talked tactics. She was sitting with Padraic, Sonja, Jason and Olivia, working on a puzzle. I pulled up a chair and greeted everyone.

By the time Hayden joined us, we were deep in a reminiscent conversation about how we all met, explaining it all to Olivia. Hayden, who had heard the whole story before, stood patiently behind me with his hand on my shoulder while we spoke. When our epic tale reached its end, he pulled up a chair and squeezed in next to me.

"D-do you know a lot about zombies?" Olivia asked shyly.

"What do you want to know?" I replied.

"Like how-how are they possible?"

Hayden scooted in even closer next to me. "A virus," he started.

"I know that," she said with a half smile. "What does it do and how did it start?"

"We don't know how it started, but I do know that it attacks the frontal lobes," Padraic said, taking the lead on this discussion. "That is the part of the brain that controls human emotions and feelings. At that stage of the virus, damage to the brain has already occurred; there is no going back. Then, parts of the brain and the central nervous system start shutting down. Basic body functions slow down significantly; metabolism, digestion, breathing, and their heart rate. Without a good oxygen supply, parts of the body start dying."

"That's when they become zombies?" she said, just as quiet as before.

"Yes. The virus has spread to more of the brain, not necessarily killing it, but greatly altering its function. Blood only goes to the most vital organs, which is why their skin starts to die and rot."

"So, are they dead?"

"Medically, yes. Their hearts still beat. With no heartbeat to pump blood—no matter how vicious it is—the cells would be depleted of oxygen and completely die. They wouldn't be able to move, since their bodies would dry up and crack apart."

"Too bad they don't," Jason added bitterly. We all nodded in agreement.

"Since when did you become such a zombie expert?" I asked Padraic.

"I did my first autopsy while you were gone," he said, wrinkling his nose at the memory.

"Sounds fun."

"There's something you forgot," Hayden told him. "Or, maybe you don't know."

"And that is...?" Padraic asked him, thinking he had thoroughly explained the zombie virus to Olivia.

"What they eat."

Padraic's face clouded with confusion for a millisecond. "Right. Stomachs. We can thank Orissa for enlightening us on that delightful bit of information." He winked at me.

"Uh, you're welcome. I only saw two though, I don't think that's enough to base it off of, is it?" I stated.

"No, but it makes sense," Hayden explained. "Think of it this way: when a wolf kills a rabbit in the wild, what does he eat? The whole thing, basically, right? And what do rabbits eat? Grass and plants. So when the wolf eats the rabbit, he's getting protein but also grains and carbs from the rabbit."

"Oh, that does make sense!" Raeya said, suddenly interested. It still didn't click right away with me. Thankfully, it didn't with Sonja either and she asked why.

"Humans need a balanced diet," Hayden went on. "We can't just eat meat. Zombies are still humans, in some messed up form."

"So crazies eat the stomachs of humans to meet nutritional needs," I finished.

"Exactly," Padraic told me with a nod.

"Are you sure? I mean, that seems very complex," I countered.

"We can't be sure about anything," Padraic admitted. "But it's a theory, and it does make sense."

"Oh, well, then, glad I helped." I unbraided my hair—which had been in a French braid—and raked my fingers through it. We worked on the puzzle until dinner; after that I hung out with Raeya while Hayden played video games with Noah, José, and Mac. As far as I knew, he was pretending Alex didn't exist.

Later I changed into pajamas and crawled into bed, surprised at how tired I was for it only being ten o'clock.

When I woke up, Hayden was in bed next to me, suggestively running his hand up and down my body. I could see his devilish smile in the dark. I held onto his hand and rolled over, bringing him closer to me. He kissed the back of my neck, but I didn't respond.

"Riss?" he asked, taken aback. I always pounced on him the moment we had a chance. "Everything ok?"

"Yeah," I mumbled. "I'm just really tired."

"Oh, ok." He wrapped his arm around me and I drifted back to sleep.

→

It was so hard to drag my ass out of bed for training the next morning. As soon as I was up and moving, I felt better. I crashed after training and slept until lunch.

"Are you feeling alright, Riss?" Hayden asked.

"Yeah, I'm just tired," I assured him. "I guess all those late night booty calls took their toll on me," I joked. He smiled and kissed me, insisting I take it easy until dinner, which is exactly what I did.

"Penwell," Ivan called as we exited our room on the way to dinner that day.

"Yeah?"

"I got your friend, Raeya, something."

"You did?"

"Yeah, I remembered what you said about her loving those dolls. I found one."

I had to bite my lip to keep from laughing. In truth Raeya was creeped out by the dolls, but a month or so earlier, I had told him different; I told him how much she loved dolls. "Wow, she's gonna be so happy. You should give it to her. Right now."

"Good idea." He disappeared into his room and came back with a box. Hayden had to turn away to hide his laughter. With the box tucked proudly under his arm, Ivan followed us into the cafeteria. We got our trays and sat in the back with the other A1s. Hayden waved Steven over, who excitedly said something to his wife and joined us. I nibbled on my food while waiting for Raeya. Impatiently, I watched her get her tray and make her way over. She was stopped by another overseer, and I was a little afraid she might sit at their table.

As if she could read my mind, Ray looked up and smiled at me. There was a time when Ray and I used to prank each other on a regular basis. I missed those days.

"Hi, Raeya," Ivan said showing off his brilliant smile. "How are you doing this evening?"

"Oh, I'm good, thanks. And yourself?"

"Glad to be back." He retrieved the box. "I saw this and it reminded me of you." He slid it toward her.

"Oh, presents!" Raeya exclaimed excitedly. "You really shouldn't have, Ivan." Her cheeks flushed just a bit as she touched the box. Carefully, she took the lid off. Her eyes bulged and a little squeak of surprise escaped her lips. She glared at me before turning on her charm.

"Thank you," she said, her voice strangled.

"Do you like it?" Ivan asked her.

"Oh yes," she said smoothly.

Hayden looked away, and I coughed to cover up my laughter.

"In fact, I like it so much I'm going to put it in my room. Riss, come with me."

"I think you can handle it," I said casually.

"Rissy!" she said in a high pitched voice, earning strange looks from our tablemates.

"Alright," I said, ducking to hide my smile.

"What the hell!?" she cried, shoving the box in my hands as soon as we were out of the cafeteria.

I doubled over in laughter. "Sorry, Ray!" I said once my laughter was under control. "The opportunity just presented itself. I couldn't help it."

She crossed her arms. "You are evil," she tried to sneer but failed and was overcome with giggles. "I'll get you back, just you wait," she warned. "And what am I going to tell Ivan? He thinks I like it!"

"Tell him the truth," I suggested.

"No, that would hurt his feelings. I'll pretend I like it."

"Yeah, so he can bring you another."

"Ugh. Don't let him!" she laughed again.

"Want me to put it upstairs? I don't want you to have nightmares over it."

"Yeah, I'd—wait, no. I don't want to be surprised by it. I'll keep it."

I narrowed my eyes. "You sure?"

"Yes. Come with me."

We hurried down the hall and into her room where she hid the doll in her dresser and went back in to finish dinner.

The compound was bursting at the seams with residents and we hoped to keep adding to our numbers. Raeya was hard at work drawing up blueprints, trying to design the simplest yet most functional cabins. It was all very old fashioned, she told me, the way it would be set up. Running water and electricity weren't a guarantee unless we were able to find the supplies we needed.

When we were kids, Raeya and I used to empty out the small shed behind my grandparents' house and play 'old fashioned days.' We would wear silly dresses, cook food over camp fires, and refuse to use anything modern for the entire day. It was fun then. The thought was scary now.

Going without heat, water, and a proper way to dispose of human waste wasn't only a huge pain in the ass, but it was a health issue, one that wasn't worth risking.

Padraic stressed he was running low on antibiotics again, too, and I didn't want to take any chances compromising anyone's health.

Two days into Alex and the others' mission, Raeya presented a very detailed list to Fuller. We went over it and were given descriptions of what to look for. Brock had worked for his uncle's construction company before joining the Marines and was familiar with the supplies we needed.

I left the meeting feeling excited about another mission and building the cabins. And Padraic had cleared Hayden to go with us! Since the cabins wouldn't offer much—if any—protection against an attack, Fuller wanted the A1s and A2s to 'test them out.' moving the A3s upstairs, allowing the Cs and Bs more room to space out.

"It's going to look like a little village," Raeya told us excitedly during dinner that night.

"I can't wait to see it!" Sonja gushed. "It looks very cute in my head!"

"Oh, it will be," Raeya agreed. "I can show you my new blueprints!" she said excitedly.

"New blueprints?" Sonja questioned. "Are they different than the ones you just showed me?"

"Yes," Raeya explained. "I had a dream about a better way to organize things."

"You dream about organizing stuff?" Jason chuckled.

I nodded. "Those are her favorite kinds of dreams," I said endearingly. "That's why we love you, Ray: you are one of a kind."

We all laughed and continued to talk about the cabins.

When the other A1s returned from their mission with five civilians, Hayden and I started getting antsy for our turn. Raeya frowned whenever the conversation turned to it and, more than once, she begged me not to go.

"I'm just so scared to lose you," she confessed one night while I sat with her in her room.

"I'll come back, I promise. And this is an easy mission. We won't be gone long."

She sighed. "I know. Still, you can't blame me." She rested her head on my shoulder. "I wish you were pregnant."

"That's a horrible thing to wish for me! What the hell would make you want *that*?"

"Then you wouldn't leave. You'd stay here where it's safe." She smiled innocently. "And Hayden probably would too, to make sure you're taken care of and healthy and whatever."

"Ray, no. Not now."

"But someday?" she asked hopefully.

"I suppose, but that's a someday in the far, far future."

"Fine. I guess you're right. I've always wanted to be an aunt, Riss. And since you're the closest I have to a sister...would you do it for me?"

"No." I couldn't help but laugh. I hugged Raeya and, once again, promised I'd be back before she knew it.

The day before we left, my little group of friends gathered around a table in the game room playing Rummy. I leaned back in my chair, my arm brushing against Hayden's.

"You know..." Raeya said as she put down a card. She smiled and looked into Hayden's eyes. "You'd make a really great dad."

"Uh," Hayden responded. "Thanks, I think."

"You're welcome. I can just see you with a baby in your arms. It would be so cute!"

"Yeah, sure," he mumbled, not knowing how to respond to that.

I glared at her.

Later that same night, I was walking around the compound looking for Hayden, who had been unable to sleep. I stepped lightly into the quiet hall, not wanting to wake anyone up.

Light spilled from Padraic's room, casting a triangle of glowing yellow into the dark hall. I was about to walk past when I heard a familiar voice.

"...no, she can make up her own mind," Hayden stated, sounding slightly irritated.

"Trust me, I know she can," Padraic told him. "I just think you should talk to her, let her know her options."

"She knows them. And look, I understand your concerns. But know that she'll be safe with us. I will take care of her."

"But you can't, not really."

"Yes, I can. I won't let anything happen to her," Hayden said sternly.

"It's nothing against you," Padraic assured him. "But you of all people know how unpredictable it is out there. You can't keep every bad thing away from her."

"Yes I can," Hayden said stubbornly.

I heard Padraic sigh. "We care about her. You should have seen Ray when she thought Orissa died. She was a wreck. I think if anyone could convince her to stay—just a little while longer—it would be you."

"Orissa knows she doesn't have to go out."

"Does she? I don't see why else she would, unless she didn't think she had a choice. And she didn't, really. You made her an A1. It wasn't her decision."

"She could have said no," Hayden said, his voice rising. "If she didn't want to go out, she wouldn't. You don't know Orissa. She's not a caged bird. She can't stay where it's safe and warm while someone else does the dirty work. She's not the kind of person that can live a life locked up."

"And how do you know that?" Padraic retorted.

"Because I'm the same way."

My heart was beating fast. I edged away from the door, afraid of being seen.

"It's not her job—" Padraic started.

"It's *mine*?" Hayden interrupted.

"Well, yeah. You're the one that joined the military."

"Right. I did. I signed up for *war*. Against people. Real live people, not the living dead. To protect your ass and ensure your freedom. I gave up my life, my time, watched my friends die for this country. And are you even an American citizen? Don't tell me what is and isn't *my* job. Do you want to go out there? I'll give you my gun right now. Have fun fighting off the zombies and seeing the rotting corpses. I brought more than half of these people here. Not because it's *my job,* but because it was the right thing to do. And Orissa feels the same."

I swallowed hard. I wasn't sure if I should step in or not. I put one foot forward and stopped, too curious to hear what the guys had to say about me.

"I didn't mean to insult you," Padraic told Hayden, though he didn't sound too sorry. "Yes, you go out there, but don't forget what I do too. How many people—yourself included—wouldn't be alive if I hadn't been here?"

"You wouldn't have any lives to save if I didn't bring them back!" Hayden countered and I rolled my eyes. Were they seriously arguing over who was more important?

"Orissa knows how important it is to keep the compound safe. She would be perfect for guarding the walls," Padraic said with slight bitterness. "You might think you know her, but don't forget I do too. She was tired of fighting them off long before we came here. Don't you think she might want a break?"

"Then she would fucking take one! No one is forcing her to go out."

"I spoke with Fuller," Padraic butted in. "I know you requested her as an A1 because you were impressed with her abilities. I know your last partner didn't die at the hands of zombies. He took his own life because he couldn't handle what it was like out there. And you wanted someone strong. You didn't stop and think what she wanted. All you thought about was yourself."

"Bullshit!" Hayden yelled. I was afraid he might go after Padraic. "Yes, Orissa is one of the best soldiers I've ever seen and yeah, it would be a waste for her not to use it. As soon as I got to know her, I knew she was more than that. It was her choice to be an A1 and it still is. That's what she wants!"

There was a moment of silence before Padraic said, "Agree to disagree?"

"Fine," Hayden spat. I pushed off from the wall and quickly padded back to my room before either guy caught me eavesdropping. I brushed my teeth and was in the process of changing when Hayden burst through the door. He rushed over to me, picked me up and kissed me. I felt his muscles relax instantly at my touch. He set me back down, ran his hands over my face and smiled.

"I love you," he whispered.

"I love you too."

"Good." He gave me another kiss and got ready for bed. He held me tightly against him. "So, I'm a bit confused," Hayden started. "Does Raeya want me to father her children?"

I laughed. "No, mine."

He raised an eyebrow. "Is this something we need to talk about?"

"No, don't worry. I don't have baby fever or anything. Ray wants me to be pregnant because that would mean I'd be stuck here and not leave on missions."

"Oh." He smiled at me. "Good, because I'm not…maybe someday, but not now."

"I totally agree." I let out a sigh of relief over him not mentioning what I had overheard. It was flattering that they both cared about me enough to fight about it, but I didn't want to have to pick sides. Padraic was a friend, a good friend, and we'd been through hell and high water together. He'd always have a place in my heart. And Hayden…I was completely in love with him.

I pushed the conflicting thoughts out of my head and wrapped my arms around my Marine, wanting to enjoy our last night together before we set out.

We loaded everything into the truck bright and early the next morning. Hayden was still horrified at the blood stains on the passenger seat.

"You should have put me in the back," he said as he ran his finger over the material. "That's what I would have done to you," he told me with a grin.

"I tried to get it out," Ivan said. "You should have seen it before."

"Thanks, man." Hayden let out a deep breath and threw his bag in the back and inspected the rest of the truck, equally unhappy about the bullet marks and holes along the back. For the first few miles, he grumbled about finding parts to replace and fix the damage. Then he and Ivan bickered over what kind of music to listen to and the guys spoke of things that happened during the war. It felt just like old times.

Brock swore he remembered passing a Home Depot before, he just couldn't remember where. We spent the morning driving around Arkansas.

"I think it was north of the compound," he told us. "And not that far north. I know I saw it."

"I remember it too," Hayden confirmed. The first thing the guys did when they got the compound up and running was canvass the state, looking for supplies and survivors.

Around noon we stopped for a lunch break in an abandoned town.

Litter and the occasional body lined the streets. The terrain was rather uneven and hilly and we were surrounded by trees. Even though we had plenty of fuel, we used this prime opportunity to fill up an extra gas can from one of the many parked cars.

A breeze blew through the trees, ridding the area of the stench of death and bringing the sweet smell and promise of spring. Birds chirped loudly, ignorant to the horrors around them. If I kept my eyes closed, I could pretend I was somewhere beautiful.

Someone grabbed my waist. I flung around and almost punched Hayden in the face; he blocked me just in time.

"Jerk," I spat, trying to look pissed. He looked behind him and quickly kissed me.

"I made you lunch."

"How sweet," I said with a smile. "What did you make me?"

"I opened a can of tuna. Yum."

EMILY GOODWIN

"I am so utterly sick of tuna."

"Aren't we all?" His hand fell into mine, letting go when we neared the truck. The four of us sat in the bed, eating and chatting.

"I haven't seen a day like this in what feels like a lifetime," Brock said with his mouthful.

"I know," I agreed, taking a deep breath. "It feels good."

"It just makes me want to get my ass to Mexico even more," Hayden said with a sigh. We all agreed and planned a hypothetical vacation. We ate slowly, enjoying the nice, early spring day. Suddenly, Brock quieted us.

"Do you hear that?"

"No," Ivan started. "I hear..." he trailed off and we all looked at each other in horror. "Nothing."

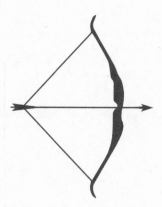

CHAPTER 11

"The birds were just chirping a minute ago," Hayden said. "Something scared them off."

We dropped our food and picked up our weapons, poised and ready for an attack. A strong breeze rattled dry branches. Twigs crunched and snapped in the woods behind us. And then somebody screamed.

It was high pitched, girly, and sounded like a child. We jumped from the truck and took off after the source. We flew down the street, hurdling over garbage and broken glass. The strap of my M16 slid down my shoulder. I yanked it up just as I noticed the blood. Too winded to talk, I pointed. Hayden nodded and shouted to Ivan and Brock.

We rounded a corner and slid to a stop in an alley. Standing a few feet in front of us was a little girl dressed in blue pajamas. She only had on one slipper, and she clutched a tie-dye teddy bear in a blood crusted hand. She turned to face us and screamed again, another high, ear-piercing yell.

Fresh blood dripped from her neck. Her lips curled into a snarl and she took a step in our direction. Her gait was steady. Hayden raised his gun but didn't pull the trigger. Sunlight glinted off the metal barrette in the crazy's hair. She screamed again, though this time it was more throaty and animal. Then she leapt forward in a full sprint.

A shot rang out, echoing against the brick walls of the buildings that boxed us in the alley. The girl crumpled to the ground, her teddy bear flying from her hand and landing in a dirty puddle. Hayden slowly lowered his gun, unable to take his eyes off the child.

"It's hard when they look normal," Ivan acknowledged, giving Hayden a pat on the back. Hayden nodded, shook himself back to reality, and re-holstered his gun.

Many things didn't seem right about this situation. But one stood out in my mind. I picked up the teddy bear and set it on the girl's chest.

"She's been bitten," I said, expecting everyone to realize the weight of my statement.

"Well, yeah. That's probably how she got in infected," Brock told me.

"No, I mean recently. Look." I pointed to the fresh set of teeth marks on her neck. "So either a vampire was after her or…"

"We can expect zombies," he finished for me. He cocked his gun. "Teams or singles?"

"Teams," Hayden and I said at the same time.

"Too bad you left the bow in the truck," Ivan said with a smile.

"I don't need it to beat you," I teased. "Game on."

We edged our way down the alley, stopping when we came to a fork; we looked around silently. Ivan motioned for us to keep moving forward. Tall brick buildings were on either side of us, tunneling us in the alley.

The four of us froze when we heard a scuffling of feet. We raised our guns, eager to get the first kill and be in the lead point-wise. I think we all fired at the same time; all four bullets hit the zombie's head in unison. His skull exploded, brains splattering the bricks. But before we had a chance to argue over whose bullet landed in the festering flesh first, a dozen zombies came staggering around the corner.

"Shit," Ivan swore and opened fire. We emptied our magazines, reloaded, emptied those, and realized we were screwed.

"We need to retreat," Hayden shouted over the moaning. I nodded, knowing that he couldn't see me. The herd moved closer, packing themselves into the alley like sardines. We whirled around, prepared to run, and stopped.

More zombies filtered in through the fork in the alley, the speed of their limping walk increasing when they caught the sight and scent of fresh food. With mouths open and hands grasping the air, they lumbered closer. We were being flanked and they were closing us in.

We stood together, going over our options.

Hayden jumped forward, grabbing onto a dumpster. He jerked it backward; it moved about a foot before the wheels jammed on loose gravel. Ivan rushed to his side and helped yank it free. They rolled it out and turned it, creating an obstacle for the zombies. It bought time but didn't provide us with anywhere to go. Brock madly beat on the back door of a building, trying to break it down. I was sure he could…if we had more time.

My eyes darted around looking for something…anything that could spare our lives. Ivan joined Brock in his attempt to break down the metal door.

"Riss, come on!" Hayden shouted and raced over to the door. I didn't move; my eyes fixed on something on the ground. "Riss!" he shouted again. I looked at him and then back at the alley. His eyes followed mine.

"It's my only idea," I blurted, knowing it was stupid, trembling with fear as the zombies came closer.

"No, it's good," Hayden said and ran over to me. He put his fingers through the grates and pulled. His face showed the pain he felt in his shoulder, but he didn't acknowledge it. The cover scraped against the gritty alley pavement. "Ivan, Brock!" Hayden yelled and climbed down the manhole. I followed, stepping on Hayden's fingers more than once. Ivan came down next and Brock barely made it in before dead hands got a hold of him.

Shaking, I jumped off the last wrung of the built in ladder. Water splashed across my shirt and the overflow went just past my boots. Hayden was also wet and covered knee-deep in standing water. It had overflowed onto the side-tiers. Hayden flicked on his flashlight, shining it around the sewer. It smelled cloying and thick and wasn't as cool as the sewer systems in movies. We stood in a narrow, rectangular room. I supposed I could call it that. Wet leaves lay in rotting clumps on the cement ground, their sweet smell a reprieve from the putrid stench of decaying flesh.

"Good thinking, Underwood," Ivan said, pulling his own flashlight out of one of the many pockets on his military issued vest.

"It was Orissa's idea," Hayden said causally.

"Good thinking, Penwell," Ivan said with the hint of a smile. Brock turned on his flashlight too. I was the only one not dressed in military clothing; I found it difficult to move with that much stuff on me, plus the extra vests were two sizes too big. Baggy clothes weren't good for running and fighting. I gave the guys major credit for their ability to do so. Hayden told me once that overseas he used to carry even more, and he did it in sweltering temperatures.

Hayden grabbed me by the waist and pulled me out of the way. An S2 had fallen down the hole; her body went limp on impact. And we were splashed with even more filthy water. I stared at her, and pulled my gun when she began to sit up. I stopped, realizing that the blast would deafen us in this small, tight space.

Brock thankfully knew that too, and he drove his knife into her eye socket. He wiped the goo on his pants and pocketed the blade.

"Now what?" he asked me.

"Uh, we walk through until we find another way out," I suggested.

Ivan nodded in agreement and took the lead. We had to walk single file through a narrow passage.

It smelled more and more like shit the farther we went. At one point we had to get on our hands and knees and crawl through sludgy water. Then the tunnel emerged into a large, catacomb-style system. I shook the slime from my hands.

Something splashed a head of us. I grabbed my gun, unsure of where to aim.

"What do you think the chances are that it's a crime fighting turtle?" Hayden asked dryly, taking a tentative step forward.

"I wish," Brock said with a laugh. "They could help us kill the sons of bitches up there."

Instead, a water-logged S3 dragged itself through the half foot of water that sat stagnant in the sewer. Its entire body was swollen, its flesh was puffy and pruney, and bits of skin literally oozed off. Its legs didn't work anymore; I assumed it was from the odd state of edema. I tipped my head with curiosity, thinking it was almost pathetic.

Ivan kicked it in the face and its skull easily broke, sending mushy brains to seep through the cracks. It fell into the thick, brown water. Someone's flashlight flicked over the body, the light glinted off a diamond earring.

Like a punch to the stomach, I was reminded that this disgusting S3 wasn't a creature. It was a human. A real human, just like me. A human with thoughts and feelings and drives and needs. I shook that thought away. I couldn't think like that; I needed to be cold if I wanted to live. And it wasn't a human, not anymore. All aspects of humanity died when the virus nestled its way into the brain.

We walked probably another mile before we turned down another tunnel. Circles of light spilled through a manhole cover. Ivan slowly climbed up and listened. Assuming the coast was clear, he shoved it open.

"It's clear," he confirmed and pulled himself out. It felt good to be above ground again. My boots were covered in brown slime and my pants needed to be burned. I grimaced, laughing internally over the fact that I was slightly happy to be covered in something other than zombie parts for once.

I blinked in the bright sunlight, holding my hand up and squinting. Ivan moved the cover back over the manhole, mumbling something about zombies in the sewers being worse than alligators. We were in the middle of a residential street; scattered abandoned houses surrounded us. With the sun centered in the sky, it was hard to tell which direction we had come from.

"This way," Hayden said confidently. With our guns at the ready, we started down the familiar street, knowing that the herd of zombies had to be close. About fifteen minutes later, we reached the town.

"Sorry, baby," Hayden said to his truck as he picked the spilled food out of the bed. I rolled my eyes and peeled off my top outer layer, careful not to swipe the soiled material across my face. Thinking it was pointless to save, I dropped my long sleeved shirt on the ground.

"You gotta take off the rest of your clothes," Hayden told me. I raised an eyebrow and glanced at Ivan and Brock, silently telling Hayden to shut up before he was overheard. "No, really. I don't want that shit in the truck. It's bad enough we've gotten blood and zombie parts all over the interior. I draw the line at human shit-juice."

"You have got to be kidding me," I said through gritted teeth. Though, truth be told, I didn't want to be stuck in a car for hours that reeked like sewage either. Remembering the drug store, I traded my M16 for the compound bow and arrows. "I'm gonna go check something," I told Hayden. He nodded as if he was ok with it but didn't take his eyes off me. I made it across the street before he jogged over.

"What are you checking?" he asked, clicking a magazine into place in his pistol.

"That store," I told him, pointing to the drug store. "I'm hoping to find soap. That way, if we find water we can actually get clean instead of just rinsing off. My skin's starting to itch."

"Another genius idea," he told me with a smile. "That's why I love you." He went in first, waving me in when he found it to be safe. "Hurry, alright? That herd isn't far."

"I will." I made a bee line to the conveniently labeled 'hygiene' aisle. There was a small display of homemade, organic soaps. I picked up a lavender-mint scented bar. It smelled wonderful, but wouldn't kill the germs we had to be covered in. Nonetheless, I picked up the little wicker basket that the soaps were displayed it and took a step down the aisle to grab something to sanitize with.

"Got enough?" Hayden questioned, looking at my basket.

"It smells good," I told him with a slight smile.

"So you need twenty?"

"First of all, it will run out eventually. And it's not all for me. Ray loves this kind of stuff. I'm gonna give half to her. Trust me, she'll be happy. What did you get?" I asked, seeing the full bag Hayden was holding. He held it up for me to look in. "And you think my soap was extensive," I joked, seeing that the bag was filled with boxes of condoms.

"This has to last us a while," he explained, unable to keep the wanting smile from his face. "Plus, we're not the only people back home who have sex. It would probably be good to have, uh, supplies."

"You're right; I hadn't really thought about it."

We walked around the store, looking for anything useful, happily discovering the unharmed display of Halloween candy. We loaded a bag full of it and went back to the truck. I put my basket in the back, and Hayden stashed his bag of goodies under his seat.

I unlaced my boots—feeling more than a little grossed out when my fingers pulled on the slimy laces—kicked them off, and tossed them in the bed. I rolled up my pants and stood in front of Hayden, who had stripped out of his shoes and outer layers as well. "Good enough?" I asked him.

"I guess," he said half heartedly. He looked guiltily at his truck before he got in.

"There's a river a mile and a half away," Brock informed us as he took off his shoes. "I saw an ad for the river that has cabins for rent hanging up in a store window. If it's safe, we can wash there. Is anyone else really itchy?"

"I am," I told him, refusing to scratch and rub the shit any deeper into my skin. I climbed in the back and Brock got in next to me. "Where is this river?"

"A little north of where we are right now. The ad had a map. I can get us there," he promised. And he did. Hayden drove past the cabins and parked as close as he could to the water's edge. Leaving the truck running, we quietly got out and assessed the surroundings.

"The herd isn't far," Hayden reminded us.

I nodded, my eyes scanning the trees.

"It seems safe—for now," Hayden said and cut the engine. We grabbed our clean clothes, pissed that we didn't have spare shoes and walked down to the water.

"How should we do this?" Brock asked, his eyes jumping from me to Hayden and then to me again. "You two go and we'll keep watch? For zombies, not watch you get naked," he added with a wry smile.

"Look but don't touch," I teased. Brock immediately looked at Hayden, as if to see his reaction. Was he expecting Hayden to be jealous? No…that would mean he would know of our couple status—which he didn't.

The rocky ground hurt my bare feet. I tip toed my way to the water, dreading how cold it was bound to be. I pulled my tank top over my head and shimmed out of my jeans, shivering instantly. Hayden stood next to me, goosebumps breaking out over his skin as the breeze blew.

"On the count of three," he said, feeling as much resistance to the cold water as I did. "One, two, three!" We stepped into the river. The water was so cold it hurt. With one hand, I splashed water up my legs, rinsing away the crusted gunk. I plunged the soap under the water and quickly scrubbed myself, then did the same with the rest of my body.

"You have crap in your hair," Hayden told me regretfully, moving out of the water to dry off and get dressed.

"Son of a bitch," I swore. "The one time I didn't put it up…" I tipped my head and let the ends of my hair dip into the water. I was shivering so badly it was hard to suds up my hair. Not sure—and not caring—if I rinsed all the soap out, I straightened up.

Something moved with the swift current, bobbing just under the surface. I narrowed my eyes, unable to descry exactly what it was. It went under and didn't resurface. I waded out into thigh-deep ice water to get a closer look.

Sunlight reflected brightly off the sparkling lake, temporarily blinding me. I held up my hand and waited for my eyes to adjust. I leaned over the strange object, only able to see my reflection on the shiny surface. Maybe it was nothing, I thought to myself.

Then it sat up. Water slimed fingers grabbed my leg and pulled. I fell into the water, scrapping my painfully cold hands on the sharp rocks that lined the river. The zombie let out a gurgled growl and pushed me under water. I grabbed a handful of small rocks and smashed them against its head. It didn't even react. My hand hit the water with a loud splash, but in water everything is weighted down and feels slow. I couldn't hit this zombie hard enough.

My hands pushed against its arms; watery flesh melted off with my touch. I scrambled back, cutting my heel on something wickedly sharp. I pushed myself to my knees and punched the zombie in the side of its face. It let out a harrowing yell right as the bullet slammed into its skull.

Arms wrapped around me.

"Orissa!" Hayden cried and embraced me.

Trembling, I leaned against him.

"Are you ok?"

"I'm alive," I said, my teeth chattering.

"Let's get you out of the water."

I nodded, wincing with each step.

"Fuck, you're bleeding," Hayden said and scooped me up.

"Put me down," I protested. "I'm fine; it's just a little scratch." Hayden didn't listen and continued to carry me. He set me down on the tailgate.

"I think I'll pass on washing up," Ivan said with a slight smile. He looked through the scope on his rifle. "The water doesn't seem so clean anymore."

"Yeah, and you always gave me hell for not liking dark water," Brock added, his eyes wide. "Are you alright, Orissa? He didn't get you, did he?"

"Nope. Just tried to cop a feel, that's all," I joked, shaking uncontrollably from the cold. Hayden took off his jacket and wrapped it around me. "You're all wet," I dumbly stated. "And y-you don't h-have any more c-clothes," I chattered.

"They'll dry," he said quietly, inspecting my hands. "I'd rather have wet clothes than have anything happen to you."

Brock tossed Hayden my clothes and turned back to face the river as I got dressed. Hayden stepped away and returned with the first aid kit. He flattened my palm and wiped an alcohol pad over the scrapes.

"I c-can do it m-myself," I told him, though I was still shivering so much I didn't know if my fingers could function.

"I'm gonna take care of you," Hayden said and I remembered his conversation with Padraic.

"Ok, thanks."

"Does this hurt?" he asked when he got to the slice on my left heel.

"A little. Honestly, I'm s-so cold I can't r-really feel anything."

He nodded and quickly disinfected the cut and bandaged it up. "You might get hypothermic," he said, sounding concerned.

"You too," I reminded him. "Your clothes are soaked." I held up his jacket. "Put it on." He closed the first aid kit and took his jacket. I hobbled into the truck and fired up the engine. Brock kept watch while Ivan quickly washed the shit off his skin. Once he was dry and dressed, Brock did the same. I rolled down the window and yelled at Hayden to get in the warm cab.

"She's right, Underwood," Ivan advised, "unless you're hoping to get into a sleeping bag with me. You know you want some of this," he joked, gesturing to his body. Hayden laughed and got into the driver's side, holding his cold hands up to the heater vents.

"You're shivering," I pointed out. "Now we're both gonna have to get naked with Ivan."

"I'll just get naked with you," he said with a grin. Body heat was the best thing for someone suffering from hypothermia. I didn't bother telling Hayden that two people with lowered temps wouldn't help each other out.

"Take your pants off," I instructed.

"Riss, not here," he said, sounding offended.

"Shut up. Take them off. They're soaking wet."

"They'll dry."

"Hayden, please. I don't want you to be cold."

"I'll be fine."

I leaned against the seat. "You're more stubborn than I am. Suit yourself and be cold then."

"I'll wash your shoes," Brock called. He picked up my boots and dunked them in the freezing water, swishing them around to clean off the shit. He tossed them to the ground and did the same with his and Hayden's.

"Thanks," I told him when he and Ivan got into the truck. "Now what?" I asked Hayden.

"We can't stay here," he said, looking at Ivan for suggestions. "I say we drive somewhere, start a fire, and dry out our shoes—and my pants. It won't kill us to wear them wet, but I'd rather not."

We all murmured in agreement. Hayden put the truck in reverse and floored it away from the river. None of us spoke as Hayden drove, all too cold to carry on a conversation. The truck slowly filled with warm air, coaxing my stiff muscles to loosen up.

Since it guaranteed safety from a large attack on one side, we stayed alongside the river and ended up in a park; Hayden stopped the truck next to a giant anchor planted in cement. I eyed it curiously for a minute and then realized it was a sundial. Ivan and I kept watch while Hayden and Brock ventured off to find firewood.

The damp ground quickly soaked through my socks. I lifted one foot up for a few seconds, temporarily alleviating the cold. I cupped my hands around my mouth and exhaled, trying to warm them.

"Soon enough," Ivan said with a half smile, "We'll be wishing for the cold."

"Not me," I told him. "I've been cold so much in the last few months. I can't wait for the day it's ninety degrees and humid out."

Ivan laughed. "The cold is tolerable. You can put more clothes on to warm up, but the heat... there's not much you can do about that."

"I'm used to hot Kentucky summers," I reminisced. "My grandparents didn't have air conditioning until I was fifteen. God, I hated it and complained every night about being too hot to sleep." With a smile I said, "When it was really hot, I'd sleep on the basement floor."

"You don't have an accent," Ivan stated.

"Stereotype much?" I said pointedly. "Not everyone does."

"Oh, sorry."

I shrugged. "A lot of people are surprised. And neither do you, Mister New Jersey."

"Very true. And we're not all drunken losers that patrol the boardwalk every night. I'm from Somerville, which isn't close to the shore."

I climbed into the bed of the truck, looking around for signs of danger. Hayden emerged from behind a tree carrying an armload of firewood. Brock was a few yards behind him with even more wood to burn. They dropped it in a pile near the truck, and I took over building the fire. Not wanting to waste time struggling with the damp branches, Ivan carefully poured a little bit of gasoline over my perfect campfire. I lit a match and tossed it in.

We stabbed sticks into the ground and set our boots on them, making sure they were close enough to dry but not so close that the rubber soles would melt. Hayden took his pants off, shivering in just his jacket and boxers, and hung them up near the fire. I stuck my cold hands over the flames, opening and closing my fists to get the feeling back into my fingers. I needed to be able to work my gun. Hayden stood next to me, doing the same. Brock poked at the fire with a stick and Ivan leaned against the truck.

When my face felt too hot, I walked over near Ivan and put the tail gate down to sit on.

"So," Ivan started, turning to face me. He crossed his arms and flashed a brilliant smile. "So, I heard you and Underwood, huh?"

My jaw might have dropped. "W-what? How...how'd...you know?" I stammered. "Ohmygod, I'm gonna kill her! Raeya is such a loudmouth!"

"No," Ivan said calmly. "You are. I *heard*. Those walls are pretty thin, ya know."

An incoherent noise escaped my lips and I gaped at Hayden. He shrugged and smiled. "I told you that you were loud," he said with fake innocence.

Brock stabbed the fire and snickered.

I glared at Hayden, annoyed with him for not caring.

"Don't worry," Ivan assured me. "We didn't tell anyone. We kinda figured you didn't want anyone to know, hence having the not so secret sex."

"How long have you known?" I asked, still feeling slightly horrified.

"Pretty much since you got back," Ivan confessed.

"And you knew they knew?" I accused Hayden.

He shook his head. "No, but I figured someone would hear us—well you—sooner or later."

I crossed my arms and pouted. "You're an ass," I spat, trying to sound mad.

"That's not what you said last night," Hayden said suggestively.

Brock stabbed at the fire once more before standing. "I don't need to hear details; I already hear enough as it is. And, holy shit, don't you people ever get tired? I'm exhausted just listening to you," he joked.

I shook my head and went back by the fire.

"I'm happy for you two," Ivan said sincerely. "It's not easy in this world anymore. It's nice to have someone. And I know Underwood's had a massive crush on you since the first time he saw you."

"Yeah," I agreed. "It took him long enough to do something about it."

"You're kind of intimidating," Hayden insisted, not entirely joking. I looped my arm though his and rested my head against him. Forgetting the fact that we were waiting for our shoes to dry because we had to escape from a herd of zombies through a sewer, I could pretend we were a normal group of friends hanging around the campfire.

We wasted two more hours letting our boots almost dry before we set off again in search of a hardware store. At least Hayden didn't have to wear wet clothing; his pants had completely dried. After three hours of blindly driving around, we realized we were in Missouri and headed south.

"So how come you're not telling anyone?" Brock asked with his mouth full of candy.

I unwrapped a peanut butter cup and looked up at the review mirror, catching Hayden's eyes. "We don't want to get separated."

"Separated?"

"Yeah, we weren't sure if Fuller would let us be roommates if he knew about us. And we thought maybe he'd worry that going on missions together wouldn't be a good idea or something."

"Good point," Brock noted. "I don't think he'd care. Not anymore at least. And we all know how much he loves Hayden."

"Shut up," Hayden said. "He doesn't treat me any differently."

"Yes he does," we all said in unison.

"I don't think it would matter to him either," Ivan told us. "Maybe before, but not now."

"I'm not gonna risk it," Hayden said, his eyes flicking up to the mirror to look at me.

"Ah, aren't you just so cute," Ivan teased.

I opened my mouth to say something catty back but abruptly stopped when something came into view.

"Uh, guys, we got company," I said, a little unsure of what I was seeing.

"We do?" Hayden asked.

"Yeah. You'll want to slow down and look. Trust me."

A naked female S2 staggered along the road. Dried blood was crusted down her front. Her blonde hair lay in a matted mess around her face and her fake boobs were bruised and discolored.

"Now there's something you don't see every day," Ivan noted with a smirk. He turned to Brock. "Finally, a girl who will like me for my brains," he joked.

The boys ogled the zombie's huge boobs for a second, all agreeing it was a shame she got infected before Hayden rolled down his window and shot her in the forehead.

"Two points," I called. "Thanks, baby."

"That doesn't count," Brock argued. "She was on his side and I'm stuck back here."

"Don't be a sore loser," I laughed. We spent the rest of our daylight driving around, trying to figure out just where the hell we were. We had a map, so once we found a sign with a town name or a major highway, we'd easily be able to get home.

At dusk, we decided to find a place to stay for the night. We pulled into a library parking lot; the small brick building was seemingly untouched. Quickly yet thoroughly we patrolled the area while Ivan picked the locks on the front door.

"I'll check upstairs," I whispered. Hayden's face twitched but he nodded.

I silently moved up and down each aisle of the children's section. A table in the back was still covered with craft supplies; a cup of Elmer's Glue had spilled across a pile of construction paper. I tapped the hardened glue, curious as to what the kids had been making.

The finished papers were lined up on the floor, probably set there to dry. Covered in glitter, glue, buttons, and beads, the point of the project was to have the kids draw a 'moral lesson' they learned from a book. I held a particularly glittery one up to the light. The child who drew this was a talented artist. Amelia, she had signed in flowing script at the bottom. She had drawn a castle and a princess holding a sword and had written "the truth is contagious" in the clouds.

"Are you still alive, Amelia?" I asked and let the paper fall to the ground. I checked behind the counter, the bathroom, the supply room and even pressed my ear against the elevator. Deeming it safe, I went back downstairs to see if Hayden had finished covering the larger first level.

I found him in the fiction section, rifle raised. I waved, making sure he knew it was me in the dark.

"Riss," he whispered. "Everything good upstairs?"

"Yeah," I whispered back. "Find anything here?"

"Nothing undead."

"Good." I took a spot by his side and combed through the rest of the library with him. He called Ivan and Brock in, who brought our sleeping bags and food. After eating a scrumptious dinner of protein bars, dried fruit, Halloween candy, and water, Hayden and I unrolled our sleeping bags and zipped them together. We only dared to remove our boots before we got inside.

"Goodnight," I whispered to Hayden as I settled into his arms.

"Night, Riss."

I kissed him once and closed my eyes. I wasn't even tired; however, I knew this was the only chance I'd get to sleep until we got back to the compound, which would hopefully be tomorrow. Ivan kept watch by the front door, occasionally moving around the downstairs to look out the back doors and the windows. Brock was upstairs doing the same.

I could hear the floor creaking as they walked around, and the sound of hushed voices floated through the empty library. Hayden ran his fingers through my hair, only getting a few inches down before they got caught on tangles.

"Sorry," he said as he yanked them out.

"I didn't think to pack a brush," I told him with a smile.

"Next time," he joked.

"Are you tired?" I asked him.

"Not really. It feels good to lie down though."

"Yeah, definitely," I agreed. The cut on my heel burned every time I put pressure on it. "Especially next to you," I added, feeling lame saying that out loud.

He laughed. "Yeah. It's good they know, see?"

"You're right. We should tell everyone else."

"Maybe," he added with hesitation.

"You're ashamed of me?" I teased.

"No, not at all." He hugged me tighter. "I don't want to risk it, Riss. I don't want Fuller to tell us we can't be together."

"Right," I agreed, not wanting to start a disagreement between us. I didn't care what the fuck Fuller told us. I wasn't going to let anything or anyone keep me from being with Hayden. "I don't want to not be with you. I'd go crazy worrying if you went out on a mission without me. I'd be so scared you wouldn't come back."

"I don't want you out of my sight," he admitted. "When that zombie grabbed you in the river, it kinda scared the shit out of me."

"You saved my life I'll have to thank you later," I said coyly.

Hayden squeezed me. "I'm not going to let anything bad happen to you, Orissa." He kissed the top of my head. "I love you."

"I love you, too." I closed my eyes, feeling as content as I could possibly feel and eventually fell asleep.

------------------------------→

The temperature had dropped considerably since the sun had sank, and, after being cuddled up next to Hayden for six hours, getting out of the sleeping bag and into the cold air was like a slap in the face.

I took the upstairs again while Hayden kept an eye out on the main floor. I turned on a flashlight and picked my way up the stairs thinking that a darkened library would make a good plot for a horror movie. A haunted library, I imagined, would be an interesting set. I pushed the thoughts of ghosts knocking books off the shelves away; I didn't have to imagine anything terrible. Real-life monsters roamed the earth.

I shoved a plastic pumpkin to the side of the counter and climbed up to look out the windows. Brock had peeled off the Halloween themed window clings, placing them in a neat pile on a desk. I looked out at the desolate town through the scope of my gun, trying to detect movement. I slowly walked to the other end of the children's section and did the same.

But this time I saw something.

She staggered along the road, tripping every now and then. Strands of her long hair fell out of the tight bun on top of her head, and her long, denim skirt was tattered and stained with blood. I held my breath, waiting to count how many followed. She crossed the street, tripping on the curb. Even with the night vision, I could see the flesh scraped off on the pavement.

She stumbled a good fifty yards in our direction. And nothing followed. I ran my hands along the window, trying to locate the locks.

"Dammit," I swore under my breath. This window was the stupid industrial kind that doesn't open. I flew down the stairs to find Hayden. "There's a lone zombie outside. I'm gonna go kill it," I told him.

"You shouldn't go out alone," he replied quickly.

"Come with then."

He nodded. "Where is it?"

"The back of the library." I pulled an arrow from the quiver I had around my shoulder. "An easy four points, I do believe."

We snuck out the front doors, Hayden leading, and made our way around the building. My breath clouded around me as I exhaled.

"Can you see her?" Hayden asked, looking through his scope.

"I see a shape," I told him and drew back an arrow. "I think it's her."

He glanced up at me. "Yeah, that's her." He held up his gun. "Aim a little higher," he said and looked through his night vision scope one more time. "If you get her in the head, I'll be thoroughly impressed."

I let out my breath, steadied myself, and let the arrow go. The string from the bow slapped my wrist; the painful sting was familiar.

"Holy shit," Hayden breathed. "You got her. Right in the eye."

I smiled triumphantly, though really I felt it was half luck. I couldn't see her *that* well in the dark. I turned on the flashlight and walked over. I put my foot on her chest and yanked the arrow out of her skull. I flicked the brain matter off and shoved it back in the quiver. Hayden and I circled the library, looking for stragglers.

Stars filled the clear night sky. I slowed my feet when we hit the sidewalk in front of the library. We hesitantly walked up the cement stairs. Suddenly, Hayden turned to me, picked me up, and pressed me against the brick wall. My legs, acting on their own accord, wrapped around him, and I pressed my mouth to his.

His tongue slipped past my lips. He forcefully kissed me. He moved one of his hands up to my hair and grabbed a tangle of it, pulling it when he closed his fist. I melted into him, wanting more. He pulled his hand down, tipping my head up. He broke away from my mouth and kissed my neck. I moaned and dug my nails into his back.

Then I smelled him.

I opened my eyes to see a S2 ascend the stairs. Fresh blood glinted off his face and bits of skin stuck in his teeth. I reached for Hayden's gun at the same moment the zombie reached for us.

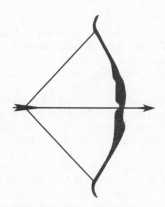

CHAPTER 12

In a swift movement, I pulled the M9 from Hayden's waist. The zombie roared and I fired.

My feet hit the ground and Hayden whirled around. He looked at the zombie and then back at me. "Nice work, Riss."

I shrugged. "Couldn't have done it without you." I put the gun back in the holster. "We should let Ivan and Brock know it's alright."

"You go," Hayden said, bending down. "This blood is fresh. I'm gonna go look for the source."

I hesitated. I didn't want Hayden out of my sight either.

"I'll be careful," he added, sensing my worry.

"Right. You will be." I nodded and jogged inside.

Brock was sitting up, finger hovering over the trigger of his gun. "It's ok!" I yelled as loudly as I dared. "Just one zombie out there that needed to be shot!"

"Told you I heard gunfire," Brock said pointedly to Ivan and flopped back down in his sleeping bag.

"Just one?" Ivan sleepily asked.

"Yeah," I lied, knowing he wouldn't be able to go back to sleep if I said otherwise. "He must have gotten separated from a herd. Or maybe never joined up. But he's dead...er. Deader, I suppose. Hayden's checking for more, but I don't think there are any," I explained quickly.

"Relax," Ivan said, running a hand over his face.

"What?"

"You're talking really fast. Underwood's fine. He's good."

I nodded, acknowledging the fact that my heart was racing. "He is."

Ivan brought his knees up and leaned forward. "It's more than just secret sex, isn't it?"

I was thankful for the dark; I knew my cheeks instantly turned red. "Yes," I said shortly.

"I knew it."

"Shut up," I snapped, unable to will myself not to smile.

"You *love* him," Ivan teased.

"Shut up," I said again. "Before I hit you."

"Mh-hm. I could take you."

"Bring it," I jeered, laughing.

He exhaled loudly. "In the morning. I'm tired. Night, Penwell."

I went up to the children's section, taking two stairs at a time. I looked out the window for movement. I didn't catch anything in the front, so I moved to the back. A dark figure swiftly ran though a thin tree line. I closed my left eye and squinted into the scope. I watched Hayden draw near, and then he moved away from my line of sight.

The doors slowly whooshed open and clinked shut. The clank of the deadbolt shooting into place let me know it was Hayden and not a crazy surreptitiously sneaking in to eat our stomach contents. I made one more round before I went back downstairs.

"Did you find anything?" I asked Hayden, who was looking out the back door.

"A dead raccoon."

"Oh, well, good." I clicked the safety on my rifle and slung it over my shoulder. "I wonder how he caught it. Those fuckers are fast."

Hayden raised an eyebrow. "I guess it doesn't matter."

"Still, it's not like zombies are stealthy, silent hunters."

Hayden laughed softly and set his machine gun down. He put his right hand on his left elbow and gently stretched his injured shoulder.

"Does it hurt?" I asked.

"It's sore, but I wouldn't say it *hurts*."

"Here," I said and stepped behind him. I gently massaged his shoulders and back.

"That feels better," he said, rolling his shoulder. "Thanks."

"Of course."

We spent the rest of the night patrolling the grounds. Hayden and I rolled up our sleeping bags and tucked them under the seats in the back of the truck, gathered up breakfast and woke up Ivan and Brock.

"Zero to ten," Hayden reminded Ivan.

"Ten? Uh, no. You guys have two."

Hayden bit off a piece of his granola bar and shook his head. "We got two last night. Both S2s. One shot with a gun, the other with an arrow."

"I don't believe you," Ivan said, narrowing his eyes.

"Want to see the bodies?"

"Yes," Ivan said stubbornly. "And that doesn't make it ten."

"Not counting the ones killed in the sewers," Hayden explained; it was best to not let 'chaos kills' count. It was too confusing to keep track. "The S2 with the jugs, the zombie in the river; four points. S2 shot with an arrow, four points, bringing it up to eight, plus the S2 on the stairs. Ten points."

Ivan grumbled about it not counting because he was asleep and didn't have a chance. I looked at Brock; he smiled and rolled his eyes. We hurried to finish eating. Hayden, having read all of the books he had back at the compound, spent a few minutes grabbing an arm load to take back with him.

We were just about to load up and take off when Hayden had an idea. I followed him back into the library and Ivan and Brock stayed outside with the truck running. We jumped behind the counter and searched for a phonebook. After only ten minutes of searching, we found it. Hayden flipped through the yellow pages and tore out the page with phone numbers and addresses for home improvement stores.

"That was brilliant," I told him as he folded the page. We got into the truck, went over the map and discovered we were only two and a half hours away from the Home Depot Brock had been talking about, which was only about an hour from the compound.

The time flew by. Brock drove, which allowed Hayden to sit in back with me. We stuffed our faces with candy and took turns picking what kind of music to listen to. Hayden likes country, Brock likes metal and alternative rock, and Ivan and I like hip hop and rap, or 'clubbing music' as Hayden referred to it.

We pulled into the parking lot of the store not a moment too soon. The tank was down to a quarter; something none of us were comfortable with. Hayden refueled while the three of us explored. An S3 limped over, blood staining the orange vest he was wearing. One of his arms had been torn off. Dried strands of muscle and ligaments dangled out of his shoulder socket.

I shot an arrow into his head. It passed through both sides of his mushy skull, hitting another gummy in the neck. He let out a gurgled groan before collapsing.

"Tell me that was on purpose," Brock said, eyes wide.

"I wish," I told him honestly.

"Best zombie kill I've seen in a while," he said back, smiling. "Too bad it's only four points."

There weren't too many zombies here, and the few that milled about were in the S3 stage. The three of us raced to get the highest score. Using the bow got me double points, but it took away time when I stopped to retrieve my arrows.

By the time Hayden had refilled the truck and siphoned enough gas from parked cars to replenish our tanks, the score had gone up twenty-eight to twenty-two, with our team still in the lead. The parking lot was open; we could easily run if we needed to.

Some of the fun in our game disappeared when Brock slid open the automatic doors.

We weren't hit in the face with the gagging smell of death. That was always a good sign.

"Do you want to do this fast and *maybe* easy or slow and safe?" Hayden asked, clicking a magazine into his Berretta.

"Fast and easy," I answered automatically.

"You would," Ivan teased.

Hayden fired a round, shattering a fluorescent light bulb. It exploded and little bits of white dust showered down on the cement floor. The bang was still echoing in my ears when the first S2 staggered out of the garden section. Brock shot him in the head before I had the chance to pull back the string of my bow. I put the arrow in place, my arm holding steady.

Three more zombies came out of hiding. Everyone fired at the same time, and a bullet hit the zombie in the head milliseconds before my arrow.

"You and Underwood hit the same one," Ivan suggested. "So that only counts as one hit for your team."

"You are such a sore loser," I laughed.

Brock knew exactly what to look for. We loaded up carts and piled everything we could possibly need near the door. Inside the store was dark and stuffy and we quickly worked up a sweat hauling and moving all of the heavy objects. We took a break for water and got back to work.

The plan was to tap into the water and electricity sources from the compound, which were powered by a combination of solar and wind power. Brock seemed to have an idea of how to do it; I didn't even attempt to pay attention as he explained it to Hayden and Ivan. He told us that he had worked on several houses that had solar panels on the roof. However, he had never installed them. If we got lucky, we'd find an engineer waiting to be rescued.

I pulled my arms through the sleeves of my sweatshirt and yanked it over my head. I tied it around my waist, wiping away the sweat that rolled down my cleavage. I flipped my head upside down and attempted—without success—to comb out the tangles in my hair. Giving up, I wadded it up in a messy bun. Hayden had stripped out of his vest and jacket. His black t-shirt stuck to his sweaty body. I admired his muscles as they flexed while he lifted a bag of cement mix, tossing it on a cart.

Finally, we were done. Having supplies at the ready made me a little more excited about the plans for expansion. It gave me hope that things could get back to an almost normal state. A Louis Vuitton purse had been dropped near the cash registered. I didn't need or want another designer purse; I still had plenty from my 'shopping spree' not that long ago. I was in search of something else. I dumped the contents on the ground.

"Yes!" I said when my fingers graced a pair of sunglasses, also designer. I put them on before we stepped out into the bright sunlight. We put our weapons in the truck and got in. We didn't even make it out of the parking lot before Hayden slammed on the brakes.

A car slowed to a stop, just feet behind us. Hayden put the truck in park.

"Wait!" I cried.

"What?" he asked.

"Maybe we should, um, approach with caution?"

Hayden's eyebrows pushed together. "Why?"

"Uh, maybe because the last two groups of living people we came across tried to kill you and held me hostage. How can we trust them?"

"Let's just talk, ok?" he soothed.

I nodded and stuck the M9 into my waistband. I swallowed hard and got out of the truck. A weathered and worn middle aged man got out of the old Ford Taurus, holding up his hands. His eyes darted to each of the three Marines, and he instantly looked relieved.

"I knew it!" he wheezed. "I knew I heard shots!" He hobbled forward on a clearly sprained ankle. "I'm Owen. I can't believe it…you're alive!"

"Hello," Hayden said formally. "I'm Sergeant Underwood." He shook the man's hand. "This is Sergeant Brewster and Lance Corporal Callias."

"Oh my, oh my God. American soldiers, thank God." He tightly gripped Hayden's hand. He turned and waved the rest of his companions out of the car. Blinking, they stepped into the sunny parking lot. I hung back, thinking there must have been a reason Hayden didn't introduce me.

Owen introduced us to the rest of his party, which consisted of an older woman named Char, Jenna, Harold, and Jared—who I guessed to be anywhere from twenty-five to thirty-five. It was hard to guess someone's age when they were malnourished, dirty, and scared shitless. The sixth person to step from the cramped car was a teenage girl named Amy. She had short black hair and dark eyes.

Owen's story was the norm with survivors: The little group escaped the initial outbreak; banded together and were constantly on the move, looking for food, shelter, and safety. They hadn't gathered too many weapons and none had any experience using them. Their group started out with seventeen and quickly dwindled down to six.

He said that he felt someone was finally looking out for them when they met up with Jared, Harold, and Amy a little over a week ago. They were the first survivors they had come across since November. And now things were looking up even more since they had stumbled into our path.

The guys explained about the compound, delivering the news like presents to children on Christmas morning. The ragged group was ecstatic.

"Follow us back," Ivan welcomed.

"Oh, we will!" Owen chattered excitedly.

Harold, who stood in the back looking oddly shifty-eyed, nodded at me.

"Who's the girl? Did you find her too?"

"Yes," I answered before Hayden had a chance to say anything else. "They just did. I'm so thankful for these handsome, brave men."

He nodded and I watched his gray eyes flick to Hayden's gun. "Hey," he said suddenly. "We have a full car. Mind if one of us ride with you?"

"Sure, in the back," I decided.

Ivan laughed. "Yes, that will be fine."

Harold put his hand on Amy's shoulder. "You're the smallest. Why don't you go?"

She nodded shyly and kept her eyes on the ground. Jared's face twitched. My heart sped up and I slowly reached behind me, my fingers brushing against the metal of my pistol. Something wasn't right. I exhaled and let my hand fall to my side when the little party crammed back into their car. Hayden drove, Ivan sat shot gun, while Brock and I got in the back with Amy in the middle.

We tried to make conversation, but she wasn't too compliant. After getting only one word responses from her, murmurs that were so quiet that it was hard to hear what she was saying, we gave up and blasted the radio. The truck flew down the road, making good time. Amy leaned forward, her body going limp. She would randomly twitch, as if she was trying to will herself not to fall asleep.

Then her body went rigid.

"Hey, are you alright?" Brock asked, gently putting his hand on her shoulder. Slowly, she turned to look at him. A growl rumbled from deep in her throat. She lunged forward and sunk her teeth into Brock's arm.

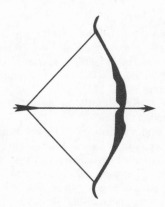

CHAPTER 13

Everything happened so fast. Brock cried out in shock and fear more than in pain. I grabbed the girls' head and yanked, unintentionally forcing her to rip a hunk of Brock's skin off in her teeth. Hayden stomped on the brakes and the truck veered off the road, bumping along the shoulder. Amy screeched and growled. I took a tangle of her hair and pulled her off Brock. I clamped my hands over her ears and twisted. Her neck snapped and her body went limp. I shoved it forward and grabbed onto Brock's arm, squeezing my hands two inches above the bite.

"Hold it down," I instructed. Air rushed in and out of my lungs at an alarming rate. I pressed as hard as I could on the veins, not wanting the virus to pump through Brock's body. The truck finally came to a stop. Hayden and Ivan jumped out and tore open the back doors. I climbed onto my knees, half on top of Amy's body. Using my thumb, I milked the blood out.

"Get the first aid kit," I barked. Ivan stared at me in horror with his mouth hanging open. Hayden raced to the back of the truck to retrieve it. I clambered over the body, moving with Brock. He held his arm out and Hayden poured an entire bottle of peroxide over the wound, even lifting the flaps of skin to thoroughly cleanse it. Brock's body twisted in my grip and he bit down to stifle a groan.

I heard a car door slam and I suddenly remembered we had others with us. My fear disappeared, turning into rage. They knew. They fucking *knew* she was infected.

"They knew all along," I said, my voice a hallow whisper. I didn't loosen my grip on Brock's arm. Ivan yanked the body out of the truck; Amy's head hit the running board with a sickening smack. Someone screamed.

"It's ok," I told Brock, though I knew it was a sad attempt at a lie. My eyes no doubt showed the pure terror I was feeling. I pushed my thumb down again before quickly moving it up and repeating the process. Brock winced in pain. He was losing a lot of blood, I knew, but I thought it was better than getting infected.

I caught movement out of the corner of my eye. I looked up to see Ivan walking over to the others, gun raised. With a rattling breath, I turned my face to Hayden. His hand flew to his M9 and he followed.

"Did you know?" Ivan demanded.

Owen's face showed true shock. With his mouth gaping, he looked at Amy's body.

"Did you know?" Ivan shouted again. "Don't tell me you put that infected bitch in the car with us on purpose."

Owen said something I couldn't hear. I turned my attention back to Brock. He was white and shaking. I leaned over him and reached my blood covered hands into the first aid kit. I wiped some of the blood off on my shirt and used my teeth to rip the plastic open around a roll of gauze. My heart raced and my hands shook. I listened to what was going on outside as I pinched Brock's skin together and rolled the gauze around the wound.

"Don't you fucking lie to me!" Ivan yelled. He thrust his hand forward, pointing the gun at Owen's face. Owen put his hands up and stumbled backwards, bumping into the hood of his car. Char screamed and covered her head. Hayden stepped forward and said something to Ivan.

"Put the gun down!" someone yelled. Trepidation pulsed through my veins and my heart jumped in horror when I saw Harold standing behind the open passenger seat door holding a pistol that was pointed at Ivan. Hayden immediately raised his gun, pointing it at Harold.

"Nobody needs to get hurt," Hayden said in a loud but level voice. "Put the weapon away. It doesn't have to end like this."

Owen slinked off the hood. Char's hands trembled as she reached for him.

"Get out of the way," Hayden ordered.

Jenna stumbled her way over.

Char wrapped an arm around her and they huddled in the middle of the road.

"Listen to him!" Owen shouted. "Harold, put the gun down! Don't do anything stupid!"

"Shut up, old man," Harold yelled back.

"Did you know?" Ivan bellowed, sounding on the brink of insanity.

"I don't know what he's talking about," Jenna cried into Char's arms.

"The girl," Hayden said through gritted teeth, "was infected. She bit my friend."

"No," Owen breathed. "I didn't know. I-I promise."

My mind raced. Why was Harold so insistent on her getting in the car with us if they didn't know? I stared Owen down.

"She seemed fine just a few hours ago," he said. "She hadn't gotten bitten—ever."

I didn't think he was lying; he had no idea Amy was infected. He looked Hayden straight in the eye when he spoke. Then his eyes cast down to Amy's body and he looked genuinely stunned and horrified. Harold kept his gun aimed at Ivan. His hand slightly shook and he held the rifle awkwardly against his chest; he didn't have the poise of someone who had handled firearms before. His finger wasn't over the trigger, leading me to believe he didn't truly intend to shoot anyone.

Jared, however, did.

He had gone unnoticed amidst the chaos and had gotten out of the car, moving around to the back. Crouched down, he closed one eye and looked through the scope on his gun. I followed the line; it led to Hayden.

Holy shit.

Harold would shoot Ivan, Jared would shoot Hayden and then…they assumed Brock was as good as dead, and I was a defenseless girl the soldiers had picked up off the side of the road. Would they steal our truck, weapons and supplies, and leave? I doubted they would take Owen, Char, and Jenna with them. What would they do with Brock and me?

I refused to be left or used…again. And I refused to let Hayden get shot—again. I smeared the blood off my hands and onto my shirt. Slowly, I unfolded my legs.

"What are you doing?" Brock whispered.

"Saving us." I looked into his eyes. "Don't move." Having been wedged in between the seat and the door, my bow and quiver had fallen out of the truck when Ivan madly opened the door. I slid my feet over the edge, silently landing on the pavement. Keeping my eyes in the direction of the guys, I crouched down and felt around for an arrow.

"I don't want to hurt you," Hayden insisted. "Put your gun down first and we will put ours down too. We'll take you back to the compound and everything will be ok."

Harold didn't move. "You first," he sneered.

"Alright," Hayden dumbly agreed. I wanted to yell at him. He lowered his Berretta slowly. "Now your turn."

I picked up my bow and one more arrow. I stuck one in my boot and held the other in my right hand. My muscles twitched with anticipation. I inched along the bed of the truck, keeping my head down and out of sight. Abhorrence threatened my usually steady shot. I rose up, strung an arrow, and pulled back.

Hayden's arms were at his sides now. And Harold hadn't backed off. Hayden stepped to the side, looking at Owen as if it would help. Ivan steadied his hand.

"Put the gun down! Now!" Owen yelled.

"It doesn't have to be this way," Hayden tried to reason.

Jared stood up. The angle of the bright sun was making it hard for him to aim at Hayden. He took a step to the side, getting ready.

And I released my arrow. It flew through the air and hit Jared in the shoulder. He cried out and fell back, accidentally pulling the trigger. Harold fired next but Ivan was faster. The rifle toppled over the car door, clanking to the ground. Harold's body slumped, unmoving in the street.

Jared writhed in pain behind the car. Time seemed to stand still. The bang of the gunfire echoed in my ears. Jenna shrieked. A cloud passed over the sun, momentarily making the day as dark as I felt. A cool breeze blew loose strands of hair across my back and neck causing me to shiver. I shook myself and sprang forward, pulling the second arrow from my boot. I strung it in place and walked around the truck.

Owen raised his hands and backed up again, his gray eyes open wide. Hayden quickly went over to Jared and picked up the gun. Ivan's face was hard. He clicked the safety on his gun and stuck it in the back of his pants.

"You missed," Ivan told me, his voice level as usual.

"No. I didn't," I assured him. "I didn't shoot to kill."

"Neither did I," he said and a chill went down my spine. I nodded and relaxed my arm. "You really had no idea, did you?" I asked Owen.

"No, I promise." His voice came out shaky.

"I told you!" Char cried. "I told you we shouldn't trust those two!" She turned to me. "Please, you have to believe us. They came up to our camp one night. I think they would have killed us if we hadn't woken up. They joined us but didn't even try to fit in. They kept to themselves, even Amy. I always felt like they were planning something."

"Ok," I said simply and looked over at Hayden.

"What should we do with him?" Ivan asked, looking at Jared with discontent.

Hayden shook his head. "He's hurt, but not bad. We...we could get him back before he bleeds out...maybe." He shot a disgusted look at Jared, who screamed in pain when he touched the arrow stuck in his shoulder.

"Shut up," Hayden demanded. "Before something hears you."

"We need to get out of here," Jenna cried. "They will hear us and smell the blood for sure. We-we need to go!" The girl seemed on the verge of a panic attack. A car door slammed and we all jumped. Brock, clutching his injured arm to his chest, made his way over. Ivan rushed to him, looking into Brock's eyes.

"You alright? You lost a lot of blood."

"I think so," Brock answered, his voice hollow. He assessed the situation that had gone from bad to worse in less than sixty seconds. He trudged into the road. "You guys go home."

"Get in the truck," Ivan told him. Brock looked away. "Callias that is an order. Get in the truck. Now."

"No. I-I can't. I can't go back. Just leave me here. It'll be easier."

Jenna raised her hand and pointed to the bloody bandage on Brock's arm. What happened must have clicked in her mind. "He's infected, isn't he? Amy bit him!"

"Yes," Brock replied gravely. "See, I can't go on with you. Just go." His stoic expression broke and emotion took over. His eyebrows pushed together with worry. "I'm not going to risk hurting you guys. You've been more like a family to me in the last few months then my family has in my whole life. Go home and carry out the mission."

"No way," Hayden said, walking over to Brock. He put his hand on Brock's shoulder.

"No!' Brock yelled and pushed Hayden away. "I was bitten!" He held up his arm. "It's only a matter of time before I snap too. Leave me here. Or...or kill me! I don't want to become one of them," his voice broke as his real fear escaped.

"We don't know if you're infected," Hayden tried to calm him down.

"I was bitten!" Brock yelled again, on the verge of hysteria. "What else do you need to know?" He took his gun from around his waist, clicked the safety off, and cocked it. "Shoot me. Do it fast and get it over with. Underwood, please! Just do it!"

"Don't listen to him," Ivan shouted. "Callias, you're going home with us. We can put you in the quarantine and if—"

"Goddammit, no!" Brock yelled and turned the gun on himself. Hayden jerked away, not knowing what to do to keep Brock from shooting himself in the head. "I'm not going to become one of them! I know what they do. I've seen too much death. I'm not going to contribute." He closed his eyes.

"Brock, no!" I cried. "Please."

"I'm disappointed, Riss. I thought you'd understand. We have to do what needs to be done."

"I've been bitten!" Hayden told him. "Twice."

"Don't lie to me, Underwood." Brock stuck the gun under his chin.

I shook.

"I'm not lying! I'm immune and so is that little boy, Parker. Padraic and Cara are working on a vaccine. That's why I get my blood taken so often," Hayden said quickly.

Brock's arm faltered. The gun lowered an inch.

"And that's why Riss and I went out on that mission alone. We had to get blood samples from zombies." He extended his arm. "Look, bite marks."

As soon as Brock's eyes shifted to Hayden's bites, Hayden moved so swiftly I almost didn't see it. With the slide of his arm, he knocked the gun out of Brock's hand. Then he quickly swung and clocked Brock in the side of the head.

Brock blacked out, falling backwards. Hayden caught him with ease, hooking his hands under Brock's armpits. He carefully lowered him to the ground and picked up the gun. Ivan rushed over, and the two Marines brought their comrade into the truck. I stripped Brock of the rest of his weapons. After I dropped them in the bed of the truck, I let out a breath and realized how fucking terrified I had been.

"What are we gonna do with him?" Hayden asked, shooting a repulsed glance at Jared.

Ivan shook his head. "Leave him?"

"You can't just leave me!" Jared shouted. He gripped the arrow and pulled. I contemplated opening my mouth and telling him that he was doing it wrong. When I remembered him turning his gun on Hayden, I opted not to.

"He won't make it long on his own," Hayden observed.

I grinded my teeth, staring at Jared. Was it wrong that I wanted to leave him too? Hayden walked over to me. I put my hand on his chest, feeling his racing heart. He took a step closer and put his hand on my waist. He looked into my eyes and shook his head. Knowing what he was thinking, I gently put my hand on his cheek.

"It'll be ok...somehow," I promised, though I felt like I was lying.

"Yeah," he distantly agreed. "Somehow."

"What are we going to do with that guy?"

"I don't know. Killing zombies is one thing; I'll shoot with no hesitation. S1's even...yeah they're alive, but they won't be for long. But killing a person, a living, uninfected person, seems wrong."

"He was going to shoot you," I reminded him. "He drew first."

Hayden shook his head ever so slightly. "No, Ivan did."

He was right. Ivan had been the first to draw his gun. I didn't even want to wonder if this whole mess could have been avoided. "He was defending his friend."

Hayden nodded and swallowed. "If it hadn't been you, I...I don't know what I would have done. It probably would have been worse."

Impulsively, I stood on my toes and kissed him. We quickly broke apart, taking a step back from one another. Hayden turned to Jared.

"It's not our decision," he said finally. "We take him back and let Fuller decide what to do with him."

Ivan nodded. "Ok."

"He's not riding with us," I stated. One, I didn't want to be around someone who tried to hurt Hayden—I might be tempted to finish what I started. Two, we didn't need any more blood in the truck. And three, there were a shit ton of weapons in our vehicle. Obviously, we couldn't trust Jared. "Stop pulling," I told him. "You won't bleed out with the arrow in you."

"Are you sure?" he asked, his voice full of fear.

"No," I answered honestly. "It's a guess," I added with a shrug.

None of us noticed the crazy until it ran up and knocked Char over.

I sprung into action, racing over and kicking the crazy in the chest. It reeled, quickly recovered, and lunged at me. I ducked, swung my leg out and kicked the crazy's feet out from under him. I didn't have any weapons on me.

A shot rang out and the crazy's brains splattered. I let out a breath and looked up; Hayden stood a few yards away with his pistol still aimed.

"Thanks," I said calmly. I rolled the crazy over, thinking no one wanted or needed to see his dead face. "Let's go."

Jared struggled to his feet. "H-how am I supposed to sit in a car with this?"

I shrugged again. "Don't know. You can figure that out. Don't lean back, I suppose."

"Take it out! It hurts!" he cried and pulled on the arrow again, yelling out as the shaft of the arrow moved. I waited, watching him yank on it some more. He only had a few inches to pull until the arrowhead hit his back. He screamed when it did.

"We need to go," Hayden instructed. "It is not secure here and..." he trailed off, casting his eyes over Brock, who lay in the truck. "Move," he instructed.

"Maybe we shouldn't," I overheard Jenna whisper. She eyed me nervously.

"Then don't," I snapped. I grabbed the crazy's ankles and dragged him off the road; we were going to have to drive this way back to the home improvement store. Ivan got in the driver's side and fired up the engine. Owen, Char, and Jenna didn't move. "Are you coming or not?" I asked impatiently.

Char looked at Owen. "How do we know we can trust you?"

"You don't," Hayden answered. "But we're going. We have to take care of our friend. You can follow or you can go on your way. No one's gonna force you." He turned his back, sighed, and got into the truck. I got in last, sitting in the back next to Brock. I gently lifted his head and resituated it against me thinking it was more comfortable for him. The truck rolled forward. Hayden turned around, watching to see if the others would follow. The car grew smaller and smaller until it was barely visible.

Hayden turned back to the road. I brushed Brock's hair off of his face and put my hand on his. I had been so focused on not losing Hayden, I never stopped to think about how much it scared me to lose anyone else. Ivan and Brock—and even Rider and Wade—were my friends too. I cared about them a lot, and, like Brock said, we were each other's family now.

Not one word was spoken as the truck sped along the road. Brock twitched and let out a groan. I held onto his hand. He blinked open his eyes.

"Orissa?" he asked when I came into his view.

"Yeah. Hi," I said dumbly, not knowing what else to say. Slowly, he sat up and looked at his arm. His face fell when he saw the bandage.

"Fuck. I hoped it was a dream." He ran a hand over his head. "Let me out."

"No," Hayden said so loudly it almost startled me. "If I have to hit you again, I will. And next time you won't wake up so soon."

Ivan's grip on the steering wheel tightened. He looked at Brock in the rearview mirror but didn't say anything. His lips were pulled into a tight line of worry.

"Were you lying?" Brock asked. "About being bitten?"

"No," Hayden said seriously. "I wasn't. Orissa knows it's true."

"She would agree with anything you say," Brock spat.

"No, I wouldn't," I told him. "But it's true. I saw it happen the second time."

Ivan took his eyes off the road. "Why would you do that? Put us all at risk?"

"Riss knew," Hayden stated. "She would have—"

"—not said anything," Ivan interrupted.

"I would have!" I retorted.

"Really?" he nearly snarled. "Then why didn't you?"

"Because I knew he'd be fine! It was the second time he had got bitten. I didn't want anyone to act irrationally."

"I can't believe you let your feelings cloud your judgment," Ivan accused Hayden. "You never would have lied before."

"I didn't lie!" Hayden argued.

"Guys!" Brock yelled. "Stop!" Silence fell over the four of us. "Things got a little…out of hand back there, but we can't fall apart."

"You're right," Ivan said. "Sorry, Underwood." He looked over his shoulder. "And Penwell. You'd do the right thing, I know it."

"Thanks, sorry too," I said.

Ten minutes crawled by.

"Look!" Brock exclaimed, turning around.

"They're coming," I said under my breath. Something sunk in my heart. Was it disappointment? I shook my head. Why did I not want the others to be safe at the compound?

"Good," Hayden said with no emotion. The rest of the ride home was awkward. Brock shifted nervously in his seat, Ivan radiated anger, and Hayden didn't say a word. When the driveway came into view Brock asked,

"What should I do?"

"Keep your mouth shut," I responded quickly.

Ivan glared at me.

"People act dumb when they're scared. Especially when they're expecting something," I reasoned.

"They'll look for symptoms," Hayden continued explaining. "And you will feel them," he told Brock. "I did."

"What if I do go crazy?" Brock wearily asked, his dark eyes big with fear.

"We will be there," Hayden assured him. "If we can handle a shit ton of zombies, we can handle one S1."

"But you're not infected," Ivan stated, being optimistic for the first time in a while.

"You might not be," I agreed. "We got to you right away. I pushed some blood out, I don't know if it did anything, but it made sense to do it to me. And Hayden poured an entire bottle of peroxide on the cut. You really could be fine."

"Do you really believe that?" he asked, his voice wavering.

"Yes," Ivan, Hayden, and I said in unison.

"Ok," Brock said, nodding, though the worry in his eyes said otherwise. He pulled on a long sleeve shirt to cover up the bite. "Riss, you're covered in my blood."

"I'm always covered in blood," I flatly stated and then laughed. "No one will suspect a thing." I leaned over Brock and grabbed a roll of gauze and several alcohol wipes. I stuffed it down my bra. I looked at Brock and smiled. "You'll be fine."

→

After we entered the compound, Brock and Hayden didn't wait around to coddle the newcomers. Ivan and I were left to explain the quarantine procedure, and we watched as they were led away, frightened and unsure. I noted that Jared was paler than before. The idiot had probably tried to remove the arrow.

When they were gone, Ivan and I went straight through to Fuller's office. When we didn't find Hayden and Brock, we decided to check the only other place they would be: the hospital ward. After missions, we went straight to our quarantine room, not interacting with anyone but other A's. Covered in crusted blood and still carrying our weapons, Ivan and I attracted a lot of attention as we strode down the halls.

I set my face and looked straight ahead, wanting to make myself look as unapproachable as possible; I was not in the mood to talk to anyone. Maybe it was our hard expressions or the lack of knowing what to say to us in this situation, but we made it to the hospital ward without having to open our mouths.

Brock was sitting on the foam bed, his sleeve rolled up and arm extended. Padraic and Dr. Cara crowded around him. Hayden and Fuller were talking in whispers down the hall. Ivan strode forward, joining his fellow Marines. I hung back, staying out of Padraic's way.

I had to remind myself to take a deep breath and stay calm. Seeing Brock under the harsh exam lights was sickening. Padraic said something to Dr. Cara, who nodded and grabbed a vial and a syringe. She jabbed the needle into Brock's vein with no hesitation.

"Oh, Orissa," Padraic said when he turned around. "I didn't know you came in here." He smiled and looked into my eyes. "I'm glad you're back." He took a step forward as if to hug me but stopped, his eyes sliding down my front. "A-are you alright?"

"Yeah," I assured him. "This isn't my blood."

Padraic nodded. "Good."

"So, what do you think?" I asked.

Knowing what my question implied, Padraic took another step closer.

"We're not sure. You acted brilliantly, pushing the blood out and stopping it from spreading," Padraic complimented honestly. "We're going to see how much of the virus is in his system."

"So you will know right away if he's infected?"

"More or less," Padraic told me. "I don't think I can confidently say we know anything for sure about the virus. We just don't have the means to run proper tests. Everything we *know* is all speculation and theory, honestly."

"And what if he has a lot of the virus in his blood?"

"Then he'll be quarantined and we wait." Padraic smiled weakly. "But let's not get ahead of ourselves."

I nodded, wanting to be optimistic like Padraic. "I was right there. I should have stopped it," I whispered, feeling a weight being lifted as I said it out loud.

"You can't stop everything bad, Riss," he reminded me.

"I know, but that doesn't mean I don't want to." I shook my head. "The last two times I've gone out, something horrible has happened to someone I care about. I think I'm cursed; I should just start going out alone."

"Or not at all," Padraic tried to joke.

I was suddenly reminded of his unfriendly exchange with Hayden before we left. I wanted to be mad at him but was too tired and upset to give a damn.

Dr. Cara pressed a cotton ball over the small hole in Brock's arm. She held the vial of blood tightly in her hand and scuttled out of the room.

"It won't be long," Padraic told me and joined her. I hopped up on the bed next to Brock. He looked like he was about to pass out or puke.

"How are you holding up?" I asked him.

"I'm wonderful," he said sarcastically. "I just want to know. One way or another. I-I don't like waiting."

"You won't have to wait alone," I told him and gently placed my hand on his.

"Thanks."

Several painful minutes ticked by. The door opened; both Brock and I jerked our heads up thinking it was Padraic or Dr. Cara with the lab results. Hayden came in first, causing my stomach to flutter in a stupid way. Ivan followed and Fuller brought up the rear. With five of us, the exam room was crowded.

"Did you find out anything?" Ivan asked.

"Not yet," Brock answered ruefully.

I looked up at Hayden, trying to send a nonverbal message to him. I met his eyes then looked at the spot next to me. He nodded ever so slightly but didn't move. He cast his eyes to Fuller. I raised an eyebrow and he shrugged. I heavily sighed and looked away.

"What's the plan?" Brock asked Fuller.

"Don't worry about that yet," Fuller said in a gentle, out of character tone. I had the feeling he didn't think Brock was going to be ok.

"Easier said than done," Brock laughed shakily. I nodded and patted his hand. Brock nervously tapped his foot against the wooden base of the bed, rattling whatever was in the built in drawers. Hayden crossed his arms and leaned against the door, his brown eyes filled will concern. Ivan's face was blank, as if he refused to process emotion. Fuller looked straight ahead, trying to appear stoic.

As much as I detested him, I had to give Fuller credit for caring about his soldiers and Marines.

Maybe it was because we were the only ones left, I thought bitterly. Several minutes later, Padraic came back into the room. We all jerked around to stare him down.

"I'm sorry, Hayden, but I need a sample to use as comparison."

"That's fine," Hayden said, straightening up and extending his arm. Padraic put on gloves, got the supplies he needed, disinfected Hayden's skin with an alcohol wipe, and very gently plunged the needle into his vein.

"Do you know anything yet?" Brock asked, his voice cracking.

"Not yet. Your lab results are done, but I want to compare your blood to Hayden's before I tell you anything." Padraic slid the cap up on the needle and pressed a piece of gauze over the little drop of blood that sat in the crook of Hayden's elbow.

"That was fast," Brock stated. "You were able to see everything already?"

Padraic looked almost confused for a second. "Oh, no. I ran your blood through a machine that tells the lab values." He smiled. "We don't have to manually test everything, just the zombie virus."

"You should name it," I said suddenly. Everyone stared at me. "You know, doctors and scientists who discover crap always name it. I think you should name it."

Padraic half smiled and turned to me. "What should I call it?"

"You're the doctor. You name it."

"Uh, alright. The...the, uh, Lazarus...Lazarus Contagium then."

"I like it."

"Not too creative. I'll think about it," he promised and left the room. We waited in silence for what seemed like eternity.

$$\longrightarrow$$

When Padraic came into the room for a second time, I knew right away that I could breathe easy. His blue eyes were clear again and he was smiling. Like Raeya, he could easily be read.

"You're clean," he told Brock.

"Are you sure?" Brock asked, on the edge of his seat.

"Yes. No traces of the virus were found in the sample we took."

"The sample," Brock repeated. "But it could be in the rest of me?"

Padraic ran his hand over his hair and the light that lit up his face died. "I can't be sure about anything related to this virus. It mutates, changes, and affects everyone differently. But I can be sure that there was none in the sample we took. As far as I'm concerned, you're not infected."

Brock's body relaxed. He squeezed my hand. "So I'm immune?"

"That," Padraic said as he leaned against the counter, "I'm not sure of. If you were resistant, like Hayden, you'd have traces of the virus in your system. And you don't." He flashed a brilliant smile in my direction. "I think you can thank Orissa for that."

Brock hugged me. "I cannot thank you enough, Riss."

"Don't worry about it," I said casually and patted his back.

"Now what?" Brock asked Fuller.

"You can be quarantined with the others if they agree to keeping watch over you."

"That's fine," Hayden answered right away.

"Fine with me too," Ivan answered.

Without giving me a chance to voice my opinion—which was the same as Ivan's and Hayden's—Fuller continued. "Alright, then. Get your stuff and go straight there. You will get an extra day off since tonight will not be restful."

The guys nodded in agreement and got up to leave. Padraic put his hand on my shoulder and nodded for me to follow him.

"Riss, I want you to be careful," he said, his eyes moving down my body. For a split second I thought he was looking at my boobs; instead, he was eyeing the dried blood.

"I am careful," I replied. "What are you talking about, Padraic?"

"I was really surprised to see the lab results," he started, rubbing the back of his neck. He sighed and let his hand drop.

"Brock's not ok?" I asked, a flicker of fear stabbing my heart.

"No, no, Brock is. It's...it's Hayden."

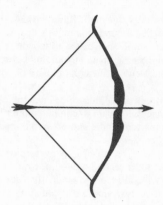

CHAPTER 14

The flicker turned into a fire. "What's wrong with him?"

"He still has a lot of the virus in his blood. I thought it would be eliminated—and some of it has—but it's taking longer than I expected."

My body went cold. "You think he could get infected?"

"Technically, he is infected. But the virus doesn't do anything to him. I don't think it will."

"Then why are you freaking me out over this?"

He put a finger on a clump of blood on my arm. "This. You used your hands, your bare hands to take care of Brock. You probably saved his life but you put yours in danger. If Hayden was injured, you'd do the same, right?"

"Of course. I'm not following, Padraic. Just say it, please."

"I think Hayden's a carrier."

My heart fell onto the floor. "A *carrier*?"

"Yes. If you came into contact with his blood, I think you could get infected."

"Oh." I already had. I'd had Hayden's blood on me more than once. And if his blood was infected then his other fluids were too…and I had been exposed to them more than once as well. And I wasn't a raging lunatic who craved the already digested meals of humans.

"Riss?" Padraic asked, putting his hand on my shoulder. "You ok?"

"Yeah," I said and snapped myself back to the here and now. "I'm tired. And stressed."

"Right. You've been through a lot."

"Did you tell Hayden? I mean, I think he should know."

"I'll talk to him once you all are released." He removed his hand. My mind was spinning thinking about the virus and blood and infecting each other. I wished Raeya's dad was around to run all sorts of tests and experiments and give us some answers, though I doubted the pharmaceutical research company he'd worked for had prepared him for anything zombie.

When we were kids, Ray and I used to get into trouble playing with test tubes and beakers we found in her dad's office. It was all fun and games then. Looking back, we were lucky we didn't pick up any weird disease or mutation.

"I shot that guy with an arrow." The words came out of my mouth just as the connection was made in my head.

"Yeah, Brock told me. You had no choice," Padraic said, thinking I felt bad for shooting a human.

"An arrow that I've used to kill zombies," I told him, my voice low.

"Oh. Oh!" Padraic exclaimed, getting what my statement implied. He shook his head. "When was the last time that arrow had zombie blood on it?"

"I'm not sure." I tried to think back. "Don't take care of him," I said selfishly. "I don't want him to hurt you."

"The virus can't live without a host for very long," Padraic assured me.

"I think I used them maybe two or three hours before I shot him." I remembered shooting down zombies in the parking lot. Padraic pressed his lips together.

"It might be ok," he assured me.

"Our weapons get covered in zombie blood," I spoke. "And we don't really clean them when we're on the road."

Padraic shook his head. "From what I've been able to tell, the virus will not survive in open air for very long; no more than a few hours at the most. I can't help the sinking feeling that my theory might not apply to all zombies."

"Oh, well, that's good," I said with a sigh of relief. "Did you find out anything else?"

"I can't say for sure since we've had limited samples to test, but it seems the virus in an S1 is the least threatening, which could be why Brock isn't infected," Padraic explained.

"What?" I asked, pushing my eyebrows together. I picked at the dried blood on my arms, which was starting to itch.

Padraic exhaled. "I don't want to tell you since I don't know for sure."

"You can tell me," I reminded him. "I want to know and I'll pester you until you tell me, so you better spit it out now."

"It seems the virus evolves. The virus in the S1 sample you brought wasn't as potent as the virus in the S3 sample. I'm not sure why yet; I have several theories." He crossed his arms and looked into my eyes. "It's a long, boring topic though. I know you're tired."

I couldn't argue with that. Today had been draining—mentally and physically. "Yeah, and I better get into the quarantine before Fuller has a heart attack." I walked to the door. "Tell Ray I'm back safe and sound and I said 'hi'."

"I will," he promised.

"Thanks, Padraic." I left the hospital ward and jogged up to my room. Hayden was waiting, with clothes for both himself and me folded over his arm.

"Slow poke," he teased.

"I was talking to Padraic about the virus," I told him grimly. "It's weird; the more I know the less confusing it should be, but it's the other way around. It's more complicated than I imagined."

"It is," Hayden agreed. "Let's not think about it now; let's just get through the next twenty-four hours."

I grabbed my shower stuff and followed Hayden down the stairs. Jones, an A3 I hadn't conversed with much, was bringing several of the dogs in. Argos broke away and raced over to me. I dropped everything I was carrying to greet the dog.

"Hi, sweetheart," I gushed, kneeling down to pet the Doberman. His stump of a tail wagged like crazy and he whined as he circled me, completely excited.

"I think he missed you," Jones said with a smile.

"Where's Greta?" Hayden asked, looking for his favorite dog of the bunch.

"She's outside," Jones told him. "You should see her in training. She's getting good at finding people."

"Awesome. When do you think she'll be ready to go out?" Hayden inquired.

"Pretty soon. I can get her, if you'd like."

"I would, but we have to get downstairs. Thanks for taking care of the dogs," he said to Jones with a smile.

I hugged Argos. "Yeah, thanks. He looks great," I agreed. I petted him one more time, thinking that he was the best looking dog I'd ever seen. I supposed it was possible I was a *little* biased. We went into the quarantine room, dropping our stuff onto the couch.

After showering, sleeping for several hours, and eating some soup, I lounged around lazily before joining Brock in a game of cards. Earlier, Hayden had given me his dog tags, and occasionally I pulled them out of my shirt and looked at them. Despite everything that had happened, having his tags around my neck made me happy. Hayden wouldn't give his tags to just anyone. Giving them to me meant he loved me enough to think we'd have a future together...even though I wasn't sure if we'd live past next week.

Twenty minutes later, Hayden got up and sat at the table with us. We ate soup, talked about past family gatherings (Brock's family was so dysfunctional it made my own messed up family seem normal), and our school experiences.

"I never got why girls are so mean to each other," Brock said as he absentmindedly shuffled the deck of cards. "I almost didn't want to have a girlfriend for the longest time because of it. You can't escape the damn drama." He and Hayden looked at me as if I knew all the answers.

"What?" I asked them.

"Come on, Riss. Don't you know some secret girl rules you can spill now that the world has gone to hell?" Brock asked.

"Not really," I told him honestly. I sighed. "Well, it's cuz girls are always judging each other."

"Why?" Hayden asked.

"Because we want to be the best." I leaned forward. "It's almost like we're hardwired to think we have to be the best or no one will like us. We try and try and if we find someone better than us—which we will—we insult her to make us feel better. Girls are jealous by nature. If another girl has better hair, a firmer ass, bigger boobs, more friends, whatever you could possibly compare, we are taught to hate her and come up with reasons to bring her down."

"You really think so?" Hayden asked.

"I know so."

"I don't see you as being the jealous type," Brock stated.

I shrugged. "I don't think I am either."

"So you wouldn't insult a girl who is better than you?" he asked.

I shook my head. "What's the point? No matter what—if you do the dumbass comparing game— you will always find someone better than you."

Brock made a face. "But you're a competitive person."

"Yeah, I am. I like challenging myself. But I learned a long time ago it's so much better if you just stop the comparing. I don't want to be brought down by society's fucking picture perfect image of what a woman should be. I'm me and if you don't like me, well, fuck you. And when you're constantly comparing and worrying about what other people think of you, they own you and you're not your own person anymore." I smiled and leaned back in the chair.

Hayden turned to Brock. "I think she's a keeper," he joked.

"And I'm sure guys do just as much comparing," I said.

Hayden and Brock immediately disagreed.

"Oh come on, you so do."

"Maybe we compare a little," Hayden admitted. "But I don't think we try to bring other dudes down."

"Yeah," Brock agreed. "Like if I saw a guy at the gym who was more built than me, I'd jealously wish I was bigger, but I wouldn't call him a whore like girls do to each other."

"Makes sense," I said and took the cards from Brock. I shuffled and dealt and started another game of Rummy.

Once twelve hours passed and Brock felt symptom free, he relaxed enough to sleep. Hayden and I cuddled up on the couch, watching movies and talking to pass the rest of the time.

I forgot to look at the clock when we first came into the quarantine. I knew we got back in the afternoon; it was currently 1:30. I ended up falling asleep while Hayden and Ivan kept an eye on Brock, though at this point we were sure he was fine. Hayden woke me up when our time was up.

Just in time for dinner, we showered and changed before going downstairs. Raeya, Sonja and Olivia raced over to me. I threw my arms around my best friend, hugging her so tightly I picked her up off the ground.

"Riss!" she exclaimed. "I missed you!"

"I missed you too," I told her and took a step back. "And see, I told you I'd only be gone for a day or two." I got my tray and joined Ray at her table filled with the people from my old group: Lisa, Sonja, Jason, and Padraic. Olivia and another teenage girl I didn't know crowded in with them. There was only one seat left. I looked at Hayden, who smiled and nodded.

Since I had just spent an entire twenty-four hours by his side, not sitting next to him for one meal wasn't going to hurt his feelings. I sat down, happy to spend time with my friends. Raeya told me that she came up with a safe system for getting everyone outside in the open air. She had come up with a 'recess timesheet' for them to follow. Fuller agreed to pull two A3s to stand guard around the dog's fenced in area while the residents were enjoying the sunshine.

"Tension is growing," she warned me. "It's almost like the gratitude for being safe is wearing off and people are becoming restless." She pushed mashed potatoes around on her plate. "Some of us have been here for months; we've grown comfortable. And with that, people seem to think they can do what they want."

"That's not good," I dumbly stated and forced myself to eat a forkful of tuna casserole. There was a time I used to enjoy that dish; having to choke it down at least once a week made me detest it with a passion.

"No, it's not. I'm afraid people are feeling like they are waiting for something that will never come."

"And what are we waiting for?" Sonja asked, having overheard us.

"For all the zombies to die," her brother pointed out as if it was the most obvious thing in the world.

"But then what?" she questioned.

Padraic took a drink of water and answered. "We start again."

"How?" Sonja pressed. "We barely have anything."

"It's been done before," I told her, Hayden's speech echoing in my mind. "Hundreds of years ago. We're smarter now; we can do it again."

"Smarter, but not tougher," Lisa said and we all laughed.

After dinner Hayden went upstairs to play video games with the other A1s. I stayed downstairs and followed Raeya into the game room. We played a board game with Lisa, Sonja, and Olivia and then I snuck Raeya upstairs and outside into the dogs' area. We found Argos and threw a tennis ball for him.

"The stars are so bright!" Raeya said, wrapping her arms around herself. Her breath clouded around her face and a cool, late winter wind blew through her hair.

"Yeah, there's no light pollution anymore." I threw the ball as far as I could and looked up. "I never realized how much there was until it was gone. Remember how dark it was when we were on the run?"

"Yeah, it was impossible to see."

"Thank God for our night vision scopes," I said with a half smile. I shivered; without the sun, the nighttime air was chilly. Raeya sat on an overturned bucket.

"I can't wait until we can spend more time out here," she sighed. "It's pretty safe, right?"

"I think so," I told her honestly. "Though, I think we've been lucky no zombies have wandered close enough to realize that there are hundreds of tasty people underground."

"They can't get to us," she reminded me, but I sensed the question in her voice.

"Right. Not downstairs at least. And the windows are bullet proof, the doors are all steel and the walls are reinforced. It would be hard for them to get inside the estate and impossible for them to get into the lower levels."

"What would we do if we were attacked?"

"Wait it out. That's what Fuller said anyway. Our livestock would be gone though. Hopefully the A2s out there would be able to get to safety. And we—the A1s—would be sent out to kill them."

"What about the A3s?"

"The watch towers they are in are high enough and sturdy enough they'd be fine. They'd just have to wait it out too."

"How long do you think that would be?"

"I have no idea. The zombies would move on eventually...I think."

She nodded and looked around the dimly lit fenced in area, no doubt planning a route of escape. "Would we know?"

"Know what?"

"If zombies surrounded the compound. Would you tell us?"

"I'd tell you," I said honestly. "But I don't think you would know as it was happening. It would create panic."

"Right, it would. And it's not like us knowing would even make a difference." She sighed heavily. "Maybe the cabins aren't a good idea after all."

"Hey," I said gently. "What's wrong?" I questioned her never faltering sense of optimism.

She shook her head. "Nothing. I-I guess I'm getting cabin fever too." She looked into my eyes. "There's just so much I miss."

"Me too," I agreed. "This dead world fucking sucks ass, but we're here and we have to make the most of it, no matter how shitty it is. I'll admit there was a time I didn't think it was worth living."

"Really?"

I nodded. "I thought I had nothing left to live for. But I have you and the others and now Hayden... I'm not good at this, Ray, but you can't give up hope. You taught me that. We're strong, we're survivors. If we've made it this far, then I think we're some pretty tough bitches who can keep going."

She smiled. "I don't think anyone but you can say so many bad words in an inspirational speech and still have it make me feel better," she laughed. "But you're right. Life isn't what it used to be, but we are alive. We can't forget that."

One of the dogs barked. I whirled around, my eyes scanning the property. Another barked and ran over to the fence. Then I heard the familiar hissing of raccoons. I let out a breath and turned back to Ray, my hands absentmindedly fiddling with the chain around my neck.

As I prepared to tell her about Brock getting bitten and the shootings, I pulled nervously on the chain.

"What is that?" she asked, unable to see it in the dark.

A smile broke out on my face. "Hayden's dog tags," I attempted to say casually but failed at keeping the happiness out of my voice.

"He gave you his tags?"

"No, I stole them while he was sleeping. Of course he gave them to me, Ray."

"Aren't soldiers supposed to wear them all the time?"

"In war yes, that's how the bodies get ID'd."

"Oh," she said but still looked at me quizzically. "So he doesn't need them anymore, right?"

"I guess not," I said, not liking the thought of needing to identify Hayden's body. I tugged on the tags, biting my lip.

"Wait," Raeya said and shot up. "Does it mean the same thing as giving someone a fraternity pin?" I nodded.

"Ohmygod, Rissy!" she squeaked. "That is so sweet!"

I waved my hand, wanting to downplay the romance. "Yeah, I guess"

"I sense a 'but' coming on."

"A butt?"

She nodded. "It is sweet *but*..."

"Oh, *that* kind of but. And yeah." I let my hand fall. "Sweet, yes, but what's the purpose? Why give me something that symbolizes wanting to be together forever when tomorrow might be as far as we get?"

"You don't know that," she told me. "And besides, you love him, don't you?"

I nodded.

"And obviously he loves you; why not hope for forever together?"

"Even if there weren't zombies, I have low expectations of forever," I reminded her.

"I know. Your parents' divorce made you have huge doubts on lasting, functional relationships," she said bluntly. "But it didn't to Hayden. It's not fair to him if you don't at least give him the chance to prove it."

I nodded again. "You make too much sense, Ray."

"That," she said with a smile, "is something I can live with. And I'm glad I'm back to giving you advice. Inspirational speeches from you are weird."

I laughed. The wind blew again and we both shivered. Deciding to take the dogs in with us, Ray and I clipped leashes on seven big dogs and scooped up the two little ones that were currently outside with us. We brought them downstairs; Raeya knew who most of the dogs belonged to.

I brought Argos up to my room with me. He trotted ahead, happy to be somewhere new. I assumed he slept with the German Shepherds that were being trained to aid us on our missions; I was sure he'd be happy to spend the night with us.

"Hey, Orissa," Gabby said. She bent down and transferred her clothes from the dyer into her laundry basket. She invited me to watch a movie with her and Jessica, the other female A1. I wanted to crash in my room with Argos and wait for Hayden to get done playing video games with the guys. But I decided to be social and accept her offer.

I watched as she tightened her blonde ponytail and picked up her basket. She could be really pretty, I thought, if she wore makeup and did something with her naturally curly and frizzy hair. "We'll start it soon, see you in a bit!"

I turned the washing machine on, grumbling to myself about having to suffer through an hour and a half of girl time watching a stupid black and white movie. Without measuring the detergent, I dumped it in and shoved my clothes inside the washing machine. I changed into pajama pants and a sweatshirt and went into Gabby and Jessica's room.

All the rooms were set up in the same way: a bed and nightstands on either side of the door, a dresser centered on the opposite wall with a window above it, a bookcase and a closet on the sides. One of the shelves on their bookcase held little glass figurines and a picture of a once happy family. It was strange to see a smile that big on Jessica's face.

Gabby patted the spot next to her. I sat on her bed, fluffing a pillow behind me.

"Have you seen this?" she asked, pressing play. *Night of the Living Dead* started playing.

"A long time ago," I told her. "You?"

"Nope. Zombie movies used to scare me. Now the real thing is so much worse."

"Yeah. They don't cover all the bases in the movies."

"Ugh. Not at all. It's all running and action and doesn't show that you still have to go on living."

Jessica came into the room carrying a bowl of popcorn. Somewhat to my surprise, she squeezed onto the bed next to me.

"At least we have an endless supply of microwave popcorn," Gabby said and grabbed a handful. We watched the movie, eating popcorn and occasionally talking. The more I got to know Gabby the more I liked her. The more I spoke with Jessica, the more I pitied her.

She was at work the day the first crazy attacked someone in her small town. As a cop, she was the first to respond. He had bitten the waitress at Sue's Diner. Another patron hit him over the head, knocking him out for only a few seconds. Then he was up again, attacking anyone who was near. He killed one person, and, by the time Jessica got there, he was feasting on his organs.

Jessica shot him on the spot.

When she came home that night, she said she knew something wasn't right with Jacob, her five-year-old son. He kept telling her his head hurt. Thinking it was a normal headache she gave him Tylenol, a kiss, and tucked him in bed.

He never woke up.

Then chaos broke out. While she and her husband were grieving the death of their child, the people of the town turned on each other. Jessica was frantically gathering weapons and supplies to make a getaway. She left her husband in the house and ran out to the garage to put a bag in the car.

When she went back to the house, the door was locked. She closed her eyes as she told me how she banged on the door, begging him to let her in. But he didn't. Finally, she gave up and broke the window in the door and reached through, cutting her arm on the broken glass.

Her husband was sitting calmly at the kitchen table. She said she yelled at him for ignoring her, but he didn't even look up. She remembered it clearly, the blood dripping on the floor. She grabbed a towel to put on her wound and raced over to check on her bleeding husband.

He had a vegetable peeler in one hand, shaving the skin off his other. Once he got a strip off, he ate it.

Gabby shivered. "Sorry," she whispered. "No matter how many times I hear it, it still gives me chills." She put her hand on Jessica's. "I wish I could go back in time," she told her. "And save them. Save everyone."

"What about you, Orissa?" Jessica asked, blinking back tears. "How did you discover everything? Did it happen all of the sudden too?"

"I think so," I told her. "I'll have to ask Padraic; I don't really know."

"Padraic?" Gabby questioned.

"Yeah. I was at the hospital; I got attacked, put in an exam room, and then got knocked out by some sort of gas. Padraic found me and brought me downstairs. We stayed in the hospital basement with close to fifty people for, shit, two weeks probably."

"So you never saw the news?" Gabby asked.

I shook my head.

"There weren't any stories at first, as if not talking about the violence made it not real," she said. "My dad told me that he thinks the news reporters weren't allowed to talk about it. He thought it has something to do with not creating panic, but I don't agree. I mean, I don't agree with the reason being to delay the panic. I fully agree with the reporters not being allowed to talk about it. And it was almost like the news reporters knew what was going on the whole time."

"I guess we'll never know," Jessica said. We turned our attention back to the movie. I was feeling a little dejected, my mind pondering the virus and the outbreak. When the movie was over, I said goodnight and went to retrieve Argos from the guys.

The following day we were back on our normal schedule. After breakfast and working out, Fuller wanted us to teach the A3s more hand-to-hand combat skills.

He told us that we needed to start being more conservative with bullets; my new go-to weapon was the bow and arrows. While on the topic of commodities, he also told us that we weren't to use the air conditioners in our cars while out on missions. The gas tanks in the barn were running low.

Gabby, Jessica, Noah, José, Alex, Mac, Wade, and Rider left that morning to bring back the supplies we gathered. They met with Sam, a pleasant middle aged man who used to be a truck driver for a demonstration on how to drive a big rig. Wade and Rider took the only semi truck we had in our possession; the large horse trailer it pulled would be great for filling with the stuff we'd need.

They were supposed to come back that night. The store was only an hour away. The moon replaced the sun and there was no sign of our missing friends. Ivan was sure that with eight of them, they'd be fine. They most likely took a wrong turn and wasted their daylight driving around on the hilly, winding roads. Hayden blankly looked ahead, nodding in agreement to what Ivan said.

It was a horrible feeling, one that dug and tunneled its way not only through my heart but also my stomach, making me sick with worry. I had let go of being pissed at Alex; he wasn't worth it anymore. And along with the six others were two of my friends. I hoped Wade and Rider really were just lost.

Hayden and I both had a hard time falling asleep that night. He tossed and turned, pulling the covers off of me more than once. I was about to suggest he get into his own bed when he finally fell asleep. Only a few hours later, he started thrashing again.

"Hayden," I said, sleepily sitting up. "Wake up. It's ok. You're here with me; you're safe." His body jerked violently. Thinking he might fall off the bed, I put my hands on his shoulders and gave them a gently shake.

He sat up so quickly his forehead whacked against mine. The pain freaked him out even more and he jumped out of bed, immediately taking a defensive stance.

"Hayden," I said calmly, heart racing. I wasn't sure what to do. "Hayden, it's me, Riss."

I carefully reached out, my fingertips touching his hand. He jerked his arm back, breath coming out in a huff. His eyes flicked over the room, seeing things that weren't really there. He jerked around, ducking.

I couldn't just sit and do nothing while Hayden was stuck in his waking nightmare. I jumped out of bed and flew to his side. I put my arms around him and he tensed, pushing me away. I didn't give up. I held him tighter and pressed my lips to his.

"Riss?" he whispered, his lips against mine.

"Yes, it's me."

"Oh. What are you doing here?" he asked and started to relax.

"We are in our bedroom, Hayden. At the compound." I ran my fingers over his hair.

He quickly inhaled and looked around the room. "Right. We are. I…I don't…"

"It's okay," I said and took his hands. We went back into bed. Hayden laid down with his head nestled between my breasts. I continued to run my fingers through his hair until he drifted back to sleep.

I was still tired when our alarm went off the next morning. I stayed up most of the night, making sure Hayden was okay. He had another nightmare, though it wasn't bad enough that I had to wake him. I hated that his mind replayed the same horrible scene of watching his best friend, Ben, die over and over again.

Groggily, we got up, dressed, and went down to breakfast. I didn't pay attention to who I was standing behind in line for food until Lauren turned around and scoffed at me. I rolled my eyes but looked away; I was too tired to deal with her.

Claudia, one of the older ladies in charge of coming up with our meal plans, put a bowl of oatmeal on Lauren's tray. Lauren wrinkled her nose and grumbled about having oatmeal—again. I was sick of it too, but I thanked Claudia for the food nonetheless. I stepped out of line, waiting for Hayden.

"You never got that hair dye did you?" Lauren asked, slowing as she walked past me to her table.

"No," I said.

"Of course you didn't." She smiled and narrowed her eyes.

"What's that supposed to mean?" I asked, my temper rising.

"Oh, nothing. It's just that I shouldn't have expected it. All you care about is yourself."

I imagined myself dropping my tray and jumping on her. Resisting that urge, I took a deep breath. "That's bullshit," I loudly told her, causing several people to turn and look at me. "I care about a lot of people."

"Mh-hm," she said and sat down. "That's why you couldn't pick up one little thing for me."

"It wasn't on our list." I leaned forward. "Because it's not important!"

"I'll have it put on a list," she jeered.

"And I'll have Raeya take it off."

She set her tray down on her table, stabbed her spoon into the oatmeal, and spun around. "You know what?" she questioned, her voice high pitched. "I'm getting really tired of you thinking you're better than everyone. You think that just because you're an A1 you get special privileges! It's not fair. And, I think I speak for more than just myself when I say it needs to stop."

I gripped my tray. "I do not think I'm better than everyone. But I am better than you, you ungrateful bitch! And special privileges—name them!"

"You get to leave here. We are stuck!" she said, looking at the residents crowded around her table. "Do you know what it's like? It's like a prison. You know how that feels, don't you? What would everyone say if they knew their beloved, brave Orissa was a felon?" she asked smugly. "Oh, you didn't tell them? Wonder why? And why are you the only ones who get to work out? And have rooms—real rooms—upstairs?"

"You want to leave? You want to go out there and see zombies and crazies and rotten bodies and burned down cities? Do you want to almost die every fucking time you leave the safety of this place? *You* remember what it was like out there—newsflash, bitch, things aren't any better! And the A's use the gym to *stay in shape* because we have to run all the damn time. Run away from zombies who want to rip our organs out and have a feast!

"And our rooms are the *least* safe place to sleep in the whole compound. Hmm, what's more important, being safe at night or having curtains? And the bathrooms—we share! And our water doesn't stay hot like it does down here. So instead of whining about how it's not fair, shut up or do something. We don't owe it to you to keep you safe. God knows I don't owe it to you to go out and gather food and supplies for *you*."

Lauren glared at me. "You better be careful, Orissa. Don't forget who you're messing with!"

"Oohh, I'm so scared of you," I huffed.

Hayden set his tray down and stood behind me, prepared to break up the argument.

"It wasn't that long ago I was the one on top," she reminded me. "Pathetic really, how in the real world you were nothing but a drunken loser from a broken home. Who knew the zombie apocalypse would be so good for you." She smiled triumphantly and clapped her hands. "Congratulations,

Orissa. I'm sure your mother would be so proud of you. Oh, that's right. She was never around. How could I forget, she preferred the company of starving, disease-ridden children thousands of miles away than to that of her own daughter."

Rage flooded my veins. "You never knew who Roger cheated on you with," I jeered. "Now you do."

Lauren jumped up. I set my tray down on the table next to me, slamming it and accidentally knocking my watered-downed juice over.

"You slut!" she screamed and pounced, attacking me from behind. Her hands grabbed a handful of my hair. Fighting her off was a joke. In one easy move, I grabbed her wrist and twisted her arm back. She grabbed onto my arm, digging her nails into my skin. I was about to slap her when someone's arms wrapped around me.

Hayden lifted me up, pulling me back. Lauren wasn't letting go and was dragged a few feet before Ivan rushed over and pulled her off. She thrashed against him, screaming to be let go.

"Calm down," Hayden whispered in my ear. "She's not worth it."

I was shaking with anger. It took everything to listen to Hayden, but I did.

"You ok?" he asked.

"Fine," I spat, panting. I marched over to the sink and got a towel. I mopped up my spilled juice, apologizing to the people who were sitting at that table. Lauren was still fighting against Ivan.

"I'll let go when you calm down," he told her.

"I hate you, Orissa!" she screamed. "And if everyone knew who you really were, they'd hate you too!"

"Ignore her," Hayden suggested. "She's trying to get to you."

I focused on cleaning up the rest of the mess I made. Forcing myself to move in a way that made me appear calm, I filled my cup up with water, took my tray and sat in the back, in between Hayden and Raeya.

"She's a bitch," Sonja immediately said, like a good girlfriend was supposed to. "I can't believe she said those horrible things about you. And we like you," she promised, looking at Jason and Olivia. They nodded.

"You're awesome," Jason said with a smile.

"Thanks," I breathed.

Ray put her hand on my shoulder and gave it a friendly squeeze. "I should have pushed her out of the attic when I had the chance," she laughed. "Did you really sleep with Roger?"

"Eww no. I made that up." Even if Lauren's ex wasn't repulsive, I would never be the other woman. I saw how devastating being cheated on was for my mother. I would never stoop so low.

"That's what I thought." She smiled. "And you know nothing she said was true, right?"

"Right," I agreed. Hayden rested his hand on my thigh, slowly moving his fingers in little circles. I didn't want to admit it, not to Hayden, Raeya, and especially not to myself, but Lauren's words cut into me, searing with the pain of truth.

"Did she hit you?" Olivia shyly asked me.

"Now you've both caused a scene in the cafeteria," Brock teased, looking from me to Hayden.

The chatter amongst the residents started up again, building back to its normal volume. When I walked to the front of the cafeteria to dump my tray, I caught Jenna, Char, and Owen staring at me. Add my squabble with Lauren to me shooting their companion a few days ago, and I'm sure they thought I was fifty shades of crazy.

$$\longrightarrow$$

Ivan, Brock, Hayden, and I worked out, trained the A3s, and then impatiently waited for the others to arrive home. We were all upstairs in Ivan and Brock's room playing video games. I couldn't get my virtual solider to walk straight. It was frustrating that I repeatedly got shot and died.

I was about to give up when someone knocked on the door. Fuller stood there, looking pissed as usual. I set the controller down and stuffed Hayden's dog tags down my shirt. Expecting him to say something about the other A1s returning, I was a little taken off guard when he asked me to follow him into the hall.

We went several doors down from the room. He took a deep breath and looked down at me.

"I understand there was an issue at breakfast today," he said.

"Yeah," I simply responded.

"Do you have anything to say for yourself?"

I smiled innocently. "Bitch got owned?"

"Orissa," Fuller bellowed. "You cannot act this way."

"Why not?" I retorted. "She deserved to get her ass beat after what she said. And *she* attacked *me*."

"I don't care what she said! And we both know she poses no threat to you; you could have avoided a physical confrontation. You have to set an example. We've already discussed this."

"Oh yeah, what a good example it sets to let someone verbally abuse you." I stared him down.

"I don't care what she *said,*" Fuller repeated. "People look up to you. If you don't stay calm and follow the rules, then why should they?"

I couldn't make a valid argument against that. "Fine," I huffed. "I'll control my temper next time."

"You better or there won't be a next time. This is your final warning."

I opened my mouth to object by telling him I didn't give a damn if he took my A1 badge and title away, I'd still go out and kill zombies but didn't get the chance because a familiar voice came over the walkie-talkie. Jason let Fuller know that the others returned—all eight of them—and that they had truck loads of supplies.

Fuller quickly turned and left. I went back into Ivan and Brock's room to relay the message, relieved that the guys got to a save point in their game and waited for the others to come up and get their clothes.

Wade jogged up the stairs first. He told us it took longer than expected to find compliable semi trucks and even longer to find enough diesel to fuel them up for the short drive back to the compound. That and several dozen zombies needed to be taken down before they could get into the store. He grabbed clothes for him and Rider and hurried back to the quarantine.

The rest of the day carried out normally, if not boring. I spent it with Ray, not seeing Hayden again until bedtime. He was playing video games with the guys; I changed into my pajamas and crawled under the covers. I was already asleep when Hayden got into bed next to me, accidentally waking me up. Lazily, I moved from the center of the bed to give him some room. As soon as I settled down, I was sleeping.

What felt like only a short while later, someone quickly stomped up the stairs, waking me up. Irritated, I rolled over and pulled the covers over my head as if that would help drown out the sound.

And then the door flew open.

"What are you doing?" Hayden sleepily asked Ivan. I sat up and blinked at the bright light that spilled in from the hall.

"It's Jessica," Ivan said, his voice a hallow whisper. "She's infected."

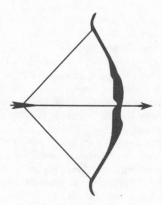

CHAPTER 15

Hayden and I both sprang up.

"What?" I asked, though I had very clearly heard Ivan.

"They're all in the quarantine. She just-just snapped." Ivan's face was blank and he spoke with little emotion.

"No," I said dumbly, as if that would make things better.

Ivan gravely nodded.

"What are we going to do with her?" Hayden asked as he pulled on his pants. I wrapped my arms around myself, suddenly cold. My heart hammered through my chest and I felt out of breath. I had just seen Jessica days ago. We sat and watched a movie together.

"She's in the hospital ward right now, tied to a bed. Wade and Alex were able to get her out of the quarantine before she hurt anyone else; she got Gabby pretty good."

"She bit her?" Hayden asked and pulled a shirt over his head.

Shaking, I put on a sweatshirt.

"Tried to but didn't. She scratched her across the face and shoved her; Gabby fell backward over a chair and hit her head. I-I think she's alright though."

"What can we do?" I asked, fumbling to put on my socks.

"I don't know." Ivan shook his head. "I just had to tell you."

Hayden held out his hand for me to take. We hurried down the hall and into the hospital ward. Gabby was lying on an exam table, holding a bag of ice to her head. Her father and a B3—who I was pretty sure was one of the veterinarians—stood behind her, talking in hushed whispers. We rushed past and into the sick ward.

The last bed must be cursed. It was where Hayden stayed when he fought for his life and now Jessica lay in it, her arms and legs tied to the bedrails. Fuller, Dr. Cara, and Padraic crowded around her. Alex and Wade stood off to the side and the remaining three A1s sat on another hospital bed across from Jessica. Brock leaned against the wall, his hand tightly closed around the bite mark on his arm.

Padraic snapped his attention up when he heard our footfalls.

"Oh, good, Hayden," he said and whisked Hayden away to take a sample of his blood to compare it to Jessica's. I heard him say something about possibly finding a way to stop the virus from progression, which sounded promising.

I knew otherwise. Padraic told me long ago that the virus kills parts of the brain. And brain damage can't be reversed. I stood close to Ivan, half curious and half afraid to look closely at Jessica. Hooked up to an IV and very subdued, she had obviously been drugged. Fuller gripped the side rails, a pained look on his face as he gazed down at his wounded soldier.

Rider got up when he saw us and walked over. His face was paler than usual and he looked terrified.

"Hey," he said quietly and pushed his messy red hair out of his face.

"Hi, Rider." I half smiled. "What's going on?"

"They're gonna run some tests, see how far along the virus is, and see if there's anything they can do," he informed us. "I don't think there is."

"Me neither," I agreed and let out a breath. I wasn't sure if Rider was aware of the possibility of a vaccine. Still, even if it was a real thing, it was too late for Jessica. Ivan nodded and crossed his arms. We sat on the edge of a bed near Jess, watching and waiting.

Dr. Cara looked like a kid on Christmas morning. With swiftness I didn't know she had, she poked and prodded at Jessica's body, taking blood, vital signs and shining a pen light in her eyes. She asked her questions and injected something into a vein in her neck.

Jessica's body went ridged before she screamed and pulled on the restraints. Fuller tensed and put his hands on Jessica's legs to hold her still. Wade and Alex rushed over to help keep her down.

"What happened?" Ivan asked Rider.

He shook his head. "I don't really know. There were a lot of S3s milling around. It took a while, but it was an overall easy kill." He let out a deep breath. "She shot one at close range and blood splattered on her face. Or at least that's all I can think of."

"Sounds likely," Ivan agreed. Hayden rejoined us, slyly hooking his arm around my body. I leaned against him and he rested his head on mine for a second before straightening up.

"Did Padraic say anything to you?" I asked Hayden.

"Nothing we don't already know; he doesn't know enough about how the virus works to really do anything at all."

I nodded and rested my head on his shoulder again. It was inevitable that one of us would get infected if not killed sooner or later. I just thought it would be later. Everything felt slightly surreal. I closed my eyes, wishing this was all a bad dream.

But I would never wake up and find everything all peachy.

"You alright?" Ivan asked softly.

"I am," Hayden sighed. "I wish she was too."

He nodded. "I hate this. I wish there was *something* we could do."

"Me too. But there's nothing," I sighed. I felt so utterly helpless. I watched as the sedative wore off and Jessica growled and bit at the air. I felt so cold and hollow…and scared. I was so preoccupied with Jess I didn't notice a second person tied to a hospital bed.

Jared, his face full of fear, was craning his neck to see around his curtain and down the aisle. He was handcuffed to the side rail for the time being. Given that we couldn't trust him, Fuller made sure that Jared posed no threat; and he would always be treated like a threat. Something boiled inside me. Dr. Cara took another vial of blood from Jessica while Alex held her arm still. She gathered up everything she had taken and strode down the aisle into the lab. I jolted forward and followed her.

"Use him," I blurted as soon as we were out of the sick wing. Dr. Cara jumped, not knowing I was behind her. "That asshole who tried to shoot at us. Test the vaccine on him. Maybe you can save Jess."

Somewhat surprisingly, Dr. Cara smiled empathically. "There's no going back now. Maybe… maybe I can stop her cells from dying. But she'll be damaged…damaged and dangerous."

I knew it was true. I was mad at myself for even saying anything. "What can you do?"

"Keep her hydrated and offer her food while she transitions."

"Transitions?"

"Into the next stage."

If my heart could sink any lower, it just did. "Into a zombie."

"Yeah." She set the vials down on the counter and pulled microscope slides out of a drawer. "I want to do experiments on her, but Fuller gets the final orders," she said, seemingly dejected.

I wanted to smack her. "Jessica was part of our team. She risked her ass for everyone and took the brunt of it. She's a human being. Why the fuck would you even fathom the thought you could do experiments on her?"

"It would give good information," she said causally and snapped on rubber gloves. She let a drop of blood fall from the vial onto the slide and stuck it in the microscope.

Angered, I spun around to leave.

"Orissa," Dr. Cara called.

"What?" I snapped.

"Can I have some blood? You heal fast. I want to see what happens if I mix your blood with the live virus."

"Sure," I sighed. "If it'll help, that's fine."

She put on clean gloves, wiped my skin with an alcohol pad and took only a syringe full of blood this time. I pressed my finger on the needle mark and left the room. I sat down next to Ivan again, waiting for Hayden to come back.

Jessica was growling and snarling now. It was so…so weird to see someone that I knew, someone I'd talked to turn into a raging monster. I remembered when Logan snapped and it still hurt to remember having to kill him. The sick ward door opened and clicked shut. Thinking it was Dr. Cara, I didn't turn to look.

Then I heard a muffled sob. I snapped around to see Gabby and her father walking down the aisle. She had three bloody claw marks running down her right cheek that would no doubt leave ugly scars that would forever remind her of Jessica.

Her father put his hand on her shoulder as they drew nearer. Tears rolled down Gabby's face. Wade moved out of the way to allow her to confront her roommate and partner.

"Jessica," Gabby whispered. "Are you in there somewhere?"

Jessica's lip quivered as she showed off her teeth like an angry dog. Gabby gently put her hand on Jess's. Jessica relaxed at the touch.

"Jess?" Gabby whimpered and leaned forward. Jessica's fingers coiled around Gabby's. Suddenly, Jessica snarled and pulled herself up, biting at Gabby.

Gabby screamed and jerked away.

Jessica growled and roared, her teeth chomping the air.

Alex pushed her down, allowing Gabby to get away. Crying, she turned to her father who protectively wrapped his arms around her and ushered her away.

We all froze, watching in horror at what had just taken place. Hayden said something to Fuller and quickly walked over.

"What's the plan?" Ivan asked, struggling to keep his voice level.

"Move her into the barn after the stall is reinforced. She'll be given food, water, and a warm, comfortable place to sleep, though I doubt she'll use it. If she needs it, she can be tranquilized and cleaned up. Then when she…she dies, we'll have a funeral for her," Hayden informed us.

I moved my head up and down, watching it play out in my mind. "Ok," I numbly said, not thinking of anything to add. I let out a shaky breath.

Fuller instructed the other A1s to go back to the quarantine and for Ivan, Brock, Hayden, and I to go back to bed. Jessica was going to stay heavily medicated and tied up until the morning. As soon as a stall was set up for her, she'd be moved.

The four of us trudged up the stairs. We paused in the hall by Ivan and Brock's door. We exchanged pained looks, all at a loss for words. I didn't know what to say to them in a situation like this.

"Night," Brock finally said and went into his room. Ivan followed suit and Hayden and I went into our own room. We changed into pajamas, brushed our teeth, and climbed under the covers. Hayden rested his head and one hand on my chest. I ran my fingers though his hair.

"Orissa," he started. "I don't want you to be an A1 anymore."

"Uh, ok," I said, not taking him seriously.

"Really. I don't."

I let my hand fall from his head. "Why?"

"It's too risky. I don't want anything bad to happen to you."

"I don't want anything bad to happen to me either. But that doesn't mean I'm going to hide in the comfort and safety of an underground bomb shelter for the rest of my life. *That* would kill me."

He rolled off me and pulled me on top of him. "Me too. Love you, Riss."

"I love you too. Night." It took forever to fall asleep that night. I had nightmares of a zombiefied Jessica roaming the halls of the compound. I startled awake and snuggled closer to Hayden, forcing away any and all bad dreams.

→

It took two weeks for Jessica to turn into a zombie. Her screams echoed through the quarantine barn and we were able to hear her from our room. It was fucking horrible. It was all we could think about, even with the extra work Fuller assigned to us; we reinforced the fence around the compound and livestock barns.

Padraic told me that—as awful as it was to watch—Jessica's death had given them a lot of insight on the virus. He spoke about it as if her death wasn't in vain, as if it had a purpose now.

Crazies don't sleep, we discovered. Several times Jessica collapsed from exhaustion. Apparently, she wasn't able to tell that she was tired. She stayed in a *sleeplike* state for several hours before springing back up and resuming her desperate, violent attempt to kill anything and anyone that walked past the stall.

She wouldn't eat the food they initially offered her, which was sweet and salty. When a can of roast beef was put on a plate, she licked it all up. She did drink some water when it was presented to her in a bucket. Padraic explained that with her decreasing body metabolism and the shutting down of body systems, she didn't need as much food or water as a 'normal' human would.

The final time she collapsed, her body went through what appeared to be a seizure. Her heart slowed to only a few beats a minute. She stopped breathing. She was officially declared dead.

Slowly, her body twitched into what Padraic called 'reanimation.' Again, she ignored any food presented and now had no interest in water. She wasn't aware of where she was. Her body moved in rigid, jerky movements. She brought herself to her feet and was just like any other S2; pale eyes, pale—and apparently clammy—skin, and blood thirsty.

Fuller was the one to pull the trigger.

We had a funeral for her the same night she died…again. Not wanting to take the chance of putting an infected body in the ground, she was wrapped in white sheets and set on a pyre. Like she well deserved, we did our best to honor her with a proper military funeral. Every single resident flooded outside. The crowd parted when Jessica's body was brought forward. Fuller stood in the front, giving commands to the soldiers. With my grandpa, I had been to more than one service for a veteran and found them to be both heartbreaking and beautiful. Of course we had to down the formalities of Jessica's funeral, much like I was forced to with Zoe's. Prayers were said, kind words exchanged, and people cried.

The bright fire was blinding. I watched it flicker and dance, sending burning embers into the cool night sky. Not caring if anyone saw, I locked my fingers through Hayden's. Behind his stoic expression I could see the hurt of losing another friend.

We stayed until the fire burned out. Once cool, the ashes would be gathered up, put in a jar and buried with a marker on top; it was inevitable that a graveyard would be started.

Fuller didn't give a single order over the next two days. I knew from Raeya that we were running low on some of our supplies. Ivan, Brock, Wade, Rider, Hayden, and I were to set out on a mission four days after the funeral.

→

The sky had been a bleak gray all of yesterday and again today. The dark clouds spit out cold rain, ruining Raeya's recess plans and lowering my spirits. When Fuller suggested we go north and see what we could find in Indiana, I immediately objected.

"I was there when the virus hit," I told him. "The cities we were in were overrun."

"That was months ago," Fuller countered. "And you didn't explore the entire state, did you?"

"No," I stubbornly admitted.

"Good. That's where you six are going," he informed us. Hayden unrolled a large map on Fuller's desk. I hadn't seen it before. Curiously, I stepped forward, putting my hands on the edge of the desk so I could lean over it.

It was a map of the United States. Black X's had been placed on what I assumed were the towns and cities explored. Pretty much all of Arkansas was X'ed out, as was the top of Louisiana, and the northwest border of Mississippi. Kentucky was speckled with several X's, as well as southern Illinois, Missouri, the eastern half of Oklahoma, South Carolina, and only one X in Kansas.

I stared at that particular X, thinking about how lucky I was that the X just happened to fall on the town I was in. If Fuller had picked a town only a few miles north or south, I wouldn't be here.

"Start here," Fuller said, drawing an X over a town in Ohio, near the Pennsylvania border. "And comb through any cities on your way back here. That way, if you find survivors, you won't have to take them farther from the compound."

"Yes sir," Hayden automatically agreed. Ivan got another map, this one was smaller, and drew out a route for us to follow. On our way back, we were to check out Columbus and Indy, though, again, I told Fuller what Indy was like. Having been avoiding big cities since the outbreak, the guys didn't know what it was like.

Fucking horrible.

Hayden assured me that we wouldn't stay if the cities were overrun, thinking I was scared of getting ambushed. I wasn't afraid; I didn't want to waste my time. We packed our crap, loaded up the truck and the Range Rover—which was weird to see in action again—and went to bed.

***

The following day, after driving for four hours, we took one bathroom break and continued on, stopping once we got to Evansville, Indiana. Having sat still for over eight hours, my legs hurt and my body was restless.

Gray clouds rolled in, covering up the pretty blue sky. The temperature was lower here and I rummaged through my bag for a long sleeve shirt. Ivan, Rider, and Hayden surveyed our surrounding area—a big, grassy field spotted with trees—while Brock and Wade helped me set up dinner.

I stood next to the truck and stretched. A gust of wind just about blew me over. I looked at the tree branches swaying in the wind. A loose branch creaked and groaned as it waved back and forth. I thought I heard something as another gust moved in. I waited, watched, and didn't see anything.

I bent over, touching my toes when Hayden snuck up behind me and slapped my ass. I glared at him from between my legs.

"What, all work and no play?" he accused, smiling.

"No, I'm just…uncomfortable from sitting still. My muscles are stiff."

"Mine too," he admitted and stretched his arms above his head. "Maybe we'll find a masseuse," he joked. I straightened up and sat on the tailgate next to Hayden while we ate. Fat raindrops spilled from the dark clouds. We hurried to finish eating and put everything away.

Our plan was to go another two hours or so until we either ran out of daylight or found a safe place for the night, whichever came first. The storm rolled in faster than we were driving. The fat raindrops increased in number and thunder boomed above us.

The rainfall became so heavy it was hard to see. Talking over the walkie-talkie, Hayden told Ivan he thought we should pull over and wait for the storm to pass. A strong gust of wind rocked the truck. I swallowed hard. The air felt electrified; this storm had power.

Ivan suggested we move off the winding and wooded road we were on, not liking the trees on either side of us. We all thought that was a good idea. Slowly, Hayden accelerated around a curve. Lightning flashed and thunder cracked like a whip.

In the summer, I used to sit on the front porch with my grandparents and watch the storms. When it got really bad, my grandma went inside and turned on the radio. When it got really, *really* bad, she'd make us come inside and hunker in the basement. When I was a kid, I used to secretly wish for the power to go out; my grandma would light candles and cook over the fire of the fireplace. I liked pretending I was in another time, someplace way more fun and exciting than central Kentucky.

Hayden slammed on the brakes so fast that the Range Rover almost rear ended us. The truck slid on the rain soaked road. We narrowly missed the tree that fell onto the road, completely blocking our way. I'd give anything for us to have a basement to hide out in.

The wind picked up, evolving from gusts to a constant, unseen source of power. Ivan's voice came over the radio, commenting on the green and fast moving clouds. My heart started beating a little faster.

I'd take a dozen zombies over a tornado any day.

"What do we do?" Wade asked Hayden.

"Move the tree," Hayden said after a moment's consideration. "We're almost to the highway." He relayed the message to Ivan. Hayden zipped up his jacket and raced out of the truck. Wade and I followed.

"Get back in the truck!" Hayden yelled over the howling wind.

"No. You need help moving this!" I told him. My hair instantly became soaked and stuck to my face. Ivan, Brock, and Rider ran over to help as well.

"Do you realize how heavy this is?" Brock shouted. He said something else but thunder interrupted him.

I didn't think it was possible but the wind blew even stronger. Leaves and branches rained down on us as the wind ripped through the trees.

"We need to get out of here!" Rider said loudly after a good sized branch hit him in the face.

"We'll turn around," Hayden shouted.

"No," Brock yelled over another clap of thunder. "Cars aren't safe during tornados!"

My heart skipped a beat. I fucking hated tornados. As much as I loved thunderstorms, they never seemed to pose a threat. Tornados, however, could kill you and destroy your home. And there wasn't a damn thing you could do about it. I hated them mostly for making me feel helpless. For forcing me to hide out while they did their damage. I couldn't shoot, threaten, or intimidate a tornado. I could only wait it out.

Hayden looked at the truck; he didn't want to leave it. And neither did I. I wasn't emotionally attached to it like Hayden was, but it was our vehicle, our way to get back home. It had our gas, our food, and our weapons inside. We needed it to survive.

The wind stopped howling and started rumbling, growling, and whistling.

"This way, go! Now!" Ivan shouted. Hayden took my hand and ran forward. We flew down a hill, over an embankment and through a thin line of trees. When we emerged from the trees, my eyes widened.

A whirling mass of destruction moved with fury at us. Ivan shouted something; his voice was lost in the wind. Branches, leaves, and random pieces of debris sliced through the air. I ducked as a piece of a plastic garbage can whizzed overhead. Hayden let go of my hand and covered his head as another piece flew above us.

Ivan looked around, madly trying to find a place to go. He pointed forward and we darted in that direction. None of us were able to look away from the tornado for long. My heart beat a million miles an hour. The rain suddenly ceased as the tornado drew closer.

We raced across the highway, staggering our way through the overgrown median. Adrenaline coursed through my body, fueling my legs to move faster than normal. The wind blew into my ears so hard it hurt. I looked back to check on Wade and Brock, who were behind me.

I didn't see the broken piece of two-by-four until it smacked into my shoulder so hard it knocked me over. Barely stopping, Rider yanked me to my feet and we were running again. I wasn't even aware of the pain in my arm. I risked another look at the tornado; it was gaining girth and picking up speed.

Then it jutted off its course, grew thinner, and disappeared into the clouds. The wind, however, didn't cease. We slowed to a jog until we reached the other side of the highway. With the wind still forcibly blowing into us, we didn't dare stop.

Hayden took my hand again and we slowed to catch our breath.

"That was close," he panted. I nodded and took a deep breath. I put my hand on my side, massaging the stitch.

"Guys!" Brock shouted. We turned and saw the funnel cloud. It was closer than before. We took off again, pushing our way through another overgrown section of land off the highway. A cluster of buildings ahead promised us safety. Our feet hit the pavement of a parking lot just as the tornado touched down.

It gained in size at a sickening rate. Hearts pounding, we looked around us.

"There!" I shouted, pointing at a parking garage. A scrap of metal got picked up in the wind, spiraling around, caught in the current before unleashing as if it was aimed at us. It clipped Rider in the head. Without hesitation, Brock and Wade raced to his side. Blood streamed down Rider's face. He pressed a hand to the cut and staggered to his feet.

With help, they half led, half dragged him into the parking garage. A minivan flipped over and scooted in the wind, upside down, along the street. We moved down toward the underground level of the parking garage but didn't want to go so far that we'd be completely in the dark.

Brock, who had stayed completely in uniform, extracted a flashlight from a vest pocket. He quickly flicked it over our surroundings; water dripped above us and the walls were covered in graffiti. Most of the parking spaces were still full.

He stepped over and shined the light on Rider's head. Rider made a strangled noise of pain when he removed his hand.

"I don't think it's that deep," Brock said, inspecting the wound. "Though there's not much skin right here. I don't know when it's considered 'deep' on a head wound." He looked at me as if I'd know.

I shook my head. "I know head wounds bleed a lot. Put pressure on it."

"It's dripping in my eye," Rider complained.

"Look down," Wade suggested. "So the blood will fall off instead of running down your face."

"No," I told him. "Won't that make it bleed more?"

"I don't know," Wade said while shaking his head.

Metal scraped on pavement; more cars must have gotten tossed around. Confident the cement garage would hold, I kept my attention on Rider.

"Do you have anything to stop the bleeding?" Ivan asked Brock. Brock patted his pockets; he had ammo for his machine gun that got left in the car as well as a shit ton of other useful things, but nothing to stop the blood.

"Hang on," I said and took the flashlight from Brock. Quickly, I picked out a newer, clean car. I yanked on the door; it was locked. I moved onto another; this one had the windows cracked a few inches. I shined the light inside the car and saw a sweatshirt on the backseat. I forced my arm through the window and unlocked the car, making the car alarm go off.

Before dealing with the blaring beep, I retrieved the shirt and tossed it to Brock. Hayden opened the driver's side door and popped the hood. He took the flashlight from me and yanked on something, making the alarm shut up.

"Come over here," Hayden suggested, opening the back door of the car so the dome light came on. Rider moved over, heavily sitting on the seat.

Brock pressed the shirt over the cut, telling Rider to hold it and look up. Something heavy moved above us. The garage trembled. I stepped close to Hayden, wishing with my whole heart that the garage wouldn't collapse on us.

Everyone else must have been thinking the same thing. We stood near the car, welcoming the little illumination the dome lights gave off. I held my breath, waiting. Pass, just fucking pass, I repeated over and over in my head. If we were lucky, this garage was new and made of reinforced steel *and* concrete.

Yeah fucking right.

Without looking at the faded and peeling paint, it was obvious this was built before I was born. Dust rained down on us. Hayden stepped close to me, protectively putting his arms over my body. Even he couldn't shield me from falling hunks of cement.

Then the place really started shaking. The dust turned into little chunks, rattled loose from the storm's wrath.

Rider stood, nervously looking around. The six of us exchanged glances, all knowing that our futures were nonexistent if the ceiling fell.

The tornado must have been right above us. Involuntarily, my body shook. Hayden pulled me closer to him. A golf ball sized piece of cement hit me on the top of the head. It hurt, but it wasn't anything serious. Hayden put his hand on the top of my head. I tried to pull away, wanting to protect him too.

My heart pounded and my palms sweated. The rattling slowed and the harrowing winds grew quieter; the tornado was passing. I felt Hayden relax considerably. I hadn't realized how tense he was.

"Holy shit," Ivan swore. "Let's not do that again!" he said.

Wade cleared his throat. "That's fine by me."

"I fucking hate storms," Rider stated, pulling the shirt off his head. Blood glistened in the weak light. He wiped what he could off his face and threw the bloody shirt on the ground. "Come on," he said, taking a step forward. "Let's find out if our cars made it."

Hayden moaned. "Don't say that."

"They're fine," I told him. "Safe and warm and happy and waiting for us."

"You think so?"

"Oh yeah," I said with a roll of my eyes. "I know so."

Hayden smiled. "Good."

But that wasn't all that was waiting for us. We rounded the corner to find a herd of zombies slowly marching, their deathly moans mixing with the howling of the wind.

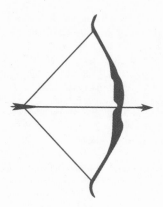

CHAPTER 16

I could hardly see them in the dark, but the groans and shuffling of feet were unmistakable. Brock held up the light. There were dozens of zombies. And there were six of us.

Six of us who were all severely under armed.

We stopped walking immediately. Already attracted to the fresh scent of blood, the zombies quickened their pace. I had my M9 with seven rounds shoved in the back of my pants. Seven. Then I'd be out. Deciding to wait and use it as a last resort, I yanked the knife from my pocket, flicking open the blade.

"We need to get out of here," Ivan whispered, his voice shaky. "This way!" he called as he turned and started running. Without giving a thought to where we were going, we followed suit. Seeing their meals suddenly flee, the herd staggered faster.

Worried Rider might falter and trip given his recent blood loss, I fell back to keep up the rear. One of the fresher S2s sprinted out of the group. I skidded to a stop, heart racing, and waited for him to rush me. I was ready; I leaned back out of his grasp and sunk the knife into his eye socket. I shoved him, flicking the eyeball off the blade.

I raced forward. The flashlight bobbed several feet ahead. Brock rounded a corner; the outlines of the soldiers faded from view. My breath caught in my chest and I pushed forward even harder. My footfalls echoed. I splashed through a puddle. I risked turning around; it was a futile attempt at best since I couldn't see anything in the dark.

My body started to tremble with adrenaline. The floor of the garage sloped down. Great; we were going even deeper underground. My hand tightened around the knife. I was certain there were dozens of zombies behind me. And I'd bet my life that there were more in front of me.

Completely blind now, I slowed. If I stayed in the center of the aisle, I'd be ok. Eventually I'd smack into a wall and figure out I'd have to turn. Then I was certain I'd see the distant glow of the flashlight. My knee hit the bumper of a car.

Wincing, I felt my way around it until my hands graced the cold, damp cement wall. Hoping I was at the end of the garage, I felt my way back and dragged my hand from car to car until I found another aisle.

The smell of death grew stronger meaning they were getting closer. I started running again, only to trip over someone…or something. I scrambled up, kicking around me until my foot hit the body again. When it didn't move, I continued on.

My breath whooshed out too loud for my liking. I stopped, spinning around, hoping my eyes would catch something—anything that would lead me out of this parking garage from hell.

"Fuck it," I swore and started jogging in a random direction. But I only made it a few yards before

I smacked into something else.

He grabbed me by the shoulders and threw me down. The wind got knocked out of me but not before my fingers touched his skin. His *warm* skin.

"Hey," I said breathlessly.

"Orissa?"

"Yeah, dumbass."

"Oh, sorry," Rider spoke and reached down in the dark to pull me up. His fingers poked my face. I swatted his hand away and stood.

"Where are the others?" I asked.

"I don't know. I-I lost them. How did you get so behind?"

"I was killing zombies."

"Oh, nice." He blindly reached out in the darkness for my hand. "Let's go."

"Go where?" I asked.

"I have no idea. Anywhere but here." We walked forward. Rider's hand shook. I squeezed his fingers. "They can't see in the dark, can they?" he asked me.

I shook my head before realizing he couldn't see the gesture. "No. They're still human. I think a lot of them can't see at all, even in the day. So they've adapted. But us...we-we rely on sight. Too much."

"Right," he agreed. Suddenly he stopped walking, yanking my hand back. I stumbled into him.

"What?" I harshly whispered.

"I thought I heard something," he whispered back. A crack of thunder echoed above us, making us both jump. I held my breath. I didn't hear anything but the distant howling of wind and water dripping in a puddle.

I'm not sure what I became of aware of next; the strong metallic smell of blood or the sound of slurping. There was a body—a fresh body—only feet in front of us, and we had no idea who it was. My mind flashed to Hayden.

No.

It wasn't him. We'd have heard screams and just...no. He wasn't dead.

"Do you have any weapons?" I whispered to Rider.

"No," he said grimly. He took a step back, bumping into a car. I nodded, internalizing what to do. The fresh body would offer a distraction. I tried to imagine how many zombies could crowd around a dead body. Would they push, and shove each other out of the way? Would the ones who didn't get a piece of meat go on? Were they even smart enough to remember that we were here?

Lightning strobed the sky, flashing ahead of us. It was startlingly bright.

"We're not as far underground as I thought," I whispered aloud to Rider. I got a millisecond look around the parking garage. While I didn't see anything—or anyone—dead on the floor, I saw that we were backed up in a corner. We needed to turn and run.

I hated holding hands while running. It slowed me down. Afraid of losing each other in the dark, I kept my fingers laced through Rider's. Seemingly out of nowhere, what had to be an S3 staggered out of the darkness, right into our path.

Rider and I both tripped over him and my knife flew out of my hand.

"Riss!" he shouted.

"I'm alright." I kicked the gummy, thinking my foot would mush through. But it didn't. My boot smacked against his sternum, which didn't break in the least. Rotting hands grasped my ankle. I thrashed and kicked.

"Come on, Riss!" Rider shouted.

"He's got me!" I shouted back. I yanked my foot forward but the gummy just came with it. I felt his teeth close around my toes. Praying the leather was strong enough to hold up to his jaw, I madly slapped the gritty cement in search of my knife.

"Where?" Rider asked frantically.

"I-I-I'm over here," I dumbly panted as I attempted to kick the S3 in the face. My foot hit something. I yanked my leg free and pulled myself along. Rider's foot hit the knife. It scraped against the floor, teasing me.

I felt around again, almost ready to give up and shoot the motherfucker. My fingers closed around something hard and kind of sticky. Without giving myself a chance to think about how gross this mystery object was, I grabbed it and whirled around just as the gummy took a hold of my ankle again.

The familiar shape of a ball point pen registered in my brain and I raised my hand. I brought it down, shoving the pen into its skull. Brain matter splattered out. I stabbed him again, trying to hit the same spot. It took five more stabs before he stopped moving.

I shoved the body away from me.

"Help me find my knife," I told Rider. I stayed on my hands and knees; the grit and dirt of the parking garage floor cut into my skin. Rider carefully walked around, hoping to find the knife by stepping on it.

"Got it!" he said loudly. I slowly got up, not wanting to stand up under the blade. I knew Rider was close, but I couldn't tell how close. I wiped the grit from my hands onto my pants. "Where are you, Orissa?"

"Here," I told him, reaching out into the darkness. My fingers brushed against his back. He took my hand and put the knife into it. "Thanks."

"No problem. Uh, now where?"

I had no idea what was around us. I couldn't see a damn thing and the scuffle with the S3 had left me a little disoriented.

"I'm not sure," I admitted. "The ground feels level right here. I can't tell which way we need to go."

"We must be on the turn then," he said. "You know, the part before the ramps. If we pick a way to walk, we'll figure out where to go."

"Yeah. Hopefully."

Ungracefully, we shuffled forward. I thought about the others: Where they were and why they hadn't come back to search for us.

"Wait," I said suddenly.

"What?" Rider asked nervously.

"There should be a door," I explained, pulling him a few steps. "Feel along the wall. The flat parts...they-they usually have a stairwell or an elevator."

"You're a genius."

"We'll see about that," I told him. I shook my head and blinked several times. I felt like I was blind. Everything about this seemed grossly unnatural. I moved feverishly, running my hands along the damp and—in some parts—slimy wall. I knew my fingers brushed over crusted gum more than once. Finally, I felt cool metal under my hands.

"Here!" I shouted. Rider rushed over, accidentally stepping on my feet. The rattle of death moans echoed. The herd was drawing in. My hand slipped off the doorknob in my hurried attempt to get through. I pushed it open and stepped in, expecting there to be four feet or so before the stairs.

I was wrong.

My foot landed heavy on the first step and I toppled down, catching myself on the rusty metal railing. I skidded down a few steps before I stopped falling.

"Riss! Shit, are you ok?"

"I'm alive," I grumbled, pulling myself up. The gun had pressed into my back when I fell and it hurt like a bitch. "And I didn't drop the knife this time," I attempted to joke. Rider carefully maneuvered down the cement steps. The stench of death was strong.

"Up or down?"

"I'm not sure," I said, shaking my head. "Up, I think. Yeah, we need to go up."

"Ok. Follow me," Rider said with a hint of laughter in his voice. I took a deep breath and walked up the stairs. Thunder clapped, echoing throughout the building.

"If you could be anywhere but here, where would you be?" I asked rather suddenly.

"Anywhere, literally," Rider told me. "Anywhere with light." We stepped onto another narrow landing. "This door?"

"Sure," I suggested. I didn't think we had gone that far down into the garage.

"Where would you be?"

"The beach. Tanning my ass with a drink in my hand."

"That does sound nice."

"It'd be better than nice," I told him, lowering my voice. "That's the first thing I want to do when this is over."

"Yeah, wait until it's over. Nothing would ruin a beach vacation more than getting sand in your drink while killing zombies. Plus you'd have that whole fighting in a bikini issue to deal with. On second thought…go. I'd like to see that."

"Pig," I joked. A bolt of lightning escaped a cloud. "The edge," I whispered to myself. "I think we're close." We picked up the pace again, running until we felt the wind. Without any glow of distant lights and with the moon and stars blocked out by thick storm clouds, the outside was just as dark and ominous as the inside of the garage.

Just as hope filled our hearts, zombies stomped it out. A fast moving S2 lumbered out of the atramentous shadows. Ready this time, I waited until he was close. I swung my fist, which collided with his face. I kicked his legs out from under him and drove the knife into what I thought was his neck.

When he kept moving, I brought the blade down again, this time in his cheek. I twisted the blade up and pulled it out, sinking it into his ear. The zombie collapsed. Rider took on another; I could hear him hitting something. I wished I could toss him the knife.

Dragging a foot, the second was easy to detect. I let out a breath and swung the knife. It whizzed over its head. Oh, it was a short zombie. I didn't want to wonder if it was a child. I kicked at where I thought the knees would be. Unsure if I actually hit my target, I sank the knife into the head of the falling zombie.

A hand closed around my wrist. I jerked away, ready to stab whoever grabbed me.

"It's me," Rider called.

"Oh." I lowered the knife. "I don't know if there are more. Let's go."

Stepping over the bodies, we took off running again.

A harrowing growl came from behind us.

"Keep going; we can out run it," Rider called.

"No. I don't like being chased in the day, I *hate* being chased when I'm blind and in the dark. I'm gonna kill it."

"You're crazy, Orissa."

"Probably," I said and let go of his hand. "Stay back. I don't want to stab you." I heard Rider scuffle his feet as he moved away. I let out my breath, rolling my neck from side to side. The zombie growled again. "I don't have all day," I jeered. "Come attack me like a good zombie."

I was expecting a typical S2 to lunge at me. I wasn't expecting him to weigh nearly three hundred undead pounds. His weight knocked my thin frame right over. I couldn't breathe. I gasped for air. My arms were pinned under him.

I rammed my knee into his stomach. It had no effect since zombies don't feel pain. The knife had stabbed him in the stomach when we fell; I could feel the vile liquid from his insides dripping out and soaking my shirt. Dragging the knife through his skin, I pried my arm free and stabbed Fatty in the ear.

I put my hands on his shoulders and shoved without success. Knowing I wasn't strong enough to push him off, I stabbed the knife into the top of his head for safe keeping. I freed my left arm and pushed against the cement, dragging myself from under the zombie's massive body. The Berretta dug into my skin but I didn't stop.

Panting, I stood, reached down for the knife and turned to where I thought Rider was standing.

"Ok, we can go," I breathed.

"Yeah," he agreed. "Easy kill? It sounded like it."

Only because I couldn't breathe the entire time. "Yeah. No biggie."

"This way?" he asked, taking my hand and tugging me forward.

"Your guess is as good as mine," I told him.

"We could be going in circles for all I know," he huffed.

"Yeah," I agreed.

"Fuck, what I wouldn't give for some light."

"I know. It's something I take for granted, I know now."

"Or night vision goggles," he added. "Or my gun. Or both."

A thought dawned on me, one so obvious I felt like a complete idiot for not thinking of it sooner. "I think I can do better than that." I held out my right hand and pulled Rider over to the parking space. "Try to find one that's unlocked."

"Uh, why?"

"We're going to drive out of here. Don't worry about the details, just do it, alright?"

"Ok. You shouldn't go too far."

"I won't," I promised. The first car I tried was locked. So were the second, the third, the fourth, and the fifth. I yanked on handle to car number six when a dome light victoriously glowed from several spots away. I raced over to Rider.

"Ohmygod, this is perfect!" I praised. I stepped past him and knelt down on the driver's side. It would be harder to do with no tools, but I wasn't leaving until I got the car started.

"Are you hot wiring the car?" Rider asked incredulously.

"I'm trying to," I informed him. "All I have is the knife, so I'll see how it goes. Keep an eye out for zombies." It took twice as long as it should to take out the screws with only a knife. Carefully, I pulled at the wires, slicing through and stripping the coating. I twisted two together and the lights and radio turned on, blasting Mariah Carey's greatest hits. I took the two remaining wires and touched them together. The engine sputtered to life. I bent the wires back so they wouldn't touch my legs; getting shocked to death would certainly put a damper on our escape.

"Get in," I told Rider as I stood and slid into the driver's seat. I put the car in reverse and grabbed the wheel. "Shit," I swore.

"What's wrong?"

"The wheel is locked." I extracted the knife from my pocket again. "It's normal when you hotwire cars and I can fix it, don't worry," I added, seeing Rider's panicked face. I jammed the knife between the back of the steering column and the steering wheel.

I let out a breath I didn't realize I was holding when the wheel smoothly turned in my hand. I backed out of the spot, turned the radio off and rolled my window down a few inches so I could hear what was going on around us.

"When did you learn how to hotwire a car?" Rider asked, his blue-gray eyes curiously drilling into me.

"I used to hang out with some, uh, not very nice people. They taught me a lot," I said, too scared to be ashamed of my past. I gently pushed on the gas; a little afraid the engine would sputter and die. I probably should have let it warm up before driving. There was a herd of zombies, we had four missing friends, and another tornado could touch down. I had no time to waste.

I passed the ramp and had to back up. I cranked the wheel and pressed on the gas.

"Oh, shit," Rider swore.

I gripped the steering wheel. "Can't we catch a break?" I yanked the gear shift into reverse once more and floored it. "There's no way this car can plow through *that*," I said, waving my hand at the herd. My mind raced. I wasn't dying today. And I especially wasn't dying by the hands of zombies.

The two dozen or more walking dead kept their steady pace of staggering up the ramp. I tapped the wheel, thinking. The herd was impassable. I wasn't sure what would happen, but I imagined zombies would either get stuck under the car or create a blockade this little car couldn't over power. Both would render us powerless and stuck in a metal deathtrap on wheels.

I pressed the pedal down again and sent us flying back. I slammed on the brakes and cranked the wheel, spinning the car. I forced the gear into drive and floored it once more.

Up. The only way we could go was up.

Several ideas flashed through my mind: We could get out and take our chances on the stairs, drive to the top level and see what could be done from up there, or peel away and pull into a parking spot and hope the zombies passed us unnoticed.

Plan C seemed the most feasible. I didn't want to give up the car, which offered a fast getaway and some light. And I sure as hell didn't want to be trapped three stories up. With my luck the storm would pick up and the car would get sucked up and flipped off the side of the garage.

"Fuck," I swore, finding a hole in my plan.

"What?" Rider asked.

"I can't turn off the car and promise to get it to start again."

"So?"

I shook my head. "I had a plan."

"What was it?"

"To pull into a parking spot and see if they pass us."

He looked behind us. "I think that's all we can do."

The silhouette of a fallen zombie became illuminated in the headlights. I actually gasped. "I have another idea."

"Ok," Rider said, waiting for me to expand. I slammed on the brakes. "I don't care how good of a plan it is, Riss, we shouldn't stop yet!"

"We're going to keep going. Get out and help me!" I raced out of the car and over to the body. It was an S2. Fresh, thick blood oozed from its face. The others must have been here. When Rider rushed to my side, I could see just how bad his head wound was. Finally scabbing over, blood stained the right side of his face and the front of his shirt.

I grabbed the zombie's ankles. "Get him on the hood," I instructed. I tightened my fingers around his fleshy, moist skin. "On three."

We hoisted the disgusting body onto the car and raced back into our seats. I had to accelerate slowly so the zombie wouldn't fly off. We went maybe fifty feet before another body lay on the gritty, damp floor. Thunder echoed and a heavy rain began to fall. When the wind gusted, we got sprayed with a cold mist.

Rider and I flopped the second body onto the hood.

"Why are we collecting zombies?" he asked.

"To hopefully cover up the smell of exhaust," I explained, easing the pedal down.

He nodded. "There's another."

The herd was close by the time we got a particularly large S3 onto the hood. I was afraid the undistributed added weight could cause a problem. We went up one more level and found one more body. I backed the car into a parking space. Rider opened his door.

"What are you doing?" I whispered, afraid the herd might see or hear us.

"Give me your knife," he whispered back.

"No! There are too many to fight. Even I'm not gonna try."

"I'm not fighting. I'm gonna cut open that S3. Ya know, for the smell."

"Oh, right." I grabbed the knife and handed it to him. "Good idea."

"Thanks," he said and rushed out of the car. I cut the lights and rolled up my window as soon as he was back in. We locked the doors and ducked our heads. My heart was beating obnoxiously loud. I couldn't see anything. I had no idea where the herd was. I wouldn't know if they discovered us until it was too late.

Though it was dark enough that I didn't need to, I closed my eyes and envisioned the zombies marching. They had to be close now. Despite my cold and wet clothes, I was sweating from nerves.

Rider reached over and took my hand, knowing how horribly wrong this situation could go. He squeezed my fingers when we heard the shuffling. Air rushed in and out of my lungs. Mentally, I began counting backwards from ten. When I got to one, I risked looking up and out the window.

Of course, I couldn't see anything. Another painful thirty seconds ticked by. The moans grew quieter and quieter until we could barely hear them anymore. I'd count once more and then flick on the lights and high tail it out of here, I told myself.

When I got to three, something pounded on the hood. Rider and I both jumped. My heart was beating so fast I thought it might burst. We waited, not yet wanting to give ourselves away. Something was on the hood.

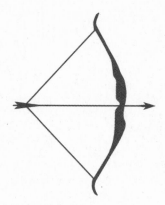

CHAPTER 17

Rider's grip on my hand tightened. The car bobbed up and down as the zombie scrambled past our decoys. Then, with a roar, it slapped the windshield. If I was a screamer, that certainly would have gotten a reaction out of me. The zombie clawed at the glass.

"We have to do something," Rider mumbled.

"Right." I sat up, felt around for the lights and turned them on. I blinked to help my eyes adjust. The zombie continued to claw the windshield. The herd had passed us—for now. One turned, apparently hearing his undead friend's attempts to get into our car for a free meal.

He let out a high pitched yell and ran at us. As if answering a call, the others slowly turned around, bumping into each other, causing some to fall. I put the car in drive and slammed on the gas. The tires squealed as we tore out of the parking spot. I jerked the wheel to try and dislodge the zombie. He got caught on one of the bodies, which was sticky with decomposition and wasn't budging.

I barely made the turn. The tail end of our car hit another. Shit. I didn't want to wreck this car yet. We needed it. The herd was closing in on us, moving faster than I expected. It was fucking terrifying.

Then another idea popped into my head.

"Take the wheel!" I shouted to Rider after I jerked it one last time. The moving zombie flew off and rolled. I pulled the Berretta from my waist band.

"You had that the whole fucking time?" Rider angrily yelled.

"Yeah," I retorted. I dropped it in my lap and took the wheel again, sliding around another turn and slowing down. "Shoot an expensive car!" I yelled.

"Why?"

"Car alarm," I explained, looking behind us. There was no way the herd could keep up if we kept moving. But that wasn't a guarantee. Rider rolled down his window and hit the back window of a yellow Hummer. The alarm instantly blared.

"I don't believe it," Rider almost laughed. "They're going right to it."

A wicked smiled pulled the corners of my mouth up. "Like moths to a flame," I joked.

"Y-you're awesome," he told me. If I could steal a glance at him, I'd assume his pale, freckled cheeks were blushing.

I always hated parking garages. Even full of lights and no zombies, they confused me. I had spent nearly fifteen minutes trying to get out of one in Indy once. I felt like a total dumbass and I still don't know how I wasn't able to find the right exit.

I paid close attention to the markers, which were luckily labeled for dummies. The big 'G' for 'ground level' helped. I slammed the gas pedal down and broke through the gate arm. The car flew over the little slope that took us from the garage to the street. We bounced over a curb, fishtailing on the wet street. I fumbled to get the windshield wipers on.

Rider let out a triumphant whoop. "We made it!"

"Holy shit, I know," I said, suddenly realizing I was out of breath. I don't think I breathed at all on the way out. The feeling of euphoria was instantly squished. "Hayden," I blurted. "And the others. W-where are they?"

Rider shook his head. "They wouldn't have left us unless…"

"No, don't even say it," I demanded. "Not all four of them. Brock was armed a hell of a lot better than I was and we made it out."

"Yeah," he agreed, though he didn't sound like he believed it. "Maybe they went back in looking for us."

"No!" I hit the wheel. "The alarm. W-what if they thought it was us signally for help—"

"—and they walked into the herd!"

I turned around. "We have to go back and make sure."

"Yes. We do."

The car's nose had just made it up the slope into the garage when we heard the shot; it came from behind us. Eager to look, I didn't bother pressing the brake. The car rolled back. Heart racing again, I had to force myself to gain control over my body. I backed up and turned the car, headlights shining in the direction of the shot.

"Oh my God," I said out loud when I saw an outline of a person running at us. Then three more joined him. I stomped on the pedal, accelerating as fast as the old car would let me. I slammed on the brake, tires sliding on the rain-slick street. I almost forgot to put the car in park.

I got out and ran to him. Hayden didn't stop running until he collided with me. His arms wrapped around me and he picked me up.

"Orissa," he panted. I hugged him tightly, not wanting to let go. He set me down, put both hands on my face and kissed me, tongue slipping past my lips. "I thought you were behind me. I had no idea," he began but stopped to kiss me again. "When I realized you weren't there. I-I panicked."

"He freaked the fuck out," Ivan said with his characteristic chuckle.

"I don't know how I lost you," I admitted. "I stopped to kill a zombie and thought I could catch up."

"I knew it," I heard Wade say. I glanced at him to see him grinning. He turned to Rider. "Didn't I say there was something going on between those two?"

Rider gave a half smile and nodded. "It was pretty obvious. How long has this been going on?"

I let out a breath and rested my head against Hayden's chest.

"Since Riss came back," Hayden said. "We didn't want people to—"

"You don't have to explain yourself," Rider said with a smile. "I'm happy for you two."

"Thanks," Hayden said and embraced me again. I heard Rider recant his story of how he got separated in the dark as well. Like us, the other guys had run past the ground level exit. They found the stairs faster since they had the light. Once they were on the street, they realized that Rider and I weren't with them. Hayden wanted to go back in right away, but Wade, Brock, and Ivan reminded him that without weapons, he'd be no use.

They were scrambling to find something that would work when they got ambushed and forced to flee. Then they heard the car alarm and came back.

"Not to ruin your romantic, reuniting kiss in the rain," Brock started, "but we need to get out of here."

Hayden and I broke apart, fully agreeing.

"How the hell did you find keys?" Wade asked me as we walked back to the car.

"I didn't," I told him. "I hotwired it. Watch out for the wires hanging down," I told Ivan, who went to the driver's side. "You could get a nasty shock." Rider, Brock, and Hayden got in the back; I sat on Hayden's lap. It was a tight fit for the three grown men, adding me made it feel like we were cramming into a clown car. Wade and Ivan took the front.

"How the hell did you learn that?" Ivan asked and put the car in drive.

"From a friend," I mumbled.

"A friend?" he questioned, stealing a glance back at me.

"Yup." I didn't want to go into detail. Other than meeting Hayden, the only good thing about the zombie apocalypse was that is made my criminal record disappear.

"You're an interesting girl, Orissa," Ivan told me.

I shrugged. "Thanks."

The rain continued to pour down on us and the wind would randomly gust, pushing against the little car. There was debris and the occasional zombie along the street. Ivan drove on the sidewalks every now and then to avoid hitting something solid and heavy.

"You have got to be kidding me," Ivan uttered aloud. The four of us in the back craned our necks to see what the problem was. "Do you think we can make it?" Ivan asked Wade.

"It looks deep," Wade speculated. "I think the tailpipe will go under."

With no one to clear crap from the gutters and sewers, the road was flooded.

"We could get out and walk," Brock suggested.

"We might have to," Wade grumbled.

"Try another street," Hayden said. Now that I was sitting still and the danger was sort of over, I was cold. I wanted to get back to the truck, take my wet clothes off and crank the heat.

"We're not that far," I reminded everyone. I knew this car couldn't make it through the tall, wet grass that lined the highway, so suggesting some off roading would be pointless.

"We'll try one more," Ivan decided and turned the car around. We went around the block, down an alley, through an intersection, and onto another street. The roof had been torn off a building, blocking our way.

"If at first you don't succeed, try again," Brock said with a sigh. We backtracked, went two blocks down and got stopped by more tornado damage.

"I think it's inevitable we're gonna have to walk," Wade grumbled. "Does anyone even remember where we came from? I wasn't paying attention," he admitted.

"If it were daylight, we'd be able to see the highway," Hayden started. "But now, I'm really not sure either." He looked out the window and shook his head. "Go back to the garage."

"The zombies might come out," Rider said. "The alarm probably stopped a long time ago. I'm not running into that herd again."

We all agreed but knew we needed to get back to the garage if we wanted to find the highway. It was the only way to retrace our steps.

"Why do they travel in herds?" Rider wondered out loud.

"Safety in numbers," I joked.

"Do you think they ever get really hungry and eat each other?" he asked no one in particular.

"No," Hayden answered. "They only want living flesh and blood. Or something that's recently dead. I think it's the, uh, nutrition they're craving."

"Interesting," Brock said.

I nodded and shivered again. Hayden put his arms around me, though, with his wet clothes and cold skin, he only made it worse.

Ivan navigated back to the garage, flooring it as we drove by. He jerked the wheel and we skidded around a turn.

"Well, wouldn't ya know?" Ivan chuckled. "The exit. We went the wrong way the first time."

Feeling relief, I relaxed against Hayden for a minute. Then the relief quickly went away when the car stopped. Tree branches littered the winding road. Hope for our vehicles surviving intact died instantly.

With the light from the car's headlights and Brock's flashlight, we were easily able to see the damage. Little braches and leaves covered the truck; the paint was scratched and nicked but that seemed to be the extent of the damage. We got weapons and flashlights before inspecting anything further.

Hayden jumped up in the bed and began removing the tree parts that had gotten jammed in the base of the machine gun. The cover had mostly stayed on, but I wouldn't be surprised if the whipping wind and rain and gotten through.

A large branch had fallen, the tip of it hitting the Range Rover above the rear, passenger side window. There was a nasty dent and a small, spider web crack in the glass.

"I don't believe it," Brock said, running his hands through his wet hair. "Did I die? This can't be real. Both cars are drivable."

"Believe it, brother," Ivan said with a smile and started up the engine of the Range Rover. I, too, smiled. If I believed that miracles were still possible in this fucked up world which was filled with undead corpses walking around trying to rip out our stomachs to feast on, I'd say the cars being practically unscathed was one.

The rain was starting to taper off but the wind still furiously blew. I opened the door to the truck, stepped close, and pulled it shut behind me. When the wind gusted, it pressed the door into me. Not wanting to get the seat wet and have to sit on the wet spot, I leaned in and grabbed my bag. I unzipped it and began digging through for dry clothes.

The door opposite me opened. Hayden smiled and pulled his bag out from under the seat. He threw socks, a pair of boxers, jeans, and a t-shirt onto the seat. He stripped out of his wet pants and jacket before hopping in and closing the door.

"Hurry up, Riss," he said impatiently. "The seat is gonna get wet."

"I'm trying," I told him and quickly dug through my bag some more.

"What's so hard? Get your stuff and get in."

"I thought I packed another bra, but I can't find it."

"Don't wear one," he suggested and took off his wet underwear.

"My boobs are too big not to wear one," I scoffed. "It's uncomfortable."

"Really? I thought you didn't like wearing them."

"Not when I'm lounging around. But running without one isn't fun." Luckily I had put a white, tight fitting tank top into my bag. I took it out.

"Oh," Hayden said excitedly. "Wear that. And stay out in the rain."

I wadded up the clothes I needed and threw them at Hayden. "That's not funny." I bent over and unlaced my soaking boots.

"No, not *funny*," he continued.

"And I'm sure Ivan, Brock, Wade, and Rider would just love it too," I informed him.

"Oh, right," he laughed.

"And sorry to disappoint you, but I'm putting a sweatshirt on over top." I kicked off my pants and got into the truck to finish getting dressed. We all put our wet clothes in the bed. I climbed into the passenger seat, turned on the truck and turned up the heat. Only blasting cold air, I switched it back off and stuck my cold hands under my legs.

Hayden, Brock, Wade, and Ivan huddled out of the rain under the open tailgate door of the Range Rover, going over the plan of action. Rider, not wanting to get his dry clothes rain soaked, rushed to the truck.

He slammed the door closed and moved my bag back under the seat.

"Oh, sorry," I told him. "I forgot I left it out."

"It's alright," he said and pulled the seat belt across himself. "I want to thank you, Orissa."

"For what?"

"Uh, for saving my life," he said as if it was the most obvious thing in the world.

"Oh, right. Thanks too. I don't think I would have been able to do that all alone," I told him and smiled.

"I didn't do much," he admitted shyly. "Don't tell anyone, ok?"

I raised an eyebrow. "Tell them what?"

He let out a deep breath and looked down. "That you found me just standing there."

Had Rider been just standing there? I couldn't see him; I had no idea what he was doing. "Why were you just standing?" I questioned.

"I gave up." The words spilled from his mouth as if he had no control. "When I fell behind, I just knew there was no way I could get out alive."

"You were injured," I reasoned.

He shook his head. "Even if I wasn't…"

He looked so ashamed. I wasn't the kind of person to give up or accept defeat; it wasn't a feeling

I was familiar with, but I assumed it was awful.

"Hey," I said gently. "It was bad back there. Stick anyone in that situation—a tornado, a total blackout, a maze-like parking garage, and a herd of zombies—and see what they do. I guarantee they'd give up as well as fall down crying."

"You didn't," he reminded me.

"No, I didn't."

"You've been through a lot. How do you do it?"

"Do what?" I asked and twisted to look him in the eye.

"Not give up."

"There were times I wanted to," I admitted. "I'd like to say that's the truth for all of us, mostly because it will make me feel better. This world…is dead. I had to find things to live for."

"Like what?"

"I promised Raeya a long time ago I'd never let anything bad happen to her. If I gave up and died, she would too. And I had my little group from the hospital to look after." And then there was Zoe; it still hurt to think about her. I remembered the way she looked at the world. She was so innocent. All she saw was the beauty around her. She had been dying for so long but was so full of life. When she died I promised myself to keep going, to live for her. I shook my head. "And now I have everyone at the compound."

"Especially Hayden," he added with a grin.

I smiled back and, for the first time, realized how young Rider looked. He couldn't be over twenty-one. "And my grandpa used to tell me that you don't give up just because something is hard. The harder it is, the more it's worth it in the end."

"Thanks," Rider said. "For talking to me."

"You're welcome. It's nice, sometimes."

"Yeah, it is."

Hayden jogged over and dashed inside the truck. He handed me the folded up map and I brushed the raindrops off and put it in the glove box.

"We've got roughly five hundred miles to go to get to the Pennsylvania border. It should take about eight hours, give or take. With the weather being this shitty, I'd say give."

"We're not driving straight through, are we?" Rider asked.

"No. We want to get away from this place and find somewhere to park for the rest of the night," Hayden told him.

"Good," Rider and I said in unison. Hayden pushed the power button on the radio and put the truck in drive. We decided to backtrack just a bit to try and avoid any more roads cluttered from the tornado. We spent a while looking for another exit and ended up making pretty good time once we got on the highway.

I unbraided my wet hair and combed my fingers through it. I had remembered to pack a brush this time. Once I retrieved it from my bag, I brushed out the remaining tangles and rebraided my hair in a tight fishtail braid. A circle of water quickly formed on my hoodie from the ends of my wet hair.

The truck was getting warm and it was making me sleepy. I closed my eyes for a minute only to open them when the truck rolled off the smooth road and bounced along the shoulder.

"What are you doing?" I asked Hayden.

"Off roading," he said, looking over at me.

The truck bumped obnoxiously over the uneven ground.

"I can see that." And I could also see the pile up of cars on the highway. If I had bothered to look before I opened my mouth, I would have seen that we were going around it. Hayden glanced over at me again. His eyes lingered a little too long and he had to quickly jerk the wheel to avoid hitting a sign.

We hit what felt like a pothole in the weedy grass. Hayden winced and patted the dashboard, apologizing to his truck. He slowed down, easing the truck through another rough patch.

I pointed to an S3 dragging itself along the road. The lights of the cars must have caught its attention; it raised a rotten hand and hissed. Hayden jerked the wheel and ran it over, its head popping like a grape under the big tires.

We drove for an hour and a half until we found an abandoned farming town. It was too dark to get out and explore. The rain picked up again, pinging rhythmically off the roof of the truck. We pulled into a parking lot of what looked like a closed Wal-Mart.

Ivan pulled the Range Rover close to the truck, its lights shining in the opposite direction as ours. As far as we could tell, this place was completely desolate. In pairs, we wandered away to pee. Hayden promised he wouldn't watch but said he didn't want me out of his sight. He still felt guilty for losing me in the garage. When we got back to the truck, I helped Wade go through the Rubbermaid bin our food was kept in. We picked out what we thought was a good combination—applesauce, peanut butter, crackers, and yogurt covered raisins—and passed it out to our friends.

We ate, made sure our guns were loaded, and got situated to sleep. Normally I would never volunteer to take the second watch but after the garage incident I was tired. I moved into the back and stretched out, pulling a sleeping bag over my body. Since it would make sense to have three sleep while three were on the lookout, Hayden and Brock also settled down for a not comfortable at all, half a night's sleep.

Five hours later, we were woken to switch. Country music softly drifted from the truck's speakers. Hayden drummed his fingers on the steering wheel. I rolled down my window and took in a deep breath of cold, night air.

The rain had ceased but the wind was still constant and strong. The air smelled fresh; I had always loved the scent of rain.

"I should have brought a book," Hayden sighed.

"Yeah, this is a little boring," I agreed.

"It's not like I could read it," he added and surveyed the surroundings.

I nodded. As dull as zombie watching could be, it was something we took seriously.

"What's your favorite animal?" he asked suddenly.

"A hawk. Why?"

He shrugged. "There's a lot of normal stuff about you I don't know."

"Oh. Black is my favorite color, dandelions are my favorite flower. I'm a Scorpio, have bitchy identical twin cousins on my dad's side that I haven't seen since I was twelve, stopped believing in Santa when I was eight, don't get poison ivy, and used to have a slight obsession with fire."

"You don't get poison ivy? I'm jealous."

"Yeah. I remember playing in a patch of it when I was just a kid. My mom freaked out and took me to the hospital thinking I was going to have some horrible, allergic reaction. When nothing happened, the doctors told us that not everyone is bothered by it."

"You don't want to know the parts of my body I've gotten poison ivy." He smiled and shook his head. "I like blue, don't care about flowers, don't know my zodiac symbol, have more cousins and second cousins than I can count. I think I believed in Santa until I was twelve—don't judge. I still have a slight obsession with fire. And I don't think dandelions are really flowers."

"Yes they are."

"They are weeds," he insisted.

"Whatever. I still like them."

"Why would anyone *like* them? They're a pain in the ass."

I folded my leg underneath me. "They're the first plants to come up in the spring and the last to die in the winter. They're tough; you can spray the suckers with weed killer and they still won't die. They grow anywhere; in a lush lawn, a dry patch of dirt or a crack in the sidewalk. Even when they're dead, they're still cool looking and offer entertainment. Don't tell me you never wished on a dandelion and then blew the seeds off. Plus, they're yellow and cheerful and edible."

"That's an interesting take," he pointed out.

I shrugged. "I suppose." I turned to face Hayden. "When is your birthday? I feel like that's something I should have known a long time ago."

"July 3rd," he told me. "Though it's not like it matters, right? We can't really celebrate it."

"You're a Cancer."

"Oh, I didn't know you liked astrology."

"I don't really," I explained. "It's interesting, I suppose. It pissed my mom and stepdad off when I took an interest in it."

Hayden nodded and smiled at me.

"I did a lot of stuff to piss people off. All I really did was piss away time I could have spent with them and doing other things."

"Don't beat yourself up over the past," he said gently and leaned over the center console. He put his hand on my cheek and kissed me. "I'm gonna risk sounding incredibly girly and lame by saying the past made you who you are today. And I think that girl is pretty awesome."

"Stop, before I barf," I teased and leaned over to kiss him again. We asked each other more random questions, just like old times, until the sun came up. The six of us got out of our cars, stretched, and ate breakfast before hitting the road again.

$$\longrightarrow$$

We were somewhere in Ohio when I suggested we go farther, maybe to the coast.

"When we get the orders to go that far, then we will," Wade said simply.

"But that won't be for a long time," Rider said, like he was trying to soothe himself; after last night I think he was ready to go home and not think about leaving for a very long time.

Not wanting to start any sort of argument, I nodded. It still seemed odd to me. I more than understood not wanting to be far from the compound. A lot of bad shit can happen close to home. And when it happened far away our chances of getting an injured comrade back in time were extremely unlikely. I shuddered when I thought of what could have happened if Hayden was shot in Texas.

Thinking of Texas reminded me of the weird symbols painted on the doors. I had forgotten about it with everything that had gone on since our discovery of the odd marks. I couldn't help but feel like there was something very obvious in their meanings that we dumbly overlooked. Part of me wanted to go back and check it out while the other part didn't want to invest my time and energy in something that might forever remain a pointless mystery.

Ivan and Hayden debated what should be done over the walkie-talkie as we drove northeast. One possibility was finding a place to bunker since none of us wanted to spend another night in the vehicle. But that would require us stopping fairly soon so we'd have time to find a safe area, check it out, and prepare a place to stay for the night. Finally it was decided we would set up camp in the daylight, rest, and then spend tomorrow looking for survivors in a fifty mile radius of our campsite.

We drove down a street filled with old, ostentatious houses that had a gazillion windows and huge doors. I'd be the first to admit I was curious to go inside the historic mansions, but I wasn't about to spend the night in a place with that many breakable glass panels.

"Oh!" I exclaimed when a nicely restored, green and white Victorian came into view. Unlike the last Victorian house I stayed in, this one was huge, inviting and welcoming. The best part about it was that the first story windows and doors appeared to be carefully boarded up.

"That'll work," Hayden agreed and radioed to Ivan. We patrolled the street for a while longer before stopping. When we didn't see any zombies, we pulled up to the house and got out, weapons at the ready. We went around the house inspecting the boards.

"They wanted to come back," Brock said, meaning the homeowners. "Whoever put these up did a good job. It's sturdy; it would take a lot to pull them apart or bust through."

"That's great and all," Wade agreed. "But how do we get in? I'd hate to break any of the boards and give the zombies a place to crawl through."

I took a step back and looked at the covered porch. "I'll climb up, go downstairs, and go through the garage."

"You shouldn't go alone," Hayden immediately objected.

"Come with me then."

"I will," he insisted. It wasn't easy hoisting ourselves and our weapons up onto the roof of the porch. Hayden broke a small, oval window and waited. "I don't hear anything," he whispered and stuck his head inside. "Or smell rotting."

He stepped through the window and told me to wait there while he checked it out. I counted to thirty before going in.

"Way to wait," he said and rolled his eyes.

"I wasn't gonna let you have all the fun," I told him and smiled. We were standing in what I could only describe as a small loft. Behind us and to the left was a characteristic Victorian tower filled with floor to ceiling paned windows. The loft connected to a circular hallway that was open to the foyer below. On either side of us were bedrooms, each with their own walk in closet and bathroom. A lucky child named Lucas, as the letters above his bed spelled out, had lived in here once.

We closed the doors behind us and went around the curved railing into the next room: A huge game room with a plasma TV mounted on the wall, bookcases filled with books and board games and tons of toys. Lucas was a lucky boy indeed. There was another bedroom with its own bathroom and large closet to check out before we reached the amazing master bedroom.

We temporarily forgot we were looking for zombies as our eyes feasted over the four post, king-sized bed. The entire room was decorated in very pleasing earth tones. The pale blue and brown comforter and matching, fluffy pillows on the bed begged me to lay down on them. The dresser was just as grand as the bed and was made out of beautiful, hand-carved wood. What must have been expensive porcelain figurines of horses adorned the top.

Beyond the bed was a sitting room, with equally regal armchairs angled between another beautiful piece of woodwork. A coffee cup had been left on top of a folded up newspaper; its contents long evaporated. I moved it and picked up the paper.

"October 23rd," I read the date out loud. "I think that's about the same time the virus hit Indy."

"Sounds about right," Hayden agreed and pushed open the bathroom door. We both longed to take a long, hot bath in the Jacuzzi tub. We quickly checked the closet and went down the stairs with Hayden insisting he go first.

I held my flashlight in one hand and rested my other on top, holding my gun. We stood in an elaborately decorated foyer. I shined the light around.

"This way?" Hayden asked and motioned to the front door. I nodded and followed him into one of the most impressive living rooms I'd ever been in. Even though our only source of light was the flashlight, I knew a fancy home living magazine would have loved to come in here and snap pictures.

I wondered if Lucas was allowed to play on the pristine white carpet or sit on the antique Victorian-styled furniture. Dust covered a grand piano.

Through the living room, we went into an equally ridiculously decorated dining room. Seriously? I looked around at the China that was set on the table. Did these people invite royalty over?

We inspected the kitchen, utility room, family room, bathrooms, and the den before we went into the four car garage. A Lexus SUV was parked nearest the door. My light wasn't enough to descry what the other two cars were. Hayden lifted the garage door open, spilling blinding light in.

"How is it?" Brock asked. I blinked when I looked at him, my eyes still adjusting to the light.

"Safe, I think," Hayden answered. "We didn't look in the basement yet."

Rider looked at the cars. There was one more Lexus and a sporty Audi. "I'm really curious to how people could afford to live like this, especially in the Depression."

Wade huffed. "Me too. It's not fair."

"Tell me about it," I agreed, recalling Aunt Jenny's cramped apartment. Surprisingly, I felt a little pang of homesickness. Not for the small and crappy apartment, but for family. I hated not knowing what happened to Aunt Jenny and my grandpa.

I shook myself back to the here and now. I offered to keep watch while the guys went into the basement. Hayden, of course, stayed with me. After ten minutes, the guys came back up telling us that the most exciting thing they found was a theater room that we couldn't use.

Rider found the keys to the three cars in the garage. With our remaining daylight, we moved all three into the yard and siphoned gas from the Audi and the car. Hayden thought it would be a good idea to take the SUV but Ivan didn't like the idea of two of us being in a car with no means of communication; we only had two walkie-talkies.

Settling on deciding later, we parked our cars in the garage and shut the door. I went around the house in search of candles. Ivan and Brock worked on starting a fire in the living and family room fireplaces with wood they had brought in from a neatly stacked woodpile out on the back, covered veranda. Hayden went through the pantry for anything useful and Wade and Rider brought in our stuff.

I closed the doors to the den and dining room; there was nothing in there we'd need. I set the whole ten candles I was able to find on the kitchen counter and got a box of matches out of my bag.

"That's better," Hayden said when the flames flickered and danced over the kitchen. He had a nice pile started on the island counter. There were numerous cans of beans, vegetables and fruit, two bags of organic potato chips, one bag of popcorn, a dozen cans of soup, a jar of pickles, chips, salsa, several boxes of cornbread, cake, and brownie mixes, and an unopened bottle of spray butter. "Do you think we need salad dressing?"

"Won't hurt to take it," I told him, carefully carrying a candle over to set down in an empty spot on the shelf in the pantry. "It can be used to flavor food. Just make sure it's not expired; we need food poisoning like we need a hole in the head."

"Right," he said and handed me the bottles to add to the pile. We finished going through the pantry, moved the candle to the counter and each took two candles to distribute throughout the house. We set two on the table by the stairs. We put a candle on a dresser in each of the four bedrooms since it would soon be dark upstairs too, one in the upstairs hallway and kept the remaining candles in the kitchen so we could use the light to see our food and make dinner.

After eating more soup, potato chips, and a can of tuna, the six of us crowded around the coffee table in the family room to a play a game of cards. I laid out our wet clothes to dry and sat with my back to the fireplace and unbraid my hair, surprised at how long it had gotten since October. I no doubt had a horrendous amount of split ends. When wet, my hair appeared jet black. Really, it was a dark espresso color and I had always liked my natural color. It was the only good thing my father had given me.

"When the world is fixed, I'm coming back here," Brock said and dealt the cards. "This house is sweet!"

"*If* the world is fixed," Rider spat bitterly.

"What do you think it will be like?" Wade asked. "When there aren't any more zombies, I mean."

"It'll be weird," Ivan laughed. "And empty."

"Who will be in charge?" Rider questioned.

"I assumed we would be," Hayden admitted. "At least with our group. We'd keep it running like how we do. I'm banking on everyone being able to go off and do their own thing while still working together as a community."

"You have more faith in people that I do," I told Hayden. "Once it's safe, I want to go back to my farm in Kentucky and not have to worry about taking care of anyone but myself and a few friends."

"How would you get food?" Ivan asked.

I shrugged one shoulder. "Farm and hunt. It wouldn't be fun but people did it before, right?"

"What about technology?" Rider continued to raise questions. "Do you think we'll have to start all over?"

"Not completely," Hayden answered. "We still have the knowledge, just not the tools or the manpower to work complex things like airports, oil rigs, and cable companies. And I think some things—like cable—are nice but are not needed to live. We'll have to go without, like we are now."

"It'll be weird," I said with a slight laugh. "When kids are born into this world we'll be telling them stories about what 3D TVs, air conditioning, and the internet were."

"And we'll have to tell them about the zombie virus," Brock added. "What will we tell them when they ask how it started? We have no idea."

"It had to be an accident," Ivan speculated. "Like in a cheesy science fiction movie where someone dropped a vial in a lab, releasing the virus to the unsuspecting public."

"Yeah," Wade agreed. "Or a science experiment gone wrong. Maybe doctors were trying to cure cancer and created cells that couldn't die or something, but they didn't expect the virus to…to mutate and create zombies."

I leaned my head back and shook out my hair to let heat get to the bottom layers. I hated sleeping on wet hair; it just annoyed me. We played another game of Rummy, talked some more, and decided to call it a night.

We were unsure if having someone stay downstairs and keep watch was worth it since no one could see a damn thing through the boarded up windows. It was unanimous that we'd all feel safer with an alert pair of ears to listen for a herd.

In sets of three again, Hayden, Brock, and I took the first watch. We sat in the family room again, eating pre-popped popcorn and talking. After three hours, I was feeling very full and very bored. My eyes were heavy and I knew I could easily fall asleep. Knowing I needed to do something to stay awake, I took my flashlight and crept up the stairs and into the game room.

I came back down with a stack of board games. The rest of our time, spent playing Loaded Questions, went by quickly, but I was still a tad bit excited when it was our turn to sleep. Yawning, I let Hayden pull me to my feet. Warm from sitting by the fire, I had removed my sweatshirt. The air upstairs wasn't cold, but it still made goosebumps break out on my arms.

I took off my boots and got under the covers of the grand bed in the master bedroom. Hayden did the same and got in next to me. I was so tired and comfortable that I fell asleep quickly and didn't open my eyes until Ivan woke us up six hours later.

We got dressed, blew out the candles, ate breakfast, and loaded up what we'd need for our day filled with searching.

<hr />

After driving around for awhile, something occurred to me. "We're less than a hundred miles from Pittsburgh," I told Hayden, tracing the road with my finger. "I think we should at least get close to see what's there."

Hayden hesitated before he answered. "There's plenty to look for here."

"But Pittsburgh is a big city and Fuller wanted us to check out the bigger cities," I insisted. "I just don't understand what the big deal is. If we find people, who cares where they came from?"

"We were given direct orders to *not* go to Pennsylvania," he reminded me.

"I know, and that makes me want to go even more," I admitted. "It's just that we are so close. I'd hate to miss a chance to find something." I leaned forward between the front seats. "Wouldn't you?"

"Yes," he answered. He ever so slightly looked at Brock, who, in return, ever so slightly shrugged.

We drove around for another hour and ran into a small town with over a dozen zombies staggering around. Almost all of them seemed in or close to being in the S3 stage. Hayden rolled down the windows and turned up the music.

Suddenly, he turned around to face me. "I'm gonna use your bow, ok?"

"Sure," I said. "But I don't think you'll hit anything. You never finished training with it."

"Teach me?" he asked with an innocent smile.

"Sure," I said again. We killed all but the slowest gummies by shooting them with our guns. Hayden took the bow and held it out. "Relax your shoulder," I instructed. "And drop your elbow a bit. It's making you hold the arrow wrong."

Hayden nodded, let out a breath, and released the arrow which lodged in the gummy's shoulder.

"Not bad, Underwood," Ivan praised. "Aim for the head this time," he teased.

I gave Hayden another arrow; this time he got the neck, severing the S3's spinal cord.

Hayden nodded with satisfaction at the fallen body. "I'll get it on my first try next time," he said with a grin. He pulled the arrows out, wiped them off, and stuffed them back in my quiver.

On foot, the six of us explored the little town. Everything seemed frozen in time; dishes with moldy food still sat on the tables inside the diner, the post office was still decorated for Halloween, business signs were still flipped to 'open,' and cars were parked within the lines in parking lots.

Besides the birds chirping, it was quiet and creepy here. We siphoned gas from several parked cars to fill our tanks, got our lunch, and sat at a picnic table in a small park.

"So," I said to Ivan. "We're pretty close to Pittsburgh."

"Hmm," he said and took a bite of beef jerky.

"Don't you want to go look?" I asked.

"Yeah, I'm curious to what it's like," he admitted causing me to smile. "But we were told not to cross the border."

I rolled my eyes. "No one would know."

"Riss," Hayden warned. "No."

I sighed but gave up. I was supposed to be a better soldier, right? I didn't bring it up any more while we ate the rest of our lunch.

The storms must have brought in the warm weather. With the sun beating down on us, I quickly got hot. I walked to the truck and pulled my brown sweater over my head.

"Jesus, Riss, what happened?" Hayden exclaimed, startling me a bit.

"Huh?" I asked not having a freaking clue what he was talking about.

He stepped over. "You're covered in bruises! How are you not feeling that?" He gently touched my side.

I winced slightly. "Oh, I sorta fell down some stairs in that parking garage and then a fat zombie landed on me."

He put his hand over the bruise. "Does it hurt?"

"Only when you touch it," I said and flinched. "I'll be fine in a day or two; I always am."

Hayden nodded. "Hopefully," he yawned.

"Tired?" I asked as I pulled a t-shirt over my head.

"Yeah, I had another nightmare," he said bitterly.

"Why didn't you wake me up?"

"You seemed content. Just having you there was enough," he said with a shy smile. I closed the truck door and walked with Hayden back to the others. Ivan was looking at the map. He tapped it with a pen and seemed to be thinking hard about something.

"I think we should go to the lake," Ivan told us when Hayden and I sat down at the table. Ivan tapped the blue mass on the map that was marked as Lake Erie. "That's my best guess for finding people."

"We won't have time today," Hayden said, looking at the afternoon sun.

"No," Ivan agreed. "How about we spend the rest of the day looking in our radius, pack our stuff, and head out early tomorrow."

"Sounds good," Hayden said with a nod. He slid the map over and turned it around. "We can go up along the border, go west along the lakeside, and drive through Cleveland. There ya go, Riss: a nice-sized city to explore."

I wrinkled my nose. I'd been to Cleveland before; it was nothing spectacular before the Depression. After…well, it wasn't exactly a tourist attraction. We loaded up in our cars and drove across the circle Ivan had drawn on the map, symbolizing our radius.

"What the…?" Hayden whispered when the truck turned onto what should have been the main street in another modest town.

"Holy shit," I said as I looked around. It looked as if a fiery tornado ripped through the town. Cars lay upside down with their tires melted off. Charred remains of houses lay in ruin. Hayden slowly drove down the road, shaking his head. When I looked over at him, his eyes were wide and full of disbelief.

We passed an apartment complex; half of it was nothing but rubble. Hayden gripped the steering wheel tightly, unable to navigate any further. He put the truck in reverse and waited for the Range Rover to back up so we could get out.

Brock, who was sitting in the passenger seat, looked very grim.

"What is going on?" I asked.

"This place has been bombed," Hayden said, his voice a harsh whisper.

"Bombed?" I asked incredulously. "No, no…why? And by *whom*?" I stammered.

Hayden shook his head again. "I-I don't know," he said and swerved the truck around and put it in drive. The Range Rover sped away. "I suppose anyone could make a bomb and it might be easy—easier at least—to get what you'd need to make one now that no one regulates…anything."

"Why?" I asked as fear crept into my heart.

"I don't know," he repeated. "Maybe the town was overrun with zombies."

"I don't see any body parts," I quietly pointed out.

"If it was done when the virus first hit," Brock started. "Then they could have decomposed by now. It's been months."

"Right," I said and swallowed the lump that was forming in my throat.

"I never thought I'd have to see this kind of damage again," Hayden mumbled to himself. Once we put a good distance between us and the bomb-ruined city, Ivan pulled over so Hayden could pull up next to him.

"Wasn't expecting that," Ivan told us with a half smile. "At least someone knows how to properly take down the zombies!"

"Yeah," Hayden agreed, not finding the humor in Ivan's statement "You think it was civilians?"

"Who else would it be?" Ivan asked. "I bet even little Miss I-can-hotwire-cars knows how to make a bomb."

Hayden twisted around to look at me and I guiltily smiled. "Kinda. I know what explodes when you mix it with fire, and Molotov Cocktails might have been included in my grandpa's life lessons. But I've never made an actual *bomb* and definitely don't know how to make one with that much destructive power."

"Really?" Ivan asked in disbelief. "I was totally joking, Penwell."

I shrugged and sank back in my seat.

"Let's start making our way back to the camp," Hayden said and rolled up his window. We looped south, driving through neighborhoods, downtowns, and rural roads and saw zero signs of life.

We reached the camp at sunset. After a quick drive up and down the block on the lookout for zombies, we retreated inside and started up the fires again.

"I wish I could shower," Wade complained, pulling at his collar. "I was sweating balls out there."

"There's a pool out back," Brock reminded us.

"Yeah, but the water is probably disgusting," Hayden said, making a face. "Unless…" he flicked on his flashlight and disappeared into the kitchen. Curious, Wade and I followed him. Hayden opened up a cabinet and clanked the pots and pans around until he found a very large soup pot. "We boil it. It won't be clean enough to ingest, but it'll be enough to use for a sponge bath at least."

"Yes!" I agreed with excitement, more than ecstatic to wash the sweat off my body. The six of us each grabbed a pot or a mixing bowl to fill with water. I assumed a professional had sealed up the pool long before the virus struck; the cover was tight and the water was surprisingly clear.

Hayden situated the large pot in the living room fire and carefully dumped the water in. I found a bottle of bathroom cleaner in the utility room and washed out the bathroom sink before rinsing it with a cup of boiled pool water and pulling the drain stopper. I dashed upstairs to get washcloths, towels and soap.

Acting like gentlemen, the guys let me wash first. Hayden poured the hot water into the sink. It steamed up the mirror and extinguished the candle. Seeing that I needed to let the water cool before I stuck my hand in it anyway, I exited the bathroom to get a match.

I removed my clothes and sat on the closed toilet while I waited for the water to cool enough to be touched. After what felt like forever, I plunged my hands in. It was at the temperature where it was uncomfortably warm but not hot enough to burn my skin. I freaking loved it.

Standing on a towel to collect the dripping water, I started with my face and then ran the wet washcloth over my body before scrubbing it with soap. After I rinsed it off, I unbraided my hair and stuck it in the sink to wash.

"I feel so much better," I said to Hayden once I was clean, not even caring that I smelled faintly of chlorine. I flopped down on the fancy settee in the living room and started combing out tangles in my hair. It took another hour to boil enough water for the guys to wash up.

We ate protein bars, dried fruit, and chips and salsa for dinner. Between the six of us, the chips and salsa went fast. I licked the salt off my fingers and wished for a margarita. We played another game of Loaded Questions before it was time to sleep in shifts.

"Who else is tired?" Hayden asked, looking for volunteers to sleep first.

"I am," Ivan said and stood. "Well then, night, sleep tight. Don't let the zombies bite."

"Ha-ha, very funny," I told him and leaned back on the family room couch. Hayden slowly got up and took a few steps before turning around to look at me.

"Are you coming, Riss?" he asked.

"Oh," I said and blinked. "Yeah, I guess." I liked first watch. I could stay up late without feeling tired. I didn't like waking up when it was still dark and watching the sun come up. Besides, I wasn't tired in the least.

I smiled at Hayden, whose hazel eyes locked with mine. After seeing the wreckage from the bombed town, I wasn't going to let him be alone tonight.

I probably only got two hours of sleep when Rider gently shook me awake. I opened my eyes and sighed, not ready to get out of bed just yet.

Hayden, Ivan, and I quietly sat in the family room. Ivan poked at the fire, Hayden propped his flashlight behind him so he could read, and I wrapped up in a blanket and sat in a very comfy armchair, trying not to fall asleep.

I failed.

Hayden woke me up in the morning, though, it was so dark in the house with the boarded up windows, I had no idea I slept until 6:30.

"You shouldn't have let me sleep," I told him as I stretched.

"Ivan and I are capable of keeping watch," he said.

"I know you are, but it's not fair. I got more sleep than anyone else." I threw the blanket on the chair. "At least I feel safe enough around you guys to sleep."

Hayden raised an eyebrow. "What does that mean?"

I reached my arms above my head. "When I was with Raeya, Padraic, and the others I was never able to let my guard down. It was constantly stressful being the only one who had experience with firearms. Yeah, Ray and Padraic are smart and resourceful and Jason wouldn't go down without a fight, but still…I felt responsible for them."

"And you don't for us?" Hayden teased.

"I do. Really, I still do. But you guys know what you're doing. You're good, you're smart, and you've been in bad situations before. And almost as awesome as I am with shooting," I said in a joking manor. "You're the one with the battle experience." I let out a deep breath. "Though I'd still prefer to keep everyone I care about locked up in a padded room where nothing will ever hurt them. Sadly, I know that's not possible…yet."

Hayden smiled. "I'd like to keep you locked up in a safe place too. Instead we're here."

"At least we're together," I said with a shy smile.

"Together," he repeated before turning and gathering up his belongings.

Not wanting to waste any daylight, we packed up our stuff, put the new food in garbage bags to keep it dry, and moved our cars out of the garage. Undecided if we would come back for the Lexus SUV, Rider pulled it back into the garage and pocketed the keys.

We got to the lake faster than I expected and drove along Lake Erie Avenue slowly in hopes of catching signs of life. After a mile or two, we turned away from the lake and tried a different road. Some of the houses had broken windows and wide open front doors. Others looked completely untouched.

Feeling dejection, Hayden cranked his music to lift our spirits. As much as I didn't like country music, there was something about Toby Keith's silly song about a cup that made me smile. We absently mindedly drove around a while longer, not ready to give up just yet.

"Holy shit!" Hayden exclaimed. Busy looking out the passenger window, I hadn't seen where we were going. The truck pulled into a high school parking lot. I audibly gasped as my eyes took in the chain link fence set up around the building.

We had found a quarantine!

A *real* quarantine.

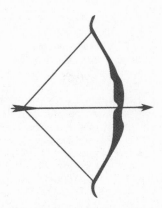

CHAPTER 18

"Oh my God," I whispered. Cars not only filled the lot, but were parked along the street and in the grass. Several fire trucks, ambulances, and police cars were parked in the front. A hand painted sign that read 'INSPECTION AREA' had an arrow pointing to the football stadium.

"I didn't think these existed," Rider said, shaking his head.

"Me neither," Hayden agreed. "It's the first we've seen," he told me. "I assumed I'd find a ton of emergency shelters when I left home. When I didn't, I realized no one had time to set anything up."

It suddenly hit me that I had no idea how the compound got started. I'd ask Hayden later.

"There must be hundreds of people here," Rider mumbled, mentally counting the cars.

"Hopefully," I added. I unbuckled my seatbelt and moved to the opposite side of the truck, peering out the window.

"Going in?" Ivan asked over the walkie-talkie.

"Yeah," Hayden responded. "Let's drive around first."

We had to stop and push open an eight-foot chain link fence. It scraped against the pavement, echoing across the empty school grounds. The fence around the football stadium was bent and broken. Bits of rotting human skin and clothing had gotten ripped off in the struggle to get over the fence. I wondered if humans escaped or if zombies got in.

The back doors to the large high school were chained shut. I squinted to see inside; the sun glared off the dark glass making it impossible to see. We continued to circle around the school. In the grassy area next to it, tents and canopies had once been set up. They were now nothing but wind ripped rags that flapped in the spring breeze.

A dumpster at the end of the parking lot was overflowing. Garbage spilled over and littered the area around it. I couldn't be sure, but I swore I saw an arm sticking out through a pile of Styrofoam cups.

"It doesn't look to promising," I sighed.

"Maybe everyone is inside," Rider suggested. "Like in the gym or the auditorium where it's safe."

"Maybe," Hayden echoed. We drove back around and parked in the narrow drive in between the parked cars. We slung our guns over our shoulders and stuffed our pockets full of ammo. Hayden flipped open his knife and stuck another in his boot.

"Only shoot if it's an emergency," he told us. "We don't know what's in there...let's not give ourselves away yet."

I resituated my M16 to rest behind my quiver. I made sure my knife was easily accessible in my pocket and gripped the bow, ready to fire an arrow if need be. Ivan led the way through a side door that opened into a dim hallway.

The dropdown security gates were locked into place. We detoured down a dark hall, making our way deeper into the school. The air was stale and heavy with humidity; I doubted any fresh air had graced these halls in ages.

"It smells like piss," Wade noted, scoffing at the scent that wafted up the hall. "I think it's coming from in there," he said, using his gun to point to a classroom. We peered inside to see the room filled with cots and sleeping bags. My eyes lingered on an elephant stuffed animal that reminded me of Raeya and I mentally smiled when I thought about seeing her again. And then I thought about the child who it belonged to and my smile disappeared.

Was he somewhere in this school? My heart wanted to believe it, but my head knew better. We walked past several more classrooms set up just the same: Cots and sleeping bags and pillows covering the floor. We turned on our flashlights and went down another hall without any windows.

Something scuffled ahead of us. I traded my flashlight for an arrow and Ivan nodded for me to take the front. Precisely moving my feet to make the least amount of noise possible, I followed the source of the scuffling. Ivan raised his flashlight up and cast the light out for me.

Something metal clanked and bounced on the ground, causing us all to jump. I took a slow, deep breath and stepped in front of a door, slowly easing it open with my foot. It creaked as it moved, instantly catching the zombie's attention.

Holding a spleen and only wearing cut off denim shorts, he roared. He was an easy shot, but I was so distracted by his grossly distended stomach I hesitated. His staggering walk waddled just a bit. When his belly hit the corner of a desk, it exploded like a water balloon.

"Sick," I whispered and released the arrow. Ivan followed me into the classroom to retrieve the arrow while the others stayed in the hall. I flicked the goo off the arrow and wiped it on the zombie's shorts before sticking it back in my quiver.

We continued our search down the dark hallway, looking in every room we went by. One was crammed with the desks taken out of the room that had been set up for sleeping, a few more held cots and blankets, another was stuffed full of duffle bags, suitcases and boxes and one was set up like a medical unit.

"There might be something useful in here," I said, using my bow to point into the med unit. "We should take a look." I gave the bow and two arrows to Hayden. I clicked on my flashlight and went into the room.

"What should I look for?" Rider asked.

"I'm not too sure. Anything that is clean or unused, I suppose. Like this," I said, holding up a box of rubber gloves.

"Jackpot," Rider said, picking up a first aid kit. "There's three more," he told me with a smile.

We stacked our stuff in a neat pile by the doorframe; Brock went back a few rooms and returned with an empty duffle bag that he began filling with the medical supplies. Along with the kits and gloves, we found an unopened box of bandages, several saline IV drip bags, ACE bandages, two bottles of iodine, and a box of snap-to-activate hot packs. The bag had to be heavy but Brock slung it over his shoulder with ease.

We went up a flight of stairs and into a hall. Every classroom door was locked. Thick dust settled on the doorknobs.

"No one has been up here," Hayden said. "No one living at least. Let's try downstairs one more time and call it." He shook his head and looked at a locker decorated with deflated pink balloons and a sign that said "Happy 17th Birthday, Dana!" in swirling purple letters.

We retraced our steps and exited through another hall that took us into the middle of the school. Her rattling death groan gave her away. I strung an arrow, prepared to let it loose as soon as the zombie stepped around the corner.

But she didn't.

"You do hear that, right?" I asked Hayden quietly.

"Yep. Definitely a zombie," he responded, loud enough to draw our attention to her.

I shrugged. "If they don't come to you, then you go to them." I stepped around the corner with the arrow aimed at head level. "What the fuck?" I said aloud.

The zombie lay on the floor like an upside down turtle. She too had a huge belly, though hers had burst. Half-chewed parts of human bodies oozed out. She held the remains of an arm clutched in her death grip, pushing the flesh into her mouth.

"She ate herself to death," Ivan said and stepped over to her. He shook his head. "Or to her un-death, I suppose." Using the heel of his boot, he stomped on her head.

"Two very full zombies," Wade said nervously. "I don't like the sound of that."

"Me neither," Hayden agreed. "I think they ate everyone here. Let's go."

All agreeing, we pushed open the doors to the cafeteria, thinking we could cut through. Dividers had been put in place, providing little privacy. The sheets on the cots were stained with blood.

"This must have been the waiting room, so to speak," Wade observed. Our footsteps loudly echoed in the empty room. We raised our weapons and went through another set of doors and into yet another hallway. I never realized how maze-like schools were until now. Bright sunlight filtered through the dirt and dust-covered glass doors at the end of a hall.

Ivan's hand pressed against the door's lever when someone screamed. It wasn't a scream of fear, more one of frustration. Springing into action, we raced in the direction it came from.

A long, blonde braid hung down her back. She was standing in the middle of where two hallways crossed, waving a broken piece of a two-by-four in the air at an oncoming zombie. We skidded to a stop right as she swung, hitting the zombie in the side of the head. When the zombie dropped, she jumped forward, kicked the feet out from under an S3 and raised the board to finish the job.

My arrow got to him first. Startled, she whirled around. Blood splattered her pretty face and was smeared across the white button up shirt she was wearing.

"Haaa," she yelled, calling to someone down the hall before pointing to us. Glaring in our direction she raised the board again.

"Hi," Ivan said calmly and holstered his gun. "I have to say I'm surprised to see someone alive in here. I'm Sergeant Brewster. We are on the same side."

Blondie didn't move. Her eyes quickly darted to whoever was walking down the hall. Ivan took a step forward, causing her to back away in fear.

"I'm not going to hurt you," he assured her. "We have a shelter—a real shelter—that we're on our way back to. You're welcome to come."

A boy with beautiful deep olive skin slinked from behind the corner. He grunted and sniffed the air. Then he turned to inspect us, revealing claw marks along the left side of his face, severing his ear from his head.

"Oh shit," Wade whispered. "He's infected."

The boy cocked his head and growled. Blondie made a gurgling noise and shushed him. She held her hand out to him; he took it and rubbed his bloody cheek against it, reminding me of a cat rubbing on its owner.

Since two adolescent crazies weren't a threat, the six of us stood rooted to the spot out of curiosity. Suddenly, Blondie snapped her attention away from the boy, growled and swung the board in the air, looking down the hall at something we couldn't see.

The telltale drag and shuffle of undead feet gradually grew louder until the zombie made an appearance. Blondie beat it to death.

"Uh, since when do S1s take down S2s?" Brock asked, shifting the weight of the heavy bag. "It's fucked up but kinda...kinda cool."

"Crazy versus zombie," I muttered and lowered my bow.

"Should we kill them?" Rider asked with his machine gun aimed at the boy.

"If they're killing zombies, I'd leave them alone," Brock suggested.

"Until they come after us," Hayden pointed out.

"Are you sure they're infected?" Wade asked, eyeing the girl who continued to stare us down.

"Hey," Ivan called. "Can you hear me? Say something."

When the girl didn't respond, Hayden shook his head. "Maybe they don't speak English." He waved his hands in the air; still no response. He walked forward six feet before the boy snarled and lunged himself at Hayden. A second later the girl followed suit, screaming a battle cry, showing her teeth, and swinging the board.

Rider quickly fired two rounds. "Definitely infected," he said. He lowered his gun and turned away. We stepped into the parking lot.

"That was not only disappointing but confusing," Wade spoke out loud. "S1s don't work together. That girl could *talk*. You heard her. She and that boy communicated somehow. But they were clearly crazy. And they killed zombies!"

I shook my head and pulled the M16 from around my neck. "I don't get it either. But it is what it is, right? Maybe Dr. Cara could make sense of it."

"She'd probably be pissed we didn't bring them home for her to do research on," Brock said with a slight smile.

"I'm seriously waiting for the day she asks us for a live sample," Wade said, shaking his head. "We already brought back the dead zombies for her to play with."

I thought about telling them how she'd asked for a monkey, but decided not to. Fortunately, she seemed to have forgotten about it.

"When did you do that?" I asked, setting my machine gun in the bed of the truck.

"When you were gone," Rider answered.

"Oh, right," I said, remembering Padraic had told me he had to do an autopsy. "I can't believe you went on a mission while you thought I was dead," I joked. "I expected everyone to be horribly grief stricken, like a teenage girl who got dumped by her first boyfriend."

"I definitely was," Ivan said with a wink. "It was a bad time; you were presumed dead, Gabby was a basket case thinking you sacrificed yourself for her, and Underwood was drugged up in the hospital ward. We were down three men."

"Men?" I asked, raising an eyebrow.

"You know what I mean," Ivan said and set his weapons down.

"No, I don't."

"Don't be such a girl," he teased and flashed his charming smile. "Men, soldiers, Marines, whatever. The way I see it, we're all equal here. We're all just as important to the team. We each have our strengths that we bring with us."

I nodded. "Well said." I set the rest of my weapons in the bed of the truck and with one last look at the failed quarantine, I got in the backseat. We headed north until we reached the shore again. Rather aimlessly, we drove around until we pulled into the parking lot of a harbor.

"Want to stop for lunch?" Hayden asked Ivan over the walkie-talkie.

"Looks clear," Ivan responded. "Yeah, let's stop."

With our cars pointing away from the water in case we needed to make a fast getaway, we got out, grabbed our weapons, and looked around. Luckily, there wasn't much to investigate. There were only a handful of boats in the dock and most were tightly sealed for the winter, making it impossible to act as a floating zombie hide out.

The six of us went back into the truck, picked out what we wanted to eat, and sat on the sun warmed boards of the dock.

"I've never been this far north," Brock said casually. "I like the lake. It'd be fun to be close to this much water; well it would be if I didn't have to worry about zombies floating by."

I laughed. "I went to college in Indiana, about two hours from Lake Michigan. On really nice days, I'd beg Ray to skip class with me, drive up north, and spend the day on the beach. We only did it a few times because gas got so expensive we couldn't afford the drive." I sighed and smiled. "It was fun. We'd pretend we were somewhere more exotic than Indiana."

"Did you live close to the coast?" Wade asked Brock.

He shook his head. "I lived in San Antonio. It's about a hundred miles to the coast. Other than going to South Carolina for training and then going overseas for the war, the most exciting place I've ever gone was Nebraska."

"I didn't get out of North Dakota until I was eighteen," Hayden said and took a bite of beef jerky. "I went to Las Vegas for my birthday, spent three days there, came home, and joined the Marines."

"My parents used to go on family vacations every summer," Rider told us. "I've been to Hawaii and Mexico a few times. Nothing too crazy but better than you two," he joked.

Wade shook his head. "My dad refused to leave the country. He said we had everything we needed right here. I've been all over the U.S. I've always wanted to go to Europe."

"I've been there," Ivan said. "Once. My sister married a British guy and the wedding was in England. The marriage didn't last long," he said with a laugh. "Guess it doesn't matter now."

"I've been all over," I admitted. "I'm partial to India, but that might be because Orissa is a city over there. My dad—my real dad that is—traveled occasionally for work. The one time my mom went with him she came home pregnant, hence my name. Anyway, Kenya is pretty cool too, kinda scary in some places though. Same with China; I met some interesting people there. I wonder if they're still alive…"

"Lucky," Wade huffed.

I shrugged. "I guess. I'm not gonna lie and say I didn't enjoy seeing the world, but I was dragged around by my mom and stepdad. They went on charity and church missions."

"That would be so—" Rider started before Hayden interrupted.

"Is that a boat?" he asked, springing up.

"Where?" we all asked in unison.

"There," Hayden said, pointing to the water. He held one hand over his eyes to shield the sun. "I think it is. And…it's moving."

I jumped up and peered onto the water. "You're right. Oh my God. There's probably people on it!"

"No shit," Brock joked, elbowing me. "Or maybe zombies learned how to drive a boat."

"Don't even joke about that," Rider said seriously. "Do you think we can catch their attention?"

"The boat's moving pretty fast," Ivan spoke. "It looks like it's going southeast. Maybe to another dock?"

"We should find out," Wade suggested. "Drive along the lake and see if we can head it off." He looked at Hayden.

"Yeah," Hayden agreed after a second. "Let's go."

We picked up our stuff and made it into our vehicles in record time. We sped down the harbor and turned left onto the main road that ran parallel to the lake. We flew down it, hoping to get ahead of the boat and flag the captain down. For a good fifteen minutes, the boat and our cars kept a steady pace.

"What if we lay on the horn?" Ivan asked over the walkie-talkie. "Do you think they'd hear it? Any hostiles around us would for sure."

"If there are people in that boat then it's worth it," Hayden said.

"Copy that," Ivan's voice crackled through. He repeatedly beeped the horn of the Range Rover. Not even a minute later, trees surrounded us on both sides.

"There're little islands in Lake Erie," Wade, who had jumped in the truck with us, said. "That'd be an almost perfect place to be. It's safe but far from supplies."

"Maybe the people are making a supplies run," I said.

"We'll go a bit farther," Hayden said with a nod. "Once we're out of the woods we'll be able to look around for another harbor."

We had crossed over the Pennsylvania border over a mile ago. Hayden kept a steady pace until we emerged onto a road with a clear view of the lake. The boat had vanished.

"There's a harbor three and a half miles from here," I said.

"How in the world do you know that?" Hayden asked, turning around to eye me.

"I used my amazing reading skills to read a sign," I told him with a smile. Hayden relayed the info to Ivan, who agreed to drive there and scope it out. More trees blocked our view of the lake and Hayden slowed down to a safer speed. We drove down a winding road that took us through the woods before emerging onto a small throughway covered in loose gravel.

The little harbor would have made the perfect background for a Hallmark card. We walked along the weathered wooden planks cautiously. There were ten spots; seven were filled.

"I don't think that boat would have fit in here," Brock stated, shaking his head.

"No," I agreed. "It wouldn't." I peered at the water and noticed something else rolling in. "We should go before the storm gets here," I suggested, pointing to the fast moving clouds.

"Not again," Hayden said with a sigh, glaring at the sky. "The boat might not fit in the spaces, but that doesn't mean they wouldn't come here. We should wait a few minutes. We might have passed them."

"True," I said and walked to the end of the dock. A few dozen small fish swam about. I tipped my head, looking at them.

"Find something interesting?" Hayden asked. He almost startled me; I was so engrossed by the fish I hadn't noticed him coming up behind me.

"Just fish."

"We should find some fishing gear and catch dinner," he said.

"These guys are small."

"Well," he began, placing his hands on my shoulders. "We can take one of the boats and go out on the lake."

"I'd like that," I told him, leaning back slightly. "I miss fishing."

His hands slid from my shoulders, down my back and around my waist. I put my hands over his and closed my eyes, resisting the urge to twist around, grab him, and kiss him.

"You can fire a gun, you know how to hunt, and you like to fish," he whispered, his breath warm on my neck. "You are the perfect woman."

I laughed. "I'm far from perfect and I'm the first to admit it."

"That guy's big," Hayden said and pointed to the water to avoid arguing with me over the different ways we viewed me.

"He is. I bet he'd taste good," I added, watching a large fish swim amongst the little ones. I was curious to see if he'd eat them. "Do you know what kind of fish that is?"

"Unfortunately, no. I was never good at ID-ing fish."

"Me neither," I admitted. "My grandma was though. She always knew. Sometimes I wondered if she just made it up because we wouldn't have known otherwise."

"Smart," Hayden chuckled. "I should have done that." He took a step closer, pressing his body against mine.

"You know what's weird?" I asked him, putting my hands over his.

"What?"

"Life has changed so much for us. Everything we knew is gone. But for animals nothing has changed. They're still going on now just as they did before zombies roamed the world."

"I never thought about it. That is weird in a way," he said softly and loosened his grip.

"Isn't it? They have no idea how different the world is."

"They're lucky," Hayden pointed out. He removed his hands from me and took a step back. I took one last look at the fish, wishing I had bread crumbs to throw in the water.

"No one's been here in ages," Ivan informed us when we rejoined the group. "Wherever that boat was going, it wasn't here."

"Should we try to fire up one of these?" Rider asked and waved his hand at the small boats in the dock. "We could try to track them down."

"I can drive a boat," Wade told us. "But I don't think we should go out with a storm coming in. Lake Erie won't get ocean-like waves, but I still don't want to be out there during a storm."

"Me neither," Brock agreed. "Two letdowns in a row: The school and the boat. Let's just go, get today over with, and have better luck tomorrow."

All agreeing, we got back into the cars. I slid into the backseat of the truck, Hayden—of course—drove and Ivan got into the passenger seat. As soon as Hayden put the truck in reverse, the roar of the boat's engine hummed in the distance. We raced back to the dock, eyes wide.

"Hey!" Ivan yelled, waving his hands. The boat veered in our direction. Ivan waved again. Excitement and anxiety swelled inside my heart. I was curious as to where this person came from and how many others they had back home.

"Shouldn't they be slowing down?" Rider asked apprehensively.

"Uh, yeah," Hayden said. "Guys, uh, let's go, get out of the way," he continued when the boat was only yards from the dock and still going full speed. We booked it away just in time for the boat to crash into the wood. The driver flew forward, toppling over the windshield, and smacking against the broken boards.

Wade got to him first, thinking he was going to help the poor man. Blood dripped down the boat driver's face. In a way that reminded me of how people moved when they were possessed in the movies, the guy sat up and growled.

"Of course," Rider spat and shook his head. "He's raging mad!"

Wade pulled out his pistol and shot the guy point blank. The body splashed into the water. Without speaking, we got into the cars and started down the winding road once again.

"Has Raeya said anything about me?" Ivan asked with a wink.

"Oh yeah, loads," I humored him.

"Is it still too soon to make a move?"

"I'm not sure. It's been…shit, I don't even know what day it is. Months. It's been months, let's put it that way. She hasn't talked about it and I don't want to bring it up."

"How did he die?" Ivan asked.

I still felt a pang of sadness over Seth's death. He was a good guy; good enough that I felt he actually deserved Ray. "Dropped dead from the virus."

"At least he didn't suffer," Hayden said to make me feel better.

"Yeah," I agreed. "I'll find out how she's doing with all that when we get back," I promised Ivan.

"Thanks," he said and smiled. "Do you think I have a chance with her? She's cute and charming, don't get me wrong, but she's the type of woman who seems like they'd have a type."

"To an extent," I informed him. Raeya liked to play it safe, know her options, and always be prepared with life and with dating. She went for the rare genuinely nice guys, preferred guys who put up with her constant planning, and needed someone she could trust. And being physically attractive was a plus.

The pickings were definitely slim in this world. But with his dazzling smile, beautiful dark skin, and muscular body, Ivan wasn't doing so bad. I'm sure in a pre-zombie world—and if Ray was single—she'd go on a date with Ivan. I wasn't sure how she'd handle a boyfriend who went out on missions. That would be the determining factor; the girl was a grand champion worrier.

"We could double date," Ivan joked. "We can all go to the cafeteria on Friday nights. It'd be so exciting!"

I laughed. "Just talk to her. Even if it doesn't work out, she's an awesome person to have as a friend."

Hayden turned on the stereo; Ivan immediately flipped through the iPod to find something other than country. Fat raindrops splattered onto the windshield. Hayden rolled up the windows and flicked the wipers on.

I leaned back in my seat, surprised that I was feeling what I would have to call homesick. I missed Raeya and Padraic. I was a little worried about Gabby since she had just lost Jessica. I hadn't been able to spend much time with Olivia, and I was really starting to feel guilty for that. I wanted to throw the tennis ball for Argos, play cards in the community room, eat bland yet warm food, shower, and most of all have some time alone with Hayden.

"Shit," Hayden said and slowed down. "Isn't this the way we came?"

"It looks like it," Ivan said, twisting around in his seat. "Didn't you go back the way we came?"

"I thought I did," Hayden sighed. "We should be on the main road by now."

"Keep going," Ivan suggested. "Even if this isn't the right way, I'm sure it will lead us back to the main road sooner or later."

"Right," Hayden said and pressed his foot on the gas again. Ten minutes later, we were even deeper in the forest.

"Where the hell are you going?" Brock's voice spoke over the walkie-talkie.

"Not sure," Hayden replied. "I thought this was the way we came."

"You're the one with the map," Brock teased.

"I'll check," Hayden said and set the walkie-talkie down. "Check the map?" he asked Ivan.

"Sure." Ivan unfolded the map. "I'd tell you where to go if I knew where we were."

"Dammit," Hayden cursed and hit the steering wheel.

"Well," Ivan cleared his throat. "If we're up here somewhere then we need to go this way." He traced a road with his finger. "We should only be a few miles from the main road."

"Alright," Hayden sighed.

I knew being in Pennsylvania bothered him. The road that we thought would be our exit was covered in fallen trees and branches. Forced to turn around and go even farther into the state, Ivan, who had been merrily chatting with me, grew quiet.

"Finally," Hayden breathed when the truck emerged from the trees. "We're on 100 West."

Ivan went over the map. "That street doesn't exist."

"I just saw the sign," Hayden countered. "One hundred and the letter 'W'. I know how to read a street sign."

"I'm not saying you don't. But I'm telling you, 100 West doesn't exist on this map."

"Maybe it was added after the map was made," I suggested. It was bound to happen.

"This map was made last year," Ivan said, shaking his head. "And this road doesn't look new. Plus, I don't think any state had money left for construction of any kind. Well, besides California and New York."

"I'll see where it goes," Hayden said through gritted teeth. "At least we can see what's around us."

The road was incredibly flat, as were the fields on either side of us. I looked intently at them; something seemed wrong. Everything was perfect and too man made. It gave off an eerie feeling. The distant low humming of giant windmills grew louder and louder.

We had three of those huge energy producing windmills back at the compound. They were kind of mesmerizing and a little scary. It was impossible to tell just how gargantuan they were until you drove up close. The humongous blades slowly spun in the wind. Amongst the windmills were dozens of identical, green pole barns. I had yet to see them in person but I recognized them right away.

"Greenhouses," I muttered. I remembered it like yesterday; my grandpa was so incredibly pissed when we first heard about them. He swore it would be the downfall of American farmers and he was right.

A greenhouse could grow crops year round and didn't rely on the weather. They could provide ten acres worth of plants in a building of just a few thousand square feet. Filled with rotating levels, fake sunlight, soil drenched in growth hormones, and the perfect amount of humidity in the air, greenhouses were guaranteed to provide America with fresh food all year round…if you could call tomatoes that never felt a ray of sunshine fresh.

Powered by the windmills, production costs were next to nothing. It was fast, cheap, and easy to harvest fruit and vegetables that grew inside a climate controlled building. The whole premise was that the low cost to grow and harvest would then be reflected in a drop in prices at the supermarket. Produce did get cheaper, just not as much as President Samael promised. The biggest difference was in the size of the crops.

Tomatoes the size of softballs, cantaloupes the size of watermelon…everyone thought they were getting a bargain, but what they were really getting was a daily dose of cancer. Or at least that's what my grandpa believed. He refused to buy anything that wasn't locally grown by someone he knew.

These greenhouse farms were placed across the country. Many of them—like this one—were near natural water sources. Supposedly they collected rain water as well. In theory, it was a great idea. But when you could spend the same amount on a five pound bag of homegrown potatoes as you could on a ten pound bag of lab grown potatoes, the choice was obvious. The economy was so bad no one could afford to eat organic.

Deciding the open space was as good as any to stop for a bathroom break, Hayden pulled the truck into the small parking lot next to a greenhouse. We quickly looked for zombies and after finding none, we got out.

I grabbed a tissue from my bag and walked around the corner of the greenhouse to pee.

"Hayden!" I called when I was done. I stood, pulling up my pants. He came running.

"Riss! You ok?"

"Yeah," I said not meeting his eyes. I swallowed and pointed to something on the ground. "Look." Still shaken, he stepped closer to me. "What?"

"Right there. Footprints."

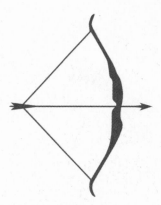

CHAPTER 19

"So?" he questioned, giving me a what-the-hell look. "I thought something was attacking you and you called me over here to look at *footprints*?"

"Yes. Someone was here."

"Someone could be anywhere, Riss. Zombies have free run over the place. I'm sure more than one has passed through here." He put his hand on mine. "Let's go."

"No," I said and pulled my hand away. "You're not looking. One set clearly walked up to the door. Not staggered or wandered. The path is straight; they meant to go inside." I moved closer to the prints. "And this set leaves the building, stepping on the ones going in. Someone went in and then out."

Hayden looked at the footprints for a second before saying, "You're right. Still, that doesn't mean much."

"Let's go in and see."

"We're not armed well enough," he reminded me. Since the tornado, none of us left the truck completely unarmed. I had my M9, two extra magazines, my knife, and a small pistol strapped to my ankle. Hayden had all that and more.

"Let me just see if the door is unlocked," I suggested.

"Ok," he agreed and stepped onto the cement pad that welcomed you to the front door. He pulled out his pistol, raised it and nodded. I put my hand on the knob and twisted.

"Dammit," I swore. "It's locked."

Hayden took his gun in his left hand and grabbed the door knob with his right. He jiggled it a few times, gave me his gun to hold and, with both hands, forced the knob to click open by breaking the lock.

I gave him his gun back. "That's why I love you," I said with a smile. Carefully, I pushed the door open. We were instantly blinded by harsh, ultraviolet lights. To be safe, I pulled out my gun, clicked the safety off and aimed it at chest level. For a full thirty seconds, we stood unmoving.

"I think the coast is clear," I whispered. "Why is the power on?"

"I'm assuming it never shut off," Hayden said, motioning to the windmills. "This place has probably been running nonstop. But there's no one to bring the water, plant seeds or harvest what grew."

Metal clinked as the top row of plants was rotated out for another row. Curiously, I peered inside. The building was tall; there were a dozen or more rows of plants with walkways in between each row. Each row was probably ten high—I didn't feel like counting—and were constantly rotated every minute.

The cement floor was swept clean. There were no dead, dried leaves, no spilled dirt or dropped vegetables. The air smelled of chemicals and not of soil and plants like a greenhouse should. At the opposite end of the greenhouse was a staircase that led to a walkway. I imagined scientists walking along it, reaching over the rails, and grabbing a piece of produce to hook up to a monitor and test.

I was about to turn and leave—the humidity was choking me—when a flash of purple caught my eye. Without thinking, I stepped from the doorframe and into the building. Following only a step behind me, Hayden kept his gun raised.

"It's an eggplant," I said. Before the row rotated, I grabbed it, twisting and snapping it off the vine. "Hayden, look." I held the football sized eggplant to my chest. "Every row." I blinked in disbelief.

"They all have plants. Growing plants," Hayden finished for me. "You were right; someone has been here."

I set the eggplant down. "We should check the other buildings. Make sure this isn't a weird fluke." Hayden nodded and took my hand. Still feeling a little stunned, we silently walked back to the cars.

"That was fast," Ivan said to us with a smile. "What, Underwood couldn't keep it up?"

I blinked, almost not catching his joke. "No, h-he can. The greenhouses work," I stammered.

"Huh?" Brock asked. He pushed himself off the Range Rover, which he had been leaning against.

"Riss saw footprints," Hayden explained. "We went into the greenhouse; I expected it to be full of dead, dried plants. But it's not, not at all. Or at least the one we went into."

"Someone's been taking care of them?" Brock asked incredulously. He ran a hand through his light brown hair. "Do you think crazy in the boat took care of them before he became infected?"

"It would make sense," Ivan stated.

Rider and Wade joined us. "What's going on?" Wade asked. Hayden quickly explained and we decided to split up in pairs and inspect the rest of the buildings. Hayden grabbed his machine gun and I slung the bow and arrows over my shoulder. We went over to the nearest building to the right. The biggest heads of lettuce I'd ever seen spilled over the top of the plastic beds.

The next greenhouse was filled with strawberries. The smell instantly made my mouth water. Hayden plucked two off and tossed one to me. I held it up; it was huge and bright red and promised to be juicy and sweet.

"What's the matter?" he asked and bit into his.

"My grandpa used to say that the hormones in these plants would cause cancer."

"Everything causes cancer," he said and picked off another. "Did you eat at restaurants?"

"Of course."

"Then you've already been exposed and you're fine. You're missing out," he told me and ate another.

Feeling silly for never thinking that restaurants would no doubt buy cheaper ingredients, I shrugged and devoured the strawberry.

"Ohmygod, this is orgasmic," I said and pulled off a few more, eager to shove them into my mouth.

"So that's all I have to do?" Hayden raised his eyebrows.

I nodded. "Right now, yeah. I think I could eat every strawberry in here. It's been months since I had fresh fruit!"

"Yeah," Hayden agreed with his mouth full. "We should bring some back for the ride home."

"I have to get some for Raeya!"

"I hate to break it to you, but we still have a while. I don't think they'd be good by then."

"Dammit," I said. "You're right."

We ate a few more before going into the greenhouse across the street. Unlike the others, this one didn't have rotating levels. Instead, it had rows of the weirdest looking trees I'd ever seen. I reached out and touched an apple.

Gleaming red and fricken huge, the heavy piece of fruit easily snapped off in my hands. I inspected it, remembering how my grandma used to take Raeya and me to the same orchard every fall to pick our own apples. I would climb up in the tree to get the best ones and then I'd throw them down to Ray. We'd spend the entire next day making apple pies, preserves, jams, and my favorite: Apple butter. When my grandma got so sick and weak that walking down the rows of trees became too much for her, Ray and I still went so we could bring her a basket of the prettiest apples we could find.

The trees in front of me were wrong, so wrong. It looked as if someone chopped off the top of the tree and stuck it on a four foot stump. The branches were held up by strong cables attached to the ceiling. I felt like a giant walking amongst the minuscule trees. It was so unnatural; I didn't like it one bit. I set the apple down and followed Hayden into another greenhouse, this one filled with radishes.

We had just stepped out of a green bean filled barn when Rider and Wade jogged over.

"Everything's fresh," Wade said. "In all of them."

I nodded. "That's how it was in the ones we looked in."

Hayden started toward the truck. Following suit, the three of us began walking with him.

"Should we load up the truck?" Rider asked. "Can you imagine how happy everyone will be when we show up with a bed full of fresh fruit?"

"It won't be all fresh by the time we get there," Hayden said grimly, eyeing the strawberries. "We still have a week."

"Oh," Rider sighed. "Right."

We walked the rest of the way to the truck in silence. Hayden jumped up in the bed and grabbed a water bottle. He drank half and offered it to me. Hot, sweaty, and thirsty, I quickly downed the warm water. I wished it were possible to keep a cooler stocked with ice.

A few minutes later, Ivan and Brock joined us, each carrying a box.

"Seeds," Brock explained and set the box next to the Range Rover. Rain started to sputter down on us again; he opened the tailgate and rearranged the items back there to make room for the seeds. Ivan told us that every greenhouse they went in had fast growing, healthy looking plants in it.

"Harvest time?" Brock asked and slammed the tailgate down.

Hayden shook his head. "Not everything will last the week's drive."

"We can't leave all this," Brock said, motioning to the greenhouses.

"No," Hayden agreed. He shifted his weight uncomfortably, his eyes moving from the truck to the greenhouses several times.

"It's your call," Brock said in a level tone. "Whatever you decide, I'll agree with."

Rider, Wade, and Ivan nodded. I didn't know Hayden officially called the shots. I wondered why he never told me that before and why he didn't use his authority more often.

"It would be a waste," Ivan agreed with Brock. "We could freeze a lot of this stuff and it could last us until our own crops grow."

"You're right," Hayden said. "We can't pass this up."

"What about the people who grew this?" Rider asked shyly. "I'm not saying they need it more than we do, but do you think we should try to find them?"

Hayden's eyes met mine. I shook my head and he nodded, getting what I implied.

"The whole situation is weird," I stated. "Why invest the time and energy to grow crops and then leave them? I would be protecting our food source with my life."

"What about the person driving the boat?" Wade brought up.

I bit my lip as I thought. "I suppose. I don't know…it still seems like a huge risk to rely on. I suppose it's possible though. Maybe they come over and set up the greenhouses once a week or something."

"And it's not like we are going to clean them out," Ivan said. "We can't fit that much into the bed of the truck."

"We're not supposed to be here," Hayden reminded us. "Let's get the food and go."

Ivan nodded. "How should we do this? I think it would be the fastest to work together with one as a look out."

"Sounds good," Hayden said and took the keys of the truck from his pocket. "Let's start at that end and work our way down."

We loaded up in our cars and drove to the first greenhouse. Brock said there were more boxes in the storage shed were they had found the seeds. Hayden suggested I be the lookout. Though picking vegetables and lugging the heavy boxes into the truck bed wasn't exactly a fun time, it beat standing in the humid drizzle.

My skin was sticky and I desperately wanted to shower. I unbraided my hair and, without even attempting to comb it out, flipped my head upside down, and twisted it into a bun. The air was too thick to have any hair touching my neck.

I flicked the safety off my machine gun and waited, carefully keeping a watchful eye. The rain and clouds had moved on by the time the guys came out of the first greenhouse. Along with the humid air, the hot sun beat down on us.

It took hours to get everything picked, packed, and loaded. Along with being hot and sweaty, the guys were now tired. Hayden complained that his back hurt from leaning over. Ivan found a working hose hooked up to a well around the back of the storage shed. We suspected it was used to fill the water tanks when the rainwater ran low. We quickly hosed off, changed into clean clothes, and got into the cars.

The bed of the truck was full. Except for a miniscule amount of room left around the machine gun, there was no space left for anything else. Paying careful attention to the map, we headed southwest.

Knowing our chances of finding survivors walking down the road were slim to none, we were all content with the thoughts of being home in half a day. We drove straight through for four hours, making good time. We had to avoid several pile ups and stalled cars on the highway and sped through a zombie infested town in northern Ohio.

We were near Columbus when the sunlight started to fade. We pulled into an empty parking lot in front of a dentist's office. Hayden used the five gummies milling about as target practice with the bow. His first shot missed, his second hit the gummy in the thigh and his third hit one in the heart.

"Relax," I reminded him. "And stop looking at the arrow; look at your target. That's what I do at least." Hayden let out his breath, refocused, and released the arrow. "See!" I said excitedly. "I'm a good teacher."

"Yes you are," he agreed and walked over to pull the arrow out of the gummy's head. He flicked the brain matter off and retrieved the other two arrows. We went around the building to find the other deteriorated humans. One was stuck in a sewage ditch—he was an easy target. Two others staggered in our direction going at snail speed.

Hayden's first arrow whizzed past, grazing the S3's head. A flap of skin peeled off, but it wasn't enough to kill the bastard. Hayden fired again and nailed him in the eye. He got the second one on his first try.

"He's not even worth shooting," I said when we walked over to the third gummy who was dragging himself along the ground. "Is it pathetic that I feel kind of sorry for him?" I asked Hayden, tipping my head to the side.

"No, I do too," he agreed. The creature in front of us only had one arm. His legs had been chewed; most of the skin was gone and the bones were splintered and broken. His face was crusted in pus and blood. Needless to say, he smelled worse than shit.

Hayden took an arrow and easily pushed it through the thing's head. His skull was about as strong as a moldy orange. He shook off the mucous and put the arrow back in the quiver. We rejoined our group who was already eating dinner. Careful not to send our boxes of fruit and veggies falling, Hayden put the tailgate down and hopped up while I grabbed us food.

"Do you have zombie crap on your hands?" I asked him before giving him the tuna and crackers I was holding.

Hayden inspected his hands. "Don't think so. And it doesn't matter for me, remember?"

"I know," I told him. "It can make you regular sick, remember?"

"Yeah," he sighed. "But we don't have soap or water. Too bad."

"Hang on," I told him and set the food down. I had forgotten that Padraic gave me a bottle of hand sanitizer several missions ago. I rooted around in my bag for it. "I know you touched those gummies," I said to Hayden and held out the bottle.

"I don't need that, Riss," he said defiantly.

"I don't need you sick," I retorted.

"I won't get sick. I haven't yet."

"Hayden, just take it. It's not hard and it won't hurt."

"I don't want it," he argued.

"Please?" I tried.

"Fine," he huffed and held out his hand. I squeezed a large drop of the hand sanitizer onto his palm.

"Underwood, you are such a baby," Ivan teased. "It's a good idea," he said and held out his hands. "We might not get infected, but think of all the nasty shit we touch. I'm surprised we haven't gotten sick more often."

We passed the bottle around, agreeing it would be a good idea to 'wash up' before eating from now on. We ate our rationed meals and really had to resist stuffing our faces full of apples, strawberries, oranges, and bananas.

Another night spent sleeping uncomfortably in the cars slowly passed. We awoke with the sun, got out to stretch, and ate a rushed breakfast. The sun was already beating down hot rays on the black truck. And we weren't allowed to use the air conditioning.

I leaned against the cool window in the backseat. The wind blowing in from Hayden's open window felt wonderful as we sped along at seventy miles an hour down a stretch of highway. He and Brock were busy talking about football. I thought it was totally irrelevant since I felt confident that at least ninety-five percent of the NFL was dead.

But I admit it was nice hearing a normal conversation. I kept my mouth shut and closed my eyes. We had to do some off roading to go around parked cars that stretched out for several miles on the highway. We splashed through a swampy cornfield and onto a gravel road. Not wanting rocks to fly up and damage the truck, Hayden drove slowly.

Sunlight glinting off the back window caught my attention immediately. It wasn't unusual in the least to see a car pulled over on the side of the road or even stopped in the middle of the road. What did strike me as odd was the mud splashed all over the navy blue Chevy Impala.

"Stop," I said suddenly.

"Why?" Hayden said and slammed on the brakes.

"That car back there," I said as I twisted in my seat. "It's dirty."

"So is everything," Hayden reminded me. "There's no one left to clean it." He took his foot off the brake.

"No, Hayden, stop. The car is dirty like it just splashed though the same mud we did. It rained yesterday remember? It would have washed it away."

"Shit," he swore and told Ivan to stop over the walkie-talkie.

"How the hell do you notice things like that?" Brock asked.

"I don't know. I just do," I admitted. "I kinda wish I didn't. Then we'd still be on our way home."

"You would have made a good detective," Brock told me. "You see things other people don't."

"Thanks. I wanted to be an actress, though. It's a selfish thing to want to be, I realize now." Even if all the zombies were killed tomorrow and the world went back to being how it was, I would never desire to be an actress again. There was no way I could sit idly by while horrible things happened. I never thought I could make a difference in this world until now.

Maybe I wasn't. Maybe taking out a dozen zombies here and there wouldn't even put a notch in the numbers. Our food supply was bound to run low, our livestock was a calling card for zombies, and our safe space was so limited it was pointless to even try and repopulate the earth. Maybe searching and saving people was a total moot point since we were all damned to die in the end.

But maybe it wasn't.

Hayden put the truck in park, cut the engine, and reached behind him to retrieve his gun from the back seat. Rider pulled himself up through the sunroof in the Range Rover and stood on its roof, looking around for zombies.

"Clear, from what I can see," he told us and hopped off the SUV. Armed, the six of us walked around the Impala. Wade opened the driver's door.

"No keys," he informed us after he searched. "But look." He pointed to the back. "Water bottles, a bag of peanuts, and some cans of food. I'd guess someone was coming back."

"Wait?" Ivan suggested.

Hayden shook his head. "That could take too long. We should try and find them."

"How?" Rider asked, looking around. "They could be anywhere."

There was about twenty yards of overgrown grass and weeds off the road that melted into a forest. My eyes scanned the grass. Once I saw what I was looking for I said, "I can track them."

"Really?" Wade asked incredulously.

"Yeah. It's not any different than tracking animals. Sometimes it's easier; people are so obvious."

"Sweet." He tipped his head slightly. "How do you know how to do that?"

"I've been hunting with my grandpa since I was seven. I picked up a few things," I explained.

"Can you teach me?" he asked almost shyly.

"I can try," I promised. I went back to the truck and pulled out a backpack to load up with supplies.

"Wait," Brock said. "Our cars. And the food." He motioned to the bed of the truck. "What if they come back and we're not here?"

"We can't leave it," Hayden stated. For a split second I thought he might order us to go straight home. "Three stay here and guard it and three go." Already deciding he was coming with me, Hayden took the keys to his truck from his pocket and held them up. "Who else is going?"

"I'll go," Wade said quickly.

Hayden tossed his keys to Brock. "Leave if need be but double back and meet us half a mile down the road. I'll keep in contact," he said and patted the walkie-talkie.

Ivan nodded. "Be careful."

"We'll be fine," Wade said and patted his machine gun. "If all else fails we'll climb a tree," he said and winked at me.

Ivan half smiled. "Remember the range isn't very far."

Hayden nodded. "I'll check to make sure we don't get past the point without letting you know. We're wasting time though, let's go."

Leading the way, I followed the trail of bent grass and weeds.

"What range are you talking about?" I asked as I slapped a mosquito off the back of my neck.

"The walkie-talkies," Hayden clarified. "After three miles the signal is lost."

"Really?" I was surprised. "I thought you guys had high tech military walkie-talkies."

"We do," Wade huffed. "But they don't work."

"Really?" I asked again.

"Yeah. They used satellite signals," Wade continued explaining. "The ones we have now use radio waves."

"Why don't the satellite signals work?" I asked.

"Wouldn't I like to know," Wade said with a sigh.

"Eventually they'd stop working," I thought out loud. "Since there's no one left to fix them. But that shouldn't have happened already." I shook my head. "Like a week after the virus hit we found out that the GPS in the Range Rover didn't work. It just doesn't make sense." I turned around just in time to see Hayden's muscles stiffen. He cast his eyes down from mine.

I turned and focused on the weeds. With some of them still dead and dry from the winter, it was easy to see where these people had gone.

"It doesn't make any sense," Wade agreed. "But if you think about the panic the initial outbreak caused it's easy to imagine someone freaking out and hitting the power button, so to speak."

"Right," I spoke but wasn't sold on the idea. Thinking about it made a knot form in my stomach. I couldn't put the puzzle together without all the pieces. I shook my head again, telling myself it wasn't worth it to worry about…yet.

The grass gave way to the leaf-covered forest floor. The trees were sparse at first but quickly became dense, no doubt blocking us from the others' view.

"I get the bent grass, but now what are you looking for?" Wade asked me.

"Foot traffic. Footprints are obvious but not always there so you have to look for other things, like this," I said and knelt down, pointing to the disturbance in the dead leaves. "See how they're all moved around? We're lucky; whoever walked through here made zero attempts to be discreet."

"I never would have noticed that," Wade admitted.

"You don't notice stuff like this," I informed him, "unless you're looking. The ground is soft here and probably even softer deeper in the woods. You can see the boot print over there."

Hayden and Wade nodded. "And there," Hayden pointed out.

"Yeah," I said. "It looks like there were three people walking through here, and one of them was big."

"How can you tell?"

I took a few steps forward until I found a clearer print. "This imprint is deeper than the others. The more you weigh, the more you sink into the mud."

"It makes so much sense I feel dumb for not picking up on it," Hayden laughed.

"Really," I said again. "It's easy not to notice stuff like this unless you're looking. And who walks with their eyes on the ground?"

"Speaking of," Hayden said and paused. "Riss, you track. Wade and I should keep an eye and ear out for zombies."

"Good idea," I agreed.

We walked a few yards before I stopped. "Seriously?" I sighed and stared at the patch of pricker bushes in front of me.

"What?" Hayden and Wade asked in unison.

"Dumbasses walked straight through those," I told them, motioning to the thorny vines. "Stay here while I go around. I'll use you as a visual to pick up the trail again."

I picked my way over a rotting log, wondering why the hell those people would choose to walk through the prickers. Even in jeans, they poked into your skin, causing little red scratches that burned and itched.

"Oh," I said aloud as soon as I got in front of the bushes. "There's a path," I called over my shoulder. If I had bothered to look up and out every now and then I would have noticed it. Once the boys joined me I asked, "Ok, without looking at the ground, can you tell which way they went?"

"That way," Hayden said, pointing to our right.

"Why?" I quizzed.

"It seems right."

I smiled. "You're actually right. Look." I took a few paces in that direction and touched an overhanging branch. "People have the tendency to snap off anything that's in their way." I put my fingers around the broken twig. "You can tell it's freshly broken by looking at where the branch is broken. See how it's fresh?"

Hayden's fingers graced mine as he felt the inside of the break. "Better than bread crumbs, right?" he asked.

"Right," I answered with a smile. We continued hiking the path following the obvious trail. At one point whoever we were tracking stopped for a snack; peanut shells littered the ground. Certain that the people stuck to the already made trail, I occasionally glanced down to make sure we were still hot on their tracks. Distracted by the distant babbling of a stream, I looked around the woods for it.

Out of the corner of my eye, it caught my attention. I stopped so suddenly that Hayden walked into me. His hand flew around my arm to keep me from falling.

"What is it?" he asked his voice almost shaky. He let go of me and raised his gun.

At a temporary loss for words, I pointed to the trampled ground and pulled an arrow from my quiver, expecting the worst.

"Holy shit," Wade swore.

I only nodded in agreement as my eyes darted around the woods. Why did the birds have to be so fucking loud? My eyes darted back to the tracks that had been left by zombies. If the scuffled leaves weren't obvious enough of the staggering dead, then the bits of flesh scraped off on tree bark were a big giveaway.

"They went that way," I whispered, pointing more or less toward the highway.

"Recently?" Hayden asked, his hand already grabbing the walkie-talkie.

There was a puddle inside one of the trenches left by a dragged foot. "I don't think so." I hurried over to a tree and poked at a chunk of flesh with my fingernail. It was crusty. "At least a day or two ago." I shook my head. "That doesn't mean they're not near." I let out a breath of relief and stuck the arrow back in the quiver, hoping it wasn't a premature move.

"And our civilians?" Wade asked.

"They walked right over the tracks. I doubt they even noticed."

Wade shook his head in disbelief. "And they say ignorance is bliss."

Hayden put his hand on the small of my back. "Keep tracking," he told me. "We'll keep an eye out. I want to find these people as fast as we can and get out of here."

I flicked another mosquito off my arm. "I wish we had bug spray," I complained and picked up the trail again. The mosquitoes grew in number the closer we came to the water, which turned out to be a shallow creek. The muddy sludge and low walls made me think it was a run off creek filled with rain water.

We kept walking, Hayden periodically checked in with Ivan to see how far we'd wandered. With no more signs of zombies, I was able to relax—only just a little—and nearly enjoy the walk through the woods.

That is until I saw something that made me stop dead in my tracks again. Hayden and Wade sprang into position. I waved my hand at them.

"No zombies," I said breathlessly, my eyes scanning a huge tree off the trail.

"Then what is it?" Hayden asked, sounding annoyed.

"I've been here before," I said hoarsely. I forced my eyes off of the huge Eastern Cottonwood tree.

"Huh?" Hayden questioned.

I shook my head. I didn't know why it shocked me so much. "I've been here before," I repeated.

"Like in a dream?" Wade asked seriously. He pushed his eyebrows together and stared at me.

"No," I spat. "Like on vacation. This is a park. Alum State Park."

"Ok," Wade said not believing me at all.

"No, really!" With both hands, I motioned to the tree. "This tree isn't something you forget. I'm telling you, I've been here before." I spun around to look at Hayden. "I used to live in Ohio, remember?"

He pulled his shoulders back and looked at the tree. "I remember." His eyes scanned the tree before locking with mine. "You sure you've been here?"

"Yes," I promised. "If we keep going north, we'll come to a campground."

"Let's go to it," he said with a smile. He tried to relay the message to Ivan, but we were too far. Ordering Wade and me to say put, he set down his backpack full of supplies and jogged back down the trail until he was close enough to reach Ivan. I hated every minute of him being out of my sight.

"He'll be fine," Wade said, playfully punching my arm.

"I'm not worried," I lied.

"Bullshit. You *look* worried."

I sighed. "Ok, I am. I don't like not knowing. Anything could happen. Zombies or even falling and twisting an ankle. And I'd never know."

"So you think you can keep bad things from happening?"

"Of course not. I wish I could, but I know I can't. If I'm with him—or anyone else for that matter—at least I know what's going on."

Wade gave me a teasing smile. "You two are good together."

I tried to force myself not to blush; I failed. "Thanks." I hit another mosquito. Even as hot as it was, I unrolled the sleeves to the blue plaid, button up shirt I had on over a pink tank top. Suddenly feeling light headed, I removed my backpack and sat on the damp ground. I took a water bottle from my bag and drank half of it thinking I'd feel better after I rehydrated.

I concentrated on what was around me; the huge tree, the leaves, forest floor greenery, birds, and the bright sunlight that filtered through the trees and checkered the path. Finally we heard Hayden's footfalls.

"All good," he told us and let out a deep breath. "It's fucking hot," he panted. "As much as we bitched about the cold, I'd rather run in it than run in the heat."

I unzipped Hayden's bag and tossed him a water bottle. While he drank it I stood up, my vision clouding with black fuzzy spots. The next thing I knew Wade put his arms around me.

"Riss?" he asked, steadying me. Hayden recapped his water and rushed over.

I shook my head. "Stood up too fast, I suppose." I took a deep breath and smiled. "Let's go."

"We can stay a while," Wade suggested, still concerned.

"I'm fine," I protested. "Don't tell me you've never had that happen."

"Only when I'm sick," he said quietly. His eyes left mine and found Hayden's, thinking Hayden would give me the order to stop and rest. I brushed mud off my ass and picked up my bag.

"Let's go," I said with too much pep.

"Orissa," Hayden said gently. "Are you sure you're alright?"

"If I wasn't I'd tell you. I'm fine now."

Wade laughed. "I told you that you were stressing," he said to me.

"Shut up," I shot back. It was apparent Hayden felt left out of the conversation.

"She wants to put a leash on you," Wade said to Hayden.

"Yes," I agreed. "A leather leash and handcuffs so I can make you my bitch," I joked. "Seriously, guys, I'm fine now."

"Ok," Hayden said with a nod. I picked up where we left off, following the footprints along the trail. Adrenaline pumped through my body and I whipped an arrow out of the quiver with record speed when I heard a rustling through the brush. I waited, swallowed, and laughed.

"Zombie bunnies," Wade said, lowering his gun. "Don't let the little fluffers fool you; they are quite deadly."

"And no one will ever suspect him," Hayden said gravely. "He'll get away and continue his reign of terror."

We laughed and continued on and soon came up to a road.

"The campground is down there," I whispered. "I know the road is curvy, but I can't remember exactly how close we are." I pointed to the muddy footprints leading down the road. "They walked down the road. Once the mud's off their shoes, I have nothing to follow. I think it'd be best to go in through the trees."

Hayden nodded. "I'll go first. If we find the people, watch them before talking to them. If they seem sketchy, leave."

"Sounds good," I told him. We went along the road a few more yards before cutting into the woods.

One of my grandpa's favorite summer pastimes was to drive out to the middle of the woods with a lawn chair, a beer, five tennis balls, and a blindfold. He'd set up his chair and place the tennis balls around it, blindfold himself, and sit back and wait. It was my job to sneak up unnoticed and take the tennis balls.

I completely failed at first. Patient, my grandpa sat in that chair for hours while I figured out how to walk in silence. And when it wasn't possible, I learned how to move in ways that mimicked forest animals. I was always scared of being mistaken for a deer and getting shot by a random hunter in the woods.

Windy days were ideal. I'd move one foot when the gust went by, masking the sound of movement. Sometimes it took forever just to move mere feet, but it worked. A flock of geese noisily flew above us; I'd move again. Loud planes were even better. Occasionally my grandpa would move, either shifting position or reaching up to scratch his back. If he moved, I moved.

It seemed so simple but was so hard to master. It was an important skill to know, my grandpa told me again and again. Not only useful for sneaking up on someone, but it was a skill that could help me get away if need be.

Precariously placing my foot down and distributing my weight from heel to toe, I slipped off the road without a sound. I bent down to avoid any contact with low hanging branches. Not only was the snapping of twigs a good way to give yourself away, but the unnatural swinging of the trees was a sure fire way to catch someone's attention.

As graceful as a cat, my body moved along with the forest. I wished my grandpa was here with me now. My heart ached and I closed my eyes; I couldn't let myself feel anything but determination right now. I took another carefully planned step.

Twigs snapped and leaves crunched. I whirled around and glared at Hayden and Wade.

"Could you be any louder?" I scolded in a hushed voice. "You're gonna give us away or they're gonna think you're a zombie lumbering through the woods."

"Sorry," Wade whispered back. I waited so I could watch them move. Hayden picked up his feet and looked before he put them down. His machine gun across his back caught on a branch, bent it back and sent it flying into Wade's face. I put my hand over my mouth to keep from laughing.

"Heel-toe," I whispered, lifting up my foot to show them. "It'll make the crunching sound less like footfalls. Stay low and don't push branches out of your way. Move out of theirs."

After his gun caught on a tree once more, Hayden took it off of his back and held it at his side. I smiled, wondering if it was dumb that I felt proud of him, and turned back around.

We continued to painstakingly pick our way through the forest, and soon we heard voices…

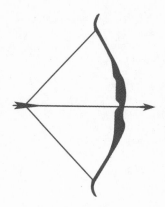

CHAPTER 20

We heard their voices right after I smelled the familiar scent of a campfire. Hayden clicked the safety off his gun and stayed close by me. I counted eight people. I assumed there were more I couldn't see. Three tents were set up in front of an RV. A silver SUV, an old Ford truck, and black sedan formed a semi circle around the campsite.

An older man with white hair poked at the fire. Two young girls dumped contents of a can into a metal pot and carried it over to the man. He set it on the fire and snatched his hand away, shaking it.

"Burn yourself, Buddy?" a female voice called.

"Singed the hairs," he replied with a smile.

A very skinny toddler ran out of a tent. Only a second later, his equally thin father dashed out and picked him up. The kid instantly started crying. His father clamped his hand over the boy's mouth, shushing him before kissing him on the back of the head.

"I know you're hungry," I heard him say. "We all are. You'll eat soon."

The group milled about, talking quietly. Every now and then we'd catch part of what they were saying. Every one of them seemed malnourished and exhausted. The two young girls clasped hands and walked away from the fire. Both had frizzy blonde hair and matching freckles across their pale faces. One was slightly taller than the other.

"Don't worry, Addison," she said to the shorter girl as she put her arm around her shoulder. "We'll find food soon. We have before, remember?"

Addison nodded and wiped a tear from her face. It was hard to guess the age of someone so filthy and starving, but I assumed Addison to be ten since she was the same height as Lisa. Her friend was maybe twelve or thirteen.

"Quinn!" the tall girl called and was immediately shushed by the others. "Quinn!" she called again in a much softer voice. The crying toddler unsteadily ran over. He too had blonde hair and freckles.

"Lizzy!" the baby's father scolded. "Don't let your brother that close to the fire. We've been over this before; you don't listen!"

"I've got him," she said and scooped him up. She spun around with him in her arms, causing Quinn to laugh. Lizzy, Quinn the baby, and Addison sat on a picnic table in front of the RV, grumbling about being hungry. I felt bad for them and remembered all too well our days spent on the run with barely any food to eat.

The RV door opened with a screech of the hinges. The camouflage uniforms immediately caught Hayden and Wade's attention. One man held a rifle and was looking at a map. I couldn't hear what they were saying. They beckoned someone named Amos over; a man the same age as my grandpa—if not older—hobbled to them.

They spoke in hushed voices as if they didn't want the others to hear. The guy with the gun looked around nervously as if he expected zombies to rush from the trees. He was smart…and scared. People do stupid things when they're scared. They act without thinking and if three bodies emerged from the forest, they would most likely shoot.

Very slowly, I turned and motioned for Hayden and Wade to follow. Once we made it fifty feet away, I whispered, "What do you think?"

"They seem harmless," Hayden responded. "Only one was armed that we saw. The others…they just look pathetic."

"We need to help them," Wade agreed.

"We should come from the road," I suggested. "Less surprise that way and less chance of being mistaken for zombies."

Hayden nodded and smiled. "I don't feel like getting shot again."

I rolled my eyes. "You're not. Never again." I smiled too and tip toed out of the forest.

"How should we do this?" Wade asked once our feet hit the pavement. "Just walk up to them. It seems like it would be kinda…kinda…"

"Awkward?" I finished for him.

"Yeah."

"Oh well," Hayden said with a shake of his head. "We'll know right away the nature of the group. I'm guessing once they learn we have food, they'll be more than welcoming. Weapons down but stay ready."

Even though I saw the pathetic state the group was in, I couldn't help the ball of nerves that formed in my stomach. The last time we picked up random strangers, Brock was bitten and two people were shot. Needless to say I wasn't in the trusting mood.

Hayden went first. "Hello!" he called out as if we weren't sure anyone was in the camp. The hush that fell over the civilians was unmistakable. Then a minute of chaos erupted when the survivors realized they weren't alone.

As I expected, the two guys in military attire approached us first. The guy holding the gun was probably no taller than my five-foot-seven frame. Sandy blonde hair fell into his eyes and he shook his head to move it out of the way. His partner was taller and at one point over weight. The way his clothes hung off his body suggested he'd recently lost a lot of it. No diet is as effective as the zombie apocalypse diet.

I fought the urge to put my fingers around the metal of my gun. I waited as the guys sized us up, wondering if Hayden was going to hold up his hands and say: 'we come in peace.' Instead, he casually said, "Hey."

Blondie lowered the gun and took a step forward. Careful to keep his hand slightly extended at his sides, Hayden also moved closer.

"I'm Sergeant Underwood. This is Lance Corporal Williams and…Orissa," Hayden introduced, turning slightly in my direction. I smiled warmly at the strangers, thinking I should come up with a fancy sounding title as well. "We have a secure base down south; we've been looking for survivors," Hayden explained.

"I'm Zack," the blonde with the gun informed us. "This is Colin." He lowered the gun and looked at us. Wade was right; this was awkward. Finally Colin shook his head.

"Wait a second, are you saying you have a safe place to stay and we're welcome?"

"That's exactly what I'm saying," Hayden said. "I can tell you more about it if you want."

"Yes!" Colin exclaimed.

I stepped up next to Hayden and spoke to the strangers. "You should probably tell your friends first. I'm sure they're wondering what the hell is going on."

"Right," Colin said and turned. Zack kept a suspicious eye on us while we followed them back to their camp site. Their buddies had gathered in a small group, peering around the trees to catch a glimpse of us. I knew right away that there were more than eight people.

"This is Underwood, Williams and Or-iss-a," Zack told his group. I was tempted to correct the pronunciation of my name. "They say they came from a zombie safe house and are looking for survivors to take back."

There was a moment of stunned silence before the group burst into questions. I hung back, keeping an eye out for zombies while Hayden and Wade explained everything. It didn't take long to convince these people to come back with us.

There were eleven in their group; half had met at an emergency shelter in Iowa when the virus first broke out and had stuck together ever since. Zack and Colin were in the National Guard and were ordered to protect the shelter. Like my soldier and Marine friends, they had no idea that zombies existed until the outbreak. The others joined up randomly here and there. In a very familiar tale, they told us about how they were staying on a farm until zombies crashed the party.

Hayden, Wade, and I stepped aside. Hayden wiped sweat off his forehead with the back of his hand.

"One of us needs to go find communication and tell the others to drive down this way. We'll feed these guys," he looked back at the eleven hungry and hopeful sets of eyes that didn't look away from us, "help them pack up their stuff and leave."

"I'll go," Wade offered.

Hayden shifted his weight and sighed. "It would make more sense for Orissa to go," he admitted, cringing as if the thought of me going off on my own was painful. "She's been here before; if she needs to run from anything she'll be able to find her way back."

He pried the walkie-talkie off his belt and reluctantly handed it to me. I took the M16 from around my shoulder and gave it to Hayden.

"I can run faster without it," I reminded him before he had a chance to object. "I'll fire one warning shot if I see a herd. I'll be fine and I'll be fast."

"I hope—I mean, I know," Hayden told me. "Be careful, Riss."

"You be careful too. I'm not sold on trusting these people yet." I looked into Hayden's hazel eyes. "Watch your back."

"I'll be ok," he promised.

I nodded. Before I turned to leave, I scanned the campground once more. When I found what I was looking for I quickly took off, jogging over to a washhouse. It wasn't working of course, and I didn't expect it to. In front of washhouses or bathrooms, campgrounds often had a posted map with a 'you are here' feature.

I pushed open the little mailbox under the large, laminated map and retrieved a slightly water damaged map. I traced my route back to the road with my finger and then followed the road to the campground.

"How far past that big tree did you have to go to have service?" I asked Hayden, holding up the walkie-talkie.

"About a quarter mile," he responded. I nodded, trying to visualize what one fourth of a mile would look like on a winding trail.

"Ok. I'll be fast. If the guys can't figure out where they are, I'll come back, tell you, and bring them the map."

"You don't have to come back just to leave again," Hayden said. "It's hotter than hell. If they can't figure it out just go and get here quick."

I nodded, folded up the map to stick in my back pocket, and took off back up the trail. I gave up jogging after a hundred yards or so. I let out a deep breath, cursing the hundreds I had l left. I wanted to take my long sleeve shirt off but didn't since the bugs were so bad and taking it off meant that I'd have to take my weapons off too; that was something I wasn't willing to do.

I stopped and listened for zombies. When I heard nothing but the normal sounds of the forest, I started running again. I had just passed the big tree when I saw a blur of dingy yellow. I slowed, unable to quickly catch my breath in this humid air and pulled an arrow from the quiver. I pulled it back on the bow and waited for the zombie to stagger closer.

Barefoot, her feet were nothing but shreds of dead skin and bone. Her once long dress that used to be yellow was filthy, covered in mud, blood, spoiled bodily fluids, and God knows what else. I let the arrow go. I nestled itself nicely in her skull and pinned her to a tree. Not wanting to waste any time yanking the arrow from the bark of the old tree, I kept moving.

"Hello?" I said into the walkie-talkie. When I got no response, I ran a few more yards. "Hello?" I repeated. Again, nothing. This time I sprinted and ended up running farther than I needed to. "Hello?" I said for the third time, panting.

"Penwell?" Ivan's calm, level voice spoke.

"Who else would it be?" I replied.

"Right. What's going on?"

"We found the people. They set up a camp. I have a map, I'll give you directions," I said shortly. I looked around once more and plopped to my butt while I waited for Ivan to go over his own map. I went over how to find the camp twice to be certain Ivan understood since we would lose communication once he started driving. I stood and, using the map as a fan, started walking back to the camp. Once I reached the big tree I decided to run despite the heat just to reach the damn camp sooner.

I was drenched in sweat by the time I got back. Hayden and Wade were sitting at the picnic table talking to Zack and Colin and the old man who I believed they called Amos. Hayden smiled and stood up when I came into view.

"That was fast," Colin stated.

"I didn't have to go far," I panted. I removed my weapons, sank down next to Hayden on the bench, and got a bottle of water from my bag. "They're on their way," I told Hayden and Wade. "It shouldn't take long." Once I caught my breath and drank half the bottle of water, I stood and unbuttoned my shirt. It stuck to my sweaty skin as I peeled it off. I sat back down and sighed, surveying our surroundings.

Colin turned his attention back to the guys. "And you've been there long?" he asked.

"I've been there since mid December," Wade said and looked at Hayden. "You've been there a little longer."

Hayden nodded. "Yeah. I think I got to the compound a few weeks before you found us," he told Wade.

"The compound?" Zack questioned.

Hayden nodded again. "I was headed to Parris Island; another sergeant and I agreed to meet there when shit hit the fan. We ran across quite a few survivors along the way and brought them with us, intending on setting up camp in South Carolina. We decided to start looking for civilians. It was pure luck we ran into Colonel Fuller.

"He knew about the bomb shelter. It was built over fifty years ago, but it's been updated and modernized. We took the people we had there, set up what we could, and started making runs for supplies, weapons and ammo, and anyone alive."

"How many have you saved?" Amos asked, his voice surprisingly strong and deep for someone his age.

"Probably close to three hundred and fifty," Wade answered after a moment's consideration. "We found people like crazy at first. It's dwindled down until now. This is the biggest group we've come across."

"We can thank Amos for that," Colin said with a nod of his head in the old man's direction. "He's been the brains of this operation."

"I couldn't do it on my own," Amos said humbly. "Buddy's been just as big of help as me. Speaking of, where is the bastard? Buddy!" he called. The white-haired man that burned his arm in the fire stepped out of the RV. Being tired, dirty, and worn had obviously aged him. When he sat down at the table with us, I guessed he was no older than forty-five.

"What are you hollering about?" Buddy asked with a wink.

"Sit your ass down and listen to these guys!" Amos said gruffly.

"I'd love to," Buddy spoke. "But I'm outta place here," he said with a smile. "I was going to leave the master planning to the military guys—and gal."

"What military?" Amos spat. "We're all that's left."

"So," Buddy said brightly. "What's the plan?"

"Eat and leave," Hayden said simply. "We want to get out of here as soon as possible. It's impossible to secure a perimeter with all the trees. What kind of weapons do you have?"

"We don't have too much, I'm afraid," Buddy informed us with a shake of his head. "And we're low on ammo."

"We can help with that," Hayden insisted.

I looked at the gun in Zack's hands, wondering where he'd acquired an AK47. "We mostly have

5.56 NATO cartridges; we prefer our M16s. I know there's a few 7.62 cal's in our supply; it'll be enough to get us home."

"Thanks," Zack said, seeming a little awe struck. "Do you have big artillery back at the compound?"

"Yeah," Wade answered. "We don't waste ammo, but I feel confident saying we won't run out any time soon."

A woman wearing a long floral-print skirt emerged from a tent carrying a small bucket of something. Curious, I watched her walk over to the fire, set the bucket down, and begin waving her hands at the flames.

She spoke softly and quickly to the fire. Then she took a handful of something in the bucket and threw it on the burning logs, causing the fire to sizzle and glow green for a split second. She raised her hands to the sky and spun around before picking up the bucket. Walking in a circle around the camp, she sprinkled white crystals onto the ground.

"What is she doing?" I asked, interrupting Hayden and Wade talking about the military aspects of the compound.

"Oh, that's Myla," Zane said in a hushed voice. "She's insane."

"No," Buddy carefully pointed out. "She's not *insane*; she just has a different view of the world than we do."

"And her view is…?" I inquired.

Zane leaned over the table. "She doesn't think the zombies are infected, dead humans. She thinks they are possessed by evil spirits."

"Are you fucking kidding me?" I asked, recoiling in disbelief.

Amos laughed, throwing his head back as he did so. "She does this every night," he chuckled. "She's our entertainment."

"Be nice," Buddy scolded. "Myla is special, I'll give you that, but she's a vital part of this group."

"Oh yeah," Amos said sarcastically. "Without those protection spells she cast, we'd all be dead." He rolled his eyes and winked at me. He laughed again, shook his head at Buddy's belittling look, and cleared his throat. "So," he began. "What and where did you all serve?"

"Marines and mostly Afghanistan," Hayden answered first. "I've been to a lot of the Middle East during my two tours."

"Also Marines; I had three years in Iraq before I got pulled," Wade said quietly. "What about you?"

"I spent my youth in Vietnam," Amos sighed. "Air Force."

My heart skipped a beat; my grandpa had also served in Vietnam in the Air Force. His image flashed in my head and I felt a pull on my heart. I wished so desperately that I could go back in time, find my Aunt Jenny, get Raeya, and take them to Kentucky where we could have waited out the outbreak.

I reached up and tugged on Hayden's dog tags. If I had done that, would I have met Hayden?

"And you?" Amos asked, pulling me out of my reverie.

I shook my head. "I'm not in the military," I told him. His eyes moved to the dog tags I was playing with. I let them fall from my hand and bounce off my chest. I put my hand on Hayden's and smiled slightly. "They're his."

Amos winked at Hayden. "Got yourself a sweetie?"

Hayden nudged me. "She's alright," he joked.

Colin shook his head. "Sorry to offend you, but why are you out here then?" he asked me.

Before I could open my mouth to answer, Brock's voice came over the walkie-talkie. I got up and walked a few feet away to respond. Obviously, the guys were close, which made the others excited with thoughts of food. An impatient silence fell over the group as they watched the road.

A few minutes later the Range Rover and the truck came into view. I set my machine gun on the back seat of the truck, grabbed an apple and a bottle of water, and went around to the other side of the RV to keep watch while the others ate. I removed the bow and the quiver from around my shoulder, rubbing the sore spots they left on my skin.

After doing a thorough scan of the surrounding woods, I sat down in the shadow of the camper. I rolled my neck to the side trying not to think about how sore my body was. I slapped a mosquito off my forearm before biting into the apple. There wasn't much talking going on between the civilians since they were eating a full meal for the first time in days—or weeks maybe. Every once in a while,

Amos would laugh and the sound would carry in the thick air.

It was stupid and I knew it. I had met Amos for all of two seconds and I liked him already. I wanted to make sure he got enough to eat and drink and that he was comfortable on the way back to the compound. He reminded me of my grandpa.

But he wasn't him.

I rarely let my mind wander. There were thoughts in my head that weren't the most pleasant. But as I looked from tree to tree searching for the living dead, I couldn't help it. I prayed he was alive. My grandpa was the most resourceful person I knew. He taught me everything; if I could make it, he could.

A little black hole in my heart burned, reminding me that he was old and suffering from the onset of dementia. His arthritis hurt when it rained and he forgot to take his blood pressure medicine even before the zombies.

I felt horribly guilty for not moving back to Kentucky after I dropped out of school. I didn't plan on staying out forever, just long enough to find a job and put some money into savings. That was my rationale for staying in Indiana, close to Purdue University.

While neither of us liked long phone conversations, I consistently called once a week to let him know I was alright. My grandpa didn't like Aunt Jenny living alone in a big city. He told me to keep her safe since he knew I could do it.

And I failed.

If Aunt Jenny was smart, she would have left and not bothered looking for me. But before smart she was compassionate. I was her favorite—yet only—niece and I knew she would never leave without trying to find me.

I would never admit it to anyone, and it embarrassed me to admit it to myself, but I secretly wished Aunt Jenny left the city, drove home to Kentucky, found my grandpa, and got away safely. If they didn't...well, then I wished they were dead and died instantly so they didn't suffer in this horrible, dead world. I wanted to believe in a better place for them to be in, but I just couldn't. If they were dead, it would at least be over for them.

"Riss?" Hayden said softly.

I snapped my attention to the left. Shit. I hadn't heard him walk over. I shook my head; now wasn't the time to space off on stupid, wishful thinking. "Yeah?"

"Go get something to eat; I'll keep watch."

I held up the apple I had only taken two bites out of. "I'm not that hungry. It's too hot."

Hayden nodded but didn't question me. "See anything?" he asked, motioning to the trees.

"Nothing undead." I smiled flatly at Hayden before turning my eyes to the forest.

"Ok," he said and sat down next to me, keeping me company while I forced myself to eat the apple and then threw the core into the weeds. "You've been quiet," Hayden observed.

I smiled and shrugged, looking quickly into Hayden's hazel eyes. My grandpa had never liked or approved of anyone I dated, though even I'll admit I never dated anyone with long term potential. Hayden, I knew for sure, would get the stamp of approval. But that would never happen. "I'm tired," I said. It wasn't a lie since I really was tired. But now wasn't the time to burden Hayden with my issues.

"Me too," he agreed. He pinched a mosquito between his fingers. "Goddammit," he swore and instantly started scratching at the insect bite on his neck.

"Here," I said and extended my hand. "Itching seems to make them worse. This is what I do." Twice I pressed my nail into the small bump, making an 'X'. "It kinda hurts at first but then it feels better...for awhile."

"Thanks," he said and let his hand fall onto my leg.

"You're welcome," I said and rested my head against the camper. I closed my eyes only to open them in less than two seconds to swat at another flying blood sucker. "Son of a bitch bit me through my jeans," I mumbled.

"Maybe there's bug spray in one of the campers," Hayden suggested. "Those guys might have already found it. Want to come with me and check?"

"Nah," I said, suddenly feeling depleted of energy. "I'll keep watch. You go."

Hayden frowned, looked at me intently for a few seconds, and got up. I stuck my hand down my shirt to wipe away the sweat that was rolling down my cleavage. An image of my mother flashed through my mind and I felt my heart break. I wished so desperately that I could go back in time and yell at myself. I was angry at my mother, but I still loved her. I always thought I'd have the time to make things better; now I would never get to.

"Got some," Hayden told me as he walked over. He held the green bottle of bug spray in the air. "Want me to spray you?"

"Yeah."

He chuckled. "You have to get up."

"Oh, right." I pulled myself up and extended my arms. "Is everyone done eating yet?"

"Almost. They're trying to eat slowly since it's been so long since they've had a real meal. Well, if you can call what we have to eat real."

I nodded and cast my eyes to the ground, looking at the patch of clovers I had been sitting on.

"Are you alright, Orissa?" Hayden asked softly. He took my hand.

"Of course," I said. "I'm tired."

"Right," he said with a nod. "Whatcha thinking about?"

"I was thinking that you guys sound so professional when you introduce yourselves," I said, coming up with that suddenly. "I think I need a title in front of my name."

"Special Agent Penwell?" he joked. I shook my head and almost laughed, recalling Jason's lie about me being in the CIA.

"I was thinking more along the lines of Queen or Princess."

Hayden raised an eyebrow.

"Duchess?" I tried.

He laughed. "Sure."

I sighed and grew quiet.

"Let's walk." He motioned to a path. "And look for zombies."

"Ok," I agreed. We went back into the camp to inform the others of where we were going. Hayden exchanged all but one of his guns for knives. Since we didn't want to risk the echoing of a gun firing in the woods unless it was absolutely necessary, I took the gun off of my ankle and locked it in the truck as well.

I wasn't familiar with this particular campground. We meandered slowly down the road, the bugs increasing in number the closer we got to the lake. Despite the heat I felt cold inside. I hated this. Before the outbreak, if I felt like this I'd call Raeya, lock myself in my room, and wait for her to talk some sense into me. She always had a way of making things seem better. Or, I'd use my lack of coping skills and go out, find a guy to buy me a drink and make me feel good about myself...for the time being.

I shook my head; what the hell had I been thinking? My life was such a serious mess. Just thinking about it made my stomach knot up. I wasn't that girl anymore, was I?

Hayden and I walked next to each other over a dirt path that broke away into the shore of the lake. The air was thicker here than back at the camp. I looked around, hoping to find a zombie so I could beat my feelings out on it. We walked along the lake until we came to a dock. Thinking it would give us a better view of the surrounding lake, Hayden led the way down.

We spent several minutes examining our surroundings. I closed my eyes and listened for anything crashing through the underbrush. I took my bow and quiver and carefully set them down on the dock. I stuck my hands in the water, feeling instant relief. I wished I could jump in.

Hayden sat down and patted the dock, signaling for me to take a seat next to him.

"Want to tell me what's really going on?" he asked once I sat down.

"Just thinking," I said simply.

"What are you thinking about?" he asked me again, though this time he was serious.

"Things I shouldn't think about. Things that make me upset."

"Tell me about them," he gently encouraged.

I shook my head and picked at a splinter on the weathered wood. "Nah. It's fine. I'll get over it."

"Riss," Hayden nearly scolded. "First of all, you're really distracted with whatever is going on inside your head. You could get hurt that way. Second—and most of all—I don't want you to be upset." He leaned back on his arms and tipped his head at me.

When our eyes met, something grew inside of me. I took a deep breath and lay down on the hot wood.

"I was thinking about my aunt and how I let my grandpa down by not taking care of her. And I feel horrible that I didn't get to my grandpa. I should have found a way out of the hospital and saved them both. I can't stop thinking about how much I failed. And it hurts *so much*. I should have done something. But I didn't."

He lay down too. "There is nothing I can say that will take the pain away. You rescued Raeya."

"I should have rescued them all. And then I keep thinking, why me? Why am I alive when they're dead?"

"You don't know they're dead."

"Be realistic, Hayden."

"Ok, we have no idea what happened. But it doesn't hurt to wish."

"Yes! Yes, it does hurt. It breaks my heart," I said exasperated. "It's all I can think about."

Hayden pushed himself up and looked into my eyes. "You have two choices: You can focus on the things that break your heart, or you can focus on the things that keep it together. No matter what, it's up to you."

I reached up and put my hand on Hayden's shoulder, running my fingers over the spot where the bullet hit. "You're right. I might have lost them, but I got you."

He got to his feet and extended a hand to pull me up. "I know this sucks, Riss. It does for all of us. Losing someone isn't easy. They say time heals everything but I think all it does is fill the wound with scar tissue; it will never heal but it won't always be the painful gaping hole it once was."

His grip on my hand tightened as he continued his speech. "Maybe we don't have much to be thankful for. But we have not only each other but the rest of our friends back home. And the compound is far from perfect but it's safe. We have fresh food, full tanks of gas, and now we have nearly a dozen people to bring back. A long time ago I promised to make you happy. I intend on keeping that promise."

"Thanks," I said shyly. Hayden took the gun from his waistband and set it on the ground.

"Did your other pair of boots ever dry?" he asked suddenly.

"Yeah, why?"

"Just curious," he replied casually. He stepped away from the water before jumping at me, his arms wrapping around my legs as he picked me up and put me over his shoulder. I didn't have time to protest before he jumped in the water.

"Hayden James Underwood!" I scolded as soon as I popped my head out of the water.

"I fell," he said innocently and splashed me.

Treading water, I laughed and splashed him back.

"Don't tell me this doesn't feel good," he said and swam on his back.

"It does," I agreed and let myself sink under the water. I swam over to Hayden. "Thanks," I told him.

"You can make it up to me later," he joked with a half smile. He took a hold of my hands and pulled me through the water until our body's touched. "I love you," he reminded me.

"And I love you," I told him. A long, deep, passionate kiss would have been ideal at that moment but making out while treading water wasn't as easy as Hollywood made it out to be.

Begrudgingly, we got out of the lake, did another sweep of the woods for zombies, and walked in wet boots back to camp. Ivan stood in the middle of the semi circle holding a machine gun. He raised an eyebrow at us.

"Fall in?" he asked with a smirk.

"We had to make sure there weren't any zombies in the water," Hayden said so seriously it was obvious he was joking. He looked out at the civilians. "Everyone ready?"

"Almost," Ivan responded. "They asked if they could rest for a while before taking off. I said it was alright since we have a long drive."

Hayden nodded. "Only a couple hours at the most. I don't feel safe here."

"Well," I said sarcastically, eyeing the salt circle. "We all know zombies are allergic to salt; we're so safe."

Ivan laughed. "Did you find anything out there?"

"No," Hayden answered. "It was quiet. But these woods are thick; it's hard to see far."

"Yeah," Ivan agreed. "I'll keep watch," he offered so Hayden and I could change into dry clothes. Once I had changed, I sat near the fire hoping the smoke would keep the bugs away and combed out my tangled hair. A young woman who looked to be about fifteen with golden, shoulder-length hair timidly joined me.

"Hi," she said shyly.

"Hey," I replied and yanked the comb through a tangle. "I'm Orissa."

"I'm Lynn."

"That's my middle name," I told her though I doubted she gave a rat's ass what my middle name was.

"What's the place we're going to like?" she asked.

"It's not bad, I promise," I told her, remembering my doubts about the compound when I first learned about it. "It's underground so it's safe. It kinda looks like a school in some ways. Bright lights, white walls, a big cafeteria, and dormitory style housing. When we left they were working on building a safe place for people to go to spend time outside, so don't worry about cabin fever."

"Good. And it's really safe? The last quarantine we were at got taken by the zombies."

"Yes. No one can get downstairs without knowing pass codes and hand scans. There are multiple steel doors that were meant to withstand a bomb. I bet my life that zombies will not get inside the shelter."

"Do you have power?"

"Power, oh, like electricity? Yeah. The compound is run by solar and wind power. We have a few of those creepy, giant windmills by our farm near the shelter."

"Is the farm safe?" She angled herself at me and looked intently and hopefully at me with brown eyes.

"No," I said since I didn't want to lie. "I think the barns are. But the fields aren't. There are fences but I don't think it would stop a herd. There are ditches dug along the livestock pastures, which work like moats. But it's still not fool proof."

"Herd?" she asked.

"A big group of zombies. They move like herds."

"Oh." She pushed her dirty hair out of her face. "We call them packs. Like a wolf pack that surrounds its prey."

"That's a good way of putting it." I smiled at her and set the comb down so I could braid my hair.

"Is he your boyfriend?" she asked, looking up at Hayden, who was talking to Zane and Amos.

"Yeah."

She looked him over before turning back to me. "Have you been together long?"

"Not really," I said right away and mentally tried to add up the months I'd known Hayden. Since time was so irrelevant during an apocalypse, I hadn't bothered to keep track of what month it was. I think I met Hayden in late December and I really wasn't sure what day let alone month it was right now. "Four or five months, give or take," I told her.

"So you met during all of this?" she asked, suddenly interested.

"Yeah."

"Did he save you? Because if he did, that would be so romantic and just like something from a movie."

I knew my eyes widened and I gave her my best what-the-fuck face. "Yes, a movie that stars the death of our family and friends while the supporting cast slowly starves to death."

Lynn swallowed hard. "Sorry."

I shook my head and cast my eyes away. "It's alright." Not wanting to talk relationships with anyone, let alone a total stranger, I got up to help the others get ready to go. It didn't take long to get their remaining items inside the cars. The Impala we spotted earlier belonged to them as well. Three had set out earlier that day in search of food but when the engine overheated and started smoking, they were forced to pull over and come back to their camp.

The six of us from the compound wandered around with weapons in our hands, ready for anything, while the civilians rested. I retrieved one of the hunting rifles from the truck and went a few campsites over, stationing myself in the shade of another RV. I held up the gun and looked through the scope, trying to locate any source of movement.

"Girls aren't supposed to know how to use guns," a voice came from behind me. I turned to see one of the young girls looking curiously at me. She was the older—or at least taller—sister, Addison.

"Why do you think that?" I asked.

She kicked at a clump of thistle in the overgrown grass. "That's what my dad told me. Girls grow up to be ladies. Ladies don't shoot things."

I flicked the safety on the gun. "Don't ladies want to live?"

"Of course they do."

"Then they better learn how to defend themselves, right?"

"Yeah," she said shyly. "I'm not allowed to use a gun."

"Maybe when you're older," I suggested, thinking her father's talk about ladies was only a way to keep her from trying to use a gun and get herself hurt. "You should go back to camp," I told her. "Before your dad gets worried."

"I'm not far," she objected. "And he's watching Quinn; he won't notice that I'm gone."

I looked through the scope again, wondering how the hell they were able to keep a toddler alive. Something moved through the trees. It was fast, too fast to be a zombie.

Dammit; it was a crazy.

"Go back to camp, now," I whispered to Addison. "Tell the guys I that I went to check something out."

Stricken with sudden fear, she nodded and had to shake herself before she could turn around and run. I traded the rifle for an arrow, muscles tense and senses on high alert. A sea of brown and green lay before me like a maze, hiding my violent enemy.

Her breath came out in a hard whoosh as her body thudded on the ground. Reluctantly taking my eyes off the forest, I turned to see Addison pushing herself up. Her foot had caught on a tangle of weeds and she tripped; and the fall caused her to bite her lip. Her hand flew to it and tears welled in her eyes.

"Shit," I swore under my breath when sunlight reflected off of the scarlet drips. I set the bow and arrow down and rushed to her side, helping her up. "Don't move," I told her and gently pushed her up against the RV.

She nodded, trying her best not to cry from the pain of her bloody lip. I turned to grab the bow and arrow when a rock struck me in the head. I recoiled in pain, stumbling over my own feet. I fell hard on my ass.

I ignored the pounding headache. My fist closed around the arrow and I felt around the tall grass for my bow. Once I had it in my grasp, I sprung up and quickly took a stance. Blood dripped into my eye, making it hard to focus. I took a step back closer to Addison, wanting to shield the girl from anything that came at us.

She screamed when the crazy galloped from the trees. He only made it a few feet before an arrow whizzed through the air and pierced his throat. His body twitched and blood bubbled from his mouth before he fell.

I immediately drew another arrow and waited, my eyes darting over the forest. A mosquito landed on my cheek. I didn't dare take my hands off my weapon. Sweat rolled down my forehead. I slowly let my breath out and stepped forward. The mosquito's needle popped into my skin. A flock of birds suddenly took flight. My muscles tensed and my heart sped up.

But nothing came out of the woods. Still not putting the bow or arrow down, I used my shoulder to wipe away the bug. Instead of flicking it away, I only smashed it on my skin. As quietly as I could, I moved a few more paces in the direction of the trees. Why did the birds have to be so loud?

I wasn't sure if I imagined the sound of leaves crunching under foot. Not wanting to leave any stone unturned, I ventured farther away from the RV. I held the arrow back until my arm grew tired. I shoved the arrow back in the quiver and shook the tension out of my arm. I let out a deep breath and dropped my guard only to raise it again at the sound of running.

In a matter of seconds I had another arrow ready. I spun around to face the source of the footfalls.

"Oh," I said aloud when Brock and Rider came into view.

"We heard the scream," Brock said and looked around to assess the situation. Rider raced over to Addison, ready to cover her if need be.

"Just one crazy," I told them. "It came from the woods." I put the arrow away, hung my bow over my shoulder, and wiped the blood and smeared bug from my face.

"Did it get you?" Brock asked, eyeing my head wound.

"Kind of," I explained and walked over to find my rifle amongst the tall grass. "It threw a rock at me."

"It what?" Rider asked, his grip on his M16 tightening.

I nodded. "It threw a rock, like he was trying to disable me."

Brock shook his head. "I don't like how the crazies are getting smarter."

I nodded in agreement. "Yeah. It's like they're evolving." I picked up my rifle and went over to the crazy to yank the arrow from its dead body. Something stringy got caught on the head of the arrow as I pulled it up; it stretched and eventually snapped, sending little bits of blood to splatter on my arm. I flicked off the goo, wiped the arrow the best I could in the grass, and put it back in the quiver.

"I don't like it here," Rider observed as he looked through the trees. "There are too many places for them to hide. If the woods aren't bad enough, we have all these abandoned campers to worry about."

"Let's get back to camp and go," Brock suggested. "If everyone is too tired to drive we should at least get to a clearing so we won't get snuck up on…again."

"Yeah, let's," I agreed. Brock led the way and Rider and I brought up the rear with Addison safely sandwiched in between. Everyone back at the camp was on edge waiting for our return, having all heard the scream.

I was pondering the effectiveness of screaming as a defense mechanism when Hayden rushed over to me.

"You're bleeding…again," he said and gently wiped away blood from my forehead. "Do you ever wonder how much total blood loss we've had? Both of us have almost bled to death."

I smiled and set the rifle down on the picnic table. "You've lost more than me."

"That was just one time. I bet if we measured it all you'd be the winner," he teased. "Sit, I'll get the first aid kit and then you can tell me what happened."

Brock and Rider spoke quietly with Ivan, Wade, and Zack. I could see by their concerned faces that they had all agreed to get the hell out of here. Hayden jogged back over and laid the first aid kit on the table. I explained how the crazy threw the rock at me while he poured peroxide on a piece of gauze. I closed my eyes and tried not to wince as he cleaned up the cut.

"It's not bad," he assured me. "And now you have matching scars on both sides of your head," he said with a smile.

I reached up and touched the shiny patch of skin I got as a result of hitting a windshield. "Gee, thanks, just what I wanted."

"I like your scars," he added quickly.

I glared at him to let him know I knew he was lying. "Sure you do." I took a deep breath and stood. "Let's go. I want out of here, and I'm dying to go home and take a shower."

"That sounds nice," Hayden said and snapped the first aid kit shut. "Are you doing alright?"

"I'm fine," I promised. I touched the bandage on my head, thinking the tape wouldn't stick since I was sweaty. "Like you said, it's not bad."

"That's not what I meant," he said gently.

"Yes," I said automatically. "Really, I am. I had my moment of weakness, but I'm back to normal now."

"It's not weakness, Riss," he reminded me and extended a hand to pull me to my feet.

"You're right. Can we talk about it when we get home?" I put my hand on his shoulder, running my fingers over the spot the bullet hit.

"Sounds good," he said and pulled the keys out of his pocket.

We made sure all four vehicles were fueled up and took off with smooth sailing for the first four hours. A derailed train blocked our path. After a quick bathroom break, we turned around to find another road home. The group had loaded into a Suburban and a truck. Hayden, Ivan, and I led the way, the two cars full of civilians followed and Brock, Wade, and Rider brought up the rear.

We ran into a herd when we crossed the Kentucky border. If the bed of the truck wasn't full of fruit and vegetables, we would have rained a storm of bullets down on the slow moving zombies with the high powered machine gun. Eager to get home, I wasn't too disappointed when Hayden decided to bypass them all together. We sped away, literally leaving the herd in the dust.

The sunlight was disappearing; a blood red sunset covered the sky. Hayden flipped through songs on the iPod, Ivan stared at the map, and I picked dirt and blood from under my nails. I looked at the clock; only a few minutes had passed since I last looked at it. I closed my eyes hoping I could fall asleep. Wide awake, I opened them only a moment later.

"If you're a hymenopterist, what do you study?" Ivan suddenly asked.

"Virgins?" Hayden supplied. Ivan shook his head and looked at me.

"I have no idea," I told him.

"Bees," Ivan answered. "What was Elmer Fudd's original name?"

"Egghead," Hayden answered after a minute.

"Correct," Ivan praised.

"What U.S. president never married?" Hayden asked.

I shook my head; I had no idea...again. When Ivan didn't answer correctly, Hayden informed us it was James Buchanan.

"What is a group of ferrets called?" I asked the guys.

"A pack?" Hayden guessed.

"Nope. A business," I told him. We continued asking each other trivia questions for another forty-five minutes.

We stopped once more before we arrived home. We pulled into an empty field, parking the cars in a semi circle to offer a small barricade if need be. Brock and I hurriedly dished out food and water bottles. The fifteen of us leaned against the cars as we ate.

"It feels so good to be somewhere warm," Lynn stated with a sigh. She picked at the orange in her hands. "I'm so over being cold."

"Why did you stay so far north?" Wade asked.

"Zombies don't fare well in cold weather," Buddy answered. "It was horrible, I won't lie. But I thought it was worth it."

"We noticed that too," Hayden informed him. "We got caught in a snow storm and barely saw any zombies. The ones we did come across were nearly frozen."

"We didn't even worry about zombies on the nights it was really cold," Buddy said. "Which was nice since we were more concerned with not freezing to death. I was afraid the warmth and light from the fires might attract them."

"How did you keep from freezing?" Hayden asked.

"If we were outside, we'd build four or five fires and stay in between them. If we were inside, we'd cram into the room that had a fireplace. The pioneers did it; I knew we could," he said with a smile. "Though they didn't have to worry about flesh-eating monsters."

Hayden nodded. "That's how I think of it. We'll pull through this. Once you guys get to our compound you'll see how we work together. We're all survivors and we'll do whatever it takes to keep it that way."

"That's a good attitude," Amos approved. He opened his mouth to say something but Myra interrupted.

"He will come for them soon. If you think things are bad now, just wait. At least we can repel the demons while they're in corporeal form," she told us in a shaky voice.

"Who is coming?" Brock asked.

"The Horsemen," she replied gravely. "The Seals have already been broken. It happened several years ago; the Mayans were right. I always knew it would happen." She wrapped her arms around herself and turned, taking several steps away from us before she started muttering in a different language.

"Too bad they were over a decade off," Brock said under his breath. "Everybody done eating?"

The kids weren't. Deciding they could finish eating in the car, we loaded up and set off again. We were fortunate enough to avoid another herd, road blocks or bad weather, making for an uneventful ride home.

My heart swelled with relief and excitement when the truck turned onto the gravel driveway. Jason's smiling face was a most welcome sight. I waved and smiled back at him and insisted he come down from the tower and grab an apple.

We parked the cars; Hayden and Ivan led the civilians to the barn, explaining the quarantine procedure. I stripped myself of my weapons, shoved a few pieces of fruit into my bag, and went inside. It was too late to find Raeya or Padraic to tell them I had made it home safely.

I quietly went up to my room, dumped my dirty laundry into my basket, and grabbed pajamas for myself and Hayden before heading to the quarantine room. Brock, Wade, and Rider were already there, bickering over who would get to take the first shower. Finally, after several games of rock-paper-scissors, the order was decided.

Not wanting to sit on the couch in my dirty clothes, I sat in the kitchenette and waited for Hayden. About ten minutes later, he and Ivan came into the room. Hayden told me that they quickly briefed Fuller on the mission. The eleven civilians were set with food, water, and blankets for the night and were extremely grateful for everything.

When the door opened a second time, I looked up expecting to see Fuller. The sight of Doctor Cara—who always looked like she just rolled out of bed—surprised me. She clutched a plastic basket full of vials. It dawned on me that after the surprise of Jessica becoming infected, we would all have our blood tested upon admission.

After we gave a blood sample, showered, and ate several bags of microwaved popcorn, we settled down for the night for some much needed sleep. With the lights off, Hayden and I assumed it would be hard to see the two of us getting into bed together.

"It feels so good to lie down," I said with a sleepy sigh.

"It will feel even better in our own room," Hayden told me. "This bed is so small."

"It is," I agreed. I really liked being in Hayden's embrace while winding down for the night. Staying in it and trying to sleep that way just wasn't comfortable. We didn't have much of a choice in the little twin bed. He kissed my neck and ran his hands over my body, making me wish we were alone.

It didn't take long for me to fall asleep. I dreamed that Hayden, Raeya, and I went on a camping trip to a place that didn't have zombies. It was an average, run of the mill, wishful thinking type of dream, the kind that leaves you wanting more when you wake up.

The wistful pain of what could have been didn't have time to settle in my heart. Someone flicked the lights on, waking me up. I pulled the blanket over my head, too tired to bitch out whoever had startled me awake.

"Orissa," Hayden said. His voice was serious and tense. My body went rigid in fear. My first thought was that I wasn't really in the quarantine room and that I dreamed that up too. Blinking, I looked around the room.

Hayden was standing next to me, and I was definitely in the quarantine room. Everyone else was up. Brock was feverishly lacing his boots. I rubbed my eyes and sat up. Gabby stood in the doorway, her face stressed.

"What's going on?" I asked.

"A herd. A herd is at the fence," she said quickly.

"Fuck," I swore and jumped out of bed. If the herd was at the fence, it wouldn't take long for them to push through and discover our barns full of animals…or the one full of innocent people.

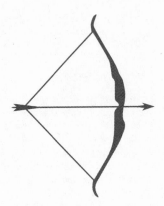

CHAPTER 21

I shoved my feet into my boots, hastily pulling at the laces. Once they were tied, I sprang to my feet and raced out of the quarantine room. Since our weapons were cleaned upon arrival, we sprinted to the weapon room on the B level to load up. The remaining A1s, A2s and A3s were moving about in a panicked fashion as well, having just been woken up like we had.

I knew Jason was working the gate tonight. My heart skipped a beat when I thought of something bad happening to him. We shoved guns and ammo unsafely into bags in a hurried attempt to leave. On impulse, I grabbed two flares and shoved them in the bag before slinging it over my shoulder. It was heavy, and the guns dug into my back.

Hayden, Rider, and I raced out of the weapon storage room. The A3s guarding the doors to the compound had left them open for us. We ran right past and were almost to the front door of the brick estate when Hayden suddenly skidded to a stop.

"Keys," he said. He dropped his load of weapons and dashed off. Rider picked up the bag and motioned for me to continue out the door. Since there was no use hiding from the zombies, the security lights were on, their harsh, artificial sunlight-strength bulbs blinding. We reached the truck in seconds.

The food and supplies had been cleared out. I set my bag down and jumped in the bed; Rider handed me the heavy bags one by one before jumping in as well. I untied the cover from the machine gun while Rider dumped the contents of the bags out. He shoved the ammo in my direction; I quickly clicked the belt into place and draped the others around my shoulder.

We had the other machine guns, rifles, and pistols loaded by the time Hayden returned. Hayden took two loaded guns and got into the driver's seat. He fired up the engine and stomped on the gas without giving Rider or me the chance to brace ourselves.

I knew there was a problem before we even reached the gate. Two A3s crouched down at the top of the tower, shooting the few zombies they could get a good aim at. Brake lights glared at us like demonic eyes. Why wasn't anyone going through?

"Orissa!" Jason shouted from the tower.

"Jason!" I called, standing up. "What's going on out there?"

"Can't open the gate! There's too many out there! They'll get in!"

Over the pounding of my heart I could hear the groaning. "How many?" I asked.

"Can't tell," he said. "A whole fucking lot!"

Rider stood. "We need to get out there. We need to start killing!"

My mind raced. I wanted—no needed—to do something. Zombies crashed into the fence, the sound of metal rattling echoing ominously in the dark night. If only we could get one car through;

they could take down the crowd that surrounded the gate while Rider, Hayden, and I cleaned up the few that would no doubt get through.

I started at the brake lights until my vision blurred red. "That's it!" I said aloud and dove to pick up the flare. Jason would be the best person to throw it since he was up the highest. I looked at the tower.

"Jason!" I shouted.

"Yeah?"

"Take this!" I said and held up the flare. "Light it and throw it as far as you can! The motherfuckers will be attracted to the light. Once they move out of the way, open the gate and let them through," I told him and motioned to the SUV in front of us. "Then close it; we'll take care of any that got through!"

The fence rippled and rattled again. The electric wire sizzled and popped as it shocked the zombies. The scent of burned rotten flesh filled the air. Oxygen entered and exited my lungs at a fast pace. I caught a glimpse of Hayden's face in the side mirror; he looked every bit as stressed and anxious as I felt.

"I'll come down and get it!" Jason shouted and his boyish face disappeared from the glassless window in the tower. I grabbed the flare and leapt out of the truck.

José, Noah, and two A2s were in the SUV in front of us. I spit out a summarized explanation to them after I handed the flare off to Jason. Hayden was speaking to someone on the walkie-talkie. I jumped back into the bed of the truck and picked up a rifle. Hayden backed the truck up, put it in park, and leaned out the window holding a gun.

Not wanting to accidentally shoot anyone with the built in machine gun, Rider flicked the safety off a pistol. We watched the flare sizzle to life and fly through the air in a perfect arc. It dimmed slightly when it landed on the ground. I held my breath and waited, praying that the zombies would notice. I considered shooting at the zombies through the fence but decided that it wasn't worth it to risk damaging the weakening fence.

It was hard to see over the SUV. My eyes were wide and my body felt like it was alive with fire. Finally, the gates opened. José stomped on the gas and the SUV flew through, hitting a zombie. Noah emerged from the sunroof, taking on a stance and fired. The A2s that I didn't know the names of rolled down the back windows and opened fire as well.

Knowing we could easily miss and hit the guys in front of us, I kept one eye on the tail lights and the other on the zombies that pushed past them. I pulled the trigger, hitting an S2 in the head. Gunfire boomed around us, echoing in the vast darkness. My ears were already ringing by the time the gate closed.

Seven zombies had gotten through. Within thirty seconds they were dead...again. The SUV raced down the street in the direction of the farm.

Hayden revved the engine of the truck and pulled forward, ready to burst through as soon as the metal hinges swung open. Rider and I held onto the side of the bed when the truck lurched.

We shot at the stragglers that staggered into the grounds of the compound. I wasn't sure if we got them all, but I didn't worry; there were still guards stationed at the entrance of the compound. Hayden jerked the wheel left, away from the farm. Rider and I began shooting at the stragglers that banged on the fence.

A walkie-talkie was shoved inside the bag of weapons. I heard muffled voices shouting and responding. Ignoring them, I continued to send bullets flying into the heads of our foe.

"Underwood!" a different voice bellowed into the walkie-talkie. I had to feel around in the bag for it since I wasn't about to take my eyes off what was in front of me. "Underwood, do you copy?"

It was Fuller's voice. I picked it up and pressed the button.

"Yes. I mean I copy. This is Orissa."

"Where is Underwood?" Fuller asked, losing his professional composure over his worry about Hayden.

"Here. He's fine," I said shortly, not thinking I should give too much attention to the conversation. I fired two shots into the open mouth of an S2 that was limping her way over.

"Get to the farm," Fuller commanded.

My heart skipped a beat; things must be *really* bad at our farm if Fuller was willing to let zombies tear down our fences.

"Ok," I said dumbly into the walkie-talkie. I set it down and relayed the message to Hayden. I tried to catch a glimpse of Jason as we sped past. If he stayed in the tower, he'd be safe. Hayden turned left, tore down the driveway, and then jerked the wheel right, remembering to slow so he wouldn't throw Rider, me, and our weapons out of the bed.

A blood red sunset crept over the horizon. Shots rang out and echoed all around us. I heard someone scream and turned just in time to see two zombies ripping into one of our soldiers. Trenches—six feet wide and ten feet deep—had been dug along the pastures surrounding the barns to protect the buildings in a similar way a moat protected a castle.

Only we didn't have a drawbridge. Two U-shaped moats surrounded the pasture, leaving two paths of land intact, enabling the animals, people, and vehicles to move in and out easily. And tonight, it enabled the undead to move in.

The gates had already been pushed through; dozens of zombie hands pounded and pushed on the metal doors of the barns. The lights on the barn shone like a neon diner sign for the zombies. It shuddered and rattled under the literal dead weight.

Hayden parked several yards from the barn and got out of the truck. Rider and I jumped out of the bed and raced to Hayden's side. Rider raised his machine gun.

"No!" Hayden said and put his hand up. "If you miss, you'll kill our animals."

"If they don't first," Rider said bitterly, shooting a disgusted glance at the undead. "What do we do?"

"Pick them off, one by one," Hayden answered and shoved a magazine into the hunting rifle he was holding. "Riss, cover us; get the strays that wander over. Rider and I will shoot the bastards at the barn."

I nodded and we rushed into position, adding to the deafening sound of gunfire. I wanted to look about and see who was still alive. I was so worried about not only my friends but anyone and everyone that it made me sick. I didn't have time for that. I had a job to do.

With my back to Hayden's, I fired at the zombies that slunk away from the barn in the direction of humans. It was mass chaos; they were everywhere. I wanted to believe there was an end to this. I wanted to believe we would win, lose nobody, and be merely annoyed with the broken fences in the morning.

But I was wrong. Turning from side to side, I continually pulled the trigger. Blood splattered in the air each time a bullet lodged itself into the putrid brain of a zombie. Their arms would flail ever so slightly before they dropped.

Smoke and gun powder hung heavy in the air. I was out of ammo. Out of habit, I reached down to pull another magazine from my pocket. Goddammit, I was wearing pajama pants. A decomposing S3 limped at me. I swung the rifle and hit it in the head. Bits of pus covered brain matter oozed out. Another zombie took his place as soon as he fell.

She reached her torn and bloody hands at me and picked up speed. Half her face had been ripped off, exposing the muscle and bones of her cheek and jaw. Blood crusted clumps hung in her black hair and she smelled worse than week old road kill in the middle of July.

I leaned back, brought my foot up, and kicked her in the chest. She stumbled backwards and fell on her ass. Using the heel of my boot, I stomped on her forehead. Her skull cracked, though not enough to kill her. I kicked her in the temple. She rolled to her side and wrapped her decomposing hands around my ankle. I raised the rifle and brought it down on her face; she released me and went limp.

I made a mad dash to the truck, cursing my stupid gray and pink polka dotted pajama pants for not having pockets. I traded the rifle for an M9, the gun I was the most familiar with. When I reached around in the dark bed for more ammo, my fingers closed around a survival knife leg strap. My heart beat so fast that my fingers almost didn't work as I quickly fashioned it around my thigh. I stole a quick glance to my left and saw Brock and Ivan battling a group of zombies.

I looked back at Hayden and Rider; they were still taking down the zombies that surrounded the barn. Nothing limped in their direction, so I rushed to Brock and Ivan. A spry S2 clocked me on my way there. We tumbled over each other and the gun flew out of my hand. He landed on top of me, his head hitting me hard in the stomach.

The red glow of the sunrise illuminated his grotesque face. Half was burned off, one eyeball loosely dangled from the socket, and maggots crawled in the rotting holes in his cheek. His boney hands were covered in thin flesh and deteriorating muscle; he moved them with surprising speed, shoving my shoulders down. He opened his mouth and roared; his breath was so foul I nearly puked.

I brought my leg up to knee him in the stomach. The zombie must have just had a feast; his very full belly popped like a balloon. Guts, bile, blood, and poorly chewed body parts spewed out all over me.

Grimacing, I put both hands on the zombie's shoulders and pushed him away. I hated how much I struggled. This piece of shit was dead with the contents of his stomach soaking through the thin tank top I was wearing. I should be stronger than him.

I brought my knee up again and desperately reached for my knife. The tips of my fingers graced it but I couldn't get a firm enough grasp to pull it out of the holder. With one hand on the zombie's chest, pushing him away, I felt around for my gun. That, too, was out of my reach.

Drainage leaked from pustules on the zombie's face. He fought against me, his large size and heavy weight almost too much to resist. I needed to do something—anything—if I wanted to live. I shoved my free hand up and inside of the zombie's open abdomen. I nearly gagged when my fingers punctured through another organ.

I pushed my hand up until I found the spine. I wrapped my hands around it and yanked it down, tearing the nerves that ran from the spine to the brain. The zombie sputtered and went limp.

Panting, I rolled him off me and wiped my hand in the grass. Not convinced he was actually dead, I pulled the knife from around my thigh, and stabbed him three more times in the head before I scrambled up. An S3 was doing her best to rush at me with two clearly broken ankles. I scooped up the M9 and shot her in the temple.

"Brock!" I shouted, not wanting to sneak up on anyone. I was covered in enough blood and guts to be mistaken for a zombie. "Brock!"

He half turned and smiled when he saw me. He and Ivan were advancing on a group of zombies that clawed at the smaller pole barn that contained our chickens. Four A2s were with them and I didn't know any of their names.

If we made it through this, I swore I would learn everyone's name. With careful aim, I fired my remaining shots into the heads of zombies. I let the empty gun fall from my grip and I yanked the knife from the leg strap once again. I turned away from the barn and rushed at a young S2 that ran at us.

I dropped to the ground, extended my leg, and spun. The zombie tripped and fell. I brought the knife down into its forehead. I put one hand on the zombie's face and forced the knife out of the bone. Not taking the time to flick the goo from the blade, I took on the next zombie that came toward us. This one was big and had dark eyes that looked almost alive. The skin around his mouth cracked and flaked from dehydration, and he had a several-inches-long cut on his arm that had blackened with necrotic, rotting tissue.

I sunk the knife into his neck, severing his spinal cord and nerves. When his body went limp, I pulled the knife back and kicked him in the chest as he fell in order to move him away from me. Another took his place. This one was a child and couldn't have been older than six or seven when she turned. She was still nothing more than a zombie. It still sickened me and hurt every fiber of my being to push the sharp blade into her eye socket.

Panting, I looked around. The sound of gunfire was decreasing. Ivan, Brock, Alex, and the A2s were finishing off the zombies at the entrance of the chicken barn. I was about to take off and go back to Hayden when I heard someone call for help.

I jerked my head around to find the source.

"Help!" I heard again. "Down here!" someone yelled.

"Oh my God," I breathed when I realized that someone had fallen into the trench. I raced over and dropped to my knees. "Hey!" I shouted. "Where are you?"

"Here!" a male voice answered. I recognized the voice but couldn't place it.

"I'll pull you out!" I called and rapidly moved down. "Give me your hand!"

Weak sunlight reflected off the blood splattered across his face. Jones, I remembered at once: A young A3, the soldier who had taken me to my room my first day at the compound.

"Are there zombies down there?" I asked

"Tons," he said. "Most are dead," his voice shook as he spoke. "I think."

"Quick, give me your hand!" I laid down on my stomach, set on pulling the kid out. He stepped on a dead zombie for leverage. His fingers locked with mine. "Ok, go!" I said, not wanting to waste time counting to three. Jones pushed off the dirt wall with his feet, and I tried to hoist him. I strained but managed to pull him up. His fingernails dug into my skin as I exhaled, taking a second to catch my breath. "Push!" I instructed, meaning for him to use the wall to propel himself upward.

His left hand slapped the ground. Not letting go of his other, I pulled back once more. He grabbed a handful of grass and hoisted himself out of the trench.

Out of breath, I rolled back. A zombie lumbered at us. We didn't have time to move out of the way.

Acting on their own accord as a reflex, my hands covered my head. The zombie's foot got caught on my side; I flattened myself and wrapped both hands around its thigh, causing it to trip and painfully land on me before toppling into the trench.

"Nice," Jones said. He rose to his feet.

"Wish I could say I planned it," I panted and got up as well. My eyes darted around in search of Hayden. When I couldn't find him, panic threatened to take over. My body momentarily froze, and I didn't know what to do. I snapped out of it and ran back toward the cattle barn, jumping over and dodging dead zombie bodies.

I didn't think it was possible to panic even more. The barn door was slightly ajar and neither Hayden nor Rider was anywhere to be seen. I wanted to scream his name and fought to keep my mouth shut. I was almost inside when the door slid shut.

I wasn't aware that Jones had been following me until we both crashed into the metal door. Knowing that if I opened the door I would likely get shot, I softly and rhythmically knocked. After only a few seconds, it opened.

"Riss?" Rider asked.

"Yes!" I desperately blurted.

He slid the door open enough for Jones and me to get through. The middle light had been turned on, creating a soft glow over the dim, dusty barn. Rider put his hand on my shoulder and I smiled at him, glad he was ok too. I immediately looked past him.

The barn was sectioned off on both sides of the aisle, creating two large, open 'stalls' that housed our few cows. They shuffled around nervously, breathing heavily. Hayden was securing the door on the opposite side.

"Hayden!" I loudly whispered. He whipped around and rushed over. I wrapped my arms around him the second he was in my reach. "Thank God."

"Don't do that again!" he spat angrily. "I didn't know where you went. One second you where there and the next you weren't! I thought you were dead!"

"I'm sorry," I soothed.

"Sorry? Riss, how many times have I asked you not to go off on your own? It's stupid and dangerous!"

"I'm fine," I told him.

He let me go. "You just don't care what it does to me, do you?"

"What? Of course I do!"

Rider cleared his throat. "There aren't many more out there, are there?"

"No," Jones answered.

"We should get back out there," Rider suggested. "Now that the back door is latched from the inside. Are you armed?"

"Not anymore," Jones said.

"Here," Rider told him and extended a pistol. "Riss, where's yours?"

"I dropped it," I explained. "I have a knife. It'll work."

Rider nodded and went to the door. He slid it open and the four of us darted out. Two zombies greeted us immediately. Rider shot one and I knifed the other in the temple. The smell of death and decay was so heavy in the air I could taste it. Staying close to Hayden, we ran to the right of the barn. Hayden shot three zombies and I stabbed another.

Steven, the A2 Fuller thought was ready to move up and go on missions, was standing next to Gabby. He pumped a shotgun and fired at the advancing zombies. The bullets peppered their faces, killing them instantly. A few yards down stood another group of soldiers. Taking the lead, Hayden ran over, joining in on the firing.

The number of zombies dwindled. One by one they dropped to the ground. Once again straying away from Hayden, I yanked a zombie by the hair. She stumbled backward and I kicked her in the face. When her skull didn't so much as crack, I bent over to bring the pointy blade of the knife into her eye.

He must have turned from crazy to zombie overnight. A tall, blonde-haired S2 ran to me, his eyes set, and his hands curled into firsts. I took on a defensive stance and waited for him to come to me. I leaned back out of his grasp and whipped the knife through the air.

It collided with his head with great force, but he didn't fall to the ground. I pulled the knife out and rammed him again. Instead of sliding smoothly through his half functioning brain like I expected it to, the blade bluntly smacked against the bone.

Son of a bitch, the tip of the blade had chipped. I swung my arm back and hit him again, sending a stinging shock up my right wrist. Blood poured from the little break I had managed to make. I dropped the nonfunctional knife and smacked the zombie in the nose with my palm, driving the bone up into the brain.

He took a bewildered step back, blood dripped from his mouth, and he fell. I jumped over the body and scrambled to Hayden's side yet again. He fired one more round before lowering his gun. He turned to me and, in the growing daylight, I could see a fine mist of zombie blood dried on his cheeks.

He let out a deep breath and took my hand.

"Underwood!" Ivan yelled.

Hayden raised his hand up and signaled to Ivan. Half a dozen shots echoed across the battlefield that used to be our farmland. Together, Hayden and I jogged over to where Ivan, Brock, Alex, Mac, José, and several A2s gathered.

Hayden and Ivan nodded at each other, silently saying 'I'm glad you're alive.' At a loss for words, we stood in silence and let the whole effect of what had just happened sink in. Steven, Gabby, and Noah joined us, followed by four more A2s, Rider and Jones.

"Where's Wade?" Rider asked, his voice a harsh, shaky whisper. I panicked when I realized he wasn't with us. I craned my neck and searched the ground but didn't see him.

"And Andy?" Steven asked.

"There are a lot missing. I don't know who all came out," Jones voiced.

Assuming the role as leader, Hayden said, "Comb the area for wounded. Make sure the dead are really dead. Who has a walkie?"

"I do," one of the A2s said and unclipped it from his belt.

"Radio in and see if they need help at the gates," Hayden instructed.

The A2 nodded. The walkie-talkie slipped from his blood covered fingers. With trembling hands, he picked it up and spoke into the walkie. "Front gate, do you copy?" A few seconds passed. "Front gate, do you copy?" he repeated, a little louder this time.

"Copy," Jason's voice spoke. I closed my eyes and mentally sighed the biggest sigh of relief.

"What is your zombie status?"

"Just strays," Jason told us. "They didn't get through the gate and the fence held," he continued. "What about you?" he asked.

"Same," the nervous A2 replied.

"Is everyone—" Jason began to ask when Fuller's voice cut him off, asking for details. Hayden told the A2 to explain everything while we combed the land for the dead...our dead. I had to close my eyes to fight off the dizziness that threatened to take over when I flipped over a body that resembled Wade in build and hair color. I couldn't bring my eyes to look at his face.

The gruesome image of the young solider getting his flesh ripped off and torn into the festering and ever-hungry mouth of a zombie made me shudder. My breath caught in my chest. I tried to suck in air but wasn't able to. I exhaled what little oxygen was left in my lungs and forced myself to take a sharp intake or air. It whooshed out too fast and my chest spasmed and I inhaled quickly again. Dammit. I was hyperventilating.

A hand settled on my shoulder. I jumped and opened my eyes. The face that looked up at me from the ground belonged to a boy who had died a long time ago and had turned into a zombie.

"Orissa," Hayden said calmly. Wide eyed, I locked eyes with him. He knelt down next to me and put both hands on my shoulders. "Hey, Riss, it's alright. Well, it's not but what else am I supposed to say?" he added with a slight smile.

Still breathing rapidly, I nodded. Hayden put his hand on my chest.

"Slow down," he instructed. "Take a deep breath."

I nodded again, closed my eyes, and tried to muster up a happy memory. Delmont's vile face flashed in my mind. No, I wasn't going to let horrible flashbacks freak me out. I remembered hitting him and smashing his balls with the butt of the shotgun.

My heart stopped racing. I recalled saving Olivia, the wonderful feeling of coming back to the compound, and seeing my friends again. I took a deep breath. I opened my eyes and looked into Hayden's.

I took another deep breath. I put my hand on Hayden's.

"Thanks," I panted. "I feel better. Sorry I freaked."

"You don't have to be sorry. I think we all are freaked." He stood and pulled me to my feet.

"No one else is panicking," I countered.

"Are you sure?" he asked.

"No," I admitted. I had no idea how anyone else was faring. Keeping a tight grip on my hand, Hayden gently pulled me forward. "What are we going to do with all the bodies?"

"Pile them up and burn them, I'd guess," Hayden said as he nudged a gummy with his boot.

"What a great bonfire," I said sarcastically. "It'll smell wonderful."

"Shit, it will. I suppose we'll have to move the bodies too; I don't think it'll be good to burn this on the grass our animals eat. I know it's not contagious to animals, but won't that make the grass bad?"

"It would make a bald spot. And yes, the rotting bodies turning to mush on the lawn is sure to give the grass a bitter taste."

He nodded, let go of my hand, and shot a zombie who crawled at us with two broken legs.

"There's another," I pointed out, seeing movement. We went over to where the thing thrashed in its attempt to get up. Having been totally eviscerated, the zombie couldn't stand because her torso had become too top heavy. Every time she pulled herself to her feet, her sliced open stomach and abs folded.

"It's almost funny," Hayden said, tipping his head and watched the zombie get up only to fall again.

"It is," I agreed. "She's determined, I'll give her that," I said with a slight laugh. Deciding to save a bullet, I waited until she fell again to break her neck.

"Help!" someone shouted.

We snapped our attention up.

"Help!" the voice called again.

Our eyes instantly went to the fence line that was dotted with trees. A strange and large figure limped down the sloping pasture. My first thought was that some horribly deformed zombie had saved his attack for last, wanting to surprise us with his disturbingly large size.

I felt like a dumbass when my brain recognized the shape as a person carrying someone over their shoulder.

Hayden and I ran over, but Ivan, Brock, and an A2 got their first. They took the body from the guy and gently laid it on the ground.

I jumped over a zombie, my boot landed in the splattered brains, and I slipped. I caught myself and kept running.

Wade was kneeling over the person on the ground with his hands pressed to a wound on the soldier's side. I wasn't sure if I should feel guilty that my friend had been the one to make it out ok.

"Get a car!" Ivan yelled as he dropped to his knees. "He needs to get into the hospital ward now!"

I recognized him as one of the A3s who guarded the front gate. His breathing was shallow and ragged; he had no doubt lost a lot of blood. Time passed incredibly slow as we waited for Jones to run off and return in a car. We kept our eyes peeled and shot three strays that meandered aimlessly around the pastures.

The wounded soldier was carefully lifted and set in the backseat of an SUV. Ivan and Jones drove him to the compound, radioing to Fuller to communicate with Padraic so he'd be ready to work a miracle.

All of the A3s at the gates were accounted for. The young man who got ripped apart was William, Steven told us, turning away to hide the falter in his voice and the tears in his eyes. The guy who Wade rescued from the fence line was Andy. He had recently asked to retest, desiring to become an A3.

Miguel, an A2, was missing. Through a chaotic mess of a radio roll call, we discovered he was the only soldier not accounted for.

"He's out here…somewhere," one of the A2s said, shaking his head. "Maybe he's injured and can't get up. We'll find him."

Under Fuller's orders, we weren't to move the zombie bodies unless we had gloves; he didn't want to risk us getting infected. I looked at my blood covered hands and wanted to tell Fuller he was a little too late on his train of thought.

There were several pairs of work gloves in the barn but not enough for all of us. Deciding to pointlessly give a damn about manners, the guys suggested Gabby and I drive the trucks while the guys with the gloves picked up the dead bodies and hoisted them into the truck beds. Hayden happily pointed out that the machine gun in the bed of his truck didn't enable us to throw the bodies into the back of it.

Still armed and on the lookout for stragglers, we drove around the pasture, picking up body after body. When the bed became full, we left the grounds of the compound and drove three miles down the street to dump the dead.

It took all morning to gather up the corpses. And we never found Miguel.

"I stopped counting how many zombies we killed after seventy," Hayden told me with a sigh. He took off the blood and pus crusted gloves and picked a piece of zombie splatter from my shoulder. "You look disgusting," he said with a half smile.

"So do you," I told him. "If my hands weren't so dirty, I'd wipe the zombie blood from your face."

He opened his mouth as if to say something—no doubt a dirty joke about me cleaning him up—but stopped. His hazel eyes locked with mine, sending that feeling through me. I took a deep breath and a step closer to Hayden. Things were far from ok, but with him, I'd be alright.

Half of the soldiers collected zombie body parts, doing their best to clean up the pasture. The other half of us fed the animals but didn't dare let them out with the broken fence and gates. I knew fixing them would now be top priority.

I dreaded that I would have to work tomorrow; I was so tired that just the thought of work wore me out.

Exhausted, shaken, saddened, and sore we got into our vehicles and drove in silence to the compound. The quarantine situation—or lack thereof—didn't hit me until we walked our bloody and muddy boot-covered feet into the fake fancy ambiance of the estate's foyer and saw Fuller in the doorway, arms crossed and looking sullen. I had never paid much attention to the first level of the house. I'd walked through the foyer to the stairs, either going up or going down, but that was pretty much it.

There was a dining room to my right; someone had even taken the time to keep the dark wooden table dusted. French doors were always closed to my left, but through the thick glass I could see the pretense of an office set up with bookshelves and desks. Fuller ushered us forward. We crossed the foyer and strode past the stairs. I officially had never gone this far into the old house.

If the scene of a young, innocent boy getting his skin torn off by hungry cannibals wasn't replaying in my mind, I would have been impressed with the grandeur of the estate. We situated in a room that was too fancy to be deemed a 'family room.' With ease, we all fit in the space.

My feet hurt and my body ached. Sitting seemed wonderful, but I didn't want to put my dirty ass on the spotless, ivory couches and armchairs. Fuller began talking, beginning with a very formal recap of events. He told us how proud he was of us and how we were an army the residents of the compound could rely on.

"Everyone will need to get their blood tested," Fuller explained. "Every single one of you was exposed. After the blood test—and regardless of the results—you will be quarantined for twenty-four hours per our standard procedure."

I shifted my weight and mentally rolled my eyes. Of course...an additional twenty-four hours of lock up. I shouldn't complain; it was damn worth it and I knew it.

"Since there are so many of you, you will be tested in alphabetical order to keep the medical staff organized. Then you will clean up and report back for quarantine instructions," Fuller informed us. As soon as he was done explaining that we were to stay up here to avoid freaking out the residents, Hayden slunk away to talk to him, no doubt giving a report on everything that happened on the mission.

I sat on the ground in the hallway. I wanted to go to sleep, wake up, and realize the attack on the farm had only been a nightmare. I didn't want to believe we had lost three of our soldiers. I hated that we had to worry about an attack. I hated that we were forced into hiding, hated that we had to get blood tests and worry about infection, running out of food, medicine, and supplies.

I wanted to find the person who created the virus—I was certain *someone* had—and hit them over the head until their skull cracked and brain and blood leaked out. Maybe I should see if they had a cure first. I shook my head. It was pointless to think like that. Whoever created the virus was probably dead anyway.

Gabby's father, Hector, emerged from the basement with a list. He read off the first five names and told them to follow him into the medical unit to be tested. I felt a little bad for Doctor Cara and really bad for Padraic for having to get up and test our blood again.

I put my head in my hands and exhaled. I heard the scuffling of feet and someone sat down next to me. I looked up, expecting to see Hayden.

"You doing alright?" Rider asked, his eyes filled with stress.

"Yeah, I guess. You?"

"Yeah," he repeated. "I hope that doesn't happen again."

"You're telling me. Our cows are getting close to mating season. Once they pop out a few we can have hamburgers again."

"That sounds good. Well, not really right now. I don't have much of an appetite at the moment."

"Me neither," I agreed and hoped he wouldn't bring up the fact that three people had lost their lives. I wasn't sure if I could emotionally handle that stoically right now. Luckily Rider closed his eyes and leaned his head against the wall. Slowly, the soft murmur of hushed voices filled the living room.

I too closed my eyes and let my head fall until it was resting on Rider's shoulder. He linked his arm through mine and laced our fingers. I gave his hand a squeeze, thanking him for his silent comfort and understanding.

I caught bits and pieces of what the others were saying. Most were talking about what had happened. A few wished they had done things differently. Muffled sobs were heard after the mention of the names of the deceased.

I tried so hard to not focus on what they were saying that I felt like I wasn't really there. Everything seemed surreal; the talking about zombies, the huge house, and the shiny hardwood floor I was sitting on. My body screamed at me to move out of the uncomfortable position I was sitting in, but I ignored it. Within a few minutes, the throbbing pain in my legs turned to numbness as the blood flow decreased.

I felt like I was spinning, getting sucked into an evil, black maelstrom of blood and violence.

"Orissa," a familiar and soothing voice called.

I snapped my head up to stare into the pretty blue eyes of Padraic.

"What are you doing?" I blurted since I assumed he was supposed to be downstairs looking at samples of our blood under a microscope. He smiled and knelt down next to me.

"I wanted to make sure you were alright."

I nodded. "I'm alright," I lied. Rider removed his hand.

"Glad to hear that," he said, not convinced. "Come on, I'll get you tested so you can get cleaned up and rest."

"My last name starts with a 'P'," I stated.

Padraic winked at me. "That's where being friends with the head doctor comes in handy." He stood and extended a hand for me. I took it and let Padraic help me to my feet. I had forgotten how soft his skin was. He had gotten his hair cut since I'd last seen him; the shorter style looked good on him. Even at the crack of dawn, Padraic looked as put together and handsome as he always did.

"I'll see you in the quarantine," I said to Rider, feeling as if I was betraying him somehow by leaving.

"Yeah, see ya," Rider said to me.

I followed Padraic through the hall and down the basement stairs. We stopped in front of the steel doors that required a hand scan and a pass code. I had to pick crusted blood from my fingertips before the scanner recognized me.

Once through the first set of doors, Padraic turned and put his hand on my shoulder.

"You have no idea how terrified I was for you," he confessed.

"Did you know what was going on?"

"Yeah. I hadn't gone back to bed since we did your first blood test. I heard running and people giving orders. You had gone out by the time I found Fuller." He stepped closer. "I wanted to go out there too, Riss. I wanted to help."

Surprised, I took a step back. "Padraic, no! You could get hurt!"

"I know the risks, Orissa."

"Then why the hell would you want to go out there?"

"Why do you?" he asked.

"Because!" I dumbly spat. "You can do so much here—inside. Where it's safe. We need you *here* Padraic! Without you…I don't even know. But a lot of people would be dead without you."

Padraic chuckled. "Don't worry. Fuller said the same thing. While I don't particularly like the guy, he does a good job running this place so I will respect his wishes."

"Good," I said and punched in the security code to get through the second set of doors.

"They don't know; Fuller is going to tell them later," Padraic whispered to me and I knew that he meant the residents. It was still early, too early for me to get up without a reason, but many of the residents were waking up to start their boring day stuck underground. I hoped they stayed in their rooms so I wouldn't have to come up with a lie to tell them.

We quickly jogged down the stairs to the B level and made a bee line for the hospital ward. Ivan and Brock sat in an exam room with three other A's, waiting for their results.

"How did you manage to cut in line?" Ivan teased as we walked past.

"Good behavior," I joked causing Ivan and Brock to laugh. Padraic and I went into the small laboratory that had been set up. Dressed in a long, yellow denim skirt and a lime green and purple stripped turtle neck sweater, Doctor Cara was bent over a microscope. She didn't so much as blink an eye at us when we walked into the room.

Padraic put on gloves and grabbed an alcohol wipe to disinfect my skin.

"Oh my," he said when he looked at my filthy arm. "Uh, can you wash your arm with soap and water first? I didn't realize just how covered in…blood you are."

"Sure," I obliged and went to the sink.

Afterward, Padraic tied a rubber band around my arm, ran the alcohol pad over the spot, and uncapped a needle. "You know," he said as he stuck the needle into my vein, "I wouldn't have called myself experienced at drawing blood before."

"That's reassuring, says the guy who has a needle in my arm."

Padraic laughed. "If my patients needed blood work, I'd order it and someone else would do it."

"Glad to be your test subject," I said sarcastically.

"I'm not that bad, am I?" he asked, his blue eyes flicked up from my arm to look into mine.

"No. I would have thought you'd been doing this your whole life," I told him honestly. "You're very…very gentle."

"Thanks," he said almost shyly. He extracted enough blood, pulled the needle out of my vein, and pressed a piece of gauze over the wound. Then he spent a few minutes looking at it under the microscope.

"I don't see any traces of the virus in your blood," he said. "You can go gets some sleep now; I'm sure you're exhausted."

"I am," I agreed. Though I was a little nervous to sleep. I didn't want the disturbing images of what had just happened flashing through my brain in dreams. "You must be too."

"I'll manage. I wasn't out on a mission like you were."

"True," I stated and walked to the door, which Padraic opened for me. We were alone in the hospital ward hall. "I feel like I haven't seen you in forever," I confessed, suddenly realizing how much I missed not only Padraic but Raeya, Sonja, Olivia, and Lisa.

"It has been a few days. Does time go by fast when you're on missions?"

"Usually, though this last one just felt long. And tiring, very tiring."

"What happened?" he asked quietly as we walked down the hall to the stairs.

I shrugged and winced at the pain the movement caused.

"What?" Padraic asked immediately. "What's wrong?"

I tried rolling my shoulder only to find it hurt even worse. "Nothing. I think I pulled a muscle in my shoulder or something."

"You are pretty banged up," he reminded me and gently touched the scab on my forehead. "What is this from?"

"A crazy threw a rock at me," I said after a moment's recall. "And this," I began and lifted up the hem of my tank top to show off the bruises on my left side, "is from falling down a flight of stairs in a parking garage while running away from a herd of zombies during a tornado."

"Holy shit, Orissa!" Padraic exclaimed. "That looks horrible!"

"You should see this then, too." I turned around so he could see the layers of skin that had been scraped off by my gun. Padraic's face was so horrified I laughed. "It's not that bad. I'll be better after a couple of days. I've been worse, you know."

"Unfortunately, you have. You're lucky you haven't been seriously hurt."

"Luck has nothing to do with it," I said. The moment the words escaped my mouth I realized that I was lucky. All the last-minute getaways, finding a car that just so happens to start...was that luck and not skill?

"Get some rest," Padraic instructed. "Doctor's orders."

"I will. Can you tell Ray I said hi and that I'm fine? I won't get to see her until tomorrow morning."

"Of course. Sleep well, Orissa."

"You too." I smiled at Padraic before going upstairs to shower and change. A few minutes later, Ivan—dressed in a towel—opened the door. He looked at me in surprise.

"I didn't expect to see you up here so soon," he confessed.

"My blood was clean," I told him.

"Good." He stepped past me. "There should still be plenty of hot water. See ya downstairs."

Once I was back in my room I moved as slow as possible since I didn't want to sit downstairs and wait. Unless Fuller pushed Hayden ahead in line, he would be one of the last of the soldiers to get their blood tested.

I lay down in my bed. The sun was shining and birds were merrily singing, unaware of the danger that surrounded us or the stain of death the day was marked with. I must have drifted off to sleep because it seemed like only a few minutes had passed when the mattress sunk down.

I opened my eyes to see Hayden; showered and clean, wearing nothing but a pair of pajama pants.

"Do we have to go to the quarantine room?" I asked, rubbing the sleep from my eyes. My throat was incredibly dry but I felt too bogged down by sleep to do anything about it.

"Nope," Hayden said and lay down next to me. "The A2 and 3s are going in there since there are more of them than there are of us."

"So where are we going?"

He wrapped his arms around me. I wormed closer to him, pressing my face against his firm chest. "We get to be locked in our rooms."

"Seriously?"

"Yeah. The door at the top of the stairs is closed and locked. Someone will bring up breakfast soon and we'll be checked on every few hours."

I closed my eyes again. "I love you, Hayden," I whispered, feeling that was something that needed to be said. Maybe Padraic was right; maybe we were only still alive because of luck. As long as I had it on my side, I was going to use it to my advantage.

But luck runs out and not everyone gets lucky. If things were to take a turn for the worst, I wanted to make damn sure the people I cared about knew exactly how much they meant to me.

"I love you, too," he whispered back and pressed his lips to mine.

"Do you think we're still alive only because we're lucky?" I asked, unable to help myself.

"No," he answered right away. "We're alive because we're smart. We know what we're doing. We don't take unnecessary risks…well, not too often. We've been more or less trained, we usually have a plan, and we have each other. And I don't mean just me and you. All of us; any of us. We all bring something different to the table. We can draw off each other's strengths. We have each other's backs. We're still alive because we're fighters; we're still alive because we want to live."

"Good," I said quietly.

"And maybe just a little lucky," he added. "I'd rather be lucky than smart. If we got lucky every mission, everything would go our way and nothing bad would happen."

"Wouldn't that be nice?"

"It would." He hugged me a little tighter. I ran my fingers up and down his arms. "I still feel lucky that we met."

"Me too," I agreed. "It's one of the few good things that came out of all this."

"It is." He kissed me once more. "Speaking of luck, am I gonna get lucky today?"

I laughed and shook my head. "Maybe later."

Hayden resituated, resting his head on my chest. I ran my fingers through his hair which almost instantly makes him relax and fall asleep. Holding the soothing words Hayden had spoken close to my heart, I closed my eyes and was able to fall into a nightmare free sleep.

Until Fuller burst into our room…

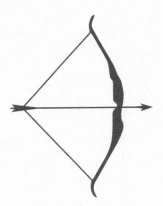

CHAPTER 22

"Sir, I can explain," Hayden spat quickly and tried to jump out of bed. His foot got caught in the sheets and he desperately pulled on the blankets to get free.

To my surprise, Fuller laughed. "I think I can figure this one out, Underwood."

Hayden picked up a shirt from the floor and put it on. "It's not what it looks like," he blurted.

"Oh, it's not?" Fuller chuckled. "What is it then?"

Hayden looked at me and knew that denying our relationship would hurt me. "Ok, it is what it looks like."

Fuller's eyes met mine for a millisecond before flashing back to Hayden's.

"Are you going to try and break us apart?" I asked, compelled to dispel Hayden's fear.

"Why would I do that?" Fuller asked, seemingly baffled.

"Because we're distracted by each other," I went on to explain.

Fuller sat on the edge of Hayden's bed and motioned for Hayden to sit back down as well. "How long has this been going on?" he asked.

"Since I got back from being abandoned," I informed him.

"I haven't noticed any drop in either of your performances," Fuller promised, his eyes practically gleaming. "And it's about time, Underwood," he said with a wink. It unnerved me to see him happy and creeped me out that his happiness steamed from seeing Hayden and I in bed together.

Hayden turned to me as if I had an answer to his unspoken question. "You knew?" he finally asked his superior.

Fuller laughed and I realized it was probably the first time I'd heard him laugh—ever. "Why else do you think I made the order not to tell you Orissa never came back from that mission? You weren't healing as well as we hoped and I knew what the news would do to you."

Hayden nodded and shrugged and agreed that thinking I was dead would more than just upset him.

"So," he said slowly. "You don't care that we're together?"

"Why would I?" Fuller asked, his voice full of amusement.

"It's unprofessional?" Hayden suggested.

Fuller crossed his arms and looked at Hayden with a very paternal I'm-going-to-give-you-advice expression. "Happiness is rare, if not extinct in this bleak world. If you find something that makes you smile, you have to hold on to that."

Fuller's words sunk my previous revelation in deeper. I felt tears bite at the corner of my eyes for some stupid reason. He smiled once more and turned to me.

"Do you love each other?" he asked so shamelessly it made blood rush to my cheeks.

"Of course," I instantly answered at the same time Hayden said 'yes.' I absently mindedly curled my fingers around the dog tags that hung from my neck. Fuller noticed the gesture and looked at Hayden somewhat incredulously. Hayden nodded, cast his eyes down, and smiled.

"Well," Fuller said and stood. "I came up to check on my soldiers and Marines. Everyone is faring as well as I hoped. We are having a service for the fallen tomorrow," he said and stepped toward the door. He paused. "Who knows?"

"Knows what, sir?" Hayden asked.

"Who knows about you two?"

"Our team," Hayden replied. "And Orissa's friend Raeya."

Fuller pressed his lips together. "Maybe it should be kept that way—for now. You know how the gossip is in this place." He smiled again. "Though it's only a matter of time; you are pretty obvious, Underwood. But be prepared for the stories and questions when you two *come out*."

Hayden laughed and walked Fuller to the door and the two stepped into the hall and spoke in hushed voices for several minutes. When Hayden came back in, he was smiling.

"Well, that was weird," I said.

"What do you mean?" Hayden closed the door and sat next to me.

"Seeing Fuller smiling and laughing and giving advice." I shook my head. "It was almost uncomfortable it was so out of character."

"Out of character? Fuller's always like that."

"No he's not," I said, raising my eyebrows.

"Yes he is. He's a nice guy."

"Are we talking about the same person here?"

"Orissa, Fuller is strict, I'll give you that. But he has to be. If he was just a resident, I think you'd see it. But he's not. He holds the weight of this place on his shoulders. It's a big responsibility. I know you two haven't exactly gotten along, and I think that's because you're not used to taking orders or respecting someone just because they are your superior. Really, he's not a bad guy."

"He freaking loves you; everybody knows that. Of course you'd sing his praises. And I'm not going to respect someone just because they have a fancy title at the beginning of their name. Respect is earned, not instantly granted."

"Respecting someone and liking someone are two different things," he countered.

"No, they're not."

He sighed. "You don't get it. Maybe it's a military thing."

"Maybe. I don't want to start an argument. I'm glad Fuller knows and isn't gonna make us change rooms."

"Me too. I feel so much better not having to hide it anymore." His arms wrapped around me and we lay back down.

"Do you think they felt much pain?" I asked when an image of the fallen soldiers flashed through my mind.

"Who?"

"The three guys that died."

"Yeah, I'm sure they did."

I glared at Hayden. "That's not what you're supposed to say."

"I'm not going to lie, Riss. You know as well as I do that having someone bite you, pull back, and rip your skin off isn't pleasant."

"I hate that they died."

He ran his fingers through my hair. "Me too. I keep thinking about how if we only got there sooner we could have saved them. But this is a war. People die in war."

"I never thought of it that way."

"In what way?"

"War."

"Oh, it's not what I'm used to," he said with a slight smile. "Thankfully the zombies don't shoot back. But they outnumber us. This isn't just some battle. This is a war; it's a fight for humanity."

"It is." I closed my eyes and was plagued with the image of a bloody pasture. I heavily exhaled and sat up, tracing Hayden's tattoo with my finger.

⟶

The next morning, we woke up on time and went down for breakfast. I eagerly looked around for my friends. When I didn't see them, I figured I missed them. Several residents thanked Hayden and me for risking our lives to keep the farm safe.

Hayden shook their hands, smiled, and thanked them for their appreciation all the while seeming so humble. He was so much better at interacting with people than I was.

I had just picked up my tray when she ran up behind me. I almost dropped my oatmeal when her arms wrapped around my body.

"Rissy!" Raeya cried. I set the tray back down and spun around.

"Ray!" I said in a stupid high pitched voice. I hugged my best friend. "I thought you already ate!"

"I did," she told me, her voice muffled by my hair. "I've been waiting forever for you to come back down! It feels like you've been gone for ages!"

"It does feel like ages," I agreed. I relaxed my grip on her. "Come, sit with us."

Hayden, Raeya, and I sat at our normal table in the back. Rider, Brock, Alex, and José were still finishing their breakfast. They smiled bleakly at us as we took our seats.

Raeya filled me in on everything I had missed while out on the mission. Everyone had finally been able to go outside at least once before a bad storm rolled in, the concepts of our fields had been put into action, and construction began on the first cabin. I knew she was itching to ask me about the details of the mission and even more so about what happened on the farm the other night. She knew better than to utter a word about it in mixed company.

After breakfast, I went with Raeya into her room. Fashioned out of what looked like an old table cloth, Raeya had made curtains and hung them centered on the wall opposite the door, giving her underground room the feeling of having a window. She checked to make sure her recluse of a roommate wasn't hiding under the covers of her bed before she shut the door and questioned me.

"How did the mission go? The weather hasn't been too nice. Did you guys run into the storm?"

"Yeah," I replied honestly. "It wasn't too bad though. We avoided it." Maybe it was wrong to lie to my best friend. But maybe it was better to not upset her with something that had already happened. "It just felt like a long ass mission for some reason." I ran my hands through my messy hair. "We found a government set up quarantine."

"Oh my God, really? Is that where the new people came from?"

I shook my head. "It was full of dead people. Well, except for a few crazies. It was bad, Ray. You don't want to know the details."

"Tell me about the fresh produce," she practically gushed.

"It was weird, that's for sure. You know those greenhouse things that replaced real farms a few years ago?"

She nodded.

"Well," I continued. "We found a greenhouse farm."

"No way," she whispered in disbelief. "A *working* greenhouse farm?"

"No, a nonworking one full of fresh fruit and veggies," I said sarcastically.

"Sorry, dumb question," she said with a smile. "You know what I mean. Can those things work without people?"

"I don't really know. It's all run mechanically; the levels rotate on their own so as long as the tanks have water and the bulbs haven't burned out, I suppose so. But the plants would be over grown. And these weren't."

"Who do you think was taking care of them?"

"We have no idea. We couldn't find any obvious signs of anyone holing up nearby."

"I wish there had been more seeds," she said.

I shook my head. "You are a city girl, Ray. You can get the seeds from the plants."

She laughed. "Right. The plants were in good shape?"

"Excellent shape," I said. "We found it because we went farther than Fuller wanted us to go. We're not supposed to cross the Pennsylvania border; it's too far or something like that. I didn't see what the big deal was, but Hayden hates disobeying orders. I think he feels guilty."

"He's a good soldier."

"Yeah he is." I gasped. "Oh, I can't believe I didn't tell you. Fuller caught us in bed together."

"What? Like *together* together?"

"We were sleeping, literally." I told her about the odd approval and encouragement Fuller gave us to be together. I summed up the rest of the mission and gave her the bare bones details of the attack on the farm. It was a bloody memory I would be happy to forget; Raeya didn't need to know about it. I knew it would upset her later.

Like the amazing friend she's always been, she could tell it struck a nerve with me too. I wasn't quite sure exactly how she knew when something upset me. I was careful to keep my body still, my voice level, and my eyes focused.

She switched the subject to something safe and we talked about Scarlet still spreading gossip, how effective training the dogs to round up the cattle had been, and whether or not we should name the baby calves this summer when they would most likely become our dinner. We wandered upstairs and played with Argos; he raced over and nearly knocked me down in his ecstatic greeting.

At 10:15, I left Raeya to find Hayden. He wasn't upstairs and Ivan told me he hadn't seen him. I went back into our room and tried to do a Sun Salutation but quit after only a few seconds. My shoulder radiated pain down my arm and back when I raised it above my head.

I opened both windows, welcoming the slight breeze that blew in. The air wasn't hot, but it was thick and sticky, carrying the scent of rain. Gray clouds were moving in fast. We could use the rain; it would wash away the blood that had been spilled on our land.

"Ready?" Hayden's voice came from behind me. I almost asked 'for what' when I remembered the service.

"No. I don't want to go. I hate stuff like this."

"Me too," he agreed. "It reminds me of how easily it could be one of us we're honoring."

I nodded. "Can I please lock you in a safe room? I promise to feed you three times a day. I'll even have sex with you at least four times a week."

"Can I have a TV?" he asked.

"Yep."

"Make it five times a week and we have a deal," he said with a smile. "But you'll have to be locked in with me. I don't want anything bad to happen to you, either."

"Well, then we're both screwed." I got off the bed and went to Hayden's side. I tucked his dog tags down the front of my shirt and followed him outside. Andy, the guy who Wade pulled from the hands of zombies, died from complications -- as Padraic explained it -- several hours after he was brought to the hospital ward. We had what was left of William's body and nothing of Miguel.

All three hundred and something residents lined up outside, raising their right hands to their foreheads in respect when the bodies were walked through. Though none of the three who died were enlisted in the military, Fuller considered them soldiers and everyone wanted them honored for their bravery and sacrifice.

I knew the twelve gun salute triggered a waking nightmare in Hayden's mind. I kept a tight grip on his hand the entire time while I fought back tears.

Hayden hadn't been asleep long that night when his body began twitching, waking me up. He was breathing heavily and drenched in sweat.

"Hayden," I said softly and cupped my hands on his face. "Hayden, wake up."

With a sharp intake of breath, his eyes flew opened and darted around the room, trying to focus on something that wasn't real.

"Hayden," I spoke again. "It's ok. It's not real. You're safe. You're with me."

With a fast, jerky movement, he grabbed me and pulled me onto him. "Orissa?"

"Yes, Hayden. It's me. It's ok."

He took a deep breath and stopped shaking. Then he suddenly startled and involuntarily squeezed me. "You don't hear it?" he asked.

I shook my head. "No, I don't. It's not real. You're safe, Hayden."

"Yes," he panted. "Safe. But it's so loud."

"What's loud?"

"The IED. Get off the road."

"We are off the road. Hayden, look at me." I sat up and put my face inches from his. "You are not on a road. You are not in Afghanistan anymore. You are in Arkansas. We are fighting zombies, not an army." That wasn't going to offer any comfort, but I wanted Hayden to come out of the dark place he was stuck in.

He opened his mouth to say something, stopped, closed his eyes, and nodded. When he opened his eyes again, I could tell he was in the present. He kept his arms wrapped tightly around me until his heart stopped racing.

"I'm sorry," he sighed.

"What are you sorry for?" I asked, not moving my head off his chest.

"For making you have to deal with that."

"You're being ridiculous, Hayden. I don't feel like I *have to deal* with anything."

"I should be over it by now."

"I don't think I'd ever get over seeing something like that. And not just Ben," I said gently. "Everything you saw over there plus all the shit we see now. It's enough to fuck anyone up."

"But I'm the only one who has nightmares," he argued, clearly upset and frustrated with himself.

"I highly doubt that," I soothed.

"It's annoying."

"Not to me. And besides," I said, sitting up so I could look into his hazel eyes. "It's your only flaw. There has to be *something* wrong with you or else you'd make me look bad."

He only nodded and ran his hands over my arms. "Are you tired?"

"Yeah," I responded with a yawn.

"Go back to sleep."

"I'll stay up with you."

"No," he said quietly. "I'm fine now. I'll read until I feel tired." He turned on the lamp next to the bed, covered the lampshade with a t-shirt to dim the light, and got a book. I resituated my pillows so my back was touching Hayden's side so I'd be able to feel if he was having another nightmare.

When I woke up at 7:30, Hayden informed me he hadn't been able to sleep most of the night and was too tired to go down for breakfast. I offered to bring him up a tray, got dressed, and went downstairs.

My shoulder was still sore. The tingling feeling in my fingers came back when I extended my arm for my tray.

"I think that can be a sign of a heart attack!" Raeya exclaimed, her voice full of concern.

I dubiously stared at her. "Yeah, Raeya, I'm having a heart attack."

"Just because you're in good shape doesn't mean it couldn't happen," she reminded me. "I know you've heard the stories of athletes dropping dead of heart attacks."

"I have and I know, but the tingling has nothing to do with my heart. It feels like my arm fell asleep."

"Exactly! It's a sign!"

"Would it make you feel better if I asked Padraic?"

She smiled. "Yeah, thanks."

Once we were done eating, the two of us went downstairs to the B level. Raeya suggested we try Padraic's room since it was his 'day off' from working in the hospital ward. Like Raeya, he too had curtains closed over a nonexistent window. Other new additions to his room included a bouquet of colorful flowers made out of paper, several drawings that were obviously done by children taped to the cinderblock walls, and a TV centered on the dresser by his bed. Dressed in green pajama pants and a thin, black t-shirt, Padraic smiled when he took in the sight of us.

"Morning. What do I owe the pleasure?" he asked, beckoning us in.

"Raeya thinks I'm having heart problems," I said calmly.

Padraic's clear blue eyes flashed with fear before he laughed. Looking at Ray, he asked, "Why do you think that?"

"She said she feels tingling," Raeya supplied.

"Which arm?" Padraic inquired, suddenly serious.

"This one," I said and held up my right arm which caused the pain to shoot down again. I winced.

"Describe your pain," Padraic said in a very doctorly way.

I described it the best I could, feeling a bit like a baby for talking about my stupid shoulder hurting when others were injured way worse than I had been.

After a few moments of gently touching, squeezing, and stretching my arm Padraic said, "I can't be certain, but I think it's a pinched nerve. They are very painful but usually go away in a week or two. Try and rest it as much as possible."

"Thanks," I told him. "See, Ray, nothing to worry about."

"You're welcome, Orissa." He turned again to Raeya. "Are we still on for part two?"

"I am if you are!" she told him with a smile.

"Yes! I'm dying to know what happens to Brooke!" he said causing Raeya to laugh. "I enjoyed my orange this morning, thanks, Orissa."

"You're welcome. I'm not the only one that deserves the thanks, though."

"You discovered the footprints, right?" he asked me. Raeya must have told him.

"Yeah, I did," I admitted.

"As weird as the situation is, I'm happy we can enjoy something fresh for a change, though I daresay it won't last long," he said.

"Sorry to rush off," Raeya began. "But I have an overseer meeting in a little bit. I'll come back as soon as it's over!"

"Sounds good," Padraic said with a smile. "See you ladies later." He walked us to the door. I waited until I heard his door click shut before I turned to Raeya.

"What are you and Padraic doing later?" I asked, hoping to sound merely curious and not disappointed that I wouldn't get to hang out with her as I had hoped.

"I've been making him watch *One Tree Hill* with me. Sofia Johnson, who is three rooms down from me, has all the seasons on DVD." She shook her head. "Sofia is lucky the guys found her. She packed more forms of entertainment than food in her bag when the virus broke out."

"Some people have no idea how to survive. It's funny...it's a skill no one thought they'd need to know."

"When this is over and things are somewhat back to normal, I think it's something we should teach the kids. A survival skills class should be mandatory," Raeya said with complete seriousness.

We walked up the stairs to the C level.

"So, have you and Padraic been hanging out a lot?" I asked carefully.

"Not any more than normal. Well, when you're gone I do. I told you, I get lonely."

She followed me back into the cafeteria to grab a tray for Hayden. "What about the other overseers?" I asked. "Don't you like them?"

"Yeah I do. But I'm like ten years younger than them. I feel awful by saying that I don't really want to hang out with them."

"Don't feel awful; it's understandable."

"What about you?" she asked. "What's it like going on missions and being with five guys twenty-four seven?"

"It's not bad at all," I confessed. "I really like the guys. I feel like those guys are family."

"I'm glad." She smiled. "Well, I'll see you at lunch." We hugged before I went into the cafeteria to get breakfast for Hayden, who was still asleep when I got back to our room.

Not wanting to sit around and do nothing, I went outside to find Argos, though my shoulder was aching so badly I didn't want to throw the ball for him. Jones was outside pouring food into bowls and distributing them amongst the begging dogs. It occurred to me that I didn't know Jones' first name.

"Hey, Orissa!" he said brightly over the sound of kibble rushing into a stainless steel bowl.

"Hi," I replied and strode over to help. The little dogs had been sectioned off for feeding and Jones stepped over the gate and set a bowl down. Instantly a fight broke out. He picked up a Chihuahua, only to quickly drop it. He shook his hand and stuck his finger in his mouth.

"It's always the little ones," I commented.

Jones inspected the teeth marks on his hand.

"He drew blood," he grumbled. "Seriously, we have how many German Shepherds? And I've never had an issue feeding them."

"Where's Argos?" I asked, looking around the yard.

"Dr. Sheehan has him. He takes him a lot, actually."

"He does?"

"Yeah. I think Argos spends more time with him than with the trainers. It's gonna make him spoiled," he laughed.

Greta, the pretty, dark sable German Shepherd that Hayden favored trotted over and licked my hand, wagging her tail.

"Sorry, girl, I don't have any treats." She stayed regardless, happy to be petted. Jones filled up several more bowls and I picked up two, setting them several feet from each other. We had to break up two more fights in the little dog section of the yard. Without being too obvious, I eyed Jones' ID tag and learned his first name was Trey.

We made small talk while the dogs ate, speaking mostly of the new tricks the canines were learning and how good Greta was at seeking out the scents of humans. In mutual agreement, we were excited to use the dogs to find people but worried to take them into such a hostile environment. Animals were innocent, Jones strongly voiced. It wasn't right for them to get killed by zombies when it could easily be avoided.

It was another humid day so we brought the dogs inside, distributing them to their owners. The military and police dogs the compound had acquired were adopted out, as Trey put it, by residents. Trey formally introduced me to Sadie, an older Shepherd who was assumed to be a former drug sniffing canine.

"They started barking a good twenty minutes before anyone saw the herd," he told me as he stroked Sadie's fur. "Being this far underground, I don't know how they sense it. Maybe it's the smell." He shook his head. "I knew something was wrong. Sadie woke me up. Then Greta started barking. It was odd; they never need to go out in the middle of the night. Then they all started whimpering and barking. That's when I knew."

I nodded. "If it wasn't for Argos, I don't know if I'd be here." The image of Logan, the first person I considered a friend during the initial outbreak, flashed through my mind. Argos saved me. I wanted to think I would have been able to get out of that situation on my own. Deep down I wasn't able to lie to myself. I would be dead if it wasn't for that dog.

Clutching my sore arm to my chest, I went down another flight of stairs to find the Doberman. Padraic's door was slightly ajar. I knocked, waited a second and then pushed it open. The stump of Argo's tail wiggled back and forth as soon as he caught sight of me.

"Hey," I called to Padraic, dropping to my knees to let Argos lick my face.

"Hi, Rissy," he said back, sitting up. He turned the volume down on the movie he was watching. "Whatcha doing?"

"I missed my dog," I told him, still petting Argos.

"Your dog?" he questioned with a laugh. "I like to call him mine."

"I found him!" I teased. "So therefore he's mine."

"Our dog?" Padraic tested.

"Fine. But he loves me more."

"Ah, I doubt it. I bring him table scraps," Padraic chuckled. On excitement overdrive, Argo slipped on the tile floor in his mad attempt to run across the room and bring me a homemade toy—a water bottle inside a sock.

Padraic sat next to me on the bed. He smiled a little too sweetly, and suddenly I felt awkward. Argos jumped up, eagerly licking my face.

"Have you met the newest residents yet?" I asked. "One of them is really weird; she thinks the zombies are possessed by evil spirits."

Padraic laughed. "I think that's the real mythology behind zombies, isn't it?"

"I don't know. It sounds right though."

Padraic's door creaked. I looked over to see who was there but saw no one. I turned back to Padraic when it creaked again and opened a few inches. He sighed and stood up.

"Looks like Petunia got out again," he said and walked to the door. He squatted and extended his hand. A dark sable ferret curiously walked over. He scooped up the little weasel and brought her over to me. Argos nosed his face into my lap, curiously sniffing the little animal.

"Oh my God! She is so freaking cute!" I exclaimed. When I was little, I wanted a ferret. I even saved up a summer's worth of allowance for one and read every book about ferrets I could get from the library. But my grandpa told me they were useless and bought me a dog instead. Two weeks later, my dog ran away, never to be seen again. "Where did she come from?"

"Cara has a few of them," Padraic explained. "I'm not really sure how many, to be honest. This little gal is a Houdini; she gets out all the time."

"Should we take her back?"

"I will," he told me. "I want to see how things are going in the lab."

"I thought today was your day off," I said.

"It is," he agreed ruefully. "I won't do any work, don't worry."

"Good, you deserve to rest too, you know."

He sighed. "I know. Now that the flu outbreak seems to be under control it has been better. That wasn't fun."

"I bet! I wouldn't want to be around sick people all the time; it's depressing."

"It can be," he agreed. "I'm not sure if this is fortunate or unfortunate, but survival of the fittest seems to be at play now. I doubt you've noticed the lack of the chronically ill here."

I tipped my head. "You're right. I never thought about it before. It's kinda sad…but I guess good too. We're not equipped to take care of really sick people."

"No, we're not at all." He turned right to go into Dr. Cara's room, shutting his door so Argos wouldn't get out. "Well, on that happy note, I'll see you at dinner."

"Yeah, see ya." I smiled and waved goodbye. I slowly walked up to my room, dug around in Hayden's snack box, and settled on a box of cookies. I fluffed the pillows and got comfortable in bed, deciding to read more of *The Hobbit* until Hayden rejoined me.

The next few days passed in a similar, uneventful fashion. Those who weren't injured went out to the farm to fix the fences, gates and work on widening the moat. Under the care of Dr. Sheehan, I wasn't cleared for labor. I played cards with Raeya, Sonja, Olivia, and Padraic while Hayden and the rest of my team went out to work under the hot sun.

Alex had a deep cut on his calf and hobbled when he walked. Still feeling slight animosity toward each other, he avoided me, sitting as far away as possible in the game room. Addison and Lizzy had become friends with Lisa and the few other children at the compound. Parker—the only person other than Hayden we knew to be resistant to the virus—was playing with Hotwheels cars with Quinn.

Scarlett buzzed around, happily introducing the new residents to everyone and retelling her story of how heroically Hayden saved her. I noticed her story got more and more farfetched every time she told it. When I asked Hayden about it, he wasn't able to recall the nitty gritty details. He said it was a regular rescue and didn't even think Scarlett's family was in immediate danger.

Sweaty and dirty, Hayden came in before lunch. I left my friends to go find him so we could shower together. Every day that passed eased the tension I still felt from the attack on the farm. When one week had passed, the hope of our survival was back in my heart. My arm didn't hurt anymore, much to Padraic's surprise. He still advised me to stay away from hard work. But with the lack of pain I was feeling, I couldn't justify my friends slaving away while I sat comfortably inside.

Zack became an A2, replacing one that we lost. Colin had the skills and know-how to be on the A level but declined any sort of position that dealt with zombies. Hayden told me Fuller was disappointed that Colin wouldn't help us out, but he said Fuller wouldn't push it; if someone didn't want to face the zombies anymore, they didn't have to. I remembered Hayden telling me a similar thing when we first met. He assured me the compound wasn't run like a prison and promised I'd still have most of my free will.

Against Sonja's protests, Jason applied to move up in the ranks. Like his sister, I preferred him to stay stowed safely away in the stone watch towers. It was sturdy and secure but still crucial to our survival. I considered asking Hayden to tell Fuller not to let Jason move up but stopped, realizing it was selfish. And, I reminded myself that I couldn't keep everyone safe forever.

As soon as the farm was not only fixed but improved, Alex and his team were given two days off to rest before they would set out on a supplies mission. Along with food, we needed household items like toilet paper, soap, cleaning products, and fans since we weren't running the air conditioner upstairs.

Back to our regular routine, Hayden and I grumbled about getting up early to work out. Fuller ventured down into the workout room, assessing our improved strength and abilities. He complimented me on my improvement since I first joined the A1 ranks. I had never considered myself to be out of shape, though I definitely noticed an increase in my strength.

I set down the weights I had been lifting and walked over to the bench my cup of water was on.

"How's your arm?" Fuller asked from behind.

I turned. "My arm?"

"Dr. Sheehan informed me you sustained an injury."

"Oh," I took a drink. "Yeah. I did. I'm better now."

Fuller nodded. "Carry on."

"Uh, ok." I resisted the urge to roll my eyes. Why Hayden thought he was so great, I'd never understand. After working out, I showered, found Raeya, Sonja, and Olivia and sat in the game room talking with them until lunch. I ate in the back with the other A1s.

<hr>

Fuller flagged Hayden down on our way out of the cafeteria. I accompanied him into Fuller's office. I spied a list on his desk, and a mixture of excitement and dread bubbled through me. We were going on a mission.

"Once the others get back and have a day or two to rest, your team will set out," Fuller told Hayden. "I want you to go on a seek mission, not just looking for people but looking to see what state the world is in. If you find a herd, do whatever it takes to bring them down. We can't risk another one passing through."

"Yes, sir," Hayden automatically said.

"Even if we find a herd and kill every last undead asshole that's in it," I said carefully. "I don't think it will help. They outnumber us ten to one, or more. Probably more."

To my surprise, Fuller didn't disagree with me. "I like to think it will help. I had imagined most of the S2s would have deteriorated into the S3 stage by now. Taking down one herd won't put a dent in the numbers, but if it stops just one person from becoming infected, then it's worth it."

"I didn't say it's not worth it," I clarified.

Hayden glanced at me out of the corner of his eye, worried I might start an argument. "And I agree; I would have thought the zombies wouldn't be so...so spry anymore."

Fuller gravely sighed and ran a hand over his head. He unrolled the big map and went over possible locations with Hayden. I noticed the Pennsylvania border had been traced with a fat, black Sharpie like that would keep us from crossing the state line next time.

They decided on Texas; it was relatively close and unexplored. The weird symbols painted on the doors of houses flashed through my mind. Months had passed since Hayden and I discovered the strange houses with running water and electricity, but it still bothered me in a way that I couldn't describe.

I was getting a little bored listening to Hayden and Fuller discuss the finer details of our mission. As far as I was concerned, the important stuff—like location and time allowed to be gone—had already been covered. Absentmindedly, I played with the silver leaf pendent I always wore.

The delicate chain had gotten tangled with the ball chain of Hayden's dog tags. I unhooked both and worked on separating the two. I put my grandma's necklace back on and examined Hayden's tags, reading over his information yet again before slipping the chain over my head.

Fuller dismissed us and walked us to the door. He paused, his dark eyes flicking from me to Hayden and then back again.

"Have you," he began, eyeing me up and down before smiling, "have you considered having kids?"

My jaw might have dropped. Incredulously I turned to Hayden, who looked just as shocked as I was.

"What?" I finally asked.

Fuller laughed softly. "Underwood is resistant to the virus. You heal very fast. I can only imagine how unique your children would be."

"And good looking," Hayden quickly joked. Unnerved, he took my hand and took a step toward the door.

"It's just a thought," Fuller said casually. "Keep it in mind."

"Yes, sir," Hayden muttered.

Awkwardly, we left Fuller's office.

"Please don't tell me you're going to take his advice," I said to Hayden when we were back in our room.

"Uh, no." He shook his head. "Don't get me wrong, Orissa, I love you and if things were different, I'd knock you up in a heartbeat." He gave me a cheeky grin. "But...no. Just no. I-I don't even want to think about it."

"Me neither. I don't want to bring a child into a world like this."

"Let's not even talk about it."

I nodded. "Good plan."

Raeya laughed when I told her about Fuller's comment during dinner. Then her face became serious and she agreed it would be a good idea. I raised one eyebrow to let her know that I hadn't forgotten her hopes of me getting pregnant so I'd be forced to not go on missions. She joked around about it for a while before she asked a question that sent a chill through me.

"Do you think Fuller wants you two to have a baby so he can do testing on it?" she asked in a hushed voice.

"Testing?"

"Yeah, like genetic testing in regards to the virus. It's almost as if he thinks you two will produce a super human. The way he pointed out your fast healing and Hayden's resistance is creepy. It just makes me wonder if he'd want to do experiments on the kid."

Suddenly not interested in my over salted vegetable medley, I pondered her question. What *would* Fuller do if Hayden and I had a kid? Why else would he think it was a good idea? Padraic pointed out more than once that he felt bad for the few pregnant women here; we didn't have any technology like ultra sound machines, fetal monitors, or a delivery room. And more concerning—to me at least—we didn't have any drugs that were safe to give a woman in labor. Padraic was a surgeon, but he had never preformed a cesarean birth before and voiced his concerns about doing a hack job. If anyone needed a C-section, they were fucked.

A week after they left, Alex and his team returned home. A nervous twist griped my gut when we headed west. I remembered exactly how to get to the field where Hayden had been shot. Out of all the horrible images that I had seen in the last few months, the memory of Hayden sinking to the ground after the bullet hit him was the worst.

Our journey started off without a hitch and the first five hours passed quickly. I had zoned out most of the trip until something caught my eye that I had to point out to Hayden and Rider. We passed an elaborately decorated yard, complete with plastic gravestones and bones sticking up from the ground. Most had fallen over in the wind and rain, but the overall effect was chilling.

The fake graveyard wasn't scary in the least. It was unnerving to see the world months behind, as it forever would be.

"I used to like Halloween," Rider huffed. "I lost my virginity on Halloween." He smiled at the memory. "Maggie Williams. I had a crush on her since middle school but it wasn't until I enlisted that she paid any attention to me."

"You didn't get laid until you were eighteen?" Hayden asked incredulously.

Not seeming embarrassed in the least, Rider said, "I was nineteen, actually. I used to want to wait until marriage; I was raised kinda strict and believed in that stuff. Then I enlisted and realized that the chance of that happening was pretty slim, since the chance of me getting out alive was pretty slim too."

"Oh," Hayden said. "That's...that's respectable."

"Thanks," Rider told him. "How old were you?"

"Fourteen."

"Seriously?" I piped up from the back. "That's young!"

Hayden shrugged. "Yeah, I guess. What about you, Riss?"

Before I got a chance to tell him, Ivan's voice came over the radio, asking if Hayden thought we should detour off the country road and explore a town. Hayden said after we crossed the Texas state line we would see what was in the first town we came across.

"Can I see the map?" I asked Rider. He opened the glove box and extracted the map, worn along the creases from being folded and unfolded so many times. It took a minute to figure out where we were; once I did, I traced the route to the street that had the houses with the weird symbols. Hayden had marked a tiny 'x' on the map to remind us that something—though it was very odd—had been looked into in that town.

"Why don't we go back here?" I asked, holding up the map and pointing to X.

"What's there?" Rider inquired. "When did you go to Texas?"

I swallowed hard and looked at the passing terrain. "Before Hayden was shot. We came out here to get zombie blood samples for Doctor Cara and Padraic to look at."

"You couldn't find any closer to home?" Rider only half teased.

I temporarily forgot the reason we had gone to Texas in the first place. It was still cold then; frost iced over the blood spilled in this dead world.

"I wanted to go south," I said. Suddenly, a red hot knife of guilt stabbed me. If I hadn't requested to go south, Hayden wouldn't have been shot. I clenched my jaw and tried not to think about it.

We stopped to eat before going to look for overrun towns. The air was warm and wonderfully dry. I sat on the hot liner in the truck bed and made peanut butter sandwiches on homemade bread for everyone.

Enjoying the nice weather and each other's carefree company, we ate in silence.

Suddenly, something moved swiftly through the overgrown grass.

We dropped our food and raised our weapons. When a large buck emerged from the underbrush, his nostrils flaring as he took in our human scents, I put my hand up to signal the guys to keep quiet.

Without taking my eyes off the deer, I felt around for my bow. Out of the corner of my eye, I saw a mop of Rider's red hair lean over and pick something up. The familiar shape of the bow graced my fingers. An arrow was given to me next.

Unobtrusively, I rose to my feet and slowly strung the arrow. The string creaked so softly only I could hear it. The buck blinked, turned and lowered his head, hiding it from my sight. I closed one eye and focused. I let out a breath, whistled a short, high pitched whistle, and let go of the arrow as soon as the deer looked up.

The arrow flew through the air and sunk into the buck's skull. His body dropped with a heavy thud, crashing into the lush, tall grass around him. I smiled triumphantly, pleased with both my skill and our luck that the buck had wandered so close.

"You make it look so easy," Rider said with a laugh. I put the bow over my neck and swung the quiver over my shoulder.

"I've been doing it for years," I reminded him. "I wasn't always good."

I jumped over the side of the truck, Hayden following suit.

"Nice shot," he complimented.

"Thanks," I said with a smile. "It was nice to shoot something that wasn't trying to eat me." I shook my head at how wrong that was.

With Hayden's help, we dragged the deer over to the truck.

"Should we take it back to the compound?" Wade asked.

Ivan shook his head. "It won't last that long. And a dead body—human or not—will only attract zombies. I say we cook him and have a feast on some real meat."

My mouth watered at the thought of venison jerky. Though, it wouldn't taste as good without being marinated in anything.

"Do you know how to skin it?" Wade asked apprehensively.

"Yeah," I told him. "But I don't have all that I need."

"What do you need?" Brock asked.

"Rope to tie it up and a saw to cut off the head and the legs."

Brock raised an eyebrow. "You've done this before?"

"Yeah," I repeated. "I've known how to hunt and how to prepare what I've killed for years."

"Interesting," Brock replied. "And I have a saw. I brought one just in case we needed to cut through fallen trees," he said with a grin. "And I think there is rope in here." He opened up a large tool box that was in the back of the SUV. "Yeah," he called, holding it up. "Is this enough?"

"Perfect!" I exclaimed. "Uh, can we find a tree? I can't really string him up without one."

We hauled the heavy carcass into the bed of the truck and drove down the road, stopping a half mile later when we spotted an accessible tree. With less grace than normal, I set to work. I had become numb to sharp objects cutting and slicing. It didn't stir any emotion in me when I cut the deer straight down the middle and let his insides tumble out.

Hayden, Wade, and Rider helped me cut up the meat and cook it over a small fire while the others kept watch. Under the shade of a small cove of trees, we sat in the tall grass and devoured our strips of cooked meat.

"It's better when it's been flavored," I said with my mouth full. I hadn't had meat that didn't come from a can or bag since Kentucky. Despite its rather bland flavor, the venison was delicious. Hayden put his arm around my shoulders and pulled me to him. I rested my head against his chest and put my hand on his.

It was beyond nice, sitting around the small fire eating with my friends. Birds and bugs filled the hot day with the sounds of summer. A comfortable silence fell over us and we relaxed for a while longer until Hayden grudgingly sighed and got up to retrieve the map.

$$\longrightarrow$$

"Are we close to the symbols?" Ivan asked. It surprised me just a bit that he remembered.

"Getting there," Hayden told him and flattened out the map. Wade and Brock curiously looked at the X.

"Symbols?" Brock questioned.

Hayden quickly explained.

Brock shrugged, not too interested. "It was months ago, do you really think whoever was using those houses is still around?"

"Nope," Hayden said and folded up the map. "But it's worth checking out, just for curiosity's sake."

I couldn't help but feel excited. Stupid anxiety built up inside me; I tried to smash it down, reminding myself that I wasn't going to get any closer to solving the mystery of who had left the symbols and why. I knew—and I repressed the notion with a passion—that I hoped to stumble upon another large, organized compound. That small groups went out on missions and marked helpful locations. If another group of several hundred people existed, the chances of human survival went up.

"We should get the rest of the supplies from that camping store," Hayden suggested to me. "We left quite a bit."

"We did," I agreed. "There was so much stuff I wanted."

"Yeah, we're going," he decided with a smile. We packed up our crap, stretched, and loaded back into the cars. Under black paint, the cab of the truck was hot. We weren't supposed to use the air conditioning either. I leaned against the door so the air from Hayden's open window blew in my face.

We turned left off of the country road we had been traveling. The landscape became more and more barren the farther west we went. Everything was overgrown and browning from the apparent lack of rain.

A faded sign for a new development beckoned us farther. Hayden turned up the radio and was singing along with Eric Church when we rolled to a stop.

"Holy shit," Rider quietly said and looked around. He held his hand up to his face to shield the sun from his eyes. "There's nothing left."

The charred remnants of the neighborhood brought a chill to my skin despite the heat. New vegetation had yet to grow over the soot and ash covered ground. Blackened boards stuck up from the rubble, a sad shadow of what they used to be. Burned skeletons of cars littered the road. If we looked long enough, I'm sure we'd find *real* skeletons in the road as well.

"Carry on?" Ivan asked over the walkie-talkie.

"Yeah," Hayden agreed. "There's obviously nothing to see here."

We drove for another few hours. When the sun was getting ready to set, we stopped to eat. We slowly looked in all directions; there was nothing but a long-forgotten, overgrown field with a giant, old oak tree a few yards from the road. I stripped myself of weapons and raised my hands above my head, breathing in and out as I stretched. My neck popped when I turned it from side to side. I reached down and touched my toes, feeling a relieving give in my calf muscles.

Not wanting to be completely weaponless, I stuck a sliver knife in my boot and wandered away from the guys so they wouldn't see me squatting in the tall grass. A grasshopper landed on me as I was zipping up my jeans. I was about to flick him off but stopped myself. I kneeled back down and more gently pushed the insect off of me. I stood and shook my head, thinking I was losing it for not wanting to be mean to a stupid bug.

The breeze rustled the knee length grass and weeds, blowing the sweet scent of clovers in my face. Despite the sinking sun, the day retained its warmth. For the first time in a while, I felt optimistic. We had survived the winter. That, in itself, was a feat.

Something snapped behind me. I extracted the knife and whirled around in a swift movement. My eyes scanned my surroundings and saw nothing. I took a steady breath and waited. My fingers tightened on the knife and I stepped forward.

He sprung up from the grass and ran. He was fast, but I was faster. I ducked out of his lunge, spun around, and planted a hard kick to the center of his firm chest. The blow stunned him, but not from the pain. A blast like that to the heart is damaging.

He countered quickly, snapping and snarling like a rabid dog. A build up of mud or blood— or more realistically both—caked his fingernails. His hands thrashed in the air, desperate to claw up my face.

When he reached out again, I was ready. I wrapped my fingers around his wrist and yanked him forward; he didn't have time to stumble in the tall weeds before the knife sunk into his temple. I let go of his arm and tilted the knife up so that it neatly slid from his head and he collapsed to the ground. Crimson stained the earth. Head wounds were always messy.

I wiped sweat off my forehead and looked back at the truck. Ivan and Wade were rummaging through our box of food in the bed. I couldn't see the other three. Using the crazy's shirt to clean the blade, I stuck it back in the sheath and concealed it once again in my boot. No one had seen the attack. I decided they didn't need to know.

"I may regret asking this," I overheard Wade saying to Ivan as I neared the truck. "But where are all the zombies? We haven't seen any in a while. Sadly, that's unsettling."

Ivan laughed. "It is. I'd guess they go where the food is. If there's no one here, they move on."

"True. So either there are no survivors here or they are well hidden," Wade rationalized.

"Sounds about right."

I pulled myself up into the bed and got a bottle of water that had warmed up from being in the sun all day. I drank it nonetheless, even though warm water made me feel even thirstier for some reason.

"Everything come out ok?" Ivan asked me with a boyish grin.

"Better than I could have hoped," I shot back, returning his youthful smile. I ripped open a protein bar and took a bite. It was supposed to taste like peanut butter but tasted like crap instead. I had to force myself to chew and swallow.

Brock joined us, looking wistfully at the landscape. His eyes held back an unspoken sadness as they gazed across the field. He was born and raised in Texas; it had to be both terrifying and welcoming to be back in the Lone Star state.

Hayden and Rider were discussing something in hushed voices and stopped talking when they reached the truck. Hayden and I made eye contact; he smiled almost shyly and diverted his eyes to the ground.

I raised an eyebrow and looked at him quizzically. He glanced at the guys, set something down, and hoped up in the truck to eat dinner.

"What are the plans for tonight?" Brock asked.

"If we can find a place to camp out, we will," Hayden told him.

"And if not?"

"Sleep in the cars," he answered grimly. We all hated sleeping in the vehicles. We ate quickly and looked at the map. "We're only half an hour away from the camping store. Let's go to that town and find a place for the night."

"Sounds good," Brock agreed. We hastily ate and packed up what we got out. Ivan, Wade, and Brock got into their SUV and Rider closed the door after he got into the cab of the truck. Hayden hung back, again acting shy.

"Riss," he said and stood. "I have something for you. Don't laugh, ok?"

"Uh, alright." What in the world would he have for me?

He jumped out of the bed and held a hand out to help me down. I didn't need his help at all but I slipped my fingers between his regardless. He picked something up that he had put on the truck's dust covered back tire. Looking absolutely adorable, he shyly held out a bouquet of dandelions.

"It's stupid, I know," he muttered.

A smile broke across my face, and I took the bundle of weeds. "No. It's beautiful."

He looked at me dubiously. "Really?"

"Ok, maybe not beautiful, but it's thoughtful and sweet and…and thank you."

He smiled and his hazel eyes looked deeply into mine. "You're welcome. I like making you happy, and you seem sad lately."

I resisted the desperate urge to jump on him and wrap my arms and legs against his body. That would have to wait. Ignoring the warmth and tingling, I smiled back and linked my fingers through his. He squeezed my hand before letting go.

I had never been overly sentimental. I didn't keep cards or flowers; what was the point? I picked the best looking dandelion from the bunch and stuck it under the driver's seat in the truck with the intention of drying and pressing it when we got home.

----->

We reached the outdoor sporting goods store at dusk. Three pathetic S3s aimlessly limped around the parking lot. Wanting to try his hand with the bow and arrow, Rider asked me to walk him through using it.

"The crossbow is much easier," I told him, eyeing its sleek black metal curved limb and the camo foregrip and stock. It had sat untouched since I took it from the camping store before Hayden had been shot.

"I don't want easy," he said and picked up my bow. "Someone once told me that the harder something is, the more it's worth it." His blue eyes met mine and his lips curved into a small smile. "She is a smart woman."

"I bet she is," I told him, smiling.

"So come on and show me how to use this thing!" He took three arrows from the quiver.

I laughed. "You really think you're gonna get them on your first try? Take the whole thing." I motioned to the quiver. "You'll need it."

"Don't bet on it. I might have beginner's luck!"

"You've shot it before," I reminded him. Fuller had made me teach a very brief course on how to use a bow and arrow. "So you're not technically a beginner," I teased. We walked a few yards from the cars. One of the gummies took notice and dragged its feet in our direction.

The skin on its face was literally dripping off. Stringy chunks of moist flesh hung off its cheeks and swung back and forth as it walked. Occasionally, one of the sticky strands would swing back and hit its neck where it would stick for a second before falling loose and flapping again.

I was unable to tell if it was a man or woman. Its clothes were soiled with mud, blood, and bodily fluids. It wasn't wearing shoes, and its left arm had been gnawed at; all the meat was gone, leaving only yellowing, dead bone.

"Lower your shoulders," I instructed. I kept one eye on Rider and the other on the approaching S3. I wasn't worried about the other zombies; the guys knew we wanted to use them as target practice but wouldn't hesitate to shoot if they got too close.

"Better?" Rider asked.

"Relax," I told him. He didn't put the arm guard on. It was a rather painful lesson to learn, but it had worked for me. "Let out your breath. Aim—you do this on your own so I can figure out what you've done right and wrong. Then let the arrow go."

He did. The arrow soared through the air and grazed the S3 in the shoulder.

"Not too bad," I told him, a proud smile forming. "You did better than I thought you would."

He beamed. "See, I told you I rock."

We laughed and Rider took another arrow. I stood behind him, watching him set up. The S3 was only a couple yards away; hardly a challenge. Rider let the arrow go, gasped when the string snapped against his skin, and reveled in his bull's-eye shot.

"Does it always do that?" he asked as he closed his fingers around the shaft of the arrow. It easily slid out of the S3's rotten head. Putrid browning brain sloshed out of the cracked skull. "I wasn't expecting it to hit my wrist."

I nodded. "That's why you wear an arm guard. And if you have long sleeves, it keeps your clothes from getting caught. It doesn't always hit you, but when it does it stings like a bitch."

"You're telling me." He flicked the nasty rotten slime from the arrow. "How is this thing still walking? Its brain is mush!"

"I wondered that too," I said, leaning over to look at the gummy. "It makes no sense. Then again, none of this does."

Rider nodded in agreement and we moved on to shoot the next S3. It took Rider five arrows to finally lodge one in the thing's throat, severing the spinal cord. He asked me to shoot the last one so he could watch and learn. I knew I wasn't the best teacher. I moved slow and deliberately, hoping he could pick up on some hint I wasn't able to verbalize.

"You make it look like a breeze," he complained.

I shrugged. "I've been doing this for years. It's second nature now. And I even miss sometimes. Rarely." I smiled.

Rider, Wade, and I checked out the front of the store while the others looked around back. It was too dark to go inside; that would have to wait until the morning.

The six of us meandered toward the dock on the lake. The water gently lapped the shore in a soporific rhythm. The purple and orange sunset reflected off the water's glassy surface.

"I have an idea," Brock said and walked briskly down the dock, his combat boots creating heavy footfalls that were muted by the water. He stopped and inspected the boats. "We should camp out in the boats. We could lengthen the ropes, drift a few feet farther from the dock and drop the anchor. We'd be untouchable."

"That's brilliant," Hayden exclaimed. "Let's get set up before nightfall." We went back to our vehicles and got our sleeping bags, food, water, weapons, and flashlights.

"Do you two want your own boat?" Ivan leered, making an obscene jester with his hands and waist.

I raised my eyebrows. "Oh yeah, baby. You know it."

Hayden laughed and nudged me. "We could, you know."

The amusement went out of my expression.

"Not *that*," he recovered quickly. "I mean just have our own boat."

"Oh, yeah. I'd like that," I agreed. We ended up splitting into twos. Hayden and I uncovered our boat of choice and tossed the inner tubes that were being stored inside to the dock. We put our stuff inside, untied the rope that tethered us to the dock, raised the anchor, and pushed off the slippery wood of the dock.

Hayden let the boat drift until there wasn't any slack left in the rope before dropping the anchor. We were still attached to the dock and could pull ourselves back to it. I doubted a crazy would be able to rationalize doing that too.

The boat had been stored with care but I was still slightly paranoid of waking up covered in spiders. Spiders beat blood thirsty—and organ hungry—zombies any day. Hayden zipped our sleeping bags together. I risked taking off my boots, unbraided my hair, and pulled the black t-shirt I was wearing off, leaving me in only jeans and a dark blue tank top.

Hayden did the same, stripping down to his pants but no shirt. Ivan and Brock took the first watch. We felt confident that we were unreachable out in our cleverly chosen boats, but we were no fools. Taking advantage of the quiet calm, Hayden put his arm around me and kissed my neck. Shivers went down my spine, creating a new kind of desire when it hit me in my core.

Giving in, I pressed myself against Hayden, feeling every hard part of his body fill with the same red hot want. We could be quiet. I was sure of it. Quiet and quick. But I wasn't about to leave the guys unmanned if a bad situation suddenly came about. I imagined Hayden and me struggling to pull apart and get our pants on in time to aid our friends.

I gave Hayden one last kiss before turning over. Relentlessly, he ran his fingers over my body, finding their way under my shirt. The rough skin on his hands sent more shivers through me when they caressed my breasts.

With a heavy sigh, he stopped rubbing me. "We should sleep," he mumbled.

"Yeah. We won't get another opportunity to feel safe at night until we're home," I speculated.

"Yup. Night." He started running his fingers over my exposed skin again but this time in a less provocative way. It felt soothing and, along with the gentle rocking of the boat in the water, helped me fall asleep.

The boat bumped against the dock, stirring us out of our restful sleep.

"Your turn," Rider muttered. I sat up ruefully and put my hands over my face. With a sigh I pulled myself out of the sleeping bag. The day was already warm. In fact, I don't think it ever cooled off completely. The twilit sky glistened on the horizon, promising another sky filled with hot, unfiltered sunshine.

I used to love days like this.

Hayden and I packed up our stuff, put it back in the truck, and sat at the dock. He took apart his guns one by one to clean, all the while staying vigilant for the undead. I swished my arrows around in the water to clear off the dried zombie crust that had built up on the tips. Once I was satisfied, I did the same with my knife.

I carefully put my weapons away and leaned back on the sun warmed wood of the deck. The dehydrated texture was uncomfortable against the dry skin of my hands. A nice shower and some lotion sounded heavenly.

Having left my sunglasses in the truck, I closed my eyes and turned my face up to the bright sun. Soon I was feeling sleepy again. Promising I'd only stay for a minute, I let myself lay down, placing my arms above my head.

"You're doing an awesome job of keeping watch," Hayden spoke.

"I'd hear them coming," I retorted.

"Yeah, and then you'd sit up and die."

"Wouldn't you save me?"

"If I could." He sounded annoyed.

I sat up, blinking in the sun. He shoved a magazine into an M4 and held it up, inspecting the accuracy of the scope. "I used to hate these," he told me. "Sand got stuck in every crevice."

"You don't have to worry about that anymore," I told him, my voice level.

"Nope," he sighed and put the gun down. "Hungry?"

"Yeah. Want me to find something?"

"I'll get it; stay here."

"Alright," I said. Knowing that if I stayed on my ass I'd feel tried and lazy, I sprung to my feet and did a Sun Salutation. Feeling much better, I walked to the end of the dock and looked out at the water. I felt the vibrations of someone walking on the dock.

I spun around, expecting to see Hayden. A tall, blonde man stood in the center of the worn wood staring at me. He cocked his head when I fluidly moved to scoop up a weapon. Before I could even touch my bow, he took off, sprinting into the parking lot.

Dammit. Hayden was there, probably not paying attention to what was going on around him because he was counting on me to keep watch. He was probably in the bed of the truck, his back turned to the world while he found something for us to eat.

I put the bow around my shoulder, grabbed two arrows and took off. I wanted to shout his name in warning but whistled a sharp, short whistle instead. Hayden looked up just in time. He jumped out of the truck right as the crazy growled and lunged at him. Hayden ducked out of the way and the crazy smacked into the side of the truck.

Hayden raised his arm and brought down his fist on the side of the crazy's head, striking him hard in the temple. The blow stunned the crazy; Hayden reached out to Blondie's head and twisted. Even from a few feet away, I heard the snap.

The body slumped to the ground. I jogged over.

"Where the hell did he come from?" Hayden asked, shoving the body away from the truck with his foot.

"I have no idea. I looked up and he was just there, watching me."

"Shouldn't they all be past this stage in the virus already?" He stepped over the body and leapt back into the truck. "Unless he just got infected."

"No, I think he's been infected," I stated and knelt down to look at the body. "Toss me the gloves," I asked.

Hayden opened the silver box and pulled out a pair of leather gloves. I put them on and rolled the body over. "He's wearing thermals under his jeans. It's been over eighty degrees in Arkansas for days now; I can only assume it's been even warmer here."

With an armload of food, Hayden got out of the truck bed and joined me. "You're right. And look at the layers of blood on his shirt. Victim after victim."

I stood. "He's been crazy for a long time."

Hayden and I exchanged uneasy glances. "Why?" Hayden asked. "Why aren't they progressing?"

"I have no clue," I shook my head. "Maybe Padraic will be able to answer that for us when we get back."

Hayden nodded. "Maybe."

We went back to the dock, mindfully quiet so we wouldn't wake up the guys, and ate breakfast. Not long after that, Brock woke up and joined us. A short time later, Ivan, Wade, and Rider arose sweating. They grumbled about the heat and Hayden laughed, reminding them that not all that long ago we were complaining about the cold. Once their stuff was put away and they ate breakfast, we armed ourselves and went into the store.

The big fish tank was even more skuzzy than before; the smell burned my nose and made my eyes water. Maggots burrowed in the liquefying flesh of the dead gummies and zombies that rotted on the floor; some were just puddles of rancid human juices.

We filled bags with clothing, the leftover weapons and ammo Hayden and I didn't have room for the first time, more camping supplies—we figured having extra sleeping bags could never hurt—water bottles with built in filters, lanterns, batteries, mosquito spray, packs, bags, night vision binoculars, boots, and fishing gear.

"There's a river near the compound," Brock pointed out while looking at the fishing rods. "If we get the crap we need, we should go fishing. I don't know about you, but fresh meat, even from a fish, sounds good."

We all agreed and loaded up what we could fit. Not wanting to completely overload the cars just yet, we carefully combed the store for anything else that would be helpful.

I gulped in a breath of fresh air as soon as I left the store. The stench of molding, rotting bodies latched onto me. I wanted to jump in the lake and wash the scent from my hair.

We split up into our usual three; Hayden drove, Rider sat shotgun, and I sat in the back. We took our chances driving south down the highway; we made it only a few minutes before getting stuck.

"Why do you think they just left their cars?" Rider asked, rolling down his window for a better look.

"Traffic jam," Hayden answered as if it was obvious.

"I get that," Rider went on. "But why? What's out there? I'd rather stay in my car."

"Maybe the jam wasn't unjamming," I supplied. "If I was stuck for hours, I'd rather get out and walk."

Rider nodded. "Maybe. I want to know where the jam starts. We never look. Do you think there are roadblocks?"

"It would make the most sense," Hayden agreed as he reversed the truck. "Though I don't know why. Mass chaos, probably. And I bet they wanted to contain the virus and keep it from spreading."

"They did a wonderful job," I stated sarcastically. Though none of us said it, the proverbial 'they' we spoke of were the authorities.

"Should we find out?" Rider asked.

"No," Hayden replied. He radioed Ivan over the walkie-talkie to get his opinion on driving parallel to the highway on a back road for a mile or two, then trying our hand at getting back on from an off exit. Ivan agreed but wasn't hopeful about being able to take the highway at all.

We sped down a road, seeing nothing but nature along the way. Rider carefully followed our path on the map and, after two miles, we exited onto the highway.

"The cars are never ending," Rider said under his breath. "Seriously, did all of Texas come this way?"

"Something must have lured them," I speculated. "Like a promise of safety."

"This highway will take us to Dallas," Hayden informed us. "There could have been a shelter set up there. I'll ask Brock if he knows of anything when we stop, which we will in just a few. I don't like being at a standstill by a pile up; there are too many things that can go wrong."

We drove another few miles southwest. Zombies started sprouting out from the scenery like unwelcomed weeds. We turned down a street lined with ornately decorated houses and discovered a herd.

Before the attack on the farm I would have called this herd large. Twenty to thirty zombies milled about; their autonomous death groans blended together creating a chilling, load moan that could be heard yards away. The sun beat down, cooking the decaying bits of human remains that littered the street.

No matter how well armed we were, it still sparked the tiniest bit of fear in me when a herd took notice of us.

"Game time," Hayden said, a wicked smile on his face. The SUV rolled to a stop next to us. Brock stuck his head out the window, also grinning.

"You're going down, Underwood!" he teased.

"You wish!" Hayden turned up his music. "Riss, will you drive? I want to kill some undead sons of bitches."

I did too, but I got into the driver's seat regardless. Hayden gave me a quick peck on the lips and jumped into the bed of the truck. He uncovered the machine gun and clicked a belt into place. He shouted at the zombies and pulled the trigger.

Making sure to stay behind the SUV so the rapid fire of the machine gun wouldn't hit our friends, I drove as fast as I could navigate through the zombies. A dozen went down within minutes. Rider leaned so far out the window I was a little afraid he might fall. Ivan and Wade did the same. As the herd thinned, I slowed down to let the guys shoot with more accuracy.

We went around the block, dropping zombies like flies. When one fell, another appeared, tripping over the limp body. It took another pass to clear the streets. Thinking we had currently rid this town of the infected undead, we pulled into a parking lot.

"You can thank me for taking care of at least seventy-five percent of them," Hayden told Brock.

"Seventy-five?" Brock questioned. "More like thirty-five. We got the rest. Our team wins."

"Bullshit," Hayden swore, acting as if he was actually mad. He gestured to the machine gun. "Do you know how many rounds per minute this thing fires?"

"It doesn't matter how many when they're not hitting anything," Wade heckled.

"Believe what you want to believe," Hayden said with a wave of his hand. He put the cover back on the machine gun and looked around. Assuming that no one would still be living in a town filled with zombies—and knowing that if there were people here, they would have heard the gunfire and sought us out—we left to search elsewhere for signs of life.

We reached another stalemate after an hour or so of driving. Having killed every zombie that crossed our path, we were ready to see someone alive. We drove even farther south. The neighborhoods grew fewer and fewer and the houses decreased in size and quality as we drove. About an hour later we stopped to eat. Hayden and I sat close together while we bit into pieces of beef jerky. Once I finished eating I unbraided my hair and let it blow in the breeze. When a loose strand fell into my face, Hayden gently pushed it behind my ear.

Ivan and Hayden got up to look at the map and decide on a definite location to check out. Brock, not satisfied with the way the new supplies were in the bed, worked on rearranging it. Wade, Rider, and I meandered up and down the dry, dusty street, keeping an eye out for zombies.

"You're lucky," Wade said, facing me.

"I am?" I asked, not sure why he would be telling me that. If Rider wasn't in front of me, I would have assumed Wade was talking to him.

"Yeah." He looked over at Hayden and then back to me. "You're lucky you got someone."

"Oh." I diverted my eyes to the ground. "Yeah, I guess."

"What do you mean you *guess*?" Rider questioned, smirking.

"I mean, I am," I explained. "Can we not talk about this?"

Rider laughed. "Are you uncomfortable talking about it? I didn't think it was possible to make you uncomfortable."

I rolled loose gravel under my feet. "I'm not uncomfortable; it's just pointless to talk about."

"How so?" Wade asked. He put the strap of his gun around his shoulder and adjusted it so that his weapon hung on his back.

"Well," I started. "What does it matter?"

"I would hope it matters to you," Rider chuckled.

"Oh it does. It does a lot. But it doesn't change anything. The world is still a fucking disaster."

"So you think it's pointless to have a relationship?" Wade guessed.

I shook my head. "Not entirely. It's not pointless for Hayden or me. We enjoy each other's company immensely—" I cut off, grinning. "Take that as you want. And don't get me wrong, I love him—so much—and I only said it was pointless to *talk* about. Does having him make it easier to deal with this shithole of a world we live in? Yes, it does, it does help a lot. And as wonderful and sappy and whatever love is, it's not the cure-all. Life isn't a fairytale; loving each other isn't going to make the bad guys go away."

"That's an interesting take on it," Wade said.

"You're the most down to earth person I've ever met," Rider admitted.

I laughed. "I am?"

He nodded. "You see things for how they are and nothing more."

I shook my head. "Thanks...I think."

"It's a compliment," Rider said and nudged me.

"I'm not sure everyone would agree with you. In fact, I'm sure plenty of people would say the opposite."

"Well," Rider told me with a smile. "Then they don't know you like we do."

"I wasn't sure about you at first," Wade confessed. "Yeah you were great when it came to killing the zombies, but you didn't have any experience working with others in battle or anything of the like."

"And I don't always play well with others," I agreed.

"No," Wade laughed. "But you do with us. I feel kind of bad for doubting you."

"Don't," I told him. "You had every right to."

"You're part of the team," Rider assured me.

"Thanks, guys," I said genuinely. I smiled at them, and thought about how close I had grown to the guys over the last few months. As I told Raeya, they really did seem like family.

Wade took the strap off his shoulder and looked through the scope of his rifle. A refreshing breeze blew his dark blonde hair into his face. We were all in desperate need of haircuts.

"Still nothing...for now," he told us. I ran my hands through my messy hair and walked over to where Hayden and Ivan were standing.

"Come up with anything?" I asked.

"Sort of," Hayden told me. "We're gonna head in the general direction of Austin and see what we can find along the way, and then explore the city."

"I'm telling you, man," Ivan said, shaking his head. "Big cities are bound to be overrun. Even with the artillery we have, we won't be able to come close to a fair fight."

"He's right," I agreed. "I told you about Indy. And when we were going from town to town, we avoided big cities. We could tell we were getting close to one just by the increase in zombies."

"Fuller wants us to kill whatever we can," Hayden reminded us.

"Not at the expense of our lives," Ivan said exasperated.

Looking irritated, Hayden folded up the map. "Let's not worry about it until we get there. If it looks like it'll be too much, we won't continue on, alright?"

"You're the boss," Ivan said almost bitterly. I didn't want to argue with Hayden. But I one hundred percent agreed with Ivan. Big cities housed more people -- more to become infected and turn into carnivorous two-legged beasts.

I folded my arms and leaned against the tailgate of the SUV. A large black shape in the sky caught my attention. I looked up to see a huge bird soaring above us. I watched it fly, wings open, just effortlessly gliding through the air. It began its telltale circling and I knew all too well that something was about to get eaten.

Another joined, circling almost in tandem. And then another. It wasn't a hawk like I thought. They were turkey vultures and turkey vultures were scavengers.

"There's something dead over there," I told the guys and pointed.

"Where?" Hayden asked, his hand flying to the M9 that was tucked into the back of his pants.

"Way over there. Do you see the turkey vultures?"

"The what?" Ivan asked.

"Those big birds flying around. They circle like that when there's something dead. I don't know if they would eat zombies or not. Maybe if they weren't horribly rotten there might be some good meat left. Or plenty of tasty bugs wiggling around in their skulls."

"Nice imagery, Penwell," Ivan told me.

"It's on our way; we can drive over and take a look," Hayden said. We all got back into the cars, not bothering to put our seatbelts on. Only a few minutes later we came across what the turkey vultures were eating.

Two birds blinked at us before taking flight, their long wings flapping as they flew to safety.

"It's just road kill," Rider said with a disappointed shake of his head. It used to be so common I almost dismissed it. Hayden snapped his head back to look at me; our eyes locked—he was thinking what I was thinking.

He put the truck in park and got out. I hurried after him. Brock rushed over too. Never before had I been so excited to see a dead raccoon in the middle of the road.

"Has it been dead long?" Brock asked me as if I would know.

I nudged it with my foot. "A few days at the most," I guessed. The vultures had done a good job picking it apart. It was honestly hard to tell if the poor little guy was fresh or not.

"There are still bloodstains," Hayden said, scuffing then with his foot. He looked down the street.

"They have to be close," Brock commented. The other three guys joined us.

"Uh, what is so significant about this?" Rider asked.

"It was hit by a car," I said, emphasizing *car*.

I could see the light bulb flick on in Rider's mind. "People were here," he said aloud.

"Let's find them!" Wade exclaimed. "Can you tell which way they went?" he asked nobody in particular.

I shook my head. Dammit. I should have paid closer attention to all those reruns of *CSI*; I was sure there was a way to tell. Ivan pulled out the map.

"This way," he pointed in the direction our cars weren't facing. "Takes us away from the city. If anyone is alive, they're best chances are in the country somewhere."

Fueled with excitement, we hurriedly got back into the cars. Hayden drove fast, so fast I almost didn't see it. We had traveled ten or fifteen miles from the dead raccoon when I yelled, "Stop!"

Hayden stomped on the brakes. "What is it?"

"Symbols," I told him and swallowed hard. "I think I saw those blue squiggly lines on the houses back there."

Hayden relayed the message to Ivan, put the truck in reverse, and turned into a subdivision off the road we were on. Sure enough, the first house was marked with blue lines.

Cautiously, we got out. Fully armed, we crept around the house. It was desolate, with no signs of the living or the dead. The front door was unlocked. The floorboards creaked under my weight. Holding a crossbow out in front of me, I took a precarious step forward.

Dust settled on the dark oak banister of the stairwell. My eyes flicked all around and, seeing nothing, I took another step in. All my senses were on high alert and my heart raced. I took a deep breath and took another step.

I shook my head and risked a look behind me. "I don't see anything," I told the guys. Then I noticed the muddy prints on the floor. "Someone has been here," I whispered. The mud was dry, my first signal that the prints were old. Second, it wasn't muddy outside. These tracks were left long ago.

"What do the blue lines mean?" Ivan asked.

"Water," Hayden told him. "Or at least that's what Riss and I think." He led the way inside to the kitchen and turned on the water.

"Holy shit," Brock swore. "You're right."

Hayden leaned over the sink. "The water has that rotten egg smell," he told me. "So it's been a few days at the least. But someone has been here and somehow turned the power on."

"Generator?" Wade asked.

I shook my head. "You'd hear it."

"What else?" Rider eagerly asked. "You said there were more symbols."

"Yeah," Hayden said and shut the water off. "A red X and a black square with a triangle; like a house."

"Any ideas what those mean?" Wade asked.

"No," Hayden and I said at the same time. "We might be able to figure them out," Hayden suggested. After turning the faucet on once more, Hayden went out the back door and looked at the back of the house for clues.

Not finding any, we moved onto the next house. This one had a red X on the door, which was also unlocked. We cautiously shuffled our way into the house, which smelled like dirty litter boxes. Ivan turned on the sink. The pipes bubbled and spit out disgusting water. He quickly shut it off.

"So red X's mean bad water?" he asked.

"Maybe," Brock said.

Curiosity got the best of me and I opened the pantry. With the exception of cans of cat food, it had been wiped clean. I opened another cabinet, one that most likely had held pots and pans. It too was empty. Maybe the X meant the place had been raided?

With Ivan and Wade keeping watch, Hayden and I went upstairs while Brock and Rider looked around the rest of the house. The bathroom had been stripped of supplies and the covers were off the beds. I sat on the mattress in the master bedroom.

The room had been nicely decorated in light blues and browns. The mattress was made out of that comfortable memory foam stuff that absorbs your weight. The dresser across from me was covered in picture frames holding images of smiling children and cats. Glass figurines took up the space between the frames. But something was off.

I stood up to inspect it. An empty space at the center of the dresser was out of place. I peered behind the dresser and saw the cable hook up. Someone took the TV. On that notion, I quickly walked to the closet. It was big and organized in such a fashion even Raeya would approve. A jewelry box lay toppled on the floor.

I knelt next to it, barely able to see in the dim light. I picked it up and shook it; it was empty.

"Find something?" Hayden asked.

"I'm not sure." I stood and put the empty jewelry box on the bed. "Why steal jewelry? How is that going to help you survive?"

"We took jewelry," he reminded me. "Just because we could, remember?"

"Yeah. Maybe that's all it was."

"Probably." We went into the other rooms and found them in a similar state. The blankets and TVs were gone and even computers were taken off desks. No closer to figuring out the meaning of the X, we left and went into the next X marked house.

Like the previous house, it had been ransacked.

"It looks like it was burglarized," Rider said, stepping over a dresser drawer that was strewn on the floor.

"It does," I agreed. Again in the master bedroom, Hayden and I discovered a lack of jewels in the jewelry box. An empty wallet lay on the floor, with only credit cards and an ID inside.

"Ok, now this is strange," Hayden said from the bathroom. He flicked his flashlight off and carried something over. "Why take necklaces but leave a first aid kit?"

I shook my head. "People are so dumb."

"They are," he agreed. "It makes me wonder how they are still alive." Keeping the first aid kit for ourselves, we joined the others downstairs. The house across the street was marked with the blue lines. The front door was unlocked and it had been stripped of most things useful and everything valuable, furthering my X-means-robbed theory. The last house on the street had a black house-like drawing on the door. And it was locked.

Not wanting to wander too far from our vehicles, we drove them to the end of the street. The road came to a 'T' with an even number of houses on either side. We didn't want to split up so we parked our cars in the driveway of the first house on the right. This one was marked with the blue lines. The front door was unlocked, the water worked and was crystal clear, and the house had been emptied.

"It makes no sense," Ivan sighed. We crossed the yard to the neighboring house. Like the other one with the black house drawing, it was locked.

"No, it doesn't," Wade agreed. "I will bet you that all the black house marked doors are locked, though."

"I think I figured it out," Hayden began. Before he could finish the distant rumble of a motor grabbed our attention. Not wanting to be mistaken for crazies, we ducked behind the house and out of sight.

Driving fast, the car quickly approached. The base was turned up, thumping an annoying echo off the walls of the house. Its sleek black paint glistened in the sun. I admired it, though it was odd to see a nicely restored classic being driven during an apocalypse. My aunt Jenny—oddly enough—had been a fan of the classics. Even with the stupid custom paint job of a skull on the front door, she would have approved of this car.

I turned around to make a catty comment and my heart skipped a beat. Brock's face was absolutely white with terror. Wade and Rider exchanged terrified looks of disbelief.

"What?" Hayden demanded.

"T-those," Brock began, his voice flat with shock. "Those are the guys that shot you."

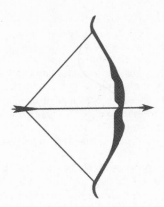

CHAPTER 23

"What?" I asked, terror creeping into my heart.

"The Imperial Lords," Wade said hoarsely. "That is their car. I remember it." He looked at Hayden with guilt in his eyes. "We thought we killed them all. I-I don't know how the last one got away. I hit him in his calf. He would have bled out unless…"

"Unless he got help in time," Rider finished for him. "But there weren't others. We made sure of it!"

My terror turned into rage. I wanted to track down the guys in the Mustang and slowly beat the life out of them. I wanted to shoot them in the shoulder so they knew how it felt. Feeling suddenly very protective of Hayden, I stepped in front of him.

Hayden bit his lip, still looking at the road. He was thinking and I could tell he wasn't sure what to do. Ivan looked just as pissed as I felt.

"Let's kill those motherfuckers," I said venomously.

Ivan nodded. "I'd love to," he agreed.

Hayden shook his head. "We don't know anything about them. They could be just as armed as we are."

"We outnumber them!" I told him, assuming it to be true. "You can't fit that many people in a Mustang."

Hayden nodded and looked at the guys. "We should follow them; keep a safe distance."

"And if we're seen?" Rider asked.

"Open fire," I answered for Hayden.

The guys nodded. "Sounds like a plan I can follow," Ivan said deviously. "Mess with my boys and you're going down."

"The one you shot who got away," I said to Wade. "I call dibs. I want to crush every bone in his face and cut off his balls and let him bleed to death."

Hayden gave me a look that said he was startled by my violence.

"You have no idea what it felt like to think you were dead," I told him. "I want them to pay for what they did. They almost killed you—almost killed me too. Do you remember the pain you were in? I'm not going to let those assholes die quickly. I want them to feel the life slipping away. I want them to bleed and I want them to hurt."

"You're scary when you're angry," Rider said after a moment of silence.

"Good," I spat. I was angry, but not at Rider. I hoped he knew that. "We're wasting time, let's go."

We rushed to the cars, which—thank God—were hidden from view by the garage. If those assholes noticed Hayden's truck, they would have stopped for sure. I sat up front, pistol at my side. We tore down the road, slowing once we figured we more or less caught up with the Mustang. Thankfully we sighted it turning onto a road lined with businesses. It was easy to track their whereabouts by the God-awful music. The base was loud enough to wake the dead.

If that was their goal, they succeeded. Hayden jerked the wheel and we flew down an alley. I imagined it going down in a drive-by fashion. The Mustang revved the engine and there was a short, rapid firing at the zombies, a few that I was too angry to pay attention to, before it sped off again.

The dumbasses managed to kill three of the seven zombies that wandered out on the streets. Four zombies weren't a threat. We could run them over if we had too.

"Oh shit," Rider said. "Don't turn around," he muttered.

Behind us, a half dozen or so crawled out of dark corners, out of broken windows, and from behind dumpsters.

"Riss, can you get them?" Hayden asked. "Where's your bow?"

"In the bed," I said grimly. "I can get out and—"

"No," Hayden interrupted. "If it comes to that, we'll run them over."

Hearts pounding, we painfully waited until the thumping base disappeared. A zombie sniffed the air and turned towards us. I removed the knife from around my ankle and waited. My window was still rolled down. I saw Hayden's fingers touch the window control buttons on his side. My grip tightened on the knife.

Half of her jaw was missing. The skin had rotted off her nose, leaving blackened holes were her nostrils should have been. Boney fingers grabbed the door. I pushed myself up and drove the knife into her forehead. I held onto the handle as she slumped down.

Her head hit the door, splattering blood on my lap and the interior of the truck. I used the hem of my shirt to wipe it up. Hayden put the truck in reverse and slowly accelerated out of the alley. We wound our way through town. Momentarily losing sight and sound of the Mustang, I felt a flicker of fear inside of me that I wouldn't get my revenge.

Then we saw it, zooming down the road, sun glinting off the chrome bumpers. Staying far behind, we slowed and only sped up once the Mustang turned off the road we were traveling. We continued our game of cat and mouse for another few miles. Then the Mustang hit the brakes and jerked a hard turn to the left.

"Stop," Brock's voice came from over the walkie.

"Why?" I answered.

"I know where that road leads," he told us.

"Where?"

"Eastmoore."

"What is that?" I asked.

"A state mental hospital."

My blood turned ice cold. "What?" I asked again, even though Brock had been perfectly clear.

"It's a mental hospital. With a maximum security ward for the criminally insane. Orissa, tell Hayden to pull over." Having heard Brock, Hayden let off the gas. The SUV pulled up next to us. "I've been here before," Brock told us. "It was a long time ago, but I didn't forget. That road leads to the hospital."

"I believe you," Hayden told him.

"What should we do?" Rider asked from the backseat.

"We should check it out," Hayden said with a nod. "Brock, do you know your way around?"

Brock shook his head. "I was here six years ago, volunteering with my psych class. I know they added to it since then. It's well built, strong, and easily guarded. Next to our compound, I would say it's the safest place to live out the outbreak."

"And?" I asked, my palms sweating. "Is there a way we can get a look at…at anything?"

"Yeah, well, I think." Brock nodded. "There is—or was—a greenhouse farm behind the hospital. It was used for therapy, like taking care of plants helps anyone," he mused and shook his head. "There was some sort of incident and two patients and a guard got killed. They shut it down and now it's empty. I know there was a story on the news about it right before I got shipped out. I don't know more details," he said apologetically.

"Can we get there on a back road? I don't want to be seen," Ivan said.

"I think so." Brock looked out the window and chewed on his lip. "We have to go back to town and turn. Then we should be able to find it."

"Or," I said, opening the glove box. "We can find out for sure."

"Let's get back into town first," Hayden suggested. "We stick out right here."

We turned around and sped into town. With trembling hands, I spread open the map, located where we were, and traced the path around the jail.

"Be prepared for anything," Hayden told me quietly. "If it's bad...Riss I don't want you there."

"If it's bad, it's because we're killing them," I told him. "Hayden, I'm getting your revenge."

He just nodded and put his hand on my thigh for a second before turning the truck around and speeding through the town and onto the road that would take us behind the hospital. My heart was hammering in my throat, my pulse bounding through my body when the greenhouses came into view.

The roof was collapsed on the closest one and another was covered in ivy. I let out a small breath of relief; they weren't being used at all. I doubted the sons of bitches who shot Hayden gave a crap about the greenhouses anymore. I put the knife back in my boot, an M9 in my waistband, an M16 around my neck, and ammo in my pockets. Ideas of what kind of pain I would inflict first flashed through my brain.

Moving slowly, we crouched our way around the greenhouses, which were all empty. The back of each greenhouse had a large, garage-style door that could manually be lifted and lowered. Thinking it would be good to keep our cars hidden we, moved the truck and the SUV inside and closed the door.

We layed down and army crawled through the trees and tall grass. My body hummed with adrenaline. The hospital was surrounded by two rows of twelve foot fencing with rolls of barbed wire at the top. Looking through the scope of my rifle, I saw a man with a gun walking the perimeter. He moved briskly down the fence, looked around, and walked just as quickly back into the hospital.

"If we can get closer we can shoot him," I whispered.

"I can shoot him from here," Hayden told me. "I just can't see him anymore."

"Look," Ivan said quietly. "There's a dry irrigation ditch. It goes around the building. If we use it, we can see what it's like on the other side."

"Ok," Hayden said. "Let's do it."

"Someone should stay here to keep watch," Brock suggested. "Since they seem to use that as an exit. The trees offer good enough cover." Using his gun, he motioned several yards over to a thicket of bushes and trees.

"I'll stay," I offered, hoping that guy would come out of the mental hospital and I could get a clear shot.

"Me too," Rider offered and clicked on his walkie-talkie. "I'll let you know if anyone comes out the door."

Ivan nodded. "Watch and report only. We're not even going to *think* about opening fire until we know just who we're dealing with." His eyes were on me.

I nodded, and as much as I wanted revenge on the people who hurt Hayden, I knew he was right.

"Be careful," I blurted, not happy that Hayden was leaving the safety of the thick tree line.

"You too," Hayden said quietly. He put his hand on my cheek and gave me a quick kiss goodbye. He went first, making sure the coast really was clear. Once in the ditch, he waved the others in. My heart beat faster and faster as they moved away. Sweat rolled down my forehead.

"Riss," Rider whispered. "Let's go."

I nodded and crawled forward, right behind Rider. He would occasionally stop and risk a look above us. We crawled, stopped, looked, and continued, going slow as we wound our way around trees. The thin forest was full of weeds, bugs, and rocks. My hands burned, but I didn't have time to think about the pain.

Rider looked up and then flattened himself to the ground. Taking the hint I did too. My breath left my lungs, seeming like a dead giveaway to where we were hiding. I took a deep breath and held it. I closed my eyes, trying to calm my racing heart. I didn't want to get spotted, and I sure as hell didn't want to get mistaken for a zombie and end up with a bullet in my head.

After what felt like eternity, Rider looked up again and slowly got to his feet. Concealed by thick, green vegetation, it would be impossible for anyone inside the hospital fence to see us. In turn, it was hard for us to see them.

I silently eased forward with painstakingly slow movements. I dropped to my knees and peered through a break in the leaves.

A deep ditch—much like our moats—was in the process of being dug around the fence. It had to be at least twelve feet deep and ten feet wide. A backhoe sat on the other side of the ditch, teasing us. *If only we had one of those*, I thought bitterly. A handmade bridge had been cast across.

I looked at Rider and pointed to the bridge. Following my finger, he narrowed his eyes.

"What do you think it leads to?" he whispered.

I shook my head. "Maybe just an *oh-shit* bridge. Ya know, in case they have to run."

Rider nodded and let his eyes run the length of the fence. "There's something over there, do you see it? It looks like a dog tunneled under the fence."

Keeping our eyes on the hospital and the area behind us, we slipped a few feet deeper into the thicket, wanting to get a better look and understanding of a possible entrance. If the guys needed that bridge to get in or out of the hospital, destroying it could work in our favor.

Something rustled.

Rider and I froze, quickly looking all around us. Rider turned to me and shook his head; he didn't see anything. I looked behind me, gazing in the direction Hayden had gone. He was far from us by now, and the greenhouses that hide our cars were probably a mile away. Carefully, Rider and I pressed forward.

It never occurred to me to look up until it was too late. Someone jumped down, landing hard on my back. I fell forward and the wind was knocked out of me. Another launched himself down at Rider. Rider dodged out of the way and rolled to my side. He kicked the guy on top of me hard in the ribs. The guy cried out and pulled a gun.

"No!" I shouted. I struggled to get my own weapon. The other guy was faster. My fingers closed on my knife right as the shot rang out. Birds took flight, the flapping of their wings echoing off the trees. Rider fell to his knees, his hands on his stomach. Blood pooled around his fingers.

"No!" I screamed again. I closed my hand around the knife and sprang up. "Rider!" I cried, rushing over to him. Tears blurred my vision.

"Riss," he muttered and started coughing. Blood bubbled from his lips.

I crawled to him, crying. He reached out for me and just as our fingers touched, I was jerked away. I swung my hand around and made contact with whoever had a handful of my hair. He yelled in pain and kicked me in the back, his foot hitting my kidney.

I thrashed forward, desperately wanting to get away and get to Rider. I raised my hand again and brought the point of the knife down on the guy's foot.

"Dumb bitch," he said and grabbed my wrist. The guy who shot Rider walked over. He laughed when he saw me struggling.

"This one seems like fun," he said and kicked the knife from my hand.

"I will kill you both!" I threatened. I elbowed the guy who was holding me in the ribs and brought my foot up to smash his balls. His grip on my hair loosened and I was able to pull away. The other guy leaned in to grab me. I reached behind me to get the M9, but it wasn't there. It must have fallen out when the bastard landed on me.

I didn't have time to get the M16 from around my neck. Something stuck me in the back of the head. Stunned, I wavered.

Then…a heavy blow to my knees.

I fell.

I made a lunge for Rider, who was coughing and gurgling up blood.

"I'm sorry," I cried. My fingers closed around his. He gave them one last squeeze. I made a mad grab for his pistol. I got it, aimed at my attacker, and pulled the trigger.

Nothing happened. Unlike me, Rider was smart and kept his safety on. From behind, someone kicked me in the side and then kicked the pistol out of my hands. He raised his foot and it came crashing down on my ribs. A horrible, biting, sharp pain flooded my body. It hurt so badly I could barely breathe.

Hands harshly grabbed a handful of my hair and pulled me back, dragging me over the rough ground. I cried out in protest and in pain when another blow came to my ribcage. Heavy, rough hands gripped my arms.

DEATHLY CONTAGIOUS

The guy who attacked Rider picked up my pistol and hit me in the temple. My vision was fuzzy and blood dripped down my face. I struggled to get away, trying to twist and sink my fingernails into my attacker's skin.

I couldn't get my feet to work properly. I was a couple yards away from Rider now. I reached up and dug my nails into the guys arm.

"Ah!" he yelled. I heard the familiar sound of a magazine sliding into a gun. The guy stopped dragging me. I felt a skull-shattering pain in the back of my head.

And then everything went black.

TO BE CONTINUED...

Emily Goodwin is the international best-selling author of the stand-alone novel STAY, The Guardian Legacies Series: UNBOUND, REAPER, MOONLIGHT (releasing 2014), The Beyond the Sea Series: BEYOND THE SEA, RED SKIES AT NIGHT (releasing 2015) and the award winning Contagium Series: CONTAGIOUS, DEATHLY CONTAGIOUS, CONTAGIOUS CHAOS, THE TRUTH IS CONTAGIOUS (Permuted Press).

Emily lives with her husband, daughter, and German Shepherd named Vader. Along with writing, Emily enjoys riding her horse, designing and making costumes, and Cosplay.

www.emilygoodwinbooks.com
facebook.com/emilygoodwinbooks

Other Books by Emily Goodwin:

The Guardian Legacies Series:
Unbound
Reaper
Moonlight

Beyond the Sea Series:
Beyond the Sea
Red Skies at Night (releasing 2015)

Dark Romance standalones:
Stay
All I Need

The Contagium Series:
Contagious
Deathly Contagious
Contagious Chaos
The Truth is Contagious